JACK HIGGINS

inside enemy lines

The Eagle Has Landed

Cold Harbour

Night of the Fox

The Eagle Has Flown

Reader's Digest Sydney London New York

This edition published by The Reader's Digest Association
Limited.
11 Westferry Circus, Canary Wharf, London E14 4HE.
www.readersdigest.co.uk

This volume was originally published by Reader's Digest
(Australia) Pty Ltd.
80 Bay Street, Ultimo, NSW 2007.
The condensations in this volume are copyright © 2007
Reader's Digest (Australia) Pty Ltd.

The Eagle Has Landed: Original full-length version
published by Collins, London. Copyright © Jack Higgins
1975. The Penguin Group (UK), London.
Cold Harbour: Original full-length version published by
Heinemann, London. Copyright © Jack Higgins 1990.
Septembertide Publishing B.V., London.
Night of the Fox: Original full-length version published by
Collins, London. Copyright © Jack Higgins 1986.
HarperCollins Publishers, London.
The Eagle Has Flown: Original full-length version published
by Chapmans, London. Copyright © Jack Higgins 1991.
The Penguin Group (UK), London.

ISBN 978–0–276–44335–0

400–364–UP0000–1

Designers: Mark Thacker, Big Cat Design; Conorde Clarke.

Photographs: front cover and page 5, top: Lambert/Hulton
Archive/Getty Images Ltd; front cover and page 5, right:
Keystone/Hulton Archive/Getty Images Ltd; pages 7, 161,
317, 469: Corbis; 8–9, 10, 165, 320, 470–1: popperfoto.com/
Emerald City Images; 162–3: Bettman/Corbis; 318–19:
Andrew Ward/Life File/Photolibrary.com; 472: Hulton-
Deutsch Collection/Corbis.

Printed in China

contents

The Eagle Has Landed

The Eagle
Has Landed

On a plan ordered by Hitler,
the message crackled through the
night: "The Eagle has landed."
It was sent from the Norfolk
coast in England by undercover
agent Liam Devlin. It was
received by Heinrich Himmler,
chief of the Nazi state police.
It meant that on this night in
1943 a mission of incredible
daring was underway: the capture
of Winston Churchill.

CHAPTER 1

OMEONE WAS digging a grave in one corner of the cemetery as I went in through the lychgate. I remember that quite clearly because it seemed to set the scene for nearly everything that followed.

Five or six black rooks lifted out of the beech trees at the west end of the church, calling angrily to each other as I threaded my way between the tombstones and approached the grave, turning up the collar of my trench coat against the driving rain.

I moved to one side of the pile of fresh earth, dodging a spadeful, and peered in. "Nasty morning for it."

An old, old man in a cloth cap and shabby, mud-stained suit, a grain sack draped across his shoulders, looked up, resting on his spade. His eyes were full of moisture and quite vacant.

I tried again. "The rain must make it difficult for you."

Some kind of understanding dawned. He glanced up at the sombre sky and scratched his chin. "Worse before it gets better."

"Maybe you can help me," I said. "I'm looking for a grave. Gascoigne—Charles Gascoigne. A sea captain."

"Never heard of him," he said. "And I've been sexton here forty-one years. When was he buried?"

"Around 1685."

His expression didn't alter. "Ah, well then, before my time. Father Vereker—now he might know something."

"Will he be inside?"

"There or the presbytery. Other side of the trees."

At that moment the rookery in the beech trees erupted, dozens of rooks filling the air with their clamour. The old man glanced up. "Noisy bastards!" he called. "Get back to Leningrad."

"Leningrad?" I said. "What makes you say that?"

"That's where they come from. They've been ringed in Leningrad and they turn up here in October. Too cold for them over there in the winter." Quite animated now, he took half a cigarette from behind his ear and stuck it in his mouth. "A lot of Germans froze to death at Leningrad during the war."

I said, "Who told you all that?"

Suddenly his face was suffused by a kind of sly cunning. "Why, Werner told me. He knew all about birds."

"And who was Werner?"

"Werner?" The vacant look appeared on his face again. "He was a good lad, Werner. They shouldn't have done that to him."

He started to dig again, dismissing me completely. I turned and worked my way through the tombstones to the church.

Inside the vestibule there was a noticeboard on the wall, the lettering in faded gold paint. CHURCH OF ST MARY AND ALL THE SAINTS, STUDLEY CONSTABLE, and underneath the times for Mass and Confession, FATHER PHILIP VEREKER, S.J.

The door was oak, held together by iron bands, studded with bolts. I turned the handle, a large ring in the mouth of a bronze lion, and the door creaked open. I had expected darkness, but instead found a medieval cathedral in miniature, flooded with light. Great Norman pillars soared up to a richly carved roof. Round clerestory windows on either side at roof level were responsible for a great deal of the light. Beside a beautiful stone font a painted board listed the priests who had served over the years, starting in 1132 and ending with Vereker, who had taken over in 1943.

Beyond was a small, dark chapel, candles flickering in front of an image of the Virgin Mary. I walked past it and down the centre aisle between the pews. It was very quiet.

Behind me a dry, firm voice said, "Can I help you?"

A tall man in a faded black cassock stood in the entrance of the Lady Chapel. He had closely cropped iron-grey hair and deep-set eyes, and the skin was stretched tight across the cheekbones. It was a face that seemed to live with pain. He came forward leaning on a blackthorn stick and dragging his right foot.

"Father Vereker?"

"That's right."

"I was talking to the old man out there, the sexton."

"Ah, yes. Laker Armsby."

"He thought you might be able to help me." I held out my hand. "My name's Jack Higgins. I'm a writer."

He hesitated slightly before shaking hands, but only because he had to switch the blackthorn from his right hand to his left. "And how can I help you, Mr Higgins?"

"I'm doing a series of articles for an American magazine," I said. "Historical stuff. I am looking for the grave of a navy captain called Charles Gascoigne who died in 1683. It seems he was brought up to Cley to be buried."

"I see," he said politely, but with a hint of impatience.

"I was at Cley yesterday," I said. "There's no trace of him there. Then I remembered that he'd been raised a Catholic, so I came to the nearest Catholic church, here at Studley Constable."

"All to no purpose, I'm afraid." He turned to go. "I've been here twenty-eight years and I can assure you I've never come across any mention of Charles Gascoigne."

"What about the church records?" I persisted.

"There is not a document connected with this church with which I am not completely familiar," he said with a certain acidity. "And now, if you'll excuse me. My lunch will be ready."

As he moved forward, the blackthorn slipped and he stumbled. I grabbed his elbow and managed to stand on his right foot.

I said, "I'm sorry, that was damned clumsy of me."

He smiled. "Nothing to hurt, as it happens." He rapped at the foot with the blackthorn.

We went down the aisle together, slowly because of his foot, and I said, "A remarkably beautiful church."

"Yes, we're rather proud of it." He opened the door for me. "I'm sorry I couldn't be of more help."

"That's all right. Mind if I look around the churchyard?"

"A hard man to convince, I see." But there was no malice. "Why not?" He held out his hand. "Good day to you, Mr Higgins."

He closed the door. The sexton had moved on and, except for the rooks from Leningrad, I had the churchyard to myself. At the end of an hour and twenty minutes I had covered the entire area. No Charles Gascoigne.

I was standing by the newly dug grave when I finally admitted defeat. The old sexton had covered it with a tarpaulin, and one end had fallen in. As I crouched down to pull it back into position, I noticed a strange thing. A yard or two away, close to the wall of the church, was a flat tombstone set in a mound of grass. Early eighteenth century, it had a superb skull and crossbones at its head and was dedicated to a wool merchant named Jeremiah Fuller, his wife and two children. Crouched down as I was, I became aware that there was another slab beneath it.

I knelt and tried to get my fingers under the tombstone, which proved to be rather difficult. But then quite suddenly it moved. "Come on, Gascoigne," I said softly. "Let's be having you."

The slab slid to one side, tilting on the mound and revealing a simple stone, with a German cross at the head. The inscription beneath it read: *Hier ruhen Oberstleutnant Kurt Steiner und 13 Deutsche Fallschirmjäger gefallen am 6 November 1943.*

My indifferent German was good enough for this. "Here lie Lieutenant Colonel Kurt Steiner and 13 German paratroopers killed in action on 6 November 1943."

I crouched there in the rain, thinking the inscription was quite absurd. An elaborate hoax on somebody's part. It had to be.

Any further thoughts on the subject were prevented by a sudden outraged cry. "*What* do you think you're doing?"

Father Vereker was hobbling towards me through the tombstones, holding a large black umbrella over his head.

I called cheerfully, "I've made a rather astonishing find."

As he drew closer I realised that his face was white and he was shaking with rage. "How dare you move that stone? Sacrilege."

"I'm sorry. But look what I've found underneath."

"I don't care *what* you've found underneath. Put it back."

I was beginning to get annoyed myself now. "Don't you realise what the inscription says? 'Here lie Lieutenant Colonel Kurt Steiner and thirteen German paratroopers killed in action on the sixth of November, 1943.' Have you seen it before?"

"No, of course not."

I didn't believe him. I said, "Who was this Steiner?"

"I haven't the slightest idea," he said. "Now will you kindly replace the original stone?"

And then I remembered something. "You took over the parish in 1943, didn't you? It says so in the church."

He exploded. "For the last time, replace that stone, and then you will oblige me by leaving at once."

There seemed little point in arguing. When I reached the path he called, "If you come back, I shall inform the police."

His threats didn't worry me. I was too excited for that. I went out through the gate and got into my Peugeot.

Studley Constable is one of those North Norfolk villages you come upon one day and can never find again, so that you begin to question whether it ever existed. There isn't much—the church, the presbytery in its walled garden, fifteen or sixteen cottages, the old mill with its massive waterwheel, the village inn.

I drove to the Studley Arms and got out. According to the plate over the entrance the licensee was one George Henry Wilde. Inside was a large, comfortable room with an open fire, several high-backed benches, a couple of tables. There were six or seven customers, with an average age of about sixty. They were countrymen to the backbone, faces weathered by exposure, tweed caps, gum boots. One old man sat by the fire playing a mouth organ. Two or three nodded at me in a cheerful way, though one massively built character with a black beard flecked with grey didn't look too friendly.

Then I saw Laker Armsby, the sexton, sitting alone, a glass of ale in front of him. I moved to his side. "Hello there. Will you have another drink?"

"I wouldn't say no." He emptied his glass in a couple of swallows. "Georgy!"

I turned to face a short, stocky man in shirt sleeves, presumably the landlord, George Wilde. He was ordinary-looking except for one feature. I'd seen enough gunshot wounds to be certain that at some time in his life he'd been shot in the face at close quarters. The bullet had scoured a furrow in his left cheek.

He smiled pleasantly. "And you, sir?"

I told him I'd have a large vodka and tonic, which brought amused looks from around the room. The drinks came and I pushed Laker Armsby's ale across to him. "Tell me about Steiner," I said.

The mouth organ stopped playing abruptly, all conversation died. Old Laker Armsby stared at me across the top of his glass with that look of sly cunning. "Steiner? Why, Steiner was—"

George Wilde cut in. "Drink up, sir. It's time, please."

I looked at my watch. It was two thirty. I said, "You've got it wrong. Another half hour till closing time."

He picked up my glass and handed it to me. "This is a free house, sir, and I say I'm closing at two thirty."

They were all looking at me, hard faces, eyes like stones, and the giant with the black beard moved across to the end of the table and leaned on it, glaring at me. "You heard him," he said. "Now drink up like a good boy and go home, wherever that is."

I drank my vodka and tonic, taking a certain amount of time over it. The tension in the air could be cut with a knife.

By now, of course, I was too far in to draw back.

I drove across a bridge, and up a few hundred yards past the church I turned into a cart track, left the Peugeot and walked back, taking with me a small camera from the glove compartment.

I found the tombstone exactly as I'd left it. I took several photos, then hurried to the church and went inside.

There was a curtain across the base of the tower and I went behind it. Choirboys' surplices hung neatly on a rail, several bell ropes trailed down through the gloom above, and a board on the wall informed the world that on 22 July 1936, a peal of five thousand and fifty-eight changes of Bob Minor was rung. Even more interesting was a line of holes cutting across the board which had at some time been filled in with plaster and stained. They continued into the masonry, for all the world like a machine-gun burst.

What I was after was the burial register. I went out through the curtain and almost instantly noticed a small door in the wall behind the font. It opened easily and I stepped inside what was obviously the sacristy, a small, oak-paneled room containing a cupboard and a large, old-fashioned desk. I tried the cupboard first and struck oil at once.

There were two deaths entered in the register during November 1943 and they were both women. Conscious of an enormous disappointment, I replaced the register in the cupboard. If Steiner and his men had been buried here, then they should have gone into the register. That was an incontrovertible point of English law.

I opened the sacristy door and stepped out, closing it behind me. There were two of them there from the pub. George Wilde and the giant with the black beard, who I was disturbed to notice carried a double-barrelled shotgun. Wilde said gently, "I did advise you to move on, sir. Now why weren't you sensible?"

The giant said, "Let's get this over with." He moved with astonishing speed for a man of his size and grabbed the lapels of my trench coat. At that moment the sacristy door opened and, surprisingly, Vereker stepped out.

"What on earth's going on here?" he demanded.

Blackbeard said, "We'll handle this, Father."

"You'll handle nothing, Arthur Seymour," Vereker said, and there was iron in his voice. "Now step back."

Seymour slowly released his grip, and Vereker said, "Don't come here again, Mr Higgins. It wouldn't be in your best interests."

It hardly seemed politic to hang around, so I hurried back to the car at a jog trot. I found Laker Armsby standing by the Peugeot.

"Ah, there you are," he said. "You got away then?"

I took out my cigarettes and offered him one. Seconds later he puffed out smoke in a cloud into the rain. "How much is it worth to you to know about Steiner?"

I took out my wallet and extracted a five-pound note. His eyes gleamed and he reached. I pulled back my hand. "Oh, no. Let's have some answers first. This Kurt Steiner—who was he?"

"That's easy," he said. "He was the German lad who came here with his men to shoot Mr Churchill."

I was so astonished that I simply stood there staring at him. He snatched the fiver, turned and cleared off.

The implications of what Armsby had said were so enormous that for the moment my mind was incapable of taking them in. I went back to my hotel in Blakeney, packed my bags, paid my bill and started home, the first stop in a journey which, although I didn't realise it then, was to consume a year of my life—a year of hundreds of files, dozens of interviews, travelling halfway around the world in search of the truth about Kurt Steiner.

CHAPTER 2

IN A SENSE, a man called Otto Skorzeny started it all on Sunday, 12 September 1943, by bringing off one of the most brilliantly audacious commando coups of World War II.

Hitler himself suddenly asked why the German military did not have commando units like the English ones which had operated so successfully, and the High Command decided to form such a unit.

Skorzeny, a young SS lieutenant, was promoted to captain and made chief of German Special Forces, none of which meant very much, which was exactly what the High Command intended.

On 3 September 1943, however, Italy surrendered. Marshal Badoglio had had Mussolini arrested. Hitler gave the seemingly impossible task of rescuing his former ally to Skorzeny.

Skorzeny learned that Mussolini was being held in a mountain hotel in the lofty Gran Sasso in Italy's Abruzzi region, guarded by two hundred and fifty men. He landed by glider with fifty paratroopers, stormed the hotel and freed Mussolini, who was flown to Hitler's East Prussian headquarters at Rastenburg.

The Führer was transported with delight and danced as he had not danced since the fall of Paris. This mood was still with him when, three days after Mussolini's arrival, he held a meeting to discuss events in Italy and the Duce's future role.

The small group of men who stood beside the long map table in the conference room included Mussolini himself; Josef Goebbels, Reich Minister of Propaganda; Heinrich Himmler, Reichsführer of the SS, chief of the state secret police; and Admiral Wilhelm Canaris, chief of Military Intelligence—the Abwehr. When Hitler entered the room they all stiffened to attention.

He descended on Mussolini and shook his hand warmly. "You look better tonight, Duce. Decidedly better."

The Italian dictator managed a weak smile and the Führer clapped his hands. "Well, gentlemen, and what should our next move be in Italy? What is your opinion, Herr Reichsführer?"

Himmler removed his silver pince-nez and polished the lenses meticulously. "Total victory, my Führer. What else?"

Hitler nodded and turned to Goebbels. "And you, Josef?"

Goebbels' dark eyes blazed. "I agree, my Führer. We have already won a moral victory, thanks to your inspired guidance."

"And no thanks to my generals." Hitler turned to Canaris. "And you, Herr Admiral. I don't wish to be too hard on you, but after all, what have your Brandenburgers accomplished?"

Canaris became pale. Hitler was referring to the Brandenburg

Division, a unique Abwehr unit established early in the war to perform special missions. "I remember hearing that the unit would be able to fetch the devil from hell. I find that ironic, Herr Admiral, because as far as I can remember they couldn't even bring me the Duce. I had to arrange for that myself."

His voice had risen to a crescendo, the eyes sparked fire, the face was wet with perspiration. "Nothing!" he shrieked. "You have brought me nothing, and yet with such facilities, you should have been capable of bringing me Churchill out of England."

Hitler glanced from face to face. "Is that not so?"

Mussolini looked hunted; Goebbels nodded eagerly. It was Himmler who added fuel to the flames by saying quietly, "Why not, my Führer? A feasibility study at the very least—surely the Abwehr can manage that?" He smiled slightly at the admiral.

"Quite right." Hitler was calm again now.

Canaris moistened dry lips. "As you command, my Führer."

Hitler put an arm around his shoulder. "Good. I knew I could rely on you as always." Then he moved forward and leaned over the map. "And now, gentlemen—the Italian situation."

WHEN CANARIS got back to Berlin it was almost dawn. The driver who picked him up at Tempelhof Airport took him to Abwehr headquarters at 74–76 Tirpitz Ufer. Canaris went straight up to his office. Unbuttoning his naval greatcoat as he went, he handed it to the orderly who opened the door for him. "Coffee," the admiral told the orderly. "Lots of coffee. Is Colonel Radl in?"

"I believe he slept in his office last night, Herr Admiral."

"Good. Tell him I'd like to see him."

The door closed. He slumped down in the chair behind the desk. The orderly brought a tray containing coffee, then withdrew. As Canaris poured a cup there was a knock at the door. The man who entered wore the uniform of a lieutenant colonel of mountain troops, with the Winter War ribbon, a wound badge, and a Knight's Cross at his throat. Even the patch over his right eye and the black leather glove on his left hand had a regulation look.

Max Radl was thirty and looked ten or fifteen years older. He had lost his right eye and left hand during the Winter War in 1941 and had worked for Canaris since being invalided home. He was at that time head of Section Three, a unit which was supposed to look after particularly difficult assignments.

"Ah, there you are, Max," Canaris said. "Join me for coffee and restore me to sanity. Each time I return from Rastenburg I feel that I need a keeper, or at least that someone does."

Radl winced, for it always made him feel decidedly uneasy when the admiral spoke in that way.

Canaris went to the window and peered through the blackout curtains at the grey morning. "You know what the Führer suggests we do, Max? Get Churchill."

Radl started violently. "Good God, he can't be serious."

"Of course not." Canaris sat down on an army cot in the corner and started to unlace his shoes. "He'll have forgotten it already." He got into the cot and covered himself with the blanket. "No, I'd say Himmler's the only worry. He backed the Führer all the way. Said that the least we could do was prepare a feasibility study. Himmler's after my blood. He'll remind the Führer about the whole affair, if only to make it look as if I don't do as I'm told."

"So what do you want me to do?"

"Exactly what Himmler suggested. A feasibility study. A nice long report that will look as if we've really been trying. Tell Krogel to wake me in one hour and a half."

Radl turned off the light and left. He was unhappy. Not because of the ridiculous assignment—that sort of thing was common—but the way Canaris talked worried him. Radl was thinking of his family. Technically the Gestapo had no jurisdiction over men in uniform, but he had seen too many acquaintances simply disappear.

When he reached his office Sergeant Hofer, his assistant, was going through the mail which had just come in. He was a quiet, dark-haired man of forty-eight, an innkeeper from the Harz Mountains, a superb skier who had served with Radl in Russia.

Radl gazed morosely at a picture on his desk of his wife and three daughters, safe in Bavaria in the mountains. Hofer, who knew the signs, gave him a cigarette. "As bad as that, Herr Oberst?"

"As bad as that." Then Radl told him the worst.

AND THERE it might have rested had it not been for an extraordinary coincidence. On the morning of the twenty-second, nearly a week later, Radl was at his desk when Hofer entered.

"I'm sorry to disturb you, Herr Oberst, but I thought this might interest you." He placed a file in front of Radl and opened it. "It's a report from an agent in England, Mrs Joanna Grey. Code name Starling. She's situated in the northern part of Norfolk on the coast. A village called Studley Constable."

Radl was suddenly enthusiastic. "Isn't she the woman who got the details of the Oboe installation?" He turned the first page.

"I've marked the interesting paragraph in red, Herr Oberst."

The report was very well put together—a general description of conditions in the area, the location of two new American B-17 squadrons south of the shallow North Sea bay between Lincolnshire and Norfolk called the Wash; all good, useful stuff without being terribly exciting. And then he came to that brief paragraph underlined in red, and his stomach contracted in excitement.

Winston Churchill was to inspect a station of the Royal Air Force Bomber Command near the Wash on Saturday, 6 November. Later that day he was scheduled to visit a factory near King's Lynn and make a brief speech to the workers. The exciting part was that instead of returning to London, he intended to spend the weekend at the home of Sir Henry Willoughby, Studley Grange, five miles outside the village of Studley Constable. It was a purely private visit, the details supposedly secret; but Sir Henry, a retired naval commander, had apparently been unable to resist confiding in Joanna Grey, who was, it seemed, a personal friend.

Radl took out the ordnance survey map of the area that Hofer had provided.

Hofer placed a finger on the Wash and ran it south along the coast. "Studley Constable, and here are Blakeney and Cley on the coast, the whole forming a triangle. A lonely coastline of vast beaches and salt marshes."

Radl sat there staring at the map for a while and then came to a decision. "Get me Starling's link man at this end. I'd like to have a word with him, only don't even hint what it's about."

"Certainly, Herr Oberst. It is Captain Meyer."

The man who entered Radl's office a few minutes later was of medium height and wore a Donegal tweed suit. His grey hair was untidy and the horn-rimmed spectacles made him seem vague. Hans Meyer was now fifty-eight years of age, and during World War I he had been a U-boat commander. From 1922 onwards he had been wholly employed in intelligence work, and he was considerably sharper than he looked.

"Sit down, Meyer, sit down." Radl indicated a chair. "I've just read the latest report from your agent Starling. Tell me about her."

"What would you like to know, Herr Oberst?"

"Everything!" Radl said.

JOANNA GREY had been born Joanna Van Oosten in March 1875 in the Orange Free State in the Republic of South Africa. Her father was a farmer and pastor of the Dutch Reformed Church. She had married, at twenty, a farmer named Dirk Jansen. She had one child, a daughter born in 1898, a year before the outbreak of hostilities with the British that became known as the Boer War.

Her father raised a mounted command and was killed in May 1900. From that month the war was virtually over, but Dirk Jansen, like others of his countrymen, fought on, a bitter guerrilla campaign.

A British cavalry patrol called at the Jansen homestead on 11 June 1901, searching for Dirk Jansen, who, unknown to his wife, had already died of wounds in a mountain camp. There were only Joanna, her mother and the child at home. Joanna refused to answer questions and was taken to the barn for an interrogation that involved being raped twice.

The British at that time were attempting to combat the guerrillas by burning farms and placing the population in concentration camps. The camps were badly run. Disease broke out and in fourteen months over twenty thousand people died, among them Joanna's mother and daughter. Joanna would have died herself had it not been for the care she received from an English doctor, Charles Grey.

Her hatred of the British was now pathological in its intensity. Yet, perhaps because she was twenty-eight, broken by life and had not a penny to her name, she married Grey when he proposed to her. That Grey loved her, there can be no doubt. He was fifteen years older and made few demands, was courteous and kind. Over the years she developed a certain affection for him.

Then in March 1925 he died of a stroke, and she was left with little more than one hundred and fifty pounds to face life at the age of fifty. But she fought on, accepting a post as governess to an English civil servant's family in Cape Town.

During this time she became interested in Boer nationalism. At one of the meetings she attended she met a German civil engineer named Hans Meyer. He was ten years her junior, yet a romance flowered briefly.

Meyer was in reality an agent of German Naval Intelligence. By chance, Joanna Grey's employer worked for the Admiralty and she was able at no particular risk to borrow from his safe certain documents which Meyer then copied. She was happy to do it because she felt a genuine passion for him, but also, for the first time in her life, she was striking a blow against England.

Meyer had gone back to Germany and continued to write to her. Then in 1929, as Europe nose-dived into a depression, Joanna Grey had a piece of genuine good fortune. Her late husband's aunt died, leaving her a cottage in the Norfolk village of Studley Constable and an income of four thousand pounds a year. There was one snag. The old lady had had a sentimental regard for the house, and the will provided that Joanna must take up residence.

To live in England! The very idea made her flesh crawl. Park Cottage, however, was a charming five-bedroom Georgian house in half an acre of walled garden. Rural Norfolk had changed little since the nineteenth century, so that in the small village she was regarded as a wealthy woman of some importance. And another, stranger thing happened. She fell in love with the place.

Meyer came to England that autumn. She showed him the endless beaches, the salt marshes. She visited him in Berlin in 1935. He showed her what national socialism was doing. She was intoxicated by the enormous rallies, uniforms, handsome boys, laughing women and children. She accepted this new order completely.

One evening as they strolled along Unter den Linden after the opera, Meyer had told her that he was with the Abwehr and asked if she would consider working for them in England.

She had said yes instantly. So, at sixty, this pleasant white-haired lady who walked the countryside in sweater and tweeds with her black retriever, Patch, became a spy with a hidden wireless transmitter, and a contact in the Spanish embassy in London who passed out her written reports in the diplomatic pouch.

Her results had been consistently good. Her duties as a member of the Women's Voluntary Services took her into many military installations. Her greatest coup had been in 1943 when the RAF had introduced Oboe, a new device for night bombing. It was amazing how much information RAF personnel at the Cromer Oboe installation had been willing to give to the kindly WVS lady who handed out library books and cups of tea.

WHEN HANS MEYER had finished, Radl laid down the pen with which he had been making notes. "A remarkable lady," he said. "Tell me—how much training has she had?"

"An adequate amount, Herr Oberst," Meyer told him. "She visited the Reich in 1936 and 1937 and received instructions: codes, use of radio, et cetera."

"What about use of weapons?"

"She was raised on the veld. Could shoot the eye out of a deer at a hundred yards by the time she was ten." Radl frowned into space, and Meyer said tentatively, "Is there something special involved, Herr Oberst? Perhaps I could be of assistance?"

"For the moment, it will be sufficient to pass all her files to this office, and no radio communication until further orders."

Meyer was aghast. "Please, if she is in danger—"

"Not in the slightest," Radl said. "I understand your concern, but there is nothing more I can say at this time."

"Forgive me, Herr Oberst, but as an old friend of the lady . . ."

He withdrew. A moment later Hofer came in.

"I've told Meyer to let you have everything he has on Starling. You take over radio communication," Radl said.

He reached for one of his Russian cigarettes. They were far too strong and made him cough. That was a matter of indifference to him; the doctors had already warned of a considerably shortened life span due to his massive injuries. Hofer produced a lighter. "Do we proceed, then, Herr Oberst?"

Radl blew a cloud of smoke. "It would appear that fate has taken a hand. When is Starling's next radio contact time?"

"This evening, Herr Oberst."

"Send her this message." Radl stared at the ceiling, trying to compress his thoughts. "Interested in your visitor of November sixth. Like to drop some friends in to meet him, hoping they might persuade him to come back with them. Your comments awaited."

FATHER PHILIP VEREKER limped out through the lychgate of St Mary and All the Saints, Studley Constable, and walked down into the village. The sun was shining, and it was a perfect autumn morning.

At that time Philip Vereker was thirty. He had entered the army as a padre in 1940 and had been assigned to the Parachute Regiment. He had seen action only once, in November 1942, when he had jumped with his unit to seize the airfield at Oudna, ten miles from Tunis. One hundred and eighty returned. Two hundred and sixty didn't. Vereker was one of the lucky ones, in spite of a bullet which had passed straight through his right ankle, chipping bone. By the time he reached a field hospital, sepsis had set in. The foot was amputated and he was eventually invalided out.

Now, four months after his discharge from a military hospital, the pain was constant. Yet he did manage a smile as Joanna Grey emerged from Park Cottage pushing her bicycle, Patch following.

"How are you, Philip?" she asked. She wore a yellow oilskin coat, and a silk scarf was tied around her white hair. With the South African tan she had never really lost, she looked charming.

"Oh, I'm all right," Vereker said. "Dying by inches of boredom more than anything else. One piece of news since I last saw you. My sister, Pamela, who's a corporal in the WAAFs, has been posted to a bomber station only fifteen miles from here. So I'll be able to see something of her. I'll introduce you."

"I'll look forward to that." Joanna climbed onto her bike.

"Chess tonight?" he asked hopefully.

"Why not? Come and have supper as well. Must go now."

She pedalled away along the stream, Patch loping behind. The radio message of the previous evening had been an enormous shock. She had lain awake, listening to the Lancasters setting out across the sea to Europe and then, a few hours later, returning.

Now, as she coasted down the hill, a horn sounded and a small sedan passed her and drew over to the side of the road. The driver had a large white moustache and florid complexion. He was wearing the uniform of a lieutenant colonel in the Home Guard.

"Morning, Joanna," he called jovially.

The meeting could have not been more fortunate. In fact it saved her a visit to Studley Grange. "Good morning, Henry," she said, and dismounted from her bike.

He got out of the car. "We're having a few people to supper on Saturday night. Jean thought you might like to join us."

"That's very kind of her. I'd love to. She must have an awful lot on at the moment, getting ready for the big event."

Sir Henry looked slightly hunted and dropped his voice a little. "I say, you haven't mentioned that to anyone, have you?"

Joanna Grey looked suitably shocked. "Of course not."

"Shouldn't have mentioned it at all actually." He slipped an arm about her waist. "Mum's the word on Saturday night, old girl, eh?"

27

He pulled away and got back into the car. "Well, I've got an area command meeting in Holt. Where are you off to?"

She'd been waiting for exactly that question. "Oh, a little bird-watching, as usual. I may go down to Cley or the marsh."

His face was serious. "Remember what I told you."

As local Home Guard commander he had all the plans of coastal defence, including details of mined beaches and those only supposedly mined. On one occasion, full of solicitude, he had shown her exactly where not to go on her bird-watching expeditions.

"I know the situation changes all the time," she said. "Perhaps you could come round to the cottage again with those maps of yours and give me another lesson. How about this afternoon?"

"After lunch," he said. "I'll be there about two," and he released the hand brake and drove rapidly away.

Joanna Grey got back on her bicycle and continued down the hill, Patch running behind. Poor Henry. She was really quite fond of him. Just like a child and so easy to handle.

Half an hour later she turned off the coast road and cycled along the top of a dyke through the marshes of Hobs End. It was a strange world of creeks and mud flats and great pale reeds higher than a man, inhabited only by the birds—curlews and redshanks and wild geese. Halfway along the dyke, behind a mouldering flint wall, was the desolate marsh warden's cottage with its large barn. The windows were shuttered. There had been no warden since 1940.

She moved onto a high ridge lined with pines, dismounted and leaned her bicycle against a stump. Beyond were sand dunes and a wide, flat beach stretching a quarter of a mile towards the sea. Across the estuary she could see the Point, curving in like a great bent forefinger, enclosing an area of channels and sandbanks that on a rising tide was probably as lethal as anywhere on the Norfolk coast. To her left were a concrete blockhouse and a machine-gun post, both with an air of decay, and in the gap near the pine trees a tank trap filled with sand. After Dunkirk there had been soldiers here. Even a year ago, Home Guard; but not now.

Joanna bent to fondle the dog's ears. "You know what it is, Patch? The English just don't expect to be invaded anymore."

She picked up a stick and tossed it straight over the line of barbed wire which prevented access to the beach, and Patch darted past the sign that said DANGER—MINES. Thanks to Henry Willoughby, to her certain knowledge there wasn't a mine on the beach. Then she produced a camera and started to take pictures.

IT WAS THE following Tuesday before Joanna Grey's photographs and report arrived at Abwehr headquarters. Radl read the report in silence. Then he said to Hofer, "Give me those Admiralty charts and the ordnance survey map."

Hofer spread them on the desk, and Radl found Hobs End and examined it in conjunction with the photos. "What more could one ask for? A perfect dropping zone for parachutists and that weekend the tide comes in again by dawn and washes away any signs of activity."

"But can you imagine one of our transport aircraft lasting for long over the Norfolk coast?" Hofer asked.

"Hardly an insurmountable problem," Radl said. "I've been told one of our night fighters recently got an RAF Dakota dropping supplies to the Dutch Resistance. Superficial engine damage only, so her pilot managed to bring her down in a ploughed field. Unfortunately for him he was near an SS barracks." Radl paused. "And, according to the Luftwaffe target chart for the area, there is no low-level radar on that particular section of the coast."

"But how do we get our raiding party out again, Herr Oberst?"

Radl looked down at the Admiralty charts for a moment. "An E-boat perhaps. There's plenty of E-boat activity in that area in the coastal shipping lanes. I don't see any reason why one couldn't slip in between the beach and the Point on a rising tide. According to Starling's report there are no mines in that channel."

"She does say that those are dangerous waters."

"Which is exactly what good sailors are for. Is there anything else you're not happy with?"

"Forgive me, Herr Oberst, but it would seem to me that there is a time factor involved which cannot be reconciled." Hofer pointed to Studley Grange on the ordnance survey map. "Here is the target, approximately eight miles from the drop zone. I would say it would take the raiding party two hours to reach it and as long to return. My estimate would be a total action span of six hours. If the drop, for security reasons, is made around midnight, this means that the rendezvous with the E-boat might not take place until after dawn, which would be completely unacceptable."

Radl had been leaning back, eyes closed. "You're absolutely right." He sat up. "The drop must be made the night before."

"Herr Oberst?" Hofer said, astonishment on his face.

"It's simple. Churchill will arrive at Studley Grange on Saturday, the sixth of November. Our party drops in the previous night, the fifth of November. Then they could be picked up before midnight on the sixth."

"There would be a grave problem of concealment on Saturday itself," Hofer pointed out.

"Right." Radl stood and started to pace the room. "But if you wanted to hide a pine tree, where would be the safest place?"

"In a forest of pines, I suppose."

"Exactly. In a remote area like this, especially in wartime, a stranger stands out like a sore thumb. Yet according to Starling's report, strangers pass through the village almost every week and are accepted without question." Hofer looked mystified and Radl continued. "Soldiers playing war games." He sat down again and reached for the report. "Here she speaks of this place Meltham House, eight miles from Studley Constable. During the past year used as a training establishment—twice by British commandos, once by a similar unit composed of Poles and Czechs with English officers and once by American Rangers. A Polish unit would do famously."

"It would certainly take care of the language problem," Hofer said. He looked at his watch. "If I might remind the Herr Oberst, the heads-of-section meeting is due to start in precisely ten minutes."

"Thank you, Hofer." Radl tightened his belt and stood up. "So it would appear that our feasibility study is virtually complete."

"Except for the most important item of all, Herr Oberst. The leader of such a venture would have to be a man of extraordinary abilities."

"Another Otto Skorzeny," Radl suggested.

"Exactly," Hofer said. "With, in this case, one thing more. Our man must be able to pass as an Englishman."

Radl smiled beautifully. "Find him for me, Hofer. I'll give you forty-eight hours." He opened the door quickly and went out.

After lunch on Thursday, Hofer placed a fresh green folder on Radl's desk. "Details of the officer who could pass as an Englishman, Herr Oberst. It took some digging. And there's a report of some court martial proceedings which I have requisitioned."

"Court martial?" Radl said. "I don't like the sound of that." He opened the file. "Who on earth is this man?"

"His name is Steiner. Lieutenant Colonel Kurt Steiner."

KURT STEINER, born in 1916, was the only son of Major General Karl Steiner, now area commander in Brittany. His mother was American, daughter of a Boston wool merchant who had moved his family to London for business reasons.

The boy had attended school in London, spending five years at St Paul's while his father was military attaché at the German embassy, and spoke English fluently. After his mother's death in a car crash in 1931 he had returned to Germany with his father, but had continued to visit relatives in England until 1938.

He entered the German army and volunteered for parachute training. He saw action in Poland and served in the Norwegian campaign. Belgium and Greece came next. In May 1941, a captain by then, he was severely wounded in the big drop over Crete.

Afterwards, the Winter War. As an acting major, Steiner had been in charge of a special assault group which led out two divisions cut off during the battle for Leningrad. He had emerged from that affair with a bullet in the right leg, which had left him with a slight limp, a Knight's Cross and a reputation for that kind of cutting-out operation.

He had been made lieutenant colonel and went to Stalingrad, where he lost half his men. In January 1943 he and the one hundred and sixty-seven survivors of his original assault group were dropped near Kiev, once again to lead out infantry divisions. There was a fighting retreat of three hundred bloodstained miles, and late in April, Steiner crossed into German lines with thirty survivors.

After an immediate award of the oak leaves to his Knight's Cross, Steiner and his men had been packed off to Germany by train, passing through Warsaw on 1 May.

He left the Polish capital with his men, under arrest by order of Jurgen Stroop, SS Brigadeführer and major general of police. There had been a court martial the following week. Only the verdict was on file. Steiner and his men had been sentenced to serve as a penal unit with Operation Swordfish on Alderney in the German-occupied Channel Islands.

RADL CLOSED the file. "What happened in Warsaw?"

"I'm not sure, Herr Oberst, but it seems that the original incident was concerned with the SS."

"All right," Radl said. "What does this unit do on Alderney?"

"Apparently it's a suicide unit which attacks Allied shipping in the Channel. They ride on a blank torpedo with a live torpedo slung underneath, which the operator is supposed to release, turning away at the last moment himself."

"Good God Almighty," Radl said in horror.

Hofer asked tentatively, "You think he could be a possibility?"

"I don't see why not. Anything should seem like an improvement on what he's doing now. Try to get me an appointment with the admiral this afternoon. Time I showed him how far we've got."

CANARIS HAD a meeting with Ribbentrop and Goebbels, and it was six o'clock before he could see Radl. He picked up a typed outline which Radl had placed on his desk, and started to read. After a while he looked up. "Very good, Max. Quite absurd, of course, but on paper it does have a kind of mad logic. Keep it handy in case Himmler reminds the Führer to ask about it."

"You mean that's all, Herr Admiral?" Radl could not believe it. "I've even got the right man for the job."

Canaris smiled and pushed the outline across the desk. "I can see that you've taken the whole thing too seriously. Plenty of other really important matters you can get on with now."

He nodded in dismissal and picked up his pen. Radl said stubbornly, "But surely, Herr Admiral, if the Führer wishes it — "

Canaris threw down his pen. "God in heaven, man, why kill Churchill when we have already lost the war?" He flushed, aware of the implicit treason in his words. Suddenly he looked old. "Trust me, Max. I know what I'm doing."

"Very well, Herr Admiral." Radl clicked his heels and went out.

RADL HAD had enough of the Abwehr for one day. Back in his office, he stuffed Joanna Grey's file and the ordnance survey map into his briefcase and put on his greatcoat. He went out the front entrance, acknowledging the sentry's salute.

As he passed under the shaded streetlight at the foot of the steps, a car pulled up. It was a black Mercedes-Benz, as black as the uniforms of the two Gestapo men who got out of the front and stood waiting. When Radl saw their insignia his heart seemed to stop beating. RFSS. Reichsführer SS — Himmler's personal staff.

The young man who got out of the rear seat wore a slouch hat and a black leather coat. His smile had the ruthless charm of the genuinely insincere. "Colonel Radl?" he said. "So glad we were able to catch you before you left. The Reichsführer presents his compliments. If you could spare him a little time, he'd appreciate it. He deftly removed the briefcase from Radl's hand. "Let me carry that for you."

Radl managed a smile. "But of course," he said, and got into the car. As the driver pulled away from the kerb, Radl noticed that the other guard had a submachine-gun across his knees.

CHAPTER 3

WHEN RADL was ushered into the office on the second floor at Prinz Albrechtstrasse, he found Himmler seated behind a large desk, a stack of files in front of him. He was wearing full uniform as Reichsführer SS, a devil in black in the shaded light, and the face behind the silver pince-nez was cold and impersonal.

The young man in the black leather coat who had brought Radl in gave the Nazi salute and placed the briefcase on the desk. "At your orders, Herr Reichsführer."

"Thank you, Rossman," Himmler said.

Rossman went out, and Radl waited while Himmler moved some files very precisely to one side of the desk and pulled the briefcase forward. At last he said, "There is not much that happens at the Tirpitz Ufer these days that I don't know about, Herr Oberst. For example, I am aware that on the twenty-second of this month you were shown a report from an Abwehr agent in England, a Mrs Joanna Grey, in which the name of Winston Churchill figures."

"Herr Reichsführer, I don't know what to say," Radl told him.

"Even more fascinating, you had all her files transferred into your custody, and relieved Captain Meyer, who had been her contact for many years, of duty." Himmler placed a hand on the briefcase. "Come, Herr Oberst, what have you to tell me?"

Max Radl was a realist. He said, "In the briefcase the Reichsführer will find all that there is to know except for one item."

"The court-martial papers of Lieutenant Colonel Kurt Steiner?" Himmler took the top file from the pile on his desk and handed it over. "A fair exchange. I suggest you read it outside." He opened the briefcase. "I'll send for you when I need you."

Radl went out into the anteroom, where Rossman sprawled in an easy chair, reading a magazine. Radl dropped the file onto a low coffee table. "It seems I've got some reading to do," he said.

Rossman smiled amiably. "I'll find us some coffee."

He went out, and Radl sat down and opened the file . . .

THE HOSPITAL train carrying Steiner and his men from the eastern front to Berlin made a brief stopover in Warsaw the morning of 1 May 1943. Orders were broadcast over the loudspeaker that no one was to leave the station. Steiner left the coach to stretch his legs, and Lieutenant Ritter Neumann, his second-in-command, joined him. Steiner's jump boots and leather coat were worn, and he was wearing a soiled white scarf and a *Schiffchen*, the boat-shaped cap more common among NCOs than officers.

Steiner and Neumann ignored orders and stepped outside the main gate. A pall of black smoke hung over the city; there was the thump of artillery and the rattle of small-arms fire. Suddenly a hand on Steiner's shoulder spun him around and he found himself facing an immaculately uniformed major of the military police.

Steiner sighed and pulled away the white scarf at his neck, exposing the collar patches of his rank and the Knight's Cross with oak leaves. "Steiner," he said. "Parachute Regiment."

"I'm sorry, Herr Oberst, but orders are orders."

"What's your name?" Steiner demanded, an edge to his voice.

"Otto Frank, Herr Oberst."

"Perhaps you would be kind enough to explain what's going on here. I thought the Polish army surrendered in '39."

"A special task force is destroying the ghetto," Frank said. "SS and other groups commanded by Brigadeführer Jurgen Stroop. Jewish bandits have been fighting from house to house for thirteen days now. So we're burning them out. Best way to exterminate lice."

During convalescent leave after Leningrad, Steiner had visited his father in France and had found him considerably changed. Six months earlier the general had seen a concentration camp at Auschwitz in Poland.

"The commander was a swine named Rudolf Hoess—a murderer

released from jail in the amnesty of 1928. Now, there he was, killing Jews by the thousand in specially constructed gas chambers, disposing of their bodies in huge ovens. Is this what we're fighting for, Kurt?"

Standing outside Warsaw Station, Kurt Steiner remembered the old general's words, and the expression on Kurt's face sent the major back a couple of steps. "That's better," Steiner said. "Make it downwind as well." Then he walked back into the station.

On the platform on the other side of the track a group of SS were herding a line of ragged and filthy human beings against a wall, where they started to take their clothes off.

"What's going on?" Steiner asked a military policeman.

"Jews, Herr Oberst. Today's crop from the ghetto. They'll be shipped to Treblinka and finished off later. They search them first."

There was brutal laughter from across the track. Steiner turned to Neumann in disgust and found the lieutenant staring along the platform to the rear of the hospital train. A young girl of perhaps fourteen, with ragged hair and smoke-blackened face, wearing a man's overcoat, crouched under the last coach. She had presumably slipped away from the group opposite and intended to ride the rods when the train pulled out. At the same moment the military policeman on the platform saw her, jumped onto the track and grabbed her. She screamed, twisted away, scrambled to the platform and ran for the entrance, straight into the arms of Major Frank. He had her by the hair and shook her like a rat.

Steiner stepped forward. "No, Herr Oberst!" Neumann cried. But Steiner gripped Frank's collar, pulled him off-balance, grabbed the girl by the hand and stood her behind him.

Major Frank scrambled to his feet, his face contorted with rage. His hand went to his holster. Steiner drew a Luger and touched him between the eyes. "You do, and I'll blow your head off."

At least a dozen armed military policemen ran forward, but paused in a semicircle a few yards away. Steiner got a hand in Frank's tunic and held him. An engine coasted through the station, hauling open coal cars. Steiner said to the girl, "If you're half the girl I think you are, you'll grab hold of one of those cars." She was gone in a flash, and he raised his voice. "Anyone takes a shot at her puts one in the major here."

The girl jumped for one of the cars, secured a grip and pulled herself up between two of them. The train moved out of the station. Steiner pushed Frank away and pocketed his Luger. The military police closed in and Neumann called out, "Not today, gentlemen."

Steiner turned and found Neumann holding a submachine-gun and the rest of his men ranged behind him, all armed.

At that point anything might have happened, but a group of SS stormed in through the main entrance, rifles at the ready. A moment later SS Brigadeführer Jurgen Stroop entered, flanked by three or four SS officers. "What's going on here, Major?"

Frank, his face twisted with rage, said, "This officer has just allowed a Jewish terrorist to escape, Herr Brigadeführer."

Stroop looked Steiner over, noting the rank badges and the Knight's Cross plus the oak leaves. "Who are you?" he demanded.

"Kurt Steiner, Parachute Regiment. And who might you be?"

Jurgen Stroop, never known to lose his temper, said calmly, "You can't talk to me like that, Herr Oberst. I'm in command here."

Steiner wrinkled his nose. "You remind me of the thing I pick up on my shoe in the gutter. Very unpleasant on a hot day."

Stroop, still icy calm, held out his hand. Steiner sighed and gave him the Luger. He looked over his shoulder. "At ease, men." He turned back to Stroop. "Is there any chance you could overlook their part in this thing?"

"Not the slightest," Stroop told him.

"That's what I thought," Steiner said. "I pride myself I can always tell a thoroughgoing bastard when I see one."

RADL SAT with the file on his knee for a long time after he'd finished reading the account of the court-martial. Steiner had been lucky to escape execution, but his father's influence must have helped. Besides, Operation Swordfish was just as certain in the long run.

Rossman sprawled in the chair opposite, apparently asleep, but when the light at the door flashed, he was on his feet. He went in without knocking and was back in a moment. "He wants you."

The Reichsführer looked up from the ordnance survey map on his desk. "What did you make of friend Steiner's little escapade?"

"A remarkable story," Radl said carefully. "An unusual man."

"I would say one of the bravest you are ever likely to encounter," Himmler said calmly. "Gifted with high intelligence, courageous, ruthless, a brilliant soldier—and a romantic fool who throws everything away for the sake of a little Jew." Then, as if dismissing the subject, he pointed to the map. "Will this plan work?"

"I think so," Radl replied.

"And the admiral? What does the admiral think?"

Radl's mind raced. "That's a difficult question to answer."

Himmler sat back, hands folded. For a wild moment Radl felt as if he were back in front of his old village schoolmaster.

"I admire loyalty, but in this case you would do well to remember that loyalty to Germany, to your Führer, comes first."

"Naturally, Herr Reichsführer," Radl said hastily.

"Unfortunately there are subversive elements at all levels in our society. In the army and in the navy, too. Indeed, I have every reason to believe that Admiral Canaris has vetoed this scheme. It would not be in accordance with his general aim, and that aim is not the victory of the German Reich, I assure you."

Radl's blood ran cold. The idea was monstrous; yet he remembered the admiral's derogatory remarks about high officials, about the Führer himself, his reaction that evening—We have lost the war.

"Herr Reichsführer," Radl said. "What do you want of me?"

Himmler actually smiled. "Why, it's really very simple. This Churchill, business. I want it carried through. I see no reason why you cannot manage without the admiral's knowledge."

"But the Herr Reichsführer must see the position this puts me in. Naturally my personal loyalty is beyond question, but what kind of authority would I have for such a project?"

Himmler took an envelope from his desk drawer and produced a letter headed by the German eagle and the iron cross in gold.

FROM THE LEADER AND CHANCELLOR OF THE STATE
MOST SECRET

Colonel Radl is acting under my direct orders in a matter of the utmost importance to the Reich. He is answerable only to me. All personnel, military and civil, will assist him in any way he sees fit.

Adolf Hitler

It was the most incredible document Radl had ever held in his hand. With such a key a man could be denied nothing.

Himmler rubbed his hands together briskly. "So, it is settled. To business then. I suggest that you see Steiner without delay."

"It occurs to me," Radl said carefully, "that in view of his recent history he may not be interested in such an assignment."

"He has no choice," Himmler said. "Four days ago we arrested his father, Major General Karl Steiner, on suspicion of treason. You might point out to Colonel Steiner that not only would it be in his own best interests to serve the Reich, but also such evidence of loyalty might well affect the outcome of his father's case." Radl was genuinely horrified, but Himmler went right on. "Now, I would like you to elaborate on this question of disguise that you mention in your outline."

Radl thought of Trudi, his wife, his three cherished daughters. For them, he thought, I've got to survive anything. He started to speak, amazed at the calmness in his voice. "The British have many commando regiments, as the Reichsführer is aware, but perhaps one of the most successful has been the unit formed to operate behind our lines in Africa. The Special Air Service. Little is known of it by the more conventional branches of the army. It is accepted that their purposes are secret, therefore it is less likely that they would be challenged by anyone."

"You would pass off our men as members of this unit?"

"Exactly, Herr Reichsführer. As members of the Polish Independent Parachute Squadron, attached to the SAS."

"And uniforms?"

"Most of these people are now wearing camouflage smock and trousers in action. They also wear the English parachutists' maroon beret with a special badge. A winged dagger with the inscription 'Who dares—wins.'"

"How dramatic," Himmler said dryly.

"The Abwehr has ample supplies of such clothing from those taken prisoner during SAS operations in the Greek Islands, Yugoslavia and Albania. Also equipment."

Himmler removed his pince-nez and stroked the bridge of his nose. "Wearing enemy uniforms is forbidden under the Geneva Convention. The penalty is the firing squad." He replaced the pince-nez and looked at Radl. "As a compromise the raiding party will wear normal uniform underneath these camouflage outfits. Before the attack they could remove these disguises. You agree?"

Radl thought it probably the worst idea he'd heard of, but realised the futility of argument. "As you say, Herr Reichsführer."

"Good. The Führer's directive will open all doors for you. Is there any question you wish to raise?"

"As regards Churchill," Radl said. "Is he to be taken alive?"

"If possible," Himmler said. "Dead, if there is no other way. Rossman will give you a special phone number. I wish to be kept in daily touch with your progress." He replaced the reports and the map in the briefcase and pushed it across.

Radl folded the precious letter, put it back in the envelope, which he slipped inside his tunic. He picked up the briefcase and his greatcoat and moved to the door.

Himmler, who had started writing in a file, said, "Colonel Radl . . ."

Radl turned. "Herr Reichsführer?"

"Remember one thing. Failure is a sign of weakness." Himmler lowered his head and continued to write.

WHEN RADL went into his office, Sergeant Hofer greeted him eagerly. "What news of the plan, Herr Oberst?"

Radl took the envelope from his breast pocket. "I want you to read this letter, Hofer."

Radl waited, peering out of the window, and turned after a

moment or so. Hofer was staring down at the letter, obviously shaken. "But what does this mean, Herr Oberst?"

"The Churchill affair proceeds. The admiral is not to know."

Hofer looked bewildered as Radl explained the situation. At last Radl took the letter back. "You and I are little men, caught in a very large web, and we must tread warily. Do you trust me?"

Hofer sprang to attention. "I've never doubted you, Herr Oberst."

Radl was aware of a surge of affection. "Good. Then let us proceed. Starling will need a man to help her. Someone with brains as well as muscle."

"A difficult combination," Hofer said.

"It always is. Who does Section One have working for them in England at the moment who might be able to help?"

Hofer shrugged. "There are perhaps seven or eight agents."

Radl turned back to the window and stood tapping one foot impatiently. His left hand was hurting, the hand which was no longer there, a sure sign of stress, and his head was splitting. Himmler's words came back to him— "Failure is a sign of weakness."

Hofer said diffidently, "Of course there is always the Irish section. The Irish Republican Army."

"Completely useless," Radl said. "The whole IRA connection was aborted long ago. A total failure, the entire enterprise."

"Not quite, Herr Oberst." Hofer took a folder from a file cabinet and laid it on the desk. Radl sat down and opened it.

"But of course . . . What does he call himself now?"

"Devlin. Liam Devlin. He is still in Berlin."

"Get him here within the hour!"

THE MAN who called himself Liam Devlin had been born in the North of Ireland in July 1908, the son of a small tenant farmer who had been executed in 1921 during the Anglo-Irish War for serving with an IRA flying column. The boy's mother had gone to keep house for her brother, a Catholic priest in Belfast, and he had arranged for him to attend a Jesuit boarding school in the south.

From there Devlin had moved to Trinity College, Dublin, where he had received a degree in English literature.

In 1931, while visiting his home in Belfast during a period of serious sectarian rioting, he had witnessed Orangemen sacking his uncle's church. The old priest had been so badly beaten that he lost an eye. From that moment Devlin had given himself completely to the Republican cause.

He had led the defence of Catholic areas in Belfast during the rioting of 1935. Later that year he had been sent to New York to execute an IRA informer who had been put on a boat to America by the police. He had accomplished the mission with efficiency.

In 1936 he had taken himself to Spain, where he'd served in the Abraham Lincoln Brigade. He had been captured by Italian troops and sentenced to life imprisonment by the Franco government. He had been freed at the instigation of the Abwehr late in 1940 and brought to Berlin, where it was hoped he might help German Intelligence to develop their Irish connection and thus ensure regular attacks on British military installations in Ulster. They discovered that Devlin, while having little sympathy with the Communist cause, was definitely anti-Fascist, a fact which made him a bad risk.

The Abwehr's hopes of developing contacts with the IRA had come to nothing. In desperation they had asked Devlin to go to Ireland, contact Captain Goertz, their best agent, and get him out. Devlin parachuted into County Meath on 18 October 1941, but before he could reach Goertz, the German was arrested by Scotland Yard's Irish Special Branch.

After months on the run, Devlin had been surrounded by police at a farmhouse in Kerry in June 1942. He wounded two of them and was himself rendered unconscious when a bullet creased his forehead. He had escaped from a hospital, got to Lisbon by boat and passed through Spain via the usual channels, until he once more stood in the offices at the Tirpitz Ufer.

From then on, the Abwehr considered Ireland a dead end. Liam Devlin was given translation duties at the University of Berlin.

IT WAS JUST before noon when Hofer came back into the office. "I've got him, Herr Oberst."

Radl looked up. Liam Devlin was scarcely five feet six. He had dark hair, vivid blue eyes and an ironic smile. He was wearing a black trench coat, and the ugly puckered scar of the bullet wound showed clearly on the left side of his forehead.

"Mr Devlin." Radl went around the desk and held out his hand. "My name is Radl—Max Radl. It's good of you to come."

"That's nice," Devlin said in excellent German. "The impression I got was that I didn't have much choice in the matter."

"Please, Mr Devlin." Radl brought a chair forward. He produced a bottle of Courvoisier and two glasses. "Cognac?"

Devlin accepted the glass, swallowed, closing his eyes for a moment. "It isn't Irish, but it'll do. Now, are you trying to lead up, in the nicest way possible, to the fact that you want me to go back to Ireland? Because if you are, you can forget it."

"Not Ireland, Mr Devlin. England," said Radl.

Devlin stared at him. "God save us, the man's mad."

"No, Mr Devlin, quite sane, I assure you." Radl pushed the Courvoisier bottle across the desk and placed Joanna Grey's file next to it. "Have another drink and read that. Then we'll talk."

He got up and walked out.

At the end of a good half hour Radl went back in. Devlin was sitting with his feet on the desk, the file in one hand, a glass in the other. The bottle looked depleted.

He glanced up and grinned. "Idea's a bloody cheek."

"You think it would work?" Radl demanded eagerly.

"It's impudent enough." Devlin threw the report down. "To, tumble the great Winston Churchill out of his bed in the middle of the night and away with him." He smiled hugely. "There is the point, however, that it won't have the slightest effect on the course of the war. On the other hand, I'd hate to miss this little jaunt."

"You mean you're willing to go?"

"I know, I'm a fool," Devlin said. "Look what I'm giving up. A nice safe job at the university with the RAF bombing by night, the

Yanks by day, food getting shorter, the eastern front crumbling."

Radl raised both hands, laughing. "No more questions."

"And then we mustn't forget the twenty thousand pounds you're going to deposit to a numbered account in a Geneva bank."

Radl felt acute disappointment. "So, you also have your price?"

"The movement I serve is notoriously low on funds."

"Very well," Radl said. "I will arrange it."

"Fine," Devlin said. "So what would my part be?"

"Starling is sixty-eight years of age. She needs a man to do the running around, to handle the rough stuff."

"And how do you get me there?"

"We'll parachute you into southern Ireland close to the Ulster border. I understand it is easy to walk across. From Belfast you'll take a boat to Heysham, then a train to Norfolk."

"No trouble there," Devlin said. "Then what?"

Radl smiled. "You will be an Irish citizen who has served with the British army. Badly wounded and given a medical discharge. That scar on your forehead will help. We'll supply you with every possible document. What do you think?"

"I'll buy it. When do I go?"

"A week, ten days at the most. For the moment, you must resign your post at the university and observe total security. Tomorrow I'm going to Alderney to see the man who will probably command the assault group. You might as well come, too."

CHAPTER 4

ALDERNEY IS the most northerly of the Channel Islands and the closest to the French coast. As the German army rolled inexorably westward in the summer of 1940, the islanders had voted to evacuate. When the first Luftwaffe plane landed on the tiny grass strip on top of the cliffs on 2 July 1940, the place was deserted. By the autumn of 1942 there was a garrison of perhaps three thousand mixed army, navy and Luftwaffe personnel and several camps employing slave labour from the Continent to work on the massive concrete gun emplacements of the new fortifications.

Radl and Devlin flew in just after noon in a Stork spotter plane. A sergeant of artillery drove them from the airfield to St Anne, the island's capital. The houses were French provincial and English Georgian, streets cobbled, gardens high-walled against winds. There were plenty of signs of war—concrete pillboxes, barbed wire and machine-gun posts—but it was the Englishness of it all that fascinated Radl. The incongruity of seeing a Luftwaffe private lighting a cigarette under a sign that said ROYAL MAIL.

Feldkommandantur 515, German civilian administration headquarters, was in the old Lloyds Bank in Victoria Street, and as the car drew up, the commandant himself appeared in the entrance. "Colonel Radl? Hans Neuhoff, temporarily in command here."

Radl said, "This gentleman is a colleague of mine."

Alarm showed in Neuhoff's eyes instantly, for Devlin, in civilian clothes and a black leather military greatcoat Radl had procured for him, obviously seemed to be Gestapo.

Neuhoff led the way into what had presumably been the manager's office. "Can I offer you gentlemen a drink?"

"Frankly, I'd like to get straight down to business." Radl took an envelope from his inside pocket and produced the letter.

Neuhoff ran his eyes over it. "The Führer himself commands." He looked up in amazement. "But what is it you wish of me?"

"Your complete cooperation, Colonel Neuhoff," Radl said. "And no questions. You have a penal unit here, I believe? Colonel Steiner, a Lieutenant Neumann and twenty-nine paratroopers."

Neuhoff corrected him. "Colonel Steiner, Lieutenant Neumann and *thirteen* paratroopers."

Radl stared at Neuhoff in surprise. "Where are the others?"

"Dead, Herr Oberst," Neuhoff said simply. "You know about Operation Swordfish? You know what they do, these men? They sit astride torpedoes and—"

"I'm aware of that." Radl reached for the Führer's directive and replaced it in its envelope. "Operation Swordfish stops now." He held up the envelope. "My first order under this directive."

Neuhoff smiled. "I am delighted to comply."

"I see," Radl said. "Colonel Steiner is a friend?"

"My privilege," Neuhoff answered. "If you knew the man, you would understand."

"Where can I find him?" Radl asked.

"Just before you get to the harbour there's an inn, a quarter of a mile from here. Steiner and his men use it as their headquarters," Neuhoff answered. "Have you any idea how long you will stay?"

"The Stork is to pick us up in the morning," Radl said.

"Would you care to dine with me tonight? My wife would be delighted and perhaps Colonel Steiner could join us."

"An excellent idea," Radl said. "I'll look forward to it."

"A NICE-LOOKING pub," Devlin said as they approached the inn. "Do you think it possible they still have a drink on the premises?"

Inside, there was a bar counter to the left, empty shelves behind it, a number of framed photographs of old wrecks on the walls, a piano in one corner. There were a dozen or so paratroopers scattered around. None came to attention at Radl's entrance, and all were remarkably unfriendly. Radl had never seen a group with so many decorations among them. There wasn't a man who didn't have the Iron Cross, First Class; and such items as wound badges and tank-destruction badges were a dime a dozen.

He stood in the centre of the room, his briefcase under his arm, his hands in his pockets. "I'd like to point out," he said mildly, "that men have been shot for this kind of behaviour."

There was a shout of laughter. Sergeant Sturm, who was cleaning a Luger behind the bar, said, "That's very good, Herr Oberst. When we reported here, there were thirty-one of us, including the colonel. Fifteen now." He shook his head. "You've been polishing a chair with your backside for so long, you've forgotten how real soldiers feel. You've come to the wrong place if you're hoping for a chorus from the 'Horst Wessel.'"

"Excellent," Radl said. "However, your completely incorrect reading of the present situation argues a lack of wit which I, for one, find deplorable in someone of your rank." He went to the bar, dumped his briefcase on the counter and took off his coat. Sturm's jaw dropped as he saw the Knight's Cross, the Winter War ribbon. "Attention!" Radl barked. "On your feet, all of you."

There was pin-drop silence as every man stood rigidly to attention. Radl said, "You think you are German soldiers, but you are mistaken." He moved from one man to another, pausing as if committing each face to memory. "Shall I tell you what you are?"

Which he did in direct terms. When he paused for breath there was a polite cough from the doorway and he turned.

Two officers were there. One said, "I couldn't have put it better myself, Colonel Radl." He held out his hand and smiled with considerable charm. "I've just been speaking to Hans Neuhoff. I'm Kurt Steiner and this is Oberleutnant Ritter Neumann."

Steiner possessed that strange quality to be found in the airborne troops of every country—a kind of arrogant self-sufficiency. He was wearing a blue-grey flying blouse with the yellow collar patches bearing the wreath and stylised wings of his rank, jump trousers and a *Schiffchen*. The rest, for a man who had every decoration in the book, was extraordinarily simple—the coveted *Kreta* cuff band, proud mark of those who had spearheaded the invasion of Crete, the Winter War ribbon, and the silver and gold eagle of the paratroopers' qualification badge. The Knight's Cross with oak leaves was partly concealed by a loose silk scarf.

"To be honest, Colonel Steiner, I've rather enjoyed putting these scoundrels of yours in their place. And now, I would like to talk to you privately on an urgent matter."

Steiner nodded. "This way, Herr Oberst."

DEVLIN AND RADL leaned on the parapet, looking down into the water, clear and deep in the pale sunshine. Steiner sat on a bollard at the end of the jetty, working his way through the contents of Radl's briefcase. Across the bay, Fort Albert loomed on the headland and below, the cliffs were splashed with birdlime, seabirds wheeling in great clouds, gulls, shags, razorbills and oyster-catchers.

Steiner called, "Colonel Radl."

Radl moved towards him and Devlin followed. "Do you think it can be done?" Radl asked.

"I don't see why not," Steiner said. "If these papers are accurate, the whole thing could go like a Swiss watch. In and out before the Tommies know what's hit them, but that isn't the point."

"What is?" asked Radl. "You and your men are dead men here. You owe it to them, to yourself, to take this chance to live."

"Colonel Radl, I'm officially disgraced. In fact, I only retain my rank because of the peculiar circumstances of this job. I don't like Adolf. He has a loud voice and bad breath. To be perfectly frank, I don't think I owe anything to anybody."

"Not even your father?" Radl said.

There was a silence, only the sea washing over the rocks below. Steiner's face turned pale. "All right, tell me."

"The Gestapo have him. Suspicion of treason."

And Steiner, remembering the week he had spent at his father's headquarters in France in 1942, remembering what the old man had said, knew instantly that it was true.

"Ah, I see now," he said softly. "If I'm a good boy and do as I'm told, it would help his case." Suddenly his face changed and he looked about as dangerous as any man could. "You bastard."

He had Radl by the throat. Devlin moved in. It took all his strength to pull him off. "Not him, you fool. He's under the boot as much as you. You want to shoot somebody, shoot Himmler."

Radl fought for breath and leaned against the parapet. Eventually he raised his dead hand. "See this, Steiner, and the eye? And other damage that you can't see. Two years if I'm lucky, they tell me. Not for me. For my wife and daughters, because of what might happen to them. That's why I'm here."

Steiner put a hand on his shoulder. "I'm sorry." He took a deep breath. "All right. I'll put it to the men."

"Not the target," Radl said. "Not at this stage."

"The destination then. They're entitled to know that. As for the rest—I'll only discuss it with Neumann for the moment."

He started to leave. Radl said, "Steiner, I must be honest." Steiner faced him. "I think it's worth a try. It won't win the war, but it may make the British think about a negotiated peace."

"My dear Radl, I'll tell you what this affair, even if successful, will buy from the British. Not a damn thing!"

He turned and walked away along the jetty.

THE BAR at the inn was full of smoke. Sergeant Hans Altmann was playing the piano and the rest of the men were crowded around. There was a sudden silence as Steiner entered, followed by Radl and Devlin. Everyone waited. "It's simple," Steiner told them. "There's a chance to get out of here. A special mission."

"Doing what, Herr Oberst?" Altmann asked.

"What you were trained to do. But it's volunteers only. A personal decision for every man here."

"Russia, Herr Oberst?" Sergeant Major Brandt asked.

Steiner shook his head. "Somewhere no German soldier has ever fought. How many of you speak English?" he asked softly.

There was a stunned silence and Neumann so far forgot himself as to say hoarsely, "You've got to be joking, Kurt."

"I've never been more serious," Steiner said. "What I tell you now is top secret. In five weeks we'd be expected to do a night drop over an isolated part of the English coast. If everything went according to plan, we'd be taken off the following night."

"And if not?" Neumann said.

"You'd be dead, so it wouldn't matter. Anything else?"

"Can we be told the purpose of the mission?" Altmann asked.

"The same sort of thing Skorzeny and the paratroopers pulled at Gran Sasso. That's all I can say."

Sergeant Major Brandt glared around the room. "If we go, we might die; if we stay, we die for certain. If you go—we go."

"I agree." Neumann snapped to attention.

Every man in the room followed suit. Steiner stood there for a long moment, then he nodded. "So be it. Do we still have that Scotch whisky?"

The group broke for the bar, and Sergeant Altmann sat down at the piano and started to play "We March Against England".

IT WAS DARK on the terrace of the commandant's house when Radl and Steiner went out to smoke a cigar after dinner. Through the blackout curtain that covered the French windows they could hear Devlin's voice, and Hans Neuhoff and his wife laughing gaily.

"A man of many qualities," Steiner said. "It will be of great assistance to have Devlin as an advance party, believe me."

Radl nodded. "You'll have movement orders within a week to ten days, depending on how quickly I can find a suitable base in Holland. Once there, you can disclose the purpose of the mission."

Radl turned to leave, but Steiner put a hand on his arm. "And my father?"

Radl said, "All that I can do is make it plain to Himmler how cooperative you are being."

"And do you honestly think that will be enough?"

"Do you?" Radl said.

Steiner's laugh had no mirth. "He has no conception of honour."

Radl was intrigued. "And you?" he said. "You have?"

"Perhaps not. Simple things like keeping your word, standing by friends. Does the sum of these total honour?"

"I don't know," Radl said. "All I can confirm with certainty is the fact that you are too good for the Reichsführer's world." He put his arm around Steiner's shoulders. "We'd better go in."

AT NOON on Wednesday, 6 October, Joanna Grey collected a large envelope deposited inside a copy of *The Times* on a bench in London's Green Park by her contact at the Spanish embassy.

Once in possession of the package, she took the train back to Norfolk. When she drove her car into the yard at Park Cottage it was almost six o'clock and she was very tired. She was greeted enthusiastically by Patch, who trailed at her heels to the sitting room, where she poured herself a large Scotch—of which, thanks to Sir Henry Willoughby, she had a plentiful supply. Then she climbed the stairs to the small study next to her bedroom.

The invisible door in the corner, designed to resemble a section of panelling, was part of the original structure. She inserted a key in the tiny keyhole and unlocked the door. A short wooden stairway gave access to a cubbyhole loft under the roof, where she had her radio receiver and transmitter. She sat down at an old card table and opened a drawer in it, pushing a loaded Luger to one side. Then she took out her code books and got to work.

When she finished an hour later her face was pinched with excitement. "My God!" she said to herself in Afrikaans. "They meant it—they actually meant it."

Then she took a deep breath, went downstairs and telephoned Studley Grange. Sir Henry Willoughby's voice warmed immediately when she spoke. "Henry—I've got a little favour to ask."

"Fire away, old girl. Anything I can do."

"Well, I've heard from some Irish friends of my late husband's. They're sending over their nephew. His name is Liam Devlin, and he was badly wounded in France. He received a medical discharge a year ago. He's quite fit now, but he needs to work outdoors."

"And you thought I might be able to fix him up?" said Sir Henry jovially. "No difficulty there, old girl. You know what it's like getting any kind of workers for the estate these days."

"Actually I was wondering about the marsh warden's job at Hobs End. That's been vacant since young Tom King went off to the army, and the house is getting very run down."

"You have something there, Joanna. Let's go into the whole thing. Are you free tomorrow afternoon?"

"Of course," she said. "It's so good of you to help, Henry. I always seem to be bothering you with my problems."

"Nonsense," he told her sternly. "Woman needs a man to smooth over the rough spots for her."

"I'd better go now," she said. "I'll see you soon."

"Goodbye, my dear."

She went back upstairs, where she transmitted a brief message to Berlin—an acknowledgment that her instructions had been received and that Devlin's employment had been taken care of.

IN BERLIN, black, cold rain was drifting across the city, pushed by a bitter wind. At Prinz Albrechtstrasse, Max Radl and Devlin were shown into Himmler's office.

The Reichsführer was at his desk. "You've done well, Radl. I'm more than pleased with the progress. This is Herr Devlin?"

"As ever was," Devlin said cheerfully. "Just a poor old Irish peasant straight out of the bog. That's me, your honour."

"What is the man talking about?" Himmler demanded of Radl.

"The Irish, Herr Reichsführer, are not as other people."

"It's the rain," Devlin said.

Himmler turned quickly to Radl. "I brought you here, in the first place, to see Herr Devlin for myself. But secondly, there seems to me one weakness in Steiner's assault group. Four or five of the men speak English to some degree, but only Steiner can pass as a native. He needs the backing of someone of similar ability."

"But such people are rather hard to find."

"I think I have a solution," Himmler said, handing Radl a file card. "There is a unit of fifty or sixty Englishmen, the British Free Corps, recruited from the prisoner-of-war camps mainly to fight on the eastern front. The SS has taken it over. Its members do have their uses. This man, for instance, Harvey Preston. When captured in Belgium he was wearing the uniform of a captain in the Coldstream Guards, and since he had the voice and mannerisms of the English aristocrat, no one doubted him."

Radl examined the card. Harvey Preston had been born in Yorkshire in 1916, the son of a railway porter. He had left home at fourteen to work as a prop boy with a touring variety company. At eighteen he was acting in repertory in Southport. In 1937 he was imprisoned on four charges of fraud. In 1939 he was sentenced to nine months on a charge of impersonating an RAF officer and obtaining money under false pretenses. The judge suspended the sentence on condition that Preston join the armed forces. He was sent to France as a clerk and, when captured, held the rank of acting corporal. His prison camp record was bad or good, according to which side you were on. Before volunteering for the Free Corps he had informed on five separate escape attempts by his comrades.

Radl handed the card to Devlin, then turned to Himmler. "And you want Steiner to take this . . . this . . ."

"Rogue," Himmler said, "who is quite expendable, but who simulates the English aristocrat quite well?"

"But Steiner and his men, Herr Reichsführer, are soldiers—real soldiers. Can you see such a man fitting in?"

"He'll do as he's told," Himmler said. "Shall we see him?"

He pressed the buzzer, and a moment later Preston entered the room and gave the Nazi salute.

He was twenty-seven, tall and handsome in a beautifully tailored field-grey uniform. He had the death's-head of the SS on his peaked cap, and wore a Union Jack shield and the insignia of the British Free Corps on his left sleeve.

"Very pretty," Devlin said to Radl.

Himmler made the introductions, and Preston inclined his head and clicked his heels like someone playing a Prussian officer onstage.

"So," Himmler said to him. "You have had ample opportunity to consider the matter of which we spoke earlier?"

Preston said carefully, in good German, "Do I take it that Colonel Radl is looking for volunteers for this mission?"

When Himmler spoke his voice was like dry leaves brushed by the wind. "What exactly are you trying to say, Untersturmführer?"

"As the Reichsführer knows, members of the British Free Corps were given a guarantee that at no time would they have to wage war against Britain—" Preston suddenly realised his mistake and tried to make amends. "I can assure you, Herr Reichsführer, that—"

Himmler didn't give him a chance. "Have you not taken an oath of sacred duty to the Führer and the Reich?"

"Of course, Herr Reichsführer."

"Then nothing more need be said. You will from this moment consider yourself to be under the orders of Colonel Radl here."

"As you say, Herr Reichsführer."

"Colonel Radl, I'd like to have a word with you in private. Herr Devlin, if you will wait in the anteroom for Colonel Radl. Untersturmführer Preston, you may go."

Preston gave him a crisp Heil Hitler, turned on heel with a precision that would not have disgraced the Grenadier Guards, and went out. Devlin followed, closing the door behind them.

Himmler turned to Radl. "I wanted to make sure that the arrangements in your office are proceeding satisfactorily."

"So far, Herr Reichsführer. My trip to Alderney I combined with Abwehr business in Paris, and I have perfectly legitimate reasons for visiting Amsterdam next week. As you know, the operation will be based on nearby Landsvoort. The admiral knows nothing."

"Good. I'm very pleased with you, Radl. Keep me informed."

"There is one other matter," Radl said. "Major General Steiner."

"What about him?"

"It was the Reichsführer himself who suggested I make it clear to Colonel Steiner that his conduct in this affair could have a significant effect on his father's case."

"That is so," Himmler said. "But what is the problem?"

"I gave Colonel Steiner an assurance that . . . that . . ."

"Which you had no authority to offer," Himmler said. "However, under the circumstances, you may give Steiner that assurance in my name. You may go now."

IN A CELL on the ground floor at Prinz Albrechtstrasse a grey-haired man of sixty or so, in a tattered shirt and military breeches, was sprawled across a bench while two muscular SS men beat him across the back with rubber truncheons. Rossman stood watching.

Eventually he stopped them, and Major General Karl Steiner crawled into a corner and crouched there, arms folded. "Not one word," he said through swollen lips. "I swear it."

RADL AND DEVLIN arrived at the Tirpitz Ufer as Hofer was emerging. Radl said, "Going off duty, Hofer? Anything for me?"

"Yes, Herr Oberst, a signal from Starling. Message received, and Herr Devlin's employment has been taken care of."

Radl turned to Devlin. "We fly to Paris tomorrow. I go on to Amsterdam. You take off Sunday night for Ireland."

CHAPTER 5

AT PRECISELY two forty-five the next Monday morning, Seumas O'Broin, aged seventy-six, a sheep farmer of Conroy in County Monaghan, was endeavouring to find his way home from a wake across a stretch of moorland. And making a bad job of it. He had consumed quantities of drink so vast that he was not certain whether he was in this world or the next; so that when what he took to be a large white bird sailed soundlessly out of the darkness overhead and plunged behind a wall, he felt only a mild curiosity.

Devlin made an excellent landing, the supply bag dangling twenty feet below from his belt hitting the ground first, warning him to be ready. He followed a split second later, rolling in springy turf, scrambling to his feet instantly and unfastening his harness. He opened the supply bag, took out a small shovel, his black trench coat, a tweed cap, a pair of shoes and a large Gladstone bag.

He quickly scraped a hole in a ditch nearby with the shovel. Then he unzipped his flying coveralls. Underneath he was wearing a tweed suit, and he transferred the Walther which he had carried in his belt to his right-hand pocket. He pulled on his shoes and then put the coveralls, the parachute and the flying boots into the bag and dropped it into the hole, raking the soil back into place quickly and tossing the shovel into a nearby copse.

He pulled on his trench coat, picked up the Gladstone bag and turned to find Seumas O'Broin leaning on the wall watching him. Devlin moved fast, his hand on the butt of the Walther. But then the aroma of good Irish whiskey told him all he needed to know.

"What are ye, man or divil?" the old farmer demanded.

"God save us, old man, but from the smell of you, if one of us lit a match right now, we'd be in hell together soon enough. As for your question, I'm a little of both. A simple Irish boy, trying a new way of coming home after years in foreign parts."

The old man laughed delightedly. "A thousand welcomes."

ON WEDNESDAY, in spite of the rainy weather, Joanna Grey went into the garden after lunch. She was digging potatoes when the garden gate creaked, and she turned to see a smallish, pale-faced man at the end of the path, wearing a black belted trench coat and tweed cap. He carried a Gladstone bag and had startlingly blue eyes. "Mrs Grey?" he inquired in a soft Irish voice.

"That's right." Her stomach knotted with excitement.

He smiled. "I shall light a candle of understanding in the heart which shall not be put out."

"Magna est veritas et praevalet."

"Great is Truth, and mighty above all things," said Liam Devlin. "I could do with a cup of tea. It's been one hell of a trip."

Minutes later Joanna Grey turned from the stove where she was making the tea and said, "Well, how was it?"

"Surprising in some ways," he said.

"How do you mean?"

"Oh, the people, the general state of things. It wasn't quite as I expected." He thought of the station restaurant at Leeds—crowded all night with travellers of every description, the rough good humour, the high spirits—and contrasted it with his last visit to the central railway station in Berlin. "They seem pretty sure they're going to win the war," he said as she brought the tea.

"A fool's paradise," she told him calmly. "They've never had the discipline the Führer has given to Germany."

Remembering the considerable portions of Berlin that were heaps of rubble, Devlin felt almost constrained to point out that things had changed since the good old days. But he got the distinct impression that such a remark would not be well received. So he drank his tea and watched her open a cupboard and take down a bottle of Scotch, marvelling that this pleasant white-haired woman in the neat skirt and Wellington boots could be what she was.

She poured two glasses and raised one in a kind of salute. "To the English Enterprise," she said, her eyes shining.

Devlin could have told her that the Spanish Armada had been so described, but remembering what had happened to that ill-fated venture, decided once again to keep his mouth shut. "To the English Enterprise," he said solemnly.

She put down her glass. "Now let me see your papers."

He produced his passport, army discharge papers and a testimonial purporting to be from his old commanding officer.

"These are really very good," she said. "Tomorrow morning I'll run you into Holt—a town about ten miles from here—and you'll report to the police. They'll give you an alien's registration form. Then you'll need insurance cards, an identity card, ration book, clothing coupons." She counted them off on her fingers.

Devlin grinned. "Heh, hold on now. It sounds like a lot of trouble to me. Three weeks on Saturday, and I'll be away from here so fast, they'll think I've never been."

"All these things are essential," she said. "It only needs one petty clerk in Holt to notice that you haven't applied for something and make an inquiry, and then where would you be?"

Devlin said cheerfully, "All right. Now what's this job?"

"Warden of the marshes at Hobs End, working for the local squire, Sir Henry Willoughby."

"And what will be expected of me?"

"Gamekeeping duties in the main, and there's a system of dyke gates that needs regular checking. Sir Henry will supply you with a shotgun, and he's allocated you one of the estate's motorbikes."

A horn sounded outside. "Here he is. Leave the talking to me."

She went out and Devlin waited. He heard the front door open and her feigned surprise. Sir Henry said, "Just on my way to a command meeting in Holt, Joanna. Anything I can get you?"

She replied much more quietly, so that Devlin couldn't hear what she said. There was a further murmur of conversation and then they came into the kitchen.

Sir Henry was in Home Guard uniform, a splash of medal ribbons for World War I above his breast pocket. "So you're Devlin?"

Devlin rose to his feet. "I'd like to thank you, sir," he said. "Mrs Grey's told me how much you've done for me."

"Nonsense, man," Sir Henry said brusquely. "You did your best for the old country. Caught a packet in France, I understand?"

Devlin nodded, and Sir Henry examined the furrow on the forehead made by an Irish Special Branch bullet. "By heavens," he said softly. "You're damn lucky to be here, if you ask me."

"I thought I'd settle him in for you," Joanna Grey said. "If that's all right, Henry? You're so busy, I know."

"I say, would you, old girl?" He glanced at his watch. "I'm due in Holt in twenty minutes. Come to think of it, you probably know more about what goes on at Hobs End than I do." He turned to Devlin. "Call at the Grange tomorrow afternoon for the bike and shotgun. Only three gallons of petrol a month, mind you, but we've all got to make sacrifices."

Joanna Grey took his arm. "Henry, you're going to be late."

"Yes, of course, my dear. All right, Devlin. See you tomorrow."

Devlin waited until they'd gone out of the front door before moving into the sitting room. He watched Sir Henry drive away and was lighting a cigarette when Joanna returned. "Tell me," he said. "Are he and Churchill supposed to be friends?"

"As I understand it, they've never met. Studley Grange is famous for its Elizabethan gardens. The Prime Minister fancied the idea of a quiet weekend and a little painting."

"With Sir Henry falling over himself to oblige."

"You're a wicked man, Mr Devlin. Come along to Hobs End."

The rain pushed in on the wind from the sea was cold, and the marsh was shrouded in mist. When Joanna Grey braked her car to a halt in the yard of the old marsh warden's cottage, Devlin got out and looked about him thoughtfully. It was a strange place, the kind that made the hair lift on the back of his head—sea creeks and mud flats, the great pale reeds merging with the mist, and somewhere out there, the occasional cry of a bird. On the very edge of the marsh was a decrepit barn of considerable age.

She opened the front door of the cottage into a flagstoned passageway. There was rising damp, and the whitewash was flaking from the wall. On the left a door opened into a large kitchen-cum-living room with a huge fireplace. Across the room were an iron cookstove and a chipped white sink. A large table flanked by two benches and an old wing chair by the fireplace were the only furniture.

"I've news for you," Devlin said. "I was raised in a cottage exactly like this in County Down. All it needs is a bloody good fire to dry the place out." He opened his Gladstone bag and took out some clothing and three or four books. Then he ran a finger through the bag's lining, found the hidden catch and removed a false bottom, to reveal his Walther, a Sten gun—the silenced version, in three parts—and a pocket-size S-phone receiver and transmitter. There was a thousand pounds in pound notes and another thousand in fivers. "To obtain the vehicles," he said.

"Where from?"

"The Abwehr has given me an address in Birmingham. I thought I'd run over there this weekend. What do I need to know?"

She sat on the edge of the table and watched as he assembled the Sten gun. "It's three hundred miles the round trip, but there's plenty of black-market petrol at three times the normal price."

Devlin checked the Sten, then took it to pieces again and replaced it in the bag. "What about the police or the security forces?"

"Oh, there's nothing to worry about there. The military would only stop you if you tried to enter a restricted area. Technically this still *is* a defence area. The police are entitled to stop you here and ask for your identity card, or on a main road as part of a spot check for misuse of petrol."

She almost sounded indignant, and remembering what he had

left, Devlin had to fight a compulsion to open her eyes. But he said, "So I shouldn't have any trouble?"

"No one's stopped me." She shrugged. "Your medical discharge papers should be enough. Everybody has a soft spot for a hero."

Devlin grinned. "Mrs Grey, I think we'll get on famously." He went and rummaged in the cupboard under the sink and returned with a rusty hammer and a nail. "The very thing." He drove the nail into the back of the smoke-blackened beam which supported the mantel, and hung the Walther up by its trigger guard. "What I call my ace in the hole."

She smiled. "Now, I'll show you the drop zone."

As they walked along the dyke road, some wild geese flew out of the mist in formation like a bombing squadron. They reached the warning DANGER—MINES. Joanna tossed a stone out over the sands, and Patch bounded through the wire to retrieve it.

"You're sure?" Devlin said.

"Absolutely."

He grinned crookedly. "I'm a Catholic. Remember that if it goes wrong."

"They all are here. I'll see you're put down properly."

He looked across the creeks and the sandbanks towards the Point. "Beautiful. The thought of leaving all this must break your heart."

"Leave? What do you mean?"

"But you can't stay. Not afterwards. Surely you must see that?"

She looked out to the Point as if for the last time, and shivered as the wind drove rain in off the sea.

DEVLIN OBTAINED a driving licence in Holt the next morning, along with his other documents, without the slightest difficulty. That afternoon he rode the motorcycle back from Studley Grange. It was a 350cc Norton that had seen better days, but when he opened the throttle wide on the straights, the needle swung up to sixty miles per hour with no trouble at all. He came down the steep hill into the village past the old mill, and slowed for a young girl with a pony and trap carrying three milk cans. She wore a blue beret and a very old trench coat two sizes too big for her. She had high cheekbones, large eyes, a mouth that was too wide, and three of her fingers poked through holes in her woollen gloves.

"Good day to you, colleen," he said cheerfully as he waited for her to cross his path to the bridge. "God save the good work."

Her eyes widened in a kind of astonishment. Then she clicked her tongue, urging the pony over the bridge.

"A lovely, ugly little peasant," he quoted softly, " 'who turned my head not once, but twice.' Oh no, Liam, me old love. Not now." He swung in towards the Studley Arms and became aware of a man glaring at him through the window. An enormous individual of thirty or so with a tangled black beard.

And what in the hell have I done to you, son? Devlin thought. The man's gaze travelled to the girl and the trap just breasting the hill by the church. It was enough. Devlin pushed the Norton onto its stand, unstrapped Sir Henry's shotgun in its canvas bag hanging around his neck, tucked it under his arm and went in.

There were only three people in the large, comfortable room. "God bless all here," Devlin announced. He put the canvas bag on the table.

A short, stocky man in shirt sleeves, who looked to be in his late twenties, smiled. "I'm George Wilde, the publican, and you'll be Sir Henry's new warden. We've heard all about you. You know how it is in the country."

"Or does he?" the big man at the window said harshly.

Wilde looked troubled, but attempted an introduction. "Arthur Seymour, and the old goat by the fire is Laker Armsby."

Laker was in his late forties, Devlin discovered later, but looked older. He was incredibly shabby.

"Would you gentlemen join me in a drink?" Devlin suggested.

"I wouldn't say no," Laker Armsby said. "A pint of brown ale."

Seymour drained his flagon and banged it down on the table. "I buys my own." He picked up the shotgun and hefted it in one hand. "The squire's really looking after you, isn't he? This and the bike.

Now I wonder why you should rate that, an incomer like you, when there's those amongst us who've worked the estate for years and still must be content with less."

"I can only put it down to my good looks," Devlin told him.

Madness sparked in Seymour's eyes. He held Devlin by the front of the coat. "Don't ever make fun of me, little man."

Wilde grabbed his arm. "Come on, Arthur," but Seymour pushed him away.

"You keep your place and we might get on. Understand me?"

Devlin smiled anxiously. "If I've given offence, I'm sorry."

"That's better." Seymour released his grip. "Only in future, remember one thing. When I come in you leave."

He went out, the door banged behind him and Laker Armsby cackled wildly. "He's bad, is Arthur."

George Wilde vanished into the back room and returned with a bottle of Scotch and some glasses. "This stuff's hard to come by, but I reckon you've earned one on me, Mr Devlin."

"Liam," Devlin said. "Call me Liam." He accepted the glass of whisky. "Is he always like that?"

"Ever since I've known him."

"There was a girl outside in a pony trap as I came in. Does he have some special interest there?"

"Fancies his chances." Laker Armsby chuckled. "Only she won't have any of it."

"That's Molly Prior," Wilde said. "She and her mother have a farm this side of Hobs End. Been running it between them since her father died last year. Laker gives them a few hours when he isn't busy at the church. Seymour does a bit for them as well."

"And thinks he owns the place? Why isn't he in the army?"

"They turned him down because of a perforated eardrum."

"Which he took as an insult to his great manhood, I suppose?"

Wilde said awkwardly, as if he felt some explanation was necessary, "I picked up a packet myself with the Royal Artillery at Narvik in April 1940. Lost my right kneecap, so it was a short war for me. You got yours in France, Mrs Grey says."

"That's right," Devlin said calmly. "Near Arras."

Laker Armsby said, "Now me, I copped my first packet on the Somme in 1916. With the Welsh Guards, I was."

"Oh, no." Devlin slapped a shilling down on the table and winked at Wilde. "Give him a pint, but I'm off. Got work to do."

WHEN HE reached the coast road, Devlin took the first dyke path at the northerly end of Hobs End marsh and drove out towards the fringe of pine trees. He opened the throttle—a hell of a risk, for one wrong move and he'd be in the marsh—but he felt exhilarated.

He throttled back to turn into another path, working his way towards the coast, when a horse and rider suddenly appeared on top of the dyke from the reeds, thirty yards to his right. It was Molly Prior. As he slowed she leaned low over the horse's neck and urged it into a gallop, racing him on a parallel course.

Devlin responded instantly, surging forward in a burst of speed, kicking dirt out in a great spray behind him. The girl had an advantage in that the dyke she was on ran straight, whereas Devlin had to work his way through a maze of paths.

She was close to the trees now, and as he skidded broadside, then found a clear run, she plunged her mount into the marsh for a final shortcut and disappeared into the pines.

Devlin left the dyke at top speed, shot up the side of a sand dune, travelled some little distance through the air and alighted in soft white sand, going down on one knee in a long slide.

Molly Prior was sitting at the foot of a pine tree, gazing out to sea, an elbow propped on her knee. She had taken off the beret, exposing short-cropped tawny hair. The horse grazed on a tuft of grass that pushed up through the sand. Devlin got the bike up on its stand and threw himself down beside her. "A fine day, thanks be to God."

She turned and said calmly, "What kept you?"

Devlin had taken off his cap to wipe sweat from his forehead. "What kept me, is it? Why, you little—"

Then she threw back her head and laughed. Devlin laughed,

too. He put a cigarette in his mouth. "Do you use these things?"

"No."

"Good for you. They'd stunt your growth."

"I'm seventeen, I'll have you know. I'll be eighteen at the end of February."

Devlin put a match to his cigarette and lay back, pillowing his head on his hands, the peak of his cap over his eyes. "Ah, a little fish, is it? Pisces. We should do well together, me being a Leo. You should never marry a Virgo, by the way. Take Arthur, now. I've a terrible hunch he's a Virgo."

"You mean Arthur Seymour?" she said. "Are you crazy?" Her eyes flashed; and then she saw his lips quiver, and leaned down to peer under the peak of the cap. "Why are you laughing at me?" She pulled off his cap and threw it away.

"And what else would I do with you, Molly Prior?" He put out a hand defensively. "No, don't answer that."

She sat back against the tree, her hands in her coat pockets. "How did you know my name?"

"George Wilde told me at the pub."

"Oh, I see now. And Arthur—was he there?"

"You could say that. I get the impression he looks upon you as his personal property."

"I belong to no man," she said, suddenly fierce.

He looked up at her from where he lay, the cigarette hanging from the corner of his mouth, and smiled. "Your nose turns up, and when you're angry your mouth goes down at the corners."

He had gone too far, touched some source of inner hurt. She flushed and said bitterly, "Oh, I'm ugly enough, Mr Devlin. I've sat all night long at dances in Holt without being asked—too often not to know my place. But you wouldn't throw me out on a wet Saturday night, I know. Anything's better than nothing."

She started to get up. Devlin had her by the ankle and dragged her down. "You know my name? How's that?"

"Don't let it go to your head. Everybody knows about you."

"I've news for you," he said, pushing himself up on one elbow and leaning over her. "You don't know the first thing about me, because if you did, you'd know I prefer fine autumn afternoons under the pine trees to wet Saturday nights." She went very still. He kissed her briefly on the mouth and rolled away. "Now get the hell out of here before my mad passion runs away with me."

She grabbed her beret, jumped to her feet and reached for the horse's bridle. She scrambled into the saddle and pulled her mount around to look at him. "I'll be at Mass, Sunday evening. Will you?"

"Do I look as though I will?"

The horse was turning in half circles, but she held it well. "Yes," she said, "I think you do," and she galloped away.

"Oh, you idiot, Liam," Devlin said softly as he pushed his motor-cycle off its stand. "Won't you ever learn?"

In Birmingham a cold wind drifted across the city, hurling rain against the window of Ben Garvald's flat. In the silk dressing gown and with the dark curly hair carefully combed, he made an imposing figure; the broken nose added a sort of rugged grandeur. A closer inspection was not so flattering, the fruits of dissipation showing clearly on the fleshy, arrogant face.

This morning he faced a considerable annoyance. The previous night one of his business ventures, a small gambling club, had been raided. Garvald was not in any danger of being arrested—that was what the front man was paid for—but three thousand pounds on the tables had been confiscated by the police.

The kitchen door swung open and Ben's younger brother, Reuben, entered. He was small and sickly-looking, one shoulder slightly higher than the other, but the black eyes in the pale face were constantly on the move, missing nothing. "There's a cheeky little mick just came in on a motorcycle." Reuben held out half of a five-pound note. "Told me to give you that. Said you could have the other half if you'd see him."

Garvald laughed quite spontaneously and plucked the torn bank note from his brother's hand. "Let's see if he's got any more."

Reuben went out, and Garvald crossed to a sideboard and

poured himself a glass of Scotch, then settled himself in an easy chair by the window.

The door opened and Reuben ushered Devlin into the room. He was wet through, his trench coat saturated.

"Take that coat off. You'll ruin the bloody Axminster carpet," Garvald said.

Devlin removed his dripping coat and handed it to Reuben, who looked annoyed but draped it over a chair by the window. "All right, sweetheart," Garvald said. "What's the name?"

"Murphy, Mr Garvald," Devlin told him. "As in spuds."

"My time's limited," Garvald said, "so let's get to it."

Devlin rubbed his hands dry on his jacket and took out a pack of cigarettes. "They tell me you're in the transport business," he said. "I need a Bedford truck. Army type."

"Is that all?" Garvald smiled, but his eyes were watchful.

"No, I also want a jeep, a compressor, plus spray equipment and a couple of gallons of khaki-green paint."

Garvald laughed out loud. "What are you going to do, start the second front on your own or something?"

Devlin took out a large envelope. "There's five hundred quid on account in here, just so you know I'm not wasting your time."

Garvald nodded to his brother, who took the envelope and checked its contents. "He's right, Ben." He handed the money over.

Garvald dropped it on the coffee table in front of him and leaned back. "All right, who are you working for?"

"Me," Devlin said.

Garvald showed he didn't believe it, but he didn't argue the point. "You must have something good lined up to be going to all this trouble. Maybe you could do with a little help."

"I've told you what I need, Mr Garvald," Devlin said. "If you don't think you can get it, I can always try elsewhere."

Reuben said angrily, "Who the hell do you think you are? Walking in here's one thing. Walking out again isn't so easy."

When Devlin looked at Reuben, the blue eyes seemed to be remote. "Is that a fact now?"

He reached for the bundle of fivers, his left hand in his pocket on the butt of the Walther.

"It'll cost you," Ben Garvald said softly. "A nice, round figure. Let's say two thousand quid."

He held Devlin's gaze. There was a pause and Devlin smiled. "Throw in fifty gallons of petrol in army jerrycans and you're on."

Garvald held out his hand. "Done. We'll have a drink on it. What's your pleasure?"

"Irish, if you've got it. Bushmills for preference."

"I got everything, boy. Anything and everything." He snapped his fingers. Reuben hesitated, his face set and angry, and Garvald said in a low, dangerous voice, "The Bushmills, Reuben." His brother went over to the sideboard and opened it.

"Where do you want to take delivery?" Garvald asked.

"Somewhere near Peterborough on the A1 highway," Devlin said.

Reuben handed him a glass. "You're bloody choosy."

Garvald cut in. "No, that's all right. You know Norman Cross? That's about five miles out of Peterborough. There's a garage called Fogarty's a couple of miles down the road. It's closed at the moment."

"I'll find it," Devlin said. "I'll take the truck, the compressor and the jerrycans on the night of Thursday the twenty-eighth, and the jeep on the next night. After dark. Say about nine."

"And the cash?"

"You keep that five hundred on account. Seven fifty when I take delivery of the truck, the same for the jeep, and I want military papers for both."

"That's easy enough," Garvald said. "But they'll need filling in with purpose and destination."

"I'll see to that myself when I get them."

Garvald nodded slowly. "Okay, you're on."

Devlin pulled on the wet trench coat and buttoned it quickly.

Garvald went to the sideboard and came back with the freshly opened bottle of Bushmills. "Have that on me."

"Thanks," Devlin said. "A little something in return." He produced the other half of the five-pound note. "Yours, I believe."

Garvald took it and grinned. "You've got the cheek of the devil, Murphy. We'll see you on the twenty-eighth."

Devlin turned at the door as Garvald sat down. "One more thing, Mr Garvald. I keep my word. See that you do." He left.

Garvald finished his Scotch. Then he went to the window and looked down into the yard as Devlin kicked the engine of his motorcycle into life and rode away. Reuben said, "What's got into you, Ben? You let that little mick walk all over you."

"He's on to something juicy, Reuben boy," Garvald said softly. "And whatever it is, I'm in, whether he likes it or not."

IT WAS HALF past four when Devlin rode down through the village past the Studley Arms. As he went over the bridge he could hear the organ playing, and lights showed dimly at the church windows, for it was not yet dark. Joanna Grey had told him that evening Mass was held in the afternoon to avoid the blackout. He pulled up outside the church. Molly Prior was there, he knew, because the pony stood patiently in the shafts of the trap, its nose in a feed bag. There were two cars and several bicycles parked also.

When Devlin opened the door, Father Vereker, in a faded rose cope, was on his way down the centre aisle sprinkling the heads of the congregation, washing them clean. *"Asperges me,"* he intoned, and Devlin slipped down the right-hand aisle and found a pew.

There were no more than seventeen or eighteen people in the congregation, including Sir Henry and a woman—who was presumably his wife. Molly was across the aisle with her mother, a pleasant, middle-aged woman with a kind face. Molly wore a straw hat decorated with fake flowers, the brim tilted over her eyes, and a flowered cotton dress. She turned suddenly and saw him. She looked at him for a second or so, then glanced away.

When later she went down on her knees on the hassock, she seemed to descend in slow motion, lifting her skirt perhaps six inches too high. Devlin had to choke back his laughter, but he sobered soon enough when he saw Arthur Seymour glaring at her.

When the service was over, Devlin was first out. He was astride the motorcycle when he heard her call, "Mr Devlin, just a minute." She hurried towards him, her mother a few yards behind her. "Don't be in such a rush to be off," Molly said. "This is my mum. We thought you might like to come back and have tea with us."

Beyond them he saw Arthur Seymour, glowering by the gate. Devlin said, "It's very nice of you, but I'm in no fit state."

Mrs Prior reached out to touch him. "Lord bless us, boy, but you're soaking. Get you home and into a hot bath."

"She's right," Molly told him fiercely.

Devlin kicked the starter. "God protect me from this monstrous regiment of women," he said, and rode away.

THE BATH was an impossibility. It would have taken too long to heat the copper kettle on the iron cookstove. He compromised by lighting an enormous log fire on the huge stone hearth; then he stripped, towelled himself briskly and dressed again. Taking a glass, Garvald's bottle of Bushmills and a book, he sat in the old wing chair and was roasting his feet by the fire when a cold wind touched the back of his neck briefly.

"What kept you?" he said, without turning around.

"Very clever. I'd have thought you could have done better than that after I've walked a mile and a quarter over wet fields in the dark to bring you your supper." She moved to the fire. She was wearing her trench coat, Wellingtons and a head scarf, and carried a basket. "A meat-and-potato pie, but I suppose you've eaten?"

He groaned. "Don't go on. Just get it in the oven."

She put the basket down, unfastened the trench coat and pulled off her boots, then the scarf. She shook out her hair. "That's better. What are you reading?"

He handed her the book. "Poetry," he said, "by a blind Irishman called Raftery who lived a long time ago."

She sat at his feet, her hand touching his arm, and peered at the page in the firelight. "It's in a foreign language."

"Irish," he said. "The language of kings." He took the book from her, read a few lines, and then translated them.

"Now, in the springtime, the day's getting longer,
On the feastday of Bridget, up my sail will go,
Since my journey's decided, my step will get stronger,
Till once more I stand in the plains of Mayo . . ."

"That's beautiful," she said. "Really beautiful."

Devlin suddenly caught hold of her hair at the back. "Jesus, Mary and Joseph aid me. Girl dear, if you don't get that pie into the oven this instant, I won't be responsible."

She laughed suddenly, leaning over for a moment, her head on his knee. "Oh, I do like you," she said. "Do you know that? From the first moment I saw you, Mr Devlin, sir, I liked you."

He groaned, closing his eyes, and she got to her feet and put his pie in the oven.

WHEN HE walked her home over the fields the clouds had blown away, leaving a sky glowing with stars. He had the shotgun over his shoulder, and she hung on to his left arm. They reached the farm-yard wall and she paused beside the gate. "I was wondering. Wednesday afternoon, if you've nothing planned, I could do with some help in the barn. You could have dinner with us."

"Why not?" he said. She reached a hand up behind his neck, pulling his face down with a fierce urgency. He said into her ear gently, "You're seventeen and I'm a very old thirty-five." He kissed her very lightly on the mouth. "Go in!"

She went without protest, and Devlin started back. He skirted the last meadow above the main road and crossed to the dyke path opposite the old wooden sign, HOBS END FARM. Suddenly there was a rustling in the reeds and Arthur Seymour bounded into his path. "I warned you," he said.

Devlin had the shotgun off his shoulder in a second and rammed the barrel under Seymour's chin. "Now you be careful," he said.

"Because I've licence to shoot vermin from the squire himself."

Seymour jumped back. "I'll get you, see if I don't. I'll pay you both out." He turned and ran into the night.

Devlin shouldered his gun. He wasn't worried by Seymour's threats, but then he thought of Molly and his stomach went hollow. "My God," he said softly. "If he harms her, I'll kill him."

CHAPTER 6

LANDSVOORT WAS a desolate little place about twenty miles north of Amsterdam between Schagen and the sea. There was an old farmhouse and barn, a hangar roofed with rusted corrugated iron, and a single runway of crumbling concrete.

On the morning of Wednesday, 20 October, Staff Sergeant Willi Scheid, from the ordnance depot at Hamburg, was demonstrating the Sten submachine-gun to Steiner and his men on the improvised firing range among the sand dunes. The MK IIS version was specially developed by the British for use by commando units, and was fitted with a silencer. It was an eerie experience to see the bullets shredding the targets at the far end of the range, five life-size replicas of charging Tommies, and to hear only the clicking of the bolt.

Scheid moved across to a groundsheet on which various weapons were displayed. "The Sten will be the main machine-gun you use. And you'll also have the Bren guns."

"What about rifles?" Steiner asked.

Before Scheid could reply, Neumann tapped Steiner on the shoulder. A Stork spotter plane was coming in low for a landing. The two men hurried to the field car, which was parked nearby, and drove to the airstrip.

Steiner lit a cigarette as they waited for Radl to disembark from the Stork. Neumann said, "He's got someone with him."

Max Radl came towards Steiner, a cheerful smile on his face. "Kurt, how goes it?"

But Steiner was looking at his companion, the tall, elegant young man with the death's-head of the SS on his cap. "Who's your friend, Max?" he asked softly.

Radl's smile was awkward. "Colonel Kurt Steiner, Untersturm-führer Harvey Preston of the British Free Corps."

THE LIVING ROOM of the old farmhouse had been converted into the nerve centre for the entire operation. Two large tables were covered with maps and photographs of the Hobs End and Studley Constable area. Radl leaned over them with interest. Neumann stood on the other side of the tables, and Steiner paced up and down by the window. He turned impatiently. "Max, do you seriously expect me to take that—that object out there?"

"It's the Reichsführer's idea, not mine," Radl said mildly. "In matters like this, my dear Kurt, I take orders, not give them."

"But he must be mad. How on earth does he expect those lads of mine to function with an outsider at this stage, especially one like Preston?" He picked up the file Radl had given him and shook it, "A petty criminal, a poseur." He threw the file down in disgust. "He doesn't even know what real soldiering is."

"He's never jumped out of an airplane," Neumann put in. "No less than six jumps go into the paratroopers' qualification badge and after that, never less than six a year if he wants to keep it."

"Very impressive," Radl said. "On the other hand, Preston has to jump only once onto what you have admitted is a perfect drop zone. I would have thought it not beyond the bounds of possibility to train him sufficiently for that single occasion."

Neumann turned in despair to Steiner. "What more can we say?"

"Nothing," Radl said, "because he goes. He goes because the Reichsführer thinks it a good idea."

"Not Preston," Steiner said. "It's impossible."

"I'm returning to Berlin in the morning," Radl replied. "Come with me and tell him yourself, if that's how you feel."

Steiner's face was pale. "You know I can't and you know why."

"Then you'll take him?" Radl said.

"Oh, I'll take him all right," Steiner said. "Only by the time I've finished, he'll wish he'd never been born." He turned to Neumann. "All right. Bring him in."

WHEN HARVEY PRESTON was in repertory he'd once played a gallant British officer in *Journey's End*. A brave, war-weary young veteran, old beyond his years, he had been able to meet death with a wry smile. When the curtain fell you simply picked yourself up and went back to the dressing room to wash the blood off.

But now this was actually happening, and suddenly he was sick with fear. It was cold in the overgrown garden and he paced up and down, smoking a cigarette. Suddenly Neumann appeared at the farmhouse door. "Preston!" he called. "Get in here."

Preston found Steiner, Radl and Neumann grouped around the map table. "Herr Oberst," he began. "I've never made a jump—"

"The least of your deficiencies," Steiner told him grimly.

"Herr Oberst, I—must protest—" Preston stammered, and Steiner cut in on him like an axe falling.

"Shut up! In future you speak when you're spoken to and not before." Preston was now standing rigidly at attention. "All you are at the moment is excess baggage, just a pretty uniform. We'll have to change that, won't we?"

Preston said hurriedly, "Yes, Herr Oberst."

"Good. We understand each other. Lieutenant Neumann will see that you're provided with parachutists' coveralls and jump smock. You'll therefore be indistinguishable from your comrades with whom you will be training. In your case, additional work will be necessary, but we'll come to that later. Any questions?"

In a choked whisper Preston said, "No questions."

"Good." Steiner turned to Neumann. "Hand him over to Brandt." He nodded to Preston. "All right, you're dismissed."

IN HER small bedroom in the farmhouse near Hobs End, Molly Prior was trying to make herself presentable for Devlin, due to arrive for his midday dinner at any moment. She had rolled on her only pair of silk stockings, each one darned many times, and she was just pulling the cotton dress that she had worn on Sunday over her head when there was the sound of a car. She peered out of the window in time to see Father Vereker drive into the farmyard in his old Morris.

As she went downstairs she ran a comb through her tangled hair. Vereker was in the kitchen with her mother, and he turned and greeted her with what for him was a surprisingly warm smile.

"Hello, Molly. How are you?"

"Hard pressed and hard worked, Father. Was it me you wanted?"

"No, it was Arthur I wanted a word with. Arthur Seymour. He helps you up here Tuesdays and Wednesdays, doesn't he?"

"Arthur Seymour doesn't work here anymore, Father. Didn't he tell you I sacked him?"

Vereker avoided a direct answer. He said, "Why was that, Molly?"

"Because I didn't want him around here anymore."

"The feeling in the village is that he's been hard done to. You should have a better reason than preference for an outsider. Hard on a man who's helped—"

"Man. Is that what he is, Father? I never realised. You could tell 'em he was always sticking his hand up my skirt." She looked at Vereker with contempt. "Don't tell me you don't know, Father. You must confess him often enough."

At a knock on the door she turned from the furious anger in his eyes, smoothing her dress over her hips. But it wasn't Devlin. It was Laker Armsby who stood there beside the tractor with which he'd just towed in a trailer loaded with of turnips.

He grinned. "Where you want this lot then, Molly?"

"In the barn, Laker. Here, I'd better show you myself."

She and Laker went across the yard, and Laker opened one of the great barn doors. Seymour was standing inside, his cap pulled low over the mad eyes, the massive shoulders straining the seams of his coat. "Now then, Arthur," Laker said warily.

Seymour shoved him backward into the mud and grabbed Molly by the wrist. "You get in here. I want words with you."

Molly kicked out furiously. "You let me go!"

"Oh, no." He pushed the door closed, shot the bolt and grabbed for her hair with his left hand. "Now you be a good girl and I won't hurt you."

His fingers were groping for the hem of her skirt when she leaned down and bit his wrist savagely. He cried out in pain, releasing his grip, but clutched at her with his other hand as she turned, dress tearing, and ran for the ladder to the loft.

DEVLIN, ON his way from Hobs End, reached the crest of the meadow above the farm in time to see Molly and Laker Armsby crossing the farmyard to the barn. A moment later Laker was propelled from the barn, to fall flat on his back, and the great door slammed. Devlin went down the hill on the run.

By the time he was vaulting the fence into the farmyard, Father Vereker and Mrs Prior were at the barn. The priest hammered on the door with his stick. "Arthur?" he shouted. "Open the door!"

The only reply was a scream from Molly. Devlin tried a shoulder and then glanced about him desperately as Molly cried out again. His eyes lit on the tractor where Laker had left it, engine running. Devlin scrambled up into the high seat and rammed the stick into gear, accelerating so savagely that the tractor shot forward, trailer swaying, turnips scattering across the yard like cannonballs. Vereker, Mrs Prior and Laker got out of the way just in time as the tractor burst the doors inward.

Devlin braked to a halt. Molly was up in the loft, Seymour down below trying to reposition the ladder, which she had obviously thrown down. Devlin switched off the engine, and Seymour gave a cry of rage and rushed at him, great hands outstretched to destroy. Devlin feinted with his right and smashed his left fist into the ugly mouth. He followed with a right under the ribs. Then he ducked in below Seymour's next wild punch and hit him under the ribs again, just as Father Vereker limped into the barn. "Footwork, timing and hitting, Father. Learn those and ye shall inherit the earth as surely as the meek. Always helped out by a little dirty work, of course."

He kicked Seymour under the right kneecap and, as the big man doubled over, put a knee into the descending face, lifting him through the door into the mud of the yard. As Devlin advanced, Seymour got to his feet and delivered a stunning blow to Devlin's forehead. He tried to rush him again, but Devlin circled, driving him relentlessly across the yard towards an old zinc water trough.

"And now you will listen to me!" Devlin said. "Never touch that girl again. Do you understand?" He punched under the ribs again and Seymour groaned. "And in future, if you are in a room and I enter, you get up and walk out. Do you understand that, too?" His right connected with the unprotected jaw, and Seymour fell across the trough and rolled onto his back.

Devlin dropped to his knees and pushed his face into the rain-water in the trough. He surfaced to find Molly crouched beside him, and Father Vereker bending over Seymour. "My God, Devlin, you might have killed him."

"Not that one," Devlin said. "Unfortunately."

As if anxious to prove him right, Seymour tried to sit up. Laker Armsby dipped an old enamel bucket into the trough and emptied it over Seymour. "There you go, Arthur," he said cheerfully. "First bath you've had since Michaelmas, I daresay."

Seymour groaned again. Father Vereker said, "Help me, Laker," and they took him between them across to the Morris.

Suddenly the earth moved for Devlin, like the sea turning over. He closed his eyes. He was aware of Molly's cry of alarm, her strong young shoulder under his arm, and then her mother was on the other side and they were walking him towards the house.

He found himself in the kitchen chair by the fire, his face against Molly's breast while she held a damp cloth to his forehead. "I'm fine," he told her.

She looked down at him, face anxious. "God, but I thought he'd split your skull with that one punch."

A few minutes later Molly's mother bustled into the kitchen, fastening a clean apron about her waist. "You must have a power-ful hunger on you, boy, after that little bout. Are you ready for your meat-and-potato pie now, then?"

Devlin looked up at Molly and smiled. "Thank you kindly, ma'am. I think I could say with some truth that I'm ready for anything."

It was late evening when Devlin returned to Hobs End. The sky was dark and thunder rumbled uneasily on the far horizon. He took the long way around to check the dyke gates, and when he finally turned into the yard Joanna Grey's car was parked by the door. She was wearing her green WVS uniform and leaning on the wall look-ing out to sea, Patch sitting beside her patiently.

She turned to look at Devlin as he joined her. There was a size-able bruise on his forehead where Seymour's fist had landed. "Nasty," she said. "Do you try to commit suicide often?"

He grinned. "You should see the other fella."

"I have." She shook her head. "It's got to stop, Liam."

He lit a cigarette, match flaring in cupped hands. "What has?"

"Molly. You're not here for that. You've got a job to do."

"Come off it," he said. "I haven't a thing to lay hand to before my meeting with Garvald on the twenty-eighth."

"People in places like this distrust strangers. They don't like what you did to Arthur Seymour. We can't afford to alienate them, so be sensible and leave Molly alone."

"Is that an order, ma'am?"

"Don't be an idiot. I'm appealing to your good sense."

When she had driven away, Devlin unlocked the door and let himself in. He lit a small fire and stood at the window, feeling sud-denly lonelier than he had ever felt in his life before.

On Sunday morning, 24 October, at Landsvoort, Steiner arranged for a demonstration of the standard British parachute in the old barn at the back of the farmhouse. After Steiner's opening remarks Brandt came forward, picked up a parachute pack and held it aloft. Neumann said, "X Type parachute used by British airborne forces and, as the Herr Oberst says, very different from ours." Sergeant Major Brandt pulled the rip cord; the pack opened, disgorging the khaki chute. "Note the way the shroud lines are fastened to the harness by shoulder straps, instead of directly to the pack."

"The point being," Steiner put in, "that you can manipulate the chute, change direction, have the kind of control that you just don't get with the one you're used to."

Neumann nodded, and Brandt said, "Let's have you all down here." There was a loft fifteen feet high at the end of the barn. A rope had been looped over a beam above it, an X Type parachute harness fastened to one end. Brandt announced, "You jump off the loft and there'll be half a dozen of us on the other end to make sure you don't hit the dirt too hard. Who's first?"

Steiner said, "I'd better claim that honour."

Neumann helped him into the harness; then Brandt and four others got on the rope and hauled him up to the loft. He paused on the edge, Neumann signalled and Steiner swung into space. The other end of the rope went up, taking three of the men with it, but Brandt and Sergeant Sturm hung on, cursing. Steiner hit the dirt, rolled over in a perfect fall and sprang to his feet. "All right. Usual formation. I've time to see everyone do it once."

He moved to the rear of the group as Neumann buckled himself into the harness. A minute later there was a roar of laughter when Neumann ended up flat on his back. Brandt went next, then the rest, with varying success. Finally it was Preston's turn.

Steiner nodded. "Up with him." The Englishman was very pale.

The five men hauled with a will, and Preston shot up until he stood on the edge of the loft, gazing down wildly. "All right, English," Brandt called. "Jump when I signal."

He turned to instruct the men on the rope, and there was a cry of alarm as Preston fell forward. Neumann jumped for the rope. Preston came to rest three feet above the ground, swinging like a pendulum, arms hanging at his side, head down.

Brandt put a hand under the chin and looked into the Englishman's face. "He's fainted. What do we do with him, Herr Oberst?"

"Bring him round," Steiner said calmly. "Then put him up again. As many times as it takes until he can do it satisfactorily, or breaks a leg." He saluted. "Carry on, please." Then he turned and went out.

WHEN DEVLIN went into the church that Sunday, Mass was almost over. Molly was on her knees beside her mother. Arthur Seymour was present also, and when he saw Devlin he simply got to his feet, slipped down the aisle in the shadows and went out.

Devlin waited, watching Molly at prayer, all innocence, kneeling there in the candlelight. After a while she turned very slowly, as if physically aware of his presence. Her eyes widened. She looked at him for a long moment, then turned away again.

Devlin left just before the end of the service. It was raining heavily by the time he reached the cottage, so he put the motor-cycle in the barn, changed into waders and an oilskin coat and got his shotgun. The dyke gates needed checking in such heavy rain, and trudging around would take his mind off things.

It didn't work. He couldn't get Molly out of his thoughts. "If this is what love is really like, Liam my boy," he said softly, "you've taken one hell of a long time finding out about it."

As he came back along the main dyke towards the cottage, woodsmoke was heavy on the damp air, and when he opened the door he could smell cooking. He put the shotgun in the corner, hung the oilskin coat up to dry and went into the living room.

She was on one knee at the fire, putting on another log. She turned to look over her shoulder gravely. "You'll be wet through."

"Half an hour in front of that fire and I'll be fine."

"Irish stew on the go. That all right?"

"Fine."

"What went wrong, Liam? Why have you been keeping away?"

He sat down in the old wing chair. "I thought it best."

"Why?"

"I had my reasons."

She reached out hesitantly and touched his hair. He seized her hand and kissed it. "I love you, you know that?"

She glowed as if a lamp had been switched on inside her. "Well at least I can go to bed now with a clear conscience."

"I'm bad for you, girl dear. There's nothing in it."

"We'll see about that," she said. "I'll get your stew."

LATER, LYING in the old brass bed, an arm about her, watching the patterns on the ceiling from the fire, he felt more at peace than he had for years. There was a radio on a table at her side of the bed. She switched it on. A song was playing.

"When that man is dead and gone . . .
Some fine day the news will flash
Satan with a small moustache
Is asleep beneath the lawn . . ."

"I'll be glad when that happens," she said drowsily.

"What?" he asked.

"Satan with a small moustache asleep beneath the lawn. Hitler. I mean, it'll all be over then, won't it?" She snuggled closer. "What's going to happen to us, Liam? When the war's over?"

"God knows."

He lay there staring at the fire after she was asleep. When the war was over. Which war? He'd been on the barricades one way or another for twelve years now. How could he tell her that? It was a nice little farm, too, and they needed a man. Oh, the pity of it. He held her close, and the wind moaned about the old house, rattling the windows.

AND IN Berlin at Prinz Albrechtstrasse, Himmler sat at his desk methodically working his way through dozens of reports on the SS extermination squads. There was a polite knock at the door and Rossman entered. Himmler looked up. "How did you get on?"

"I'm sorry, Herr Reichsführer, he won't budge. I'm beginning to think he might be innocent after all."

"Not possible. Earlier this evening I received a signed confession from his orderly, who engaged in work prejudicial to state security on Major General Karl Steiner's direct order."

"So what now, Herr Reichsführer?"

"I'd still prefer a signed confession from General Steiner himself. Let's try a little psychology. Clean him up, get an SS doctor to him, plenty of food. You know the drill."

"I'll do as you suggest, Herr Reichsführer," Rossman said.

CHAPTER 7

AT FOUR o'clock on Thursday, 28 October, Joanna Grey drove into the yard of the cottage at Hobs End and found Devlin in the barn working on the motorcycle. "I've been trying to get hold of you all week," she said. "Where have you been?"

"Out and about," he said cheerfully, wiping grease from his hands on a rag. "I've been having a look at the countryside."

"So I've heard. Riding around on that motorcycle with Molly Prior. You were seen in Holt at a dance on Tuesday night."

"A very worthy cause," he said. "Wings for Victory. Actually your friend Vereker turned up and made an impassioned speech about how God would help us crush the bloody Hun."

"I told you to leave Molly alone."

"It didn't work. Anyway, what did you want? I'm busy getting this thing in perfect working order for my run to Peterborough tonight."

"American Rangers have moved into Meltham House," she said.

He frowned. "Meltham House—isn't that the training place?"

"That's right. It's about eight miles up the coast road."

"I see. Should it make any difference, their being here?"

"Not really. It's a factor to be considered, that's all."

"Fair enough. Let Radl know, and there's your duty done."

She got back into her car and drove away, and he returned to his work on the motorcycle. Twenty minutes later Molly rode up out of the marsh, a basket hanging from her saddle. She dismounted and tethered the horse. "I've brought you a shepherd's pie."

"Yours or your mother's?" She threw a stick at him and he ducked. "It'll have to wait. I've got to go out tonight. Put it in the oven for me and I'll heat it up when I get in."

"Can I go with you?"

"Not a chance. It's business." He slapped her behind. "A cup of tea is what I crave, so off with you and put the kettle on."

She grabbed her basket and ran for the cottage. In the living room the Gladstone bag was on the table, and as she passed she caught it with her arm, knocking it to the floor. It fell open, disgorging packets of bank notes and the Sten gun parts.

She knelt there, stunned. There was a step in the doorway and Devlin said quietly, "Put them back, now, like a good girl."

Her voice was fierce. "What does this mean?" She held up a packet of fivers.

"Nothing for little girls." Devlin took the bag from her, stuffed the money and the weapon inside and replaced the bottom. Then he opened the cupboard under the window, took out a large envelope and tossed it to her. "Size ten. Was I right?"

She opened the envelope and there was an immediate look of awe on her face. "Silk stockings. Where did you get these?"

"Oh, a man I met in a pub in Holt."

"The black market, that's what you're in, isn't it?"

There was a certain amount of relief in her eyes, and he grinned. "The right color for me. Now would you kindly hurry with the tea? I want to be away by six and I've still got work on the bike."

She hesitated. "Liam, it's all right, isn't it?"

"And why wouldn't it be?" He kissed her briefly, turned and went out, cursing his own stupidity.

REUBEN GARVALD opened the peephole in the workshop door of Fogarty's garage and peered out. Rain swept across the cracked concrete, where the two rusting petrol pumps stood forlornly.

The garage had once been a bar and was surprisingly spacious.

In spite of a wrecked car in one corner, there was still plenty of room for the Bedford truck and the van in which Garvald and his brother had travelled from Birmingham.

Ben Garvald himself walked up and down impatiently, occasionally beating his arms together. It was bitterly cold. "What a dump," he said. "Isn't there any sign of that little mick?"

"It's only a quarter to nine, Ben," Reuben told him.

"I don't care what time it is." Garvald turned on a large, hefty young man in a sheepskin flight jacket who leaned against the truck, reading a newspaper. "You get me some heat in here tomorrow night, Sammy boy, or I'll send you back to the army."

Sammy, who had long, dark sideburns and a cold, dangerous-looking face, said, "You're a card, Mr Garvald. A real card."

Reuben called from the shop door. "He's just turned in."

Garvald tugged at Sammy's arm. "Open the door."

Devlin entered in a flurry of rain and wind. He wore oilskin leggings with his trench coat and an old leather flying helmet. His face was filthy, and when he pushed up his goggles there were great white circles around his eyes. "A dirty night for it, Mr Garvald," he said as he shoved the Norton on its stand.

"It always is, son." Garvald shook hands warmly. "Nice to see you. This is Sammy Jackson, who drove the Bedford over for you." There was an implication that Jackson had done him a great personal favour.

Devlin responded, putting on the Irish. "Sure and I appreciate that," he said, wringing Sammy's hand.

Garvald said, "Here's your truck. What do you think?"

The Bedford's paintwork had seen better days, but the tyres weren't too bad and the canvas covering was almost new. Devlin noted the army jerrycans, the compressor and the paint. "It's all there." Garvald offered him a cigarette. "Check the petrol, if you want."

"No need. I'll take your word for it." Garvald surely wouldn't try any nonsense at this stage. He wanted him to return the next night. Devlin lifted the hood. The engine seemed sound.

"Try it," Garvald invited. Devlin switched it on and tapped the accelerator, and the engine broke into a healthy roar. He jumped down and noted the truck's military registration.

Garvald snapped a finger. "Give him that form."

Reuben produced it from his wallet and said sullenly, "When do we see the colour of his money?"

"Don't be like that, Reuben. Mr Murphy's as sound as a bell."

"No, he's right enough." Devlin passed a fat envelope to Reuben. "You'll find seven hundred and fifty in there, as agreed."

He pocketed the form Reuben had given him after glancing at it, and Garvald said, "Aren't you going to fill that thing in?"

"And let you see where I'm going? Not bloody likely, Mr Garvald. If someone could give me a hand with my bike, I'll be off."

Garvald nodded to Jackson, who dropped the tailboard of the Bedford and found an old plank. He and Devlin ran the Norton up and laid it on its side, and Devlin clipped the tailboard in place. "That's it then, Mr Garvald. Same time tomorrow."

"Pleasure to do business with you, old son." Garvald beamed, wringing his hand again. "Get the big doors open, Sammy."

Devlin climbed behind the wheel, started the engine and drove out into the night. As soon as Sammy and Reuben got the doors closed, Garvald's smile disappeared. "It's up to Freddy now."

"What if he loses him?" Reuben asked.

Garvald patted him on the face. "Then there's tomorrow night."

DEVLIN, A half mile down the road, was aware of dim lights behind him. A vehicle had pulled out of a lay-by, exactly as he expected, a minute or so earlier as he passed.

An old ruined windmill loomed on his left, with a flat stretch of ground in front of it. He switched off all his lights, drove into the area blind, and braked. The other vehicle continued, increasing its speed, and Devlin jumped to the ground, went to the back of the Bedford and removed the bulb from the taillight. Then he got in, turned the truck onto the road and only switched on his lights when he was driving back towards Norman Cross.

A quarter of a mile before Fogarty's he took a side road, stopping outside Doddington. He replaced the bulb, then got out the form and filled in his destination as the RAF radar station at Sheringham, ten miles beyond Hobs End on the coast road.

It was just after midnight when he reached the cottage and drove inside the barn. There were only a couple of loft windows, and it had been easy to black those out. He lit two oil lamps, checked outside, then went back in and took off his coat.

Within half an hour he had the truck unloaded and washed down. When it was clean he masked the windows with newspapers and tape. Then he put the spraying equipment together and mixed some paint. He started on the tailboard first, taking his time, but within five minutes he had covered it with a glistening new coat of khaki green. He moved around and started on the side panels.

AFTER LUNCH on Friday, Devlin was touching up the numbers on the truck with white paint when he heard Joanna Grey's car arrive. He opened the barn door and led her in. She was obviously impressed. "This looks really good, Liam. Did you have any trouble?"

"He had someone try to follow me, but I soon shook him off. The big confrontation should be tonight."

"Can you handle it?"

"This can." He picked up a cloth bundle lying on a packing case, unwrapped it and took out a Mauser with a strange bulbous barrel. "The SS use them. Only really efficient silenced handgun I've ever come across." He went to the door with her. "If everything goes according to plan, I should be back around midnight."

Her face was tense and anxious. She put out her hand impulsively and he held it tight for a moment. "Don't worry. It'll work. I have the sight, or so my old granny used to say."

"You rogue," she said, and kissed him affectionately on the cheek. "I sometimes wonder how you've survived so long."

"That's because I've never particularly cared whether I do. Tomorrow I'll be round to check with you first thing. You'll see."

In Fogarty's garage it was even colder than it had been on the previous night, in spite of Sammy Jackson's punching holes in an old oil drum and lighting a coke fire. The fumes it gave off were quite something. Ben Garvald, standing beside it, retreated hastily. "What are you trying to do, poison me?"

Jackson, who was sitting on a packing case nursing a sawn-off, double-barreled shotgun across his knees, put it down and stood up. "Sorry, Mr Garvald. It's the coke — too bloody wet."

Reuben, at the peephole, checked his watch. "Just on nine. He should be here any moment."

If they had but known it, Devlin until five minutes earlier had been standing in the rain at the boarded-up rear window. His vision through a crack had been limited, but he'd heard every word. Then he'd worked his way through the yard to the road and back to where he'd left his motorcycle.

Reuben called suddenly, "Here, I think he's coming."

"Get that gun out of the way, Sammy," Garvald said quickly, "and remember, you don't make your move till I tell you."

Sammy put the shotgun under a piece of sacking beside him and hurriedly lit a cigarette. They waited as the sound of the approaching engine grew louder. Reuben turned from the peephole excitedly. "It's definitely him."

"Okay, get the door open," Garvald said.

The wind, when Devlin entered and shoved the motorcycle up on its stand, had the coke crackling like dried wood. Devlin's face was plastered with mud, but when he pushed up his goggles he was smiling cheerfully. "Hello there, Mr Garvald."

"Here we are again," Garvald said.

Devlin looked at the jeep. Like the Bedford, it needed paint badly, but otherwise it was fine. It had a canvas top and a machine-gun mount. The registration, in contrast to the rest of the vehicle, had been freshly painted, and when Devlin looked closely he could see traces of another underneath. "Now, Mr Garvald," he said. "Would some Yank airbase be missing one of these?"

"Look here, you—" Reuben put in angrily.

Devlin cut him off. "Come to think of it, Mr Garvald, there was a moment last night when I thought someone was trying to follow me. Nerves, I suppose. Nothing came of it."

Garvald's anger, contained with considerable difficulty, overflowed now. "You need a lesson in manners, sweetheart," he said.

He started to unbutton his overcoat, and Devlin said, "Is that a fact now? Well, before you start, I'd just like to ask Sammy boy here if that shotgun he's got under the sacking is cocked or not, because if it isn't, he's in big trouble."

In that moment Ben Garvald suddenly knew that he'd just made the worst mistake of his life. "Take him, Sammy!" he cried.

Jackson had already grabbed for the shotgun under the sacking — too late. Devlin's hand was inside his trench coat and out again. The silenced Mauser coughed once; the bullet smashed into Jackson's left arm, turning him in a circle. The second shot shattered his spine. In death his finger tightened convulsively on the shotgun triggers, discharging both barrels into the roof.

The Garvald brothers backed away slowly towards the workshop door. Devlin said, "That's far enough."

Garvald said, "All right, I made a mistake."

"Worse than that, you broke your word," Devlin said. "And where I come from, we have an excellent specific for such people."

"For God's sake, Murphy—"

There was a dull thud as Devlin fired again. The bullet splintered Garvald's right kneecap. He fell with a stifled cry and rolled over, clutching at his knee with both hands.

Reuben crouched, hands raised in futile protection, head down. When he finally had the courage to look up, he discovered Devlin positioning an old plank at the side of the jeep. The Irishman ran the Norton up into the rear. He opened one garage door. Then he snapped his fingers at Reuben. "The papers."

Reuben produced them from his wallet with shaking fingers and handed them over. Devlin checked them, then took out an envelope, which he dropped at Garvald's feet. "Seven hundred and fifty quid. I keep my word. You should try it sometime." He drove off.

LATER THAT night, in a tiny operating room in a nursing home near Birmingham, Ben Garvald lay back on the padded table, eyes closed. Reuben stood beside him while Dr Das, a tall, cadaverous Indian in an immaculate white coat, cut away the trouser leg with surgical scissors.

"Is it bad?" Reuben asked him, his voice shaking.

"Yes, very bad," Das replied calmly. "He needs a first-rate surgeon if he is not to be crippled. There also may be sepsis."

"Listen, you," Ben Garvald said, eyes opening. "It says surgeon on that fancy brass plate of yours, doesn't it?"

"True, Mr Garvald," Das told him calmly. "I have degrees from the universities of Bombay and London, but you need a specialist."

Garvald pushed himself up on one elbow. Sweat was pouring down his face. "You listen to me and listen good. A girl died in here three months ago. What the law would call an illegal operation. I know enough to put you away for seven years at least, so if you don't want the coppers in here, get moving on this leg."

Das seemed unperturbed. "Very well, Mr Garvald, on your own head be it. I'll have to give you an anesthetic."

"Give me anything you bleeding well like, only get on with it." Garvald closed his eyes.

Das opened a cupboard, took out a gauze face mask and a bottle of chloroform.

THE FOLLOWING morning Devlin rode over to Joanna Grey's. He parked his motorcycle and went to the back door. She opened it instantly and drew him inside. She was still in her dressing gown.

"Thank God, Liam." She took his face between her two hands and shook him. "I hardly slept a wink. I've been up since five o'clock drinking whisky and tea alternately. A hell of a mixture at this time in the morning." She kissed him warmly. "You rogue you."

Patch swung his hindquarters frantically from side to side, anxious to be included. Joanna Grey busied herself at the stove and Devlin stood before the fire. "How was it?" she asked.

"All right." He was deliberately noncommittal.

She turned, surprise on her face. "They didn't try anything?"

"Oh, yes," he said. "But one look at my Mauser was enough. They're not used to guns, the English criminal fraternity. Razors are more their style."

She carried the breakfast things on a tray across to the table. "Oh, the English. Sometimes I despair of them."

"I'll drink to that in spite of the hour. Where's the whisky?"

She got the bottle and a couple of glasses. "This is disgraceful at this time of day, but I'll join you. What do we do now?"

"Wait," he said. "I've got the jeep to fix up. You'll need to squeeze old Sir Henry dry right up to the last moment, but other than that, all we can do is bite our nails for the next six days."

"Oh, I don't know," she said. "We can always wish ourselves luck." She raised her glass. "God bless you, Liam, and long life."

"And you, my love."

Suddenly something moved inside Devlin like a knife in his bowels, and he knew the whole thing would go as wrong as it could.

PAMELA VEREKER had a thirty-six-hour pass from the bomber station that weekend, and her brother had driven over to pick her up. At the presbytery she got into jodhpurs and a sweater. Then she cycled six miles along the coast road to Meltham Vale Farm, where the tenant had a stallion in need of exercise.

Once over the dunes behind the farm, she gave the stallion his head and galloped up the track through the tangled gorse towards a wooded ridge. On the crest of the hill there was a pine tree across the track, a windfall no more than three feet high, and the stallion took it in its stride. As it landed on the other side, however, a figure stood up in the undergrowth. The stallion swerved. Pamela Vereker lost her stirrups and was tossed to one side.

She was winded and lay there fighting for breath, aware of American voices. She opened her eyes and saw a ring of soldiers, all heavily armed, in combat jackets and helmets, faces daubed with camouflage cream. Kneeling beside her was a large, rugged master sergeant. "You all right, miss?" he asked anxiously.

She frowned and shook her head, and suddenly felt rather better. "Who are you?"

He touched his helmet in a kind of half salute. "Name's Garvey. Master sergeant. Twenty-first Specialist Raiding Force. We're based at Meltham House for field training."

A jeep arrived at that moment, skidding to a halt, and the driver, a young officer, demanded, "What's going on here?"

"Lady got thrown from her horse, Major Kane," Garvey replied. "Krukowski jumped out of the bushes at the wrong moment."

She scrambled to her feet. "I'm all right, really I am."

She swayed, and Major Harry Kane took her arm. "I don't think so. Do you live far, ma'am?"

"Studley Constable."

He guided her to the jeep. "We've got a medical officer down at Meltham House. I'd like him to make sure you're okay."

The five acres of garden at Meltham House were surrounded by an eight-foot flint wall, with barbed wire at the top. Harry Kane and Pamela strolled towards the small seventeenth-century manor house. He had spent an hour showing her the estate and she had enjoyed every minute of it. "How many of you are there?"

"About ninety. Most of the men are in the camp area I pointed out on the other side of the woods."

As they went up the steps to the terrace, an officer came out through the French windows. He stood facing them, slapping a riding crop against his knee, full of a restless animal vitality. Kane saluted. "Colonel Shafto, allow me to present Miss Vereker."

Robert Shafto was at that time forty-four years of age, a handsome, arrogant-looking man in polished boots and riding breeches. He wore a forage cap and two rows of medal ribbons. Perhaps most extraordinary was the pearl-handled Colt .45 he carried in an open holster on his left hip.

He touched his riding crop to his brow and said gravely, "I was distressed to hear of your accident, Miss Vereker. If I can do anything to make up for the clumsiness of my men ..."

"That's most kind of you," she said. "However, Major Kane here has very kindly offered to run me back to Studley Constable, if you can spare him, that is."

"The least we can do." He saluted again with the riding crop. "And now you must excuse me. I have work to do."

At six o'clock in the evening of the same day, in his private room in the nursing home, Ben Garvald lost consciousness. His condition was not discovered for an hour. It was eight before Dr Das arrived in answer to the nurse's urgent phone call, ten past when Reuben walked in.

He had been back to Fogarty's on Ben's instructions, and the unfortunate Jackson had just been disposed of at a local private crematorium in which the Garvalds had an interest.

Ben's face was bathed in sweat and he groaned, moving from side to side. Reuben caught a glimpse of the knee as Das lifted the dressing. He turned away, fear rising into his mouth like bile. "How bad is it?" he asked.

"Very bad."

Reuben made his decision. "You get an ambulance round here quick. I'm putting him in a hospital."

"But that will mean the police, Mr Garvald," Das pointed out.

"Do you think I care?" Reuben said hoarsely. "I want him alive, understand? He's my brother. Now get moving!"

He opened the door and pushed Das out. When he turned back to the bed there were tears in his eyes. "I promise you one thing, Ben," he said brokenly. "I'll have that little Irish bastard for this if it's the last thing I do."

At the same moment in Landsvoort the Dakota lifted off the runway and turned out to sea. Her pilot was Captain Peter Gericke, recruited from Night Fighter Group 7 on the Dutch coast, where he had recently made his thirty-eighth kill against the RAF. Gericke took the Dakota up to a thousand feet, banked to starboard and dropped towards the coast. Inside, Steiner and his men, dressed in British paratroop gear, prepared for their practice jump.

"All right," Steiner called.

They all stood and clipped their static lines to the anchor-line cable, each man checking the comrade in front of him, Steiner seeing to Harvey Preston, who was last in line. Steiner could feel the Englishman trembling as he tightened his straps for him.

"Fifteen seconds," he said, and walked to the head of the line, where Neumann checked his straps. Steiner slid back the door as the red light blinked above his head, and there was the sudden roaring of wind.

Gericke throttled back and went in low over the beach. The green light flared above Steiner's head and he slapped Neumann on the shoulder. The young Oberleutnant went out, followed by the rest, ending with Brandt. Preston stood there, mouth gaping, staring out into the night.

"Go on!" Steiner grabbed for his shoulder.

Preston pulled away, holding on to a steel strut. He shook his head, mouth working. "Can't!" he finally managed. "Can't do it!"

Steiner grabbed him by the right arm and slung him towards the open door. Preston hung there, bracing himself with both hands. Steiner put a foot in his rear and shoved him out into space. Then he clipped on to the anchor line and went after him.

Preston was aware of himself somersaulting, the sudden jerk, the slap of the chute catching air, and then he was swinging beneath the dark khaki umbrella.

It was fantastic. The moon pale on the horizon, the creamy line of the surf. He could see an E-boat and a row of collapsed parachutes along the beach. He glimpsed Steiner above him, and then seemed to be going in fast. The supply bag, below him, hit the sand with a thump. He went in hard, rolled, and miraculously found himself on his feet, the parachute billowing like a flower.

He moved in quickly to deflate it as he had been taught and suddenly paused on hands and knees, a sense of overwhelming joy, of personal power sweeping through him of a kind he had never known in his life before.

"I did it!" he cried. "I showed them."

CHAPTER 8

AT FORTY-FIVE, Chief Inspector Jack Rogan of the Irish Special Branch at Scotland Yard had been a policeman for nearly a quarter of a century—a long time to work a three-shift system and be disliked by the neighbours. But that was the policeman's lot, as he frequently pointed out to his wife.

It was nine thirty on Tuesday, 2 November, when he entered his office, having spent a lengthy night interrogating members of an Irish club. There was a little paperwork to clear up, and he'd just settled down at his desk when there was a knock at the door and his assistant, Detective Inspector Fergus Grant, entered. Grant was one of the new breed from Hendon Police College. In spite of this, he and Rogan got on well together.

"Sir," Grant said, "we've had a rather unusual report from the Birmingham police. They thought it might interest you."

"All right." Rogan pushed back his chair and started to fill his pipe from a worn leather pouch. "Tell me about it."

"Ever hear of a man called Garvald, sir?"

Rogan paused. "Ben Garvald? He's been bad news for years."

"He died early this morning. Gangrene as the result of a gunshot wound. The hospital got their hands on him too late. He was shot in the right kneecap, by an Irishman."

Rogan stared at him. "That *is* interesting. The statutory IRA punishment for a double cross. What was this Irishman's name?"

"Murphy, sir."

"It would be. Is there more?" Rogan said.

"You could say that," Grant told him. "Garvald has a brother who's so cut up about his death that he's singing like a bird. He wants friend Murphy nailed to the door."

Rogan nodded. "What was it all about?"

Grant told him in some detail, and by the time he had finished,

Rogan was frowning. "An army truck, jeep, and khaki-green paint? What did Garvald's brother make of it?"

"He seemed to think Murphy was organising a raid on a commissary. You know—drive in dressed as soldiers in an army truck."

"And drive out again with fifty thousand quid's worth of Scotch and cigarettes," Rogan said. "I'd accept that if it wasn't for the bullet in the kneecap. That's pure IRA. No, Fergus, I think we could be on to something."

"All right, sir, what's the next move?"

"I'm not having Birmingham botch this up for us," said Rogan. "Book a car from the pool and get up there today. Take the files with you, photos, the lot. Every known IRA man not under wraps. Maybe Garvald can pick him out for us."

"Right, sir," Grant said. "I'll get moving."

IT WAS EIGHT that evening when General Karl Steiner finished dinner in a room on the third floor at Prinz Albrechtstrasse. A chicken leg, potatoes fried just as he liked them, a tossed salad and a half bottle of Riesling served ice-cold. And real coffee.

Things had certainly changed since the final interrogation, when he had collapsed. The following morning he had awakened between clean sheets in a comfortable bed. No sign of Rossman and his Gestapo bullyboys. Just one guard, a decent type, full of apologies. A dreadful mistake had been made. False information had been circulated. The Reichsführer himself had ordered a full inquiry. In the meantime, he regretted that the Herr General had to be kept under lock and key, but this would only be for a few days. He was sure he understood.

Which Steiner did perfectly. All they had ever had against him was innuendo. They were hanging on to him now to make sure he looked good when they released him. The bruises had almost faded. They'd even given him a new uniform.

He poured more coffee. The key rattled in the lock and the door opened. There was an uncanny silence. Rossman stood in the doorway, a Gestapo man on either side of him. "Hello, Herr General," Rossman said. "Did you think we'd forgotten you?"

Something seemed to break inside Steiner. "You bastard!" he said, and threw the cup of coffee at Rossman.

"The cellars," Rossman said simply, and went out.

The two Gestapo men moved in quickly, got an ankle apiece and followed, dragging the general behind them face down.

MAX RADL knocked at the Reichsführer's office and went in. Himmler was drinking coffee at his desk. He put down his cup. "I had hoped that you would have been on your way by now."

"I leave on the overnight flight for Paris," Radl told him. "From there I have a flight for Amsterdam tomorrow morning."

Himmler nodded. "I've read your report. Your Irishman seems to have earned his wages. The rest is up to Steiner."

"I don't think he'll let us down," Radl said. "May I be permitted to inquire after his father's health?"

"I last saw Major General Steiner yesterday evening," Himmler replied with perfect truth, "although I must confess he did not see me. At that time he was working his way through a meal consisting of roasted potatoes, mixed vegetables and a rather large rump steak." He sighed. "If only these meat eaters realised the effect on the system of such a diet. Do you eat meat, Herr Oberst?"

"I'm afraid so."

"And smoke sixty or seventy of those vile Russian cigarettes a day, and drink brandy?" He shook his head as he piled his papers in front of him. "Ah, well, in your case I don't suppose it matters. What time do they leave on Friday?"

"Just before midnight. A one-hour flight, weather permitting."

Himmler looked up instantly, eyes cold. "Colonel Radl, Steiner and his men go in as arranged, weather or no weather. This is not something that can be postponed until another night. From Friday morning you will communicate with me hourly until the operation is successfully concluded."

"I will, Herr Reichsführer."

Radl turned for the door and Himmler said, "One more thing. I have not kept the Führer informed of our progress in this affair for many reasons. The destiny of Germany rests on him. I would like this to be—how can I put it?—a surprise for him."

Radl choked back an insane desire to laugh.

"It is essential that we don't disappoint him," Himmler concluded. Then he flipped up his right arm in a rather negligent party salute. "Heil Hitler!"

Radl, in what he afterwards swore was the bravest action of his life, gave him a punctilious military salute and left.

When he went into his office at the Tirpitz Ufer, Hofer was packing a suitcase for him. "Herr Oberst, I've ordered your car for nine fifteen."

"You know what our esteemed Reichsführer has just let slip, Karl? He hasn't told the Führer how far along we are with this thing. He wants to surprise him."

"Herr Oberst, for God's sake."

Radl opened the desk drawer and took out a sealed envelope. "This is for my wife. See that she gets it."

"Surely the Herr Oberst doesn't think . . ."

"My dear, good Karl," Radl told him. "I think nothing. I simply prepare for any unpleasant eventuality. If this thing goes wrong, your own line should be to deny all knowledge of the affair."

"Herr Oberst, please," Hofer said, tears in his eyes.

IN THE sitting room of Park Cottage, Sir Henry was playing bezique with Father Vereker and Joanna. He had had a considerable amount to drink. "Let me see now, I had a royal marriage—forty points—and now a sequence in trumps. Two ninety altogether."

"Wait," Vereker said. "He's got a ten above the queen."

"But I explained that earlier," Joanna told him. "In bezique, the ten *does* come before the queen."

Philip Vereker shook his head. "I'll never understand this game."

Sir Henry laughed delightedly and jumped up. "Mind if I help myself, Joanna?"

"Of course not, my dear," she said brightly.

"You seem pleased with yourself tonight," Vereker remarked.

Sir Henry, warming his backside in front of the fire, grinned. "I am, Philip, I am, and good cause to be." It all came flowing out of him in a sudden burst. "Don't see why I shouldn't tell you. You'll know soon enough now."

The old fool! Joanna Grey's alarm was genuine as she said hastily, "Henry, do you think you should?"

"Why not?" he asked. "If I can't trust you and Philip, who can I trust?" He turned to Vereker. "Fact is, the Prime Minister is coming to stay the weekend on Saturday."

"Good heavens!" Vereker was astounded. "I didn't realise you knew Mr Churchill, sir."

"I don't," Sir Henry said. "Thing is, he fancied a quiet weekend, painting the gardens at Studley. Downing Street got in touch, and I was only too delighted."

"Naturally," Vereker said.

"Now you must keep it to yourselves, I'm afraid," Sir Henry admonished. "Villagers can't know till he's gone."

Vereker said, "I suppose he'll be quite heavily guarded."

"Not at all," Sir Henry replied. "Wants as little fuss as possible, but I've arranged for a platoon of my Home Guard chaps to guard the perimeter of the Grange while he's there."

"Is that so?" Joanna said.

"Yes. I'm to go up to King's Lynn on Saturday to meet him. We'll come back by car." He belched and put down his glass. "I say, would you excuse me? Don't feel too good."

"Of course," said Joanna.

After he'd gone out of the room, Vereker said, "That's one for the book." He stood up, groping for his stick. "I'd better run him home. He's not fit to drive."

Joanna steered him to the door. "That would mean going for your car. I'll take him." She helped him into his coat.

"If you're sure, then?"

"Of course." She kissed his cheek.

He limped away and she closed the door. Sir Henry reappeared from the cloakroom and weaved an unsteady path to a chair by the fire. "Must go, old girl."

"Nonsense," she said. "Always time for another." She poured two fingers of Scotch into his glass and sat on one arm of the chair. "You know, Henry, I'd love to meet the Prime Minister. I think I'd like that more than anything in the world."

"Would you, old girl?" He gazed up at her foolishly and she smiled back.

IT WAS very quiet that night in the cellars at Prinz Albrechtstrasse as Himmler went down the stairs. Rossman was waiting at the bottom. His sleeves were rolled up and he was very pale. "He's dead, I'm afraid, Herr Reichsführer."

Himmler was not pleased. "Careless of you, Rossman."

"With all due respect, Herr Reichsführer, it was his heart which gave out. Dr Prager has just confirmed it."

Himmler removed his pince-nez and gently rubbed between his eyes. "Very well, Rossman," he said. "He was guilty of treason against the state, of plotting against the life of the Führer himself."

"Of course, Herr Reichsführer." Rossman clicked heels in the party salute as Himmler left.

ON WEDNESDAY morning Fergus Grant laid a card on Chief Inspector Rogan's desk with a photo of Liam Devlin and several different names typed underneath. "That's Murphy, sir."

Rogan whistled softly. "Him? Are you sure?"

"Reuben Garvald is."

Rogan sat still for a moment. "He's one of the few top liners in the movement I've never met. Always the mystery man."

"He was arrested at Kerry in June last year, after a gunfight in which he shot two policemen and was wounded himself," Grant said. "He escaped from the hospital the following day, and the last Special Branch information was that he'd made it to Lisbon."

"And now he's back; but what for?"

IT WAS PRECISELY eleven fifteen on Friday morning at Meltham House when Harry Kane, in answer to an urgent summons, knocked at his colonel's door and went in. Shafto was standing at the window, riding crop in hand. "What is it, sir?"

"Those bastards at Combined Operations who've been trying to get me out of here have finally succeeded. When we finish next weekend, I'm to go back stateside. Instructor at Fort Benning."

Kane said, "Isn't there anything you can do about it, sir?"

Shafto turned on him. "Do about it!" He picked up the order and pushed it into Kane's face. "See the signature? Eisenhower himself." He crumpled it into a ball and threw it away.

AT HOBS END, Devlin was lying in bed writing in a notebook. Molly came in from the kitchen, wearing Devlin's trench coat and carrying a tray, which she put down on the table beside the bed. "There you are, O lord and master. Tea and toast, and two boiled eggs, four and a half minutes, as you suggested."

Devlin stopped writing and looked at the tray. "Keep up this standard and I might take you on permanently."

She took off the trench coat. Underneath she was wearing only panties and a bra, and she picked up her sweater and denim pants from the end of the bed and put them on. "I'll have to get moving. I told Mum I'd be in for my dinner."

He poured himself a cup of tea and she picked up the notebook. "What's this?" She opened it. "Poetry?"

He grinned. "A matter of opinion in some quarters."

She found the place where he had been writing. *"There is no certain knowledge of my passing, where I have walked in woodland after dark."* She looked up. "Why, that's beautiful, Liam."

"I know. Like you keep telling me, I'm a lovely boy."

She kissed him fiercely. "You know what today is? Guy Fawkes Day, only we can't have no bonfire because of rotten old Adolf."

"What a shame," he jeered.

"Never you mind. I'll come round tonight and cook you supper and we'll have a nice little bonfire all our own."

"No, you won't," he said. "Because I shan't be here." He kissed her lightly. "I probably won't get back till tomorrow afternoon. I'll call for you—all right?"

She nodded reluctantly. "If you say so."

There was the sound of a horn outside. Molly darted to the window and came back in a hurry. "It's Mrs Grey."

Devlin laughed as he pulled on his clothes. Molly reached for her coat. "See you tomorrow, beautiful. Can I take this to read?" She held up his notebook.

"God, but you must like punishment," he said.

She kissed him, and he opened the back door for her, standing watching her run to the dyke, knowing that this could be the end. "Ah, well," he said softly. "The best thing for her."

A moment later he greeted Joanna Grey. "What's the news?"

"I transmitted directly to Radl at Landsvoort last night." Her eyes were shining. "Come hell or high water, Steiner and his men will be here at approximately one o'clock."

STEINER HAD finished giving the assault group their final briefing, with Max Radl present. Later, as the two colonels walked along the beach, Radl said, "Well, is it going to work, Kurt?"

At that moment Lance Corporal Werner Briegel and Private Gerhard Klugl came over the sand dunes. They were wearing ponchos, and Briegel had field glasses slung around his neck.

"Let's try them out," Steiner suggested, and called out in English, "Private Kunicki! Private Moczar! Over here, please!" The two doubled across without hesitation. Steiner continued, "Who am I?"

"Lieutenant Colonel Howard Carter, in command of the Polish Independent Parachute Squadron, Special Air Service Regiment," Briegel replied in good English.

Radl turned to Steiner with a smile. "I'm impressed."

Steiner said, "What are you doing here?"

"Sergeant Major Brandt—" Briegel began, and hastily corrected himself. "Sergeant Major Kurczek told us to relax. We're looking for shore larks, Herr Oberst."

"Shore larks?" Steiner said.

"Yes," Briegel explained. "They're quite easy to distinguish. A most striking black and yellow pattern on face and throat."

Steiner exploded into laughter. "You see, my dear Max? Shore larks. How can we possibly fail?"

As DARKNESS fell at Landsvoort the ex-RAF Dakota stood in the hangar. Her pilot, Captain Gericke, inspected the airstrip repeatedly, but despite heavy rain the fog was as thick as ever.

Steiner and Radl waited in the hangar. "There's still no wind," Gericke informed them at ten thirty. "That's what we need now."

"Are you trying to say you can't take off?" Radl demanded.

"No problem there," Gericke told him. "I can take off blind. But I can't just drop those men and hope for the best. We could be a mile out to sea. I need to see the target, however briefly."

Bohmler, Gericke's observer, peered in through the aperture in one of the big hangar doors and beckoned.

Gericke moved to join him. "What is it?" Bohmler had switched on the outside light, and Gericke could see the fog swirling in strange patterns. Something touched his cheek coldly. "Wind!" he shouted. "We've got wind."

Suddenly the wind tore a gap in the fog curtain and he could see the farmhouse for a moment. "Do we go?" Bohmler demanded.

"Yes," Gericke said. "But it's got to be now."

In THE SECRET cubbyhole in the loft of her cottage, Joanna Grey sat by the radio receiver reading a book. At eleven o'clock her earphones started to buzz. She dropped her book, reached for a pencil and a pad. It was a brief message, decoded in seconds.

She went downstairs and got her sheepskin coat. The retriever sniffed at her heels. "No, Patch, not this time," she said.

Because of the fog it was twenty minutes later when she drove into the yard at Hobs End. Devlin opened the door and she slipped in. "I've just received a message from Landsvoort, timed eleven o'clock exactly," she said. "The Eagle has flown."

"They must be crazy. It's like pea soup up there on the beach."

"It seemed a little clearer to me as I turned along the dyke."

He had assembled the silenced Sten gun, and he handed it to her. "You know how to work these?"

"Of course."

He picked up a bulging rucksack and slung it over his shoulders. "Right, then. We've got work to do. They should be here in forty minutes." He opened the door and they plunged out into the fog.

IN THE Dakota they talked in low tones with all the calm of veterans. As nobody had been allowed to have German cigarettes on his person, Steiner moved among them, handing them out singly. He came to Preston. "A cigarette, Lieutenant?" he said in English.

"Thanks very much, sir." Preston's clipped voice suggested he was playing the Coldstream Guards captain again.

"How do you feel?" Steiner asked.

"In excellent spirits, sir," Preston told him calmly.

Steiner retreated to the cockpit. They were at two thousand feet. Through occasional gaps in the clouds, stars could be seen and a pale sickle moon. Fog covered the sea like smoke in a valley.

"Another thirty minutes," Gericke said.

At that moment Bohmler, huddled over his observer's equipment, gave an excited gasp. "I've got something, Peter."

They entered a cloud. Steiner said, "What's it likely to be?"

"Probably a night fighter, as he's on his own," Gericke said. "Better pray it isn't one of ours. He'll blow us out of the sky."

They emerged from the cloud and Bohmler tapped Gericke's arm. "Coming in like a bat out of hell on the starboard quarter."

Steiner turned his head and could plainly see a twin-engined aircraft levelling out to starboard.

"Mosquito," Gericke said. "Let's hope he knows a friend when he sees one."

The Mosquito held course for only a few more moments, then waggled its wing tips and swung away to starboard, disappearing into heavy cloud.

"See?" Gericke smiled up at Steiner. "All you have to do is live right. Better make sure your men are ready to go. I'll call you when we pick up Devlin on the S-phone."

IT WAS COLD on the beach in Norfolk and the tide was about two-thirds in. Devlin walked up and down to keep warm, holding the receiver, the channel open. It was almost ten to twelve and Joanna Grey, who had been sheltering among the trees from the light rain, came up. "They must be close now."

As if in reply, the S-phone crackled and Gericke's voice came through: "This is Eagle. Are you receiving me, Wanderer?"

Devlin spoke into the S-phone. "Loud and clear."

"Please report conditions over nest."

"Visibility poor," Devlin said. "One hundred to one hundred and fifty yards. Wind freshening."

"Thank you, Wanderer. Estimated arrival, six minutes."

Devlin shoved the S-phone into Joanna Grey's hand. "Hang on to that while I lay out the markers."

He hurried along the beach, taking cycle lamps from his ruck-sack and putting them down at intervals of fifteen yards in a line following the direction of the wind, switching each one on. Then he made a parallel line at a distance of twenty yards.

"Oh, this damn fog," Joanna said when he rejoined her. "They'll never see us. I know they won't."

It was the first time he'd seen her crack in any way, and he put a hand on her arm. "Be still, girl."

In the distance there was the rumble of engines.

THE DAKOTA was down to a thousand feet. Gericke said over his shoulder, "One pass, that's all I'll get, so make it good."

"We will," Steiner told him. He clapped Gericke on the shoulder and went out. He nodded to Neumann, who gave the order. Brandt slid back the exit door and Steiner moved down the line, checking each man personally.

Gericke went in so low that Bohmler could see the white of

breakers. Ahead was fog and more darkness. Then, as if some unseen power had decided to take a hand, a sudden gust of wind revealed Devlin's parallel lines of cycle lamps, clear in the night.

Gericke nodded. Bohmler pressed the switch, and the red light in the cabin flashed above Steiner's head.

Gericke banked to starboard, throttled back until his airspeed indicator stood at a hundred, and made his pass along the beach at three hundred and fifty feet. The green light flashed. Neumann jumped into darkness, Brandt followed, the rest of the men tumbled after them. Steiner could feel the wind on his face, smell the salt tang of the sea, and he waited for Preston to falter. The Englishman stepped into space without a second's hesitation. It was a good omen. Steiner was the last man out.

Bohmler, peering back from the cockpit, tapped Gericke on the arm. "All gone. I'll close the door."

Gericke swung out to sea. A few minutes later the S-phone crackled and Devlin said, "All fledglings safe in the nest."

Gericke said to Bohmler, "Pass that on to Landsvoort at once. Radl must have been walking on hot bricks for the past hour."

IN HIS office at Prinz Albrechtstrasse, Himmler worked alone in the light of the desk lamp. There was a discreet knock and Rossman entered. Himmler looked up. "What is it?"

"We've just heard from Radl at Landsvoort, Herr Reichsführer. The Eagle has landed."

IN THE MARSH warden's cottage, Devlin, Steiner and Joanna Grey were examining a large-scale area map. "Look here, behind St Mary's," Devlin said. "Old Woman's Meadow. It belongs to the church, and the barn with it, which is empty at the moment."

"You move in there tomorrow," Joanna said. "See Father Vereker first and tell him you're on exercises."

"And you're certain he'll agree?" Steiner asked.

Joanna nodded. "That sort of thing happens all the time."

"Vereker was a paratrooper padre," Devlin added, "so he'll

lean over backward to assist when he sees those maroon berets."

"There's another point in our favor," Joanna said. "Sir Henry is giving a small dinner party for the Prime Minister tonight, and I'm invited. I'll go only to make my excuses. Say that I've been called on night duty for the WVS. It's happened before, so Sir Henry and Lady Willoughby will accept it. Then I'll be able to describe the immediate situation at the Grange to you."

"Excellent," Steiner said. "It seems more plausible by the minute."

Just then the door opened and Neumann entered. He was wearing a camouflaged jump jacket and trousers, and there was an SAS winged dagger badge on his maroon beret.

"Everything all right out there?" Steiner asked.

Neumann nodded. "Everyone bedded down for the night. Only one grumble. No cigarettes."

"Of course. I left them in the car." Joanna Grey hurried out.

She was back in a few moments with two cartons of Players.

"Holy Mother," Devlin said in awe. "Did you ever see the like? They're like gold, those things. Where did they come from?"

"WVS supplies." She smiled. "And now, gentlemen, I must leave you. We'll meet tomorrow, by accident, of course, in the village."

CHAPTER 9

IT WAS JUST after ten on Saturday morning when Molly, on a sudden impulse and in spite of her promise to Devlin to wait until he called for her, rode down through the fields towards Hobs End.

In the barn, Brandt and Altmann were supervising the mounting of a Browning M2 heavy machine-gun on the jeep. Preston watched, giving the impression of being in charge.

Werner Briegel and Klugl had partially opened one of the rear shutters, and Werner was surveying the birds of the marsh through his field glasses. "There's a green sandpiper."

He continued his trajectory and Molly jumped into view. "Hell, we're being watched."

In a flash Preston was at his side. "I'll get her," he said, and ran out.

Devlin and Steiner had been to the beach to make certain that the tide had covered all traces of the previous night's activities. Devlin had also shown Steiner the pickup area for the E-boat. They were on their way back when Preston emerged from the marsh, with the girl, kicking and shouting, slung over his shoulder.

"What is it?" Steiner demanded.

"It's Molly Prior, the girl I told you about." Devlin started to run, reaching the cottage yard as Preston did. "Put her down, damn you!" Devlin shouted.

Preston turned. "I don't take orders from you."

But Steiner called in a voice like iron, "Lieutenant Preston, you will release the lady now." Preston set Molly down, and she promptly slapped his face.

There was immediate laughter from inside the barn and she turned to see, through the open door, a line of grinning faces, the truck beyond, the jeep with the Browning machine-gun mounted.

"Liam," she said in bewilderment. "What's going on?"

But it was Steiner who handled it, smooth as silk. "Lieutenant Preston, you will apologise to this young lady at once."

Preston said, "Humble apologies, ma'am, my mistake." Then he turned and went into the barn.

Steiner said, "I can't tell you how sorry I am."

"This is Colonel Carter, Molly," Devlin explained.

"Of the Polish Independent Parachute Squadron," Steiner said. "We're here for tactical field training and I'm afraid Lieutenant Preston gets rather carried away when it comes to security."

She was more bewildered than ever. "But Liam—" she began.

Devlin took her by the arm. "Come on, let's catch that horse." He pushed her towards the edge of the marsh, where her mount peacefully nibbled grass. "Now look what you've done," he scolded her. "Didn't I tell you to wait for me to call?"

"But I don't understand," she said. "Paratroopers here, and—"

He gripped her arm fiercely. "Security, Molly. They've a very special reason for being here, but for the moment it's top secret and you mustn't mention seeing them to a living soul. As you love me, promise me that."

"I see the way of it now," she said. "All these things you've been doing, the trips at night and so on. You let me think it was the black market. But—you're still in the army, aren't you?"

"Yes," he said with some truth. "I'm afraid I am."

Her eyes were shining. "Oh, Liam, can you ever forgive me thinking you some cheap spiv peddling stockings round the pubs?"

Devlin took a deep breath, but managed a smile. "I'll think about it. Now go home like a good girl and wait until I call."

"I will, Liam. I will." She kissed him, and swung up into the saddle. "You can rely on me."

IN LONDON, Rogan was clearing his desk, thinking about lunch, when Grant entered, his face tense with excitement. "Just in over the teleprinter, sir." He slapped the message down in front of Rogan. "We've got him. He's up on the coast near Studley Constable."

"So he's calling himself Devlin," Rogan said when he had read the message. "How far is this place?"

"A couple of hundred miles."

"It's a while since I've had a weekend in the country."

"You've got an appointment at the attorney-general's office after lunch," Grant reminded him. "The Halloran case."

"I'll be out of there by three o'clock. You get a car from the pool and we can get straight off."

Grant had a hand on the door when Rogan added, "And Fergus, draw a couple of Browning Hi-powers from the armoury. This character shoots first and asks what you wanted afterwards."

JUST BEFORE noon Philip Vereker went down to the presbytery cellar. His foot was giving him hell and he had hardly slept during the night, but Pamela was coming for the weekend, and that was something. Furthermore, Major Harry Kane was picking her up.

At the bottom of the steps, Vereker opened an ancient oak cupboard, stepped inside and closed the door. He switched on a torch, felt for a hidden catch, and the back of the cupboard swung open to reveal a long, dark tunnel with Norfolk flint walls that glistened with moisture. It was a priest's tunnel linking the presbytery with the church, a relic of the days of Roman Catholic persecution under Elizabeth Tudor. For Vereker it was simply a great convenience.

He passed through the tunnel, mounted a flight of stone steps and paused, listening. Someone was playing a Bach prelude on the organ, and very well indeed. He opened a door (which was in fact a section of the panelled wall in the sacristy), closed it behind him and went through into the church.

Sergeant Altmann was thoroughly enjoying himself. Then in the organist's mirror he saw Vereker at the bottom of the chancel steps. He stopped playing abruptly. "I'm sorry, Father, but I just couldn't help myself. One doesn't often get the chance in my present occupation." His English was excellent, but with a definite accent.

Vereker said, "Who are you?"

"Sergeant Emil Janowski, Father. I came in here looking for you with my CO, who's now gone to try the presbytery."

The great door creaked open and Steiner entered, a leather swagger stick in one hand, his beret in the other. His boots rang on the flagstones, and the shafts of light from the clerestory windows touched with fire his fair hair. "Father Vereker?"

"That's right."

"Lieutenant Colonel Howard Carter, in command of the Polish Independent Parachute Squadron of the Special Air Service Regiment." He turned to Altmann. "You behaving yourself, Janowski?"

"As the colonel knows, the organ is my principal weakness."

Steiner grinned. "Cut along and wait outside with the others."

Altmann departed, and Vereker looked Steiner over. "I was a paratrooper myself. Padre to the First Parachute Brigade."

"Were you?" Steiner said. "It's a pleasure to meet you."

Vereker smiled. "What can I do for you?"

"Put us up for the night, if you will. You've a barn in the field next door that's had similar use before, I believe."

"You're on exercise?"

Steiner explained, and it worked, exactly as Joanna Grey had predicted. Philip Vereker said, "I'll be only too happy to help."

ALTMANN WENT down the road to where the Bedford stood at the entrance to Old Woman's Meadow. The jeep waited near the lych-gate, Klugl at the wheel, Werner Briegel behind the Browning M2.

Werner had his field glasses trained on the rookery in the beech trees. "Let's take a closer look," he said to Klugl.

They got out and went through the gate. Laker Armsby was digging a grave at the west end of the church. Seeing them coming, he stopped and took a half-smoked cigarette from behind his ear.

"Hello, there," Werner said.

Laker squinted. "Foreigners, eh? Thought you was British boys in them uniforms."

"Poles," Werner told him. "My friend doesn't speak English." Laker fiddled ostentatiously with the cigarette butt until the young German produced a pack of Players. "Have one of these."

"Don't mind if I do. What's your name then?"

"Werner." There was a nasty pause as he realised his mistake and added, "Kunicki."

"Oh, aye," Laker said. "Always thought Werner was a German name. I took a prisoner once in France in 1915. He was called Werner. Werner Schmidt."

"My mother was German," Werner explained.

"Not your fault that," Laker replied.

Werner asked, "How long has the rookery been here?"

Laker, puzzled, stared up at the trees. "Since I were a lad, that is a fact. Go on, you aren't interested in these tatty old rooks?"

"Certainly I am," Werner told him. "Many arrive during the late autumn and winter from as far afield as Russia."

"Get away," Laker told him.

"No, it's true. Many rooks in this area before the war were found to have been ringed around Leningrad, for example."

There was a shout, "Kunicki—Moczar, we're leaving," and they turned and found Steiner and the priest standing outside the church vestibule. Werner and Klugl doubled back to the jeep.

Steiner and Father Vereker started down the path together as another jeep came up the hill from the village and parked on the opposite side of the road. Pamela Vereker and Harry Kane got out and joined them at the gate.

Pamela reached up to kiss her brother on the cheek. "Sorry I'm late, but Harry wanted to see a little more of Norfolk."

"And you took him the long way round?" Vereker said affectionately. "I'd like you both to meet Colonel Carter of the Polish Independent Parachute Squadron. He and his men are on exercise in this district. My sister, Pamela, Colonel, and Major Harry Kane."

Kane shook hands. "We've one or two Polish guys in our outfit. Krukowski, for instance. Born and raised in Chicago, but his Polish is as good as his English. Maybe we can get together."

"I'm afraid not," Steiner said. "I'm under orders to move on and join up with other units tomorrow. You know how it is."

"I do." Kane glanced at his watch. "In fact, if I'm not at Meltham House in twenty minutes, the colonel will have me shot."

Steiner said, "Nice to have met you. Miss Vereker. Father." He got into the jeep with Klugl and Werner, and they drove away.

"Try to remember it's the left-hand side of the road you drive on here, Klugl," Steiner said calmly.

AFTER SETTLING his men in Vereker's barn, Steiner walked down the track and leaned on the gate. Joanna Grey was toiling up the hill on her bicycle, Patch running along behind.

"Good afternoon, ma'am." Steiner saluted.

She dismounted. "How's everything?" She held out her hand as if introducing herself formally. At a distance it must have looked very natural. "And Philip Vereker?"

"Couldn't be more helpful. You were absolutely right."

"What happens now?"

"You'll see us playing soldiers round the village. Devlin said he'll be up to see you at six thirty."

"Good." She held out her hand again. "I'll see you later."

Steiner saluted and Joanna remounted her bicycle.

IN LONDON, as Big Ben struck three, Rogan came out of the Royal Courts of Justice and hurried along the pavement to where Fergus Grant waited at the wheel of a Humber sedan.

At the same moment Molly, on her way to help Pamela Vereker decorate the church for Sunday, tethered her horse and went through the back gate into the graveyard. As she approached the church a shouted command drifted up the hill, and she looked down towards the village, where the paratroops were advancing in the direction of the old mill by the stream, their maroon berets very clear against the green of the meadow. Inside the church, she found Pamela on her knees at the altar polishing the brass rails.

"Hello, Molly," Pamela said. "Wouldn't you think there was enough war without them having to play their stupid games? Is my brother down there?"

"He was when I came in."

"I wonder sometimes if he resents being out of it all now." Pamela shook her head. "Men are strange creatures."

DOWN IN the village, Ritter Neumann had split the assault group into three sections of five, all linked to each other by field telephone. He and Harvey Preston were deployed among the cottages with one section each. Preston was rather enjoying himself. He crouched by the wall at the side of the Studley Arms, revolver in hand, and gave his section a signal to move forward.

George Wilde leaned on the wall, watching, and his wife, Betty, called from the doorway, "Wish you was back in action?"

Wilde shrugged. "Maybe."

"Men," she said in disgust. "I'll never understand you."

The third section consisted of Brandt, Sergeant Sturm, Corporal Becker and Privates Jansen and Hagl. They were deployed in the meadow opposite the old abandoned mill. Usually the massive waterwheel stood still, but the stream, flooded by heavy rain, had snapped the locking bar, and the wheel was moving again.

Steiner, sitting in the jeep, noted the wheel as it churned the water into foam, then turned to watch Brandt correcting young Jansen's technique in the prone firing position. On a footbridge upstream from the dam, Father Vereker, George Wilde's eleven-year-old son, Graham, and little Susan Turner also watched.

"What are they doing now, Father?" Graham asked Vereker.

"Well, Graham," Vereker said, "it's a question of having the elbows in the right position to get a steady aim."

Five-year-old Susan Turner was bored. She was a pretty, fair-haired child, an evacuee from Birmingham living with her grandparents, Ted and Agnes Turner, who ran the post office and general store.

She crossed the footbridge, ducked under the rail and squatted at the edge. The river rushed past two feet below. She dangled a doll, chuckling as water splashed its feet. Then, clutching the rail above her head, she dipped the doll's legs below the surface. The rail snapped, and with a scream she went into the water.

Before the priest could move she was swept under the bridge. Graham, more by instinct than courage, jumped in after her, grabbed the tail of her coat and hung on tight. His feet were scrabbling for the bottom, but there was no bottom, and he cried out in fear as the current swept them down towards the dam.

Graham's cry alerted Brandt and his men instantly. As they turned to see what the trouble was, the two children went over the dam and slid down the concrete apron into the mill pool.

Sergeant Sturm ran for the edge of the pool, tearing off his equipment. The children, with Graham still hanging on to Susan, were being carried relentlessly into the path of the waterwheel. Sturm, without waiting to unzip his jump jacket, plunged in and struck out towards them. He grabbed Graham by the arm. Brandt plunged waist-deep into the water behind him. As Sturm pulled Graham in, the boy's head dipped momentarily under the water. He panicked, releasing his grip on the girl. Sturm swung him around in an arc so that Brandt could catch him, then plunged on after Susan. He pulled her into his arms and tried to stand. But he went right under, and when he surfaced again, he felt himself being drawn inexorably towards the waterwheel.

He was aware of a cry above the roaring, turned and saw Brandt back in the water again and pushing towards him. Sturm summoned up everything he had and hurled Susan through the air to Brandt's arms. A moment later he was swept under the wheel.

George Wilde had seen the children go over the dam. He called to his wife and ran across the road to the bridge. Preston and his men, who had also witnessed the mishap, followed.

Except for being soaked to the skin, Graham Wilde seemed none the worse for his experience. The same held true for Susan, though she was crying hysterically. Brandt thrust her into George Wilde's arms and ran along the bank to join Steiner and the others searching beyond the waterwheel for Sturm. Suddenly Sturm floated to the surface in calm water, and Brandt plunged in to get him.

Sturm's eyes were closed, his lips slightly parted. Brandt waded out of the water holding him in his arms, and everyone seemed to arrive at once — Vereker, then Preston and his men and finally Mrs Wilde, who took Susan from her husband.

"Is he all right?" Vereker demanded.

Brandt ripped the jump jacket open and got a hand inside the blouse, feeling for the heart. He touched a bruise on the forehead, and the skin was immediately suffused with blood, the flesh and bone soft as jelly. He looked up at Steiner and said in fair English, "I'm sorry, sir, but his skull is crushed."

For a moment the only sound was the mill wheel's eerie creaking. It was Graham Wilde who broke the silence, saying loudly, "Look at his uniform, Dad. Is that what the Poles wear?"

Beneath the open jacket was revealed Sergeant Sturm's normal uniform with all his decorations, as per Himmler's instructions.

"Oh, my God," Vereker whispered.

The Germans closed around in a circle. Steiner said in German to Brandt, "Put Sturm in the jeep." He snapped his fingers at Jansen, who was carrying one of the field telephones. "Let me have that. Eagle One to Eagle Two," he called. "Come in, please."

Neumann and his section were on the far side of the cottages. He replied almost instantly. "Eagle Two. I hear you."

"The Eagle is blown," Steiner said. "Meet me at the bridge now." He passed the phone back to Jansen.

Betty Wilde said in bewilderment, "What is it, George? I don't understand."

"They're Germans," Wilde said. "I saw uniforms like that in Norway. But I don't know what they want here."

"You poor stupid bastard," Preston jeered. "Don't you know Mr Lord-God-Almighty-Winston-bloody-Churchill himself is staying at Studley Grange tonight?"

Wilde stared at him in astonishment. "You must be cracked. I never heard such nonsense in all my life. Isn't that so, Father?"

"I'm afraid he's right." Vereker got the words out slowly and with enormous difficulty. "Very well, Colonel. Do you mind telling me what happens now? These children must be chilled to the bone."

Steiner turned to Betty Wilde. "Mrs Wilde, you may take your son home now, and take Susan to her grandparents. They run the post office and general store, is this not so?"

"Yes, that's right."

Steiner said to Preston, "There are only six telephones in the general village area. All calls come through a switchboard at the post office and are connected by either Mr or Mrs Turner."

"Shall we rip it out?" Preston suggested.

"No. Someone might send a repairman. When the child is changed, send her and her grandmother up to the church. Keep Turner on the switchboard. If there are any incoming calls, he's to say that whoever they want isn't in. Now, get to it."

Preston turned to Betty Wilde. Susan had stopped crying, and he held out his hands. "Come on, beautiful, I'll give you a piggyback."

The child responded instinctively with a delighted smile. "This way, Mrs Wilde, if you'd be so kind."

Betty Wilde, after a desperate glance at her husband, went after him, holding her son by the hand. The rest of Preston's section— Privates Dinter, Meyer, Riedel and Berg—followed.

Wilde said hoarsely, "If anything happens to my wife . . ."

Steiner ignored him. He said to Brandt, "Take Father Vereker and Mr Wilde up to the church and hold them there. Becker and Jansen can go with you. Hagl, you come with me."

Preston met Neumann and his section at the bridge and was obviously telling the Oberleutnant what had happened.

Vereker said, "Colonel, I've a good mind to call your bluff. If I walk off now, you can't afford to shoot me. You'll arouse the whole village."

Steiner faced him. "My sergeant major will put a knife under your ribs in just the right way to kill you instantly and without a sound. Then we walk you to the jeep between us and drive off." He turned and hurried towards the bridge. Hagl had to trot to keep up with him.

Neumann came to meet them. "What do you want us to do?"

"You send a man up for the truck, then start at one end of the village and work your way through, house by house. I want every-body out and up in that church within twenty minutes. And set up a roadblock at each end of the village. We'll make it look nice and official, but anyone who comes in stays."

"What about Mrs Grey?"

"She needs to be free to use the radio. I don't want anyone to know she's on our side until it's necessary. I'll see her myself." He grinned. "A tight one, Neumann."

"We've known them before, Herr Oberst."

"Good." Steiner saluted and started up the hill to the church.

MOLLY AND PAMELA had created a display of reeds and marsh grasses for the altar. Pamela said, "It needs some ivy."

She went out through the vestibule and plucked some leaves

from the vine on the tower. Just then there was a squeal of brakes, and she turned to see a jeep draw up. Her brother and George Wilde got out, and it occurred to her that a huge sergeant major was covering them with the rifle he held braced against his hip. She would have laughed at the absurdity of it had it not been for Becker and Jansen, who followed carrying Sturm's body.

Pamela retreated through the partly opened door, bumping into Molly. "What is it?" Molly demanded.

Pamela hushed her. "I don't know. Something's wrong. Quick, in here . . ." She opened the sacristy door. They slipped inside and she slid home the bolt. A moment later they heard voices.

Vereker said, "All right, now what?"

"You wait for Colonel Steiner," Brandt told him. "On the other hand, I don't see why you shouldn't fill in the time by doing what's right for poor old Sturm."

"Bring him to the Lady Chapel," Vereker said.

The footsteps died away, and Molly and Pamela crouched against the door. Footsteps echoed hollowly on the flags of the vestibule, and the outer door creaked open. Pamela put a finger to her lips.

Steiner paused by the font, tapping his swagger stick against his thigh. "Father Vereker," he called. "Down here, please." He moved towards the sacristy and tried the door. As Vereker limped down the aisle, Steiner said, "This seems to be locked. Why?"

The door had never been locked to Vereker's knowledge, because the key had been lost for years. That could mean only that someone had bolted it from the inside. Then he remembered that he had left Pamela working on the altar when he had gone to watch the paratroopers. The conclusion was obvious.

He said clearly, "It is the sacristy, Herr Oberst. I'm afraid the key is over at the presbytery. Sorry for such inefficiency. I suppose you order things better in the SS?"

"Do you imagine all German soldiers serve in the SS?"

"No, perhaps it is just that they behave as if they do."

"Like Sergeant Sturm, I suppose." Vereker could find nothing to say to that. Steiner added, "For the record, we are not SS. We are paratroopers."

"So you intend to assassinate Mr Churchill tonight?"

"Only if we have to. I'd prefer to keep him in one piece."

"And now the planning's gone slightly awry?" Vereker said.

"Improvisation is the essence of our kind of soldiering."

"For heaven's sake, man, you've had it. No element of surprise."

"There still will be," Steiner told him calmly. "If we hold the entire village incommunicado."

"But that is impossible!"

"Not at all. My men are at this very moment rounding up everyone at present in Studley Constable. There are only sixteen houses, Father. Forty-seven people in all. My men will be up here within fifteen minutes. We control the telephone system and the roads." Steiner looked at his watch. "Sir Henry Willoughby and the Prime Minister were due to leave at three thirty from King's Lynn on the Walsingham road. Which, give or take a minute or two, is right now."

"You seem to be very well informed."

"Oh, I am." Steiner held out his hand. "I'll have the keys of your car. It might come in useful."

"I haven't got them with me—" Vereker began.

"Don't waste my time, Father. I'll have my lads strip you."

Vereker reluctantly produced his keys, and Steiner slipped them into his pocket. "Right. I have things to do."

He raised his voice. "Brandt, I'll send Preston to relieve you. Then report to me in the village." He went out, and Private Jansen came and stood against the door with his M1.

"So now we know," Pamela said. "We've got to get out of here."

"But how?"

Pamela moved to the other side of the room, found the concealed catch, and a section of the panelling swung back to reveal the entrance to the priest's tunnel. Molly was gaping in amazement.

"Come on," Pamela said impatiently as she picked up the torch that her brother had left on a table.

When they exited into the presbytery cellar and went up to the hall, Pamela said, "If I could only get down to Mrs Grey's."

"Then what would you do?"

"I'd borrow her car and go straight to Meltham House," Pamela said. "There are American Rangers there. They'd show Steiner's bunch a thing or two. Let's see if we can take the field path back of Hawks Wood and get to Mrs Grey's without being seen."

Molly didn't argue. They darted across the road into the shelter of the wood. Pamela led the way down the hidden path until they came out on the opposite side of the stream from Park Cottage. There was a narrow footbridge, and the road seemed deserted.

Pamela said, "All right, let's go. Straight across."

Molly grabbed her arm. "I've changed my mind. You try this way. I'll get my horse and try another. Two bites of the apple."

Pamela nodded. "That makes sense." She kissed Molly on the cheek impulsively. "Only watch it! They mean business."

Molly turned and started to run back up the track to the presbytery. Oh, Devlin, she thought, I hope they crucify you. By the time she reached her horse, the tears, slow, sad and incredibly painful, were oozing from her eyes.

WHEN PAMELA went to the rear of the cottage, Joanna's car was outside, keys in the ignition. She started to get in, and heard an indignant voice. "Pamela, what on earth are you doing?"

Joanna Grey was standing at the back door. Pamela ran towards her. "I'm sorry, Mrs Grey, but something absolutely terrible has happened. This colonel and his men who are exercising in the village. They're not SAS at all. They're German paratroopers here to kidnap the Prime Minister."

Joanna Grey drew her into the kitchen. Patch fawned about her knees. "Now calm down," Joanna said. "This really is a most incredible story." She turned to her coat hanging behind the door, fumbled in the pocket.

"Yes, but he will be this evening," Pamela said. "Sir Henry is bringing him back from King's Lynn."

Joanna turned and brought out her Luger. "You have been busy, Pamela." She reached behind and got the cellar door open. "Down you go."

Pamela was thunderstruck. "Mrs Grey, I don't understand."

"And I don't have time to explain. Let's just say we're on different sides. Now get down those stairs. I won't hesitate to shoot if I have to."

Pamela went down, Patch scampering in front of her, and Joanna followed. She switched on a light at the bottom and opened a door to a dark storeroom filled with junk. "In you go."

Patch, circling his mistress, managed to get between her feet. She stumbled against the wall. Pamela gave her a violent push through the doorway. As she fell back, Joanna Grey fired the Luger. Pamela was aware of the explosion that half blinded her, the sudden touch of a white-hot poker against the side of her head, but she managed to slam the door and bolt it.

There was a desperate air of unreality to everything as Pamela stumbled upstairs to the kitchen and out to the car. Then, as in a dream, she found herself getting in behind the wheel of the car, driving out of the yard.

As he walked towards Park Cottage, Steiner saw the car leave and assumed that Joanna Grey was driving. He swore softly and went back to the bridge, where he had left the jeep with Werner Briegel and Klugl.

At that moment the Bedford came back down the hill from the church, with Neumann standing on the running board. He jumped down.

"Twenty-seven people up at the church now, Herr Oberst."

"Devlin estimated a present population of forty-seven," Steiner said. "If we allow for Turner at the switchboard and Mrs Grey, that leaves about eight people who are certain to turn up at some time." Steiner mentioned seeing Mrs Grey in her car.

"Perhaps she's gone to see Devlin?"

"That's a point. We'll have to let him know what's happening anyway." He slapped the swagger stick against his palm.

There was a crash of breaking glass, and a chair came through the window of Turners' store. Steiner and Neumann drew their Brownings and ran across the road.

CHAPTER 10

FOR MOST of the day Arthur Seymour had been felling trees. Mrs Turner had given him an order for some logs only that morning. Now, back in the village, he kicked open the Turners' kitchen door and walked in, a sack of logs on his shoulder—and came face-to-face with Dinter and Berg, who were sitting drinking coffee. "Here, what's going on?" he demanded.

Dinter, who had his Sten slung across his chest, moved it on target. At the same moment Preston appeared in the other doorway. He stood there, hands on hips, looking Seymour over. "My God," he said. "The original walking ape."

Something stirred in Seymour's dark, mad eyes. "You watch your mouth, soldier boy."

"It can talk as well. All right, put him with the others." Preston turned to go back into the post office, and Seymour tossed the sack of logs at Dinter and Berg and jumped on Preston, one arm clamping around his throat, a knee in his back. Berg got to his feet and slammed the butt of his M1 into Seymour's kidneys. The big man cried out in pain, released Preston, and launched himself at Berg with such force that they went through the open door into the store, a display cabinet collapsing beneath them.

Berg lost his rifle, but he got up and backed away as Seymour advanced on him. He managed to pick up a chair. Seymour knocked it aside in mid-flight and it went out through the store window. Berg drew his bayonet and Seymour crouched. Preston moved in from behind, Berg's M1 in his hands, and drove the butt into the back of

Seymour's skull. The big man grabbed for support and brought a shelf and its contents down on top of him as he slid to the floor behind the counter.

Steiner and Neumann burst into the store at that moment, guns ready. The place was a shambles. Dinter appeared in the kitchen doorway, swaying slightly, a streak of blood on his forehead. Old Mr Turner was hovering in the side door to the post office, tears in his eyes. "And who's going to pay for that lot?"

"Send the bill to Churchill," Preston said brutally.

The old man slumped down in a chair, and Steiner said, "All right, Preston, I won't need you here anymore. I'll send Altmann to man the switchboard. Get on up to the church and take that specimen behind the counter with you. Relieve Brandt. Tell him to report here to Oberleutnant Neumann."

Preston kicked Seymour in the backside and hauled him to his feet. "Come on, ape."

AT THE CHURCH, the terrified villagers sat in pews as instructed, talking to each other in low voices. Vereker moved among them, bringing what comfort he could. Corporal Becker stood guard near the chancel, a Sten gun in his hands, Private Jansen at the door.

After Brandt had departed, Preston found a length of rope in the bell room, lashed Seymour's hands and ankles together, then dragged him on his face to the Lady Chapel. There were gasps of horror, particularly from the women. Vereker limped forward and grabbed Preston by the shoulder. "Leave that man alone."

"Man?" Preston laughed in his face. "This isn't a man, it's a thing." Vereker reached down to touch Seymour, but Preston knocked him away and drew his revolver.

One woman choked back a scream. Preston raised the weapon. A moment in time. Vereker crossed himself, and Preston laughed again and lowered the gun. "A lot of good that will do you."

"What kind of man are you?" Vereker demanded.

"A special breed," Preston said. "The finest fighting men that ever walked the earth. The Waffen SS, in which I have the honour to hold the rank of Untersturmführer." He walked up the aisle, turned and took off his jump jacket, revealing the tunic underneath.

It was Laker Armsby, sitting beside George Wilde, who said, "Here, he's got a Union Jack on his sleeve."

Vereker frowned, and Preston held out his arm. "Yes, he's right. Note the insignia—British Free Corps. Don't any of you realise? I'm English, like you, only I'm on the right side."

George Wilde came out of his pew and deliberately stood looking up at Preston. "The Jerries must be damned hard up, because the only place they could have found you was under a stone."

Preston shot him in the face. As Wilde fell back bleeding, there was pandemonium. Women were screaming. Preston fired a shot into the air. "Stay where you are!"

There was a frozen silence. Vereker got down on one knee awkwardly and examined Wilde, who groaned and moved his head. Betty Wilde ran up the aisle, followed by her son, and dropped to her knees beside her husband. "He'll be all right, Betty," Vereker told her. "See, the bullet has just gouged his cheek."

At that moment the church door crashed open and Neumann rushed up the centre aisle. "What's going on here?"

"Ask your colleague from the SS," Vereker suggested.

Neumann glanced at Preston, then knelt to examine Wilde. "Don't touch him, you bloody German swine," Betty said.

Neumann stood up and took a field dressing from one of his breast pockets. "Bandage him with that. He'll be fine."

The door opened again and Joanna Grey ran in. "Herr Oberleutnant," she called in German. "Where's Colonel Steiner?"

Her face was streaked with dirt and her hands were filthy. Neumann went to meet her. "He's gone to see Devlin. Why?"

Vereker said, "Joanna?" There was dread in his voice.

She ignored him and said to Neumann, "I don't know what's been going on here, but about forty-five minutes ago Pamela Vereker turned up at the cottage, and she knew everything. Wanted my car to go to Meltham House to get the Rangers."

"What happened?"

"I tried to stop her and ended up locked in the cellar. I only managed to break out five minutes ago. What will we do?"

Vereker put a hand on her arm and pulled her around to face him. "Are you saying you're one of them?"

"Yes," she said impatiently. "Now will you leave me alone? I've work to do." She turned back to Neumann.

"But why?" Vereker said. "You're British—"

She rounded on him then. "British? Boer, damn you! Boer! How could I be British? You insult me with that name."

There was horror on every villager's face. The agony in Philip Vereker's eyes was plain. "Oh, my God," he whispered.

Neumann took her by the arm. "Back to your house, fast. Contact Radl at Landsvoort. Keep the channel open."

She nodded and hurried out.

HARRY KANE was supervising a course in field tactics in the wood behind Meltham Vale Farm when he received Shafto's urgent summons to report to the house with the training squad.

As he arrived, sections which had been training on various parts of the estate were all coming in together. He could hear the revving of engines from the motor pool at the rear. Several jeeps turned into the gravel drive and drew up in front of the house.

Kane went up the steps on the run. The outer office was a scene of frenzied activity. Master Sergeant Garvey paced up and down outside Shafto's door, nervously smoking a cigarette.

"Is something wrong?" Kane demanded.

"Don't ask me, Major. All I know is that lady friend of yours arrived in one hell of a state about fifteen minutes ago, and nothing's been the same since."

Kane opened the door and went in. Shafto, in breeches and riding boots, was standing at the desk with his back to him. When he swung around, Kane saw that he was loading the pearl-handled Colt. His eyes sparkled.

"Fast action, Major. That's what I like."

He reached for belt and holster, and Kane said, "What is it, sir? Where's Miss Vereker?"

"In my bedroom. Under sedation and badly shocked. She took a bullet in the side of the head." Shafto buckled his belt, easing the holster low down on his hip. Then in a few brief sentences he quickly filled in the picture. "Well, Major Kane, what do you think?"

"We should notify the War Office and the general officer commanding East Anglia—"

Shafto cut in. "Have you any idea how long I'd be on the phone with those chair-bound bastards?" He slammed a fist down on the desk. "No, dammit. I'm going to nail these Krauts myself, here and now. Action this day!" He laughed harshly. "Churchill's personal motto. I'd say that's rather appropriate."

Kane saw it all then. To Shafto it must have seemed like a dispensation from the gods themselves—not only the salvaging of his career but also the making of it. The man who had saved Churchill. A feat of arms for the history books.

"Look, sir," Kane said stubbornly. "This must be just about the hottest potato of all time. If I might respectfully suggest, the British War Office won't take too kindly—"

Shafto's fist slammed down on the desk again. "What's got into you? It's already four fifteen. That means the Prime Minister must be getting close. We know the road he's coming on. You take a jeep, head him off and bring him back here. Now get moving and take Master Sergeant Garvey with you."

As Kane opened the door he heard Shafto say, "Get me Captain Mallory in here on the double."

TEN MINUTES later eight jeeps crammed with forty men, under the command of Colonel Shafto and Captain Mallory, roared down the drive and through the massive front gate. A couple of hundred yards down the road, Shafto, in the lead jeep, waved them to a halt and told his driver to pull in close to the nearest telephone pole. He turned to Sergeant Hustler in the rear seat. "Give me that Thompson gun."

Hustler handed it over. Shafto cocked it, took aim and sprayed the top of the pole, reducing the crossbars to matchwood. The telephone lines parted, springing wildly through the air. Shafto handed the Thompson back to Hustler. "I guess that takes care of any unauthorised phone calls for a while." He slapped the side of the vehicle. "Okay, let's go, let's go, let's go!"

MASTER SERGEANT Garvey, with Kane beside him, drove like a man possessed. Even then they almost missed their target, for as they came along the final stretch to join the Walsingham road, the small convoy flashed past at the end of the lane—two military policemen on motorcycles, then two Humber sedans, and two more policemen bringing up the rear. "It's him!" Kane cried.

The jeep skidded into the main road and Garvey rammed his foot down hard. As they roared up behind the convoy, one of the policemen at the rear waved them back.

Kane said, "Sergeant, pull out and overtake, and if they won't stop, you have my permission to ram that front car."

Garvey grinned. "Major, if this goes wrong, we'll end up in the stockade so fast you won't know what day it is." He swerved out past the motorcyclists and pulled alongside the rear Humber. Kane couldn't see much of the man in the back seat because the side curtains were pulled forward. The driver, who was in dark blue chauffeur's uniform, glanced sideways in alarm, and the man in the grey suit in the front passenger seat drew a revolver.

"Try the next one," Kane ordered, and Garvey pulled alongside the front Humber, blaring his horn.

There were four men in the car, two in army uniform. One of them turned in alarm, and Kane found himself looking at Sir Henry Willoughby. There was instant recognition, and Kane shouted to Garvey, "Okay, pull out in front. I think they'll stop now."

Garvey accelerated, overtaking the military policemen at the head of the small convoy. A horn blared a signal, and when Kane looked over his shoulder the convoy was pulling up at the side of the road. Garvey braked, and Kane jumped out and ran back.

The police had Sten guns trained on him, and the man in the grey suit was out of the rear car, revolver in hand.

A staff colonel got out of the first car, Sir Henry at his heels. The staff colonel said curtly, "My name is Corcoran, chief Intelligence officer, East Anglia District. Will you kindly explain yourself, sir?"

"The Prime Minister mustn't go to Studley Grange. The village has been taken over by German paratroops—"

"Good God," Sir Henry interrupted. "What nonsense!"

Corcoran waved him to silence. "Can you substantiate that, Major?"

"What does it take to convince you guys?" Kane shouted. "Won't anybody listen?"

A voice from behind, a voice that was entirely familiar to him, said, "I will, young man. Tell your story to me."

Harry Kane turned slowly, leaned down at the rear window, and was finally face-to-face with the great man himself.

WHEN STEINER reached the cottage at Hobs End, Devlin was just riding the Norton across the network of narrow dyke paths. He turned into the yard, shoved the bike up on its stand and pushed up his goggles.

After Steiner had filled him in, Devlin smiled. "I know one thing. My fingernails will be down to the quick by nine tonight."

Steiner jumped into the jeep. "I'll keep in touch."

From the wood across the road, Molly stood beside her horse and watched Steiner depart and Devlin unlock the front door. She had intended to confront him, filled with the desperate hope that even now she might be mistaken, but the sight of Steiner and his two men in the jeep was the ultimate truth of things.

A HALF MILE outside Studley Constable, Shafto waved the column to a halt and gave his orders. "Captain Mallory, you take three jeeps and fifteen men, cross the fields to the south of the village and circle round till you come out on the Studley Grange road just below the water mill. Sergeant Hustler, the moment we reach the edge of the village, you dismount and take a dozen men on foot up through Hawks Wood to the church. The remaining men stay with me. We'll plug the road by the Grey woman's house."

There was silence. It was Sergeant Hustler who finally broke it. "Begging the colonel's pardon, but wouldn't some reconnaissance be in order?" He tried to smile. "I mean, from what we hear, these Kraut paratroopers ain't exactly shrinking violets."

"Hustler," Shafto said coldly. "You ever query an order of mine again and I'll have you down to private so fast you won't know your own first name." A muscle twitched in his right cheek. "Hasn't anybody got any guts here?"

"Of course, sir," Mallory answered. "We're right behind you."

"Well, you'd better be," Shafto said. "Because I'm going in there now on my own with a white flag."

"You mean you're going to invite them to surrender, sir?"

"Surrender, my backside, Captain. While I do some talking, the rest of you will be getting into position and you've got exactly ten minutes."

DEVLIN WAS hungry. He heated a little soup, fried an egg and made a sandwich of it with two thick slices of Molly's own bread. He was eating it in the chair by the fire when the door opened, and she stood there. "So there you are?" he said cheerfully. "I was having a bite before coming looking for you."

"You dirty swine!" she said. "You used me."

She flung herself on him, hands clawing at his face. He grabbed her wrists and fought to control her. "What is it?" he demanded. Yet in his heart he knew.

"I know all about it. Carter isn't his name—it's Steiner, and he and his men are bloody Germans come for Mr Churchill. And what's your name? Not Devlin, I'll be bound."

He pushed her away. "No, Molly, it isn't. You weren't meant to be any part of this, my love. You just happened."

"You bloody traitor!"

He said in a kind of exasperation, "Molly, I'm Irish. That means

I'm as different from you as a German is from a Frenchman. I'm a soldier of the Irish Republican Army."

She needed to wound him then. "Well, friend Steiner's finished or soon will be. You next."

"What are you talking about?"

"Pamela Vereker was with me up at the church when he and his men took her brother and George Wilde up there. We overheard enough to send her flying off to Meltham to get those Yankee Rangers."

He grabbed her by the arms. "How long ago?"

"You go to hell!"

"Tell me, damn you!" he shook her roughly.

"I'd say they must be there by now, so there isn't a thing you can do except run."

He released her and said wryly, "Sure and it would be the sensible thing to do, but I was never one for that."

He pulled on his cap and goggles and his trench coat. He crossed to the fireplace and felt under a pile of old newspapers. There were the two hand grenades which Neumann had given him. He now placed them carefully inside the front flap of his trench coat. He put the Mauser into his right pocket and lengthened the sling on his Sten almost to waist level so that he could fire it one-handed if necessary. Finally he checked that his Walther was where he always kept it, hanging inside the hearth.

Molly said, "What are you going to do?"

"Into the valley of death, Molly my love. Did you think I'd leave Steiner in the lurch?"

"You can't go up there." There was panic in her voice now. "Liam, you won't stand a chance." She caught hold of his arm.

"Oh, but I must, my pet." He kissed her on the mouth and pushed her firmly to one side. He turned at the door. "For what it's worth, I wrote you a letter. It's on the mantelpiece."

The door banged, she stood there rigid, frozen. Somewhere in another world the engine roared away. She found the letter and opened it feverishly.

Molly, my own true love,

I came to Norfolk to do a job, not to fall in love for the first and last time in my life with an ugly little peasant girl that should have known better. By now you'll know the worst of me, but try not to think it. To leave you is punishment enough. As they say in Ireland, we knew the two days.

Liam

Tears blurred the words. She stuffed the letter into her pocket and stumbled outside. She scrambled onto her horse and urged him into a gallop towards the village.

BRANDT SAT on the parapet of the bridge and lit a cigarette. "So what do we do, run for it?"

"Where to?" Neumann, who had just come from his encounter with Joanna Grey at the church, looked at his watch. "Twenty to five. It should be dark by six thirty. If we can hang on until then, we could fade away in twos and threes and make for Hobs End. Maybe some of us could catch that E-boat."

"The colonel could have other ideas," Altmann said.

Brandt nodded. "Only he isn't here, so it seems to me we'd better get ready to do a little fighting."

Neumann said, "And we fight only as German soldiers." He took off his maroon beret and jump jacket, revealing his *Fliegerbluse*. From his hip pocket he produced his *Schiffchen* and adjusted it to the correct angle. "All right," he said to Brandt and Altmann, "you'd better get moving to your posts."

Neumann tried to raise Steiner on the field telephone. "Come in, Eagle One. This is Eagle Two." There was no reply. He handed the phone back to Private Hagl, who lay in the shelter of the bridge parapet, the barrel of his Bren protruding through a drainage hole. A stack of ammunition was beside him.

Hagl stiffened. "I hear a jeep."

The vehicle came around the corner by Park Cottage. A white handkerchief fluttered on the radio antenna. There was one occupant only. Neumann moved forward and waited, hands on hips.

Shafto took a cigar from one of his shirt pockets and put it between his teeth. He took his time lighting it, then got out of the jeep. He stopped a yard or two from Neumann and stood, legs apart, looking him over.

Neumann noted the collar tabs and saluted formally. "Colonel."

Shafto returned the salute. His glance took in the uniform with its decorations. "So, no more pretense, Herr Oberleutnant? Tell Steiner that Colonel Robert E. Shafto, in command Twenty-first Specialist Raiding Force, would like to speak with him."

"I am in charge here, Herr Oberst. You must deal with me."

Shafto's eyes took in the barrel of the Bren poking through the bridge parapet, swivelled to the post office, then to the second floor of the Studley Arms, where two bedroom windows stood open. Neumann said politely, "Is there anything else, Colonel?"

"Has Steiner run out on you?" Neumann made no reply. "Okay, son. If I have to bring my boys in here, you won't last ten minutes. Why not throw in the towel?"

"Sorry, but I forgot to put one in my overnight bag."

"Ten minutes, that's all I'll give you. Then we come in."

"I'll give you two," Neumann said, "to get the hell out of here." There was the metallic click of weapons being cocked.

Shafto looked at the windows. "Okay, sonny, you asked for it."

He stamped the cigar very deliberately into the ground and walked back to the jeep. As he drove away he reached for the mike on the field radio. "This is Sugar One. Twenty seconds and counting. Nineteen, eighteen, seventeen . . ." He was passing Park Cottage at twelve, disappeared around the bend in the road on ten.

Joanna Grey, who had witnessed the entire scene from her bedroom window, went to the study, opened the door to the secret cubbyhole loft and locked it behind her. She climbed the stairs, sat down at the radio, took the Luger from the drawer and laid it on the table. She wasn't in the least afraid.

THE LEAD JEEP in Shafto's section roared around the corner into the straight. There were two men in front, and two stood in the rear working a Browning machine-gun. As the Rangers passed the cottage next to Joanna Grey's, Dinter and Berg stood up together, Dinter supporting a Bren gun across his shoulder while Berg did the firing. He loosed one long, continuous burst that knocked the two men at the Browning off their feet. The lead jeep bounced over the grass bank and came to rest upside down in the stream. The next jeep in line swerved away wildly. Berg continued to fire short bursts, driving one of the jeep's gun crew over the side and smashing its windshield before it rounded the corner to safety.

In Stalingrad, Dinter and Berg had learned that the essence of success in such situations was to make your hit, then get out fast. They exited immediately through a wrought-iron gate in the wall and worked their way back to the post office.

Shafto, who had watched the debacle from a rise in the wood down the road, ground his teeth with rage. The jeep which had just been shot up had pulled in at the side of the road and a sergeant was putting a field dressing on its driver's face. Shafto shouted, "Dammit, Sergeant Thomas, what are you playing at? Go forward with three men on foot and take care of that machine-gun."

Krukowski, behind him, winced. *Five minutes ago we were thirteen. Now it's nine. What does he think he's doing?*

There was heavy firing from the other side of the village. Shafto snapped his fingers and Krukowski passed him the field phone. "Captain Mallory, do you read me? What's going on up there?"

"They've got a strong point set up in the mill. They knocked out my lead jeep. I've already lost four men."

"Then lose some more," Shafto yelled into the phone. "Get in there, Mallory. Burn them out. Whatever it takes." The firing was very heavy now as Shafto tried the other section. "You there, Sergeant Hustler?"

"Colonel, this is Hustler." His voice sounded faint.

"I expected to see you on the hill at that church by now."

"It's tough going, Colonel. We got tangled up in a bog. Just approaching the south-east end of Hawks Wood now."

"Well, get the lead out!" He handed the phone back to Krukowski just as Sergeant Thomas and his three men returned.

"Nothing to report, Colonel. Just these." Thomas held out a handful of .303 cartridge cases.

Shafto struck his hand violently, spilling them to the ground. "Okay, I want two jeeps out in front, two men to each Browning. I want that bridge plastered. I want you to lay down such a fire that even a blade of grass won't stand up."

"But, Colonel—" Thomas began.

"And hit that post office by the bridge. Krukowski stays with me." Shafto slammed his hand on a jeep's bonnet. "Move it!"

BRANDT HAD Corporal Walther, Meyer and Riedel with him in the mill. For defence, it was perfect: the ancient stone walls were three feet thick, and downstairs the oak doors were bolted and barred. The windows of the second floor commanded an excellent field of fire, and Brandt had a Bren gun set up there.

Below, a burning jeep blocked the road, one man inside, two more sprawled in the ditch. From behind hedges the Americans poured considerable fire into the mill walls, to little effect.

"I don't know who's in charge down there, but he doesn't know his business," Walther observed as he reloaded his M1.

Brandt held up his hand. "Everyone stop firing."

"Why?" Walther demanded.

"Because they've stopped." There was a deathly silence, and Brandt said softly, "I'm not sure I believe this, but get ready."

A moment later, with a rousing battle cry, Mallory and eight or nine men emerged from shelter and ran for the mill, firing from the hip. In spite of the fact that they were getting covering fire from the two remaining jeeps, it was an incredible act of folly.

Brandt put a long, almost leisurely burst into Mallory and killed him instantly. Three more went down as the Germans all fired at once. One American picked himself up and staggered to the safety of the first hedge as the survivors retreated.

In the quiet which followed, Brandt reached for a cigarette. "I make that seven. Eight if you count the one by the hedge."

"Suicide," Walther said. "All they have to do is wait."

MAJOR KANE and Colonel Corcoran sat in a jeep two hundred yards down the road from the main gate at Meltham House and looked up at the shattered telephone pole. "Good God!" Corcoran said. "What on earth was he thinking of?"

Kane could have told him, but refrained. He said, "I don't know, Colonel. Maybe some notion he had about security."

A jeep turned out of the main gate and drove up to them. Garvey was at the wheel. "We just got a radio message. Krukowski says it's a mess down there. Dead men all over the place."

"And Shafto?"

"Krukowski was pretty hysterical. Kept saying the colonel was acting like a crazy man. Some of it didn't make much sense."

Kane said to Corcoran, "I think I should get down there." He turned to Garvey. "What's left in the motor pool?"

"A White Scout car and three jeeps."

"All right, we'll take them, plus a detail of twenty men. That leaves twenty-five here to protect the Prime Minister."

"Twenty-six, with me," Corcoran said. "Perfectly adequate."

CHAPTER 11

THE VILLAGE was still a good mile and a half away when Steiner first became aware of the persistent electronic buzz from the field phone. Someone was on channel, but too far away. "Faster," he told Klugl. "Something's wrong."

When they were a mile away the rattle of small arms fire in the distance confirmed his worst fears. He cocked his Sten gun and looked up at Werner. "Be ready to use that thing."

As they drew closer to the village, Steiner tried to make contact on the field phone but with no better success.

A moment later they topped the rise at Garrowby Heath, three hundred yards west of the church, and the whole panorama was spread below.

Steiner raised his field glasses and took in the remainder of Mallory's detail, behind the post office and the Studley Arms, and Neumann, Hagl beside him, pinned behind the bridge by the machine-gun fire from the Brownings of Shafto's jeeps, firing from over Joanna Grey's garden wall.

Werner tapped him on the shoulder. "Below, Herr Oberst, in the wood on the right. Soldiers."

Steiner swung his field glasses. Sergeant Hustler and his men were halfway along the track through Hawks Wood. Steiner made his decision. "We're Fallschirmjäger again, boys."

He tossed his maroon beret away and took off his jump jacket. Klugl and Werner followed his example. Steiner said, "Down that track through the wood, across the footbridge for a few words with those jeeps. I think you can make it, Klugl, if you go fast enough, then on to Oberleutnant Neumann at the main bridge." He looked up at Werner. "And don't stop firing."

Steiner's jeep was doing fifty as it went down into Hawks Wood, bounced over a slight rise, and there was Sergeant Hustler with his men, no more than twenty yards away, strung out on the track. Werner started to fire. A front wheel bounced over a body and then they were through, leaving Hustler and seven of his men dying behind them. The jeep emerged from the wood like a thunderbolt, shot straight across the footbridge and up the bank to the road.

The machine-gun crew of one jeep alongside Joanna Grey's garden wall swung their Browning too late; Werner raked the wall with a burst that knocked them both off their feet. But the crew of the second jeep had two or three precious seconds to react. They had their Browning around and were already firing as Klugl hurtled towards the main bridge. Werner got in a quick burst that caught one of them, but the other kept on firing. Bullets hammered into the Germans' jeep, shattering the windshield. Klugl gave a sharp cry and fell forward across the steering wheel; the jeep swerved wildly, smashed into the parapet at the end of the bridge, then tipped over slowly.

Klugl lay huddled in the shelter of the jeep and Werner crouched over him, blood on his face from flying glass. He looked up at Steiner, his eyes wild. "He's dead, Herr Oberst." He reached for a Sten gun and started to stand.

Steiner dragged him down. "Pull yourself together, boy. He's dead, you're alive. Get this Browning set up."

Werner nodded dully. "Yes, Herr Oberst."

Neumann crawled out from behind the parapet, carrying a Bren. "You certainly created hell back there." Then he nodded to where Hagl's boots protruded from behind the parapet. "He's done for, I'm afraid."

Steiner said, "All right, Herr Oberleutnant. I think it's time we regrouped. Where is everybody?"

Neumann gave him a quick rundown on the general situation. Steiner nodded. "You get Altmann and his boys, and I'll see if I can get through to Brandt."

Werner gave Neumann covering fire with the Browning as the Oberleutnant darted across the road, and Steiner tried to raise Brandt on the field phone.

On the second floor of the mill, Riedel had just switched on during a lull in the fighting. "It's the colonel," he cried to Brandt, and said into the phone, "This is Eagle Three, in the water mill. Where are you?"

"At the bridge," Steiner said. "What is your situation?"

Riedel turned to the others. "He's at the bridge. Trust Steiner to pull us out." He crawled along to the loft door and kicked it open.

"Come back here," Brandt called.

Riedel peered outside. He laughed excitedly and raised the field phone to his mouth. "I can see you, Herr Oberst, we're—"

There was a heavy burst of automatic fire from outside, blood and brains sprayed across the wall and Riedel went headfirst out of the loft, still clutching the field phone.

Brandt flung himself across the room and peered over the edge. Riedel had fallen on top of the waterwheel. It kept turning, carrying him with it, down into the churning waters. When it came around, he was gone.

NEUMANN EMERGED from the post office with Altmann, Dinter and Berg. Within seconds all four had reached the parapet, and Steiner said, "I've lost them in the mill. I want the rest of you to make a run for the church. You've good cover, if you keep to the hedge. You're in charge, Neumann."

"What about you?"

"I'll cover with the Browning, then I'll follow."

"But Herr Oberst—" Neumann began.

Steiner cut him off short. "No buts about it. Today's my day for playing hero. Now get to hell out of it."

Neumann hesitated, but only fractionally. He nodded to the others. "All right. When I give the word, we all go together."

A moment later they dashed across the road to the hedge. A Ranger on a Browning at the other end of the village saw them cross, too late. In frustration, he raked the hedge.

Berg and Dinter died as bullets shredded the foliage, hammering them both back across the meadow in a last frenzied dance. Werner turned with a cry, and Altmann grabbed him by the shoulder and pushed him after Neumann.

SHAFTO, WITH Krukowski behind him on the field telephone, crouched in the shelter of the wall in Joanna Grey's front garden, stunned by the enormity of the news one of the survivors of Hustler's section had just brought. In a little over half an hour he had lost more than twenty men, dead or wounded—half his command. The consequences were appalling.

He looked up. At that moment Joanna Grey peered from behind the bedroom curtain. She drew back too late. Shafto growled deep in his throat, "That damned woman is still in the house."

He scrambled to his feet, drawing his Colt. "Come on, Krukowski," he cried, and ran to the front door.

Joanna hurried to the secret door, locked it behind her and went quickly up to the loft. She sat down at the radio and started to transmit to Landsvoort. She could hear doors being flung open downstairs and furniture knocked over as Shafto ransacked the house.

He was very close now, stamping about in the study. She heard his cry of rage as he left that room.

A voice from below. "Hey, Colonel, there was a dog locked in the cellar. He's comin' up now like a bat out of hell."

Joanna reached for the Luger and cocked it, continuing to transmit. In the hall, Shafto stood to one side as Patch scurried past him. He followed the retriever into the study and saw him scratching at the panelling in the corner.

Shafto quickly found the keyhole. "She's here, Krukowski!" There was a savage joy in his voice. "I've got her!"

He fired three shots at the keyhole. The lock disintegrated, and the door swung open just as Krukowski entered the room.

"Take it easy, sir," Krukowski said.

"Like hell I will." Shafto started up the stairs, the Colt held out in front of him as Patch flashed past.

As Shafto's head rose above floor level, Joanna Grey shot him between the eyes. He tumbled back down into the study. Krukowski poked the barrel of his M1 around the corner and loosed off an eight-round clip. The dog howled, there was the sound of a body falling, and then silence.

DEVLIN BRAKED to a halt at the church as Neumann, Altmann and Werner Briegel were retreating through the tombstones towards the porch. "It's a mess," Neumann said. "And the colonel's still down there by the bridge."

Devlin looked down to the village, where Steiner continued to fire the Browning from behind the damaged jeep, and Neumann grabbed his arm and pointed. "My God, look what's coming!"

Beyond Joanna Grey's cottage were a White Scout car and three jeeps. Devlin revved his motor. "Sure and if I don't go now, I might think better of it, and that would never do."

He went straight down the hill and skidded broadside to a halt behind Steiner. Steiner didn't say a word. He simply stood up, holding the Browning in both hands, and emptied it in a long burst before tossing it to one side and swinging a leg over the pillion. Devlin gunned the motor, swerved across the bridge and went straight back up the hill as the White Scout car nosed around the corner of Joanna Grey's cottage.

Neumann and his two comrades were still firing from behind the tombstones when Devlin and Steiner arrived on the scene. The Irishman ran the motorcycle through the lychgate and up the path to the church. Corporal Becker had the door open. When all five men had passed inside, he bolted it shut. The villagers huddled together, tense and anxious.

Philip Vereker limped down the aisle to confront Devlin. "Another damned traitor!"

Devlin grinned. "Ah, well," he said. "It's nice to be back amongst friends."

IN THE MILL it was quiet. "I don't like it," Walther said.

"You never do," Meyer said, and frowned. "What's that?"

There was the sound of a vehicle approaching. Brandt tried to peer out of the loft entrance over the road and immediately came under fire. He drew back.

The White Scout car was doing at least forty when Garvey swung the wheel and smashed it straight through the mill doors. Kane stood in the back behind a Browning anti-aircraft machine-gun and was already firing enormous .50-calibre rounds up through the wooden ceiling, ripping the planking to pieces. He was aware of the cries of agony but kept on firing, working the gun from side to side, only stopping when there were gaping holes in the ceiling.

A bloodstained hand showed at one of them. It was very quiet. Garvey took a Thompson gun and went up the steps in the corner. He came down almost instantly.

"That's it, Major."

Kane's face was pale, but he was completely in command of himself. "All right," he said. Now for the church."

MOLLY ARRIVED on Garrowby Heath in time to see a jeep drive up the hill, a white handkerchief fluttering from its radio antenna. It stopped at the lychgate, and Kane and Garvey got out. As they went through the churchyard, the church door opened and Steiner moved out of the vestibule. Devlin leaned against the wall behind him, smoking a cigarette. Harry Kane saluted formally. "We've met before, Colonel."

Steiner said calmly, "What can I do for you?"

"Surely that's obvious. Surrender. There's no point in further bloodshed. The men you left in the mill are all dead. The Prime Minister is safe, under as heavy a guard as he's likely to see in his lifetime. It's all over."

Steiner nodded, his face very pale. "Honourable terms?"

Before Kane could reply, Vereker pushed past Becker at the door and limped forward. "No terms!" He shouted it aloud, like a cry to heaven. "These men came here in British uniform—"

"But did not fight in them," Steiner cut in. "We fought only as German soldiers. The other was a legitimate *ruse de guerre.*"

"And a direct violation of the Geneva Convention," Vereker answered. "Which prescribes the death penalty for the wearing of an enemy's uniform."

Steiner saw the look on Kane's face and smiled gently. "Don't worry, Major, not your fault. The rules of the game and all that." He turned to Vereker. "Well now, Father, your God is a God of wrath indeed. You would dance on my grave, it seems."

Kane said, "You'll let the villagers go?"

Steiner looked faintly amused. "Why not? Did you think we'd hold the entire village hostage or come out fighting, driving the women in front of us? The brutal Hun? Sorry I can't oblige." He turned. "Send them out, Becker, all of them."

The door swung open and the villagers started to pour through. Betty Wilde came last with her son, Graham, and Neumann supported her husband, who looked dazed and ill. Garvey hurried back up the path and got an arm around him and Betty Wilde reached for Graham's hand and turned to Neumann.

"He'll be all right, Mrs Wilde," the young Oberleutnant said. "I'm sorry about what happened in there, believe me."

"It wasn't your fault," she said. "Would you tell me your name?"

"Neumann," he said. "Ritter Neumann."

"Thank you. I'm sorry I said the things I did." She turned to Steiner. "And I want to thank you and your men for Graham."

"He's a brave boy," Steiner said.

The boy stared up at him. "Why are you a German?" he demanded. "Why aren't you on our side?"

Steiner laughed. "Get him out of here, before he completely corrupts me."

She took the boy by the hand and hurried away.

Steiner turned to Kane. "So, Major, the final act. Let battle commence then." He saluted and went back into the vestibule, where Devlin was still standing. "I don't think I've ever heard you silent for so long before," Steiner said.

Devlin grinned. "To tell you the truth, I couldn't think of a damned thing to say except *Help*. Can I go in now and pray?"

FROM HER vantage point on the heath Molly watched Devlin disappear inside the church with Steiner, and her heart sank. Oh, God, she thought, I must do something. At the same moment a dozen Rangers, headed by Master Sergeant Garvey, cut across the road from the wood and worked through the presbytery garden. She watched the sergeant jump for the guttering and pull himself over, then scramble up the ivy to the roof. Once there, he uncoiled a rope and tossed the end down, and the other Rangers followed. Seized by a new determination, Molly swung into the saddle and urged her horse down to the wood behind the presbytery.

IT WAS very cold inside the church, a place of evening shadows, with only the flickering candles, the ruby light of the sanctuary lamp. There were eight of them left, including Devlin—Steiner, Neumann, Werner Briegel, Altmann, Jansen, Corporal Becker and Preston. There was also Arthur Seymour, who, still in the darkness of the Lady Chapel, had managed to push himself into a sitting position against the wall and was working on his wrists, his mad eyes fixed on Preston.

Steiner stood in the aisle to face his men. "Well, all I can offer you is another fight."

Preston said, "How can we fight? They've got the men, the equipment. We couldn't hold this place for ten minutes."

"We don't have any choice," Steiner said. "We have put ourselves gravely at risk by wearing British uniforms. If it's to be a bullet, rather now than from a firing squad later."

"I don't know what you're getting so worked up about anyway, Preston," Neumann said. "The English have never held traitors in particularly high regard. They'll hang you so high the crows won't be able to get at you."

Preston sank down in a pew, head in hands.

The organ rumbled into life, and Hans Altmann, sitting high above the choir stalls, called, "A choral prelude of Johann Sebastian Bach, entitled 'For the Dying.'"

Just as the music swelled, one of the clerestory windows high up in the nave smashed. A burst of automatic fire knocked Altmann off the seat into the choir stalls. Werner turned, crouching, firing his Sten. A Ranger pitched headlong through the window and landed between two pews. Several more clerestory windows crashed in, and heavy fire was poured down into the church. Werner was hit in the head and fell without a cry. Someone was using a Thompson gun up there now, spraying it back and forth.

Steiner crawled to Werner, turned him over, then dodged up the chancel steps to check on Altmann. He returned to the rear of the church, where Devlin asked, "What's the situation up there?"

"Altmann and Werner Briegel both gone."

"It's a bloodbath," Devlin said. "We don't stand a chance. Neumann's been hit in the legs and Jansen's dead."

Neumann was lying on his back, binding a field dressing around one thigh. Preston and Becker crouched beside him.

"Are you all right, Neumann?" Steiner asked.

"They'll run out of wound badges, Herr Oberst." Neumann grinned, but he was obviously in great pain.

All firing stopped, and Garvey called from high above, "You had enough yet, Colonel?"

Preston cracked then, jumped to his feet and ran out into the open by the font. "Yes, I'll come! I've had enough!"

"Bastard!" Becker cried. He ran out of the shadows and rammed his rifle butt against Preston's skull. Garvey's Thompson gun rattled, its short burst driving Becker headlong through the curtains at the base of the tower. He grabbed at the ropes in dying, as if trying to hang on to life itself, and somewhere overhead a bell tolled sonorously for the first time since 1939.

There was silence again, and Garvey called, "Five minutes."

There was an eerie creaking, and straining his eyes, Devlin saw that someone was standing in the entrance to the sacristy. A familiar voice whispered, "Liam?"

"It's Molly," he said to Steiner. "Where in the hell did she spring from?" He crawled across the floor to her, and was back in a moment. "Come on!" he said, getting a hand under Neumann's arm. "The little darling's got a way out for us!"

They slipped through the shadows, Neumann between them, and moved into the sacristy. Molly waited by the secret panel. Once they were inside, she closed it and led the way down the stairs and along the tunnel. It was very quiet when they came up into the hall at the presbytery. "Now what?" Devlin said. "We'll not get far with Neumann like this."

"Father Vereker's car is in back," Molly told them.

Steiner put a hand in his pocket. "And I've got his keys."

They were all the way down to the coast road when shooting began again at the church.

AFTER THE tiny click of the panel door in the sacristy closing, there was a stirring in the Lady Chapel, and Arthur Seymour stood up, hands free. He padded down the north aisle without a sound, holding in his left hand the coil of rope with which Preston had bound his feet. He leaned down to satisfy himself that Preston was still breathing, picked him up and slung him over one massive shoulder. Then he turned and walked straight up the centre aisle towards the altar.

On the roof, Garvey was beginning to worry. It was so dark down there that you couldn't see a damn thing. Suddenly the private on his right grabbed his arm. "Look, Sergeant, near the pulpit. Isn't someone moving?"

Garvey took a chance and flashed his torch. The young private gave a cry of horror. Garvey ran the torch quickly along the south aisle, then spoke to Kane on the field phone. "I don't know what's happening, Major, but you'd better get in there."

A moment later a burst from a Thompson gun shattered the lock on the main door. It crashed back and Harry Kane and a dozen Rangers moved in fast, ready for action. But there was only Arthur Seymour kneeling in the guttering candlelight, staring up into the hideously swollen face of Harvey Preston, hanging by his neck from the centre pole of the rood screen.

CHAPTER 12

THE PRIME MINISTER had taken the library overlooking the rear terrace at Meltham House for his personal use. When Harry Kane came out at seven thirty, Colonel Corcoran asked, "How was he?"

"Very interested," Kane said. "He wanted chapter and verse on the whole battle. He seems fascinated by Steiner."

"Aren't we all. What I'd like to know is where the damn man is now, and that Irish scoundrel."

"Nowhere near the cottage he's been living in, that's for sure. I've had a radio report from Garvey. It seems that when they went to check out the cottage they found two inspectors from Special Branch waiting for him."

"How on earth did they get on to him?"

"Some police investigation or other. Anyway, it's highly unlikely he'll turn up there now. Garvey is staying in the area and setting up a couple of roadblocks on the coast road, but we can't do much till we get more men."

"They're coming in, my boy, believe me," Corcoran said. "Since your chaps got the telephones working again, I've had several lengthy discussions with London. Another couple of hours should see the whole of North Norfolk sealed up tight. And it will certainly stay that way until Steiner is caught."

Kane nodded. "There's no way he could get anywhere near the Prime Minister. I've got men on his door, on the terrace and in the garden."

The door opened and a young corporal entered, typewritten sheets in his hand. "I've got the final lists, Major."

He went out and Kane looked at the first sheet. "Everyone is accounted for except Steiner, his second-in-command, Neumann, and the Irishman, of course. The other fourteen are all dead."

"But how did they get away? That's what I'd like to know."

"My theory is that when Pamela and the Prior girl got out through this priest's tunnel, they were in such a hurry they didn't close the secret door properly."

"I suppose so. Anyway, what about casualties on your side?"

Kane glanced at the second list. "Including Shafto and Captain Mallory, twenty-one dead, eight wounded." He shook his head. "Out of forty. There's going to be a big squawk when this gets out."

"*If* it gets out. London is already making it clear they want everything played down. They don't want to alarm the people, for one thing—Fallschirmjäger dropping into Norfolk to seize the Prime Minister, Englishmen in the SS! Can you imagine how *that* would look in the papers? And look at it from the Pentagon's point of view. A crack American unit takes on a handful of German paratroopers and sustains seventy per cent casualties."

"It's expecting a hell of a lot of people to keep quiet."

"There's a war on, Kane," Corcoran said. "And in wartime people can be made to do as they are told."

IN THE North Sea area generally, as the weather report had it, the winds were three to four knots, with rain squalls and some sea fog persisting till morning. By eight o'clock the E-boat was through the minefields and into the main coastal shipping lane.

Lieutenant Koenig, her captain, looked up from the chart table, where he had been plotting their course with great care. "Ten miles due east of Blakeney Point, Erich."

Petty officer Muller, who was at the wheel, nodded, straining his eyes into the murk ahead. "This fog isn't helping."

"You might be glad of it before we're through," Koenig said.

The telegraphist entered with a message from Landsvoort. Koenig read it in the light of the chart table. He looked at it for a long moment, then crumpled it into a ball. "The Eagle is blown. We are to proceed as I see fit … Of course, it's always possible some of them might make it. Just one or two."

SINCE JOANNA GREY'S final message, Radl had insisted on staying in the radio room while the operator tried to raise Koenig.

At five minutes to eight the operator smiled. "I've got them, Herr Oberst. Message received and understood."

"Thank God," Radl said, and fumbled to open his cigarette case. He took out the last of his Russian cigarettes and lit it.

The operator was writing feverishly on his pad. He tore off the sheet and turned. "Reply, Herr Oberst."

Radl felt strangely dizzy. He said, "Read it, please."

"'Will still visit nest. Some fledglings may need assistance. Good luck.' Why does he add that, Herr Oberst?"

"Because Koenig is a very perceptive young man, who suspects I'm going to need it as much as he does." Radl braced himself. "Now you can get me Berlin."

THERE WAS a decaying cottage on the northern boundary of the Priors' farm, at the back of the wood across the main road to Hobs End marsh. It provided some shelter for the Morris.

It was twenty past eight when Devlin and Steiner left Molly there to look after Neumann and went down through the trees to make a cautious reconnaissance. The marsh warden's cottage at Hobs End was in darkness, but on the main road there were two jeeps, one on either side of the road. It was raining hard, and several Rangers were sheltering under the trees. A match flared in Garvey's cupped hands, lighting his face for a moment.

Steiner and Devlin retreated. Steiner said, "The master sergeant who was with Kane, waiting to see if you show up."

"Why not at the cottage?"

"He probably has men out there, too."

"Not so good," Devlin said.

"You don't need to go to the cottage. You and Neumann can cut through the marsh on foot and still reach that beach in time."

"For what?" Devlin sighed. "I've a terrible confession to make, Colonel. I went off in such a devil of a hurry that I left the S-phone at the bottom of a carrier bag filled with spuds that's hanging behind the kitchen door. I can't call Koenig without it."

"My friend, even if Koenig fails to get a signal from you, he will still come in to that beach. What you need is a diversion."

"Such as?"

"Me in a stolen car passing through that roadblock. I could do with your trench coat, if you'd consider a permanent loan."

"You're not going with us." It was a statement of fact.

"I think you know where I must go, my friend."

"Meltham House?" Devlin sighed. "You won't even get close. They'll have more men round him than there are flies on a jam jar."

"In spite of that, I must try."

"Why? Because you think it might help your father's case back home? Face up to it. Nothing can help him if that devil at Prinz Albrechtstrasse decides otherwise."

"You're probably right. I think I've always known that."

"Then why?"

"Because I find it impossible to do anything else. Think of this game you play. Trumpets on the wind. Up the Republic. But tell me this, my friend. In the end, do you control the game, or does the game possess you? Can you stop, if you want, or must it go on the same until the day you lie in the gutter with a bullet in your back?"

Devlin said hoarsely, "God knows; I don't."

"But I do, my friend. And now, I think we should rejoin the others. You will naturally say nothing about my personal plans. Neumann could prove difficult."

"All right," Devlin said reluctantly.

They moved back through the night to the ruined cottage. Molly was in the car rebandaging one of Neumann's thighs. "How are you doing?" Steiner asked him.

"Fine," Neumann answered, but when Steiner put a hand on his forehead, it was damp with sweat.

Molly joined Devlin in the angle of the two walls, where he sheltered from the rain, smoking a cigarette. "He's not good," she said. "Needs a doctor, if you ask me."

"You might as well send for an undertaker," Devlin said. "But never mind him. It's you I'm worried about now. You could be in serious trouble from this night's work."

She was curiously indifferent. "Nobody saw me get you out of the church; nobody can prove I did. As far as they're concerned I've been sitting on the heath in the rain, crying my heart out at finding the truth about my lover."

He said awkwardly, "I haven't thanked you."

"It doesn't matter. I didn't do it for you. I did it for me. I love you. That's why I got you out of that church tonight. Not because it was right or wrong, but because I couldn't have lived with myself if I'd stood by and let you die." She turned to go back. "I'd better check on how the lieutenant is getting on."

She walked over to the car, and Devlin swallowed hard. Wasn't it the strange thing? The bravest speech he'd ever heard in his life, a girl to cheer from the rooftops, and here he felt more like crying at the tragic waste of it all.

Steiner came and stood beside him. "I'll have that trench coat now," he said.

Devlin couldn't see his face in the darkness and suddenly didn't want to. He unslung his Sten gun, took off the trench coat and handed it over. "You'll find a silenced Mauser in the right-hand pocket and two extra magazines."

"Thank you." Steiner took off his *Schiffchen* and pushed it inside his *Fliegerbluse*. He pulled on the trench coat and belted it. "So, the final end of things. We'll say goodbye here, I think."

"Tell me one thing," Devlin said. "Has it been worth it?"

"Oh, no." Steiner laughed lightly. "No more philosophy, please." He held out his hand. "May you find what you are searching for, my friend."

"I already have, and lost it in the finding," Devlin told him.

"Then, from now on, nothing really matters," Steiner said. "A dangerous situation. You will have to take care."

They got Neumann out of the car and pushed it to where the track started to slope downhill to the road. "Do we go now?" Neumann asked bravely.

"You, not me," Steiner told him. "There are Rangers down there on the road. I thought I might arrange a small diversion while you get across. I'll catch up with you later."

Neumann grabbed his arm, and there was panic in his voice. "No, Kurt, I can't let you do this."

Steiner said, "Oberleutnant Neumann, you are undoubtedly the finest soldier I've ever known. From Narvik to Stalingrad, you've never shirked your duty or disobeyed an order of mine, and I haven't the slightest intention of letting you start now."

Neumann tried to straighten up, bracing himself on a stick that Steiner had cut for him. "As the Herr Oberst wishes."

"Good," Steiner said. "Go now, Mr Devlin, and good luck."

He opened the car door, and Neumann called softly, "Herr Oberst?"

"Yes."

"A privilege to serve with you, sir."

"Thank you, Herr Oberleutnant." Steiner got into the Morris, released the brake, and the car started to roll down the track.

DEVLIN AND MOLLY went through the trees, Neumann between them, and paused at the side of the road. Devlin whispered, "Time for you to go, girl."

"I'll see you to the beach, Liam," she said firmly.

He had no chance to argue, because the car engine started forty yards up the road and the Morris's dim headlights were turned on. One of the Rangers took a red lamp from under his cape and waved it. Devlin had expected the German to drive straight on, but to his astonishment, he slowed. Steiner was taking a coldly calculated risk, something designed to draw every last man there. There was only one way. He waited for Sergeant Garvey's approach, his left hand on the wheel, his right hand holding the Mauser.

"Sorry, but you'll have to identify yourself." Garvey switched on a torch, picking Steiner's face out of the darkness.

The Mauser coughed once as Steiner fired at point-blank range, but a good two inches to one side. The wheels skidded as he stamped on the accelerator and was away.

"That was Steiner!" Garvey cried. "Get after him!"

There was a mad scramble as everyone jumped to get on board. Garvey's jeep was away first, the other hard behind. The sound dwindled into the night.

The 1933 Morris was virtually worn out, and although she suited Vereker's requirements adequately enough, they were not those of Steiner that night. With his foot flat on the boards, the needle obstinately refused to move beyond forty.

As he debated the merits of stopping suddenly and taking to the wood on foot, Garvey's jeep started to fire its Browning. Steiner ducked over the wheel, bullets hammered through the body, the windshield dissolved in a snowstorm of flying glass.

The Morris swerved to the right, smashed through some wooden railings and lumbered down a slope of young firs. Steiner opened the car door and tumbled out. He was on his feet in a moment, moving away as the Morris went into the flooded marsh below.

The jeeps skidded to a halt on the road above. Garvey was first out, the torch ready in his hand. As he reached the bank, the muddy waters of the marsh closed over the roof of the Morris. He took off his helmet and started to unbuckle his belt, and Krukowski, sliding down after him, grabbed him by the arm. "Don't think it. That isn't water. It's mud, deep enough to swallow a man whole."

Garvey nodded slowly. "Yes, I suppose you're right." He played his torch on the surface of the muddy pool where bubbles broke through, then turned and went back up the slope to radio in.

KANE AND Colonel Corcoran were having supper in the ornate front drawing room when the corporal from the radio room rushed in with the message. Kane looked at it briefly, then slid it across the polished surface of the table.

"My God, and he was pointing in this direction, you realise that?" Corcoran frowned. "What a way for such a man to go."

Kane felt curiously depressed. He said to the corporal, "Tell the motor pool to send a recovery vehicle. I want Colonel Steiner's body out of there."

The corporal went out, and Corcoran said, "What about the other one, and the Irishman?"

"I don't think we need worry. They'll turn up, but not here." Kane sighed. "No, in the end it was Steiner on his own, I think."

"Will you tell the Prime Minister or shall I?" Corcoran asked.

"Your privilege, I guess, sir." Kane managed a smile. "I'd better let the men know. They can phase the guard system now, so they get time off in turns for a hot meal and so on."

THE COTTAGE at Hobs End was in total darkness as Devlin, Molly and Neumann paused. Devlin, thinking of the S-phone, whispered, "You two keep moving along the dyke. I'll catch you up."

Before either of them could protest, he had slipped across the yard and was listening at the window. The front door opened with a slight creak and he moved inside, the Sten gun ready.

The living-room door stood ajar, a few embers from the dying fire glowing on the hearth. He stepped inside. The door slammed behind him, the muzzle of a Browning was rammed into the side of his neck and the Sten plucked from his hand. "Hold it right there," Chief Inspector Jack Rogan said. "All right, Fergus, let's have a little light on the situation."

A match flared as Fergus Grant lit the oil lamp. Rogan put his knee into Devlin's back and sent him staggering across the room. "Let's have a look at you."

Devlin half turned, a foot on the hearth. He put a hand on the mantelpiece. "I haven't had the honour."

"Chief Inspector Rogan, Inspector Grant, Special Branch." Rogan sat on the edge of the table, pointing his Browning.

"The Irish section, is it?"

"That's right. You've been a naughty boy from what I hear."

"Do you tell me?" Devlin said, leaning a little farther into the hearth, knowing that even if he got to the Walther, his chances were of the slimmest.

"Yes, you really give me a pain, you people," Rogan said. "Why can't you stay back there in the bogs where you belong?" He took out a pair of handcuffs. "Get over here."

A stone crashed through the window, and both policemen turned in alarm. Devlin reached for the Walther hanging at the back of the chimney beam. He shot Rogan in the head, knocking him off the table, but Grant got off one wild shot that caught the Irishman in the right shoulder and Devlin fell into the easy chair, still firing, shattering the inspector's left arm.

Grant fell back against the wall and slid down to the floor. He seemed in deep shock. Devlin picked up the Browning and stuffed it in his waistband, then went to the door, took down the carrier bag and emptied the potatoes on the floor. The small canvas bag at the bottom contained the S-phone and a few other odds and ends, and he slung it over his shoulder.

"Why don't you kill me as well?" Fergus Grant said weakly.

"You're nicer than he was," Devlin said. "I'd find a better class of work, son, if I was you."

He went out quickly. When he opened the front door, Molly

was standing outside. "Thank God!" she said, but he put a hand to her mouth and hurried her away. They reached the wall where Neumann waited. Molly said, "What happened?"

"Special Branch detectives. I killed one, wounded another."

"I helped you do that?"

"Yes. Will you go now, Molly, while you still can?"

She turned from him suddenly and started to run back along the dyke. Devlin hesitated and then, unable to contain himself, went after her. He caught her within a few yards and pulled her into his arms. Her hands went to his neck, she kissed him with a passion that was all-consuming. He pushed her away. "Go now, girl, and God go with you."

She ran into the night, and Devlin went back to Neumann. "A very remarkable young woman," the Oberleutnant said.

"That's the understatement of the age," Devlin told him. He got the S-phone out of the bag and switched it on. "Eagle to Wanderer. Eagle to Wanderer. Come in please."

On the bridge of the E-boat his voice sounded as if he were just outside the door. Koenig reached for the mike, his heart beating. "Eagle, this is Wanderer. What is your situation?"

"Two fledglings still in the nest," Devlin said. "Can you come immediately?"

"We're on our way." Koenig turned to Muller. "Switch to silencers and break out the White Ensign. We're going in."

As DEVLIN and Neumann reached the trees, the Irishman cursed suddenly at the searing pain in his shoulder, now that the shock was beginning to wear off.

"Are you all right?" Neumann asked.

"Bleeding like Mrs O'Grady's pig, but nothing like a sea voyage to cure what ails you."

They went past the warning notice, picked their way gingerly through the barbed wire and started across the beach. Neumann was gasping with pain at every step, yet he never faltered. They stumbled across the sands, and as the tide flowed in, the water grew deeper—first knee-deep, then up to their thighs. They were well out into the estuary now and Neumann groaned and fell to one knee. "It's no good, Devlin. I've had it. I've never known such pain."

Devlin crouched beside him and raised the S-phone to his mouth again. "Wanderer, this is Eagle. We are waiting for you in the estuary a quarter of a mile offshore. Signalling now." From the canvas bag he took out a luminous signal ball and held it up in the palm of his right hand.

Twenty minutes later the water was up to his chest. He had never been so cold in his life. He stood on the sandbank, legs apart, his left arm supporting Neumann, his right hand holding the signal ball high, the tide flowing around them.

"It's no good," Neumann whispered. "I can't feel a thing. I'm finished. I can't take any more."

"Don't give in now," Devlin said. "What would Steiner say?"

"Steiner?" Ritter coughed, choking a little as saltwater slopped over his chin and into his mouth. "He'd have swum across."

Devlin forced a laugh. "That's the way, son. Keep smiling." He started to sing at the top of his voice, *"And down the glen rode Sarsfield's men all in their jackets green."*

A wave passed over his head. This is it, he thought. But when it had rolled on he still managed to find his feet.

Three minutes later the E-boat slid out of the darkness and a torch shone down on them. A net was thrown over, and willing hands reached for Neumann. "Watch him," Devlin urged.

When he went over the rail himself and collapsed, Koenig knelt beside him with a blanket. "Drink some of this." He passed him a bottle. "I am glad to see you both. A miracle."

"The only one you're likely to get this night."

Koenig stood up. "Then we will go now. Please excuse me."

Devlin got the cork out of the bottle and sniffed at the contents. Rum! Not one of his favourites, but he swallowed deep and huddled against the stern rail, looking back towards the land.

In her bedroom at the farm, Molly sat up suddenly, then moved across the room and drew the curtains. She threw the windows open and leaned out into the rain, a tremendous feeling of elation filling her, and at that very moment the E-boat moved from behind the Point and turned out towards the open sea.

IN HIS OFFICE at Prinz Albrechtstrasse, Himmler worked at his eternal files in the light of the desk lamp. There was a knock, and Rossman entered. "I'm sorry to disturb you, Herr Reichsführer, but we've had a signal from Landsvoort. The Eagle is blown."

Himmler showed no emotion. He laid down his pen carefully and held out his hand. "Let me see." Rossman gave him the message and Himmler read it through. After a while he looked up. "I have an errand for you. Take two of your most trusted men. Fly to Landsvoort at once and arrest Colonel Radl."

"Of course, Herr Reichsführer. And the charge?"

"Treason against the state. That should do for a start."

JUST BEFORE nine o'clock Corporal George Watson of the military police ran his motorcycle to the side of the road a couple of miles south from Meltham House and pushed it up on its stand. He was almost soaked to the skin, in spite of his long dispatch rider's coat—bitterly cold and very hungry. He was also lost.

He leaned down to check his map in the light of his headlamp. A slight movement to his right made him look up. A man in a trench coat was standing there. "Hello," he said. "Lost, are you?"

"I'm trying to find Meltham House," Watson told him.

"Here, let me show you," Steiner said.

Watson leaned down to examine the map again; the Mauser rose and fell across the back of his neck, and Steiner pulled his dispatch case over his head. There was only one letter. It was addressed to Colonel William Corcoran, Meltham House.

Steiner dragged Watson into the shadows. A few moments later he was wearing the dispatch rider's long raincoat, helmet and goggles and leather gauntlets. He pushed the motorcycle off its stand, kicked the engine into life and rode away.

AT THE SIDE of the road they had placed a spotlight, and as the recovery truck's winch started to revolve, the Morris came up out of the marsh onto the bank. Garvey waited above on the road.

The corporal in charge had the door open. He peered inside and looked up. "There's nothing here."

"What in the hell are you talking about?" Garvey moved down through the trees quickly. He looked inside the Morris. "Oh, my God," he said, and he scrambled up the bank and grabbed for the mike on his jeep's radio.

STEINER HALTED at the gate of Meltham House, which was closed. The Ranger on the other side shone a torch on him and called, "Sergeant of the guard."

The sergeant came out of the lodge. "What is it?"

Steiner held out the letter. "Dispatch for Colonel Corcoran."

The sergeant nodded, and the Ranger unbolted the gate. "Straight up to the house. One of the sentries will take you in."

Steiner rode up the drive and turned away from the front door, following a branch that finally brought him to the motor pool at the rear of the building. He left the motorcycle beside a parked truck, then followed the path to the garden. He stepped into the shelter of the rhododendrons and removed the crash helmet and goggles, the raincoat and gauntlets. He took his *Schiffchen* from inside his *Fliegerbluse* and put it on. He adjusted the Knight's Cross at his throat and moved off, the Mauser ready.

He paused on the edge of a sunken garden below the terrace to get his bearings. The blackout wasn't too good, chinks of light showing at several windows. He took a step, and someone said, "That you, Corporal?"

Steiner grunted. A dim shape moved forward. The silenced Mauser coughed in his right hand. There was a startled gasp as the Ranger slumped to the ground. In the same moment a curtain was pulled back, and light fell across the terrace above.

The Prime Minister was standing at the balustrade smoking a cigar.

155

WHEN CORCORAN came out of the Prime Minister's room he found Kane waiting. "How is he?" Kane asked.

"Fine. Just gone out on the terrace for a cigar before bed."

They moved into the hall. "He probably wouldn't sleep too well if he heard my news, so I'll keep it till morning," Kane told him. "They hauled that Morris out of the marsh, and no Steiner."

Corcoran said, "Are you suggesting he got away? How do you know he isn't still down there? He might have been thrown out."

"It's possible," Kane said. "So I'm doubling the guard."

The front door opened and the sergeant of the guard came in. "You wanted me, Major?"

"Yes," Kane said. "When they got the car out, Steiner was missing. We'll double the guard. Nothing to report from the gate?"

"Only that military policeman with the dispatch for Colonel Corcoran."

Corcoran stared at him, frowning. "That's the first I've heard of it. When was this?"

"Maybe ten minutes ago, sir."

"Oh, my God!" Kane said. "He's here! Steiner's here!" Tugging at his Colt automatic, he ran for the library door.

STEINER WENT up the steps to the terrace slowly. The scent of the good Havana cigar perfumed the night. As he put his foot on the top step it crunched in gravel. The Prime Minister turned sharply and looked at him. He removed the cigar from his mouth, that implacable face showing no kind of reaction. "Oberstleutnant Kurt Steiner of the Fallschirmjäger, I presume?"

"Mr Churchill." Steiner hesitated. "I regret this, but I must do my duty, sir."

"Then what are you waiting for?" the Prime Minister said.

Steiner raised the Mauser, the curtains at the French windows billowed and Harry Kane stumbled through, firing wildly. His first bullet hit Steiner in the right shoulder; the second caught him in the heart, killing him instantly, pushing him over the balustrade.

Corcoran arrived on the terrace a moment later, revolver in

hand. Below in the sunken garden, Rangers appeared from the darkness on the run, to pause and stand in a semicircle. Steiner lay in the pool of light from the open window, the Knight's Cross at his throat, the Mauser still gripped in his right hand.

"Strange," the Prime Minister said. "With his finger on the trigger, he hesitated. Whatever else may be said, he was a fine soldier and a brave man. See to him, Major." He turned and went inside.

CHAPTER 13

ALMOST A YEAR to the day after I had made that astonishing discovery in the churchyard at St Mary and All the Saints, I returned to Studley Constable, this time by direct invitation of Father Philip Vereker. I was admitted to the presbytery by a young priest with an Irish accent.

Vereker was sitting in a wing chair in front of a huge fire in the study, a rug about his knees, a dying man if ever I've seen one. The skin seemed to have shrunk on his face, exposing bone, and the eyes were full of pain. "It was good of you to come."

"I'm sorry to see you so ill," I said.

"I have cancer of the stomach. Nothing to be done. The bishop has been very good in allowing me to end it here, arranging for Father Damian to assist with parish duties, but that isn't why I sent for you. I hear you've had a busy year."

"I don't understand," I said. "When I was here before, you wouldn't say a word. Drove me out, in fact."

"It's really simple. For years I've only known half the story. Now I have an insatiable curiosity to know the rest before it is too late."

So I told him, and by the time I had finished, shadows were falling across the grass outside and the room was half in darkness. "Remarkable," he said. "How did you find it all out?"

"Not from any official source, believe me. Just from talking to people, those who are still alive and who were willing to talk. The biggest stroke of luck was in being privileged to read a diary kept by the man responsible for the organisation of the whole thing, Colonel Max Radl. His widow is still alive in Bavaria. What I'd like to know now is what happened here afterwards."

"There was a complete security clampdown. Every single villager involved was interviewed by Intelligence. The Official Secrets Act invoked. Not that it was really necessary. These are a peculiar people. Drawing together in adversity, hostile to strangers, as you have seen. Did you know that Arthur Seymour was killed last February — driving back from Holt one night drunk?"

"What happened to him after the other business?"

"He was quietly certified. Spent eighteen years in an institution, until the mental health laws were relaxed."

"And the tombstone? Who erected that?"

"The military engineers who were sent here to clean up the village, repair damage and so on, placed all the bodies in a mass grave in the churchyard. We were told it was to remain unmarked."

"But you thought differently?"

"Not just me. All of us. Wartime propaganda was a pernicious thing then, however necessary. Every war picture we saw at the cinema, every book we read, every newspaper, portrayed the German soldier as a ruthless barbarian, but these men were not like that. Graham Wilde is alive today, Susan Turner married with three children, because one of Steiner's men gave his life to save them. And at the church, remember, he let the people go."

"So a secret monument was decided on?"

"That's right. Old Ted Turner was a retired monument mason. It was laid, dedicated by me at a private service, then concealed from the casual observer as you know. The man Preston is down there, too, but was not included on the monument."

"And you all agreed with this?"

He managed one of his rare, wintry smiles. "As some kind of personal penance, if you like. Dancing on his grave was the term Steiner used, and he was right. I hated him that day."

"Because it was a German bullet that crippled you?"

His face was completely in shadow. I found it impossible to see his expression. "I am more used to hearing confessions than making them, but I worshipped Joanna Grey. Oh, not in any silly superficial way. To me she was the most wonderful woman I'd ever known. I can't even begin to describe the shock I experienced on discovering her true role."

"So in a sense, you blamed Steiner?"

"I think that was the psychology of it." He sighed. "Do you still intend to publish?"

"I don't see why not."

"It didn't happen, you know. No stone any more, and have you found one single official document to substantiate any of it?"

"Not really," I said cheerfully. "But I've spoken to a lot of people and they've told me what adds up to a pretty convincing story."

"It could have been." He smiled faintly. "If you hadn't missed out on one very important point."

"And what would that be?"

"Look up any one of two dozen history books on the last war and check what Winston Churchill was doing during the weekend in question. But perhaps that was too simple, too obvious."

"All right," I said. "You tell me."

"Getting ready to leave in HMS *Renown* for the Teheran Conference. Called at Algiers on the way, and arrived at Malta on the seventeenth of November, where he invested Generals Eisenhower and Alexander with special versions of the North Africa ribbon."

It was suddenly very quiet. I said, "Who was he?"

"He was George Howard Foster, known on the stage as the Great Foster. He was an impressionist. The war was his salvation."

"How was that?"

"He not only did a more than passable imitation of the Prime Minister, he even looked like him. After Dunkirk he started doing a special act, a grand finale to the show. 'I have nothing to offer but blood, toil, tears and sweat.' The audiences loved it."

"And Intelligence pulled him in?"

"On special occasions. If you intend to send the Prime Minister to sea at the height of the U-boat peril, it's useful to have him publicly appearing elsewhere." He smiled. "He gave the performance of his life that night. They all believed it was him, of course. Only Colonel Corcoran knew the truth."

"All right," I said. "Where's Foster now?"

"Killed, along with a hundred and eight other people when a flying bomb hit a little theatre in Islington in February 1944. So you see, it's all been for nothing. It never happened. Much better for all concerned."

He went into a bout of coughing that racked his entire body. The door opened and a nun entered. She leaned over him and whispered. He said, "I'm sorry. It's been a long afternoon. I think I should rest. Thank you for coming and filling in the gaps." He started to cough again, so I left as quickly as I could.

I lit a cigarette and leaned on the flint wall of the churchyard. I knew that Vereker was telling the truth. I looked towards the porch where Steiner had stood that evening so long ago in confrontation with Harry Kane, thought of him on the terrace at Meltham House, the final hesitation. *And even if he had pulled that trigger, it would still all have been for nothing.*

There's irony for you, as Devlin would have said. Ah, well, in the final analysis there was nothing I could find to say that would be any improvement on the words of a man who had played his own part so well on that fatal night.

"Whatever else may be said, he was a fine soldier and a brave man." Let it end there. I turned and walked away through the rain.

Cold
Harbour

Cold
Harbour

An American war hero in the
uniform of the German SS elite.
An RAF ace at the controls of
a Luftwaffe fighter plane. A
young Englishwoman beguiling
Nazi officers at a French
château. For the schemers at
Cold Harbour, no stratagem is
too daring, no risk too great.
And nothing, ever, is what it
appears to be.

CHAPTER 1

HERE WERE bodies all around, clear in the moon-light, some in life jackets, some not. Way beyond, the sea was on fire with burning oil, and as Martin Hare lifted on the crest of a wave he saw what was left of the destroyer, her prow already under the water. There was a dull explosion, her stern lifted, and she started to go. He skidded down the other side of the wave, buoyant in his life jacket, and choked, half fainting as he struggled for breath, aware of the intense pain from the shrapnel in his chest.

The sea was running very fast in the slot between the islands, six or seven knots at least. It seemed to take hold of him, carrying him along at an incredible rate; the cries of the dying faded into the night behind. Again he was lifted higher on a wave, paused for a moment, half blind from the salt; then he was swept down very fast and cannoned towards a life raft.

He grabbed at one of the rope handles and looked up. A man crouched there, a Japanese officer in uniform. His feet were bare. They stared at each other for a long moment, and then Hare tried to pull himself up. But he had no strength left.

The Japanese officer crawled forward without a word, reached down, caught him by the life jacket and hauled him onto the raft. At the same moment the raft spun like a top, caught by an eddy, and the Japanese pitched head first into the sea.

Within seconds he was ten yards away, his face clear in the moonlight. He started to swim back towards the raft, and then, behind him, cutting through the white froth between the waves, Hare saw a shark's fin. The Japanese didn't even cry out, simply threw up his arms and disappeared. And it was Hare who screamed, as he always did, coming bolt upright in the bed, his body soaked in sweat.

THE DUTY NURSE was McPherson, a tough, no-nonsense lady of fifty, a widow with two sons in the marines. She came in now and stood looking at him, hands on hips.

"The dream again?"

Hare swung his legs to the floor and reached for his dressing gown. "That's it. Who's the doctor tonight?"

"Commander Lawrence, but he won't do you any good. Another couple of pills so you'll sleep some more."

"What time is it?"

"Seven o'clock. Why don't you have a shower? You can come down to dinner. It'll do you good."

"I don't think so."

He looked in the mirror and ran his fingers through the unruly black hair that was streaked with grey. The face was handsome enough, pale from months of hospitalisation. But it was in the eyes that the lack of hope showed—no expression there at all.

He opened a drawer in the bedside locker, found his lighter and a packet of cigarettes and lit one. He was already coughing as he walked to the open window and looked out over the balcony to the garden.

"Wonderful," she said. "One good lung left, so now you're trying to finish what the Japs started."

There was a thermos filled with coffee by the bed. She poured some into a cup and brought it over. "Time to start living again,

Commander. As they say in the movies, for you the war is over."

He sipped his coffee. "So, what do I do?"

"Back to Harvard, Professor." She smiled. "The students will love you. All those medals. Wear your uniform on the first day." He smiled in spite of himself, but only briefly.

"God help me, Maddie, but I don't think I could go back. I've had the war, I know that."

"And it's had you, angel." She walked to the door, opened it and turned. "Only I would suggest you comb your hair and make yourself respectable. You've got a visitor."

He frowned. "A visitor?"

"Yes. He's with Commander Lawrence now. Very top brass. A Brigadier Munro of the British army, though you'd never think so. Doesn't even wear a uniform."

She went out, closing the door. Hare stood there for a moment, bewildered, then hurried into the shower.

BRIGADIER DOUGAL Munro was sixty-five and white-haired, an engagingly ugly man in an ill-fitting suit of Donegal tweed. He wore a pair of army-issue steel-rimmed spectacles.

"But is he fit, Doctor?" Munro was saying.

Lawrence wore a white surgical coat over his uniform. He opened the file in front of him. "He's forty-six years of age, Brigadier. He took three pieces of shrapnel in his left lung and spent six days on a life raft. It's a miracle he's still around."

"Yes, I take your point," Munro said.

"Here's a Harvard professor, a naval reserve officer and a famous yachtsman with all the right connections, who gets himself in patrol torpedo boats at the age of forty-three, when the war starts." He leafed through the pages. "Every battle area in the Pacific. Lieutenant commander, and medals—including two Navy Crosses—and then that final business at Tulugu in the Solomon Islands. That Japanese destroyer blew him half out of the water, so he rammed her and set off an explosive charge. He should have died."

"As I heard it, nearly everyone else did," Munro observed.

Lawrence closed the file. "You know why he didn't get the Medal of Honor? Because it was General MacArthur who recommended him, and the navy doesn't like the army interfering."

"You're not regular navy, I take it?" Munro said.

"Am I, hell."

"Good. I'm not regular army, so, plain speaking, is he fit?"

"Physically—yes. Mind you, the medical board has indicated no more seagoing duty. He has the option of taking a medical discharge now."

Munro tapped his forehead. "And what about up here?"

Lawrence shrugged. "He's had reactive depression, but that passes."

"So, he's fit to leave?"

"Oh, sure. With the proper authorisation, of course."

Munro took a letter from his inside pocket, opened it and passed it across.

Lawrence read it and whistled softly. "It's that important?"

"Yes." Munro put the letter back into his pocket.

Lawrence said, "My God, you want to send him back in."

Munro smiled gently. "I'll see him now, if you please."

MUNRO LOOKED OUT across the balcony to the lights of the city in the falling dusk. "Very pleasant, Washington, this time of year." He turned and held out his hand. "Munro—Dougal Munro."

"Brigadier?" Hare said.

"That's right."

Hare was wearing slacks and an open-necked shirt, his face still damp from the shower. "Forgive me for saying so, Brigadier, but you are the most unmilitary man I ever saw."

"Thank God for that," Munro said. "Until 1939 I was an Egyptologist by profession, at Oxford. My rank was to give me, shall we say, authority in certain quarters."

Hare frowned. "Do I smell intelligence here?"

"You certainly do. Have you heard of SOE, Commander?"

"Special Operations Executive," Hare said. "Don't you handle agents into occupied France and so on?"

"Exactly. I'm in charge of Section D at SOE, more commonly known as the dirty tricks department."

"And what would you want with me?" Hare demanded.

"You were a professor of German literature at Harvard. Your mother was German. You spent a great deal of time in Germany as a boy, even did a degree at Dresden University. You speak the language fluently, or so your naval intelligence service tells me, and your French is quite reasonable."

"Are you trying to recruit me as a spy or something?"

"Not at all," Munro told him. "You see, you really are unique, Commander. It's not just that you speak fluent German. It's the fact that you're a naval officer with a vast experience in torpedo boats who also speaks German that makes you interesting."

"I think you'd better explain."

"All right." Munro sat down. "This is classified, but I can tell you that at the urgent request of your own Office of Strategic Services you are to be transferred to the English Channel to land and pick up agents on the French coast."

"Me?" Hare said in amazement. "You're crazy. I'm all washed up. They want me to take a medical discharge."

"Hear me out," Munro said. "In the English Channel the British MTBs, motor torpedo boats, have had a very rough time with their German counterparts."

"What the Germans call a *Schnellboot*," Hare said. "A fast boat. An apt title."

"Yes. Well, we call them E-boats. As you say, they're fast—too damn fast. We've been trying to get hold of one ever since the war started, and we finally succeeded last month."

"You're kidding," Hare said.

"I think you'll find I never do, Commander," Munro told him.

"One of the S-eighty series. Had some engine problem on a night patrol off the Devon coast. When one of our destroyers turned up at dawn, the crew abandoned ship. Naturally her captain primed a charge to blow the bottom out of her, but it failed to explode. Interrogation of his radio operator indicated that their final message to their base was that they were sinking her, which means we have their boat and the German navy, the Kriegsmarine, don't know." He smiled. "You see the point?"

"I'm not sure."

"Commander Hare, there is in Cornwall a tiny fishing port called Cold Harbour. No more than two or three dozen cottages and a manor house. It's in a defence area, so the inhabitants have long since moved out. My department operates a couple of planes from there, German planes. A Stork and a JU eighty-eight S night fighter. They still carry Luftwaffe insignia, and the man who flies them— gallant RAF pilot though he is—wears a Luftwaffe uniform."

"And you want me to do the same thing with this E-boat?"

"Exactly. A Kriegsmarine boat needs a Kriegsmarine crew."

"Which is contrary enough to the rules of war to put the same crew in front of a firing squad if caught," Hare pointed out. "It's crazy."

"The S-eighty usually carries a complement of sixteen. The Admiralty thinks you could manage with ten. As it's a joint venture, both our people and yours are searching out the right people. I've already got the perfect engineer. A Jewish German refugee who worked at the Daimler-Benz factory. They manufacture the engines for all E-boats."

There was a long pause. Hare turned and looked out across the garden to the city. It was quite dark now. When he reached for a cigarette, his hand shook, and he turned and extended it to Munro.

"Look at that. And you know why? Because I'm scared," Hare said hoarsely. "I won't do it."

"Oh, but you will, Commander," Munro said. "And shall I tell you why? Because there's nothing else you can do. You certainly can't go back to the classroom after all you've been through. We're both in the same boat—men who've spent most of our lives living in the mind. And then the war came, and do you know what, my friend? You've enjoyed every golden moment."

"What if I say no?"

"Oh, dear." Munro extracted the letter from his inside pocket. "I think you'll recognise the signature at the bottom—Commander in Chief of the American armed forces."

Hare looked at it in stupefaction. "Good God!"

"Yes, well, he'd like a word before we go. Be a good lad and get into your uniform. We haven't got much time."

THE OVAL OFFICE was shadowed, the lamp on the desk, which was littered with papers, the only light. President Roosevelt was in his wheelchair at the window, staring out, a cigarette in his usual long holder, glowing in the darkness.

He swivelled around in the chair. "There you are, Brigadier."

"Mr President."

"And this is Commander Hare?" He held out his hand. "You're a credit to your country, sir. As your President, I thank you. That Tulugu business was quite something."

"Better men than me died sinking that destroyer, sir."

"I know, son." Roosevelt held Hare's hand in both of his. "Better men than you or me are dying every day, but we just have to press on and do our best. The brigadier's filled you in on this Cold Harbour business? You like the sound of it?"

Hare glanced at Munro, hesitated, then said, "An interesting proposition, Mr President."

Roosevelt tilted back his head and laughed. "A neat way of putting it." He wheeled himself to the desk and turned. "To wear the enemy uniform is totally against the terms of the Geneva Convention. But correct me if I get my history wrong, Brigadier. Isn't it a fact that during the Napoleonic Wars, ships of the British navy occasionally attacked under the French flag?"

"Indeed it is, Mr President, and usually when they were sailing French ships taken as prizes of war."

"So, there is a precedent for this type of action as a legitimate *ruse de guerre*," Roosevelt observed.

"Certainly, Mr President."

Hare said, "It's a point worth making that in all such actions it was customary for the British to hoist their own flag just before battle commenced."

"I like that." Roosevelt nodded. "If a man must die, it should be under his own flag." He looked up at Hare. "A direct order from your Commander in Chief. You will at all times carry the Stars and Stripes on this E-boat of yours, and if you find yourself sailing into battle, you will hoist it in place of the Kriegsmarine ensign. Understood?"

"Perfectly, Mr President."

Roosevelt held out his hand again. "Good. I can only wish you Godspeed." They both shook hands with him, and as if by magic, a young aide appeared and ushered them out.

As their limousine turned down Constitution Avenue, Hare said, "A remarkable man."

"The understatement of the year," Munro said. "What he and Churchill have achieved between them is amazing." He sighed. "I wonder how long it will be before the books are written proving how unimportant they really were."

"Second-rate academics out to make a reputation?" Hare said. "Just like us?"

"Exactly." Munro looked out the window. "I'm going to miss this town." He grunted. "There's something I forgot to tell you. In view of the circumstances, your navy has decided to promote you."

"To full commander?" Hare said in astonishment.

"Yes, but Fregattenkapitän is the equivalent rank in the Kriegsmarine, so that's what it is from now on."

Hare leant back against the seat, aware of a sudden fierce exhilaration. It was as if he'd been asleep for a long time and was awake again.

CHAPTER 2

As CRAIG OSBOURNE reached the edge of St Maurice, there was a volley of rifle fire, and rooks in the beech trees beside the village church lifted into the air in a dark cloud, calling to one another angrily. He was driving a Kübelwagen, the German army's equivalent of the jeep. He parked it by the gate to the church cemetery and got out, immaculate in the grey field uniform of a Standartenführer in the Waffen SS.

It was raining softly, and he took a greatcoat of black leather from the rear seat, slipped it over his shoulders and went forward to where a gendarme stood watching events in the square. There were a handful of villagers down there, an SS firing squad, and two prisoners waiting hopelessly, hands manacled behind their backs. A third lay face down on the cobbles by a wall. As Osbourne watched, an elderly SS general appeared, wearing a long greatcoat with silver lapel facings. He took a pistol from his holster, leant down and shot the man on the ground in the back of the head.

"That's General Dietrich, I suppose?" Osbourne asked in perfect French.

The gendarme, who had not noticed his approach, answered automatically. "Yes. He likes to finish them off himself, that one." He half turned, became aware of the uniform and jumped to attention. "Excuse me, Colonel. I meant no offence."

"None taken. You and I are, after all, fellow countrymen." Craig raised his left sleeve, and the gendarme saw the cuff title of the French Charlemagne Brigade of the Waffen SS. Whatever his private thoughts concerning a countryman serving the occupying enemy, the gendarme kept them to himself, face blank.

"This happens often?" Osbourne asked. The gendarme hesitated, and Osbourne nodded encouragingly. "Go on, man, speak your mind."

It surfaced then — the anger, the frustration. "Two or three times a week. A butcher, this one."

One of the two men waiting was positioned against the wall; there was a shouted command, another volley.

"And he denies them the last rites. You see that, Colonel? No priest, and yet when it's all over, he comes up here like a good Catholic to confess to Father Paul."

"Yes, so I've heard," Osbourne told him.

He turned away and walked back towards the church. The gendarme watched him go, wondering, then turned to the square as Dietrich went forward again, pistol in hand.

Craig Osbourne went up a path through the graveyard, opened the great oak door of the church and went inside. It was dark in there, a little light filtering down through stained-glass windows. As Osbourne approached the altar, the door of the sacristy opened and an old white-haired priest emerged. He wore an alb and a violet silk stole over his shoulders. He paused, surprise on his face.

"May I help you?"

"Perhaps. Back in the sacristy, Father."

The old priest frowned. "Colonel, I must hear confession."

Osbourne glanced across the empty church to the confessional boxes. "Not much custom, Father, but then there wouldn't be, not with that butcher Dietrich expected." He put a hand on the priest's chest firmly. "Inside, please."

The priest backed into the sacristy, bewildered. "Who are you?"

Osbourne pushed him down onto the wooden chair by the desk, took a length of cord from his coat pocket. "The less you know, the better, Father. Let's just say all is not what it seems." He tied the old man's wrists firmly behind his back. "I'm granting you a clean bill of health with our German friends." He took out a handkerchief.

The old priest said, "My son, I don't know what you plan, but this is God's house."

"Yes, well, I like to think I'm on God's business," Craig Osbourne said, and gagged him with the handkerchief.

He left the old man there, closed the sacristy door and crossed to the first of the confessional boxes, switched on the tiny light above the door and stepped inside. He took out his Walther, screwed a silencer onto the barrel and watched; the door was open a crack so that he could see down to the entrance.

After a while Dietrich entered with a young SS captain. They stood talking for a moment, then the captain went back outside and Dietrich walked along the aisle between the pews, unbuttoning his greatcoat. He took off his cap, entered the confessional box and sat down. Osbourne turned on the small bulb that illuminated the German on the other side of the grille, remaining in darkness himself.

"Good morning, Father," Dietrich said in bad French. "Bless me, for I have sinned."

"You certainly have, you bastard," Craig Osbourne told him, pushed the silenced Walther through the flimsy grille and shot him between the eyes.

Osbourne stepped out of the confessional box, and at the same moment the young SS captain opened the church door and peered in. He saw the general lying on his face, the back of his skull a sodden mass of blood, and Osbourne standing over him. The young officer drew his pistol and fired twice wildly, the sound deafening between the old walls. Osbourne returned the fire, catching him in the chest, knocking him back over one of the pews, then ran to the door.

He peered out and saw Dietrich's car parked at the gate, his own Kübelwagen beyond. Too late to reach it now, for already a squad of SS, rifles at the ready, were running towards the church, attracted by the sound of the SS captain's pistol shots.

Osbourne turned, ran along the aisle and left from the back door by the sacristy. He raced through the cemetery at the rear of the church and, vaulting a low stone wall, started up the hill to the woods above.

They began shooting when he was halfway up, and he ran, zigzagging wildly. He was almost to the woods when a bullet plucked at his left sleeve, sending him sideways to fall on one knee. He was up again in a second and sprinted over the brow of the hill. A moment later he was into the trees.

He ran wildly, both arms up to cover his face against the flailing branches, and where in the hell was he supposed to be running to? No transport and no way of reaching his rendezvous with the Lysander aircraft that was to pick him up. But Dietrich was dead.

There was a road in the valley below. He went sliding down through the trees, landing in a ditch, picked himself up and then, to his total astonishment, a Rolls-Royce came around the corner and braked to a halt.

René Dissard of the black eye patch was at the wheel in his chauffeur's uniform. The rear door was opened, and Anne-Marie looked out. "Playing heroes again, Craig? You never change, do you? Get in, for heaven's sake, and let's get out of here."

As THE ROLLS moved off, Anne-Marie nodded at the blood-soaked sleeve of Craig's uniform. "Bad?"

"I don't think so." Osbourne stuffed a handkerchief inside. "What are you doing here?"

"Grand Pierre was in touch. He says that Lysander pickup isn't on. Heavy fog and rain moving in from the Atlantic. I was supposed to wait for you at the farm and tell you, but I had a bad feeling about this one. Decided to come along and see the action. We were by the station. Heard the shooting and saw you running up the hill. René said you were bound to come this way."

"Good thing for me," Osborne told her.

She lit a cigarette and crossed one silken knee over the other, elegant as always in a black suit, a diamond brooch at the neck of the white silk blouse. The black hair was cut in a fringe across her forehead and curved under on each side, framing high cheekbones and a pointed chin.

"What are you staring at?" she demanded petulantly.

"You," he said. "Too much lipstick, as usual, but otherwise, perfectly marvellous."

"Oh, get under the seat and shut up," she told him.

She turned her legs to one side as Craig pulled down a flap, revealing space beneath the seat. He crawled inside, and she pushed the flap back into position.

A moment later they went around a corner and discovered a Kübelwagen across the road, half a dozen SS waiting.

"Nice and slow, René," she said.

"Trouble?" Craig Osbourne asked, his voice muffled.

"Not with any luck," she said softly. "I know the officer. He was stationed at the château for a while."

René stopped the Rolls, and a young SS lieutenant walked towards them. "Mademoiselle Trevaunce. What an unexpected pleasure."

"Lieutenant Schultz." She opened the door and held out her hand, which he kissed gallantly. "What's all this?"

"A wretched business. A terrorist has just shot General Dietrich in St Maurice," Schultz told her. "A terrible thing. Murdered in the church during confession." He shook his head. "That there are such people in this world passes belief."

"I'm so sorry." She pressed his hand in sympathy. "You must come and see us again soon. The countess had rather a fondness for you. We were sorry to see you go."

Schultz actually blushed. "Please convey my felicitations, but now I must delay you no longer."

He shouted an order, and one of his men reversed the Kübel-wagen. Schultz saluted, and René drove away.

"Mam'selle has the luck of the devil," he observed.

Craig Osbourne said softly, "Wrong, René. She is the devil."

AT THE FARM, they parked the Rolls-Royce in the barn while René went in search of information. Osbourne removed his tunic and ripped away the blood-soaked sleeve of his shirt.

Anne-Marie examined the wound. "Not too bad. It hasn't gone through, simply ploughed a furrow. Nasty, mind you."

René returned with a change of clothes and a piece of white

sheeting, which he proceeded to tear into strips. Anne-Marie set about the task of bandaging Osbourne's arm.

"There's a message from Grand Pierre," René said. "London says they're going to pick you up by torpedo boat off Léon tonight. Grand Pierre can't make it himself, but one of his men will be there. Blériot. Know him well. A good man."

Osbourne went around to the other side of the Rolls and changed. He returned wearing an old tweed cap, corduroy jacket and trousers, and broken boots. He put the Walther into his pocket and gave the uniform to René, who went out.

"Will I do?" he asked Anne-Marie.

She laughed out loud. "With three days' growth on your chin, perhaps, but you still look like a Yale man to me."

René returned and got behind the wheel. "We'd better get moving, mam'selle. It'll take us an hour to get there."

She pulled down the seat flap. "In you go, like a good boy."

Craig did as he was told and peered out at her. "I'm the one who's going to have the last laugh. Dinner at the Savoy tomorrow night. The Orpheans playing, dancing girls."

She slammed the flap shut, and René drove away.

Léon WAS a fishing village so small that it didn't even have a pier, most of the boats being drawn up onto the beach. There was the sound of accordion music from a small bar—the only sign of life— and they drove on, following a rough track to a tiny bay. A heavy mist rolled in from the sea, and somewhere in the distance a foghorn sounded forlornly. René led the way down to the beach, a torch in his hand.

Craig said to Anne-Marie, "You don't want to go down there. You'll only spoil your shoes. Stay with the car."

She took off her shoes and tossed them into the back of the Rolls. "Quite right, darling. However, thanks to my Nazi friends, I do have an inexhaustible supply of silk stockings. I can afford to ruin one pair for the sake of friendship." She took his arm, and they went after René.

"Friendship?" Craig said. "As I recall, in Paris in the old days, it was rather more than that."

"Ancient history, darling. Best forgotten."

She held his arm tight, and Osbourne caught his breath sharply, aware that his wound was really hurting now. Anne-Marie turned and looked at him.

"Are you all right?"

"Damned arm hurting a bit, that's all."

They approached René and another man standing beside a small dinghy, an outboard motor tilted over on its stern.

"This is Blériot," René said.

"Mam'selle." Blériot touched his cap.

"This is the boat?" Craig demanded. "And what do I do with it?"

"Around the point you will see the Grosnez light, monsieur."

"In this fog?"

"It's very low lying." Blériot shrugged. "And there's this." He took a luminous signal ball from his pocket. "SOE supply these. They work very well in the water."

"Which is where I'm likely to end up, from the look of the weather," Craig said as waves lapped hungrily across the beach.

Blériot took a life jacket from the boat and helped him into it. "You have no choice, monsieur. You must go. They are turning the whole of Brittany upside down for you."

"Have they taken hostages yet?"

"Of course. Ten from St Maurice, including the mayor and Father Paul. Ten more from farms in the surrounding area."

"My God," Craig said softly.

Anne-Marie lit a Gitane and passed it to him. "The name of the game, lover. You and I both know that. Not your affair."

"I wish I could believe you," he told her as René and Blériot ran the dinghy down into the water. Blériot started the outboard.

Anne-Marie kissed Craig briskly. "Off you go, like a good boy, and give my love to the dancing girls."

Craig got into the dinghy and turned to Blériot, who held the boat with René. "Pickup by MTB, you say?"

"Or gunboat. British navy or Free French, one or the other. They'll be there, monsieur. They've never let us down yet."

"So long, René. Take care of her," Craig called as they pushed him out through the waves, and the tiny outboard motor carried him on.

ROUNDING THE POINT and facing the open sea, he was soon in trouble. The waves lifted in whitecaps, and water slopped over the sides of the dinghy. He could see the Grosnez light through gaps in the fog and was steering towards it when suddenly the outboard motor died. He worked at it frantically, pulling the starting cord, but the dinghy drifted helplessly, pulled in by the current.

A heavy wave, long and smooth and much larger than the others, swept in, lifting the dinghy high in the air, where it paused in a kind of slow motion, water pouring in.

The dinghy went down like a stone, and Craig Osbourne drifted helplessly in the water, buoyed up by his life jacket. It was intensely cold, biting into his arms and legs like acid, so that even the pain of his wound faded.

Not good, my boy, he told himself. Not good at all. And then the wind tore another hole in the curtain of the fog, and he heard a muted throbbing of engines, saw a dark shape out there.

He raised his voice and called frantically, "Over here!" And then he remembered the luminous signal ball that Blériot had given him, got it out of his pocket, fumbling with frozen fingers, and held it up in the palm of his right hand.

The curtain of fog dropped again, and the throb of the engines seemed to be swallowed by the night.

"Here!" Osbourne cried, and then a torpedo boat drifted out of the fog like a ghost ship and bore down on him.

He had never felt such relief in his life as a searchlight was switched on and picked him out in the water. He started to flail towards it, forgetting his arm for the moment, and stopped suddenly. There was something about the craft, something wrong. Then the flag on the jack staff flared out with a sharp crack in a gust of wind, and he saw the swastika plainly. A German E-boat. As it slid alongside, he saw painted on the prow LILI MARLENE. He floated there, sick at heart, looking up at two Kriegsmarine sailors. And then one of them threw a rope ladder over the rail.

"All right, my old son," he said in ripest Cockney. "Let's be having you."

THEY HAD TO help him over the rail. The German sailor with the Cockney accent said cheerfully, "Major Osbourne, is it?"

"That's right."

"You're losing a lot of blood from that arm. Better take a look at it for you, sir. I'm the sick-berth attendant."

Osbourne said warily, "What goes on here?"

"Not for me to say, sir. That's the skipper's department. You'll find him on the bridge."

Craig Osbourne fumbled at the straps of his life jacket, took it off, stumbled to the small ladder and went up. In the wheelhouse, there was a helmsman at the wheel. Another man sat at the chart table and wore a Kriegsmarine captain's cap. He turned to look at Osbourne, his face calm and expressionless.

"Major Osbourne," he said in good American. "Glad to have you aboard. Excuse me for a moment. We need to get out of here."

He turned to the coxswain and said in German, "Leave silencers on. Course two one zero. Speed twenty-five knots."

"Hare," Craig Osbourne said. "Professor Martin Hare."

Hare took a cigarette from a tin of Benson & Hedges and offered him one. "You know me?"

Osbourne took the cigarette, fingers trembling. "I'm from Boston. After Yale I was a journalist. Worked for *Life* magazine. Paris, Berlin. I went home for a vacation. April '39. A friend told me about a series of lectures you were giving at Harvard. Supposedly on German literature, but very political, very anti-Nazi. I went to four of them."

The door opened, and the Cockney appeared. He was holding a blanket. "I thought the major might need this. I would also point out to the Herr Kapitän that he is wounded and needs attention."

"Then do your job, Schmidt," Martin Hare told him.

Osbourne watched as Schmidt expertly bandaged the wound. "A little morphine, guv'nor, just to make things more comfortable." He jabbed a syringe into Osbourne's arm.

Craig said to him, "Who are you? No German, that's for sure."

"My parents were German Jews who thought London might be more hospitable than Berlin. I was born in Whitechapel myself."

"Schmidt, you have a big mouth," Hare said in German.

Schmidt sprang to attention. "*Jawohl, Herr Kapitän.*"

"Go on, get out of here."

"*Zu Befehl, Herr Kapitän.*" Schmidt grinned and went out.

"This is a mixed crew," Hare said. "Americans and Brits, but everyone speaks fluent German. We play this game to the hilt. Normally only German is spoken, only Kriegsmarine uniform worn, even back at base. It's a question of staying in character."

"And where's base?"

"A little port called Cold Harbour, near Lizard Point, in Cornwall. We'll have you there by morning. We take our time on the way back. Our people warn us in advance of the Royal Navy MTB routes each night. We like to keep out of their way."

"I should imagine you do. A confrontation would be most unfortunate. Whose operation is this?"

"Officially it's Section D of the SOE, but it's a joint effort. You're OSS, I hear. A tricky way to make a living."

"You can say that again."

Hare grinned. "Let's see if they've got sandwiches in the galley. You look as if you could do with some nourishment." And he led the way out.

IT WAS JUST before dawn when Osbourne went on deck. There was quite a sea running, and spray stung his face. When he entered the wheelhouse, he found Hare on his own, his face dark and brooding in the compass light. Osbourne sat by the chart table and lit a cigarette.

"Can't you sleep?" Hare said.

"The boat's too much for me, but not for you, I think?"

"No, sir," Hare told him. "I can't remember when boats didn't figure in my life. I was eight years old when my grandfather put me to sea in my first dinghy."

There was a faint grey light around them now, the sea calmer, and land loomed before them.

"Lizard Point," Hare said.

"You like all this, don't you?" Osbourne asked. "You wouldn't want to go back to how it was before. Harvard, I mean."

"Perhaps." Hare was solemn. "Will any of us know what to do when it's over? What about you?"

"Nothing to go back to. You see, I have a special problem," Osbourne told him. "It would seem I have a talent for this. I killed a German general yesterday. He was head of SS intelligence for the whole of Brittany. A butcher who deserved to die. I killed him, so they took twenty hostages and shot them. Death seems to follow at my heels, if you know what I mean."

Hare didn't answer, simply reduced power and opened a window, allowing rain to drift in. They rounded a promontory, and Osbourne saw an inlet in the bay beyond, a wooded valley above. A small grey harbour nestled at the foot of it, and two dozen cottages around. There was an old manor house in the trees.

"Cold Harbour, Major Osbourne," Martin Hare told him.

CHAPTER 3

HARE AND OSBOURNE walked along the cobbled quay. "The houses all look pretty much the same," Craig observed.

"I know," Hare told him. "The whole place was put together in one go by the lord of the manor, a Sir William Chevely, in the mid-eighteenth century. Cottages, harbour, quay, everything—except the pub, which has been here for donkey's years. This is it by the way. The boys use it as their mess."

It was a low, squat building with high gables, timber inserts and mullioned windows. Craig looked up at the inn sign over the door. "The Hanged Man," he said.

"Rather appropriate." Hare clambered into a jeep that stood outside. "Come on, I'll take you up to the manor."

As they drove away, Craig turned to look at the sign again. It depicted a young man hanging by his right ankle from a wooden gibbet. The face was calm, the head surrounded by a halo.

"Did you know that's a tarot image?" he said.

"Oh, sure. The housekeeper at the manor arranged it. Madame Legrande. She's into that kind of thing."

"Legrande? Would that be Julie Legrande?" Craig asked.

"That's right." Hare glanced at him. "Do you know her?"

"I knew her husband before the war. He lectured in philosophy at the Sorbonne. Later he was mixed up with the Resistance in Paris. I came across them there in '42. Helped them get out when the Gestapo were on their backs."

"Well, she's working here now for SOE."

"And her husband, Henri?"

"He died of a heart attack in London last year."

"I see."

They were passing the last of the cottages. Hare said, "This is a defence area. All civilians moved out. We use these as billets. Besides my crew, we have RAF mechanics to service the planes."

"You have aircraft here? What for?"

"The usual. Drop agents in or bring them out."

"I thought the squadron at Tempsford handled that."

"They do, or at least the normal cases. Our operation is a little more unusual. I'll show you. We're just coming up to the field."

The road curved through trees, and on the other side was an enormous meadow with a grass runway. A prefabricated hangar stood at one end. Hare turned the jeep in through the gate, bumped across the grass and stopped.

A Fieseler Stork spotter plane taxied out of the hangar, the Luftwaffe insignia plain on its wings and fuselage, and the two mechanics who followed it wore black Luftwaffe overalls. Behind, in the hangar, there was a JU 88S night fighter.

The pilot of the Stork clambered out and came towards them. He wore flying boots and baggy, comfortable trousers in blue-grey, as worn by Luftwaffe fighter pilots. The short Fliegerbluse gave him a dashing look. He wore his silver pilot's badge on the left side, Iron Cross first class above it, and the Luftwaffe national emblem on the right.

"Everything but the bloody Knight's Cross," Osbourne said.

"Yes, he is a bit of a fanatic," Hare told him. "Also something of a psychopath if you want my opinion. Still, he did pull in two DFCs in the Battle of Britain."

The pilot approached. He was about twenty-five, the hair beneath the cap straw blond, almost white. Although he smiled, there was a touch of cruelty to the mouth, and the eyes were cold.

"Flight Lieutenant Joe Edge—Major Osbourne, Office of Strategic Services."

Edge held out his hand. "Brigandage a specialty, eh?"

Craig Osbourne didn't like him one little bit, but tried not to show it. "You've got quite a set-up here."

"Yes, well, the Stork can land and take off anywhere. Better than the Lysander in my opinion."

"Rather unusual camouflage, the Luftwaffe insignia."

Edge laughed. "Useful on occasions." He turned to Hare. "Give me a lift up to the manor, will you, old boy?"

"Hop in," Hare told him.

Edge got into the back. As they drove away, Craig said, "You said Section D of SOE was running this thing. Isn't that Dougal Munro's old dirty tricks department?"

"That's right. You know him, too?"

"Oh, yes," Craig said. "I worked for SOE in the beginning. We've had dealings, me and Dougal. A ruthless old bastard."

"Which is how you win wars, old boy," Edge commented.

"You're an anything-goes man, are you?" Craig asked.

"Thought we all were in our business, old son."

Hare said, "Munro hasn't changed. The motto really is 'Anything goes'. You'll see for yourself soon enough."

He turned in through cross gates and braked to a halt in a flagged courtyard. The house was grey stone, three storeys high. Very old, very peaceful. Nothing to do with war at all.

Hare said, "Grancester Abbey." He got out of the jeep. "We'll beard the ogre in his den if he's here."

BUT AT THAT precise moment Brigadier Dougal Munro was being admitted into the library at Hayes Lodge in London, the house that General Dwight D. Eisenhower was using as temporary headquarters. The general was enjoying coffee and toast and an early edition of *The Times* when a young army captain ushered Dougal Munro in and closed the door behind him.

"Morning, Brigadier. Coffee, tea—anything you want is on the sideboard." Munro helped himself to tea. "How's this Cold Harbour project working out?"

"So far, so good, General."

"You know, war is a little like the magician who fools people into watching his right hand while his left is attending to the real business of the day." Eisenhower poured more coffee. "Deception, Brigadier. Deception is the name of the game. Intelligence tells me that Rommel has done incredible things since they put him in charge of the Atlantic Wall."

"Quite true, sir."

"This E-boat of yours has taken engineers in by night to the French coast to get beach samples on so many occasions that you must have a pretty good idea where we intend to go in?"

"That's right, General," Munro said calmly. "All the indications would seem to predict Normandy."

"All right. So we're back with deception," Eisenhower said, and walked to a wall map. "I've got Patton heading a phantom army up here in East Anglia. Fake camps, fake planes—the works."

"Which would indicate to the Germans our intentions to invade in the Pas-de-Calais area," Munro observed.

"Which they've always expected because it makes military sense." Eisenhower nodded. "We've already got things moving to reinforce that idea. The air force will raid the area frequently, make it look as if we're trying to soften it up. Resistance groups will constantly attack the railways; double agents will transmit the right false information to headquarters."

He stood there staring at the map, and Munro said, "Something worrying you, sir?"

Eisenhower moved to a bay window and lit a cigarette. "Let me be explicit with you, Brigadier. We can only succeed with this invasion by having every advantage. More men than the Germans, more tanks, more planes—everything. You know why? Because in every engagement fought in this war on equal terms, the Germans have always won. Unit for unit they usually inflict fifty per cent more casualties."

"I'm aware of that unfortunate fact, sir."

Eisenhower turned. "Brigadier, I've always been sceptical of the exact worth of secret agents in this war. But you sent me a report last week I hardly dare to believe. You said that there was to be a staff conference headed by Rommel himself quite soon. A conference concerned solely with Atlantic Wall defences."

"That's right, General. At a place called Château de Voincourt, in Brittany."

"You further stated that you had an agent who could penetrate that conference?"

"Correct, General." Munro nodded.

Eisenhower said, "If I was a fly on the wall at that meeting. To know Rommel's thoughts, his intentions . . ." He put a hand on Munro's shoulder. "You understand how crucially important this could be?"

"Perfectly, General."

"Don't let me down, Brigadier." He turned and stared at the map.

Munro let himself out quietly and went to his car. Munro's aide, Captain Jack Carter, sat in the rear. Carter had a false leg, courtesy of Dunkirk.

"Everything all right, sir?" he asked as they drove away.

Munro pulled the glass panel across, cutting them off from the driver. "The de Voincourt conference has assumed crucial importance. I want you to get in touch with Anne-Marie Trevaunce. She can go on another false trip to Paris. Arrange a Lysander pickup. I need to talk with her face to face."

"Right, sir."

"Anything new I need to know?"

"Message came in concerning Cold Harbour, sir. Seems an OSS agent knocked off General Dietrich in Brittany. Due to bad weather their Lysander pickup had to be aborted, so they asked us for help. Commander Hare picked up the agent concerned. Major Craig Osbourne."

Munro turned in astonishment. "Craig Osbourne? Is he still around? His luck must be good. The best man I ever had at SOE. Is he at Cold Harbour now?"

"Yes, sir."

"Right. Stop at the nearest phone. Call the CO at RAF Croydon. Tell him I want a Lysander within the hour. Priority one. I'll fly down to Cold Harbour and see Craig Osbourne."

"You think he could be useful, sir?"

"Oh, yes, Jack. I think you could say that." And Munro turned and looked out the window, smiling.

CRAIG OSBOURNE, stripped to the waist, sat on a chair in one of Grancester Abbey's large old-fashioned bathrooms. Schmidt, a medical kit open on the floor, sat beside him and worked on the wounded arm.

Julie Legrande leant at the doorway, watching. She was in her late thirties and wore slacks and a brown sweater. Her blonde hair was tied back severely, a contrast with the calm, sweet face.

"How does it look?" she asked.

"So-so." Schmidt shrugged, priming a hypodermic. "This new penicillin drug is supposed to work wonders with infection."

Julie said, "Let's hope so. I'll get some coffee."

She left as Schmidt administered the injection. He put a dressing pad in place and bandaged the arm expertly.

"I think you're going to need a doctor, guy," he said.

"We'll see," Craig told him. He stood up, and Schmidt helped him put on a clean khaki shirt. He managed to button it himself and went into the adjoining bedroom as Schmidt repacked his medical kit.

The room was very pleasant, though a little shabby. It had a mahogany bed, and a table and two easy chairs in the bay window. Craig went and looked out. There was a terrace below and, beyond that, an unkempt garden, beech trees, a small lake in a hollow. It was very peaceful.

Schmidt came out of the bathroom, kit in hand. "I'll check you out later." As he opened the door Julie Legrande entered with a tray bearing coffee, toast and marmalade. She placed the tray on the table at the window. She sat opposite Craig.

As she poured coffee she said, "I can't tell you how good it is to see you again, Craig."

"I was sorry to hear about Henri," he said, taking the coffee cup she handed him. "A heart attack, I understand."

She nodded. "He died in his sleep. But at least he had that last eighteen months in London. We have you to thank for that."

"Nonsense." He felt strangely embarrassed.

"The simple truth. Without you we'd never have evaded the Gestapo that night. You were a sick man, Craig. Have you forgotten what those animals did to you? And yet you went back that night for Henri, when others would have left him." She was suddenly emotional, tears in her eyes. "You gave him a life, Craig. I'll always be in your debt for that."

He lit a cigarette and looked out the window. "I left SOE after that affair. My own people were starting OSS. They needed my kind of experience, and to be honest, I'd had enough of Dougal Munro."

"I've been working for him down here for four months," she said. "A hard man. But it's a hard war."

He nodded. "A strange set-up, this place, and even stranger

people. The pilot Edge, for example, swaggering around in his Luftwaffe uniform."

"Yes. Joe's quite mad, even on a good day," she said. "I sometimes think he really imagines he is Luftwaffe. He gives all of us the willies, but you know Munro—always ready to look the other way if a man is truly excellent at what he does. And Edge's record is extraordinary."

"And Hare?"

"Martin?" She smiled. "Ah, Martin is a different story. I think I'm a little bit in love with Martin."

The door opened, and Edge entered without knocking. "So there we are. All very tête-à-tête." He leant against the wall and put a cigarette in the corner of his mouth.

Julie said wearily, "You really are a rather unpleasant little rat at heart, aren't you, Joe?"

"Touched a nerve, did I, sweetie? Never mind." He turned to Osbourne. "The boss has just flown in."

"Munro?"

"Must want to see you bad, old boy. He's waiting in the library now. I'll show you the way."

He went out. Osbourne turned and smiled at Julie. "See you later," he said, and followed him.

THE LIBRARY WAS an imposing room, its walls crammed with books from the floor to a ceiling of beautiful Jacobean plasterwork. Munro was standing in front of the fire, cleaning his spectacles carefully as Craig Osbourne entered the room. Munro adjusted the spectacles and looked at Osbourne calmly. "Good to see you, Craig."

"I can't say it's mutual," Craig told him, and sat down, lighting a cigarette. "We go back too far."

"Don't be bitter, dear boy. It doesn't suit."

"Yes, well, I was always just a blunt instrument to you."

Munro sat opposite. "Colourfully put, but apt. Now then, what about this arm?"

"Schmidt thinks I might need a doctor, just to make sure."

"No problem. We'll have that taken care of. This Dietrich business, Craig. Really quite something, if I might say so. It's going to give Himmler and the SD severe problems."

"And how many hostages did they shoot in reprisal?"

Munro shrugged. "It's that kind of war. Not your affair."

Craig said, "Anne-Marie used the exact same phrase."

"Ah, yes. I was delighted to hear she was of assistance to you. She works for me, you know."

"Then God help her," Craig said forcefully.

"And you, dear boy, you're on the strength as of right now."

Craig leant forward, tossing his cigarette into the fire. "Like hell I am. I'm an American officer. You can't touch me."

"Oh, yes, I can. I operate under the direct authority of General Eisenhower. The Cold Harbour project is a joint venture. Hare and four of his men are American citizens. You'll join me, Craig, because you're an officer in the armed forces of your country, just like me, and you'll obey orders." Munro stood up. "No more nonsense, Craig. We'll go down to the pub, see Hare and tell the boys you're now a member of the club."

He turned and walked to the door, and Craig followed him, feeling curiously light-headed, despair in his heart.

THE HANGED MAN was a typical English village pub. It had a stone-flagged floor, a log fire on an open hearth, ironwork tables that had seen years of use, and high-backed wooden benches. The one incongruous thing was Julie pulling pints behind the bar for the men in Kriegsmarine uniforms leaning against it.

As the brigadier entered, followed by Osbourne, Hare stood up and called in German, "Attention. General officer present."

The men clicked heels. Munro said in fair German, "At ease. Carry on." He held out a hand and said to Hare, "Congratulations. Good job last night."

"Thank you, sir."

Munro warmed his backside at the fire. "But do try to clear things with me in future."

Joe Edge said to Hare, "Good point, old boy. For all you knew, the gallant major might have been expendable."

Something flared in Hare's eyes, and he took a step towards Edge, who backed off, laughing, and turned to the bar.

"Calm down, Martin," Munro said. "Let's all have a drink." He turned to Craig. "It's not that we're alcoholics, but as the lads work by night, they do their drinking in the morning." He raised his voice. "Listen, everybody, this is Major Craig Osbourne of the Office of Strategic Services. As of right now, he will be one of us here at Cold Harbour."

There was a moment's silence. Julie, at the bar, paused in the act of pulling a pint, face grave; then Schmidt raised his glass of ale. "Gawd help you, guv'nor."

There was a general laugh, and Munro said to Hare, "Introduce everyone, Martin." He turned to Osbourne. "Under their assumed identities, of course."

The chief petty officer, Langsdorff, who had been at the wheel, was American. So were Hardt, Wagner and Bauer. Wittig and Brauch, like Schmidt, were English Jews.

Craig sat down, feeling more than light-headed now. He was sweating, and his forehead was hot. "It's warm in here," he said.

Hare looked at him curiously. "Are you okay?"

Edge approached with two glasses. He gave one to Munro and the other to Craig. "You look like a gin man to me, Major. Get it down. It'll set the old pulses roaring. Julie will like that." Craig took the glass and drank. Edge squeezed onto the bench beside him.

"You are an unpleasant little swine, Joe," Martin Hare said.

Edge glanced at him, managing to look injured. "Intrepid bird-man, old boy, that's me. Gallant knight of the air."

"So was Hermann Göring," Craig said.

"Quite right. Brilliant pilot."

Craig's voice sounded to him as if it came from someone else. "You must feel right at home in the JU eighty-eight."

"JU eighty-eight S, old boy. Let's be accurate. Its engine-boosting system takes me up around four hundred."

"He forgets to tell you that his boosting system depends on three cylinders of nitrous oxide. One hit in those tanks, and he ends up in a variety of very small pieces," Martin Hare said.

The voices faded as Craig Osbourne plunged into darkness and rolled onto the floor. Schmidt ran across from the bar and crouched down as the room went silent. He looked up at Munro.

"Sir, he's got a raging fever. That's quick. I only checked him out an hour ago."

"Right," Munro said grimly, and turned to Hare. "I'll take him back to London in the Lysander. Get him into hospital."

Hare nodded. "Okay, sir." He stood back as Schmidt and two others picked Osbourne up and carried him out.

CRAIG OSBOURNE awoke from a deep sleep feeling fresh and alert. No sign of any fever at all. He struggled up on one elbow and found himself in what seemed to be a small hospital room with white painted walls. He swung his legs to the floor and sat there as the door opened and a young nurse came in.

"You shouldn't be up, sir."

She pushed him back into bed, and Craig said, "Where am I?"

She went out. A couple of minutes passed, and a doctor in a white coat, a stethoscope around his neck, entered.

He smiled. "So, how are we, Major?" he said, and took Craig's pulse. He had a German accent.

"Who are you?"

"Dr Baum is my name."

"And where am I?"

"A small nursing home in north London. Hampstead, to be precise." He put a thermometer in Craig's mouth, then checked it. "Very good. No fever at all. This penicillin is a miracle. The chap who treated you gave you a shot, but I gave you more. Lots more."

"How long have I been here?"

"This is the third day. You were quite bad. Frankly, without the drug . . ." Baum shrugged. "You have some tea, and I'll ring Brigadier Munro. Tell him you are all right."

He went out. Craig got up, found a dressing gown and went and sat by the window looking out at a high-walled garden. The nurse came back with a pot of tea on a tray. After a while there was a knock at the door, and Jack Carter limped in, a walking stick in one hand, a briefcase in the other. "Hello, Craig."

Craig, truly delighted, stood up. "Jack, how great to see you after all this time. So, you still work for that old bastard."

"Oh, yes." Carter sat down and opened the briefcase. "Dr Baum says you're much better."

"So I hear."

"Good. The brigadier would like you to do a job for him, if you feel up to it, that is."

"Already? What's he trying to do? Kill me off?"

Carter raised his hand. "Please, Craig, hear me out. It's not good, this one. This friend of yours—Anne-Marie Trevaunce."

"What about her?"

"The brigadier needed to see her face to face. Something very big. A Lysander pickup was arranged to bring her out, and I'm afraid things went very badly wrong." He passed a file across. "See for yourself."

Craig opened the file and started to read. After a while he closed it, great pain on his face.

Carter said, "I'm sorry. It's pretty bad, isn't it?"

"About as bad as it could be. A horror story."

He sat there thinking of Anne-Marie, the lipstick, the arrogance, the good legs in the dark stockings, the constant cigarette. So irritating and so perfectly marvellous and now . . .

Carter said, "Did you know of the existence of this twin sister, this Genevieve Trevaunce, in England?"

"No." Craig handed back the file. "She was never mentioned in all the time I knew Anne-Marie. I knew there was an English father, but I always thought he was dead."

"Not at all. He's a doctor. Lives in Cornwall. North Cornwall. A village called St Martin."

"And the daughter? This Genevieve?"

"She's a nurse at St Bartholomew's Hospital, here in London. She was recently rather ill with influenza. She's on extended sick leave, staying with her father at St Martin."

"So?" Craig said.

"The brigadier would like you to go and see her." Carter took a large white envelope from his briefcase and passed it across. "This will explain just how important it is."

Craig opened the envelope, took out the typed letter and began to read it slowly.

CHAPTER 4

JUST BEHIND the village of St Martin there was a hill that had been some kind of Roman-British fort in ancient times. It was Genevieve Trevaunce's favourite place. From its crest she could sit and look out to where the surf washed in over treacherous shoals, with only the seabirds to keep her company.

She had climbed up there after breakfast for what was to be the last time. She was well again, and the raids on London, according to the BBC news, had intensified. They would need everyone they could get in the casualty wards at Bart's now.

It was a fine, soft day, the sky very blue, and she felt at peace with herself. She turned and looked down at the village below, saw her father working in the garden of the old rectory. And then she noticed a car some distance away. As it drew nearer she saw that it was painted the drab military green.

It stopped outside the rectory gate, and a man in some sort of uniform got out. Genevieve started down the hill at once. She saw her father put down his spade and go to the gate. A few words were exchanged, and then he and the other man went up the path together and went inside the house.

It took her no more than three or four minutes to reach the bottom of the hill. As she did so, the front door opened and her father came out and started down the path. They met at the gate.

His face was working terribly, a glazed look in his eyes. She put a hand on his arm. "What is it? What's happened?"

His eyes focused on her for a moment, and he recoiled, as if in horror. "Anne-Marie," he said hoarsely. "She's dead."

He pushed past her, making for the church. He went through the graveyard in a grotesque limping half run and entered the porch. The great oak door closed with a hollow boom.

She stood there, suddenly ice cold. No emotion at all, only an emptiness. Footsteps approached behind.

"Miss Trevaunce?"

She turned slowly. The olive-drab uniform was American. A major, with a surprising number of medal ribbons for such a young man. The forage cap was tilted across gold hair with red highlights in it. A smooth, blank face gave nothing away, eyes the same cold grey as the Atlantic in winter. He opened his mouth slightly, then closed it again, as if unable to speak.

She said, "You bring us bad news, I believe, Major?"

"Craig Osbourne." He cleared his throat. "Dear God. I'm sorry, Miss Trevaunce, for a moment there it was like seeing a ghost."

SHE SHOWED HIM into the parlour, then put her head around the kitchen door. "Could we have some tea, Mrs Trembath? I have a visitor. Father's in church. I'm afraid we've had bad news."

The housekeeper turned from the sink, wiping her hands on her apron—a tall, gaunt woman, the strong Cornish face very still, blue eyes watchful. "Anne-Marie, is it?"

"She's dead," Genevieve said simply, and closed the door.

Craig was standing at the mantel, looking at a photo of Anne-Marie and Genevieve as children.

"Not much difference, even then," he said. "It's remarkable."

"You knew my sister, I take it?"

"Yes. I met her in Paris in 1940. I knew she had an English father, but she never mentioned you."

Genevieve Trevaunce made no comment. She sat down in one

of the wing chairs by the fire. There was an awkward pause, but it could be put off no longer. "How exactly did my sister die?"

"In a plane crash," Craig told her. "In France."

"How would you know that?" Genevieve asked. "France is occupied territory."

"We have channels," he said. "The people I work for."

"And who would they be?"

The door opened, and Mrs Trembath came in with a tray, which she placed carefully on a side table. She glanced at Osbourne briefly and departed. Genevieve poured the tea.

"I must say you're taking this remarkably well," he said.

"And you've just managed to avoid answering my question, but never mind." She handed him a cup of tea. "My sister and I were never close. She went to live in France when my mother died, in 1935. I stayed with my father. It was as simple as that. Now, who do you work for?"

"OSS—Office of Strategic Services," he said.

"Commandos?"

"Not really. Most of our people wouldn't go in wearing uniform."

"Are you trying to tell me that my sister was involved in that sort of thing?" she asked.

He produced a packet of cigarettes and offered her one. She shook her head. "I don't smoke, but you may if you wish."

He lit one, got up and walked to the window. "I met your sister when I was working for *Life* magazine and I did a feature on the de Voincourts, which meant I had to interview the countess—"

"Hortense?"

He turned, a wry smile on his face. "Quite a lady, that one. She'd just lost her fourth husband when I saw her. An infantry colonel, killed at the front."

"Yes. And my sister?"

"Oh, we became"—Craig paused—"good friends." He came back to the fireplace and sat down. "And then the Germans took Paris. I had to exit rather quickly. I came to England. America wasn't at war at that time, so I worked for a British outfit at first—SOE.

Same kind of work as OSS. I transferred to my own people later."

"And how did my sister come to be involved?"

"The German high command started to use your aunt's château. Generals—those sort of people—putting up there for a few days' rest, a conference or two. It was good propaganda to have the countess and her niece acting as hostesses."

Genevieve was angry then. "You expect me to believe that Hortense would allow herself to be used in this way?"

"Hold on a minute and let me explain," Craig said. "Your sister was allowed to travel back and forth to Paris whenever she wished. She got in touch with the Resistance and offered to work for us. She was in a unique position to do that."

"So, she became an agent," Genevieve said calmly.

"You don't seem very surprised."

"I'm not. She probably thought it rather glamorous."

"War," Craig said quietly, "is not in the least glamorous."

"I'm a staff nurse at St Bartholomew's Hospital, in London, Major," Genevieve said. "Military ward ten. You don't need to tell me much about the glamour of war."

He didn't answer, simply stood up and paced restlessly around the room. "We got information about a special conference the Nazis were going to hold at the château. It was necessary to talk to Anne-Marie face to face. She arranged a holiday in Paris, and a Lysander aircraft was sent to pick her up. The idea was that she would be brought to England for a briefing, then flown back. She was supposed to be driving to St Maurice to catch the Paris train. But in reality she was taken to the field where the Lysander was to put down."

"What went wrong?"

"According to our Resistance sources, they were shot down by a German night fighter as they took off."

"I see," Genevieve said.

He stopped pacing and said to her angrily, "Don't you care? Do you even give a damn?"

"When I was thirteen, Major Osbourne," she told him, "Anne-

Marie broke my right thumb in two places." She held it up. "See, it's still crooked. She wanted to see how much pain I could stand. She used a walnut cracker. She told me I must not cry out, however much it hurt, because I was a de Voincourt."

"My God," he whispered.

"And I didn't. I simply fainted when the pain became unbearable, but by then the damage had been done."

"What happened?"

"Nothing. A playful prank turned sour, that's all. Where my father was concerned, she could do no wrong." She poured herself more tea. "How much of this have you told him, by the way?"

"I said your sister had been killed in a car accident."

"But why tell me and not him?"

"Because you looked as if you could take it; he didn't."

He was lying, she knew, but at that moment her father walked past the window. She stood up. "I must see how he is."

As she got the door open, Craig said gently, "None of my business, but I'd say you're the last person he'd want to see right now." And that hurt, really hurt, because in her heart she knew that it was true. "Having you around will only make it worse for him. Every time he sees you, he'll think it's her for just a split second."

"Hope it's her, Major Osbourne," Genevieve corrected him. "But what would you suggest?"

"I'm driving back to London now, if that would help."

And then she saw, knew beyond any shadow of doubt. "That's why you're here, isn't it? I'm what you came for?"

"That's right, Miss Trevaunce."

She turned and went out, closing the door behind her.

Her father was gardening again, digging weeds. He straightened and said, "You'll be off on the afternoon train from Padstow?"

"I thought you might want me to stay on for a while."

"Would it alter anything?" His hands were shaking slightly.

"No," Genevieve said wearily, "I suppose not."

"Then why stay?"

"Major Osbourne has offered me a lift back to London."

"Kind of him. I'd take it if I were you."

He returned to his digging, looking at least twenty years older than he had an hour earlier. As if he had already crawled into the grave with his beloved Anne-Marie.

GENEVIEVE TOOK a last look around her tiny bedroom, making sure she hadn't forgotten anything, picked up her case and went out.

Craig Osbourne took the case from her without a word and put it on the rear seat of the car. She took a deep breath and approached her father. He looked up, and she kissed him on the cheek. "I'm not sure when I'll be back. I'll write."

He hugged her hard and then turned away quickly. "Go back to your hospital, Genevieve. Do some good for those who can still be helped."

She went to the car then without another word, aware of the strangest sense of release in his rejection of her.

After driving a while, Craig said, "Are you okay?"

"Would you think I was crazy if I told you I felt free for the first time in years?" she said.

"No. Knowing your sister as I did and after what I've seen here this morning, I'd say that makes a certain wild sense."

He lit a cigarette and wound the window down. "Your father — a country doctor, yet according to that plate on the gate back there, he's a fellow of the Royal College of Surgeons."

She leant back. "My father came out of Edinburgh University in 1914 with a talent for surgery, which he put to good use in the field hospitals of the western front in France. In 1918 he was wounded. You probably noticed that he still limps. Château de Voincourt was used as a convalescent home. You see how much of a fairy story it's beginning to sound? My grandmother, holder of one of the oldest titles in France and proud as Lucifer; the elder sister, Hortense, sardonic, witty, always in control; and then there was Hélène, young and wilful and very very beautiful."

"Who fell in love with the doctor from Cornwall?" Craig asked. "I shouldn't imagine the old girl liked that."

"She didn't, so the lovers fled away by night. My father became established in London, and all was silent from France."

"Until *la belle* Hélène produced twins?"

"Exactly." Genevieve nodded.

"So, you started to visit the old homestead?"

"My mother, Anne-Marie and me. It worked very well. We fitted in. My mother raised us to only speak French in the house, you see."

"And your father?"

"Oh, he was never made welcome. He did very well over the years. A senior surgeon at Guy's Hospital."

"And then your mother died?"

"That's right. Pneumonia. We were thirteen at the time."

"And Anne-Marie chose France, while you stayed with your father? What was all that about?"

Genevieve shrugged, looking suddenly very French. "Grandmère was dead, and Hortense, who couldn't have children, was the new Countess de Voincourt—a title held by the eldest female in our family since the days of Charlemagne."

"And Anne-Marie was next in line?" Craig asked.

"By eleven minutes. Oh, Hortense had no legal claim on her, but my father gave Anne-Marie free choice in the matter."

"He hoped she'd choose him—right?"

"Poor Daddy." Genevieve nodded. "Anne-Marie knew exactly what she wanted. For him it was the final straw. He sold up in London, moved back to St Martin and bought the old rectory."

Craig flicked his cigarette out the car window. "So, you're the new heir?"

Genevieve's face suddenly drained of colour. "God help me, but I hadn't thought of that—not for a moment."

He put an arm around her. "Hey, come on now. It's okay. I understand."

She suddenly looked very tired. "When we get to London, you'll tell me the truth? The whole truth?"

"Yes," he said. "I think I can promise you that."

"Good."

After a while she slept, turned sideways on her seat, her head pillowed on his shoulder.

The perfume was different. Anne-Marie, yet not Anne-Marie. Craig Osbourne had never felt so bewildered in his life, and drove onwards to London glumly.

As THEY approached London it was dark, and there were hints of fire and the crunch of bombs on the horizon. In the city, there were signs of bomb damage everywhere from the previous night's raid. When Genevieve wound down the window, she could smell smoke in the damp air. People were crowding into the tube stations, whole families carrying blankets and suitcases, ready for another night underground. It was 1940 all over again.

"I thought we'd finished with all this," she said bitterly.

"Somebody forgot to tell the Luftwaffe," Craig said.

There were flames over to the right of them, and a stick of bombs fell close enough for Craig to swerve from one side of the street to the other. He pulled in at the kerb, and a policeman in a tin hat emerged from the gloom.

"You'll have to park here and take shelter in the tube."

"I'm on military business," Craig protested.

"You could be Churchill himself, old son. You still go down the bleeding tube," the policeman said.

They got out and locked the car and followed a motley group into the tube station. The platforms were crowded, people sitting everywhere, wrapped in blankets, their belongings around them. Women's Voluntary Service ladies were dispensing refreshments from a trolley.

"People are marvellous," Genevieve said. "Look at them. If Hitler could see this right now, he'd call off the war."

At that moment an air-raid warden in a tin hat, his face covered in dust, appeared in the entrance.

"I need half a dozen volunteers. We got someone trapped in a cellar up the street."

A couple of middle-aged men sitting nearby got up. "We'll go."

Craig hesitated, touching his wounded arm, then joined them. Genevieve followed, and the warden said, "Not you, love."

"I'm a nurse," she said crisply. "You might need me."

He shrugged wearily, turned and led the way out. There was a stench of acrid smoke in the air. About fifty yards from the entrance to the tube, a row of shops had been blasted into rubble. The warden said, "I heard someone crying out over here. I think there's someone in the cellar."

They attacked the pile of bricks with their hands, burrowing deep, until the top of the steps appeared. There was barely room for a man to enter head-first. While they were crouching to inspect the opening, one of the men cried out in alarm, and they scattered as a wall crumpled into the street.

The dust cleared, and they stood up. "Madness to go down there," one of them said.

Craig handed his trench coat and cap to Genevieve. "I only got this uniform two days ago," he said, dropped on his belly and slithered into the slot above the steps.

Everyone waited. After a while they could hear a child crying. Craig's hands appeared holding a baby. Genevieve ran forward to take it from him. A little later a boy of about five years of age crawled out. Craig emerged behind him, took the boy's hand and crossed the street to join Genevieve. Someone cried a warning, and another wall cascaded down in a shower of bricks, completely covering the entrance.

"Blimey, guv'nor, you're in luck," the warden said as he comforted the crying child. "Anyone else down there?"

"A woman. Dead, I'm afraid." Craig gave Genevieve a tired grin. "There's nothing like a really great war, that's what I always say, Miss Trevaunce."

She held the baby close. "The uniform," she said. "It's not so bad. It should clean up very well."

"Did anyone ever tell you you're a great comfort?" he enquired.

LATER, DRIVING ON, she saw a street sign, HASTON PLACE, and Craig stopped outside a pleasant Georgian terrace house.

"Where are we?" she asked.

"About ten minutes' walk from SOE headquarters, in Baker Street. My boss has the top-floor flat here."

"And who might this boss be?"

"Brigadier Dougal Munro."

"Now that doesn't sound very American," she observed.

He opened the door for her. "We'll take anything that comes to hand, Miss Trevaunce. Now, if you'd follow me, please."

CHAPTER 5

JACK CARTER was waiting on the landing, leaning on his walking stick. He held out his hand.

"Miss Trevaunce. A great pleasure. My name's Carter. Brigadier Munro is expecting you."

They went in. The sitting room was very pleasant. A coal fire burning in the grate, a great many antiques on display, all of them an indication of Munro's original career as an Egyptologist. As they entered, Munro stood and came around the desk.

"Miss Trevaunce." He nodded. "Quite a remarkable likeness. I wouldn't have believed it. My name is Dougal Munro."

"Brigadier." She nodded in acknowledgment.

He turned to Craig. "Good God, you are in a state. What on earth have you been up to?"

"A little tricky getting through town tonight," he said.

Genevieve said, "He saved the lives of two children trapped in a cellar. Crawled in and got them out himself."

"Dear me," Munro observed. "I wish you wouldn't indulge in heroics, Craig. You really are too valuable to lose at this stage. Please sit down, Miss Trevaunce, or may I call you Genevieve? Your sister was always Anne-Marie to me."

"If you like."

"A drink, perhaps?"

"No, thanks. Do you think we could get down to business?"

"A little difficult to know where to begin."

Jack Carter and Craig sat by the fire. Munro opened a silver box and held it across the desk to Genevieve. "Cigarette?"

"No, thanks. I don't smoke."

"Your sister did—this brand. Gitanes. Try one."

There was a persistence to him now that she didn't like. She said impatiently, "No, why should I?"

"Because we'd like you to take her place," he said simply.

She stared at him. "You're mad," she said. "You want me to go to France in my sister's place?"

"On Thursday. The moon is right that night for a Lysander drop."

She turned to look at Craig. He was sprawled in the chair, face calm as ever. No help there, and she turned back to Munro. "This is nonsense. You must have any number of trained agents far better qualified than I to take on this job."

"No one else who can be Anne-Marie Trevaunce, niece of the Countess de Voincourt, at whose château this coming weekend some of the German high command will be holding a conference to discuss the Atlantic Wall defence system. We'd like to hear what they have to say. It could save thousands of lives."

"I'm disappointed in you, Brigadier," she said. "That one went out years ago."

He leant back in his chair, fingertips pressed together, a slight frown on his face as he considered her. "Your aunt will be in a difficult position when Anne-Marie fails to materialise from that trip to Paris on Friday. German intelligence hasn't the slightest idea who was in that Lysander, you see."

"Did my aunt know about Anne-Marie's activities?"

"No. But if your sister vanishes completely, the Germans will start to dig. They're very thorough. It would only be a question of time before they'd turn to your aunt, and she's not exactly up to the kind of pressure they'd put on her. I understand her heart's not been too good for some time now."

Genevieve took a deep breath. "What would they do?"

It was Craig who answered. "They have camps for people like her. Very unpleasant places."

"Major Osbourne has had personal experience of such a situation," Munro said. "He knows what he's talking about."

She sat there staring at him. She could feel a rising panic. "I can't play Anne-Marie. It's been four years since I last saw her."

"She was your twin sister," he said remorselessly. "Same face, same voice. We have only a few days to prepare you. Her hairstyle, clothes, make-up, perfume. We'll tell you how she handled herself at the château. We *will* make it work."

"But it wouldn't be enough, can't you see? It would be a house of strangers. New servants since I was there, plus the Germans. I wouldn't know who was who." Suddenly the nonsense of the whole business made her laugh. "I'd need a still, small voice whispering in my ear every step of the way, and that isn't possible."

"Isn't it? Your aunt has a chauffeur called René Dissard. He was Anne-Marie's right hand. He's in the next room now."

She stared at him in astonishment. "René? Here?"

Craig Osbourne opened the far door, and René Dissard entered slowly—the same old René, one of the eternal figures from childhood. Small, broad-shouldered, iron-grey hair and beard, the black patch, evidence of the wound that had cost him an eye as a young soldier at Verdun. He recoiled for a moment at the sight of her, as if the dead walked, but he recovered quickly.

"Mademoiselle Geneviève. It is so wonderful to see you."

She held his hands tightly. "My aunt is well?"

"As well as may be expected in the circumstances," he said. "Things are very different at the château these days."

"You know what they want me to do, René?"

"*Oui, mam'selle.* It would complete what she started," he said gravely.

She nodded and turned away.

"All right?" Munro said.

And then a sudden revulsion hit her. Something in her protested totally at being manipulated in this way.

"No, it isn't," she said. "I've already got a job, Brigadier. I'm in the business of saving lives when I can."

"Strangely enough, so are we, but if that's how you feel . . ." He turned to Osbourne. "You'd better take her to Hampstead and get this whole thing wrapped up."

She said, "Hampstead? What are you trying to pull now?"

He looked up, a mild surprise on his face. "Your sister's personal effects will be handed over to you. A document or two to sign, just for the records, and you can forget this whole sorry business."

He picked up a pen as if dismissing her. She turned, thoroughly angry now, walked past Osbourne and went out.

THE HOUSE IN Hampstead was a late-Georgian affair, with high walls and a metal gate that was opened by a man in some sort of blue uniform. A board on the gate said ROSEDENE NURSING HOME. At the front door Craig pulled on an old-fashioned bell chain, and they waited.

Genevieve heard footsteps approaching. There was the sound of a bolt being withdrawn. The door opened to reveal a young fair-haired man in a white lab coat. He stood back, and Craig led the way inside without a word.

The hall was dimly lit, and there was a strangely antiseptic smell that reminded her of a hospital ward. The young man bolted the door carefully behind them and said, "Herr Dr Baum will be with you in a moment. This way, please."

He opened a door at the end of the hall, let them pass in and closed it again. It was like a dentist's waiting room—shabby chairs, a few magazines—and was rather cold, in spite of the electric fire.

"Herr Dr Baum," she said to Craig. "German?"

"No. Austrian."

The door opened. The man who entered was small, balding, and wore a white doctor's jacket, a stethoscope around his neck.

"Hello, Baum," Craig said. "This is Miss Trevaunce."

The eyes were small and anxious, and suddenly there was the same touch of fear that she had seen with René and her father.

"Fräulein." He bowed and took her hand.

There was a long silence. Baum, sweating profusely, took out a handkerchief to mop his brow.

"Major Osbourne tells me that you have some things for me that belonged to my sister," Genevieve said.

"Yes, that is so." His smile was ghastly.

There was a photo on the mantelpiece of a young girl of sixteen or seventeen, gently smiling. She had a kind of ethereal beauty.

Genevieve said instinctively, "Your daughter?"

"Yes."

"Still at school, I suppose?"

"No. She is dead." The sad, quiet voice seemed to echo in her ears. "It was the Gestapo—Vienna, in 1939. You see, I am an Austrian Jew. One of the luckier ones who got away."

"And now?"

"I do what I can against her murderers." The voice was so gentle, and yet the pain in those eyes was terrible to see.

Craig said, "You'd better get started. I'll wait for you here."

"I don't understand . . ." Baum looked extremely agitated. "I thought you were going to handle this."

There was contempt on Craig's face. "Okay, Baum, okay."

He opened the door and stood to one side, waiting for her.

"Look, what game are you playing now?" she demanded.

"Something I think you should see," Craig said gravely. He went out, and in spite of herself, she went after him.

At the end of the hall, they descended a dark stairway. There was a long corridor at the bottom, brick walls painted white, doors on either side. Where the corridor turned a corner she could see a man sitting on a chair, reading a book. A rhythmic banging started, and as they reached the end of the corridor it increased to unbearable proportions. The man on the chair glanced up briefly, then returned to his book.

"He's quite deaf," Craig said. "He needs to be."

Craig stopped at a metal door. The banging had ceased, and it was very quiet. He moved a small panel, glanced in, then stood to one side. She moved forward and peered in through the bars. She could barely make out the outline of a small bed. And then a movement, just out of sight, caught her eye.

There was something in a rag of clothing crouched in the far corner. Impossible to tell whether it was male or female. It made a moaning sound and clawed at the wall. As if becoming aware that someone was watching, it raised its face slowly, and Genevieve gazed in terror upon her own face, twisted, broken, as if seen in one of those distorting mirrors in a penny arcade.

She couldn't even scream—fear was cold inside her. They seemed to stare at each other for ever, that ruin of a face and Genevieve; and then there were fingers reaching out through the bars, hooking into claws. Craig pulled Genevieve back, slamming the panel shut, cutting off the high-pitched animal scream.

She struck him across the face then, backhand, with all her strength. Once, twice, and then his hands were on her like iron, holding her still.

"It's all right," he said calmly. "We'll go now."

THEY GAVE her brandy, and she sat beside the electric fire, shaking like a leaf, hanging on to the glass for dear life.

"What happened?" Genevieve whispered.

"René was to accompany your sister to Paris by train. She went to the station as arranged, changed clothes and started across country to the pickup point on foot. He had gone off to contact the local Resistance. She was stopped by an SS patrol looking for partisans. Her papers—false, of course—seemed perfectly in order. To them she was just a good-looking village girl. They dragged her into the nearest barn. René found what was left of her wandering the countryside afterwards. That's what the Lysander brought back two days ago."

"You lied," Genevieve said. "All of you—even René."

"To spare you if we could, but you left us no choice."

"Does she really have to stay in that horrible place?"

It was Baum who answered. "No. She is on a course of drugs that should gradually reduce her violence, but it will take two weeks. Then we will transfer her to a suitable establishment."

"Is there any hope?"

He mopped his brow. "Fräulein, what do you want me to say?"

She took a deep breath. "My father must know nothing about this—you understand me? It would kill him."

"Of course." Craig nodded. "He has his story."

She stared down into the glass. "I never really had any choice from the beginning, did I? And you knew that."

"Yes," he said gravely.

"Right, then." She swallowed the brandy, which burned the back of her throat. "What happens now?"

"Tomorrow we'll fly you down to Cold Harbour, in Cornwall. It's the place used to prepare people in our line of work. Munro and I will accompany you."

"Then let's get on with it." And she led the way out.

CHAPTER 6

CROYDON, USED AS a fighter station in the defence of London, was thick with mist, and a heavy rain was falling. Nothing seemed to be landing or taking off as Genevieve peered out the window of the rather cheerless Nissen hut. The Lysander—a squat, ugly, high-wing monoplane—was standing outside.

René was sitting by the stove drinking tea, and Munro moved across to Genevieve as rain spattered against the window. "Damn weather," he said.

"Doesn't look good, does it?" she said.

"No," he said.

The door opened, and Craig came in with their pilot. He was

quite young, with a light moustache, dressed in RAF blue, flying jacket and boots.

"Flight Lieutenant Grant," Craig said to Genevieve.

The young man smiled and took her hand.

Munro said testily, "Are we going to be delayed?"

"It's not the weather here that's the problem, Brigadier," said Grant. "We can take off in pea soup as long as it's clear up above. It's landing, and visibility is limited at the Cold Harbour end. They'll let us know as soon as there is a change."

"Damn!" Munro said. He opened the door and went out.

Craig said to Genevieve, "Grant will be flying you across to France on Thursday night. You're in good hands. He's done that kind of thing before, haven't you, Grant?"

"That's right," Grant said. "Piece of cake, really. We take off at eleven from Cold Harbour. Estimated time of arrival, two o'clock. Major Osbourne will be coming with us for the ride."

He was so calm, so terribly offhand about it all, and Genevieve realised that she was shaking a little.

"We'll be landing in a field about fifteen miles from the railway station at St Maurice," said Craig. "The chap who'll be waiting to take you in charge—Grand Pierre is his code name—is English. He'll deliver you to the station before dawn. He's holding Anne-Marie's suitcases. The night train she was supposedly taking back from Paris arrives at seven thirty a.m."

He had spoken without looking at her directly, apparently very calm, and yet a muscle twitched in his right cheek. She couldn't help liking Craig Osbourne—it was as simple as that, and where was the harm? A little warmth against the dark. Anything to blot out the memory of her sister's ravaged face.

"Hey," she said, and put a hand on his arm, "don't tell me you're starting to worry about me?"

Before he could reply, the door was flung open, and Munro roared in. "The station commander has given us permission to leave now. Only takes an hour. If we can't land, we'll just have to come back. You have enough fuel, haven't you?"

"Of course, sir," Grant told him.

"Then we're off."

Everything seemed to be happening at once, and Genevieve found herself running through the rain to the Lysander. Craig bundled her up into the rear of the glass cabin, and he and René crowded in beside her. Munro followed, taking the observer's seat behind Grant. She was so busy strapping herself in that she was hardly aware of the deepening engine note and the sudden lurch as they lifted off.

IT WAS A bad trip, noisy and confusing, the roar of the engine making it difficult to conduct any kind of conversation. Outside, slate-grey rain dashed against the hood. The whole aircraft seemed to shake constantly, and every so often they dropped alarmingly in an air pocket.

After a while she must have dozed off, for she became aware of a hand shaking her and realised that her legs were covered with a blanket.

Craig had a thermos in one hand. "Coffee?"

She was very cold, and her legs seemed to have lost all feeling. The coffee was just what she needed, hot and strong and very sweet.

Grant had the radio speaker on. She heard a crackling voice say, "Lysander Sugar-Nan Tare. Ceiling six hundred."

Munro turned and said cheerfully, "All right, my dear?"

"Fine." She was lying, because suddenly she was shaking like a leaf as they were going down. And then there was a sudden roaring as the Lysander rocked violently in the slipstream of a great black bird that came out of a cloud from nowhere, passing so close that she could see the swastika on its tail.

"Bang, bang, you're dead, old boy!" A voice crackled over the loudspeaker, and the Junkers vanished as quickly as it had appeared.

Grant turned with a frown. "Sorry about that. Joe Edge, even more crazed than usual."

"Stupid young idiot," Munro said, and then they broke through the mist and cloud at six hundred feet before Genevieve could ask what it was all about. Below was Cold Harbour, the JU 88 already dropping down on the grass runway.

"Right on target," Grant called over his shoulder. The Lysander dropped in over a line of pine trees and landed, taxiing towards the hangar. The JU 88 had already come to a halt. Joe Edge got out of the cockpit.

"The uniform," Genevieve said, and clutched at Craig's sleeve.

"It's okay," he told her. "We haven't landed on the wrong side of the Channel. Let me explain."

IN THE BAR of The Hanged Man, still a little bewildered by it all, Genevieve sat at one of the tables in the window with the brigadier, Craig and Martin Hare, eating bacon and eggs cooked by Julie Legrande in the back kitchen and served by Schmidt. The crew of the *Lili Marlene* lounged around the fire.

Martin Hare poured Genevieve a cup of tea. "All this must seem very weird to you."

"You can say that again." She had liked him at once. "You must feel pretty strange yourself when you look in the mirror and see that uniform. Do you ever wonder which side you're really on?"

"Only when I have to deal with Joe Edge."

"He's totally unbalanced," Craig said. "Grant told me a pretty unsavoury story that just about sums him up. During the Battle of Britain a JU eighty-eight lost one engine and surrendered to two Spitfire pilots, who took up position on either side and started to shepherd it to the nearest airfield. It would have been quite a coup. But Edge came up on his rear, laughing like a maniac over the radio, and blew the Junkers out of the sky."

"That's terrible," Genevieve said. "Surely his commanding officer should have had him court-martialled?"

"He tried, but he was overruled. Edge was a Battle of Britain war hero. It wouldn't have looked good in the papers."

"The one bit you left out," Hare said, "was that Edge's commanding officer was an American. Edge never forgave him, and he's hated Americans ever since."

"Yes, well, he's still the best pilot I ever saw," Munro told them.

The door opened, and Edge came in, an unlit cigarette dangling from the corner of his mouth. "Everybody happy?" There was a sudden silence as he came across to the table. He leant so close to Genevieve she could feel his breath on her ear. "Settling in all right, are we, sweetie? If you need any advice, Uncle Joe's always available."

She pulled away, angry, and stood up. "I'll see if Madame Legrande needs any help in the kitchen."

Edge laughed as she walked away. Hare glanced at Craig with lifted brows. "Not fit to be out, is he?"

Julie was washing dishes, elbow-deep in the sink, when Genevieve entered.

"Madame Legrande, let me help."

"Julie, *chérie*," the other woman said with a warm smile.

Genevieve suddenly remembered that her aunt Hortense had always called her *chérie*. Never Anne-Marie; only her. She picked up a tea towel and smiled.

"Everything all right?"

"I suppose so. I like Martin Hare. A remarkable man."

"And Craig?"

Genevieve shrugged. "Oh, he's all right, I suppose."

"Which means you like him a lot?" Julie sighed. "An easy thing to do, *chérie*."

"Tell me about him," Genevieve said.

"His father was an American diplomat, his mother French," Julie told her. "As a child he lived for years in Berlin and Paris. In 1940 he became involved in smuggling Jews out through Spain until the Germans discovered what he was up to. That's when he joined the English secret service—SOE."

"Where did he go?"

"He operated a sabotage unit in the Loire Valley for several months before they were betrayed. The Gestapo took him to their Paris headquarters, at the Ministry of the Interior."

"Go on!" Genevieve turned pale.

"He was interrogated for three days. Notice his hands some time. His fingernails are misshapen because they were torn out."

Genevieve felt slightly sick. "But he escaped?"

"Yes. He was lucky. A car in which he was being transferred was involved in a collision with a truck. He got away in the confusion, hid in a church. The priest got in touch with my husband, who was leader of the underground movement in that part of Paris. Craig could hardly walk because they'd done things to his feet also." She held Genevieve's right hand tightly for a moment. "This is how it is over there. And things like this—they could also happen to you. This you must face now. After Thursday it will be too late."

Genevieve stood there staring at her. "What happened to Craig after that?"

"The French made him a commander of the Legion of Honour; his own people gave him the Distinguished Service Cross and made him join OSS. The irony now is that he is back in Munro's clutches."

"What's wrong with him?" Genevieve asked.

"He is, I think, a man who looks for death," Julie said. "Sometimes I think he would not know what to do with himself if he survived this war."

"That's nonsense," Genevieve said, but shivered all the same.

The door opened, and Edge came in. "Women at the kitchen sink. A lovely sight and so proper."

"Why don't you go and play with your toys, Joe?" Julie told him.

"Plenty to play with here, darling." He moved in behind Genevieve and slipped his arms about her waist.

"Leave me alone," she said, struggling against his grip.

"Look, she likes it," he taunted.

"Like it? You make my flesh crawl," Genevieve told him.

She continued to struggle, and then Edge gave a cry of pain, and Martin Hare was there, had him by the arm, which he continued to twist even after Edge had released Genevieve.

Schmidt appeared from nowhere and got the back door open. Hare simply threw Edge through it. The pilot fell to one knee. He got to his feet and turned, his face contorted.

"I'll pay you back for this, Hare!" He hurried away.

Schmidt closed the door. "A real time bomb, if I may say so, sir."

"Couldn't agree more. Now, get out to the boat and find Miss Trevaunce a pair of sea boots."

Genevieve was still shaking with rage. "Sea boots?" she demanded. "What for?"

"We'll go for a walk." He smiled. "Salt air, the beach. Nothing like the beauties of nature to get things into perspective."

AND HE WAS right, of course. They followed the narrow beach beyond the end of the quay where the inlet widened into a maelstrom of white water spray lifting high into the air.

Genevieve said, "This is wonderful. Every breath you take in London stinks of war, death and destruction."

"The sea washes things clean," Hare told her. "Ever since I was a boy, I've sailed. No matter how bad things are, you leave everything behind on the shore at your point of departure."

"Does your wife think the same way?" Genevieve asked.

"Used to," he said. "She died of leukaemia, in 1938."

"I'm so sorry." Instinctively she took his arm. They had rounded the point now, and the beach was much wider, following the cliffs. "It's been a long war for you, I think."

"Not really. I take it day by day, and that's all I expect—today." He smiled, suddenly looking immensely charming.

"And Craig? Does he think in the same way?"

"You like him, don't you?" He squeezed her arm against him. "Don't. There's no future for people like me and Craig."

"That's a terrible thing to say." She turned to face him, and he put his hands on her shoulders.

"Listen to me, Genevieve Trevaunce. War, played the way people like Craig and I play it, is like going to Monaco for a weekend's gambling. What you have to remember is that the odds are always against you. The house wins—you lose."

She pulled away. "I can't accept that."

But he ignored her now, looking beyond her, a frown on his

face. She turned and saw a man in a life jacket a few yards away, bouncing about in the surf. Hare ran past her and into the water, waist-deep, secured a grip on the life jacket and returned, towing the body behind him.

"Is he dead?" she called.

He nodded. "Oh, yes." And pulled the corpse up onto the beach.

It was a young man in black overalls, with the German eagle on his right breast. His feet were bare. He had fair hair, and his eyes were closed as if in sleep. He looked remarkably peaceful. Hare searched the body and found a wallet sodden with water. He examined it. "German seaman. Twenty-three years of age."

A sea gull swooped overhead, cried harshly and flew out to sea. The surf washed in. Genevieve said, "Even here, in a place like this, the war touches everything."

"The house always wins, remember." He put an arm around her. "Come on. I'll arrange for someone to bring him in."

THE ROOM Julie Legrande had given her was very pleasant. It had a four-poster bed, Chinese carpets on the floor, and a view of the garden at the rear of the house from the bay window.

Genevieve stood there now, staring out, as Julie turned down the bed. "You're sad, *chérie*?"

"That boy on the beach—I can't get him out of my mind," Genevieve said.

"To you he was a boy, but to people like me . . ." Julie shrugged. "If you could see what the *Boche* have done to my country . . . Believe me, the Nazis must be beaten. We have no choice."

The door opened, and Craig came in. "Ah, there you are."

"You didn't bother to knock," Genevieve said. "Don't I get any privacy around here?"

"Not really," he said calmly. He sat by the window and lit a cigarette. "From now on we only speak French. Just to get you back into the habit. That includes me."

He seemed different, a hard, tough edge to him, and Genevieve was annoyed. She said in French, "All right. What's next?"

"We have three main tasks. Number one — to familiarise you with the present situation at the château: the staff, both French and German. This will involve lengthy sessions with René, and we've got a lot of photographic material to show you."

"Then?"

"You'll need to fully understand the purpose of your mission so that you know what to look for, what's relevant, what isn't."

"That sounds complicated."

"It won't be. I'll take care of it, and Munro will help. The third is of a more practical nature. Can you shoot?" She stared at him. "Handguns," he said. "Have you ever fired a pistol?"

"No."

"Don't worry. It's easy when you know how. You just make sure you're standing close enough and pull the trigger." He glanced at his watch. "I'd better get moving."

He went out. Julie made a face. "It begins, *chérie*."

"So it would appear," Genevieve said.

CHAPTER 7

THE NEXT morning Munro sat by the library fire, working his way through a sheaf of papers on his knee. The table in the centre was covered with maps, photos and an array of documents. René sat on one side; Craig and Genevieve sat together opposite him.

Craig said, "The most important thing to remember is that when you drive into that château, you *are* Anne-Marie Trevaunce. On appearance alone, everyone who knows you will accept that without hesitation. Now, let's start with a few basic things Anne-Marie would be familiar with. German uniforms, for instance." He opened a book of illustrations.

She flipped through a few pages. "Goodness, do I have to learn all these?"

"Just a few. The Kriegsmarine is simple, and you've seen Joe

Edge's Luftwaffe uniform — blue-grey, with yellow rank patches."

She stopped at one page, an illustration of a combat soldier in three-quarter-length camouflage smock. "What's he? Doesn't even look like a German. The helmet's all wrong."

"He's a Fallschirmjäger — a paratrooper. They wear a special rimless steel helmet, but you don't need to bother about that. Here's an important one."

He indicated a German soldier with a metal plate suspended from his neck. " 'Feldgendarmerie'," she read.

"That metal plate means military police. The guy who stops your car on the road or stands guard at the château gates."

"And I must always be nice to them?"

"Well, let's say a hint of stocking getting out of the car wouldn't come amiss." Craig didn't even smile. "The other group of importance to you is the SS, because there're plenty of those at the château. You'll always recognise anyone in the SS by the silver skull-and-crossbones badge on his cap. All right?"

Genevieve nodded. "Yes, I think so."

Craig said, "Then let's have a look at the château."

They had a large-scale map of the surrounding countryside and a plan of the house itself, in finest detail. As Genevieve looked closely, it all came flooding back, every stairway and passage. There was a sudden excitement at the thought of returning. She'd forgotten quite how much she'd loved the place.

René said, "The perimeter wall has been wired along its entire length to provide an electric warning system. The gate is guarded at all times, and the Germans have installed the usual swing barrier system. For the rest, their security depends upon a system of what they call prowler guards. These are all Waffen SS, and they are good, mam'selle. Make no mistake. They know their job."

"Now, let's get to the really important details," Craig Osbourne said. "The way you wear your hair might suit you, but not Anne-Marie. See for yourself. This photo was taken a month ago."

Genevieve wore her hair to her shoulders; Anne-Marie's was much shorter, sliced in a very straight fringe just above her eyes.

Genevieve again, but a different Genevieve, with an arrogant smile on her mouth, as if telling the whole world to go to hell. Unconsciously Genevieve copied that expression and turned to look at Craig.

He didn't like it. For the first time she felt she had really got through to him in some strange way, as if for the moment he was afraid of what he saw. He snatched the photo from her roughly.

"Let's move along, shall we?" He placed another photo in front of her. "You know this woman?"

"Yes. Chantal Chevalier, my aunt's personal maid."

Dear Chantal of the rough tongue and hard hand, who had served Hortense for more than thirty years.

"She won't like me," Genevieve said. "She never did."

René nodded. "She never cared for Mam'selle Anne-Marie. But with you, mam'selle, it was different."

"Your maid could be a problem," Craig said. "Here she is."

She was small, dark-haired, pretty enough in her own way. "Maresa Ducray," René commented crisply. "Pretty clothes, men and money are the important things in her life."

"You can read her family background later," Craig said, and handed her another photo. "This is the commandant at the château, Major General Carl Ziemke."

It was a blow-up from a group photo. He was the wrong side of fifty, army, not SS, silver in the hair and the clipped moustache, and a little too fleshy. He had nice eyes with laugh lines around them, but no smile. He looked tired.

"A good man once," Craig said. "But now they've put him out to grass. He and your aunt are lovers."

Genevieve handed the photo back to him calmly. "If you were trying to shock me, you're wasting your time. My aunt always did need to have a man around, and Ziemke looks rather nice."

"He's a soldier," René said grudgingly, "I'll say that for him. And so is this bastard."

He pushed a photo across to her. There was a shock of recognition. She had never seen this man before, and yet it was as if she had known him all her life. Black hair cut short, a strong craggy face, eyes that seemed to look right through her. Not a handsome face, and yet one you would turn to look at again, even in a crowd.

"Sturmbannführer Max Priem," Craig said. "That means major, to you. Knight's Cross holder and a thoroughly dangerous man. He's in charge of security at the château. He took a bullet in the head in Russia last year. They had to put a silver plate in his skull."

"And how did he get on with Anne-Marie?" Genevieve asked.

"They fought as equals, mam'selle," René said. "He did not approve of her, and she did not like him. Her relationship with General Ziemke was excellent. She flirted with him outrageously, and he treated her like a favourite niece."

"Which all paid off very nicely, with passes for those trips to Paris, freedom to come and go," Craig said. "But I must stress how much the Germans value the de Voincourt connection. You and your aunt are collaborators, make no mistake about that. You continue to live in luxury while thousands of your countrymen toil in labour camps. And with your friends—the French industrialists and their wives who often make up the parties at those weekend conferences—you are among the most hated people in France."

"You've made your point."

"One more individual to be noted with particular care," he went on. The photo wasn't nice. A young SS officer with very fair hair, narrow eyes, a generally vicious look to him that wasn't at all pleasant. "Hauptsturmführer—that's captain—Hans Reichslinger. He's Priem's assistant."

"An animal." René spat into the fire.

Craig picked up a large brown envelope and handed it to her. "You'll find background information on every individual in there. Study it as if your life depends on it, because it does."

There was a knock at the door, and Julie looked in. "The hairdresser is here."

"Good," Craig said. "We'll carry on later."

As Genevieve started to move away, he added, "Before you go—just one more picture. Chief architect of the Atlantic Wall defence system. The man you'll be playing hostess to this weekend at the château."

He placed, very carefully, on the table in front of her a photo of Field Marshal Erwin Rommel. She stood there staring down at it in astonishment, and Munro stood up and crossed to her.

"So, you see, my dear Genevieve, I wasn't exaggerating when I said that what you could accomplish for us this weekend might very well affect the course of the entire war."

As SHE AND Julie watched in the mirror, Genevieve changed into Anne-Marie minute by minute. Not just the hair—that was easy. The hairdresser, a small, rather dapper middle-aged man formerly employed as a senior make-up artist by a film studio, knew exactly what he was doing. There was the shade of lipstick, the rouge, the mascara and the perfume, Chanel No. 5—one that Genevieve never used herself.

The complete transformation took about an hour and a half. When he had finished, he nodded, obviously satisfied. Genevieve sat looking at herself. Me and yet not me, she thought.

Julie offered her a cigarette. "Have a Gitane."

Genevieve began to refuse, and Julie said, "Anne-Marie would. You'll have to get used to the idea."

Genevieve took the cigarette and light, and coughed as the smoke caught the back of her throat.

"Good," Julie said. "Now, go and show yourself to Craig. He's in the basement, at the shooting range, waiting for you."

THE DOOR to the cellar was next to the kitchen, and when Genevieve opened it, she could hear the sound of shooting.

The far end of the firing range was brilliantly lit to reveal a row of cardboard figures resembling German soldiers against sandbags. Craig Osbourne was standing at a table loading a revolver, several other weapons laid out before him. He glanced over his shoulder casually, then froze. "Good God!"

"Which obviously means I'll do."

His face was quite pale. "Yes, I think you could say that. Quite astonishing." He snapped the revolver shut. "You've never done any shooting?"

"I fired an air rifle once at a funfair."

He smiled. "Nothing like starting from scratch. I'm not going to do more than explain the two handguns you're most likely to come across and how you should fire them." He placed the revolver down and picked up two other guns. "The Luger and the Walther are automatic pistols used a great deal by the German army."

He spent twenty minutes patiently showing her how to load a cartridge clip, ram it home and cock the gun for firing. Only when she could do that did he take her to the other end of the range.

It was a Walther she was using now, with a Carswell silencer on the end. When fired, it made only a strange coughing sound. It was very heavy, which surprised her, but her hand fitted around the butt quite easily.

They stopped a yard from the targets. "Close to your man," he said. "But not too close, in case he tries to grab you. Now, hold it waist-high, shoulders square, and squeeze."

She closed her eyes when she fired, and when she opened them again, saw that she'd shot the target in the stomach.

"Very good," Craig said. "Didn't I tell you it was easy as long as you stand close enough?"

SHE SPENT the late afternoon and evening going over those background notes again and again until she really felt she knew all those people. Afterwards there was dinner in the kitchen with Craig, Munro and René, and Julie's cooking was superb. They had steak-and-kidney pudding, roast potatoes and cabbage, a very good red Burgundy and apple pie.

"A superbly traditional English meal." Munro kissed Julie on the cheek. "What a sacrifice for a Frenchwoman." He turned to Craig. "I think I'll take a walk down to the pub. Care to join me?"

"I don't think so," Craig said. He seemed moody.

"How about you, René? Fancy a drink?"

"Always, *mon général*." René laughed, and they left together.

Craig and Genevieve went up to the Blue Room, a pleasant sitting room next to the library, with comfortable furniture and a fire burning and a rather nice grand piano.

Genevieve lifted the lid, fitting the rod carefully under it. She started to play a Chopin prelude—deep, slow, crashing chords in the bass and the infinitely sweet crying of death at the top.

Craig came forward and leant on the end of the piano, watching. His eyes were questioning as she started to play "Clair de Lune", beautifully, achingly sad.

She played well—better, she told herself, than she had done in a long time. When she finished and looked up, he had gone. She hesitated, put the lid down and went after him.

She found him on the terrace, in the dark, smoking. She leant against the parapet.

"You were good," he said.

"As long as I stand close enough?" Genevieve asked.

"All right," he said. "So I've given you a hard time, but that's how it's got to be. You don't know what it's like over there."

"What do you want, absolution?" she said. "I've got to go; you said so yourself. There's no choice, because there is no one else. It's not your fault. You're just an instrument."

Craig put out his cigarette. "We've a full day tomorrow," he said. "You're to see Munro again in the morning. Time for bed."

"Yes." She reached for his sleeve. "And thanks for acting like a human being for once."

His voice, when he replied, was strange. "Don't be kind to me now, not now. We haven't finished with you yet."

He turned and went inside quickly.

THEY CAME for her in the night. Torchlight in her eyes, the bedclothes thrown back, and then she was pulled upright.

"You are Anne-Marie Trevaunce?" a voice demanded harshly in French.

"Who do you think you are?" She was thoroughly angry, tried to get up, and received a slap across the face.

"You are Anne-Marie Trevaunce? Answer me."

Then she realised that both the shadowy figures were in German uniform, and the reason for the nightmare struck her.

"Yes, I'm Anne-Marie Trevaunce," she said in French.

"That's better—much better. Now, put your gown on and come with us."

"You are Anne-Marie Trevaunce?"

It must have been the twentieth time they had put that question to her as she sat in the library, blinded by the hard white lights in her face.

"Yes," she said wearily. "How many times do I have to tell you?"

"Your maid, Maresa. Tell me about her family."

She took a deep breath. "Her mother has a small farm about ten miles from the château. Maresa has a brother called Pierre, who is a corporal in a French tank regiment."

"And General Ziemke. Tell me about him."

"I've told you all about him at least four times."

"Tell me again," the voice said patiently.

Suddenly it was over. Someone switched the main light on. There were two of them in German uniform.

Craig Osbourne was standing by the fire, lighting a cigarette.

"Not bad. Not bad at all."

"Very funny," she said.

"You can go to bed now."

As she headed towards the door, he called, "Oh, Genevieve?"

She turned to face him again. "Yes?" she said wearily.

There was a heavy silence; they looked at each other. She'd fallen for the oldest trick in the book.

"Sorry."

"Try not to do that over there, won't you?" he said calmly.

CHAPTER 8

IN THE MORNING it seemed like a nightmare, something that had never happened. One of the most frightening things about it had been the mingling of personalities that she had begun to feel. The constant insistence that she *was* Anne-Marie Trevaunce was something that she'd almost come to believe herself during the moments of most intense strain.

She sat at the window, smoking a Gitane, coughing a little less now, and gradually it grew lighter, and the first orange-yellow of the sun glinted on the lake down there in the hollow.

The door opened, and once again Craig Osbourne walked in without knocking. "There you are."

"It gets worse," Genevieve said. "Still no privacy."

He ignored the remark. "Munro would like to see you as soon as possible. He's flying back to London this morning. I'll be in the library."

He went out, closing the door. Genevieve shrugged. Munro could wait.

THE HOUSE was quiet, no sign of anyone else around as she went down the stairs after dressing. Craig was standing by the library fire reading a newspaper.

He glanced up. "You'd better go straight in. The last door."

She walked to the other end of the library, paused at the leather-covered door and knocked. There was no reply. She hesitated, opened it and went in. Munro's overcoat was draped over a chair, and there was a briefcase on the desk, holding down one end of a large-scale map. She could see what it was at once—a section of the French coast. The heading said "Preliminary Targets, D-day." As she stood looking down at it, a door in the far corner opened, and Munro came in.

"So, there you are." And then he frowned, crossed the room quickly and rolled up the map. He put it in the briefcase and closed it. "Amazing how different you look."

"Isn't it."

"Have they been giving you a hard time?" He smiled. "No, don't answer that. I know how Craig operates." He stood at the desk with his hands behind his back, suddenly serious. "I know this hasn't been easy for you, any of it, but I can't impress the importance of it too much. When the big day comes, when we invade Europe, the battle is going to be won on the beaches. Once we get a foothold, the final victory is only a matter of time. We know that and so do the Germans."

It sounded as if he were making a speech to his officers.

"That's why they put Rommel in charge of coordinating their Atlantic Wall defences. You can see now why any information you can get us from that conference this weekend could be vitally important."

"Of course," she said. "I can win the war for you at one fell swoop."

"That's what I like about you, Genevieve. Your sense of humour." He reached for his overcoat. "Well, I've got to go."

"Haven't we all," she said. "Tell me, Brigadier, do you enjoy your work? Does it give you job satisfaction?"

He picked up his briefcase, and when he looked at her, his eyes were bleak. "Goodbye, Miss Trevaunce," he said formally. "I look forward to hearing from you." And he walked out.

CRAIG WAS still standing by the library fire. Looking at her gravely, he moved to the table. "I've got something for you."

He passed her a cigarette case made of silver and onyx. It was really very beautiful. She opened it and found it was neatly packed with Gitanes.

"A going-away present?" she asked.

"Rather a special one." He took the case from her. "See here in the back?" He pushed his thumbnail in, and a wafer-like flap of silver fell down to show the tiniest of lenses and a camera mechanism. "It takes good, sharp pictures even in poor light. So if you see any documents or maps, all you have to do is point it and pull this thing here."

"Always remembering to stand close enough?"

Somehow she'd hurt him now—she could see that. She could have bitten her tongue, but it was too late.

He gave her the cigarette case back and moved to the table, all business again.

"The rest of the day I suggest you go over your photos and case histories until you're word perfect."

"And tomorrow?"

"I'll go over everything again with you until you know it backwards. Tomorrow night we take off a little after eleven. You and René will be picked up at the drop-off point by the local Resistance people, who will transport you to St Maurice by road. You'll wait there in the stationmaster's house until the night train from Paris has passed through. Then René will go and collect your car, as if you've just got off the train, and drive you home to the château."

"Where I'll be on my own?"

"You've got René," he said. "He has a radio. He can contact us here through the coastal booster station."

They stood there, a silence between them. Finally he said, strangely gentle, "Is there anything I can do for you?"

"Anne-Marie. I'm worried about her. If anything happens . . ."

"I'll take care of it. I give you my word." He lifted her chin with a finger. "And nothing is going to happen to you. You've got luck. I can tell."

She was almost in tears, suddenly vulnerable. "And how can you know a thing like that?"

"I'm a Yale man," he said simply.

SHE WORKED on the papers all morning. Julie had told her she would be going down to the pub at lunch time, so just after noon Genevieve stopped work and walked down to the village.

Everyone seemed to be at The Hanged Man. The entire crew of the *Lili Marlene*, Craig, even Joe Edge at the end of the bar. She joined Craig and Martin Hare at a table by the window. Julie was passing hot Cornish pasties from the kitchen, which Schmidt was dispensing with his usual good humour. "Nothing kosher about these, but they smell bloody marvellous," he said.

Craig and Hare exchanged jokes and drank beer with their pasties, while Genevieve tried another Gitane. She didn't like to admit it, but she was actually beginning to enjoy them.

Craig said, "Excuse me for a moment. I need to see Julie about something."

He went behind the bar and into the kitchen. Genevieve was aware of Edge at the end of the bar, watching her, eyes glittering. She began to feel uncomfortable and said to Hare, "Actually I could do with some air. I think I'll go for a walk."

She went out, aware of Edge following her with his eyes. She was angry then, for it was as if he'd driven her out, and she started to walk fast, following a path up through the trees. A moment later Edge emerged from the pub and hurried after her.

Martin Hare, by the window, took another pasty Schmidt passed to him and turned at the same moment to see Genevieve disappear into the trees, Edge running after her. He put the pasty down.

"I think I'll leave this till later."

"I think it might be an idea, sir," Schmidt said.

Hare went out quickly and hurried along the path.

Schmidt went into the kitchen, where Craig was talking quietly with Julie. "Excuse me, guv'nor," he said.

"What is it?" Craig demanded.

"A little potential drama, I think. Miss Trevaunce went off to the wood. Then we see Edge running after her. The commander didn't think too much of that. He went after them — and he's only got one good lung. I mean, if it gets physical . . ." But Craig was already on his way out the door, moving very fast indeed.

IT STARTED to rain a little as Genevieve moved on through the trees. She came into a clearing and found a half-ruined building, a relic of the tin-mining explorations of the previous century. She hesitated in the entrance, then moved inside. It was very dark and mysterious in there.

"Whither away, oh maiden?" She turned, and saw Edge leaning in the doorway. When she moved to pass him, he put up an arm to bar her way. "What does it take to make you just a little more friendly?"

"Nothing you have to offer."

He grabbed her by the hair, pulling her close. She cried out and beat at his face with a clenched fist. He slapped her, backhand, and she staggered, catching her foot on a stone, and fell down. In a second he was on her.

"Now then," he said. "Let's teach you your manners."

Martin Hare's heart was pounding, and he was gasping for breath as he ran in through the entrance. He had just enough energy to grab Edge by the hair and pull him off.

Edge, on his feet, turned with a cry of rage and punched him high on the right cheek. Hare keeled over, and Edge raised a knee in his face. Genevieve grabbed Edge from the rear, and he cursed and struck out at her as Hare fell to his knees.

Edge turned and had Genevieve by the throat as Craig Osbourne arrived on the run. Craig delivered a thoroughly dirty blow, knuckles extended, to Edge's kidneys. Edge screamed, and Craig grabbed him by the neck and ran him out the doorway.

As he turned, Genevieve was helping Hare to his feet. The commander smiled ruefully. "A fat lot of use I turned out to be."

"You'll always be a hero to me," Genevieve told him.

"See," Craig said, "it's the thought that counts. Come on. I'll buy you a drink. And you"—he turned to Edge—"try anything like that again and I'll personally see you court-martialled."

They went out, leaving Edge on his hands and knees gasping for breath, and walked back towards the pub.

JULIE LAID the table for a special dinner in the library and decked it with the best Grancester Abbey could provide. Silverware, linen tablecloth, exquisite plates of bone china. It was a wonderful atmosphere, the only illumination coming from the flickering candelabra and the log fire.

Julie, very attractive in the typically French little black dress, her hair tied with a velvet bow, insisted on handling everything in the kitchen herself, helped only by René, who acted as waiter.

Dinner was exquisite. Champagne, a liver pâté with toast, a leg of lamb with herbs, some Cornish early new potatoes, a green salad and, afterwards, a concoction of fruit and whipped cream that melted in the mouth.

"I thought there was supposed to be a war on," Craig observed as he went around the table refilling the glasses.

Martin Hare sat beside Genevieve, still playing the officer of the Kriegsmarine, a medal at his throat.

She reached across to touch it. "What is that decoration?"

"The Knight's Cross, similar to our Congressional Medal of Honor. It usually means the wearer should really be dead."

"Doesn't Max Priem have one of those?" she asked.

"With oak leaves and swords," Craig said. "That means three awards. He really is on borrowed time, that boy."

"A brave man, though," she said.

Craig raised his glass. "To brave men everywhere."

Julie bustled in with coffee on a tray. "Wait for me," she called, put the tray on the table and picked up her glass.

The fire flared up as in a sudden draught. Genevieve shivered, the champagne ice cold as she swallowed. She could see the french windows reflected in the great mirror above the fire, curtains drawn, and then they billowed outwards, came apart, and three men stepped through and stood there, just inside the room.

They were German paratroopers, in rimless steel helmets and long camouflage jackets. Two of them held machine pistols at the ready, hard, dangerous-looking men. The one in the middle held a Walther with a silencer on the end in his right hand.

"Finish your drinks, ladies and gentlemen, by all means. I'm sure you don't mind if I join you."

He crossed to the table and poured himself a glass of champagne.

"My name is Sturm, Hauptmann; Special Duty Squadron; Ninth Parachute Regiment." His English was quite reasonable.

"And what can we do for you?" Craig Osbourne asked.

"Why, exactly as you are told, Major. The special duty tonight is to convey you, the young lady here and the Fregattenkapitän to territory occupied by the Reich as fast as possible."

"Really? I don't think you'll find that so easy."

"I don't see why not." Sturm savoured the champagne. "The parachute drop was the difficult part. Much simpler to slip out to sea in the E-boat you've so thoughtfully provided."

Genevieve saw it all then and barely stopped herself from laughing. But she forced herself to react as Anne-Marie would and turned towards Osbourne, a cynical smile on her face.

Only Craig wasn't smiling, and René, his face contorted with rage, thrust a hand inside his coat and pulled out a pistol. "*Sale Boche!*" he cried.

Sturm's hand swung up, the Walther coughed once, and René fell back into his chair, dropping the pistol, a hand to his chest. He looked at the blood on it in a kind of wonder, turned to Genevieve in mute appeal, then slid to the floor.

Julie cried out in fear, her hands to her face; she turned and started to run towards the door. Sturm's arm swung up.

"No!" Genevieve called.

His Walther coughed again. Julie seemed to trip, lurched to one side and fell on her face. Sturm walked the length of the room and knelt beside her.

"Dead, I'm afraid. A pity."

"You butcher!" Genevieve said.

"I suppose that depends whose side you are on." Sturm turned to Hare. "Is your crew on board the E-boat at the present time?" Hare made no reply, and Sturm said, "Come now, Commander. We'll find out soon enough when we get down there."

"All right," Hare said reluctantly. "I believe the engineer is doing some work below, and Obersteuermann Langsdorff is keeping watch."

"Then I'm sure that you can put to sea with no difficulty." He turned to Craig. "I understand you have a reputation for action, Major Osbourne. I would most earnestly advise against it on this occasion." He took Genevieve by the arm and touched the silencer to her cheek. "The consequences for Fräulein Trevaunce could be severe. Do I make myself plain?"

"Perfectly," Craig told him.

"Good. Then we go now, I think."

He took Genevieve by the hand and led the way out through the french windows. Craig and Hare followed, menaced by the machine pistols of the other two paratroopers.

It was cold, and Genevieve shivered as they passed through the garden into the wood and reached the first cottages at the edge of the village.

What could have gone so disastrously wrong? she thought. They were passing The Hanged Man now, curtains drawn at the windows, only a chink of light showing. There was laughter and singing, all curiously remote.

There was only a dim light up in the wheelhouse of the *Lili Marlene*, and the deck was shrouded in darkness. They went down the gangplank one by one.

The door to the companionway was flung open, light flooded out, and Schmidt appeared. He was laughing, as if he'd just been talking to someone, but now the laugh faded.

"Here, what the bleeding hell is going on?" he demanded.

Again Sturm's Walther swung up, and the German shot Schmidt at close quarters, sending him back down the companionway.

Sturm gestured to one of his men. "Get below and watch the engineer. The rest of you—on the bridge."

Sturm went first. Genevieve, Hare and Craig followed, covered from behind by the other paratrooper. Langsdorff was seated at the chart table, and he looked up, then stood in amazement.

"Get this thing moving," Sturm said.

Hare nodded. "Do as he tells you."

There was a slight pause. Langsdorff called down to the engine room. A moment later the engines rumbled into life, and the *Lili Marlene* drifted out into the harbour.

"See how simple life can be?" Sturm said. "Only one thing, and it's been annoying me. Brave men have died for that medal, Commander. I object to your use of it. It's not for play actors."

He tore the Knight's Cross from Hare's neck, and Hare, in the same movement, grabbed his wrist, forcing the Walther to one side. There was a dull thud as it discharged.

Genevieve ran her nails down Sturm's face and kicked him in the shins.

"Get her out of it, Craig. Now!" Hare cried as he and Sturm swayed together.

Craig wrenched open the door, reaching for Genevieve's hand, pulling her after him. She lost a shoe, stumbled, and below on the afterdeck the other paratrooper fired his machine pistol. Craig pushed her to the rail. "Jump, for God's sake! Now!"

He lifted her up, a hand to her back, and then she was falling, hit the water and went under. He vaulted over to land beside her as she surfaced. The E-boat was already slipping away into the darkness. There were sudden stabbing fingers of flame as the machine pistol fired again, ineffectually, and then silence. Genevieve and Craig floated there alone.

"You all right?" he asked her, coughing.

"Yes, I think so. But Martin, Craig?"

"Never mind that now. This way. Follow me."

They started to swim through the darkness. It was bitter cold. Then she heard the rumble of the E-boat's engines again.

"It's coming back," she said in a panic.

"Never mind. Keep swimming."

The engines were quite close now. She thrashed forward, and then suddenly a searchlight picked them out of the water, and then another light was turned upon the quay. There was a ragged cheer. She floated, looking up. The crew of the *Lili Marlene* were up there, as was Dougal Munro, in a heavy overcoat. "Well done, Genevieve," he called.

The *Lili Marlene* coasted in beyond them. Lines were thrown to the quay. Martin Hare was standing beside Sturm and Schmidt at the rail.

She turned to Craig, laughing. "Oh, you bastard."

Willing hands reached down to help them up the ladder to the top of the quay. Someone gave her a blanket, and Munro came forward, Sturm and Hare behind him.

"Excellent, Genevieve. Good as a film. Allow me to introduce Captain Robert Shane, Special Air Service."

Shane grinned and said, "Pleasure to do business with you." He put a hand to his scratched face. "Some of the time."

Julie came through the crowd, René behind her. "I thought we were all pretty damn good," she said. "Now, let's get inside before you catch pneumonia. Scotch all round, I think."

They turned and walked towards The Hanged Man. Craig put an arm around Genevieve's shoulders. "Just a taster," he told her, "of how rough things might get. You did well."

"Don't tell me you're proud of me?" she said.

"Something like that." And he opened the door of the pub and ushered her inside.

CHAPTER 9

IT WAS JUST after seven on the following morning when Heinrich Himmler entered Gestapo headquarters at Prinz Albrechtstrasse in Berlin. Guards sprang to attention as he entered; clerks hurriedly busied themselves over meaningless pieces of paper. He wore black full-dress uniform as Reichsführer-SS, and the face behind the silver pince-nez was a blank, as usual.

He went up the marble stairs and entered his office suite. In the anteroom his secretary, a middle-aged woman in the field-grey uniform of an SS auxiliary, stood up behind her desk. Himmler had personnel working shifts twenty-four hours a day.

"Send for Hauptsturmführer Rossmann at once," he said.

Himmler went into his office, placed his briefcase and cap on his desk and went to the window, where he stood, hands behind his back. After a while there was a knock at the door. A young captain entered and clicked heels.

"At your order, Reichsführer."

"Ah, Rossmann." Himmler sat behind his desk. "I was with the Führer last night. He raised the matter of this conference which is to take place at Château de Voincourt, in Brittany, this weekend. He is concerned, and rightly so. There is devilry afoot." He sat back. "I have always been able to count on your loyalty?"

"To the death, Reichsführer." Rossmann sprang to attention.

"Good. Then I will tell you now of things I've had to keep very private. Generals of our own high command, men who have taken a holy oath to serve the Führer, are engaged in a conspiracy to assassinate him."

"My God!" Rossmann said.

Himmler took a sheet of paper from his briefcase. "This list may surprise you."

Rossmann looked over the list in astonishment. "Rommel?"

"Yes. The people's hero, the good field marshal himself. As the Führer said, we must suspect that this conference at Château de Voincourt might be a cover for something more. Atlantic Wall conference. What nonsense!" Himmler laughed entirely without mirth. "A cover, Rossmann. This General Ziemke, for example, who's in charge of the place. I'm sure he is involved."

Rossmann nodded eagerly. "There is one thing in our favour about the de Voincourt set-up, Reichsführer."

"And what is that?"

"That security there is in the hands of the Waffen SS."

"Really?" Himmler looked up. "You're sure of this?"

"Oh, yes, Reichsführer. The officer responsible is Sturmbann-führer Max Priem. He wears the Knight's Cross, with oak leaves and swords."

"I see." Himmler tapped his fingers on the desk while Rossmann waited nervously. "Yes," Himmler said. "I think this Major Priem will serve our purpose very well. Get him on the phone, Rossmann. I'll speak to him personally."

AT THAT precise moment Max Priem was running through the woods on the other side of the lake from Château de Voincourt. He was an inch under six feet, the short black hair tousled, sweat on his face. He wore athlete's shorts, a scarf around his neck, and an Alsatian guard dog ran with him.

"Remember," the surgeon had told him on the day of his release from the hospital, "for a man with a silver plate in your head, you've done very well, but walk, don't run, from now on."

Well, to hell with that, Priem told himself, and went across the lawn to the main entrance in a final burst of speed, with the Alsatian, Karl, hard on his heels.

He went up the steps, past the sentries, who saluted, and into the great entrance hall. He went along the corridor, aware of the phone ringing in his office. He opened the door and found Hauptsturm-führer Reichslinger, his aide, who had come through from his own office, answering the phone.

"Yes, this is Sturmbannführer Priem's office. No, but he's just come in." He paused, then turned to Priem, his narrow eyes widening. "It's Reichsführer Himmler himself."

Priem held out his hand for the phone, his face giving nothing away. He pointed to the office next door. Reichslinger went through, closed the door, then hurried to his desk and picked up his phone gently. He heard Himmler say, "Priem?"

"Yes, Reichsführer."

"You are a loyal member of the SS brotherhood? I may rely on your help and discretion?"

"Of course, Reichsführer." What's the bastard got up his sleeve now? Priem wondered.

"Listen to me attentively," Himmler said. "The life of our Führer could be in your hands."

Priem listened, fondling the Alsatian's ruff as it sat beside him.

"So, what would you wish me to do, Reichsführer?" he asked when Himmler was finished.

"I'm convinced the conference this weekend is spurious. General Ziemke seems heavily suspect to me, and as for Rommel—the man is a disgrace to the officer corps."

In spite of having heard Germany's greatest war hero dismissed in such a fashion, Priem stayed calm. "We are not talking arrests here, I take it, Reichsführer?"

"Of course not. Total surveillance, a log of everyone present, and a record of all telephone calls. This is a direct order, Priem."

"*Zu Befehl, Reichsführer,*" Priem said automatically.

"Good. I look forward to your report."

The phone went dead, but Priem still had the receiver to his ear. There was the faintest of sounds. He glanced at the adjoining door, smiled slightly, put his phone down gently and crossed the room, followed by the Alsatian. When he opened the door, Reichslinger was just replacing the receiver. He turned, guilt written all over his face.

Priem said, "Listen, you miserable toad. If I catch you doing that again, I'll give Karl here permission to rip you into little pieces."

The Alsatian stared fixedly at Reichslinger, its tongue hanging out. Reichslinger, face ashen, said, "I meant no harm."

"You are, however, now privy to a state secret of the utmost gravity." Priem suddenly barked, "Heels together, Reichslinger."

"*Zu Befehl, Sturmbannführer.*"

"You took an oath to protect your Führer. Repeat it now."

Reichslinger gabbled, "I will render unconditional obedience to the Führer of the German Reich, Adolf Hitler, supreme commander of the armed forces, and will be ready, as a brave soldier, to stake my life at any time on this oath."

"Excellent. Keep your mouth shut or I'll have you shot."

As Priem turned to leave, Reichslinger called, "I would remind the major of one thing."

"And what would that be?"

"You also took the oath."

MAX PRIEM went upstairs to his room, showered and changed, inspecting himself in the mirror when he was ready. Except for the silver death's-head on his cap and his SS badge, his uniform was all paratrooper. Field-grey flying blouse, and jump trousers tucked into boots. A gold wound badge, Iron Cross first class, and a gold-and-silver paratrooper's badge studded his left breast. The Knight's Cross hung from his neck. He went out and walked across the landing above the great hall, then up the steps leading to the Countess de Voincourt's suite. He knocked on the door, opened it and went into the anteroom. Chantal was sitting in a chair by the bedroom door. She looked, as always, thoroughly unfriendly.

"Yes, Major?"

"See if the countess will receive me."

She opened the door, went in and closed it. After a while she returned. "You may go in now."

Hortense de Voincourt was propped up against pillows. She wore a silk gown, and a kind of cap covered the red-gold hair. She had a tray in front of her and was eating a buttered roll.

"Good morning, Major. Did I ever tell you that you look like the devil himself in that preposterous uniform?"

Priem liked her immensely. He clicked heels and gave her a salute. "You are as radiant as the morning, Countess."

She sipped champagne and orange juice from a tall crystal glass. "What piffle! If you want Carl, he's reading on the terrace. I will not allow a German paper to be read in this house."

Priem smiled and went out through the french window. Ziemke was seated at a small table reading a two-day-old copy of a Berlin newspaper. He looked up and smiled.

"What is it, Max?"

"I've had a phone call from Reichsführer Himmler," Priem said. "It seems that Château de Voincourt is a hotbed of conspiracy. Not only yourself, but most other generals who stay here, including Rommel, are suspected of designs on the Führer's life."

Ziemke folded his paper. "My thanks for telling me, Max." He got up and put a hand on Priem's shoulder. "My poor Max. A hero of the SS, and yet you're not even a Nazi. It must make life terribly difficult."

"Oh, I manage," Priem told him.

There was a murmur of voices inside, and Chantal appeared a moment later. "An orderly left this, General."

Ziemke read the signal, then laughed out loud. "Reichsführer Himmler is buying your services in advance, Max. You are promoted to the rank of Standartenführer." Ziemke pushed him into the bedroom. "What do you think, darling?" he said to the countess. "Max here has been promoted. He's now a full colonel."

"And what does he have to do for that?" she demanded.

Priem smiled ruefully. "I look forward to your niece's return. Tomorrow, I think."

"Yes. Anne-Marie has been staying at the Ritz," she said.

"I know," he told her. "I've rung three times—she's always out."

"What do you expect? Shopping in Paris is still shopping in Paris, in spite of this dreadful war."

"Yes, well, I must be about my duties." Priem saluted and left.

Hortense looked up at Ziemke. "Trouble?"

He took her hand. "Nothing I can't handle, and not from Max. He's caught in the middle."

"A shame," she said. "You know, Carl, I like that boy."

"So do I, *liebling*." And he took the champagne from the bucket and refilled her glass.

AT COLD HARBOUR, rain was drumming relentlessly against the kitchen window of Grancester Abbey. It had been raining all day. Julie and Genevieve sat at the table, and the Frenchwoman was shuffling a pack of tarot cards. The gramophone was playing "A Foggy Day".

"Very appropriate, considering the weather," Julie said.

"What happens now?" Genevieve asked.

"They'll come up with something." She held up the tarot cards. "They tell me I have a gift for these things. Shuffle them and give them back with your left hand."

"You mean you can foretell my future? I'm not sure I want to know." But Genevieve did as she was told.

Julie closed her eyes for a moment, then spread the cards face down on the kitchen table. She looked across. "Three cards, that is all you need. Select one and turn it over."

Genevieve did as she was told. The painting was dark and sombre, the title in French. There was a pool guarded by a wolf and a dog. Beyond it, two towers, and in the sky above, the moon.

"This is good, *cherie*, for it is in the upright position. It betokens a crisis in your life. Reason and intellect have no part—only your own instincts will bring you through. You must, at all times, flow with your own feeling. This alone will save you."

"You've got to be kidding." Genevieve laughed uncertainly.

"No, this is what the card says to me," Julie told her earnestly. "It also tells me you will come back. Choose another."

The card was the hanged man—a replica of the inn's sign.

"It does not mean what you think. Destruction and change, but leading to regeneration. You go forward as your own person for the first time, owing nothing to others."

There was a pause. Genevieve took a third card. It was a knight on horseback, a baton in his hand.

Julie said, "This is a man close to you. Probably a soldier."

Genevieve shrugged. "Crisis, change, a soldier. What does it all add up to?"

"The fourth card will tell. You should draw it now."

Genevieve hesitated, then pulled out the card. Julie flipped it over. Death stared up at them—a skeleton with a scythe.

Genevieve tried to laugh. "Not too good, I presume?"

Before Julie could reply, Craig came in. "Munro wants us in the library now. It's decision time." He paused, smiling. "Have you been messing around with those things again, Julie? You'll be getting yourself a tent next at the spring fair at Falmouth."

Julie smiled and scooped up the cards. "An interesting idea."

She got up, came around the table, and squeezed Genevieve's hand as they followed him.

MUNRO AND HARE were in the library with Flight Lieutenant Grant examining a chart of the Channel. René sat by the fire smoking a little cigar, simply awaiting orders.

Munro looked up. "Ah, there you are. The weather, as you can see, hasn't improved, and the weather boys still can't guarantee that it will in time for takeoff at eleven."

Grant said, "We were supposed to have a moon tonight and dry weather. Ideal conditions, but this stinks. You see, it isn't just the visibility. We land in ordinary fields. If they get waterlogged by heavy rain, it would be impossible to take off again."

The door opened, and Joe Edge came in. Munro said, "Any further word?"

"I'm afraid not, Brigadier," Edge told him.

Genevieve glanced at Edge. His face was blank, no expression, but the eyes said it all—only hatred there.

Munro said, "That does it. You have to go, my dear. We can't delay. If there's no plane, it will have to be a fast boat by night." He turned to Hare. "You're sailing now, Commander."

"Fine, sir." Hare nodded. " We leave at eight. The fog is perfect for a nice invisible run."

"We'll call Grand Pierre with the new arrangement," Craig said. "He'll be waiting with suitable transport. You'll still be at St Maurice on schedule."

Genevieve felt strangely calm. "That's it, then," she said softly.

CHAPTER 10

GENEVIEVE, CRAIG and René stayed below, at Hare's request, as the *Lili Marlene* left the harbour. Sitting at the table in the tiny wardroom, Genevieve found herself reaching for a Gitane almost as a reflex action. Craig gave her a light.

"You're really enjoying those things now, aren't you?"

"A bad habit." She nodded. "I've had the horrible idea that it might haunt me all the years of my life—should I live that long."

After a while a door opened, and Schmidt glanced in. "The guv'nor says you can come up top if you want to."

"Fine." Genevieve turned to Craig. "Coming?"

He looked up from his newspaper. "Later. You go."

Which she did, going up the companionway. When she opened the door, the wind dashed rain into her face. The boat seemed full of life, the deck heaving beneath her feet as she held on to the lifeline and struggled towards the ladder to the bridge. Totally exhilarated, she pulled herself up and got the wheelhouse door open.

Langsdorff was at the helm, Hare at the chart table in a swivel chair. He stood up. "Sit here. You'll be more comfortable."

She did as she was told. "This is nice. Exciting."

"It has its points." He said to Langsdorff in German, "I'll take over for a while. Take a coffee break."

"*Zu Befehl, Herr Kapitän*," he said, and went out.

Hare increased speed. The fog was patchy, so that at times they travelled in a private dark world and at others burst out into open water. For the moon was clear on occasion in spite of rain squalls.

"The weather doesn't seem to know what to do," she said.

"It never does in this part of the world."

She found another Gitane. "But we'll just have to soldier on, I suppose."

"Not quite the right phrase for a flight officer."

"A what?" Genevieve asked, the lighter flaring in her hand.

"All women agents going into the field are sent as officers of one sort or another. As I understand it, you were commissioned as a flight officer in the Women's Auxiliary Air Force yesterday."

"Munro didn't say a word to me about this."

Hare shrugged. "A devious old dog, but there's method in his madness. It gives him personal control over you. Disobey an order in wartime, and you could be shot."

"I sometimes think there was never any other time," she said.

"I know the feeling well."

The door opened, and Craig came in. "How's it going?"

"Fine," Hare said. He turned to Genevieve. "I'd go below if I were you. Try and catch a little sleep. Use my cabin."

"All right. I think I will."

She negotiated the heaving deck and went down to his tiny cabin. So much had happened and it was all whirling around in her head, and yet, in spite of that, she drifted into sleep after a few minutes.

OFF THE COAST of Brittany, it was still foggy in patches as the *Lili Marlene* eased in towards the shore, her silencers on. The crew were at battle stations, manning the guns fore and aft.

Langsdorff had the helm, and Hare and Craig surveyed the shore with night glasses, while Genevieve and René waited behind them. There was a sudden pinpoint of light dead ahead.

"There they are," Hare said. "Easy now. Dead slow."

The pier at Grosnez loomed out of the darkness—a tall, skeletal structure. The boat bumped against the lower jetty, and some of the crew were instantly over the side with lines.

There was a light at the top of the pier, and a voice called in French, "Is that you?"

"Grand Pierre," Craig said. "Let's move it."

Genevieve and René went ahead, and Craig followed with Hare. On the jetty, Craig moved close.

"Present for you." He gave her a Walther and a spare clip. "Stick those in your pocket. No girl should be without one."

"Not in these parts," Hare said, and put an arm about her. "You take care now."

Craig said calmly, "Okay, angel, up you go. The greatest performance of your career. As they say in show business, break a leg."

She turned quickly, almost in tears, and went up the steps to the upper level, René following. There was a truck, shapes moving in the darkness, and then a villainous-looking man stepped out to confront them. He wore a cloth cap, dirty old moleskin jacket and leggings, and a collarless shirt. The three-day stubble on his chin didn't help, nor did the scar on his right cheek.

"Grand Pierre?" René called.

Genevieve put a hand in her pocket to find the Walther. "This can't be our man," she whispered urgently to René.

Scarface paused a yard or so away and smiled. "Sorry to disappoint you, old girl," he said in a beautiful Oxford accent, "but if it's Grand Pierre you're looking for, then I'm your man."

Behind him a dozen or so more men moved out of the darkness, carrying rifles and Sten guns. They stood there silently.

Grand Pierre clapped his hands. "Come on, you rat pack," he called in French. "Let's get moving, and watch your language. We have a lady with us, remember."

GRAND PIERRE drove the truck quite fast, whistling tunelessly between his teeth.

She said, "What if we run into a German patrol?"

"Not round here. They only move about during the day and in strength. Ever get up to Oxford at all?"

"No, I'm afraid not."

They came over the brow of a hill, and at the same moment the clouds parted to reveal the moon. In its light she could see the cluster of houses that was St Maurice.

"Pity," he said. "I used to shoot up there. Near Sandringham. Lovely place."

"Do you miss it?"

"Not really. Pretend I do, just to keep me going."

"What did you do before?"

"Taught literature at a rather second-rate public school."

"You enjoy doing this sort of thing?"

"Oh, yes—scouting for boys and all that. The worst sores in life are caused by crumpled rose leaves, not thorns, Miss Trevaunce, wouldn't you agree?"

"I'm not even sure I understand."

"That's exactly what my pupils used to say."

They were entering the village now, and he started to slow. They turned in between massive gateposts, rattled across a cobbled yard to the house in the corner. A door opened; someone peered out.

René scrambled down. Genevieve followed.

"Thanks very much," she said.

"We aim to please." Grand Pierre smiled down at her. "Crumpled rose leaves. You think about it."

He drove away, and she turned and followed René inside.

GENEVIEVE SAT in front of the mirror in the small bedroom of the stationmaster's house, Anne-Marie's suitcases on the bed, her papers beside them. There was her French identity card, the German Ausweis, ration cards, a driver's licence.

The door opened, and the stationmaster's wife, Madame Dubois, entered. She was a small, careworn woman in a shabby grey dress. She didn't approve, Genevieve could see, of the finery displayed on the bed. The navy-blue suit from Paris with the pleated skirt, the silk stockings, the oyster satin blouse.

Remembering who she was supposed to be, Genevieve said sharply, "Next time, knock first. What do you want?"

Madame Dubois shrugged defensively. "The train, mam'selle. It has just come in."

"Good. Tell René to fetch the car. I'll be down soon."

The woman withdrew. Genevieve dressed quickly—underwear, stockings, slip, blouse, skirt—all Anne-Marie's. As she put on each item it was as if she were removing another layer of herself.

She wasn't afraid as she checked herself in the mirror, simply coldly excited. She really did look rather good, and she knew it. She snapped a suitcase shut, draped a caped greatcoat of blue worsted over her shoulders and went out.

She found Henri Dubois in the kitchen with his wife. He was a small, sallow-faced man, very ordinary looking, the last person one would have imagined to involve himself in such a business.

"René is bringing the car now, mam'selle."

She took the silver-and-onyx cigarette case from her handbag and selected a Gitane. She lit the cigarette and walked to the window, aware of the woman's hostile eyes on her, but that didn't matter. Nothing mattered now except the job at hand.

The Rolls-Royce emerged from one of the goods sheds and came up to the door to meet her. René, wearing a chauffeur's uniform now, got out and opened the door for her without a word. She got into the rear seat.

Dubois appeared with the suitcases, placed them in the boot, then came around to the window as René got behind the wheel. "You will convey my respects to the countess, mam'selle?"

Genevieve didn't reply, simply wound up the window and tapped René on the shoulder, aware of his eyes in the mirror, watching her, a touch of fear in them. And now it really does begin, she thought, and leant back, filled with restless excitement.

As THEY DROVE, the countryside became increasingly familiar, green fields and forest, the mountains capped with snow, the river gleaming in the early morning sun in the valley below. They moved down towards Pougeot, a small village she remembered well. As they drove through it she found the streets strangely deserted. "Not many people about," she said to René.

"Most able-bodied men have been shipped off to labour camps in Germany. The women run the farms. They'd even have taken an old dog like me if it had not been for the countess."

"And she could not do anything for the others?"

"What she can, she does, mam'selle, but in France these days most things are difficult."

They came around a bend in the road and became immediately aware of a black Mercedes on the grass verge. The bonnet was raised, and a German soldier was working on the engine. An officer stood beside him, smoking a cigarette.

"It's Reichslinger," René said as the officer turned and raised a hand. "What shall I do?"

"Stop, of course," Genevieve said calmly.

"Anne-Marie has nothing but contempt for this one, mam'selle, and shows it."

"Good. Let's see how we get on, then, shall we?"

She opened her handbag, took out the Walther and slipped it

247

into her right-hand pocket. The car slid to a halt, and she wound down the window as Reichslinger approached.

He was exactly like his photo. Fair hair, narrow eyes, a generally vicious look. He smiled, contriving to look even more unpleasant. "Mademoiselle Trevaunce. My luck is good," he said in French, and gestured towards the car. "The fuel pump is giving trouble, and this fool of a driver is unable to do anything about it. Under the circumstances I must beg a lift from you."

She let it hang there for a moment, made him wait, his sallow cheeks flushing slowly, then said, "The master race being masterful? What can I say except yes."

He hurried around to the other side, scrambled in beside her, and René drove away.

She took out a cigarette, and he hastily produced a lighter. "I trust you had a pleasant stay in Paris?"

She said, "Not really. Service is abominable now, and one is constantly stopped and searched, which is very inconvenient. Still, you soldiers have to play at something, I suppose."

"Mam'selle, I can assure you, my SS comrades in Paris have considerable success in tracking down terrorists."

"Really? I'm surprised all those soldiers haven't succeeded in putting down the Resistance movement entirely."

He was angry then, but she gave him one of her sister's beautiful smiles and had the satisfaction of seeing him swallow hard.

"How is Major Priem?"

"Standartenführer since yesterday."

"Colonel? That's nice." She laughed. "He does take himself rather seriously, but he is most efficient, you must admit."

Reichslinger scowled. "With others to do the work for him."

"Yes. It must get very boring for you. Why don't you apply for a posting in Russia? Lots of honour and glory there."

She was actually enjoying herself now because it was working; he had totally accepted her as Anne-Marie. In a sense, running into him had been the luckiest thing imaginable.

"I go where the Führer sends me," he said stiffly.

At that moment they came around a corner, and René had to swerve violently to avoid an old woman leading a cow along the road. Genevieve was thrown into the corner, Reichslinger with her, and she became aware that his hand was on her knee.

"Are you all right, mam'selle?" His grip tightened.

She said icily, "Please remove your hand, Reichslinger."

René, scenting trouble, started to pull in at the side of the road.

Reichslinger moved his hand a little higher. "What's wrong?" he demanded. "Aren't I good enough? Is that it? I'll show you I'm as good a man as Priem."

"The colonel is a gentleman, which you are very definitely not. To be perfectly honest, I find you just a little beneath me, Reichslinger."

"I'll show you, you arrogant—"

Her hand came out of her pocket holding the Walther. She slid off the safety catch in one smooth movement as Craig had taught her and pushed the muzzle into his side.

"Get out of this car!"

René braked. Reichslinger got the car door open and stumbled out. She closed it behind him, and René drove away instantly. She looked back and saw Reichslinger standing at the side of the road looking strangely helpless.

"Did I do well?" She asked René.

"Your sister would be proud of you, mam'selle."

"Good." She leant back and lit a Gitane.

THEY CAME over the hill, and she saw it half a mile away, nestling at the foot of the mountains, among the trees. Château de Voincourt, grey and still in the morning sun. House of nobility, survivor of religious wars, of revolution. As always since childhood, whenever she had returned to this place, there was the same feeling of calm. Of total happiness just at the sight of it.

The gates stood open, but the way was blocked by a swing bar. There was a guardhouse just inside and a sentry holding a machine pistol. He was only a boy, in spite of being SS. He said uncertainly, with a heavy accent, "Papers?"

"But I live here," she said. "Don't you know me?"

"My orders are firm, mam'selle. I must see your papers."

"All right," she said. "I'll give myself up. I'm a British agent and I've come to blow up the château."

A quiet voice cut in, speaking in German. She didn't understand a word, but the sentry did, running to lift the barrier at once. She turned to the man who had emerged from the guardhouse, the SS colonel, Knight's Cross at his throat. She didn't need René to tell her who this man was.

"Max, how nice."

Max Priem opened the door and got in. "Drive on," he told René. He said in French, "The boy has only been here for three days." He kissed her hand. "I'll never understand the pleasure you get from baiting my soldiers. It's bad for morale. Reichslinger gets very upset about it."

"Not at the moment," she commented. "He has other things on his mind."

The vivid blue eyes were suddenly very alert. "Explain."

"His car broke down near Pougeot. I gave him a lift but had to put him out near Dauvigne. I don't know where he did his training, but it certainly didn't include how to behave in the company of a lady."

His mouth was smiling, but his eyes were not. "And he went quietly? Reichslinger? Is this what you are telling me?"

"With a gentle prod from my friend here."

She produced the Walther, and he took it from her. "This is German army issue. Where did you get it?"

"A friendly barman in Paris. A girl needs all the protection she can get these days."

"Paris, you say?"

"Now, don't expect me to tell you the name of the bar."

He weighed the pistol in his hand for a moment, then returned it to her, and she slipped it into her handbag.

"So, you enjoyed your trip?" he said.

"Not really. Paris isn't what it was."

"Is that so?"

There was, for some reason, a certain irony to his voice, and she glanced at him quickly, out of her depth a little and not understanding why. They stopped at the front door, and René went around to the boot and got her suitcases.

"I'll take those," Priem said.

"You really are mortifying the flesh today," she told him. "An SS colonel with a bag in each hand, like a hotel porter? I should have a camera. They'll never believe it in Paris."

"To the men of the SS, nothing is impossible."

Inside, there was a sentry on each side of the door, but the hall was exactly as she remembered, right down to the ornaments. They ascended the wide marble staircase together.

She said, "How is the general?"

"His bad leg is a little stiff. All the rain we've been having."

They reached the top corridor. She paused outside the Rose Room—Anne-Marie's room—and waited. He sighed, put down one suitcase and opened the door for her.

As a child she had slept in this room often. It was light and airy, tall french windows opening onto a balcony. The polished mahogany furniture was completely unchanged.

Priem pushed the door shut, came across and put the suitcases on the bed, then turned. There was a slight grave smile on his mouth, a strange air of expectancy, as if he were waiting for something.

"Well?" she said.

"Well, yourself." He smiled. "Was Paris really that bad?"

"I'm afraid so."

"Then we'll have to try and make it up to you." He clicked his heels formally. "But later. Duty calls."

She was aware of an overwhelming surge of relief as the door closed behind him. She tossed her coat onto the bed, opened the french windows and went out onto the balcony.

There was an old rocking chair of hand-carved beech that she remembered well. She sat down in it, gently rocking, the sun warm on her face. She couldn't help wondering how often Anne-Marie had done this.

PRIEM WALKED across the landing and paused at the top of the staircase, aware of the boots of the SS sentries slamming in salute outside. A moment later Reichslinger entered the hall below.

"Reichslinger!" Priem called.

"Standartenführer?" Reichslinger looked up.

"My office. Now."

Reichslinger looked hunted as he walked across the hall and into the corridor. Priem went down the steps slowly. When he entered his office, the young Hauptsturmführer was standing at his desk. Priem closed the door.

"I get the impression you didn't try hard enough to be the gentleman with Mademoiselle Trevaunce."

"She had a pistol, Standartenführer. A Walther."

"Which you provoked her into using?"

"The penalty for a civilian found in possession of a weapon is death, as the Standartenführer well knows."

"Reichslinger," Priem said patiently, "there are wheels within wheels here. Things you know nothing about. In other words, mind your own business."

And Reichslinger, unable to hold his anger, said viciously, "That the Trevaunce girl is your business I understand only too well, Standartenführer Priem."

Priem seemed to go very still, his face calm, and yet suddenly Reichslinger was afraid. The colonel went around his desk and took a document from his IN tray. "A signal from Berlin. Rather depressing. SS battalions in Russia are desperately short of officers. They enquire if we can spare anyone."

Reichslinger's throat went dry. "Standartenführer," he whispered, "I'm sorry, sir. I didn't mean—"

"I know exactly what you meant," Priem said. "If you ever speak to me like that again, step out of line just once . . ." He held up the signal.

Reichslinger's face was ashen. "Yes, sir."

"Now, get out." The young man hurried to the door and got it open. Priem added, "And Reichslinger."

"Standartenführer?"

"Interfere with Mademoiselle Trevaunce again in such a way, and I will most certainly have you shot."

SITTING IN the rocking chair on the balcony of the Rose Room, Genevieve realised that she'd always had a fear of being swallowed up by Anne-Marie, just as she'd always had the feeling that in some strange way she should never have been born. Each had always had a kind of resentment of the fact of the other's existence.

Strange how this quiet place could cause such thoughts, and then she became aware of movement in the room. She stood up and went in. Black dress, white apron, dark shoes—the perfect lady's maid. Maresa was leaning over her suitcases.

"Leave them!" Genevieve ordered. Her voice was angry, for inside she was a little scared. Here was another to convince, someone else who knew her intimately.

"I want to sleep," she said. "You can unpack later."

For a moment she thought she saw hatred in the dark eyes and wondered what Anne-Marie could have done to earn that.

She closed the door behind Maresa and leant against it, hands shaking. Another hurdle passed. She glanced at her watch and saw that it was just after noon. Time she braved the lioness in her den. She smoothed her skirt, opened the door and went out.

CHAPTER 11

WHEN GENEVIEVE went into her aunt's sitting room, it was like entering another world. One wall was entirely covered by an exquisite Chinese mural. Heavy blue silk curtains hung from ceiling to floor. Genevieve knelt on the faded chaise lounge by the window and looked down into the garden.

She saw General Ziemke sitting on a bench. His hair was more silver than in the photos, his face more arresting at a distance, giving him the air of a man still in his prime. He appeared to be deep in thought.

"What do you want?"

Genevieve turned, and there she was—her grim, ugly face totally unchanged since the last time she had seen her. Chantal. "To see my aunt, of course."

"She's resting. I won't let you disturb her."

Genevieve said patiently, "Do as you're told for once, Chantal. Ask Hortense nicely if she'll see me. If you won't, then I'll go in anyway."

The door behind her was slightly ajar. As Genevieve turned to it, she heard the voice, so familiar in spite of the years, and her heart beat a little faster.

"She must want something badly. Let her in."

As Chantal pushed the door open, Genevieve could see Hortense sitting up in bed reading a newspaper. Genevieve smiled sweetly as she went past. "Thank you, dear Chantal."

But once inside she found herself totally at a loss. What would Anne-Marie say? She took a deep breath and went forward. "Why do you put up with her?" she asked, flinging herself down in a chair by the fireplace.

She felt the most intense excitement, wanting only to tell her aunt that it was she, Genevieve, come back after all these years.

"Since when have you cared?" She was a disembodied voice behind the newspaper. Now she lowered it, and Genevieve had one of the greatest shocks of her life. She was still Hortense, but infinitely older from when she had last seen her. "You want something?" Hortense said.

"Do I?"

"Usually." She sat back against the cushions, staring at Genevieve. "Now, tell me what you're up to and give me a cigarette."

Genevieve came over to the bed, and Hortense reached for her handbag, had it open before Genevieve could stop her, and rummaged inside. There was a pause; then Hortense took out the Walther.

"Be careful," Genevieve said, and reached for it, the wide silk sleeve of her blouse sliding up her arm.

Hortense hesitated, her eyes blank. She dropped the pistol and grabbed Genevieve's right wrist, a grip of incredible strength, so that she was pulled forward onto her knees beside the bed.

"Once, when you were a little girl of eight, you waded into the fountain in the lower garden—the boy with a trumpet. You told me later that you wanted to climb up to drink the water as it spouted from his mouth." Genevieve shook her head dumbly. The grip tightened. "One of his bronze fingers was broken. You slipped and caught your arm. Later, here in this very room, you sat on my knee holding me tight as Dr Marais repaired the damage. How many stitches was it—five?"

"No!" Genevieve struggled wildly. "That was Genevieve."

Hortense traced a finger along the thin white scar clearly visible on the inside of the right forearm. "I saw you arrive, *chérie*," she said. "From my window." Her grip slackened; a hand stroked Genevieve's hair. "From the moment you stepped out of the car— from that moment. Did you think I would not be able to tell?"

There were tears in Genevieve's eyes. She threw her arms about her.

Hortense kissed her gently on the forehead, then said softly, "And now, *chérie*, the truth."

WHEN GENEVIEVE had finished, she still knelt by the bed. There was a long pause; then Hortense patted her hand. "I think I would like a glass of cognac. Over there—the cabinet in the corner."

"But is that wise?" Genevieve said. "They told me you'd had trouble with your heart. Brigadier Munro said you were in poor health."

"What nonsense. Do I look ill to you?" She was almost angry.

Genevieve said, "No. You look marvellous, if you really want to know. I'll get your brandy."

She went to the cabinet and opened it. So, another piece of Munro's dishonesty, and Craig had gone along with it. She poured some Courvoisier into a crystal glass and carried it to her aunt.

Hortense took it down in one quick swallow and looked into the empty glass pensively. "Poor Carl."

"Why do you say that?"

"Do you think I could bear to have his hands on me now, knowing what those animals did to Anne-Marie?" She placed the glass down on the bedside cabinet. "We lived in a state of armed conflict, Anne-Marie and I. She was selfish, totally ruthless where her own desires were concerned, but she was my niece, my blood, my flesh. A de Voincourt."

"And acted like one these past few months."

"Yes. And we must see that what she did is not wasted."

"Which is why I am here."

Hortense snapped her fingers. "Tell Chantal to run my bath. I'll soak for an hour and think about what can be done to pay a little back on account. Come back in an hour, *chérie*."

AT COLD HARBOUR, Craig went into the kitchen at Grancester Abbey in search of Julie. She took in the fact of his uniform, the trench coat.

"You're leaving?"

"I'm flying up to Croydon with Munro." He put an arm around her. "Are you okay? You don't seem yourself."

She smiled wanly. "I know I amuse you with my tarot cards, Craig, but I do have the gift. I get feelings. I just know when something isn't as it should be."

"Explain," he said.

"Genevieve and her sister. There's more to this than meets the eye. Much more. I don't think Munro is telling the truth."

And he believed her, his stomach contracting into a knot, his hands tightening on her shoulders.

"Craig, I'm afraid."

"Don't be. I'll sort it. I intend to do some digging when I get to London." He kissed her on the cheek. "Trust me. You know what a wild man I am when I get angry."

CRAIG SAT beside Munro when they took off. The brigadier produced papers from his briefcase and studied them. No point in a frontal attack at this stage, Craig knew.

He said, "She'll be well into things by now."

"Who will?" Munro glanced up.

"Genevieve. She should be at the château by now."

"Oh, that." Munro nodded. "We'll have to see how it goes. She is an amateur, of course. One must remember that."

"That fact didn't bother you before," Craig told him.

"Yes, well, one mustn't expect too much. Two thirds of all women agents we've put in the field have come to a bad end."

He returned to his documents, unperturbed, and Craig sat thinking. Julie was right. There *is* more. He tried to analyse everything step by step. Central to it all was Anne-Marie, of course. If what had happened to her hadn't happened . . . Craig thought of her as he'd last seen her and shuddered. And then there was Baum, who couldn't bear to go near her himself. Strange, that. Very strange. A doctor afraid to go near his own patient. There had to be an answer.

"THE CONFERENCES are always held in the library," Hortense told Genevieve. "The rest of the time Priem uses it as his main office. He even sleeps there on a camp bed. He has a smaller office next to Reichslinger, but that's for routine business. Important papers are always kept in the library safe, behind the portrait of Elizabeth, the eleventh countess."

"How can you be sure?"

"Sooner or later, *chérie* any man in my life discloses all. Carl is no different. You see, he is not a Nazi. He doesn't approve, which means when he gets angry, he talks. A kind of release."

"You know that Rommel is coming the day after tomorrow to discuss their coastal defence system? That's what I'm here for. Any information I can get."

"Which means getting into the safe. That's where anything worth looking at will be. When they first came, I was compelled to hand over the key. They asked for the spare, too. They're very thorough, the Germans. On the other hand . . ." She opened the drawer of her bedside cabinet, took out a trinket box and lifted the lid. She produced a key. "I didn't give them the spare to the spare."

Genevieve said, "That's marvellous."

"Only a beginning. Such papers would soon be missed."

"I have a camera." Genevieve took out the silver-and-onyx cigarette case, fiddled at the back until the flap dropped. "See?"

"Ingenious." Hortense nodded. "So, the conference is to be held during the afternoon. In the evening there will be a ball, after which Rommel will return to Paris. If you are to see the contents of the safe, it will have to be during the ball itself."

"But how?"

"I'll think of a way, *chérie*. Depend on it." Hortense patted her cheek. "Now leave me for a while. I need to rest."

"Of course." Genevieve kissed her and crossed to the door.

As she reached for the handle Hortense said, "One more thing."

Genevieve turned. "What's that?"

"Welcome home, my darling. Welcome home."

WHEN GENEVIEVE got back to her room, she found that she was really tired. She lay down fully clothed on the bed.

She woke to find Maresa shaking her gently by the shoulder. "I thought Mam'selle would wish a bath before dinner."

"Yes, thank you," she said.

Maresa was obviously slightly bewildered by the gentleness of her tone, and Genevieve realised at once she wasn't playing her part.

"Well, go on, girl!" she said sharply.

"Yes, mam'selle."

Maresa disappeared into the bathroom, and Genevieve heard the sound of running water. She wasn't sure about Maresa at all. She was not stupid. And there had been that look of hate in her eyes when Genevieve had first arrived.

She luxuriated in the hot water, and after a while there was a discreet knock.

"It's half past six, mam'selle. Dinner is at seven."

After her bath Genevieve sat down in front of the dressing table, and Maresa immediately started to brush her hair, something Genevieve had always found intensely irritating, but she forced herself to sit there as Anne-Marie would have done.

"And what will Mam'selle wear tonight?"

"God knows. I'd better have a look."

Which was the only sensible solution, for the wardrobes were crammed with dresses of every description. Her sister had expensive tastes, no doubt about that. In the end she slipped into something in chiffon, subdued blues and greys, floating and elegant. She glanced at the clock. It was five past seven. "Time to go, I think."

Maresa opened the door. As Genevieve went past, she could have sworn the girl was smiling to herself.

CHANTAL APPEARED from the stairway, carrying a covered tray.

"What's this?" Genevieve demanded.

"The countess has decided to eat in her room tonight." She was angry, as usual. "He's in there."

Genevieve opened the door for her. Hortense was sitting in one of the wing chairs by the fire, wearing a spectacular Chinese housecoat in black and gold. General Ziemke was behind the chair, resplendent in full uniform. When he turned and saw Genevieve, his face broke into a smile of welcome that was very real.

"At last," Hortense said. "Now perhaps I can get a little peace."

Ziemke kissed Genevieve's hand. "We've missed you."

"Oh, get out of here, both of you," Hortense said impatiently. She beckoned to Chantal to bring the tray forward.

Ziemke smiled. "An essential quality for any good general is to know when it pays to retreat." He opened the door for Genevieve, inclined his head, and she went out.

THERE WERE about twenty people at the dining table, mostly men. There were a couple of women who looked like secretaries and wore evening gowns, and two rather pretty girls in uniform. Max

Priem sat opposite Genevieve, and she noticed Reichslinger at the far end of the table. When he glanced towards her, his eyes glittered with hate, reminding her strangely of Joe Edge. A couple of order-lies in dress uniform and white gloves came around with wine, and she remembered that Anne-Marie was capable from an early age of putting away far larger amounts than Genevieve ever could.

Ziemke, who sat next to her, leant close. "I trust the countess will feel in better spirits tomorrow?"

"You know her moods as well as I do."

"The day after, Field Marshal Rommel himself visits us. If the countess were to have one of her headaches, it would be most unfortunate."

"I understand you perfectly, General." Genevieve patted his hand. "I'll do my best."

"I would be loath to order her to be there. In fact," he added frankly, "I'd be afraid to. The day Priem and I arrived here . . . How she ran rings around us. Isn't that so, Priem?"

"I fell in love with her instantly," the colonel said.

"People have the habit of doing that," Genevieve told him.

She found his smile so disquieting that she had to look away from the penetrating blue eyes, her heart beating quickly. She had the strongest feeling that he could see right through her.

The general was speaking again. "The day we came, you were in the village, as I recall. Your aunt barred the door to us for quite some time. When we finally gained admittance, there were several conspicuous spaces on the walls."

He laughed delightedly, and for the rest of the meal was in the highest of spirits. As for Genevieve, the strain of playing her role was beginning to make her tense.

"Coffee in the drawing room," Ziemke finally announced.

There was a momentary confusion as everyone rose.

Ziemke steered her across the room and out to the terrace. "That's better," he said. "Fresh air. Cigarette?"

As she took it she said, "You're worried about this conference. Is it so important?"

"Rommel himself, my dear. What would you expect?"

"No. It's more than that," Genevieve said. "You don't agree with them—not any more. Isn't that it?"

"You make it too complicated," he said. "We'll be talking about defences, and I know what most of the others think."

This, of course, was exactly the kind of conversation she'd come to hear. "And you disagree?"

"I do. Unless the Führer changes it all, we will lose the war."

She reached for his hand. "I wouldn't say that too loudly."

He held her hand and stared out into the dark grounds, seemingly lost in thought. She didn't mind—that was the strange thing. He was kind and unhappy and she liked him, and that hadn't been part of the scheme at all. There were footsteps, and she pulled away.

"Sorry to disturb you, Herr General," Max Priem said, "but there's a call from Paris."

The general nodded heavily. "I'll come. Good night, my dear." He kissed her hand and went back in.

Max Priem stood to one side. "Fräulein," he said formally. She caught the mocking look in his eyes and, strangely, something else, too. Anger.

CHAPTER 12

HORTENSE SENT for Genevieve just after breakfast. She was in her bath when Genevieve went in.

"I've decided to go to Mass this morning. You will come with me," her aunt said. "It is necessary."

"For the salvation of my immortal soul?"

"No. To give Maresa a chance to search your room. Chantal overheard Reichslinger giving her instructions late last night."

Genevieve said, "He suspects me, then?"

"Why should he? You made a bad enemy there, that's all. This is probably just a way to get back at you. An RAF propaganda leaflet would be enough for that one to denounce you as an enemy of the Reich. We must make his little plan backfire."

"What do I do?"

"When you return, you will make the unpleasant discovery that your diamond earrings are missing, which they will be, because by then Chantal will have transferred them to some suitably stupid hiding place in Maresa's bedroom. You will naturally raise the devil. Go straight to Priem, who is, after all, in charge of security. He will find the earrings in Maresa's bedroom very quickly. She will protest her innocence, but the facts will speak for themselves. It is at that point that the silly girl will begin to cry ...."

"And confess that she was only acting under Reichslinger's instructions?"

"Exactly."

"You could beat the devil himself at cards."

"Of course."

"But will Priem believe her?" Genevieve said.

"I think we may rely on it. He'll deal with Reichslinger. This colonel of yours is a hard man when he has to be."

"Mine? Why do you say that?"

"Poor Genny." Nobody had called her that for years. "Since you were old enough to climb on my knee, I have been able to read you like an open book. He fills you with unease, this man. Yes? Your stomach turns hollow with excitement just to be near him."

Genevieve took a deep breath to steady herself, and stood up.

"I'll do my best to resist the temptation. I think you can rely on that. Have you told Chantal?"

"Only that Anne-Marie is up to her neck in subversive activities. I think she will smile on you more warmly now."

"All right," Genevieve said. "Now, as to a plan of campaign."

"All sorted out. We'll discuss it later. Be a good girl and tell Maresa to inform René that I'll need the Rolls."

Genevieve did exactly as she was told. But when they went out the front door, there was no sign of René or the Rolls—only Max Priem and a black Mercedes.

He saluted gravely. "Your car is out of order this morning, Countess. In the meantime I am wholly at your service. You wish to go to church, I believe?"

Hortense hesitated, then got inside, and Genevieve followed her.

He drove them himself, and Genevieve had to sit there, uncomfortably aware that Priem was watching her in the driving mirror, his eyes full of laughter. Hortense noticed, too.

At the church, Priem turned the car in beside the gate, got out and opened the rear door. "If you please, ladies."

Hortense turned to Genevieve. "No need for you to come in. Pay your respects to your mother. I shan't be long."

She pulled down her veil and went up the path between the gravestones to the porch of the ancient church.

Priem said, "A remarkable woman."

"I think so." There was a slight pause as he stood there, hands clasped behind him.

She said, "If you'll excuse me, I'd like to visit my mother."

"But of course."

She entered the churchyard. After a moment he followed. It was an ideal setting in the far corner, shaded by a cypress tree. Her mother's headstone was beautifully simple—as Hortense had intended it to be—and there were fresh flowers in a stone vase.

"Hélène Claire de Voincourt Trevaunce," Max Priem said, moving close, and then he did a strange thing. He saluted briefly, a perfect military salute, nothing Nazi about it. "Well, Hélène Claire," he said softly, "you have a very beautiful daughter. You would be proud of her, I think." He turned to Genevieve. "And of the sister of whom you so seldom speak? Genevieve, isn't it?"

She was frightened then at the fact that he knew so much, and she was aware of a desperate feeling of being balanced on some dangerous edge. She was saved because of a sudden shower. As it burst upon them he seized her hand.

"Come. We must run."

They reached the shelter of the church porch and sat down on a stone bench.

He sighed, his face softening a little. "Always since I was a boy I have loved the rain."

"Me, too," she said.

He smiled gravely. "Good. Then we have something in common."

They sat there waiting for Hortense as the rain increased, and her aunt had been right, as usual, for she had never felt so excited in her life.

IN A SPY FILM Genevieve had seen, the hero had placed a hair across a door so that he could tell later whether his room had been entered. She had employed the same ruse with the drawers in her dressing table. It was the first thing she checked when she got back from church. They'd been opened.

She went in search of Priem. She found him at his desk in the library, Reichslinger at his side, going over some papers.

They both looked up. She said, "It really is too much, Colonel. That your security people should search our rooms is something we must regrettably take for granted. But I am not prepared to overlook the disappearance of a pair of very valuable diamond earrings."

"Your room has been searched?" Priem said calmly. "How can you be sure?"

"A dozen different ways. And the earrings, of course."

"Perhaps your maid was simply tidying up. Have you spoken to her?"

"Not possible," Genevieve said impatiently. "I gave her the morning off before leaving for church."

He said to Reichslinger, "Do you know anything about this?"

Reichslinger's face was pale. "No, Standartenführer."

Priem nodded. "After all, there would be no question of your undertaking such a search without my authority."

Reichslinger stayed silent. Genevieve said, "Well?"

"I'll deal with it," Priem told her, "and come back to you."

"Thank you, Colonel." She turned and walked out.

Priem lit a cigarette and looked up at Reichslinger. "The truth, man. Five seconds is all you've got."

"Standartenführer, I was only doing my duty. The Walther—it worried me. I thought there might be other things."

"So, you force Mademoiselle Trevaunce's maid to search her mistress's room, and in the process she gets sticky fingers? Very helpful, Reichslinger."

"Standartenführer, what can I say?"

"Nothing," Priem said wearily. "Just bring Maresa to me."

GENEVIEVE WAITED in her room nervously, trying to read. In an hour there was a knock at her door, and Priem entered.

He crossed the room and dropped the earrings into her lap. "Your maid took them. You see, I was right."

"The ungrateful little slut. It's back to the farm for her."

"An impulse of the moment, I would say. A stupid girl who persisted in her innocence of the charge in spite of the fact that I had discovered the earrings in her room. In any case, she could hardly have hoped to get away with such a thing."

"Are you suggesting that I give her another chance?"

"That would require a little charity, a commodity in short supply in these hard times." He smiled. "You will excuse me now?"

"Of course."

The door closed behind him. She waited for a couple of minutes, then left herself, quickly.

"MARESA IS having an affair with one of the soldiers," Hortense said, "or so Chantal informs me." She glanced up at her grim old maid. "You may bring her to me now."

"You intend to use Maresa in some way?" Genevieve asked after Chantal left the room.

"Naturally." Hortense allowed herself a tiny smile. "Maresa's soldier is on guard duty on the terrace outside the library tomorrow night. If you are to get into the library, it must be during the ball. The catch on the third french window is broken. If you push hard enough, it will open. How long will it take you to open the safe and use this camera of yours? Five minutes? Ten?"

"But the guard outside," Genevieve said. "On the terrace."

"Ah, yes. Maresa's young man. I think we can rely on her to take him off into the bushes for a reasonable length of time."

Maresa arrived then, shepherded by Chantal, her face swollen, ugly with weeping.

"Please, mam'selle," she pleaded. "I didn't take your earrings. I swear it."

"But you searched my room on Reichslinger's orders."

Her mouth gaped in shock. She was too shaken to deny it.

"You see, we know everything, you stupid girl, just like Colonel Priem," Hortense said. "He made you tell him the truth, didn't he, and then told you to shut up about it?"

"Yes, Countess." Maresa dropped to her knees. "Reichslinger's a terrible man. He said he'd have me sent off to a labour camp if I didn't do as he told me."

"Get up, girl, for goodness' sake." She did as she was told, and Hortense continued, "You want me to send you back to the farm? Disgrace your mother, eh?"

"No, Countess—please. I'll do anything."

Hortense reached for a cigarette and smiled up at Genevieve coldly. "You see?" she said.

THE OFFICERS were holding a small party at the château that evening as a preparation for the great event.

Genevieve was dressed and ready to go down just before seven when there came the lightest of taps on the door. She opened it and found René standing there, holding a tray.

"The coffee mam'selle ordered," he said gravely.

Her hesitation was only fractional. "Thank you, René," she said, and stood back.

She closed the door; he put down the tray and turned quickly. "Mam'selle, I've received word to go and visit one of our contacts. A message from London perhaps. It goes well?"

"Perfect so far."

"I'll contact you tomorrow, but I must go now, mam'selle."

He opened the door and went out. She was conscious of a feeling of real unease. She poured some of the coffee he'd brought and sat by the window to drink it.

THEY WERE using the old music room for dancing. Two young officers spent the first hour seeing to the gramophone but soon relinquished the task to one of the orderlies, and the music became a little more lively. There was quite a crowd.

. Genevieve played the aristocrat to the hilt, a way of keeping at a distance people she was probably supposed to know. Max Priem, a glass of cognac in one hand, kept his face very straight as he talked to an army colonel, but there was wry amusement in those blue eyes when he glanced at Genevieve briefly.

She watched Priem for a while, this man who was nothing at all like what she had expected. All Germans were Nazi brutes, like Reichslinger. She had believed that because that was what she was supposed to believe.

But Priem was different. When she looked at him, she shivered slightly. Such thoughts were stupid. She was here for a purpose and must hold on to that fact.

The music was a curious mixture and not always German. There were French tunes and even a little American boogie-woogie. Tomorrow would be nothing like this. The music would be dignified, an orchestra. They would drink lots of champagne and punch from silver bowls, and soldiers would wait upon them in white gloves, dress uniforms.

A young lieutenant approached and asked her to dance so diffidently that she flashed him Anne-Marie's most brilliant smile and said she'd be delighted. He was a beautiful dancer, probably the best in the room, and blushed when she complimented him.

While the record was being changed, she stood chatting, and a voice said, "May I have this dance?"

As the music began, Max Priem took her hand. He was an excellent dancer, and suddenly it was all rather pleasant. And yet she was a spy, surrounded by the enemy. If they found out, what would they do to her? Those Gestapo cellars in Paris, where Craig Osbourne had suffered?

"Of what are you thinking?" Priem murmured.

"Nothing very special."

It was rather marvellous drifting there, the light swimming in a haze of smoke. The music throbbed, and then she realised it was Al Bowly singing "Little Lady Make Believe". A curious choice. Last time she'd heard the song was during the London blitz, at one of the clubs, with an American pilot.

Priem said, "You may have noticed the music has stopped."

"Which shows how tired I am. I think I'll go to bed."

An orderly appeared with a message for him. He took the piece of paper and read it, and curiosity made her stay just to see if it was important. Not a muscle moved in his face. He slipped the paper into a pocket.

"Good night, then," he said.

"Good night, Colonel."

She felt dismissed and had a strange feeling about that paper, as if it meant something she ought to know.

CHAPTER 13

IN LONDON, Craig Osbourne had found himself trapped for most of that day at headquarters. It was evening before he arrived at the nursing home in Hampstead. The guard didn't open the gate, simply spoke through the bars.

"What can I do for you, sir?"

"Major Osbourne," he said. "I'm here to see Dr Baum."

"I believe he's out, sir."

"Damn," Craig said, and started to turn away.

"If it's urgent, sir, I think you'll find him at The Grenadier. Just down the road. He's there most nights."

"Why, thank you," Craig told him, and hurried away.

The Grenadier was on the corner of a cobbled mews. When Craig went in, he found himself in a typical London pub. It wasn't too busy. Behind the bar a middle-aged blonde in a tight satin blouse looked up from the magazine she was reading. Her eyes brightened at the sight of his uniform.

"What can I get you, love?"

"Scotch and water," he told her. "I was hoping I might find a friend of mine here. A Dr Baum."

"The little foreign doctor from the nursing home?"

"That's right."

She was filling a glass. "He's in the snug, through that door, love. In there most nights. Likes to be on his own."

"Thanks." Craig paid her and took his drink.

She said, "He ain't half putting it away these days—the booze, I mean. See if you can get him to slow down."

"Been drinking hard, has he?"

"I should say so. Used to come in every night, same time, sit on the stool at the end of the bar, read *The Times*, drink one glass of port, then go."

"So, what happened?"

"Well, his daughter died, didn't she?"

"But that was some time ago. Before the war."

"Oh, no, love. You're wrong there. It was about six months ago. I remember it well. Dreadfully upset, he was. Went in the snug and leant on the bar with his head in his hands. Crying, he was. He said he'd just heard his daughter had died."

Craig managed to stay calm. "I obviously got it wrong. Never mind. I'll have a word with him now."

He opened the Victorian frosted-glass door and found himself in a long private room. The main bar extended into it. In other days it had been intended for ladies only. Leather benches fringed the wall. Baum was sitting beside a small coal fire, a glass in his hand. He looked seedy and neglected.

Craig said, "Hello, Doctor."

Baum looked up in surprise. "Major Osbourne. How are you?"

His speech was slightly slurred, his eyes tired-looking and bloodshot.

"I'm fine." Craig leant against the bar. "I promised Genevieve Trevaunce I'd check on her sister."

Baum ran a hand across his face, frowned and then nodded.

"How is she?" Craig asked.

"Not too good, Major." Baum shook his head and sighed. "Poor Anne-Marie. And Miss Genevieve—have you heard from her?"

"Heard from her?" Craig asked.

"From over there. The other side."

"You know about that, then?"

Baum assumed an expression of cunning. "Not much I don't know. Fast boat, passage by night."

Craig just let it flow, nice and easy. "The barmaid was telling me your daughter died six months ago."

Baum nodded, maudlin now, his eyes filling with tears. "My lovely Rachel. A terrible thing."

"But if she was in Austria, how could you find out?" Craig said gently. "The Red Cross?"

"No," Baum answered automatically. "It was my own people. The Jewish underground." He suddenly looked worried. "Why do you ask?"

"It's just that I understood your daughter died before the war, when you fled to this country."

"Well, you're wrong." Baum seemed to have sobered up. He got to his feet. "I must go. I have work to do."

"What about Anne-Marie? I'd like to see her."

"Some other time perhaps. Good night, Major."

Baum went into the bar; Craig followed. The barmaid said, "He went off like a rocket."

"Yes, he did, didn't he?"

Craig smiled with total charm and went out.

IT WAS half past nine when Craig went up the steps to the door at the Haston Place house and rang the bell of the basement flat. "It's Craig, Jack," he said into the intercom.

When the door opened, he went in and walked along the corridor to the basement stairs. Carter was standing at the bottom.

"Come on." Carter turned and went into the flat, and Craig followed him. "Drink?" Carter asked.

"No, thanks. I'll have a smoke if you don't mind." He lit a cigarette. "I've just seen Baum."

"Really?" Carter was making himself a scotch.

"Yes. I found him at the local pub. He's really pouring the stuff down these days. Apparently started six months ago, when he got word that his daughter had died in German hands."

"Yes, well, I think that would be enough to start me drinking." Carter spoke without thinking.

"Only one thing wrong," Craig said. "As I understood it, Baum got out of Austria just before the war, after the Nazis had killed his daughter. Munro told me that himself. He told me Baum offered his services to intelligence. He wanted revenge."

"Yes, I believe that's true," Carter said.

"What's true, what's false, Jack? Did his daughter die in '39 or six months ago?"

"Look, Craig, there's a lot you don't know about this."

"Try me," Craig said. "No. Let me try you. How about this? The Nazis hold Baum's daughter and suggest that if he wants her to continue to exist, he flees to British intelligence, continuing to work for them, or else."

"You've been reading too many spy stories," Carter said.

"And then something goes wrong. The girl dies in the camps. Baum's masters don't tell him, but the Jewish underground does. Now Baum really wants revenge. So, he goes to Munro and confesses all. No question of punishment. He's too valuable as a double agent."

Carter said nothing.

"But there's more. Anne-Marie and Genevieve. There's more to it than meets the eye. What is it, Jack?"

Carter sighed, went and opened the door. "My dear Craig, you're overwrought. Get yourself a decent night's sleep."

"You're a good man, Jack, a decent man." Craig shook his head. "But that one upstairs worries me. He really does believe the end justifies the means."

"Don't you?" Carter asked.

"No way. Because if it does, it makes us just as bad as the people we're fighting. Night, Jack."

He went upstairs, and Carter immediately picked up the house phone by the door and rang Munro in his flat. "Brigadier, Osbourne is on to something. The Baum business . . . Right. I'll come up."

The door was slightly ajar. In the darkness of the passage above, Craig had heard everything. Now, as Carter ascended the stairs, Craig tiptoed to the front door and let himself out quietly.

IT WAS RAINING hard and just after ten when Craig arrived back at the nursing home. No point in trying the gate. Baum, frightened, would have left orders that he was not to be admitted.

Craig tried a lane at one side. There was a two-storey building at the end, an iron staircase going up one side. He went up quietly. The wall of the nursing home was no more than three feet away. It was ridiculously easy to climb over the rail, step across and drop down into the garden.

He moved cautiously towards the home, avoiding the front door. Around to the rear, light showed through a crack in the curtains of a room looking out over a terrace.

He went up the steps to the terrace and peered through the gap in the curtains. Inside, Baum sat at a desk, head in hands, a bottle of scotch in front of him. Craig thought for a moment and then knocked on the french window smartly. Baum looked up in surprise.

Trying to sound as English as possible, Craig called, "Dr Baum. It's the gate guard."

He stepped back and waited. A moment later the window opened, and Baum peered out. "Johnson. Is that you?"

Craig moved in fast, had a hand around Baum's throat in an instant and pushed him back into the room and into the chair.

"Are you crazy?" Baum demanded hoarsely.

"No." Craig said. "It's question-and-answer time."

"I've nothing to say," Baum quavered. "You're mad. When the brigadier hears about this, it will mean your commission."

"Fine." Craig held up his left hand. "See how crooked they are? The Gestapo did that in Paris. They broke each finger in turn and pulled out the nails with pincers."

"My God," Baum whispered.

"I've been there, Baum. I stopped caring a long time ago." He grabbed Baum by the chin and squeezed painfully. "Genevieve Trevaunce is infinitely more important than you are. I'll do whatever is necessary to make you talk, so why not go easy on yourself and just answer the questions."

Baum was utterly terrified now. "Ye- yes," he stuttered.

"You didn't escape from the Nazis. They held your daughter hostage and told you to claim political asylum, pretend she was dead and offer your services to British intelligence."

"Yes," Baum moaned. "It's true."

"How did you communicate?"

"I had a contact at the Spanish embassy. He sent out messages in the diplomatic pouch. Bomb damage, troop movements. That sort of thing. For emergencies there was a woman who lives in a village in Romney Marsh. She has a radio."

"And you got away with it until the Jewish underground told you six months ago that your daughter really was dead?"

"That's right." Baum mopped sweat from his face.

"So, you went to Munro and spilt the beans?"

"Yes." Baum nodded. "He ordered me to carry on as if nothing had happened. They even left the woman in Romney Marsh in place. Ruth Fitzgerald. She's a widow. Married to an Irish doctor. Hates the English."

Craig stood up and walked to the other side of the desk. "And Anne-Marie Trevaunce? What's the truth there?" Baum looked wildly from side to side, and Craig picked up an old-fashioned mahogany ruler from the desk and turned. "The fingers of your right hand for starters, Baum. One at a time."

"For God's sake, it wasn't my fault," Baum said. "I just gave her the injection. I was doing what Munro told me."

Craig went very still. "What injection?"

"A new kind of truth drug. They decided to try it on every agent who came in from the field. It's excellent when it works."

"And for her it didn't," Craig said grimly.

Baum's voice was almost a whisper. "An unfortunate side effect. The damage to the brain is irreversible. The only good thing is that she could die at any time."

"Is there more?"

"Yes," Baum said wildly. "I was ordered to blow the Trevaunce girl's cover."

Craig stared at him. "Munro told you to do that?"

"Yes. I sent a message to the Fitzgerald woman at Romney Marsh three nights ago to transmit on the radio, letting them know about Genevieve." Behind Craig the door opened quietly, but Baum didn't see. "He wants her caught, Major. I don't know why, but he wants them to take her."

"Oh, dear me, what a loose tongue we have," Dougal Munro said.

Craig turned and found the brigadier standing there, hands in the pockets of his old cavalry coat. Jack Carter stood beside him, leaning on his walking stick, Browning in hand.

"You bastard," Craig said.

"A sacrificial lamb is required occasionally, dear boy. You don't really think an amateur like Genevieve would stand an earthly chance of getting hold of that information from Rommel. No, Craig. Deception is the name of the game. It is essential that the Germans think we're invading where we're not. Various little projects will reinforce the suggestion."

"So?" Craig said.

"I had a rather bright thought, which was the real reason I sent for Anne-Marie. When Genevieve had to take over, we kept to the same plan. I allowed her to see—by accident—a plan on my desk at Cold Harbour. It was of the Pas-de-Calais area, headed 'Preliminary Targets, D-day'. The brilliance of that little stroke is that she doesn't appreciate the importance of that false information. It will make it seem all the more genuine when they sweat it out of her, which they will."

"You'd have sold Anne-Marie out, too?" Craig's face was terrible to see. He took a step towards Munro. Carter raised the Browning.

"Stay where you are, Craig."

Craig said to Munro, "You'd do anything, wouldn't you? You and the Gestapo have a lot in common."

"Sacrifices are sometimes necessary." Munro sighed. "Put him in the cellar, Jack. Lock him up and tell Arthur to take extra care. We'll have words in the morning."

Carter's face was troubled. "Come on, old son. Don't give me any fuss."

Craig walked ahead of him and down the back stairs to the basement. It was very quiet, no sound from Anne-Marie. Deaf Arthur, in his white coat, sat on his chair reading a book.

Carter stayed well away from Craig as they paused at a cell door. "Inside. There's a good chap." Craig did as he was told, and Arthur stood up and came forward. Carter spoke full into the man's face so that he could lip-read. "Keep an eye on the major for me, Arthur. The brigadier and I will be back in the morning. And take care. He's a dangerous man."

"Aren't we all?" Arthur said in a strangely metallic voice as he locked the door.

Carter started to turn away, and Craig called, "Jack, just one thing. René Dissard? Where did he fit in?"

"We told him Anne-Marie'd had a mental breakdown. The rape story was necessary to motivate Genevieve. The brigadier persuaded Dissard to go along with that story."

"So, even her old friend René let her down."

"Good night, Craig."

Carter's footsteps faded, and Craig turned to inspect his quarters. There was an iron camp bed with a mattress and nothing else. No window and no blankets. The door's construction was of the strongest. No way out there.

He sat on the bed, which sagged alarmingly. He pulled the mattress back and saw that the heavy coiled springs had rusted with age. It gave him an idea. He took a small penknife from the pocket of his tunic and started to work.

It was almost six o'clock in the morning when Anne-Marie started to scream. Craig got to his feet and went to the door, the heavy coil of bedspring swinging from his hand. Five minutes passed, and then he heard the sound of approaching footsteps. He saw Arthur coming, an enamel mug in one hand.

Craig stuck a hand out. The man turned and looked at him. "I need the lavatory," Craig said. "I haven't been all night."

Arthur didn't reply, simply walked away. Craig's heart sank, and then a few moments later the man reappeared, the key in one hand, an old Webley service revolver in the other.

"All right. Out you come, and watch it," he said in that strange voice. "One wrong move and I'll break your arm."

"I wouldn't be such a fool," Craig told him as they moved into the corridor. Then he swung on one foot, the coiled spring lashing across the hand holding the revolver. Arthur cried out, dropping the weapon, and the coiled spring arched, catching him across the side of the head. Craig grabbed the man's arm and ran him head first into the cell. He slammed the door shut and turned the key. As he went along the corridor Arthur started to shout, and beyond him, in the other cell, Anne-Marie's voice rose to a crescendo, drowning him out. Craig closed the padded door at the end of the corridor, cutting off the sound, and went upstairs.

The house was very quiet. He slipped into Baum's study, closed the door gently, picked up the phone and called Grancester Abbey. Julie answered, her voice full of sleep.

"It's Craig. Sorry if I got you out of bed, but it's urgent."

"What is it?" she asked, suddenly alert.

"You were right. Something's wrong, but you can't imagine how wrong in your wildest dreams. Listen carefully . . ."

When he was finished, she said, "What are we going to do?"

"You spell it out to Martin Hare. Tell him I need a fast passage to France. I'll be there as soon as I can. See you soon."

He replaced the receiver, took out his wallet and found his SOE security card. He smiled softly. It always did pay to go in hard. Nothing to lose, anyway. He let himself out by the french window, slipped through the shrubbery to the wall, pulled himself on top and stepped across to the iron staircase. A moment later he was hurrying down the lane and into the main road. His luck was good. As he reached the next corner a taxi driver starting his shift spotted him and pulled over.

"Where to, guv'nor?" He grinned. "I bet you've had a good night. Gawd, you Yanks."

"Baker Street," Craig told him, and got in.

He was gambling now that his dispute with Munro was still private. At SOE headquarters, he produced his pass and was checked through by security. He went up the back stairs two at a time and entered the transport office. His luck was still good. The night duty officer, Wallace, was still on. Craig had known him since his early days with SOE.

"Hello, Osbourne," Wallace said in surprise. "What brings you out so bright and early?"

"Big flap on. Munro wants to go down to Cold Harbour in a hurry. I'm meeting him at Croydon. Give me the usual authorisation, then phone through to Croydon to tell them to expect us. We'll need the Lysander. Oh, and you'd better give me a chit for the motor pool."

"We're trying to win the war in a hurry again, are we?" Wallace filled in the documents and handed them to him.

Craig said, "Thanks—I'd better get moving. You'll phone through to Croydon?"

"Of course," Wallace said, reaching for the phone.

IT WAS RAINING steadily at Croydon, but visibility was good as Craig, in the passenger seat of a jeep, was passed through the main gate. He dismissed his driver and found Grant in his flying clothes having a cup of tea with the orderly officer.

Grant said, "Hello, old son. Where's the brigadier?"

"He's going to come down later," Craig told him. "There's your authorisation."

He passed it over and the orderly checked it. "Fine. Everything's in order."

"All right, old boy. Might as well get going," Grant said, and he and Craig went out and ran together through the rain to the Lysander.

MUNRO HAD worked for most of the night, catching up on paperwork. He was having a late breakfast when the phone rang. "Get that," the brigadier said to Carter.

Carter picked it up, listened, then held the phone to his chest, the slightest trace of a smile on his face. "Baum, sir. It would appear our Craig is on the loose."

Munro flung down his napkin. "Just tell Baum I'll handle it. And get the car, Jack."

At Baker Street, Carter and Munro found Wallace going down the front stairs as they were coming up.

"Morning, sir," Wallace said to Munro. "Change of plans?"

"What on earth are you talking about?" Munro demanded.

Wallace told him.

JOE EDGE stood outside the hangar at Cold Harbour and watched the Lysander lift off into the fog as Grant started the return journey to Croydon. The telephone began to ring in the small glass office in the hangar.

Edge went in and lifted the receiver. "Yes?"

"Is that you, Edge? . . . Munro here. Any sign of Osbourne?"

"Yes, sir. Landed half an hour ago. Hare picked him up in one of the jeeps. Julie was with him. They went down to the pub."

"Now, listen carefully, Edge," Munro said. "Osbourne may have some wild idea of persuading Hare to make an unauthorised trip to France. You must prevent that."

"How, sir?"

"Good God, man, any way you know how. Use your initiative. As soon as Grant's back, we'll be down there."

He rang off. Edge replaced the receiver, a smile on his face — not a nice smile. Then he opened a drawer and took out his Walther. He went out quickly, got into his jeep and drove down through the village, stopping some fifty yards from the pub. He went into the back yard and peered through the kitchen window. It was empty. He opened the door quietly and went in.

THE CREW of the *Lili Marlene* leant against the bar listening to what Hare was saying.

"You've heard the facts. Miss Trevaunce is in about as bad a spot as she could be, and it's all Munro's doing. The major and I intend to do something about that, but I've no authorisation. If any man feels he can't come, I won't hold it against him."

"For God's sake, guv'nor, what are we wasting time for?" Schmidt said. "We've got to get ready."

"He's right, Herr Kapitän," Langsdorff said stolidly. "If we leave at noon, we'll be at Grosnez by six."

Craig and Julie sat behind the bar watching. In the kitchen Edge could hear everything clearly.

Hare turned to Craig. "There you go, then."

Craig said, "I'll take Julie up to the house. I need some things from costume, and she can radio to Grand Pierre."

Edge was already out the back door and running to his jeep.

FROM THE COSTUME rack Craig selected the black dress uniform of a Standartenführer in the Charlemagne Brigade of the Waffen SS. "I prefer the black when the going gets rough," he told Julie. "It puts the fear of God into everyone."

"What shall I say to Grand Pierre?"

"He must be at the pier at Grosnez by six, and he must provide me with the right kind of German military transport."

The door creaked, and as they turned, Edge appeared, the Walther at the ready.

"Actually, old son, you aren't going anywhere. Munro just gave me strict orders to hang on to you."

"Is that a fact?" Craig said, and swung the SS tunic over Edge's hand, smothering the Walther and smashing his arm against the wall, so that he dropped the weapon. Craig punched him very hard on the side of the jaw.

The pilot doubled over. Craig handcuffed his arms around one of the legs of a big work table and said, "Leave him until Munro and Jack Carter get here."

Julie leant up and kissed him. "Take care, Craig."

"Don't I always?" He went out then, the door slammed, and a moment later she heard the jeep start up.

Half an hour later Julie went out to the end of the garden from where she could see all the way down to the village. Fog rolled in from the sea. It was going to be a dirty crossing. As she watched, the *Lili Marlene* left harbour, the scarlet-and-black Kriegsmarine ensign on her jack staff vivid as she was swallowed by the mist like a ghost.

CHAPTER 14

As THE *Lili Marlene* left Cold Harbour, Field Marshal Erwin Rommel was arriving at Château de Voincourt, and Genevieve waited at the front door to welcome him with her aunt, Max Priem, and Ziemke and his staff.

The convoy was surprisingly small—three cars and four military policemen on motorbikes. Rommel was in an open Mercedes, a short, stocky man in a leather greatcoat, the famous desert goggles he affected pushed up above the peak of his cap. Genevieve watched him salute and shake hands with General Ziemke, and then Ziemke introduced her aunt. A moment later it was Genevieve's turn.

His French was excellent. "An honour, mademoiselle." He looked straight into her eyes, as if sizing her up, and she was conscious of the power, the enormous drive. He raised her hand to his lips.

They moved into the hall. Hortense said to Ziemke, "We'll leave you now, General. You have important matters to discuss. Field Marshal, we meet again this evening, I believe?"

"I look forward to it, Countess." Rommel saluted courteously.

As they went up the stairs Hortense said to Genevieve, "I want to talk to you. The old summerhouse in fifteen minutes."

IT WAS PLEASANT in the garden, with a hint of spring in the air. Genevieve went through an archway in the grey stone wall and found Hortense sitting on the edge of the fountain, the white summerhouse behind her. One of the guards passed a few yards away, a machine pistol slung from his shoulder, an Alsatian straining on a steel chain.

Hortense shivered in distaste. "Life becomes daily more unpleasant. I wish to God the Allies would hurry up and make this landing we've all been promised for so long. Still, what about tonight? You know exactly what you are about?"

"I think so."

"Not 'think', child. You must know."

Hortense shaded her eyes and looked up to the Rose Room. "From your balcony to the terrace is what? Twenty feet? You are certain you can manage it?"

"Since I was ten years of age," Genevieve assured her, "and in the dark. The brickwork stands out like the steps in a ladder."

"Very well. The ball is supposed to commence at seven. I shall come down just before eight. I suggest you slip away to your room as soon after that as you can."

"Maresa has arranged to meet her guard, Erich, here at eight."

"Well, whatever her charms, I wouldn't count on her holding him for more than twenty minutes," Hortense said. "Chantal will be waiting in your room to give you any assistance you need."

"If everything works, I should be in the library, take my pictures and be out again inside ten minutes," Genevieve said. "Back at the ball by eight twenty, the safe locked behind me and nothing missing, and no one will know a thing about it."

"Except us," Hortense said with a cold smile. "And that, my love, I find eminently satisfying."

IT WAS JUST before six, the light fading, as the *Lili Marlene* sailed boldly in towards the deserted pier at Grosnez. Langsdorff was at the wheel, and Hare checked the shore with glasses.

"Yes, there they are." He laughed softly. "Now, there's cheek for you. He's brought two vehicles. Looks like a Kübelwagen and a black sedan, and three men in uniform."

He passed the glasses to Craig. The men were in German army uniforms standing by the Kübelwagen. Grand Pierre leant against it, smoking a cigarette.

"He's got style, this one—you have to admit that," Craig said, buttoning the tunic of the Waffen SS uniform.

Hare lit a cigarette. "You feel okay about this?"

Craig said, "In all those books I read in my teens, the hero always went back for the girl. It kind of programmed my thinking." He put on his cap. "Will I do?"

"Who is going to query you in uniform like that?" Hare said, and led the way out of the wheelhouse.

As they coasted in to the lower jetty Grand Pierre came down the steps to meet them, looking as disreputable as usual. He smiled. "Good heavens, takes me back to costume parties when I was at Oxford. You do look dashing, Osbourne."

"I want to make one thing clear," Craig said. "We've come for the girl on our own initiative."

"Save it, old son. Julie Legrande managed to put me in the picture. I've got you a rather elegant Mercedes and a Kübelwagen with three of my lads in uniform to escort you. They'll peel off when you get to the château."

Craig said, "You're going to hang around?"

"Why, yes. Up there in the woods. Does the boat stay?"

"We'll be here." Hare smiled.

Craig gave the crew a punctilious salute. "Men," he said in English, "it's been an honour to serve with you."

Those on deck sprang to attention. Only Schmidt replied. "Good luck, guv'nor. Walk all over the bastards."

Craig and Grand Pierre went up to the cars. Grand Pierre said in French to the three in German army uniform, "Right, you rogues, look after him. If you mess up, don't come back."

They grinned and got into the Kübelwagen. Craig slid behind the wheel of the Mercedes.

Grand Pierre said, "It's a ball they're having tonight, by the way. Sounds fun. Wish I could join you, but I don't have my dinner jacket with me."

The Kübelwagen moved away.

Craig switched on the ignition of the Mercedes and followed, the figure of Grand Pierre growing smaller in the driving mirror, disappearing altogether as Craig started up the hill.

THE DRESS was really beautiful, a white silk-jersey material that was more than flattering. Maresa helped Genevieve into it.

"Have you seen René today?" Genevieve asked casually.

"I don't think so, mam'selle. He wasn't in the servants' hall for his evening meal. Shall I send someone to look for him?"

"No. It's not important. You've got enough to think about. You know what you have to do?"

"Meet Erich in the summerhouse at eight and keep him there as long as I can."

"Which means at least twenty minutes," Genevieve said. She patted the girl's cheek. "Don't look so worried, Maresa. A joke we're playing on the general, that's all."

Genevieve smiled reassuringly and went out.

The ball was being held in the long gallery, and when Genevieve went in, everyone seemed to be there already. The chandeliers gleamed, there were flowers, and a small orchestra played a Strauss waltz.

There was no sign of Rommel, but General Ziemke was there.

When he saw Genevieve, he excused himself and crossed the dance floor.

"Your aunt," he said anxiously. "She is coming down?"

"As far as I know. What about the field marshal?"

"He was here a moment ago but was called away for a phone call from Berlin. The Führer himself, apparently." Ziemke wiped sweat from his forehead with a handkerchief. "We have many people here that you know. The Comboults, for instance."

There they were, on the opposite side of the room. Maurice Comboult with his wife and daughter. The richest man in the district, growing even richer out of collaborating with the Germans. Genevieve swallowed her anger, just barely.

Field Marshal Rommel appeared in the doorway, Priem beside him, and Ziemke said, "Excuse me for a moment."

She stood by a pillar, waiting for Hortense to appear, and Priem said from behind, "I would not have thought any improvement possible, but you look especially beautiful tonight."

The orchestra began to play another waltz. He took her in his arms without a word, and they started to dance. The music seemed to go on for ever, and there was an air of total unreality to everything. There were just the two of them, the rest clockwork figures only. The waltz came to an end, and there was no sign of Rommel now, but Ziemke beckoned to Priem, who excused himself and left.

It was at that moment that Hortense chose to make her entrance in a gown of midnight-blue velvet, her beautiful red-gold hair piled high on her head. Conversation died as people turned to look, and Ziemke hurried along the length of the gallery to meet her, bowing over her hand.

Genevieve glanced at her watch. It was five minutes to eight, and as the orchestra struck up again, she backed through the crowd, opened the door to the music room and slipped inside.

She had intended it as a short cut to the hall and instead received the shock of her life, for Field Marshal Rommel was seated in a chair by the piano, smoking a cigar.

"Ah, it is you, mademoiselle." He stood up. "Had enough?"

"A headache only," she said, her heart pounding, and unthinkingly ran a hand across the piano keys.

"Ah, you play. How charming," Rommel said.

"Only a little."

She sat down, because it seemed the natural thing to do, and started to play "Clair de Lune". It made her think of Craig, of that evening at Cold Harbour. Rommel leant back in the chair, a look of pleasure on his face.

It was fate that saved her, for suddenly the door opened and Max Priem appeared. "Oh, there you are, sir. The telephone again, I'm afraid. Paris, this time."

"You see, mam'selle? They will not leave me in peace." Rommel smiled charmingly and went out. Priem went after him. Genevieve hurried across to the other door, let herself out into the hall and went up the great stairway quickly.

CHANTAL WAS waiting when she entered the bedroom. "You're late," she scolded. "It's ten past eight."

"Never mind that now. Just get me out of this dress."

The magnificent white creation slipped to the floor, and Genevieve stepped into a pair of dark slacks and pulled a black sweater over her head. She slipped the cigarette case into one pocket with the key to the safe, put a torch in the other, and turned.

"Into battle, then."

Chantal kissed her roughly on the cheek. "Go on. Be off with you and get it done, Genevieve Trevaunce."

Genevieve stared at her. "How long have you known?"

"I was changing your nappies before you were a year old, my girl. You think I can't tell the difference by now?"

Genevieve smiled, slipped out through the curtains to the darkness of the balcony. It seemed very quiet, standing there, the sound of music far away. She was twelve years old again and sneaking out by night with Anne-Marie to go riding in the dark. She climbed over the balcony, got a firm hold on the brickwork and descended quickly.

When she peered around the corner, the terrace lay quiet and deserted. It was exactly eight fifteen. She moved along to the third french window, placed a hand on the centre where the doors met, and pushed. There was resistance, but it gave in the end.

The library was quite dark, the sound of music a little louder here. She switched on her torch and found the portrait of Elizabeth, the eleventh Countess de Voincourt. Genevieve swung the portrait back on its hinges, revealing the safe behind. The key turned smoothly in the lock; the door swung open.

The safe was stuffed with papers. Her heart sank as she gave way to genuine panic, and then she saw the leather briefcase with the inscription ROMMEL stamped on the flap in gold leaf.

She opened it quickly. It contained only a single folder, and when she opened that, the photos of beach defences told her that she had found what she had come for.

She put the briefcase back in the safe for the moment, laid the folder on Priem's desk and switched on the desk lamp. Then she took out her cigarette case. In the same moment she heard Priem's voice quite distinctly outside the door.

She had never moved faster in her life. She got the safe door closed, although there was no time to lock it, pushing the painting back into position. Then she switched off the desk lamp and picked up her torch and the folder.

As the key started to turn in the lock, she slipped through the curtains and pulled the french window together. The door opened, and the light was switched on. She peered in and saw Priem enter the room.

She stood there thinking in the darkness of the terrace, but she simply didn't have any other choice. She slipped around the corner and climbed back up to her balcony.

CHANTAL DREW the curtains together behind her. "What's happened?" she demanded. "Did something go wrong?"

"Priem turned up. I didn't get a chance to take my pictures. I'll see to that now." She laid the file down on her dressing table.

"Then what will you do?"

"Go down again. Hope that he's gone back to the ball so I can return this before it's missed."

"And Erich?"

"We'll just have to put all our faith in Maresa."

Genevieve picked up the silver case, opened the flap and started to take pictures, exactly as Craig Osbourne had shown her. Twenty exposures—there were more pages than that. Still, it would have to do.

As she finished, there was a knock at the door. They froze. Chantal whispered, "I locked it."

The knock came again; the doorknob rattled. Genevieve pushed Chantal towards the bathroom. "Stay in there."

Genevieve slipped the Rommel file into the nearest drawer and turned to reach for her dressing gown. A key rattled in the lock. The door opened, and Max Priem walked in.

HE SAT ON the edge of the table, swinging one leg, regarding her gravely, then held out his hand. "Give it to me."

"What on earth are you talking about?"

"The file you have just taken from Field Marshal Rommel's briefcase. I can have the room searched, but it has to be you. Why else your interesting change in dress—"

"All right!" she cut in on him sharply, opened the drawer and took out the file.

He placed it beside him. "I'm sorry it worked out this way."

"Then you are in the wrong business." She picked up her cigarette case and selected a Gitane.

"I didn't choose it, but one thing we'd better get straight from now on, Miss Trevaunce. I know who you are."

She inhaled deeply to steady herself. "I don't follow you."

"It's in the eyes, Genevieve," he said softly. "They're exactly the same colour as hers, and yet, the light inside . . . totally different. Like everything else about you two—the same and yet not the same at all."

She stood there waiting for the axe to fall.

"They taught you everything about her," he said. "Provided our friend Dissard as a guide but, in the end, left out one essential fact—the most important of all. The one that told me from the first that you could not be Anne-Marie Trevaunce."

"And what would that be?"

"Why, that she was working for me," he said simply.

SHE SAT DOWN, curiously calm, perfectly in control, or so she told herself. Priem parted the curtains and rain tapped against the window with ghostly fingers, as if Anne-Marie were out there trying to get in. He continued to speak without turning to face her.

"I was tipped off about your true identity, even before you got here, by one of our agents in London, a mole in the SOE."

She was truly shocked. "I don't believe you."

"True, I assure you, but let's talk about your sister. When we first set up house here, I decided to provide London with an agent, and who more suitable than Anne-Marie?"

"Who in exchange could continue to live in the manner to which she was accustomed. Is that what you're trying to say?"

"Not quite. She was never cheap, whatever else she was. She gave the SOE enough information to keep everyone happy; most of it relatively unimportant, of course. I even allowed her to draw in Dissard to complete the picture. Then London found out about a rather important conference and took an unprecedented step. They sent for her, and I said she must go."

"And she always did what you told her?"

"But of course. We had Hortense, you see. Anne-Marie's one weakness is this love for her aunt." Genevieve stared at him blankly. "Her only reason from the beginning—don't you see that?" He sighed. "I don't think you ever knew her at all, this sister of yours."

The rain tapped more insistently than ever. Genevieve sat there unable to speak, so great was her emotion.

"Knowing you were playing games with me, it seemed prudent to have words with Dissard."

"René?" she whispered.

"Yes. The message that took him away so urgently—I arranged that. When he reached his destination, Reichslinger and his men were waiting."

"Where is he now? What have you done with him?"

"He shot himself," Priem said, "before they could disarm him. To protect you, I should imagine. Not that it mattered. Our mole at SOE—a certain Dr Baum—had provided all the necessary information. Of course, I've known for some time he was working for the other side. I have a more reliable source in London, you see."

"You're lying," Genevieve said.

"Your sister is at this very moment in the cellar of a house at one hundred and one Raglan Lane, in Hampstead. She is, I understand, quite mad."

Her reply came boiling out of her, instinctive, hot with rage. "And you swine made her like that. It was an SS patrol that ruined her, those animals. Did you know that?"

"Not true," he said. "It was your own people—no one else."

The room was very quiet, and she was horribly frightened. "What do you mean?" she whispered. "What are you saying?"

"My poor Genevieve," he said. "I think you'd better listen."

WHAT HE TOLD her, although she did not know it, was substantially what Baum had told Craig Osbourne. The truth, the real truth about her sister, the good doctor, Rosedene Nursing Home and Munro.

When he was finished, she sat there gripping the arms of her chair for a while; then she reached for the cigarette case and got a Gitane. She turned to face him. "Why should I believe you? How could you know all this?"

"Through Baum's contact—a Mrs Fitzgerald. After Baum told the British about her, she was given a choice to work as a double agent or face execution. Naturally she chose the sensible course, or appeared to. In fact, she warned us of Baum's defection. We know he tells us only what they want us to know. In this case they wanted us to know about you."

"What nonsense," Genevieve said, and yet, with some horror, she saw the terrible truth.

"What was the purpose of your mission? Rommel's conference? Plans for the Atlantic Wall?" He shook his head. "It couldn't have been. They sent you here to be betrayed by Baum."

"But why would they do that?"

"They expected you to break. They've told you something, something you can't even remember yourself for the moment. Something that would apparently be of supreme importance."

She remembered Munro in his study at Cold Harbour, the map on the desk that he had so quickly put away after allowing her to glimpse the D-day landing areas.

Priem had been watching her intently. Now he smiled. "You've got it, I see."

She nodded, suddenly very tired. "Yes."

"Would you tell me?"

"I'd try not to, just in case I'm wrong. You've proved very effectively that there are people on my side as rotten and unscrupulous as you are, but I'd still rather see my side win." She took a deep breath. "What happens now?"

"You will change into your gown and return to the ball."

She was beginning to feel light-headed. "You can't be serious?"

"Oh, but I am. Field Marshal Rommel will leave for Paris in one hour. You will be among those who will smile and wish him well. You will exchange a few words. He will drive safely away into the night, and you, my dear, will continue dancing. You might seize some chance, however slight, to slip away, but that would mean leaving the countess in our hands, which would be unfortunate. You follow my thinking?"

"Completely."

"Perfect trust between us, then." He kissed her hand. "I've fallen in love with you a little, I think. Just a little. You were never her, Genevieve. Always yourself alone."

He started to open the door. Genevieve said, "You really thought you knew her, didn't you?"

He turned, slightly surprised. "Anne-Marie? As well as anyone, I think."

Her anger was so great now that she could not contain herself. "Does the name Grand Pierre mean anything to you?"

He went very still. "Why do you ask?"

"A very important Resistance leader, am I right? I'm sure you'd give a great deal to get your hands on him. Would it surprise you to know that my sister had dealings with him?"

His face was quite pale now. "Yes, to be perfectly frank."

"You failed to catch General Dietrich's assassin. You know why? Anne-Marie spirited him away from under the noses of your precious SS, hidden under the rear seat of her Rolls-Royce." She smiled fiercely. "So, you see, Colonel Priem, she was never completely what you thought she was at all."

He looked at her for a long moment, turned and went out, closing the door softly.

She hurried across to the bathroom door and said, "Stay in there until I've gone."

"All right," Chantal whispered.

The rain drifted against the window, and Genevieve stood there listening. So, this was how it ended. Out of her hands now, all of it, and no way out.

She took a deep breath and started to dress.

CHAPTER 15

SHE DRIFTED down the stairs on Priem's arm as if in a dream. "Prepare to make your entrance," he said. "And smile."

An orderly opened the door, and they passed inside. For the moment the orchestra had stopped playing, but there were raised voices and laughter, a general air of well-being.

Hortense was sitting in one of the gold chairs on the opposite side of the room, an infantry colonel leaning attentively over her.

She was laughing at something he'd just said, and then her eyes briefly met Genevieve's. There was a pause, and then she smiled brightly again and looked up at her colonel.

"May I speak to my aunt?" Genevieve asked Priem.

"Certainly. After all, she should know the state of the game."

Genevieve walked unhurriedly through the crowd. As she arrived, Hortense smiled. "Having a nice time, *chérie?*"

"But of course." Genevieve perched on the arm of her chair.

Hortense handed her empty glass to the colonel. "Would you mind?"

He clicked his heels obediently and moved away. She said casually, "Something's wrong. I can see it in your eyes."

"Priem arrived at the wrong moment. He knows everything."

Hortense smiled gaily, waving to someone on the other side of the room. "That you are not Anne-Marie?"

Genevieve nodded and said softly, "I was sent here by Munro to be betrayed. I've just learnt that from Priem. René is dead, by the way."

That got through to Hortense as nothing else had, wiping the smile away instantly.

Genevieve gripped her hand. "Hang on, my love, very tightly. It's going to be a long, long night."

The colonel was now back beside them, gallantly offering Hortense her drink. Genevieve patted her aunt's cheek. "Behave yourself," she told her, laughing, and turned away.

The music started again at that moment, a waltz. Priem appeared and inclined his head, bowing slightly. "A turn around the floor, perhaps?"

"Why not?"

He held her lightly as they circled. She remembered to smile at the general as they passed, noticed Field Marshal Rommel talking politely with her aunt.

"At the end of the evening," Priem said gravely, "when the field marshal has departed, you and your aunt will be escorted to your rooms. I will post a guard outside your doors."

"Naturally."

Out of the corner of her eye she seemed to catch sight of a shadowy figure on the fringe of things, like an elusive memory that wouldn't go away. The familiar tilt of a head as someone lit a cigarette. But that was impossible — totally impossible.

She saw him clearly now, leaning against the wall, a haze of smoke around his head. He smiled delightedly, as if seeing her for the first time, then started across the dance floor.

Craig Osbourne, immaculate in the black dress uniform of a colonel in the SS Charlemagne Brigade.

Which didn't make any sense, for if what Max Priem had told her was true, there was no reason on this earth why Craig Osbourne should be here like this. They stopped dancing as he arrived, Priem frowning slightly.

"Anne-Marie, how marvellous. I hoped you might be here." His French was perfect. He turned to Priem. "You will excuse me if I cut in? Mademoiselle Trevaunce and I are old friends." He took her hand and kissed it lightly. "July of '39. The long, hot summer a thousand years ago."

Priem's expression had changed to one of sardonic amusement, and she realised he must imagine her truly caught now, playing Anne-Marie with an old friend whose name she couldn't possibly know.

"Henri Legrande," Craig said smoothly. "Colonel . . .?"

Priem clicked his heels. "Priem. At your service, Standarten-führer." He withdrew.

Craig took her firmly in his arms, and they commenced to dance. "Do you come here often?" he asked.

Strange, considering what she knew about the whole thing now, and yet her immediate concern was only for him. "You must be mad."

"I know. My mother used to say that all the time. Don't look so worried. Keep that dazzling smile of yours firmly in place." His arm tightened across her back. "It was a set-up, angel. Munro put your head in the noose. Try anything, and they'll be waiting for you."

"Old news," she said. "I tried this evening, and I was caught. Priem knows, Craig. Told me everything. Baum, Anne-Marie, the whole rotten affair. I'm only out now on a leash, don't you realise? He's watching every move I make."

Craig stopped dancing and slipped her arm through his. "Let's give him something to think about, then."

He guided her firmly through the crowd and out through a french window. There was a slight chill to the air, and they stayed under the colonnade because of the rain.

"The occasional laugh would be a good idea," he said. "And a cigarette would help."

She glanced up as the match flared in his cupped hands, illuminating his strong face.

"Why, Craig? Why?"

"What did Priem tell you?"

"That Anne-Marie worked for him."

He whistled softly. "That means you didn't stand a chance, not from the start."

"Are you trying to tell me that you didn't know? I can't believe that. You used me, Craig, just like you used Anne-Marie. I know the truth about that now."

"I see. And René?"

"Dead. Shot himself to protect me. They were on to him."

There was silence. Craig said, "Now, you believe me or you don't, but this is how it was. The business with the drug and your sister was an accident, a new gimmick they were going to try on every agent fresh in from the field, only it went wrong. I only found that out from Baum last night. The story they sold you—the SS-atrocity thing—was Munro's idea to give you the urge to do your bit. I was told the same yarn."

"And Baum?"

"I didn't know the first thing about his connection with German intelligence until last night. What you were told, I was told. That you were coming here to fill your sister's place and get any information you could on Rommel's Atlantic Wall conference."

"Then why has Munro allowed you to come here like this?"

"He hasn't. I'm here strictly on my own."

And suddenly, with a tremendous feeling of relief, she believed him. Believed him completely.

"Martin Hare and his boys brought me over on the E-boat. The boat's waiting at Grosnez. Now, tell me exactly what the situation is here."

She covered that side of things in a few brief sentences and then said, "They're watching me every second. Just go, Craig, while you can."

"Not on your life. Do you think I could leave you to that lot in there? We go together or not at all."

"Not possible. I wouldn't leave Hortense even if I could."

He said urgently, "What do you think I'm doing here? Were you really so blind back there at Cold Harbour? Did you think it was Anne-Marie I saw every time I looked at you?"

Which left Genevieve only one way out, for his sake now, not her own. She took it, turning swiftly and going back through the french window before he realised what was happening.

Priem was by the fire, smoking a cigar. He tossed it into the flames and came forward. "Abandoned the poor colonel already?"

"You might say that. An old lover of my sister's who still has the urge. The memory of me was all that got him through Russia."

"These French," he said, "are so romantic. The field marshal, by the way, is leaving soon. You are all right now?"

"Of course. I think I'll have some champagne now."

FIELD MARSHAL Rommel left Château de Voincourt, and Genevieve stood with Hortense and smiled and wished him well, as Priem had told her she would. No sign of Craig Osbourne.

The crowd started to fade, and Priem turned to her and Hortense. "Time to retire, ladies. A long night."

"So thoughtful, isn't he?" Hortense said.

Genevieve gave her an arm. They started up the stairs, followed by Priem and a lieutenant who carried a Schmeisser machine pistol.

"At the first opportunity, you will get out of here. Do you understand me?" Hortense murmured.

"And leave you?" Genevieve said. "Do you imagine for one moment that I can do that?"

They reached the top corridor, Priem nodded, and the young lieutenant brought a chair forward, which he positioned where he could watch the doors of both bedroom suites.

"You really are concerned about our welfare tonight, Colonel," Hortense observed.

"Lieutenant Vogel is merely on call should you need him, as is the man stationed under your balcony. I wish you a peaceful night." Hortense hesitated, glanced at her niece and went in.

Priem turned to face Genevieve. "The field marshal enjoyed himself, I think," he said. "Of course, if he had been aware that a certain file had temporarily disappeared from his briefcase, he would not have been so pleased. But that we can keep to ourselves." He opened her door. "Good night, Miss Trevaunce."

She could have told him to go to hell, but there would have been little point. So, she simply went in, closed the door and leant against it. The bolt had been removed. And, of course, the gun, with which she'd so carefully practised, was gone.

She changed into slacks and sweater again, then stepped out onto the balcony. She listened for sounds of the guard down below, and after a few moments heard a cough. So, that was that.

She returned to the bedroom and picked up the silver case. Not a single cigarette left, only the spool of film in its secret compartment and useless now. She felt tired and cold, and put on Anne-Marie's hunting jacket and slipped the cigarette case into the pocket. She settled into the chair by the window, leaving the light on, like a little girl afraid of the dark.

SHE DOZED off for a while, came to, stiff and miserable, and saw the curtains stir. Craig Osbourne moved into the room, a Walther in his right hand. He was still in SS uniform.

"We'll take your aunt as well. Satisfied?"

Genevieve was filled with sudden cold excitement. "How did you get up here?"

"Climbed up to your balcony."

"I thought they had a man down there?"

"Not any more." He padded across to the door and listened. "What have they got outside?"

"A young lieutenant with a machine pistol."

"Get him in here. Tell him you've heard something suspicious on the balcony. Anything."

He holstered the Walther and took something from his pocket. There was a sharp click; a blade gleamed dully in the light. She stared, fascinated, and he gave her a little push. She moved to the door, knocked lightly, then opened it.

Vogel was across the corridor in an instant.

Her throat was so dry that she could hardly speak, and yet she forced herself, turning and pointing towards the curtains that lifted in the slight breeze. "Out there, on the balcony. I think I heard something."

Vogel hesitated, then came forward. Craig Osbourne moved too, an arm around the throat, knee up into the spine, arching Vogel backwards like a bow. Genevieve never saw the knife slide home, heard only the faintest of groans as she turned away, sick to her stomach. Craig dragged the body to the bathroom. When he returned, he was holding the Schmeisser.

"Let's go, then," he said.

HORTENSE WAS sitting up in bed, a shawl about her shoulders, reading a book. She showed no surprise at all.

"So, you would appear to have made a friend, Genevieve."

"Major Osbourne, ma'am."

"You've come for my niece, I presume?"

"You, too, ma'am. She won't leave without you."

Hortense got a Gitane from the box on the bedside cabinet and lit it. Genevieve took out her empty cigarette case and filled it from the box quickly. Hortense blew out smoke in a long plume.

"We're rather short on time, ma'am," Craig said patiently.

"Then I suggest you go, Major, while you still can."

Genevieve, filled with panic, reached forward to pull the bed-clothes back. Hortense grasped her wrist with surprising strength. "Listen to me." There was iron in her voice. "You once told me you knew I had a bad heart."

"But that wasn't true. Just another lie they fed me."

"Anne-Marie believed it. An invention of my own to explain certain dizzy spells. I kept the truth to myself. One has one's pride. Dr Marais didn't pretend. He's too old a friend for that. I have only a month now, perhaps two, and it will be painful."

"Not true." Genevieve was angry now. "Not any of it."

"Did you ever wonder where your eyes come from, *chérie*?" She had both of Genevieve's hands now. "Look at me."

Green and amber, flecked with golden light and filled with love, more love than Genevieve could ever have believed existed. Hortense was telling the truth; she knew that.

"For me, Genevieve." She kissed her on both cheeks gently. "Do this for me. Always you have given me your love—total, unselfish. The most precious thing in my life. Would you deny me the right to give less?"

Genevieve backed away, hands shaking, unable to reply.

Hortense said, "You'll leave me one of your guns, Major." Craig took out his Walther and placed it beside her on the bed.

"Go now," she said. "Very quickly, please."

Craig got the door open, started to pull Genevieve through. The last view she had of her aunt was of her sitting up in bed, one hand on the Walther, and she was smiling.

THEY MOVED silently down the great staircase. The hall was a place of shadows. Nothing stirred.

"Where would Priem be?" Craig whispered.

"In his office in the library. He sleeps there too."

A light showed under the door. Craig paused, the Schmeisser ready, turned the handle very gently, and they went in.

Priem was still in uniform, working on some papers in the light of a desk lamp. He glanced up but showed no surprise.

"Ah, the lover. Not quite what he seemed."

"Get his pistol," Craig told Genevieve in English.

Priem stood up, hands on the desk. Genevieve moved behind him and took the Walther from its holster. Priem sighed. "So, what happens now?"

"We leave by the side door," Craig told him. "Then we take a walk down to the back courtyard. I noticed a Mercedes there earlier. That should do very nicely."

Priem addressed Genevieve. "You'll never get away with it. Reichslinger himself is on duty at the gate."

"You'll tell him the field marshal left important papers," Craig said. "If anything goes wrong, I'll kill you, and if I don't, she will. She'll be behind us."

Priem looked faintly amused. "You think you could, Genevieve? Now, that I doubt."

No more than she did. Her fingers, wrapped around the butt of the Walther in the right-hand pocket of her hunting jacket, trembled, her palm already damp with sweat.

"No more talk," Craig said. "Now, put on your cap, nice and regimental, and let's get out of here."

It was amazingly still outside, walking through the rain across the cobbles of the courtyard. When they reached the Mercedes, Genevieve opened the rear door and crouched down in the darkness, between the seats, holding the Walther ready. Priem got behind the wheel, Craig beside him. There was not a word spoken. The engine roared into life; they moved away. It wasn't long, of course, before they rolled to a halt. She heard the sentry's challenge, the click of his heels as he sprang to attention.

"Your pardon, Standartenführer."

Priem hadn't needed to say a word. There was a slight creaking as the barrier was raised, and then, quite suddenly, another voice, calling sharply from the guardhouse. Reichslinger.

Genevieve held her breath as his feet crunched across the

gravel. He leant down, saying something to Priem in German.

Priem spoke to him. The only word she recognised was Rommel. Reichslinger replied; his boots crunched in the gravel again. She glanced up cautiously. To her horror she saw his face above, peering in at her through the side window.

As he jumped back, tugging at his pistol, Craig raised the Schmeisser and fired straight through the window, showering her with glass, driving Reichslinger back in a mad dance. Then he had the barrel hard against Priem's neck.

They surged forward into the night, Priem working the wheel, swerving furiously as the sentry behind started to fire. And then the darkness swallowed them up, and they were away.

"You okay back there?" Craig asked.

There was blood on her right cheek, which had been sliced by a sliver of flying glass. She wiped it away casually.

"Yes, I'm fine."

They took the mountain road. "A pointless exercise," Priem said. "Within an hour there will be a roadblock at every point."

"Long enough for our purposes," Craig told him. "Just keep driving and do as you're told."

HORTENSE DE VOINCOURT lay propped against the pillows, aware of the pandemonium on the grounds outside that had followed the sounds of firing down at the main gate. There was shouting in the hall below, footsteps a moment later pounding along the corridor and then a thunderous knocking. Her door was flung open, and Ziemke appeared, a pistol in his hand, an SS corporal behind him holding a Schmeisser.

"Why, Carl," she said, "you do look agitated."

"What's going on?" he demanded. "I've been informed that Anne-Marie, Priem and that French Standartenführer just drove out of the main gate. Reichslinger's dead. That damned Frenchman shot him."

"The best news I've heard in ages," she informed him. "I never did like Reichslinger."

He went very still, a slight frown on his face. "Hortense? What are you saying?"

"That the party's over, Carl. That it's high time I acted like a de Voincourt and remembered that you and your kind are occupying my country. You're a nice man, but you're also the enemy." Her hand came out from under the bedclothes. "Goodbye, my dear."

She fired the Walther twice, catching him in the heart, driving him out into the anteroom. The SS corporal ducked out of sight, poked the barrel of the Schmeisser around the door and fired in return on full automatic, emptying the magazine. For Hortense de Voincourt the darkness was instant and merciful.

St Maurice was quiet as the grave as they drove through. Twenty minutes later they reached the coast road and Léon.

The moon came out from behind a cloud at the moment they reached the woods on the cliffs above Grosnez.

Craig tapped Priem on the shoulder. "Stop here."

The German braked to a halt, switched off the engine. "What now? A bullet in the head?"

"Nothing so easy." Craig smiled. "You're coming to England with us. There's someone I'd like you to meet. I'm sure he'll find you a mine of information."

He got out of the car. There were men carrying guns moving down out of the woods. Grand Pierre came forward.

Priem had a fixed smile on his face as he looked at Genevieve in the rear-vision mirror. "There's blood on your cheek."

"It's nothing. Just a cut."

"I'm glad."

Craig opened the driver's door, and Priem reached under the dashboard of the car. His hand came out clutching a Luger, and she reacted instinctively, in blind panic, ramming the Walther against his spine, pulling the trigger twice.

His body jerked; there was the stench of cordite in her nostrils. Very slowly he half turned, surprise in his eyes, then slumped across the wheel.

Craig reached for her as she scrambled out, but she pushed him away. "No. Leave me alone!"

He stood there staring at her, his face dark, then turned and nodded to one of Grand Pierre's men, who leant across Priem's body and released the hand brake. The Mercedes rolled over the edge of the cliff, crashing down into the sea below.

"He never thought I could do it," she whispered. "And when it comes right down to it, neither did I."

"So, now you know what it feels like," Craig said. "Welcome to the club."

Grand Pierre went with them down the steps to the lower jetty, where the *Lili Marlene* waited.

Schmidt called, "Bleeding hell, he's done it. He's got her."

There was an excited murmur from the crew, and Hare called down from the bridge, "Congratulations. Now, let's move it."

The engines rumbled into life. Craig stepped over the rail, turned to give Genevieve a hand.

She said to Grand Pierre, "Thank you for everything."

"Crumpled rose leaves, Miss Trevaunce. I warned you."

"Will I ever get over what I just did?"

"Everything passes. Now, off you go."

She reached for Craig's hand. As she touched the deck the lines were cast off, and the *Lili Marlene* slipped out to sea through the darkness.

CHAPTER 16

IT WAS STILL dark as Dougal Munro walked down in the rain from Grancester Abbey to the village. Light showed through the drawn curtains of The Hanged Man, the sign swinging to and fro in the wind, creaking eerily.

When he opened the door and went in, he found Julie Legrande sitting by the fire, a glass in her hand.

"Ah, there you are," he said. "Can't sleep, eh, just like me?"

"Any news?" she asked.

"Not so far. Jack's standing by in the radio room." He took off his overcoat and hat. "What are you drinking?"

"Whisky, a little lemon, some sugar and boiling water," she said. "When I was a child, it was a remedy my grandmother employed against the flu. Now it's just a remedy."

"Little early in the day."

"For a lot of things, Brigadier."

"Now, don't let's start all that again. I've already forgiven your part in this wretched affair. No recriminations, please."

There was the sound of a vehicle drawing up outside. The door opened; a gust of wind blew in, followed by Jack Carter and Edge.

"Well?" Munro said.

Carter was smiling, a kind of awe on his face. "He did it, sir. Craig actually pulled it off. Got her out of there."

Julie leapt to her feet. "You're certain?"

"Absolutely." Carter unbuttoned his wet trench coat. "We had a message from Grand Pierre fifteen minutes ago. The *Lili Marlene* left Grosnez just after midnight. With any luck they could be here in an hour and a half."

Edge went behind the bar and poured himself a large gin. His face was quite composed, but anger showed in the eyes, touched by more than a bit of madness.

Julie laughed harshly. "Craig spoilt your rotten little scheme, didn't he, Brigadier? It would have suited you far more if he hadn't managed to get back at all. If none of them had."

"It's a thought, I suppose, but a slightly hysterical one." Munro picked up his overcoat and put it on. "I've things to do at the house." He turned to Edge. "You want a lift?"

"No, thanks, sir. I'll walk back. I need the air."

Carter and Munro went out and drove away. Edge took a bottle of gin from behind the bar and put it into his pocket. "I'm for a little shut-eye," he said. "It's been a long night."

When he let himself out, the wind was freshening. He went to the edge of the quay and looked out to sea. He uncorked the bottle of gin and drank deeply.

"Damn you, Osbourne," he said softly. "Damn the lot of you!"

He put the bottle back into his pocket, turned and started up the cobbled street through the village.

At Grancester Abbey, he sat drinking gin from a tin mug until more than half the bottle was gone, and he was drunk in an angry, excited way. Not long now and the *Lili Marlene* would be entering the harbour. He thought of Craig and the way the American had humiliated him, and his rage boiled over. He poured another shot of gin, and as he raised it to his lips he paused, because suddenly he saw the perfect way to pay them back. All of them.

"It's beautiful." He laughed drunkenly. "I'll put the fear of God into the bastards."

He picked up the phone, called his chief mechanic, Sergeant Henderson, and told him to get the Junkers ready.

THE SEA was lifting into whitecaps, rain driving in as the *Lili Marlene* raced onwards to the Cornish coast, like some greyhound unleashed. Dawn was staining the sky in the east when Schmidt came in from the galley with tea for Genevieve and Craig. "England, home and beauty. Not long now." He was wearing a life jacket over his yellow oilskin.

"What's all this?" Craig demanded, pointing to the life jacket.

"Skipper's orders. He thinks it's going to get a bit nasty." Schmidt put the mugs on the table. "You'll find yours in the locker under the bench."

He went out. Genevieve swung her legs out of the way, and Craig opened the locker and produced a couple of life jackets. He helped her into one, then pulled on the other himself. He sat down opposite her and drank his tea.

She offered him a Gitane. "I suppose I should take care with this." She held up the silver-and-onyx case. "It wouldn't do to get water in and ruin the film."

"No chance," he said. "Designed by a genius, that thing."

She said, "What happens now, Craig?"

"Who knows? The situation's changed. You actually filmed those Atlantic Wall plans, and what's more important, the Germans don't know. They won't change a thing. Makes you something of a heroine, doesn't it? And if Martin and I hadn't gone for you ..." He shrugged and patted her hand. "Let's go topside and get some air."

Water cascaded beneath the canvas screens of the rail as they negotiated the deck. Genevieve climbed the ladder to the bridge, Craig behind her, and went into the wheelhouse. Langsdorff was at the helm, while Hare was plotting the final approach.

"How are we doing?" Craig demanded.

"Fine. The sea's behind us." Langsdorff looked out. "Going to get worse before it gets better, but we'll get there."

Craig put an arm around her. "I've had a really great idea. Dinner at the Savoy, champagne, dancing."

Before she could reply, Martin Hare said, "I've had an even better one." He searched his pocket and found half a crown. "I'll flip you to see who gets the first dance."

SERGEANT HENDERSON had just moved the Junkers out of the hangar when Edge drove up in a jeep. Edge pulled on his flying helmet and goggles and adjusted the chin strap as he walked forward, swaying slightly.

"Everything all right, Sergeant?"

"All ready to go, sir."

Edge staggered, and Henderson reached out to steady him. "You okay, sir?" In the same moment he got a whiff of gin.

"Of course I'm okay, you idiot," Edge told him. "Going to have some fun. I'm going to teach an E-boat a lesson." He laughed. "By the time I've finished, Hare and Osbourne will know who the real hero is around here. And won't Munro just be properly grateful?"

He turned to the plane, and Henderson grabbed his arm. "Just a minute, sir. I don't really think you should be flying."

Edge pushed him away violently and drew his Walther from his service holster.

"Get away from me!"

He fired wildly into the ground at the sergeant's feet; Henderson ran, taking cover. Then he heard the door clang shut in the fuselage. A moment later the twin radial engines rumbled into life. The aircraft started to move. Henderson ran inside the hangar and made for the telephone.

AT GRANCESTER ABBEY, Munro and Jack Carter were just finishing their tea when there was a roaring overhead. The brigadier moved to the window in time to see the JU 88S sweep low over the harbour and start to climb into the grey morning.

"What's going on, Jack?" he demanded.

The library phone started to ring. Carter answered it. Munro watched the aircraft go, then turned and saw Carter replacing the phone, face troubled.

"That was Sergeant Henderson, sir. It seems Joe Edge is going to beat up an E-boat. Edge said that by the time he was finished, Hare and Osbourne would know who the real hero was and that you'd be properly grateful."

Munro was astonished. "He must be mad."

"Also drunk, sir. So drunk that he fired his pistol into the ground at Henderson's feet when he tried to restrain him."

Munro's face was white. "What are we going to do?"

"Nothing we can do, sir. The *Lili* never uses her ship-to-shore radio. That's always been a strict rule. You didn't want the Royal Navy or the coastguard listening in. Impossible to warn her. If we drive up to the headland, we can see the approach at least."

"Then let's get moving, Jack."

Munro struggled into his overcoat, and they hurried out.

AS THEY approached The Hanged Man, Julie came out. Carter slowed down, and she said, "What's going on? What's Joe up to?"

"Get in!" Munro ordered.

She scrambled into the rear, and as Carter drove away he said, "Edge appears to have blown his top."

"We don't really know that, Jack," Munro said. "He's had a few drinks, that's all. It's going to be all right."

They breasted the hill and bumped over the grass towards the edge of the cliff. Carter braked to a halt. "There's a pair of binoculars here." He fumbled under the dashboard. "Here they are."

They got out of the jeep and went forward. There was some mist at sea level, but the wind kept blowing great gaps in it. It was rough now, the waves breaking on the beach below.

Suddenly Julie pointed. "There they are."

The *Lili Marlene* came out of the grey morning about a mile away, moving towards Cold Harbour at speed, the Kriegsmarine ensign standing out vividly, and then the Junkers simply swept out of a black cloud like some bird of prey and raced towards the E-boat. A moment later there was the sound of cannon fire.

EDGE FIRED wide of the *Lili Marlene* and banked to starboard. Craig and Genevieve were still with Hare in the wheelhouse.

"It's Edge," Craig said. "What's he playing at?"

Hare turned to the radio, which was normally never used, flicked on the loudspeaker and picked up the hand mike. "Come in, Edge! Come in! What's going on?"

The Junkers had banked, was coming straight for them, and again cannon shell churned up the sea.

"Bang, you're dead!" Edge's voice was clear over the radio's loudspeaker, and he was laughing hysterically. "Can you hear me, Hare?" The plane rose overhead. "You've really given us a lot of problems. The poor old brigadier was most concerned. Far better if you hadn't come back at all."

Hare opened a locker, took out a bundled flag and pushed Langsdorff to one side.

"I think we have trouble here. Have a man haul down the ensign and put that in its place."

"Still there?" Edge's voice sounded again from the loudspeaker. "Try again, shall we? See how close I can get."

He banked again, closing on the stern no more than fifty feet above the water as the Kriegsmarine ensign on the jack staff was hauled down.

A moment later the Stars and Stripes streamed out bravely, and the sight inflamed Edge even more. "Bloody Yanks!" he screamed.

He was very close now, opened up with his machine gun this time and got it badly wrong, ripping up the afterdeck on the starboard side, killing two crewmen instantly, driving them both over the rail into the sea.

"He's gone mad!" Craig said.

Already Wagner and Bauer were working the Bofors gun on the afterdeck, and Wittig was hammering at Edge with the 20-mm ack-ack gun in the foredeck well.

The Junkers staggered as cannon shell punched holes in the starboard wing. Edge cursed and flung the aircraft to port. "All right, you bastards," he cried. "If that's the way you want it."

He went down then, dangerously low, and came in towards the stern again. Hare was giving the *Lili Marlene* everything she had, crisscrossing from one side to the other at better than forty knots. Edge closed at over four hundred miles an hour, no more than thirty feet above the waves.

Craig grabbed Genevieve by the arm. "Down!" he cried, and flung himself on top of her.

Edge used his machine gun again, ripping up the afterdeck, mowing down both Wagner and Bauer at the Bofors gun, shattering the wheelhouse windows, catching Langsdorff in the back, driving him head first through the door.

Suddenly the *Lili Marlene* was slowing in the water. Craig stood up, and as Genevieve joined him she saw Hare slumped forward, blood on his reefer jacket. Half the controls had been shot away, and down on the foredeck Wittig was hanging over the ack-ack gun, supported only by its shoulder rests.

"You're hurt, Martin." She put a hand to his shoulder.

The Junkers came in on the port side, raking the ship. The *Lili Marlene* was on fire now, and through the smoke she saw Schmidt clamber across the foredeck to pull Wittig away so that he could get at the gun.

Hare said, "We've had it. Get Genevieve off."

Craig pushed her ahead of him. There was already water slopping across the deck as Hare followed them. He and Craig uncoupled a dinghy stowed on the afterdeck and got it over the rail.

Craig held the line. "Go on, get in," he told Genevieve.

She did as she was ordered, and in the same moment Edge came in very low towards the stern.

Hare said, "I'm going to get him," and turned and plunged towards the Bofors gun.

Craig released the line to the dinghy, and before Genevieve knew it, there was ten yards between her and the E-boat. "Craig!" she screamed, but by then it was too late.

He was beside Hare at the Bofors, already knee-deep in water. "Concentrate on his belly," Craig shouted. "Remember those nitrous-oxide tanks."

The Junkers came in hard, Edge giving them everything he had. The Bofors gun hammered in reply, and Genevieve saw Martin Hare lifted up, blown back. And now Craig was at the gun, swinging to follow the Junkers as it passed overhead.

The explosion, when it came, was the most catastrophic thing she had ever seen. The Junkers simply disintegrated into an enormous ball of fire as its nitrous-oxide tanks exploded like a bomb.

A great wave pushed the dinghy up. Genevieve was already fifty yards away and moving fast when she saw the prow of the *Lili Marlene* lift high out of the water. There was no sign of Craig Osbourne or Schmidt, no one in the water that she could see. The prow lifted even higher, the Stars and Stripes flowering for a moment, and then the *Lili Marlene* went down by the stern and slid under the surface.

ON THE CLIFF top, Dougal Munro slowly lowered the binoculars, his face ashen. Julie Legrande was crying.

"What now, sir?" Carter asked. "I think I saw a dinghy."

"Inform the coastguard. It won't take the lifeboat long to get here from Falmouth. There's always a chance."

But he didn't sound as if he believed that, even to himself.

THE DINGHY was pitching violently. The sky was blacker than ever, and it was raining heavily. Not that it mattered. With a foot of water in the dinghy Genevieve was soaked to the skin anyway, and she just lay there, head pillowed on the side, as miserable as any human being could be.

It was perhaps three hours after the *Lili Marlene* had gone down that she heard the sound of an engine approaching. She pushed herself up and saw the Falmouth lifeboat bearing down on her. Five minutes later she was inside its cabin, wrapped in blankets, a crewman handing her a mug of coffee.

A man in oilskins came in, middle-aged, with a pleasant face. "I'm the coxswain, miss. We haven't found anyone else."

"I don't think you will," she said dully.

"Well, we'll look for another hour, then take you into Cold Harbour. He hesitated, then asked, "What went on out here, miss?"

"I'm not sure," she said. "I think it was a game that went wrong. A sort of ultimate stupidity, just like the war."

He frowned, not understanding, and went out. Genevieve wrapped her hands about the mug, seeking comfort from its warmth, and sat there staring into space.

GENEVIEVE LAY in the hot bath Julie had provided, until the water started to cool. She got out and dried herself carefully. There were bruises all over her body, but she felt no pain. In fact, she didn't feel anything. Julie had left underwear on the bed for her, a heavy sweater, corduroy slacks and jacket. She dressed quickly and was just finishing when Julie entered.

"How are you, *chérie*?"

"Fine." She hesitated and then said calmly, "Any news?"

"I'm afraid not. But I've just seen Carter. He said the film turned out to be perfect. He asked me to give you this."

She handed her the silver-and-onyx case. Genevieve smiled slightly and took it.

"An interesting souvenir."

"Munro would like to see you in the library."

"Good," Genevieve said. "I'd like to see him."

She started to walk to the door, stopped and picked up Anne-Marie's hunting jacket. She felt in the pocket and took out Priem's Walther.

"Another interesting souvenir," she said, slipped it into her pocket, opened the door and went out.

Julie stood there for a moment, frowning anxiously; then she went after her.

MUNRO WAS sitting by the fire sipping brandy from a crystal goblet. Carter was standing at the dresser pouring a scotch, when Genevieve entered the library.

The brigadier said, "Ah, Genevieve, come in. Let's have a look at you. You've heard the splendid news about the film. A major coup. You've shown real talent for this kind of work. I can use you at SOE, my dear, very definitely. You should do well."

"Like hell I will."

"Oh, yes, Flight Officer Trevaunce. You'll obey orders and do exactly as you are told. The Lysander will be here in a while. You'll come back to London with us."

"Just like that?"

"Naturally there will be some sort of decoration for you, and well deserved. The French will probably give you the Legion of Honour. I think we can manage a Military Cross. Unusual for a woman, but not unprecedented."

"I know about my sister," she said.

"I'm sorry," Munro said calmly. "An accident of war."

She said, "You sit there calmly swilling brandy, and yet you set me up quite cold-bloodedly from the beginning. And you know what's so funny about that, Brigadier?"

"No, but I'm sure you'll tell me."

"You didn't need to have Baum sell me out. It seems Anne-Marie was working for the other side, so I didn't stand a chance with Max Priem from the beginning. I shot him dead, by the way. With this." She took the Walther from her pocket.

Munro said, "You see? You have an aptitude for this work. You're certain about Anne-Marie?"

"Oh, yes. And this Fitzgerald woman at Romney Marsh who you've been running as a double. She's fooled you. She still works for German intelligence."

"Does she indeed?" Munro went very still for a moment, then glanced at Carter. "Get on to Special Branch at Scotland Yard." He turned back to her. "Ike will be delighted about the copies of Rommel's Atlantic Wall plans, and the beauty of it is, Rommel doesn't know."

"Wonderful," she said. "Do you get a cigar?"

He said calmly, "All right, so I'm a bastard—the kind of bastard who wins wars."

"Using people like me?"

"If that is what it takes."

She walked to the table and turned, the Walther heavy in her hand. "You know, I was going to make a speech. All about honour and how if you didn't have rules, even in a stupid game like this, you're as bad as the people we're trying to beat."

"My dear Genevieve," he said calmly, "time is limited. What exactly are you trying to say?"

"That since you're as bad as the Gestapo, maybe I should treat you like the Gestapo."

The Walther swung up in her hand. Munro didn't flinch, and it was Julie, hidden in the shadows at the back of the library, who cried, "No, Genevieve. He isn't worth it!"

Genevieve stood there, very pale, the Walther steady in her hand.

"Well, get on with it," Munro said impatiently. "Make your mind up, girl."

"Damn you, Brigadier!" She sighed and put the Walther down on the table beside her.

Jack Carter came forward and placed a tumbler of whisky in her hand. He picked up the Walther and put it into his pocket.

Munro said, "Very sensible. I'd drink that if I were you. You're going to need it."

"More bad news?"

He said, "Your sister died last night."

She closed her eyes, and then there was only the dark and Carter's anxious voice.

"Are you all right?"

She opened her eyes again. "How?"

"I ordered a post-mortem. It was the heart."

"Another side effect of that drug of yours?"

"Very probably."

"Where is she? I want to see her."

"She'll be buried in an unmarked grave, six a.m., the day after tomorrow. Highgate Cemetery."

"Where is she now?"

"An undertaker in Camberwell. Jack can take you."

The phone rang, and Carter answered it. He turned. "The Lysander just landed, sir."

"Good." Munro stood up. "We'll be off, then."

"But there still might be a chance," Genevieve said. "Craig . . . the others."

"Yesterday's news," Munro said. "So, let's get going."

CHAPTER 17

ON THE AFTERNOON of the following day Jack Carter delivered her to the undertaker in Camberwell. He waited outside while she went in. It was pleasant enough—a small oak-panelled waiting room smelling of beeswax polish and candles, a sheaf of white lilies in a brass container by the door. The man who attended was very old, his hair snow white.

"Ah, yes," he said. "The party in number three. There is a gentleman in there already."

She brushed past him and entered the small corridor beyond. A green baize curtain was drawn across the third cubicle. A voice murmured softly the prayers for the dead in Hebrew. She'd heard them often enough in the wards at Bart's during the blitz.

She pulled the curtain aside, and Baum swung to face her, clutching a prayer book. Tears coursed down his cheeks.

"I'm sorry, so sorry. As God is my witness, I never meant for such a thing."

Beyond him she could see Anne-Marie, hands folded across her breast, the face—her own face—framed in the shroud, peaceful now in the candlelight.

She took his hand in hers and held it tightly, saying nothing, for there was nothing to say.

It was a grey morning, fog in the air, at Highgate Cemetery. She was delivered to the gate, once again by Jack Carter, in a limousine.

"No need to wait," she told him. "I'll find my own way back."

He didn't argue, but drove away.

She saw them up in the far corner soon enough. The old man from the undertaker's, in a black overcoat, bowler hat in hand, two grave diggers leaning on their spades while a minister in black cassock worked his way through the burial service.

She waited until he'd finished and only went forward herself as the grave diggers started to shovel in earth. They glanced up, old men, long since past the age for military service.

One of them paused. "Someone you knew, miss?"

She glanced down at the plain pine coffin partially covered with dirt. "I thought I did once. Now I'm not so sure."

"You all right, miss?"

"Perfectly, thank you," Genevieve said.

She turned and found Craig Osbourne standing a few yards away, watching her.

HE WAS in uniform. His medal ribbons made a brave show in the grey morning, as did the double wings on his right sleeve. He slipped his trench coat over her shoulders without a word. They walked down the path between the gravestones, and fog swirled, shrinking the world until it encompassed only the two of them.

"I'm sorry," he said, "about Anne-Marie. Munro only told me last night."

"They didn't tell me that you were safe. Even Jack Carter didn't mention it."

"It was after midnight when I got in. They told me you'd be here this morning. I wanted to tell you myself."

"What happened to you?" she asked.

"I drifted away when the *Lili* went down. Finally washed up on a beach near Lizard Point."

"And Martin?"

"Gone, Genevieve. They're all gone."

She nodded, took out her case and selected a Gitane. "What's going to happen to you now? Munro can't have been too pleased."

"At first he was madder than hell. Said he was shipping me out to China. There's an OSS project starting there."

"And then?"

"The supreme commander took a look at the blow-ups of those photos of yours."

"And everything changed?"

"That's about the size of it. It's coming soon now, Genevieve — the big day. It's been decided to drop in Special Air Service and OSS units far behind German lines in France, to cause as much disruption as possible."

"In other words Munro needs you again."

He didn't reply to that, simply said, "Jack tells me the old bastard wants you for SOE?"

"So it would appear."

"Damn him to hell!" He put his hands on her shoulders. "You were always yourself alone, never her. Remember that."

Priem had said that to her. Amazing how alike they had been. She nodded. "I will."

He stood there looking at her. "That's it, then?"

"I suppose so."

He walked away suddenly; the greyness swallowed him, and that was no good, no good at all. There was a war on. You lived for today and took what there was. It was as simple as that.

She ran forward, calling his name. "Craig!"

He turned. "Yes?"

"Didn't you say something about dinner at the Savoy?"

Night of the Fox

Night of the Fox

In April 1944, a wounded
American serviceman is washed
ashore on Nazi-occupied Jersey.
He knows about the coming
D-Day, so he must be rescued by
Allied security before the
truth is tortured out of him.
There is just one man for the
job. One man cunning enough
to pass himself off as an SS
officer. Harry Martineau.

CHAPTER 1

Jersey 1985

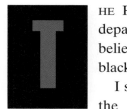HE ROMANS used to think that the souls of the departed stayed near their tombs. It was easy to believe that, on a cold March morning with a sky so black that it seemed as if night was about to fall.

I stood in the granite archway and looked in at the graveyard. The noticeboard said "Parish Church of St Brelade" and the place was crammed with headstones and tombs. I noticed a winged angel on the far side; and then thunder rumbled on the horizon and rain swept in across the bay.

I put up my umbrella and ventured out from under the arch. Last Sunday in Boston I'd never heard of the British Channel Islands, or the island of Jersey. Now it was Thursday, and here I was, having travelled halfway round the world to seek the final answer to something that had taken three years out of my life.

As I moved through the tombstones towards the old granite church, pausing to look out over the bay, I heard voices. Turning, I saw two men in cloth caps, sacks over their shoulders, crouching under a cypress tree by the far wall. They stood up and walked away, and I noticed they were carrying spades. They disappeared round the back of the church and I crossed to the wall.

There was a freshly dug grave, covered with a new tarpaulin. I don't think I've ever felt so excited. It was as if it had been waiting for me to find it.

I turned and walked through the headstones to the entrance of the church, opened the door and went inside. I'd expected a place of darkness and gloom, but for some reason lights were on, and it was very beautiful, the vaulted ceiling unusual in that it was constructed of granite, no evidence of wooden beams at all. I walked towards the altar and stood for a moment looking round, aware of the quiet. There was the click of a door opening and closing. A man stepped out of the shadows.

He had white hair and eyes of the palest blue. He wore a black cassock and carried a raincoat over one arm. His voice was dry and very old and there was a hint of Irish to it when he spoke. "Can I help you? My name is Cullen. Canon Donald Cullen."

I shook hands. He had a surprisingly firm grip. "Alan Stacey."

"You're an American?"

"Yes," I said. "My first visit to Jersey. Until a few days ago I never knew the place existed. Like most Americans, I'd only heard of New Jersey."

He smiled, and we moved towards the door. "You've chosen a bad time of the year for your first visit. Jersey can be one of the most desirable places on earth, but not usually during March."

"I didn't have much choice," I said. "I came because you're burying someone here today. Harry Martineau."

He had started to pull on his raincoat and paused in surprise. "That's right. At two o'clock this afternoon. Are you a relative?"

"Not exactly, although I sometimes feel as if I am. I'm an assistant professor of philosophy at Harvard. I've been working on a biography of Martineau for the past three years."

"I see." He opened the door and we went out into the porch.

"Do you know much about him?" I asked.

"Very little beyond the extraordinary way he met his end."

"And the even more extraordinary circumstances of his last rites," I said. "After all, Canon, it isn't often you get to bury a man forty years after his death."

CANON CULLEN'S bungalow was at the other end of St Brelade's Bay, close to L'Horizon Hotel, where I was staying. It was small and unpretentious, but the living room was surprisingly large, and two walls were lined with books. Sliding windows looked out onto a terrace, a small garden and the bay beyond. The wind was lifting the sea into whitecaps, and rain rattled against the window.

My host came in from the kitchen and put a tray on a small table by the fire. He poured me a cup of tea and pushed it towards me as I sat down. The silence hung between us. He raised his cup and drank precisely, waiting.

"You're comfortable here," I said.

"Yes," he said. "I do very well. Lonely, of course. The great weakness of all human beings, Professor Stacey, is that we all need somebody." He refilled his cup. "I spent three years in Jersey as a boy and grew to love the place. When I retired it seemed an obvious choice."

He took out a pipe and started to fill it from a worn leather pouch. "So," he said briskly. "Tell me about friend Martineau."

"Do you know much about him?"

"I'd never heard of the man until a few days ago when my good friend, Dr Drayton, came to see me and told me the body was being shipped from London for burial here."

"You're aware of the manner of his death?"

"In a plane crash in 1945."

"January 1945, to be precise. The RAF had a unit called the Enemy Aircraft Flight during the Second World War. They flew captured German planes, to evaluate their performance and so on. Harry Martineau worked for the Ministry of Economic Warfare, and in January 1945 he went missing when he was travelling as an observer for the Enemy Aircraft Flight in an Arado 96, a German training plane. It was always believed to have gone down in the sea, but two weeks ago it was found during excavations in an Essex marsh. An RAF unit recovered what was left of it."

"And Martineau and the pilot were still inside?"

"What was left of them. For some reason the authorities kept a low profile on the affair. News didn't filter through to me until last weekend. I caught the first plane out. Arrived in London on Monday."

He nodded. "You say you've been working on a biography of him. What makes him so special? I had never even heard his name before."

"Nor have the general public," I said. "But in the thirties he was considered one of the most brilliant minds in his field."

"Which was?"

"Moral philosophy."

"An interesting study," the canon said.

"For a fascinating man. He was born in Boston. His father was in shipping. Wealthy, but not outrageously so. His mother, although born in New York, was of German parentage." I got up and walked to the window, thinking hard as I peered out. "Martineau went to Harvard, did a doctorate at Heidelberg and was a Rhodes scholar at Oxford. He was made a fellow of Trinity College and Croxley Professor of Moral Philosophy at the age of thirty-eight."

"A remarkable achievement," Cullen said.

I turned. "But the strange thing is that here was a man who was questioning everything, turning his whole field upside down. Then the Second World War broke out, and the rest is silence."

"Silence?"

"Oh, he left Oxford, we know that. Worked for the Ministry of Defence and then the Ministry of Economic Warfare, as I told you. Many academics did that. But the tragedy is that he seems to have stopped academic work altogether after September 1939. No more papers, and the book he'd been writing for years was left unfinished." I went back and sat down.

The clock on the mantelpiece struck twelve. Cullen got up, moved to the sideboard and poured whisky into two glasses. He came back and handed me one. "And so, Professor, what about the rest?"

"The rest?"

"Priests are supposed to be ingenious souls who know nothing of the reality of life," he said. "Rubbish, of course. After fifty-two years as an ordained priest, one learns to know when someone is not telling one everything." He put a match to his pipe and puffed away. "Which applies to you, my friend, unless I'm much mistaken."

I took a deep breath. "He was in German Luftwaffe uniform when they found him. Both he and the pilot."

"How do you know that?"

"I have a friend who's with the CIA at our embassy in London. They get to know things, these people. And he found out something else. The newspaper report about that Arado being from the Enemy Aircraft Flight. That's suspect, too."

"Why?"

"Because they always carried RAF roundels and this one still had Luftwaffe markings."

The old man frowned. "And you say you couldn't get any more information from official sources?"

"None at all. I ran into roadblocks, if you know what I mean. Martineau and that flight are still covered by some wartime security classification. All I *did* discover was that Martineau was awarded the Distinguished Service Order in January 1944. No information about what he'd done to earn it." I shrugged. "Nothing makes much sense. Martineau and Jersey for example. To the best of my knowledge he never visited the place, and he died five months before it was freed from Nazi occupation. He has no living relatives, and he never married. So tell me, who is this Dr Drayton of yours? He must have a lot of pull with the Ministry of Defence to get them to release the body to him."

"You're absolutely right." Canon Cullen poured me another whisky. "In all respects but one. Dr Drayton," he said as he raised his glass to toast me, "is not a he, but a she. Dr Sarah Drayton, to be precise."

I AM THE Resurrection and the life, saith the Lord: he that believeth in me, though he were dead, yet shall he live.

Cullen sounded more Irish as he lifted his voice against the heavy rain. He wore a dark cloak over his vestments and one of the undertaker's men stood beside him, holding an umbrella. There was only one mourner, Sarah Drayton, standing on the other side of the open grave.

She looked perhaps forty-eight or fifty although, as I discovered later, she was sixty; small and with a figure still trim, in a black suit and hat. Her hair was short and iron-grey. She was not in any way conventionally beautiful, with a mouth that was rather too large, and hazel eyes above wide cheekbones. But it was a face of considerable character, and there was an extraordinary stillness to her.

I stayed back under what shelter the trees provided as Cullen concluded the service, moved towards her and spoke briefly. She kissed him on the cheek and he turned and walked away towards the church followed by the undertakers.

She stayed at the graveside for a while, and the two grave-diggers waited respectfully a few yards away. She ignored me as I moved forward, picked up a little damp soil and threw it down on the coffin.

"Dr Drayton?" I said. "I'm sorry to intrude. My name is Alan Stacey. I wonder if I might have a few words?"

Her voice was calm and beautifully modulated. She said, without looking at me, "I know very well who you are, Professor Stacey. I've been expecting you at any time these past three years." She turned and smiled, and suddenly looked enchanting and about twenty years of age. "We really should get out of this rain before it does us both a mischief. My car is in the road outside. I think you'd better come back for a drink."

THE HOUSE was no more than five minutes away. It was Victorian, and it stood in about an acre of well-tended garden, surrounded by beech trees through which one could see the bay far below. As we went up the steps the door was opened instantly by a sombre-looking, silver-haired man in a black alpaca jacket.

"Ah, Vito," Dr Drayton said as he took her coat, "this is Professor Stacey."

"*Professore.*" He bowed slightly.

"We'll have coffee later," she said. "I'll see to the drinks."

"Of course, Contessa." He turned and left us.

"Contessa?" I asked.

"Oh, don't listen to Vito." She dismissed my query politely, but firmly. "He's a terrible snob. This way."

She opened a double mahogany door and led the way into a large library. The walls were lined with books and french windows looked out to the garden. There was a fireplace with a fire burning brightly in the basket grate and a grand piano, the top crammed with photos.

"Scotch all right for you?" she asked.

"Fine."

She busied herself at the drinks tray and handed me a glass. "I've known about you ever since you started work on Harry."

"Who told you about me?"

"Oh, friends," she said. "From the old days. The kind who get to know things."

"You must have influence," I said. "Nobody seems to want to answer any of my questions at the Ministry of Defence, and yet they released the body to you."

She sat in a wingback chair by the fire, crossing slim legs. "Have you ever heard of SOE, Professor?"

"Of course," I said. "Special Operations Executive. Set up by British Intelligence in 1940 on Churchill's instructions, to coordinate resistance in Europe."

"Set Europe ablaze, that's what the old man ordered." Sarah Drayton took a cigarette from a silver box and lit it. "I worked for them."

I was astonished. "But you can't have been more than a child."

"Nineteen," she said. "In 1944."

"And Martineau?"

"Look on the piano," she said. "The end photo, the one in the silver frame."

I crossed to the piano and picked up the photo. Her face jumped out at me, strangely unchanged except in one respect. Her hair was startlingly blonde and marcelled—that is the term I think they used to use. She wore a little black hat and one of those coats from the wartime period with big shoulders, tight at the waist.

The man standing next to her was of medium height and wore a leather military overcoat, hands thrust deep into the pockets. The eyes were dark, no expression in them at all, and his smile had a kind of ruthless charm. He looked thoroughly dangerous.

Sarah Drayton got up and joined me. "Not much like the Croxley Professor of Moral Philosophy at Oxford there, is he?"

"Where was it taken?" I asked.

"In Jersey. Not too far from here. May 1944."

"But Jersey was occupied by the Germans at that time," I said.

"Very much so."

"And Martineau was here? With you?"

She crossed to a Georgian desk, opened a drawer and took out several old snaps. She passed one to me. "This one I don't keep on top of the piano for obvious reasons."

She was dressed pretty much as she had been in the other photo and Martineau wore the same leather trenchcoat. The only difference was the SS uniform underneath, the silver death's-head badge in his cap. "Standartenführer Max Vogel," she said. "Colonel, to you. He looks rather dashing, doesn't he?"

"Dear God!" I said. "What is all this?"

She didn't answer, but passed me another photo. A group of German officers. In front of them stood two men on their own: one was Martineau in SS uniform, but it was the other who took my breath away. Field Marshal Erwin Rommel. The Desert Fox himself.

"Was that taken here too?"

"Oh yes."

She put the photos back in the desk and picked up my glass. "I think you could do with another drink."

"Yes, I believe I could. Do I get an explanation?"

"Why not?" she said and turned as rain drummed against the french windows. "I can't think of anything better to do on an afternoon like this, can you?"

CHAPTER 2

London 1944

IT STARTED, if one can ever be certain where anything starts, with a telephone call received by Brigadier Dougal Munro at his London flat, ten minutes walk from SOE headquarters in Baker Street. As head of Section D at SOE Munro had two phones by his bed, one routed straight through to his office. It was this which awakened him at four o'clock on the morning of 28 April 1944.

He listened, face grave, then swore softly. "I'll come over."

Within five minutes he was hurrying along the deserted street. He was sixty-five, a squat, powerful-looking man with white hair, his round face set off by steel-rimmed spectacles. He wore an old raincoat and carried an umbrella.

At the entrance in Baker Street he nodded to the guard and went straight upstairs. When he reached his office Captain Jack Carter, his night duty officer, was seated behind his desk.

"Is there any tea, Jack?"

"Thermos flask on the map table, sir."

Munro unscrewed the flask, poured a cup and drank. "God, that's foul; but at least it's hot. Right, get on with it."

Carter got up and walked over to a map of southwest England on the table, showing Devon, Cornwall and the English Channel.

"Exercise Tiger, sir," he said. "You remember the details?"

"Simulated landings for Overlord."

"That's right. Here in Lyme Bay in Devon there's a place called Slapton Sands. It bears enough similarity to the beach we've designated Utah in the Normandy landings to make it invaluable for training purposes. Last night's convoy consisted of eight landing craft. Under naval escort, of course. They were to do a practice beach landing at Slapton."

There was a pause. Munro said, "Tell me the worst."

"They were attacked at sea by German E-boats."

"And the damage?"

"Two landing craft sunk. Others torpedoed and damaged. Around two hundred sailors and four hundred and fifty soldiers missing."

"Are you trying to tell me we lost six hundred and fifty men last night? And we haven't even started the invasion of Europe?"

"I'm afraid so."

Munro walked restlessly across the room and stood at the window. "Were there any Bigots amongst those officers lost?"

"One or two, sir."

"Dear God, I warned them. I warned them about this," Munro said. "No Bigot to undertake hazardous duty of any kind."

Some months previously it had become clear that there had been serious breaches of security in connection with the projected invasion of Europe. The Bigot procedure had been brought in as an answer to the problem. It was an intelligence classification above Most Secret. Bigots knew what others did not; in many cases, the details of the Allied invasion of Europe.

"Has Eisenhower been told?"

"He's in town, sir, at Hayes Lodge. He wants to see you at breakfast. Eight o'clock."

Munro shook his head, staring down at the map. "It'd be ironic if the greatest invasion in history had to be called off because one man with all the right information fell into the wrong hands."

"I don't think it's likely that any of those missing were picked up by the Germans, sir. I gather the E-boats attacked at a range of fifteen hundred yards, then got the hell out of it fast. A lot of darkness and confusion on both sides. And the weather isn't too good. Wind force 5 to 6 and freshening. But I'm informed that the way the currents are, most of the bodies will come ashore."

"I pray that you're right, Jack. I pray that you're right," Dougal Munro said fervently.

AT THAT precise moment, Colonel Hugh Kelso was more afraid than he had ever been in his life, cold and wet and in terrible pain. He lay huddled in the bottom of a life raft about a mile off the Devon coast, a contrary current carrying him fast towards Start Point on the southernmost tip of Lyme Bay. Beyond lay the open waters of the English Channel.

Kelso was forty-two, married, with two daughters. A civil engineer by profession, he had been chief executive of the family firm of construction engineers in New York for several years and had a high reputation. Which was why he had been drafted into the engineering corps in 1942. His experience of the engineering problems involved in beach landings on various South Pacific islands had earned him a transfer to the Supreme Headquarters Allied Expeditionary Forces (SHAEF) in England to work on the preparation for the Normandy landings.

Six weeks previously, under cover of darkness, Kelso had actually visited the Normandy beach code-named Utah, to check on the suitability of the terrain for vehicles. It had therefore seemed sensible to have him aboard when LST (tank landing ship) 31 sailed from Plymouth to take part in Exercise Tiger.

Like everyone else on board, Kelso had been taken by surprise by the attack. A number of flares had been noticed in the distance, which had been assumed to come from British motor torpedo boats (MTBs). Then the first torpedo had struck and the night had become a living hell of burning oil and screaming men.

Kelso had been blown off his feet by the force of the explosion and thrown into the sea. His life jacket kept him afloat, but he had lost consciousness, coming to his senses to find himself being towed through the icy water.

The flames were a hundred yards away and in the reflected light he had become aware of an oil-streaked face.

"You're okay, sir. Just hang on. There's a life raft here."

The life raft loomed out of the darkness; a round, fat, orange sphere, riding high in the water and intended to carry as many as ten men. There was a canopy on top to protect the occupants from wind and weather. The entrance flap was open.

"I'll get you in, sir, then go back for some more. Up you go."

Kelso felt curiously weak, but his unknown friend was strong. He pushed hard, shoving Kelso head first through the flap. And then Kelso was aware of the pain in his right leg, worse than anything he had ever known. He screamed and fainted.

When he came to he was numb with cold, and it took him a few moments to work out where he was. There was no sign of his unknown friend. He peered out through the open flap. No light anywhere, only the dark and the wind. He checked the luminous dial of his waterproof watch. It was almost five a.m. Then he remembered that these life rafts carried an emergency kit. As he turned to feel for it in the darkness, the pain in his leg started again. He gritted his teeth as his hands found the box and opened the lid.

There was a waterproof torch inside. He switched it on. He was alone, as he had thought, in the orange cave, water slopping around him. His trousers were torn below the right knee and when he gingerly put his hand inside he could feel the raised edges of broken bone under the skin.

There was also a Very pistol in the box and he fingered it for a moment. It seemed the obvious thing to do, to send up a flare, but then he paused. What if the German naval units which had attacked them were still in the area? He couldn't risk being picked up by the enemy; in a matter of weeks an armada of six thousand ships would sail across the narrow waters of the English Channel, and Kelso knew times and places. No, better to wait until dawn.

His leg was really hurting now. He rummaged in the box and found the medical kit with its morphine ampoules. He jabbed one in his leg and, after a moment's hesitation, another. Then he found the bailer and wearily started to throw water out through the open flap. God, but he was tired. Too much morphine perhaps, but at least the pain had dulled. He leaned back and was suddenly asleep.

On his right, a few hundred yards away, was Start Point. A freshening wind drove the life raft past that final headland and out into the cold waters of the English Channel.

EISENHOWER WAS seated in the Regency bay window of the library at Hayes Lodge having a breakfast of poached eggs, toast and coffee, when a young aide showed Dougal Munro in.

"Leave us, Captain," the general said, and the aide withdrew. "Have you eaten?"

"I haven't eaten breakfast for years, General."

For a moment, Eisenhower's face was illuminated by that famous and inimitable smile. "Which shows you aren't an old military hand. You prefer tea, don't you? You'll find it on the sideboard behind you—special order. Help yourself, then tell me what you know of this wretched business."

Munro helped himself to tea, sat in the window seat and gave Eisenhower a brief résumé of the night's events.

"But surely the naval escorts should have been able to prevent such a thing happening," the general said. "It's past belief."

Munro shrugged. "We've had Royal Navy torpedo boats hanging around off Cherbourg during these exercises because Cherbourg, as you know, is the most important E-boat base on the French coast. But there was a sea mist, and the Germans obviously slipped out with their silencers on and their radar switched off. They fired off parachute flares, so the people in the convoy assumed they were ours."

"Goddammit, you never assume anything in this game. I'm tired of telling people that." Eisenhower stood up and went to the fire. "Bodies coming ashore by the hundred, so they tell me."

"I'm afraid so."

"Needless to say, this whole thing stays under wraps. If it got out, so close to the invasion, it could have a terrible effect on morale."

"I agree." Munro hesitated and said carefully, "There is the question of the Bigots, General. There were three in all. Two of the bodies have already been recovered. The third, this man," Munro took a file from his briefcase and pushed it across, "is still missing."

Eisenhower read the file quickly. "Colonel Hugh Kelso." His face darkened. "I know Kelso personally. He checked out a beach in Normandy only weeks ago." The American general sighed. "He knows both when we're going and where."

"We've men on the beaches around Slapton looking for him now, General. I think his body may well turn up with the rest of them."

Eisenhower said sharply, "Some of those bodies will never come in on the tide. I know that and so do you, and if Kelso is one of them, we can never be certain that he wasn't picked up by the enemy." Rain dashed against the window. "What a day," he said morosely.

HITLER WAS beside himself with rage, pacing up and down in the map room at Wolf's Lair, his underground headquarters deep in the forests of East Prussia. "Again and yet again they try." He turned on Rattenhuber, commander of the resident SS guard. "And you, Oberführer? What about you? Sworn to protect my safety."

"My Führer," Rattenhuber stammered. "What can I say?"

"Nothing!" Hitler turned on the other officers in the room. "You say nothing of use to me—none of you."

In the shocked silence, it was Heinrich Himmler, Reichsführer of the SS, who spoke. "That there has been negligence is true, my Führer, but surely in the failure of this dastardly attempt we see further proof of the certainty of your own destiny. Further proof of Germany's inevitable victory under your inspired guidance."

Hitler's eyes blazed, his head went back. "As always, Reichsführer, *you* see. You are the only one who does." He turned on the others.

"Get out, all of you. I wish to talk to the Reichsführer alone."

They went without a murmur, while Hitler stood staring down at the map desk, hands clasped behind him.

"In what way may I serve my Führer?" Himmler asked.

"There is a plot, am I not right?" Hitler said. "A general conspiracy to destroy me?"

"Not so much a general conspiracy as a conspiracy of generals, my Führer."

Hitler turned sharply. "Are you certain?"

"Oh, yes. But proof—that is something else."

Hitler nodded. "So this Captain Koenig, the traitor who tried to bring a time bomb into my headquarters this morning, was simply an agent? I am told he was an aide to General Olbricht. Is Olbricht one of those you suspect?" Himmler nodded. "And the others?"

"Generals Stieff, Wagner, von Hase, Lindemann. Several more, all being closely watched."

Hitler stayed remarkably cool. "Traitors each and every one. No firing squad. A noose each when the time comes. No one higher, though? It would seem our field marshals are loyal, at least."

"I wish I could confirm that, my Führer, but there is one who is heavily suspect. I would be failing in my duty if I did not tell you."

"Then tell me."

"Rommel."

Hitler smiled a ghastly smile that was almost one of triumph. "So, the Desert Fox wishes to play games."

"I'm almost certain of it."

"The people's hero," Hitler said. "We must handle him carefully, wouldn't you say?"

"Or outfox him, my Führer," Himmler said softly.

"Outfox him. Outfox the Desert Fox," Hitler smiled delightedly. "Yes, I like that, Reichsführer. I like that very much indeed."

HUGH KELSO slept until noon, and when he awakened he was very sick. He turned over in the violently pitching life raft and pulled down the zip of the entrance flap. His heart sank. The sky was black, heavy with rain and there was no hint of land anywhere. He was well out in the English Channel, so much was obvious. If he drifted straight across he'd hit the coast of France, possibly the Cherbourg peninsula. Below that, in the Gulf of St Malo, were the Channel Islands. He didn't know much about them, except that they were British and occupied by the enemy.

He got the Very pistol out, and fired a distress flare. There was seldom any German naval traffic in the Channel in daylight. They tended to keep to the inshore run behind their minefields. He fired another flare and then water cascaded in through the flap and he hurriedly zipped it up. His leg was on fire again. He got out another morphine ampoule and injected himself. After a while, he pillowed his head on his hands and slept.

Outside, the sea lifted as the afternoon wore on. By five o'clock the wind was blowing southwesterly, turning him away from the French coast and the Cherbourg peninsula, so that by six o'clock he was ten miles to the west of the Casquets lighthouse, off Alderney.

Kelso was aware of none of these things. He woke around seven o'clock with a high temperature, washed his face with a little water, was sick again, and dropped into something like a coma.

CHAPTER 3

AS COMMANDER of Army Group B, Field Marshal Erwin Rommel was responsible for the Atlantic Wall defences, and his sole task was to defeat any Allied attempt to land in northern France. Since taking command he had strengthened the coastal defences to an incredible degree, tramping the beaches, impressing his own energetic presence on everyone, from divisional commanders to the lowliest soldier.

His headquarters seemed permanently on the move and he had an uncomfortable habit of turning up unexpectedly, in his familiar black Mercedes, accompanied only by his driver and his most trusted aide from his Afrika Corps days, Major Konrad Hofer.

About the time that Hugh Kelso was drifting past the west coast of Alderney, Field Marshal Rommel was sitting down to dinner with the officers of the 21st Parachute Regiment in a château some ten miles from St Lô in Normandy.

His primary reason for being in the area was sound enough. The high command believed that the Allied invasion, when it came, would take place near the Pas-de-Calais. Rommel disagreed and had made it clear that if he were Eisenhower, he would strike for Normandy. None of this had done anything for his popularity in Berlin, but Rommel didn't give a damn about that any more. The war was lost. The only uncertainty was how long it would take.

Which brought him to his second reason for being in Normandy. He was involved in a dangerous game and it paid to keep on the move. Since taking command of Army Group B he had renewed old friendships with General von Stulpnagel, military governor of France, and General Alexander von Falkenhausen. Both were involved, along with Colonel Klaus von Stauffenberg, in the conspiracy to assassinate Hitler. It had not taken them long to bring Rommel round to their point of view.

They had all been aware of the projected assassination attempt at Rastenberg that morning. Rommel had already sent Konrad Hofer to General Olbricht's headquarters in Berlin to await the outcome, but so far there had been no news from him.

Now, Colonel Halder, commanding officer of the 21st Parachute Regiment, stood to offer a toast. "Gentlemen—to Field Marshal Erwin Rommel, the Desert Fox himself, who does us so much honour tonight."

They drained their glasses, then applauded him, cheering wildly. Rommel was immensely touched.

Colonel Halder said, "The men have arranged a little entertainment in your honour, Field Marshal. We were hoping you might be willing to attend."

"But of course. Delighted."

A door opened at the back of the room and Konrad Hofer entered. He looked tired and badly needed a shave.

"Ah, Konrad, there you are," Rommel called. "Come and have a glass of champagne. You look as if you could do with it. Good flight?"

"Terrible." Hofer swallowed the champagne gratefully.

"My dear boy, have a shower and we'll see if they can make you a sandwich." Rommel turned to Colonel Halder. "See if you can delay this little show the men are putting on for half an hour."

"That will be no problem, Field Marshal."

"Good—we'll see you later then." Rommel picked up a fresh bottle of champagne and walked out, followed by Hofer.

As soon as his bedroom door was closed, Hofer turned in agitation. "It was the worst kind of mess. All that fool Koenig managed to do was blow himself up outside the main gate."

"That seems rather careless of him," Rommel said dryly. "Now calm yourself, Konrad. Get under the shower and take it slowly."

Hofer disappeared into the bathroom. While he waited, Rommel straightened his uniform, examining himself in the mirror. He was fifty-three, stocky and thickset with strong features, and there was a power to the man, a force that was almost electric. His uniform was simple enough, his only decorations, the Pour le Mérite, the famous Blue Max and the Knight's Cross with Oak Leaves, Swords and Diamonds, which hung around his neck. One hardly needed anything else if one had those.

Hofer emerged in a bathrobe, towelling his hair. "Olbricht and the others are furious, and I don't blame them. The Gestapo or the SD could be on to this at any time."

"How was von Stauffenberg?" Rommel asked.

"As determined as ever. He suggests you meet with Generals von Stulpnagel and Falkenhausen within the next few days."

"I'll see what I can do."

"I'm not so sure it's a good idea. If Himmler does have his suspicions about you, you could be under surveillance already."

"I'll think of something," Rommel said. "Now, hurry up. The men are putting on a little show for me, and I don't want to disappoint them."

THE SHOW WAS presented on a small stage in the main hall of the château. Rommel, Hofer and the regimental officers sat on chairs at the front, the men stood behind them.

A young corporal came on, bowed, sat down at a grand piano and played a selection of light music. There was polite applause. Then the curtains parted to reveal the regimental choir, singing lustily. There were cheers from the back of the hall and everyone started to join in, including the officers. The curtain came down to a storm of clapping and there was a pause.

"Brilliant," said Rommel. "Is there more?"

"Oh yes, Herr Field Marshal. Something very special."

There was a steady, muted drum roll. The curtain rose to reveal subdued lighting. As the choir started to sing the song of the Afrika Corps from the side of the stage, Rommel walked on. It was unmistakably him: the cap with the desert goggles, the white scarf carelessly knotted at the neck, the old leather greatcoat, the field marshal's baton in one gloved hand, the other arrogantly on the hip. The voice, when he spoke, was perfect, as he delivered a few lines of his famous battlefield speech before El Alamein.

"I know I haven't offered you much—sand, heat, and scorpions—but we've shared them together. One more push and it's Cairo, and if we fail . . . well, we tried—together."

There was total silence from the hall as Colonel Halder glanced anxiously at Rommel. "Field Marshal, I hope you're not offended?"

"Offended? I think he's marvellous," Rommel said, and jumped to his feet. "Bravo!" he called, and behind him the entire audience joined in the chorus of the Afrika Corps song, cheering wildly.

IN A MAKESHIFT dressing room next to the kitchen, Corporal Erich Berger slumped down into a chair and stared at himself in the mirror. His heart was beating fast and he was sweating. It was a hell of a thing for any actor to perform in front of the man he was taking off. And such a man. The most popular soldier in Germany.

"Not bad, Heini," he said softly. "*Mazel tov.*" He took a bottle of schnapps from the drawer, drew the cork and swallowed some.

A Yiddish phrase on the lips of a German corporal might have seemed strange to anyone who had overheard. His secret was that he wasn't Erich Berger at all, but Heini Baum, Jewish actor and cabaret performer from Berlin.

His story was surprisingly simple. He had performed in cabaret all over Europe. He had never married, and had continued to live in Berlin, even when the Nazis came to power, because his ageing parents had always lived there and would not believe that anything terrible could happen.

But then came that terrible night in 1940 when he had arrived at the end of his street after the cabaret in time to see the Gestapo taking his parents from the house. He had turned and run, like the coward he was; but there was nowhere to go, for his papers told the world he was a Jew.

So he'd caught a train to Kiel, with the wild idea that he might be able to get a ship from there to somewhere—anywhere. He'd arrived just after one of the first, devastating, RAF raids on that city, and had stumbled through the chaos and flames searching for shelter.

Lurching down into a cellar he'd found the bodies of a man, a woman and a twelve-year-old girl—Erich Berger, his wife and daughter, as Baum discovered when he examined their identity cards. And one thing more. In Berger's pocket were his call-up papers, ordering him to report for military duty the following week.

What better hiding place for a Jew who was afraid to be a Jew than in the German army? To swap the photos of the two identity cards was simple enough, so that the body he dragged out to leave in the rubble of the street was that of Heini Baum.

It was the paratroops he'd been inducted into. He'd been everywhere since then: Crete, Stalingrad, North Africa, a nice flashy hero in his Luftwaffe blouse and baggy paratroopers' pants, and he'd got the Iron Cross Second and First Class to prove it. He took another pull at the schnapps bottle and silently toasted his good fortune.

ROMMEL LEANED on the mantelpiece and stirred the fire with his boot. "So, the others would like me to talk with von Stulpnagel and Falkenhausen?"

"Yes, Herr Field Marshal," Hofer said, "but, as you pointed out, secrecy would be essential."

"And opportunity," Rommel said. "Secrecy and opportunity." The clock on the mantelpiece chimed twice and he laughed. "Two o'clock in the morning. The best time for crazy ideas."

"What are you suggesting, Herr Field Marshal?"

"Quite simple, really. What if we arranged a meeting next week, at some agreed rendezvous, with von Stulpnagel and Falkenhausen, while I was actually supposed to be somewhere else? Jersey, for example?"

"The Channel Islands?" Hofer looked bewildered.

"The Führer himself suggested not two months ago that I inspect the fortifications there." He turned and smiled. "The Führer is right. As commander of the Atlantic Wall defences, I should certainly inspect such an important part of it."

Hofer nodded. "I see that, Herr Field Marshal, but how can you be in two places at once? Meeting Falkenhausen and Stulpnagel in France and inspecting fortifications in Jersey?"

"You saw me in two places earlier this evening," Rommel said calmly, "both in the audience and on stage at the same time."

"My God," Hofer whispered, "are you serious?"

"Why not? That man Berger even fooled *me* when he came on stage."

"But would he be intelligent enough to carry it off? I mean, being a field marshal is rather different from being an orderly-room corporal."

"He seems intelligent enough to me," Rommel told him. "A brave soldier to boot. Iron Cross First and Second Class. And he'd have you at his shoulder every step of the way."

Suddenly Rommel sounded impatient. "Where's your enthusiasm, Konrad? Let's see, it's Saturday now. How about descending on Jersey next Friday. Only for thirty-six hours or so. You can be back in France on Saturday night, or Sunday at the latest. If Berger can't carry it off for that length of time, I'll eat my hat."

"Very well, Herr Field Marshal. I'll notify the Channel Islands authorities that you'll be arriving next Friday."

"No, you won't," Rommel said. "We'll box more cleverly than that. Who's the military commander in Jersey?"

Hofer took a file from his briefcase and worked his way down a list. "Yes, here we are. Colonel Heine."

"Good," said Rommel. "This is what we do. Send the commander-in-chief, General von Schmettow, a signal ordering him to hold a meeting in Guernsey next Saturday to consider the implications for the islands of the threatened invasion of France this summer. I want them all there. The military commander, Heine, and whoever's in charge of the navy and Luftwaffe contingents on the islands."

"Which will leave only junior officers in command on the other islands."

"Exactly. I'll fly in on Friday in the Stork, or rather, you and Berger will. The first they'll know about your arrival is when you ask the tower for permission to land at the airfield."

"And what will von Schmettow think?"

"That the whole thing has been a deliberate ploy so that I can make a snap inspection of the military situation on the island."

"That's really rather clever," Hofer said.

"Yes, I think it is." Rommel started to unbutton his tunic. "Meanwhile, I'll meet Falkenhausen and Stulpnagel at some quiet spot." He yawned. "I think I'll go to bed. Oh, and speak to Colonel Halder tomorrow. Tell him I'm much taken with Corporal Berger and want to borrow him for a while. I don't think he'll make any difficulties."

DOUGAL MUNRO slept that night on a small military bed in the corner of his office at Baker Street. It was about three o'clock in the morning when Jack Carter shook him gently awake. Munro opened his eyes instantly and sat up. "What is it?"

"Latest lists from Slapton, sir. You asked to see them. Still over a hundred bodies missing."

"And no sign of Kelso?"

"I'm afraid not. But General Montgomery has had an assurance from the navy that the E-boats couldn't have picked up survivors. They were too far away."

"The trouble with life, Jack, is that the moment someone tells you something is impossible, someone else promptly proves that it isn't. Order a car for eight o'clock. We'll take a run down to Slapton and see for ourselves."

AT SIX O'CLOCK on that same morning, Kelso woke up feeling very cold. His feet and hands were numb, and yet he was sweating.

He unzipped the flap and peered out into the grey light of dawn. Not that there was anything much to see for he was shrouded in a dense sea fog. Somewhere in the distance he heard a foghorn. Although he didn't know it, it was the Corbière lighthouse on the tip of the southernmost coast of Jersey, already behind him as the current swept him along.

He could hear waves breaking on an unseen shore and then, as the current carried him into St Aubin's Bay, he glimpsed cliffs with concrete gun emplacements on top. All around him was white foam, rocks showing through. And then there was a voice, high and clear, and the fog rolled away to reveal a small beach. A man was running along the shore, in a woollen cap, heavy coat and rubber boots.

The life raft slewed broadside on in the surf and smashed against rocks, pitching Kelso into the water. He tried to stand up, but screamed as his right leg collapsed under him, and then the man was knee-deep in water, holding him. It was only at that moment that Kelso realised it was a woman. "All right, I've got you. Just hang on."

He wasn't sure what happened after that until he came to in the shelter of some rocks. The woman was trying to drag the life raft out of the water. When he attempted to sit up, she came towards him. Kelso asked as she knelt down, "Where am I, France?"

"No," she said. "Jersey."

He closed his eyes for a moment and shivered. "You're British?"

"I should hope so. My name's Helen de Ville. Where did your plane come down?"

"It didn't. I'm an American army officer. Colonel Hugh Kelso."

"An *army* officer? Where on earth have you come from?"

"England. I'm a survivor of a ship that was torpedoed in Lyme Bay." He groaned suddenly as pain knifed through him.

She opened his torn trouser leg and frowned. "That's ghastly. You'll have to go to hospital."

He clutched at the front of her coat. "No—no Germans."

She eased him back down. "Just lie still, I'm going to leave you for a little while. We're going to need a cart."

"Okay," he said. "But no Germans. You must promise."

She leaned over him, face set, and said, "The Jerrys aren't going to have you—that's a promise. Now, wait for me."

She turned and hurried away. He lay there on that fog-shrouded shore, trying to get his bearings, and then the leg started to hurt again. Seconds later he plunged into darkness.

CHAPTER 4

HELEN DE VILLE took a short cut from the beach, scrambling up the steep hillside through the pine trees. She was strong and wiry after four years of enemy occupation and food restrictions. She often joked that it had given her back the figure she'd enjoyed at eighteen, an unlooked-for bonus at forty-two.

She stood at the edge of the wood and looked across at the house. De Ville Place was very old, constructed of Jersey granite, weathered by the years. There were rows of french windows at the front on either side of the entrance, and a granite wall divided the house from a courtyard at one end.

She paused, for there was an old Morris parked in the courtyard, one of those requisitioned by the enemy. For two years she'd had

German naval officers billeted in the house. They came and went, of course, sometimes staying only a night or two.

As she started across the lawn, the front door opened and one of them came out. He wore a white sweater, old reefer coat and seaboots, and carried a duffel bag in one hand. The face beneath the salt-stained naval cap was good-humoured and recklessly handsome. He wore a white top to his cap, usually an affectation of German U-boat commanders, but then Lieutenant Guido Orsini was a law unto himself, an Italian on secondment to the German navy, trapped in the wrong place at the wrong time when the Italian government had capitulated. Helen de Ville had long felt considerable affection for him.

"Morning, Guido."

"Helen, *cara mia.*" He blew her a kiss. "I'm the last as usual."

"Where to today?"

"Normandy. Granville, to be precise. Should be fun in this fog. Can I give you a lift to St Helier?"

"No thanks. I'm looking for Sean."

"I saw him not ten minutes ago walking down towards his cottage. See you tomorrow. I must fly. *Ciao, cara.*"

The moment she heard the Morris start up and drive away, she crossed the courtyard, went through a field gate and ran along the track through the trees to Sean Gallagher's cottage. She could see him now, in old corduroy trousers and riding boots, the sleeves of his checked shirt rolled up above muscular arms as he split logs.

"Sean!" she called and stumbled, almost falling.

He lowered the axe and turned towards her, pushing a lock of reddish brown hair from his eyes.

Sean Gallagher was fifty-two and, as an Irish citizen, officially neutral in this war. He was born in Dublin, but his Jersey-born mother died in childbirth, so the boy grew up spending long summers in Jersey with his grandparents, and the rest of the year in Dublin with his father. His ambition was to be a writer and he took a degree in English literature. But the exigencies of life made him a soldier, for as he finished at university, the First World War began.

He joined the Irish Fusiliers, and by 1918 was a very old twenty-six: a major with a Military Cross for gallantry on the Somme. He continued his military career back in Ireland, and by the age of thirty he'd been made a general. But he was sick of war, so he set off to travel the world, finally settling in Jersey in 1930. Ralph de Ville had been a boyhood friend, and Helen he had loved hopelessly from the first moment they had met. His home in the parish of St Lawrence was requisitioned by the Germans in 1940, and Helen, with Ralph away serving with the British army, needed a strong right arm, so he had moved into a cottage on the estate. He still loved Helen, and still quite hopelessly.

GALLAGHER AND Helen negotiated the track down to the beach with an old cart that had seen better days and a horse that was considerably leaner than it should have been.

"If they find out you're helping this man," Sean said gravely, "it won't just be a prison sentence. It could mean a firing squad."

"And what about you?" Helen asked.

"I'm a neutral, don't I keep telling you that?" He smiled mischievously, his grey eyes full of humour. "They've got to handle me with kid gloves."

She laughed. "I love you, Sean Gallagher. You always make me feel good at the worst times."

"As a brother," he said. "You love me as a brother, as you often remind me, so keep your mad passion in your pocket, woman, and concentrate. Colonel Hugh Kelso, he said? An American army officer torpedoed off Devon?"

"That's right."

"And what was all that about how the Germans mustn't get their hands on him?"

"I don't know. He was half out of his mind and his leg's in a terrible state, but at the suggestion he might have to go to hospital he went crazy."

"A fine old mess from the sound of it," Gallagher said, and led the horse down onto the fog-shrouded beach.

Hugh Kelso lay face down on the sand, unconscious. Gallagher turned him over gently and examined the leg.

He gave a low whistle. "He needs a surgeon, this lad. I'll get him in the cart. You gather as much driftwood as you can, and hurry."

Helen ran along the beach and Gallagher lifted the groaning Kelso onto the sacks in the cart and draped a few of them across him. He turned as Helen came back with an armful of wood. "Cover him with that while I see to the life raft."

It was still bumping around in the shallows. He waded into the water, removed the emergency kit, then took out a spring-bladed gutting knife and slashed at the life raft's skin. As the air rushed out, he rolled it up and shoved it onto the rack underneath the cart.

"I'll stop in the paddock and we'll put the life raft down the old well. Let's get moving."

They started up the track, Helen sitting on the shaft of the cart, Sean leading the horse.

"Where do we take him?" she demanded. "There'll be no one at de Ville Place at the moment. I gave Mrs Vibert the day off. There's always the Chamber."

During the English civil war, Charles de Ville, the Seigneur of the manor at the time, had espoused the Royalist cause. He'd had a room constructed in the roof of de Ville Place, and it became known to the family over the years as the Chamber. It had saved de Ville's life during Cromwell's rule, when he was sought as a traitor.

"No, too awkward at the moment," said Sean. "He needs help, and quickly. We'll take him to my cottage first. Now, hang on while I get this life raft down the well."

He tugged it out and moved into the trees. Helen sat there, aware of the sound of her breathing in the silence of the wood. Behind her, under the sacking and the driftwood, Hugh Kelso groaned and stirred.

AT SLAPTON SANDS, just before noon, the tide turned and a few more bodies came in. Dougal Munro and Carter sat in the lee of a sand dune, having had an early lunch of sandwiches and beer.

Soldiers tramped along the shoreline, occasionally venturing into the water to pull in another body.

A young American officer approached and saluted. "Thirty-three since dawn, sir. No sign of Colonel Kelso." He hesitated. "Does the brigadier wish to view the burial arrangements?"

"No thank you," Munro said. "I think I can do without that."

The officer saluted and walked away. Munro got up and helped Carter to his feet. "Come on, Jack. I've got a bad feeling about this. A very bad feeling. Let's get back to London."

"SO, BERGER, you understand what I am saying to you?" Konrad Hofer demanded.

Heini Baum stood rigidly to attention in the office at Campeaux which had been loaned to the field marshal and his aide. Rommel stood at the window looking out into the garden.

"I'm not sure, Herr Major. I think so," Baum replied.

Rommel turned. "Don't be stupid, Berger. You're an intelligent man, and a brave one." He tapped the Iron Cross First Class with the tip of his baton. "I'm a plain man, so listen carefully. You did a very professional impersonation of me last night."

"Thank you."

"Now I require a second performance. On Friday, you will fly to Jersey for the weekend, accompanied by Major Hofer. You think you could fool them in Jersey for that long, Berger? Would you like that?"

Baum smiled. "Actually, I think I would, sir."

Rommel said to Hofer, "There you are. Sensible and intelligent, just as I told you. Now, make the arrangements, Konrad, and let's get out of here."

GALLAGHER'S COTTAGE on the de Ville Estate was built in the same kind of granite as the house. There was one large living room, with a beamed ceiling and a dining table and half a dozen chairs in a window alcove. The kitchen was on the other side of the hall. Upstairs, there was one large bedroom, a boxroom and a bathroom.

Gallagher had laid Kelso on the sofa in the living room. The American was still unconscious and Gallagher found his wallet and opened it. Inside were his security card, some snaps of a woman and two young girls, obviously his family, and a couple of personal letters. Kelso opened his eyes and noticed the wallet in Gallagher's hand.

"Who are you?" He grabbed at it weakly. "Give it back to me."

Helen came in and sat on the sofa and put a hand on his forehead. "It's all right. Just be still. You're burning up with fever. Remember me, Helen de Ville?"

He nodded slowly. "The woman on the beach."

"This is a friend, General Gallagher. Do you remember where you are?"

"Jersey." He managed a smile. "I'm not quite out of my mind, not yet anyway."

"All right, then listen to me," Sean said. "Your leg is very bad indeed. You need hospital and a good surgeon."

Kelso shook his head. "Not possible. As I told this lady earlier, no Germans. It would be better to shoot me than let them get their hands on me."

"Why?" Sean Gallagher demanded bluntly.

"She called you General. Is that true?"

"I was once in the Irish army, and I served with the Brits in the last war. Does that make a difference?"

"Perhaps."

"All right, what's your unit?"

"Engineers—assault engineers to be precise. We specialise in beach landings."

Sean Gallagher suddenly saw it all. "Is this something to do with the invasion?"

Kelso became extremely agitated. Helen soothed him, easing him down.

"It's all right, I promise you."

"Is George Hamilton coming?" Gallagher asked her.

"He was out when I telephoned. I spoke to his housekeeper and told her that you wanted to see him urgently. I said you'd cut your leg and thought it needed a stitch or two."

"Who's Hamilton?" Kelso demanded.

"A doctor," Helen said, "and a good friend. He'll be here soon to see to that leg of yours."

Kelso was shaking again as the fever took hold. "You must speak to your Resistance people here. Tell them to notify Intelligence in London that I'm here. They'll have to try and get me out."

"But there *is* no Resistance movement in Jersey," Helen said. "Nothing like the French Resistance, if that's what you mean."

Kelso stared at her in astonishment and Gallagher said, "This island is approximately ten miles by five. There are something like 45,000 civilians. The population of a good-size market town, that's all. How long do you think a Resistance movement would last here? No mountains to run to, nowhere to take refuge."

"Then what about France?" Kelso asked desperately. "Granville, St Malo? They're only a few hours away across the water, aren't they? There must be a local unit of the French Resistance in those places, surely?"

There was a pause, then Helen turned to Gallagher. "Savary could speak to the right people in Granville. He has contacts."

"True."

"Guido told me they are trying for Granville this afternoon. Taking advantage of the fog." She glanced at her watch. "They won't have the tide until noon. You could take the van. There are those sacks of potatoes to go into St Helier for the supply depot and the market."

"All right," Gallagher said. "But it's taking one hell of a chance."

"We don't have any choice, Sean," Helen said simply.

GALLAGHER DROVE through the tiny, picturesque town of St Aubin and followed the curve of the bay towards St Helier in the distance.

They only had the old Ford van as a special dispensation because the de Ville farmlands supplied crops for the use of the German forces. The size of the petrol ration meant the van could only be used two or three times a week, even if Gallagher stretched the petrol by acquiring a little black market fuel. He checked his watch. It was just before eleven. Plenty of time to catch Savary before the *Victor Hugo* left for Granville, so he turned left into Gloucester Street and made his way to the market.

There weren't too many people about, mainly because of the bad weather, and above the town hall entrance the scarlet and black Nazi flag with its swastika hung limply in the damp air. He parked outside the market in Beresford Street, took two sacks of potatoes from the van, kicked open the gate and went inside. He made straight for a stall on the far side where a large, genial man was arranging swedes in neat rows under a sign which read "D. Chevalier".

"So, it's swedes today?" Gallagher said as he arrived.

"They're good for you, General," Chevalier said.

"Is that so? Mrs Vibert gave me swede jam for breakfast the other day." Gallagher shuddered. "I can still taste it. Two sacks of spuds for you here."

Chevalier's eyes lit up. "I knew you wouldn't let me down, General. Let's have them in the back."

Gallagher dragged them round to the back of the stall and Chevalier opened a cupboard and took out an old canvas bag. "Four loaves of white bread."

"Goodness," Gallagher said. "Who did you kill to get those?"

"A quarter pound of china tea and a leg of pork. Okay?"

"Nice to do business with you," Gallagher said. "See you next week."

His next stop was at the troop supply depot in Wesley Street, where a burly Feldwebel (Sergeant) called Klinger was sitting in the glass office eating a sandwich. He waved, and came down the steps. "Herr General," he said genially.

"God, Hans, but you do well for yourself," Gallagher said, in excellent German, and prodded the ample stomach.

Klinger smiled. "A man must live."

"Some better than others," said Gallagher.

Klinger shrugged. "You have something for me?"

"Two sacks of potatoes for the official list and another sack for you, if you're interested."

"And in exchange?"

"Petrol."

The German nodded. "One five-gallon can."

"Two five-gallon cans," Gallagher said.

"You're so unreasonable." Klinger turned to a row of British army-issue petrol cans, picked two up and brought them to the van. "What if I turned you in?"

"Prison for me and a holiday for you," Gallagher said. "They say the Russian Front's lovely at this time of the year."

"As always, a practical man." Klinger pulled the three sacks of potatoes out of the van.

Survival was what it was all about, mused Gallagher as he drove away. This was an old island and, with his Jersey blood, he was fiercely proud of that. Over the centuries it had endured many things. As he passed German naval headquarters, he looked up at the Nazi flag hanging above the entrance and said softly, "And we'll still be here when you bastards are long gone."

CHAPTER 5

GALLAGHER parked the van at the weighbridge and walked along the Albert Pier. He looked down into the harbour. As always, it was a hive of activity. There were craft of various kinds, from Rhine barges to large minesweepers, and several cargo vessels, among them the SS *Victor Hugo*, were moored against the Pier.

Built in 1920, the *Victor Hugo* had definitely seen better days. Her single smokestack had been punctured in several places by cannon shell from RAF Beaufighters during an attack two weeks previously. Robert Savary was the master, with a crew of ten Frenchmen. The anti-aircraft defences consisted of two machine-guns and a Bofors gun, manned by seven German naval ratings commanded by Guido Orsini.

Gallagher walked towards the hut further along the pier which served as a café. It was not busy: four French seamen playing cards at one table, three German sailors at another. Robert Savary, a large, bearded man in a reefer coat and cloth cap, sat on his own.

"Robert, how goes it?" Gallagher demanded and sat down.

"Unusual to see you down here, *mon Général*. Which means you want something."

"Ah, you cunning old peasant." Gallagher passed an envelope under the table. "There, have you got that? Just put it in your pocket and don't ask questions. When you get to Granville, there's a bar in the walled city, called Sophie's. You know the good Sophie Cresson and her husband Gérard?"

Savary was already beginning to turn pale. "Yes, of course I do."

"Then you'll know that they not only shoot the *Boche*, but they also like to make an example of collaborators. So if I were you, I'd be sensible. Take the letter and give it to Sophie with my love. I'm sure she'll have a message for me."

"Damn you," Savary muttered, as he put the envelope in his pocket.

"You know my telephone number at the cottage. Ring me as soon as you get back."

Savary got up and they went outside.

"I'll be off then." Savary made a move to walk towards the gangway of the *Victor Hugo*.

Gallagher said softly, "Let me down on this one and I'll kill you, my friend. Understand?"

Savary turned, mouth open in astonishment, and Gallagher smiled cheerfully and walked away along the pier.

DR GEORGE HAMILTON was a tall, angular man whose old Harris tweed suit looked a size too large. At one time he had been a distinguished consultant at Guy's Hospital, but he had retired to a cottage in Jersey just before the outbreak of war.

He pushed a shock of white hair back from his forehead and stood looking down at Kelso on the sofa. "He should be in hospital. I really need an X-ray to be sure, but I'd say at least two fractures of the tibia. Possibly three."

"No hospital," Kelso said faintly.

Hamilton made a sign to Helen and Gallagher and they followed him into the kitchen. "As there is no open wound, no bone sticking through, it might be possible simply to set the leg and plaster it. Traction may not be necessary."

"Can you handle that?" Helen demanded.

"I could try, but I certainly wouldn't dream of proceeding without an X-ray." He hesitated. "There is one possibility. There's a little nursing home in St Lawrence, run by Catholic Sisters of Mercy. They have X-ray facilities and a decent operating theatre. Sister Maria Teresa, who's in charge, is a good friend. I could give her a ring."

"Do the Germans use it?" Helen asked.

"Now and then. Usually young women with prenatal problems, which is a polite way of saying they're in for an abortion. The nuns, as you may imagine, don't like that one little bit, but there isn't anything they can do about it."

Gallagher said, "You're taking one hell of a risk helping us like this, George."

"I'd say we all are," Hamilton told him dryly.

"It's vitally important that Colonel Kelso stays out of the hands of the enemy," Helen began.

Hamilton shook his head. "I don't want to know, Helen, and I don't want the nuns to be involved either. As far as they're concerned, our friend must be a local man. It would help if we had an identity card for him, just in case."

Gallagher went to a pine desk in the corner of the kitchen, pulled out the front drawer, then reached inside and produced a small box-drawer of the kind used to hide valuables. There were several blank identity cards in it, signed and stamped with the Nazi eagle.

"Where on earth did you get those?" Hamilton asked in astonishment.

"An Irishman I know, barman in one of the town hotels, has a German boyfriend, if you follow me. A clerk at the Feldkommandatur. I did him a big favour last year. He gave me these in exchange. I'll fill in Kelso's details and we'll give him a good Jersey name. How about Le Marquand?" He took out pen and ink and sat at the kitchen table. "Henry Ralph Le Marquand. Residence?" He looked up at Helen.

"Home Farm, de Ville Place," she said.

"Fair enough. I'll enter his occupation as fisherman. That way we can say it was a boating accident. And one more thing, George."

"What's that?" Hamilton asked, as he lifted the phone.

"I'm going with you."

HAMILTON STOOD in the operating theatre at the nursing home examining X-ray plates. "Three fractures," Sister Maria Teresa said. "He should be in hospital, doctor, but I don't need to tell you that."

"Sister," Hamilton said, "if he goes down to St Helier our German friends will want to know how it happened. And Le Marquand was fishing illegally when the accident took place."

Gallagher cut in, "Which could earn him three months in jail."

"I see." She shook her head. "I wish I had a bed to offer, but we're quite full."

"Any Germans about?"

"Two of their girlfriends," she said calmly. "The usual thing. One of the army doctors handled that yesterday. Major Speer."

"I've worked with him on occasion," Hamilton said. "I've known worse. Anyway, Sister, if you'd care to assist me, we'll get started."

She eased him into a robe and he went to scrub up at the sink in the corner. "A short term anaesthetic only. Chloroform on the pad will do." He moved to the operating table and looked down at Kelso. "All right?"

Kelso gritted his teeth and nodded. Hamilton said to Gallagher, "You'd better wait outside."

Gallagher turned to leave and at that moment the door opened and a German officer walked in.

"Ah, there you are, Sister," he said in French, then smiled and changed to English. "Doctor Hamilton, what a surprise."

"Major Speer," Hamilton replied, gloved hands raised.

"I've just looked in on my patients, Sister. Both doing well."

Speer was a tall, handsome man with a good-humoured, rather fleshy face. "Anything interesting, doctor?"

"Fractures of the tibia. An employee of General Gallagher here."

"I've heard of you, General. It's a pleasure to meet you." Speer moved to the X-rays and examined them. "Not good."

"I know hospitalisation and traction would be the norm," Hamilton said. "But there isn't a bed available."

"Oh, I should think it perfectly acceptable to set the bone and then plaster." Speer smiled with great charm and took off his great-coat. "But Herr Professor, this is hardly your field. It would be a pleasure to take care of this small matter for you."

He was already taking a gown down from a peg on the wall. "If you insist," Hamilton said calmly. "There's little doubt this is more your sort of thing than mine."

From the corner, Gallagher watched, fascinated.

SAVARY WASN'T feeling too pleased with life as he walked along the cobbled streets of the walled city in Granville. The trip from Jersey in the fog had been lousy and he was distinctly unhappy at the situation Gallagher had placed him in. He turned into a quiet square and walked slowly and reluctantly into Sophie's Bar.

Gérard Cresson sat in his wheelchair playing the piano, a small man with the white, intense face of an invalid. He'd broken his back in an accident two years before the war, and would never walk again.

There were a dozen or so customers scattered around the bar. Sophie sat on a high stool behind the marble counter, reading a newspaper. She was in her late thirties, dark hair piled high on her head, black eyes, face sallow, mouth painted bright red.

"Ah, Robert, it's been a long time. How goes it?"

"It could be worse, it could be better."

As she poured him a cognac, he slipped the letter across. "What's this?" she demanded.

"Your friend Gallagher uses me as a postman now. I don't know what's in it and I don't want to, but he expects an answer. We sail tomorrow at noon. I'll be back." He swallowed his cognac and left.

She came round the counter and called to one of the customers, "Hey, Marcel, look after the bar for me."

Her husband stopped playing and asked, "What was that all about?"

"Let's go in the back and find out."

She pulled his wheelchair from the piano, turned it and pushed him into the sitting room behind the bar.

Gérard Cresson sat at the table and read Gallagher's letter, then pushed it across to Sophie, his face grave.

She read it quickly. "He's in a real mess this time, our friend the General. Maybe the British will ask us to get this Yank out of Jersey."

"Difficult at the best of times," Gérard said. "Not possible with the state he's in. Take me to the storeroom. I must radio London."

MAJOR SPEER turned from the sink, towelling his hands, and crossed to the operating table. He looked down at the unconscious Kelso.

"An excellent piece of work," George Hamilton said.

"Yes, I must say I'm rather pleased with it myself." Speer reached for his greatcoat. "I'm sure you can handle the rest. I'm already late for dinner at the officers' club. Do let me know how he progresses, Herr Professor." He turned and went out.

Hamilton stood looking down at Kelso, who moaned a little as he started to come round and said softly, "Janet, I love you."

The American accent was unmistakable. Sister Maria Teresa glanced sharply at Hamilton and then at Gallagher.

"He seems to be coming round," Hamilton said lamely.

"So it would appear," she said. "Why don't you and General Gallagher go to my office. One of the sisters will get you some coffee. Sister Bernadette and I will put the cast on for you."

"That's very kind of you, Sister."

Gallagher and Hamilton went out and along the corridor to the office. Hamilton sat behind the desk and Gallagher gave him a cigarette and went and sat in the window seat.

"The moment when Speer came through the door will stay with me for ever," the Irishman said.

"He's not a bad sort," Hamilton said. "And he's a damn fine doctor."

"You think Kelso will be all right?"

"I don't see why not. We should be able to move him in an hour or so. We'll have to watch him closely for the next few days. The possibility of infection mustn't be discounted."

"Sister Maria Teresa—she knows things aren't what they seem."

"Yes, I feel bad about that," Hamilton said. "She won't tell, of course. It would be contrary to every belief she holds dear."

"She reminds me of my old aunt in Dublin when I was a lad," Gallagher said. "Incense, candles and Holy Water." He stood up. "I think I'll sample the night air for a while," and he opened the door and went out.

George Hamilton rested his head on his arms on the desk and yawned. It had been a long day.

IT WAS JUST after ten p.m. and Dougal Munro was still working away in his office when Jack Carter walked in, his face grim. He placed a signal on the brigadier's desk.

"Brace yourself, sir. Message just in from our Resistance contact in Granville."

Munro started to read and straightened up. "I don't believe it."

"I warned you, sir."

"It couldn't be worse. There isn't a Resistance movement in Jersey. No one to call on. This de Ville woman and the Gallagher man, how long can they manage, especially if he's ill?"

"You'll think of something, sir, you always do," Carter said gently.

"Thanks for the vote of confidence." Munro stood up and reached for his coat. "Now you'd better phone Hayes Lodge and get me an immediate appointment with General Eisenhower."

HELEN DE VILLE had been waiting anxiously for the sound of the van returning, and when it drove into the courtyard at the side of de Ville Place, she ran out. As Gallagher and Hamilton got out of the van, she cried, "Is he all right?"

"Still doped up, but the leg's doing fine," Gallagher told her.

"There's no one in at the moment. They're either at sea or at the officers' club, so let's get him upstairs."

Gallagher and Hamilton got Kelso out of the van and carried him across the wide panelled hall and up the great staircase. Helen opened the door of the master bedroom and led the way in. Beside the four-poster bed, carved shelving from wall to ceiling was crammed with books. Her fingers found a hidden spring and a section swung back to disclose a stairway. She led the way up and Gallagher and Hamilton followed with some difficulty, but finally made it to the room under the roof where there was a single bed under a window in the gable end.

They got Kelso onto the bed and Helen said to him, "The only entrance is from my room, so you should be quite safe."

"All I want to do is sleep," Kelso said, his face strained.

She nodded to Gallagher and the old doctor and they went downstairs.

Hamilton said, "I must be off. I'll look in tomorrow."

Gallagher took his hand for a moment. "George, you're quite a man."

"All in a doctor's day, Sean." Hamilton smiled. "I'll see you tomorrow.'

Gallagher went through to the kitchen. He was putting the kettle on the stove when Helen came in.

"Is Kelso all right?" he asked.

"Fast asleep already. Now what do we do?"

"Nothing we can do until Savary gets back from Granville with some sort of message. So sit down and have a nice cup of tea."

She shook her head. "We've a choice of either bramble or beet tea, and tonight I just can't face either."

"Oh, ye of little faith."

Gallagher produced the packet of china tea which Chevalier had given him that morning at the market.

She started to laugh helplessly, and put her arms round his neck. "Sean Gallagher, what would I do without you?"

EISENHOWER was in full uniform, for he'd been attending a dinner party with the prime minister when he'd received Munro's message. He paced up and down the library at Hayes Lodge. "Is there no way we can put someone in?"

"If you mean a commando unit, I don't think so, sir. It's the most heavily defended coast in Europe."

"For God's sake, Munro, everything could hang on this! The whole invasion. Months of planning."

Jack Carter, standing respectfully quiet by the fire, coughed. "There is one way, General."

"What's that, Captain?" Eisenhower enquired.

"The best place to hide a tree is in a wood. The people who are most free to come and go are the Germans themselves. I mean, new personnel must be posted there all the time."

Eisenhower turned sharply to Munro. "He's got a point. Have you got any people capable of that kind of work?"

Munro nodded. "Here and there, sir. It's a rare skill. Not just a question of speaking fluent German, but of thinking like a German too."

Eisenhower said, "I'll give you a week, Brigadier. One week and I expect you to have this matter resolved."

"My word on it, sir."

Munro walked out briskly, Carter following behind. "Radio Cresson in Granville and tell him to relay a message to Gallagher in Jersey saying someone will be there by Thursday. I must say, that was a masterly suggestion of yours, Jack," Munro said cheerfully.

"Thank you very much, sir."

"German personnel moving in and out all the time. What would one new arrival be among many?"

"It would take a very special man, sir."

"There's only one man for this job. You know it and I know it. Only one man capable of playing a Nazi to the hilt. *And* he's ruthless enough to put a bullet between Kelso's eyes if the worst comes to the worst. Harry Martineau."

"I must remind you, sir, that Colonel Martineau was given a promise that his services wouldn't be required again. His health alone would make it impossible."

"Nonsense, Jack. Harry could never resist a challenge. Find him. And another thing. Check SOE files. See if we've got anyone with a Jersey background."

CHAPTER 6

THE MORNING after Dougal Munro's meeting with Eisenhower, Harry Martineau was walking along the seashore not far from Lulworth Cove in Dorset, occasionally throwing stones into the incoming waves. He was forty-four, of medium height, with good shoulders under his old paratrooper's jacket. His face was pale, with the kind of skin that never seems to tan, his eyes so dark that it was impossible to say what their true colour was. His mouth was mobile, with a slight ironic smile permanently in place: the look of a man who found life more disappointing than he had hoped.

He'd been out of hospital for three months now. He didn't get the chest-pain any more, except when he overdid things, but the insomnia was terrible. He could seldom sleep at night. Too many years on the run, danger constantly at hand.

He was no use to Munro any more, the doctors had made that clear. He could have returned to Oxford, but that was no answer.

Neither was trying to pick up the threads of the book he'd been working on in 1939. So, he'd dropped out as thoroughly as a man could. The cottage above the cliffs, books to read, space to find himself in.

"And where the hell have you gone to, Harry?" he asked morosely as he started up the cliff path, "because I'm damned if I can find you."

"So HE'S IN Dorset, is he?" Munro said. "Doing what?"

"Not very much from what I can make out." Carter hesitated. "But sir, he did take two bullets in the left lung, during that business in Lyons . . ."

"No sad songs, Jack, I've other things on my mind. You've had a look at my ideas on a way of getting him into Jersey? What do you think?"

"Excellent, sir. I would have thought it was all pretty foolproof, at least for a few days."

"And that's all we need. Now, what else have you got for me?"

"As I understand it from your preliminary plan, sir, what you're seeking is someone to go in with him, to establish his credentials. Someone who knows the island and the people and so on?"

"That's right."

"Well, there's Sarah Anne Drayton, sir: age nineteen; born in Jersey; left the island just before the war to go out to Malaya where her father was a rubber planter. He sent her home a month before the fall of Singapore."

"Which means she hasn't been back in Jersey since when?" Munro looked at the file. "1938. Six years. That's a long time at that age, Jack. Girls change out of all recognition. So with luck no one will recognise her. Where did you find her?"

"She was put forward for SOE consideration two years ago, mainly because she speaks fluent French, with a Breton accent. Naturally, she was turned down then because of her youth."

"Where is she now?"

"Probationer nurse right here in London, at the Cromwell Hospital."

"Excellent." Munro stood up and reached for his jacket. "We'll go and see her."

BY EIGHT O'CLOCK on that Sunday evening, the casualty department at the Cromwell Hospital was working flat out. Sarah Drayton should have come off duty at six. She had now been on duty for fourteen hours without a break. She worked on, helping with casualties laid out in the corridors, trying to ignore the crump of bombs falling nearby, the sound of fire engines.

She was a small, intense girl, dark hair pushed up under her cap, her face very determined, hazel eyes serious. She helped the matron sedate a panic-stricken young girl who was bleeding badly from shrapnel wounds, and said, "I thought night raids were a thing of the past?"

"Tell that to the casualties," Matron said. "Right, clear off, Drayton. You'll be falling down soon from fatigue."

Sarah walked wearily along the corridor, aware that the sound of the bombing now seemed to have moved south of the river.

The night clerk was talking to two men. She said, "Actually, this is Nurse Drayton coming now."

Jack Carter said, "Miss Drayton, this is Brigadier Munro, and I'm Captain Jack Carter."

"What can I do for you?" Her voice was low and very pleasant. Munro was much taken with her at once.

Carter said, "Do you recall an interview you had two years ago? An intelligence matter?"

"With SOE?" She looked surprised. "I was turned down."

"Yes, well if you could spare us some time we'd like a word with you." Carter drew her over to a bench beside the wall and he and Munro sat on either side of her. "You were born in Jersey, Miss Drayton?"

"That's right."

He took out his notebook and opened it. "Do you by any chance know a Mrs Helen de Ville?"

"I should do. She's my mother's cousin, although she was always Aunt Helen to me."

"And Sean Gallagher?"

"The General? I've known him since I was a child."

"When did you last see him, or your aunt?" Munro asked.

"Nineteen thirty-eight. When my mother died my father took a job in Malaya and I went out to join him." She frowned at him for a moment. "What's this about?"

"It's quite simple really," Dougal Munro said. "I'd like to offer you a job with SOE. I'd like you to go to Jersey for me."

She stared at him in astonishment, but only for a moment and then she started to laugh helplessly, close to hysteria. It had, after all, been a long day. "But Brigadier," she said, "I hardly know you!"

"STRANGE CHAP, Harry Martineau," Munro said. "I've never known anybody quite like him."

"From what you tell me, neither have I," Sarah said.

The car taking them down to Lulworth the next day was a huge Austin, with a glass partition separating them from the driver. Munro and Carter were in the back, side by side, and Sarah Drayton was sitting on the jump-seat opposite. She was wearing a tweed suit, black brogues and a cream blouse with a black string tie at the neck. She looked extremely attractive, cheeks flushed, eyes flickering everywhere. She also looked extremely young.

"It was his birthday the week before last," Carter told her.

She was immediately interested. "How old was he?"

"Forty-four."

"What they call a child of the century," Munro told her. "Born on the 7th of April 1900."

"Aries," she said.

Munro smiled. "That's right. Before the advent of our so-called enlightened times astrology was a science. Did you know that? The

Ancient Egyptians always chose their generals from Leos, for example."

"I'm a Leo," she said. "27th of July."

"Then you *are* in for a complicated life. Something of a hobby of mine. Take Harry, for instance. Very gifted, professor at Oxford at thirty-eight. Then look at what he became in middle life."

"How do you explain that?" she demanded.

"Well, Aries is a warrior sign, but very commonly those born around the same time as Harry are one thing on the surface and something else underneath. On one level, you're Harry Martineau, scholar, philosopher, poet, full of sweet reason, but on the dark side . . ." He shrugged. "Cold and ruthless. Yes, there's a curious lack of emotion to him, wouldn't you agree, Jack?"

Carter said, "Just in case you're getting a rather bad impression of Harry Martineau, two things, Sarah. Although his mother was born in the States, she was of German parentage and Harry spent a lot of time with his grandparents in Dresden as he grew up. His grandfather, who was a professor of surgery, died in a fall from the balcony of his apartment. A nasty accident."

"Aided by two Gestapo thugs taking an arm and a leg each to help him on his way," Munro put in.

"And then there was a Jewish girl named Rosa Bernstein. Harry met Rosa when she did a year at Oxford in 1932. Both his parents were dead. His father had left him reasonably well off and as an only child, he had no close relatives."

"But he and Rosa never married?"

"No," Munro said. "You'll often find prejudice on both sides of the fence, my dear. Rosa's parents were Orthodox Jews and they didn't like the idea of their daughter marrying a Gentile."

"What happened?"

It was Carter who answered. "She was active in the socialist underground. Went backwards and forwards from England to Germany as a courier. In May 1938 she was apprehended by the Gestapo. She was brutally interrogated and executed."

There was a long silence. Sarah seemed abstracted, staring out of the window into the distance. "So Harry Martineau doesn't particularly care for Germans?" she said, finally.

"He doesn't like Nazis. There's a difference."

She felt on edge, and it was all to do with Martineau, this man she had never met. He filled her mind. Would not go away.

"One thing we didn't ask," Carter interrupted. "I hope you don't mind my being personal, but is there anyone in your life at the moment? Anyone who would miss you?"

"A man? Good heavens, no! I never work less than a twelve hour shift at the Cromwell. That leaves just about enough time to have a bath and a meal before falling into bed." She shook her head. "No one to miss me at all. I'm all yours, gentlemen." She delivered the speech with an air of bravado and calm sophistication that was strangely moving in one so young.

Munro, unusually for him, felt uncomfortable. "This mission is important, believe me." He leaned forward, put a hand on her arm. "We wouldn't ask you if it wasn't."

She nodded. "I know, Brigadier, I know." She turned and stared out of the window again at the passing scenery.

HARRY MARTINEAU awoke that morning with a dull headache. Only one answer to that. He pulled on an old tracksuit, grabbed a towel and ran down to the sea.

He stripped and ran out through the shallows, plunging into the waves. The sky was slate grey and there was rain in the wind, yet quite suddenly he experienced one of those special moments. Sea and sky seemed to become one for a little while. Nothing mattered. Not the past nor the future. Only this present moment. As he turned on his back in the water, it started to rain.

A voice called, "Enjoying yourself, Harry?"

Martineau turned towards the shore and saw Munro standing there in an old tweed coat and battered hat, holding an umbrella over his head. "My God!" he said. "Not you, Dougal?"

"As ever was, Harry. Come on up to the cottage. There's someone I'd like you to meet."

Munro turned and walked back across the beach; Martineau floated for a while, thinking about it. Dougal Munro wasn't just paying a social call, that was for sure, not all the way from London. Excitement surged through him and he waded out of the water. He towelled himself briskly, pulled on the old tracksuit and ran across the beach and up the cliff path. When he reached the cottage, Jack Carter was standing in the porch.

"What, you too, Jack?" Martineau smiled and took the other man's hand. "Does the old devil want me to go back to work?"

"Something like that." Carter hesitated, then said, "Harry, I think you've done enough."

"No such word in my vocabulary, Jack." Martineau brushed past him and went inside.

Munro was sitting by the fire, reading a notepad he'd found on the table. "Still writing bad poetry?"

"Always did." Martineau took the pad from him, tore off the top sheet, crumpled it up and tossed it into the fireplace. Then he became aware of Sarah Drayton standing in the kitchen doorway.

"I'm making tea. I hope that's all right, Colonel Martineau. I'm Sarah Drayton." She didn't hold out her hand, for it would have trembled too much. Her stomach was hollow with excitement.

At first he responded, his face illuminated by a smile of great natural charm. Then the smile faded and he turned to Munro with anger in his voice. "My God, Dougal. You're using schoolgirls now?"

"THE OTHER month we knocked off a man called Braun in Paris," Munro said. "Jack has the details. I think you'll find it all very interesting."

"What was he, Gestapo?" Martineau asked.

"No, SD." Carter turned to Sarah Drayton sitting on the other side of the fire. "That's the Secret Intelligence Department of the SS, responsible only to Himmler himself."

"Go on about Braun," Martineau said.

"Well, according to his papers, he was a member of Himmler's personal staff." He passed a piece of paper to Martineau. "It seems

Braun was a kind of roving ambassador, empowered to make his own investigations wherever he pleased. Read that letter."

Martineau took it. The heading was embossed in black:

DER REICHSFÜHRER – SS   Berlin, 9 November 1943
SS–Sturmbannführer BRAUN Erwin, SS-Nr 107863

This officer acts under my personal orders on business of the utmost importance to the Reich. All personnel, military and civil, must assist him in any way he sees fit.

H. Himmler

A remarkable document in itself. Even more astonishing was that it was countersigned across the bottom by Adolf Hitler himself.

"He obviously had a certain amount of influence," Martineau said dryly, handing it back to Carter.

"Well, he's dead now, but our Paris people got some useful information out of him."

"I bet they did," Martineau said, and lit a cigarette.

"Himmler has a dozen or so of these special envoys floating around Europe, putting the fear of God into everyone wherever they turn up. All highly secret. Nobody knows who they are. I've got the forgery department preparing a complete set of papers for you, including an SD identity card and a copy of that letter. Name of Max Vogel. We thought we'd give you a little rank, so it's Standartenführer." Munro turned to Sarah. "Colonel to you."

"I get the picture," Martineau said. "I arrive in Jersey and frighten the hell out of everyone."

"You must admit you do a very good Nazi, Harry."

"And Sarah?" Martineau enquired. "Where does she fit in?"

"You need someone with you to establish your credentials with Mrs de Ville and this chap Gallagher. Sarah is related to one and knows the other. Another thing, she was last in Jersey six years ago, aged thirteen, all plaits and ankle socks, I shouldn't wonder. Helen de Ville and Gallagher might still recognise her, but she'll pass as a stranger among other people, especially when we've finished with her."

"And what's that supposed to mean?"

"Well, there's a fair trade in ladies of the night between France and Jersey."

"You're not suggesting she plays a French tart?"

"Most senior German officers in France have French girlfriends. Why should you be any different? Sarah speaks excellent French with a Breton accent. By the time our people at Berkley Hall have finished with her, changed her hair colour, her clothes . . ."

"And when are we supposed to go in?"

"Thursday. A Lysander drop near Granville, in Normandy. Afterwards, you will use your authority to cross to Jersey on one of the night boats. Once over there, you've got till Sunday at the outside."

"And what if it's impossible to get him out?"

"Up to you. I'll back whatever you decide to do."

"I see. I play executioner for you again?" He turned on Sarah. "What do you think about all this?"

He was angry, his face whiter than ever, his eyes very dark. Yet Sarah still remained calm. "Oh, I don't know," she said. "It sounds as if it could be rather exciting."

He opened his mouth as if to speak, then changed his mind, turned and poured himself a Scotch instead. He raised his glass and toasted them all. "Here we go then. Berkley Hall next stop."

CHAPTER 7

THE INDOOR firing range at Berkley Hall was in the basement. The armourer was an Irish Guards staff sergeant named Kelly. The place was brightly lit at the target end, where cutout replicas of charging Germans stood against sandbags. Kelly and Sarah Drayton were the only people on the firing line. They'd given her battledress to wear, slacks and blouse of blue serge, the kind issued to girls in the Women's Auxiliary Air Force. She'd tucked her hair up inside the peaked cap, leaving her neck bare. It somehow made her look very vulnerable.

Kelly had various weapons laid out on the table. "Have you ever fired a handgun before, miss?"

"Yes," she said. "In Malaya. My father was a rubber planter. He used to be away a great deal so he made sure I knew how to use a revolver."

"That's good. Obviously in more normal circumstances you'd be given a thorough grounding in weaponry as part of your course, but in your case, there just isn't time. What I'll do is familiarise you with some basic weapons you're likely to come across. Then you can fire a few rounds."

He went through the submachine-guns with her, then the hand-guns, both revolvers and automatics. When she tried with a Smith & Wesson, arm extended, she only managed to nick the shoulder of the target once out of six shots.

"I'm afraid you'd be dead, miss."

As he reloaded, she said, "What about Colonel Martineau? Is he any good?"

"You could say that, miss. I don't think I've ever known anyone better with a handgun. Now, try this way." He crouched, feet apart, holding the gun two-handed. "See what I mean?"

"I think so." She copied him, the gun out in front of her in both hands.

"Now squeeze, with a half breath of a pause between each shot."

This time she did better, hitting the target once in the shoulder and once in the left hand.

"Terrific," Kelly said.

"Not if you consider she was probably aiming for the heart."

Martineau had come in quietly behind them. He wore a dark polo-neck sweater and black corduroy pants. "As I'm going to have to look after this infant, and as time is limited, do you mind if I take a hand?"

"Be my guest, sir."

Martineau picked up a pistol from the table. "Walther PPK, semi-automatic. Seven-round magazine goes in the butt, like so. Pull the slider back and you're in business. It's not too large, but it's a man-stopper. Now come down the range."

They moved so close that the targets were no more than ten yards away.

"You should never be further away than you are now. Simply throw up your arm and point the gun at him. Keep both eyes open and fire very fast."

She hit the target six times in the general area of the chest and belly. "Oh, my word," she said, very excited. "That wasn't bad, was it?"

As they walked back to the firing line he said, "Yes, but could you do it for real?"

"I'll only know when the time comes, won't I? Anyway, what about you? The Brigadier told me you were ruthless. Are you?"

There was another Walther on the table with a round cylinder of polished black steel screwed on to the end of the barrel. "This is what's called a Carswell Silencer," Martineau told her, ignoring her question. "Specially designed for use by SOE agents."

His arm swung up. He didn't appear to take aim. He fired twice, shooting out the eyes of his target. The only sound had been two dull thuds and the effect was quite terrifying.

He laid the gun down and turned, eyes blank in the white face. "I've got things to do. Dougal wants us in the library in half an hour. I'll see you then." He walked out.

There was an awkward silence. Sarah said to Kelly, "He seemed angry."

"The Colonel gets like that, miss. I don't think he likes what he sees in himself sometimes. Last November he killed the head of the Gestapo in Lyons. Man called Kaufmann. A real butcher. Colonel Martineau took two bullets in his left lung before he got away. They brought him back from there in a puddle of blood, in a Lysander. He's been different since then."

"In what way?"

"I don't know, miss." Kelly frowned. "Here, don't go getting silly ideas about him. I know what you young girls can be like. Just remember he's got twenty-five years on you."

"You mean he's too old?" Sarah said. "Isn't that like saying you can't love someone because they're Catholic or Jewish or something? What's the difference?"

"Too clever for me, that kind of talk." Kelly opened a drawer and took out a cloth bundle which he unwrapped. "A little present for you, miss." It was a small black automatic pistol, very light, almost swallowed up in her hand. "Belgian. Only .25, but it'll do the trick when you need it." He looked awkward.

She reached up and kissed him on the cheek. "I think you're wonderful."

"You can't do that, miss, you being an officer. It's against regulations."

"But I'm not an officer, Sergeant."

"I think you'll find you are, miss. Probably one of the things the Brigadier wants to tell you. I'd go to the library now, if I were you."

MUNRO, CARTER and Martineau were already in the library at Berkley Hall having afternoon tea when Sarah· went in.

"Ah, there you are," Munro said. "Do join us."

As Carter poured her a cup of tea, Sarah said, "Sergeant Kelly said something about my being an officer now. What was he talking about?"

"Yes, well, we do prefer our women operatives to hold some sort of commissioned rank. In theory it's supposed to help you if you fall into enemy hands," Munro told her.

"In practice, it doesn't do you any good at all," Martineau interrupted.

"However, for good or ill, you are now a flight officer in the WAAF," Munro said. "Now, let's look at the map."

They all got up and went to a table where several large-scale maps were spread out, making a patchwork that included the south of England, the Channel Islands, Normandy and Brittany.

"The flight will take no more than an hour and a half," Munro explained. He indicated a spot on the coast of Normandy. "You'll land not far from Granville and the local Resistance people will be on hand to take care of you. We find the early hours of the morning best. Say four or five o'clock."

"Then what?" Sarah asked.

"The evening of the same day, you'll leave Granville by ship for Jersey. Most German convoys go by night." He turned to Martineau. "Naturally, the question of passage is a matter for you, in your role as Standartenführer Max Vogel. I doubt whether anyone is likely to do anything other than run round in circles when they see your credentials." Martineau nodded.

"As regards your dealings with Mrs de Ville and General Gallagher, well, you have Sarah to vouch for you."

Munro picked up the phone at his side. "Send Mrs Moon in now." He put the phone down and said to Sarah, "We're very lucky to have Mrs Moon. We borrow her from Denham film studios. There's nothing she doesn't know about make-up, dress and so on."

Hilda Moon, when she arrived moments later, was a large, overweight woman with a Cockney accent who wore too much lipstick.

"Yes." She nodded, walking round Sarah. "Very nice. Of course, I'll have to do something with the hair."

"Do you think so?" Sarah asked in alarm.

"Girls who make a living from pleasing men, the way you're supposed to do in this part, dear, have to make the best of what they've got. You trust me, I know what's best for you." She took Sarah by the arm and led her out.

As the door closed, Martineau said, "We probably won't recognise her when we see her again."

"No." Munro smiled. "But that's the general idea."

IT WAS EARLY that same evening when the phone rang in Sean Gallagher's cottage. He was in the kitchen, working through farm accounts, and answered it instantly.

A familiar voice said "Savary here. The matter of the package we discussed."

"Yes."

"My contact in Granville was in touch with head office. It seems someone will be with you by Thursday, to give you the advice you need."

"You're certain of that?"

"Absolutely."

The phone went dead. Gallagher sat thinking for a moment, then put on his old corduroy jacket and went up to de Ville Place.

AS MRS MOON worked on Sarah, she talked incessantly. "I've been everywhere. Denham, Elstree, Pinewood. I do all Miss Margaret Lockwood's make-up and Mr James Mason's. Now he *is* a real gentleman."

When Sarah came out from under the dryer, she couldn't believe what she saw. Her dark hair was golden blonde and marcelled tight against her face. Then Mrs Moon started with the make-up. "Plenty of rouge, dear. A little too much, if you know what I mean, and lots of lipstick. Now, what do you think?"

Sarah sat looking into the mirror. It was the face of a stranger.

"We'll try one of the dresses. Of course, the underwear and every individual item will be of French origin, but you only need the dress at the moment, just for the effect."

It was black satin, very tight and rather short. She helped Sarah into it and zipped it at the back.

Sarah pulled on a pair of high-heeled shoes and looked at herself in the mirror. She giggled. "I look the most awful tart."

"Well, that's the idea, love. Go and see what the brigadier thinks."

Munro and Carter were still sitting in the library talking in low tones, when she went in.

It was Carter who looked up first. "Good God!" he said.

Munro was far more positive. "I like it. Like it very much indeed. Yes, they'll go for you in the German officers' club in St Helier."

The door opened and Martineau entered. She turned to face him, hands on hips in a deliberate challenge. "Well?" she demanded.

"Well, what?"

She sighed in exasperation. "You can be a most infuriating man, Colonel Martineau. Is there a village near here with a pub?"

"Yes."

"Will you take me for a drink?"

"Like that?"

"You mean I don't look nice enough?"

"Actually, you transcend all Mrs Moon's efforts. You couldn't be a tart if you tried. I'll see you in the hall in fifteen minutes." He turned and went out.

THE BAR WAS crowded but they managed to find a couple of seats in the corner by the fire and he ordered her a shandy and had a Scotch himself. "Well, what do you think of it so far?" he asked.

"It makes a change from the wards at the Cromwell."

"In other circumstances you'd be trained for about six weeks," he said. "The Scottish Highlands to toughen you up; courses in unarmed combat and so on; twelve days of killing someone with your bare hands."

"That sounds very gruesome. Can you do that sort of thing?"

"Anybody can be taught to do it. It's brains that are important in this game."

"But you don't hesitate, do you? I noticed that in the firing range this afternoon. I think I understand now what the brigadier meant about you being ruthless. You have an aptitude for killing."

"Words," he said. "Games in the head, that's all I had for years. Nothing but talk, nothing but ideas. Let's have some facts. Let's stop playing games in black satin dresses with our hair bleached. You know what the first technique is that the Gestapo employ in breaking down any woman agent who falls into their hands? Multiple rape. If that doesn't do the trick, the electric shock treatment comes next. I used to have a girlfriend in Berlin. She was Jewish."

"I know. Carter told me about her."

"How they tortured her, then murdered her in the Gestapo cellars?" Martineau shook his head. "He doesn't know everything. He doesn't know that the head of the Gestapo in Lyons, whom I killed last November, was the man responsible for Rosa's death in Berlin in 1938."

"I see now," she said softly. "You hated that Gestapo chief for years and when you finally took your revenge, you found it meant nothing."

"All this wisdom." He laughed coldly. "All I've learned for certain is that going over there and taking on the Gestapo isn't like one of those movies they make at Elstree studios. There are fifty million people in France. You know how many we estimate are active members of the Resistance?"

"No."

"Two thousand, Sarah. Two lousy thousand." He was disgusted. "I don't know why we bother."

"Then why do you? Not just for Rosa, or your grandfather."

He turned briefly and she said, "Oh, yes, they told me about him, too."

There was a silence. "It's something I've never talked about," Martineau began. "I was due to go to Harvard in 1917. Then America joined the war. I joined up on sheer impulse and ended in the trenches in Flanders." He shook his head. "Whatever you mean by hell on earth, that was the trenches."

"It must have been terrible," she said.

"And I loved every minute of it. Can you understand that? I lived more in one day, felt more, than in a year of ordinary living. Life became real, bloody, exciting. I couldn't get enough."

"Like a drug?"

"Exactly. That was what I ran away from, back to Harvard and Oxford and the safe world of classrooms and books."

"And now the war has come round again."

"Yes, and Dougal Munro has yanked me back out into the real world. The rest, as they say in the movies, you know."

CHAPTER 8

THE FOLLOWING day just after noon at Fermanville on the Cherbourg peninsula, Karl Hagan, the duty sergeant at the central strong point of the 15th Coastal Artillery Battery, was idly leaning on a parapet in the sunshine when he observed a black Mercedes coming up the track. No escort, so it wouldn't be anyone important, and then he noticed the pennant fluttering on the bonnet. He was inside the operation room in a flash, where Captain Reimann, the battery commander, sprawled at his desk reading a book.

"Someone coming, sir. Looks like top brass to me. Surprise inspection perhaps."

"Right. Klaxon alarm. Get the men to fall in, just in case."

Reimann buttoned his tunic and adjusted his cap to a satisfactory angle. As he went out on the redoubt, the Mercedes pulled in below. The driver got out, followed by an army major with staff stripes on his trousers. The next man out was Field Marshal Erwin Rommel, in leather trenchcoat, white scarf knotted carelessly at his neck, desert goggles pulled up above the peak of his cap.

Reimann had never been so shocked in his life. As he hurried down the steps he heard Sergeant Hagan's voice, and the battery personnel started to run out into the courtyard below, to take up their positions.

Reimann moved towards Rommel and saluted. "Herr Field Marshal. You do us a great honour."

Rommel tapped the end of his field marshal's baton against the peak of his cap. "Your name?"

"Reimann, Herr Field Marshal."

"Major Hofer, my aide." Rommel indicated the man at his side.

Hofer said, "The field marshal will see everything, including the subsidiary strong points. Please lead the way."

"First, Major, I'll inspect the troops," Rommel told him. "An army is only as strong as its weakest point, always remember that."

"Of course, Herr Field Marshal," Hofer said.

Rommel moved down the line of soldiers, stopping here and there. Finally he turned. "Good turnout. Highly satisfactory. Now we will go."

For the next hour he tramped the cliff top from one strong point to another as Reimann led the way. Radio rooms, men's quarters, ammunition stores. Nothing escaped his attention.

"Excellent, Reimann," he told the artillery officer. "First-rate performance. I'll endorse your field unit report personally."

Reimann almost fainted with pleasure. He called the honour guard to attention. Rommel tapped the baton against his cap again and got into the Mercedes. Hofer joined him on the other side and as they were driven away, checked that the glass partition separating them from the driver was tightly closed.

"Excellent," Hofer said. "I think you carried that off very well, Berger."

"Really, Herr Major?" Heini Baum said. "I get the booking then?"

"One more test, I think. Something a little bit more ambitious. Dinner at some officers' mess, perhaps. Then you'll be ready for Jersey. Now, back to the field marshal to report."

WHEN SARAH and Harry Martineau went into the library at Berkley Hall on the evening of their departure, Jack Carter was sitting with the maps spread before him.

"Ah, there you are," he said. "Brigadier Munro has gone up to London to report to General Eisenhower, but he'll be back tonight to see you off. Here are your papers, Sarah. Ration cards. French identity card with photo." He handed her a slip of paper. "There are your personal details. Your name is Anne-Marie Latour. We've kept to your own age and birth date. Born in Brittany, naturally, to explain your accent. We've made your place of birth Paimpol, on the coast. I believe you know it well?"

"Yes, my grandmother lived there. I spent many happy holidays with her."

"One more thing. Your relationship with Standartenführer Vogel must at all times seem convincing. You do appreciate what that could entail?"

"Sharing a room?" She smiled. "No problem, Captain."

"All right. Then read this, both of you. Regulations, Sarah."

It was a typical SOE operations order, in cold, no-nonsense language. It laid out the task ahead of them, procedure, communication channel via the Cressons in Granville. There was a code name for the operation: JERSEYMAN. At the end of the flimsy it said, NOW DESTROY.

Martineau struck a match and touched it to the paper, dropping it into the ashtray. "That's it then," he said. "I'll go and do my packing. See you later, Sarah."

On the bed in his room, the wardrobe people had laid out a three-piece suit in light grey tweed, shoes, some white shirts, two black ties. There was also a military overcoat in soft black leather, of a kind worn by many SS officers.

The grey-green SS uniform hung behind the door. He checked it carefully. On the left sleeve was the RFSS cuff-title of Himmler's personal staff, an SD patch above it. The oak leaves of his collar patches indicating his rank were in silver thread.

He decided to try it on. Everything fitted to perfection. He picked up the cap and examined the silver death's head badge, running his sleeve across it. He put it on his head at a slight angle. From behind, Sarah said quietly, "I get the feeling you like uniforms."

"I like getting it right," he said. "It's important, Sarah. You don't get second chances."

There was a kind of distress on her face and she moved close and gripped his arm. "I'm not sure if it's you any more, Harry."

"It isn't, not in this uniform. It's Standartenführer Max Vogel, of the SD. Feared by his own side as much as the French. You'll see. This isn't a game any more."

She shivered. "I know, Harry, I know."

HORNLEY FIELD had been an aero club before the war. It was now used for clandestine flights to the continent, mainly Lysanders and the occasional Liberator. The commanding officer was a Squadron Leader Barnes, an ex-fighter pilot.

It was two thirty in the morning but warm enough in a hut near the runway where a stove was roaring away.

"Can I offer you some more coffee?" Barnes asked Sarah.

She turned and smiled. "No thanks."

Martineau stood by the stove, hands in the pockets of his leather trenchcoat. He wore the tweed suit and a dark slouch hat.

"You're going to have to get moving, I'm afraid," Barnes said. "Just the right conditions at the other end if you go now. Too light if you wait."

"I can't imagine what's happened to the brigadier," Carter said.

"It doesn't matter." Martineau turned to Sarah. "Ready to go?"

She nodded and carefully pulled on her leather gloves. She was wearing a black coat nipped in at the waist with wide shoulders, all very fashionable.

Martineau picked up their two suitcases and they went out and crossed to the Lysander where the pilot, Flight Lieutenant Green, waited. "Any problems?" Martineau asked.

"Coastal fog, but only in patches. Slight headwind." Green glanced at his watch. "We'll be there by four thirty at the outside."

Sarah went first and strapped herself in. Martineau passed up the suitcases then shook hands with Carter. "See you soon, Jack."

"You've got the call sign," Carter said. "All Cresson has to do is send that. No message needed. We'll have a Lysander out to the same field at ten p.m. on the same day to pick you up."

Martineau climbed in next to Sarah and fastened his seat belt. He didn't look at her, but he took her hand as Green climbed into the pilot's seat and the sound of the engines shattered the night. They taxied to the end of the runway. As they started to roll between the twin lines of lights, gradually increasing speed, an Austin turned in through the main gate, hesitated for the sentry's inspection, then bumped across the grass towards the hut. As

Dougal Munro got out, the Lysander lifted over the trees at the far end of the field.

"Damnation!" he said. "Held up at Baker Street, Jack. Something came up. Thought I'd just make it."

"They couldn't wait, sir," Barnes told him. "Might have made things difficult at the other end."

"Of course," Munro said.

Barnes walked away and Munro said, "The ball's in Harry Martineau's court now. All up to him."

"And Sarah Drayton, sir."

"Yes. I liked that young woman." Aware suddenly that he had spoken in the past tense, Munro shivered, as if at an omen.

THE FLIGHT was uneventful, mainly because Green was an old hand, with more than forty such sorties under his belt. When the Lysander crossed over the Cherbourg peninsula, he turned the plane slightly towards the south, and spoke over the intercom. "Fifteen minutes, so be ready."

"Any chance of running into a night fighter?" Martineau asked.

"Unlikely. There's a maximum effort strike by bomber command on various towns in the Ruhr tonight. Jerry will have scrambled every night fighter in France to go and protect the Fatherland."

"Look!" Sarah cut in. "I can see lights."

"That's it," Green told them. "I've landed here twice before, so I know my stuff. In and out very fast. You know the drill, Colonel."

And then they were drifting down over the trees into the meadow. As they rolled to a halt, Sophie Cresson ran forward, waving. She held a Sten gun in one hand. Martineau got the door open, threw out the suitcases and jumped down. He turned to help Sarah, while behind her, Green slammed the door shut, locking the handle.

The engine note deepened to a full-throated roar as the Lysander raced across the meadow and took off.

Sophie Cresson gathered up the three torches which she had used as landing lights, and said, "Come on, let's get out of here.

Bring your suitcases." They followed her to an old Renault van and she opened the rear door. In the back were several dead chickens and a few pheasants.

"There's just enough room for both of you. Don't worry, I know every *flic* [policeman] in the district. If they stop me, all they'll do is take a chicken and go home."

"Some things never change," Sarah said.

"Hey, Breton girl?" Sophie flashed her torch on Sarah's face and grunted. "My God, now they send little girls." She shrugged. "In you get and let's be out of here."

Sarah crouched among the dead fowl, her knees touching Martineau's as Sophie drove away. So, this is it, she thought, the real thing. No more games now. She opened her handbag and felt for the butt of the little automatic pistol that Kelly had given her. Would she be able to use it if necessary? Only time would tell. She leaned back against the side of the van feeling wonderfully, marvellously alive.

IT WAS NOON before she woke, yawning and stretching her arms. The small bedroom under the roof was plainly furnished, but comfortable. She threw back the sheets and crossed to the window. The view of Granville harbour was really quite special. Behind her the door opened and Sophie came in with a pot of coffee on a tray.

"So you're up."

"It's good to be back." Sarah took the tray from her and sat on the window seat.

"You've been here before?" Sophie asked.

"Many times. My mother was half-Jersey, half-Breton. I used to come over to Granville from Jersey when I was a little girl. There was a fishermen's café on the quay that had the most wonderful hot rolls."

"Not any more," Sophie said. "The war has changed everything. Look down there." The harbour was crammed with shipping: Rhine barges, three coasters and a number of German naval craft.

"They're definitely sailing for the islands tonight?" Sarah asked.

"Oh yes. Some for Jersey, the rest, on to Guernsey. Now, get dressed and come downstairs and we'll have lunch."

AT GAVRAY, in what had once been the country house of the count of that name, Heini Baum sat at one end of the table in the officers' mess of the 41st Panzer Grenadiers and smilingly acknowledged the cheers as the officers toasted him. When they were finished, the young colonel of the regiment said, "If you could manage a few words, Herr Field Marshal? It would mean so much to my officers."

There was a worried look in Hofer's eyes, but Baum disregarded it and stood up, straightening his tunic. "Gentlemen, the Führer has given us a simple task. To keep the enemy off our beaches. Yes, I say *our* beaches. Europe, one and indivisible, is our goal. There is no possibility of losing. The destiny of the Führer is God-given. So much is obvious to anyone with a grain of sense." His irony was lost on them as they gazed up, enraptured. He raised his glass. "So, gentlemen, to our beloved Führer, Adolf Hitler."

"Adolf Hitler!" they chorused.

Baum tossed his glass into the fire and with a stirring of excitement, they all did the same. Then they applauded again, forming two lines as he walked out, followed by Hofer.

"Rather heavy on the glasses, I should have thought," Hofer said, as they drove back to Cressy, where Rommel had established temporary headquarters at the old castle.

"You didn't approve?" Baum said.

"I didn't say that. Actually, the speech was rather good. It was exactly what they wanted to hear."

Crazy, Baum thought. Am I the only sane man left alive?

They drew into the courtyard of the castle and he went up the steps fast, acknowledging the salutes. Hofer trailed him all the way up to the suite on the first floor.

Rommel had locked himself in his study and only came out when he heard Hofer's knock. "How did it go?"

"Perfect," Hofer said. "He passed with flying colours. You should have heard the speech you made."

"Excellent." Rommel nodded. "Everything progresses in the Channel Islands? You spoke to von Schmettow in Guernsey?"

"Personally, Herr Field Marshal."

"Good." Rommel frowned. "One thing occurs to me. You and Berger flying in with all that RAF superiority in the area." He turned to Baum. "What do you think about that, Berger?"

"I think it could be interesting if the Herr Major and I went down in flames into the sea. The Desert Fox is dead." He shrugged. "That could lead to some strange possibilities, Herr Field Marshal."

GÉRARD CRESSON sat in his wheelchair in the sitting room and refilled the glasses with red wine. "I hate to dispel your illusions," he said to Sarah, "but out on Jersey, just as in France and every occupied country in Europe, the real enemy is the informer. Without them the Gestapo couldn't operate."

"But I was told that there was no Gestapo in Jersey," Sarah said.

"Officially they have a Geheime Feld Polizei set-up there. That's the Secret Field Police, and they're controlled by the Abwehr. Military Intelligence. The whole thing is part of the ruling-by-kindness policy, a cosmetic exercise aimed at fooling the people. The implication is 'because you're British we won't stick the Gestapo onto you'."

"Which is rubbish," Sophie put in, "because several of the GFP men in Jersey are Gestapo operatives on secondment."

"Mind you," Gérard added, "Here on Jersey it's a Mickey Mouse operation compared to what goes on in Lyons or Paris, but watch out for a Captain Muller. He's in command, and his chief aide's an inspector called Kleist."

"Are they SS?" Martineau asked.

"I don't know. Probably not. They're probably seconded from the police in some big city. Full of themselves, like all *flics*. Out to prove something." He shrugged. "You don't have to be in the SS to be in the Gestapo."

"True," Martineau said. "Anyway, how do you rate our chances of bringing Kelso over from Jersey?"

"It will be difficult. They are very tight on civilian traffic. It would be impossible in a small boat at the moment."

"And if he can't walk ..." Sophie shrugged expressively.

"We'll think of something," said Martineau.

"Like a bullet in the head maybe?" Cresson suggested. "I mean, if this man is as important as they say ..."

Martineau shook his head. "He's entitled to a chance. If there's any way I can pull him out I will. They'll be standing by at SOE for a call from you any time this weekend. The Lysander is due to pick us up on Sunday night. Now, what's the procedure for booking a passage to the island tonight?"

"There's an officer in the green hut on the quay. He issues the passes. There'll be no difficulty in your case."

"Good," Martineau said. "That seems to be about it, then."

Sophie picked up her glass. "I'm not going to wish you luck, I'm just going to tell you something."

"What's that?" Martineau enquired.

She put an arm round Sarah's shoulders. "You bring the kid back in one piece, because if you don't and you show your face here again, I'll put a bullet in you myself."

She smiled genially and toasted him.

CHAPTER 9

DARKNESS WAS already falling and Granville harbour was a scene of frenzied activity as the E-boat convoy got ready to leave. Chief Petty Officer Hans Richter, checking the 40mm Bofors gun in the stern of his boat, paused to watch dockers working on the *Victor Hugo* which was moored next to them. Her holds were crammed full, and they were dumping sacks of coal and bales of hay on her decks.

Richter could see the master of the *Hugo*, Savary, on the bridge

talking to the officer in command of the gun crew, the Italian lieutenant. Orsini was as flamboyant as usual, with a red scarf at his
neck. As Richter watched, Orsini went down the gangway to the
quay and walked towards the port officer's hut. Richter turned back
to the gun and a voice called, "Petty Officer!"

Richter looked over the rail. Standing a few feet away was an SS
officer, a black leather trenchcoat over his uniform, the silver
death's head on his cap gleaming dully in the evening light. When
Richter saw the oak leaf collar patches of a full colonel his heart
sank. He clicked his heels together quickly. "Standartenführer.
What can I do for you?"

The young woman standing at the colonel's shoulder was pretty
in her little black beret and belted raincoat, her hair very fair. Too
young for an SS bastard like this, Richter thought.

"Your commanding officer is Kapitänleutnant Dietrich, I understand?" Martineau said. "Is he on board?"

"Not at the moment. He is in the port officer's hut, Standartenführer."

"Good. I'll have a word with him." Martineau gestured to the
two suitcases. "See that these go on board. We'll be travelling with
you to Jersey."

Richter watched them walk away, then nodded to a young seaman who'd been listening with interest. "You heard the man. Get
those cases."

"He was SD," the sailor said. "Did you notice?"

"Yes," Richter said. "As it happens I did. Now get on with it."

ERICH DIETRICH, at only thirty years of age, was never happier than
when he was at sea and in command, especially in E-boats. Just now,
leaning over the chart table with the port officer, Lieutenant
Schroeder, and Guido Orsini, he was in the best of humours.

"Winds three to four, with rain squalls. Could be worse."

Schroeder said, "Intelligence expect big raids on the Ruhr
again tonight, so things should be clear for us down here as
regards the RAF."

"If you believe that, you'll believe anything," Orsini said.

"You're a pessimist, Guido," Erich Dietrich told him. "Expect good things and they'll always fall into your lap."

The door opened behind him, Schroeder's face dropped and Guido stopped smiling. Dietrich turned and found Martineau standing there, Sarah at his shoulder.

"Kapitänleutnant Dietrich? My name is Vogel." Martineau produced his SD identity card and passed it across, then he took Himmler's letter from its envelope. "If you would be kind enough to read this also."

Dietrich read the letter, then handed the document back. "Your credentials are without doubt the most remarkable I've ever seen, Standartenführer," Dietrich said. "In what way can we serve you?"

"I need passage for myself and Mademoiselle Latour to Jersey. As you are convoy commander I shall naturally travel with you. I've already told your petty officer to take our cases on board."

"Happy to oblige, Standartenführer," Dietrich said smoothly. "There is one problem however. Naval regulations forbid the carrying of civilians on a fighting ship at sea. I can accommodate you, but not, alas, this charming young lady."

It was difficult to argue with him because he was right. Martineau tried to handle it as a man like Vogel would have done, arrogant, demanding. "What would you suggest?"

"One of the other convoy ships perhaps. Lieutenant Orsini here is in command of the gun crew on the SS *Victor Hugo*. You could go with him."

But Vogel would not have allowed himself to lose face completely. "No," he said calmly. "It is good that I should see something of your work, Kapitänleutnant. I shall travel with you. Mademoiselle Latour, on the other hand, can proceed on the *Victor Hugo*, if Lieutenant Orsini has no objections."

"Certainly not," said Guido, who had hardly been able to take his eyes off her. "A distinct pleasure."

"Unfortunately Mademoiselle Latour speaks no German."

Martineau turned to her and spoke in French. "We must separate for the journey across, my dear. A matter of regulations. I'll keep your luggage with me, so don't worry about that. This young officer will take care of you."

"Guido Orsini, at your service, signorina," he said gallantly, and saluted. "Come with me and I'll see you safely on board. We sail in thirty minutes."

She turned to Martineau. "I'll see you later then, in Jersey." He nodded calmly.

As she went out, Orsini holding the door open for her, Dietrich said, "A charming girl."

"I think so." Martineau leaned over the chart table. "Are we to enjoy an uneventful run tonight? I understand your convoys are often attacked by RAF night fighters."

"Frequently, Standartenführer," Schroeder told him. "But the RAF will be busy elsewhere tonight." He gathered up his charts. "Now, if you will follow me, we'll go on board."

THE CONVOY, eleven ships in all, left Granville just after ten o'clock. On the bridge of the *Victor Hugo* it was like being in a safe and enclosed world, rain and spray drifting against the glass. Savary stood beside the helmsman. Sarah and Guido Orsini leaned over the chart table.

"This is the convoy route, what the navy call Weg Ida, from Granville east of the Chausey Isles."

She liked Orsini. He was certainly good-looking. Too handsome, really, in a way that Latins could be, but there was strength there too.

"Come to the saloon," he said. "I'll get you a coffee and you can use my cabin if you'd like to lie down."

Savary turned. "Not just now, Count. I want to check the engine room. You'll have to take the bridge." He went out.

"Count?" Sarah said, raising her eyebrows.

"There are lots of counts in Italy. Don't let it worry you."

He offered her a cigarette and they smoked in companionable

silence, looking out into the night, the noise of the engines a muted throbbing. "I thought Italy capitulated last year?" she said.

"Oh, it did, except for those fascist fanatics who decided to fight on under the Germans."

"Are you a fascist?"

He looked down into the appealing young face. "To be honest, I'm not anything. I loathe politics. It reminds me of the senator in Rome who's supposed to have said, 'Don't tell my mother I'm in politics. She thinks I play the piano in a brothel.'"

She laughed. "I like that."

"Most of my former comrades are now working with the British and American navies. I, on the other hand, was seconded to serve with the 5th E-boat Flotilla in Cherbourg. When Italy decided to sue for peace there wasn't a great deal I could do. I didn't fancy a prison camp. Of course, I'm not allowed to command an E-boat any more. I suppose they think I might roar across to England."

"Would you?"

Savary returned to the bridge at that moment and the Italian said, "Right, let's go below now and get that coffee."

CAPTAIN KARL MULLER, the officer in command of the Secret Field Police in Jersey, sat in his office in the Silvertide Hotel at Havre des Pas and worked his way through a bulky file. It was wholly devoted to anonymous letters, the tip-offs that led to whatever success his unit enjoyed. It was all small beer, of course. Nothing to what it had been like at Gestapo headquarters in Paris. Unfortunately, a young Frenchwoman he had been interrogating there had died without disclosing any names. She had been involved with the principal Resistance circuit in Paris, and in the eyes of his superiors he'd botched things badly. The posting to this island backwater had followed. Now he was seeking any way he could to get back into the mainstream of things.

He stood up, a tall man, a shade under six feet, with hair that was still dark brown in spite of the fact that he was in his fiftieth year.

He stretched, went to the window to look out at the weather, and the phone rang. He picked it up. "Yes."

It wasn't a local call, he could tell by the crackling. "Captain Muller? This is Schroeder, port officer at Granville."

TEN MINUTES later, there was a knock on Muller's door. The two men who entered, like Muller, were in civilian clothes. The GFP never wore uniforms if they could help it. The one who led the way was broad and squat with a Slavic face and hard grey eyes: Inspector Willi Kleist, Muller's second-in-command, also seconded from the Gestapo. They had known each other for years. The man with him was much younger with fair hair, blue eyes and a weak mouth. This was Sergeant Ernst Greiser, who had been transferred from the army's field police to the GFP six months earlier.

"An interesting development," Muller said. "I've had Schroeder on the phone from Granville. Apparently an SD Standartenführer presented himself on the quay with a young Frenchwoman and demanded passage to Jersey. He's travelling under a special warrant from Reichsführer Himmler. According to Schroeder it's counter-signed by the Führer."

"My God!" Greiser said.

"So, my friends, we must be ready for him. You were going to take care of the passenger checks when the convoy ships get into St Helier, isn't that so, Ernst?" he enquired of Greiser.

"Yes, Herr Captain."

"Inspector Kleist and I will join you. Whatever his reason for being here, I want to be in on the action. I'll see you later."

They went out. He went to the window and stared out into the darkness, more excited than he had been in months.

IT WAS JUST after eleven when Helen de Ville took the tray up to her room, using the back staircase that led from the kitchen. None of the officers ever used it. They kept strictly to their own end of the house. In any case, she was careful. Only one cup on the tray.

Everything for one. If she chose to have a late supper in her room that was her affair.

She went into the bedroom, locking the door behind her, then crossed to the bookshelves, opened the secret entrance and moved inside, closing it again before going up the narrow stairway.

Kelso was sitting up in bed, reading by the light of an oil lamp. He looked up and smiled. "What have we got here?"

"Not much. Tea, but at least it's the real stuff, and a cheese sandwich. I make my own cheese these days so you'd better like it. What are you reading?"

"One of the books you brought up. Eliot. *The Four Quartets.*"

"Poetry, and you an engineer?" she sat on the end of the bed.

"I certainly wasn't interested in that kind of thing in the old days, but this war . . ." He shrugged. "Like a lot of people, I want answers, I suppose. What's it all mean?"

"Well, if you find out, don't forget to let me know." She noticed the photo of his wife and daughters on the bedside locker and picked it up. "Do you think of them often?"

"All the time. They mean everything to me. My marriage really works. I never wanted anything else. Then the war came along and messed things up."

"Yes, it has a bad habit of doing that."

"Still, I can't complain. Comfortable bed, decent cooking, and the oil lamp gives things a nicely old-fashioned atmosphere."

"They cut off the electricity at nine o'clock sharp," she said. "That's why you've got that oil lamp."

"Are things really as bad as that?"

"Yes, they are. You're lucky to have that cup of tea. Elsewhere in the island it would be a rather inferior substitute made from blackberry leaves. Not one of life's great experiences."

She smiled, and plumped up his pillows. "I'm going to bed now."

"The big day tomorrow," he said.

"If we're to believe the message Savary brought." She picked up the tray. "Try and get some sleep."

ORSINI HAD given Sarah his cabin. It was very small, hot and stuffy, and the noise of the engine which churned directly below gave her a headache. She lay on the bunk, closed her eyes and tried to relax. The ship seemed to stagger. An illusion, of course. Then there was an explosion.

Things appeared to happen in slow motion after that. The ship was perfectly still, and there was another violent explosion which caused the walls to tremble. She cried out and tried to stand up and then the floor tilted and she fell against the door. Her handbag was thrown from the locker top. She picked it up automatically and attempted to open the cabin door, but it was stuck fast. She shook the handle desperately, and then the door opened so unexpectedly that she was hurled back against the opposite wall.

Orsini stood in the entrance, his face wild. "Move!" he ordered. "We've been hit twice. Torpedo attack. We've only got minutes. This old tub will go down like a stone."

They went up the companionway to the deserted saloon. He took off his reefer coat and held it out to her. "Get this on." She did as she was told, stuffing her handbag into one of the coat's ample pockets. He pulled her arms roughly through a life jacket, and put one on himself as he led the way out onto the deck.

There was a scene of indescribable confusion as the crew tried to launch the boats and, above them, the machine-gun crew fired into the night. Fire arced towards them in return, raking the bridge where Savary stood shouting orders. He cried out in terror and jumped over the rail, bouncing off some bales of hay below. Cannon shell ripped into one of the lifeboats a few yards away, tearing great holes in it.

Orsini pushed Sarah down behind some sacks of coal. As he did so there was another explosion, and a portion of the deck disintegrated, flames billowing into the night. The entire ship tilted sharply to port and the deck cargo started to break free, sacks of coal, bales of hay, sliding down against the rail.

It had not been possible to launch a single boat, so rapidly had disaster struck, and men were already going over the rail, Savary leading the way. Sarah fell and felt herself slide down the slippery deck. Then the rail dipped under and she was in the water.

THE E-BOAT surged forward within seconds of the first explosion, and Dietrich scanned the darkness with his night glasses. Martineau almost lost his balance at the sudden burst of speed and hung on grimly. "What is it?"

"I'm not sure," Dietrich said. Then flames blossomed in the night five hundred yards away, and he focused on the *Victor Hugo*. A dark shape flashed across the patch of light like a shadow, and then another. "British MTBs. They've hit the *Hugo*."

He pressed the button on the battle stations alarm and the ugly sound of the Klaxon rose above the roaring of the engines. Already the crew were moving to their stations. The Bofors gun and the welldeck cannon started to fire, lines of tracer curving into the night.

The only thing Martineau could think of was Sarah. He grabbed Dietrich by the sleeve. "We must help the people on that ship."

"Later!" Dietrich shrugged him aside. "This is business. Now keep out of the way."

SARAH KICKED desperately to get as far from the ship as possible. There was burning oil on the water towards the stern, and men were swimming to get away from it as it advanced relentlessly.

She moved awkwardly because of the life jacket, and the reefer coat was bulky, saturated with water. But she realised now why Orsini had given it to her, as the cold started to eat at her legs. Where was he?

There was wreckage floating everywhere, the bales of hay from the deck cargo buoyant in the water. A hand grabbed her life jacket from behind; she turned and Orsini was there. He towed her towards one of the bales and they clung on to its binding ropes. "Who were they?" she gasped.

"British MTBs."

There was a mighty rushing sound in the night and machine-gun bullets churned the water as an MTB carved its way through men and wreckage. A tracer flashed through the darkness in a great arc. A moment later, a parachute flare illuminated the scene.

My God, Sarah thought, what a way to go. My own people trying to kill me. She hung on to the rope and said, gasping, "Did they have to do that? Machine-gun men in the water?"

"War, *cara*, is a nasty business. It makes everyone crazy. Are you managing?"

"My arms are tired."

A hatch drifted by and he swam to it and towed it towards her. "Let's get you onto this."

It was a struggle, but she finally managed it. "What about you?"

"I'll be fine hanging on." He laughed. "Don't worry, I've been in the water before. My luck is good, so stick with me."

She laughed shakily. "There's nothing like the Channel Islands for a holiday at this time of the year. Perfect for sea bathing," and then she realised, to her horror, that she'd spoken in English.

He floated there, staring up at her, and then said in excellent English, "I knew there was something different about you from the first moment, *cara*," he laughed. "Which means there's also something unusual about the good Standartenführer Vogel."

"Please," she said desperately.

"Don't worry, *cara*, I fell in love with you the moment you came through the door of that hut on the quay. I like you, I don't like them—whoever they are. We Italians are a very simple people."

There was the sound of a throttled-down engine approaching, and a moment later, an armed trawler was looming above them, a net over the side. Two or three German sailors clambered down, reaching for Sarah, and pulled her up. Guido followed and collapsed on the deck beside her.

A young lieutenant came down the ladder from the bridge and hurried forward.

"Guido, is that you?" he said in German.

"As ever was, Bruno," Guido answered in the same language.

"And you, Fräulein, are you all right? We must get you to my cabin."

"Mademoiselle Latour, Bruno, and she speaks no German," Guido told him in French. He smiled at Sarah and helped her to her feet. "Now, let's take you below."

CHAPTER 10

As SARAH pulled a heavy sweater over her head there was a knock on the door of Bruno's cabin. She opened it and a young rating announced in French, "We're entering St Helier harbour."

He left, and she went to the basin and tried to do something with her hair. The effects of the salt water had made it a tangled mass.

The contents of the handbag that she had stuffed into a pocket of Orsini's reefer before leaving the *Victor Hugo* had survived surprisingly well. Her identity card and other papers had been soaked, of course. She had laid them out on the hot water pipes to dry, and now she replaced them all in her handbag and retrieved the small pistol from under the pillow.

There was a knock and Guido came in. "How are you?" he asked in French.

"Fine," she said, "except for the hair. I look like a scarecrow."

He was carrying a Kriegsmarine reefer coat. "Put this on. It's a damp morning out there."

Up on the bridge of the trawler, Sarah looked down upon a scene familiar from her childhood. St Helier harbour, Elizabeth Castle on her left, the Albert Pier, the sprawl of the town itself. The same and yet not the same. Military strong-points everywhere and the harbour more crammed with vessels than she had ever known it. Dockers were already starting to unload the barges, and there seemed to be soldiers everywhere.

"Where's the E-boat?" she asked Guido as she leaned on the bridge rail beside him and Bruno Feldt.

"Probably having a last look for survivors," he said, as they nosed in towards the Albert Pier. "No sign of Savary," he added.

"Someone else may have picked him up," said Bruno Feldt. "I see the GFP are ready and waiting."

"GFP?" Sarah asked in a deliberate display of ignorance. "What's that?"

"Geheime Feld Polizei," Guido told her. "The tall one, Captain Muller, is on loan from the Gestapo. So is the thug next to him, the one built like a brick wall. That's Inspector Willi Kleist. The young one with the fair hair is Sergeant Ernst Greiser."

The three GFP officers hurried up the gangway when it went across, and Muller was first on the bridge, followed by Kleist.

"Herr Leutnant." Muller nodded to Feldt. "You had quite a night of it, I hear?" He wore an old raincoat and felt hat and there was something curiously gentle about him as he turned to Sarah and said in French, "You were a passenger on the *Hugo*, mademoiselle . . .?"

"Latour," Orsini put in. "We were in the water together."

"A remarkable escape," Muller nodded. "You lost your papers?"

"No," she said. "I have them here." She took the handbag from her pocket and started to open it.

Muller held out his hand. "The bag, if you please, mademoiselle."

There was a moment's pause. Everyone waited. Then Sarah handed it to him. "Of course."

Muller turned to Bruno Feldt. "We'll use your cabin for a few minutes, if we may."

Guido squeezed Sarah's arm and whispered quickly, "I'll wait for you, *cara*, and if the colonel doesn't arrive you can come up to my billet at de Ville Place. My landlady will look after you."

Muller followed Sarah down the companionway and back into Lieutenant Feldt's cabin. Kleist leaned against the open door.

"So, mademoiselle." Muller sat on the bed, turned the handbag upside down and emptied it. Her papers fell out, her make-up case, and also the pistol. He made no comment. He opened her identity card, examined it, then replaced everything carefully in the bag. Only then did he pick up the pistol. "You are aware that there is only one penalty for a civilian caught in possession of any kind of firearm?"

"Yes," Sarah said.

"This is yours, I take it?"

"Certainly. It was a gift from a friend. He was concerned for my safety. These are troubled times, Captain."

"And what kind of friend would encourage you to break the law so flagrantly?"

There was a footstep outside, and a cold voice said in German, "Perhaps you should address that question to me."

Harry Martineau stood in the doorway. He presented a supremely menacing figure in the SS uniform and black leather trenchcoat.

Karl Muller knew the Devil when he met him face-to-face and got to his feet very fast indeed. "Standartenführer."

"You are?"

"Captain Karl Muller, in charge of Geheime Feld Polizei here in Jersey. This is my second-in-command, Inspector Kleist."

"My name is Vogel." Martineau took out his SD pass and handed it over. Muller examined it and passed it back. Martineau produced the Himmler warrant. "Read that."

Muller did as he was told, folded the letter and handed it back. "In what way can I serve you, Standartenführer?"

"Mademoiselle Latour travels under my protection." Martineau picked up the pistol and put it back in her handbag. "She has done me the honour of choosing my friendship. There are those amongst her countrymen who do not approve. I prefer that she should be in a position to defend herself should any unfortunate situation arise."

"Of course, Standartenführer."

"Good, then kindly wait for me on deck."

Muller didn't even hesitate. "Certainly, Standartenführer." He nodded to Kleist and they went out.

Martineau closed the door and turned. He smiled suddenly, changing from Vogel into Harry. "You look awful. Are you all right?"

"Yes," she said, "thanks to Guido."

"Guido, is it?"

"He saved my life, Harry. It was awful. Burning oil, men dying." She shuddered. "And the British MTBs machine-gunned us in the water. I thought it was only the Germans who were supposed to do that! We've got a problem," she added. "At one point when we were in the water I spoke to Guido in English."

"Good God!"

She put up a hand defensively. "It was very confusing out there. Anyway, he speaks good English himself."

"Stop!" Martineau said. "It gets worse. You *have* been careless."

"He's no fascist, Harry. He's an Italian aristocrat who doesn't give a damn about politics, stuck here because he happened to be in the wrong place when the Italian government capitulated."

"But why should he go to all this trouble for you?"

"He likes me. You know what these Latins are like." She smiled mischievously. "Another thing. Guido's billeted with Aunt Helen at de Ville Place. He was going to take me up there if you hadn't arrived."

"Perfect," Martineau said. "As for the other business, we'll tell him your mother was English, and that you've kept quiet about it during the occupation years in case it caused you any problems."

"Will he believe it?"

"I don't see why not. Are you going to be all right for clothes?"

"Yes. I've got everything I need in the large case. I'm glad it travelled with you on the E-boat."

They went up the companionway. Muller was standing on the bridge talking to Feldt and Orsini.

Martineau spoke to Orsini in French. "Anne-Marie tells me you are billeted in most congenial circumstances. Some country house called de Ville Place?"

"That's right, Colonel."

Martineau turned to Muller. "It sounds as if it would suit my needs exactly. Would there be any objection?"

Muller, eager to please, said, "None at all, Standartenführer. It has, by tradition, been allocated to officers of the Kriegsmarine, but Mrs de Ville, the owner, is currently seven or eight below her full complement."

"I'll take you up there now if you like." Orsini offered. "I have a car parked at the end of the pier."

"Good." Martineau said. "I suggest we get moving, then."

They went down the gangway to the pier and a Kriegsmarine rating picked up the two suitcases and followed. Orsini and Sarah walked in front, Martineau followed with Muller at his side.

"Naturally, once I'm settled in, I'll return to town to pay my respects to the military commandant, Colonel Heine. I will need a vehicle. A Kübelwagen would be best in case I wish to use it over rough country." The Kübelwagen was the German army's equivalent of the jeep.

"No problem, Standartenführer. I will also be happy to provide one of my men as a driver."

"Not necessary," Martineau said. "I prefer to do things for myself. I'll find my way about this little island of yours, believe me."

"Could I have some idea of the purpose of your visit, Standartenführer?"

"I am here on special instructions from Reichsführer Himmler himself, countersigned by the Führer. You have seen my orders," Martineau told him. "Are you querying them?"

"Certainly not."

"Good." They had reached Orsini's Morris saloon and a sailor was stowing the suitcases in the boot. "You will be informed of my movements if and when necessary. In the meantime, have that Kübelwagen delivered to me."

Sarah was already in the back seat, Orsini behind the wheel. Martineau got into the front passenger seat and the Italian drove away. As they drove along Victoria Avenue, Martineau said to Orsini, "I believe there's a misunderstanding to be cleared up.

Anne-Marie has a Breton father, but an English mother. She felt it sensible to keep quiet about this in case it caused problems with the occupying powers."

"You may rely on my discretion," Orsini said. "The last thing I would wish to do is embarrass Mademoiselle Latour in any way."

"Good," Martineau said. "I felt sure you'd understand."

BACK IN his office at Silvertide, Muller sat behind his desk, thinking. After a while, he flipped the intercom. "Ask Inspector Kleist and Sergeant Greiser to come in."

He went to the window and looked out. The tide, still advancing, blanketed the rocks on the shore with white foam.

The door opened and the two policemen entered. "You wanted us, Herr Captain?" Kleist asked.

"Yes, Willi." Muller sat down, and leaned back in his chair. "Your brother used to work at Gestapo headquarters in Prince Albrechtstrasse in Berlin, Ernst?"

"Peter? Yes, Herr Captain, but now he's at Stuttgart headquarters, in charge of criminal records," Greiser said.

"He must still have connections in Berlin. Book a call to him. Ask about Vogel. I remember being told when I was a young detective that no matter how good an egg looks, if it smells, there's something wrong. And this smells, Ernst. I'd like to know more about Standartenführer Vogel. I want to know just how important he is."

"I would remind you, sir, that calls for Germany are routed via Cherbourg and Paris. They've been taking fifteen or sixteen hours recently, even at priority level."

"Then book one now, Ernst." The young man went out and Muller said to Kleist, "See about a Kübelwagen. Have it delivered to de Ville Place. Let's keep him happy for the time being."

IN THE KITCHEN at de Ville Place, Helen was rolling out pastry made from potato flour when Gallagher came in. "Good, you can clean the fish for me," she said.

There were some plaice on a marble slab beside the sink. Gallagher took a knife from his pocket. When he pressed one end, a razor-sharp double-edged blade sprang into view.

"I loathe that thing," Helen said.

"When my grandfather was twelve he made his first trip in a schooner from Jersey to Newfoundland, to fish for cod. This knife was his father's gift to him. He left it to me in his will. Knives, guns—it's how they're used that's important, Helen."

At that moment there was the sound of a car drawing up outside. "That's probably Guido," Helen said.

There were steps in the passageway, and Guido came in carrying two suitcases.

"A good passage?" Helen asked.

"No, the *Hugo* was torpedoed, Savary is missing, three crew members dead and four of my gun crew." Sarah stepped in through the door, followed by Martineau. Orsini carried on, "This is Anne-Marie Latour. She was a passenger on the *Hugo*, and this is Standartenführer Vogel."

Helen looked bewildered. "What can I do for you?"

"Put us up, Mrs de Ville," Martineau spoke in English. "I'm in Jersey for a few days. We need quarters."

"Impossible," Helen told him. "This is a billet for officers of the Kriegsmarine only."

"And you are well short of your full complement," Martineau told her. "If you would be kind enough, therefore, to show us to a suitable room."

Helen was angrier than she had been in years: with the ice-cold assurance of the man, the SS uniform, and the silly little tart with him.

Guido said hurriedly, "Right, I'm going to have a bath and catch up on a little sleep. I'll see you all later."

The door closed behind him. Helen pushed Gallagher out of the way angrily, washing the potato flour from her hands under the tap. She was aware of the SS officer still at the door.

Very softly, a voice said, "Aunt Helen, don't you know me?"

Helen went quite still. Gallagher was looking over her shoulder in astonishment. "Uncle Sean?" And then, as Helen turned, "It's me, Aunt Helen. It's Sarah."

Helen moved forward and grabbed her by the shoulders, gazing at her searchingly. With recognition, there were sudden tears in her eyes. She ran her fingers through the girl's hair. "Oh, my God, Sarah, what have they done to you?" Then they were in each other's arms.

LATER, WHEN Sarah had washed her hair, using some homemade soap Helen had provided, she still looked a mess. Helen came into the bathroom and said, "It's no good. You need a hairdresser."

"Are there still such things?"

"Oh, yes. Most of the shops in St Heliers still function."

She tried combing the girl's hair into some semblance of a style, and Sarah said, "What's life been like for you here on Jersey?"

"Not too bad if we behave ourselves. A lot of the time the Germans are all right, but step out of line and see what happens. You have to do as you're told, you see." She finished combing. "There, that's the best I can do."

She helped Sarah pull her dress over her head and zip it up. "You and Martineau? What's the situation there? He's old enough to be your father."

"My father he very definitely is not." Sarah smiled as she pulled on her shoes. "He's probably the most infuriating man I've ever met, but he's also the most fascinating."

"And to think that the last time I saw you, you had pigtails! Now let's go and have some tea."

In the kitchen, Helen put two spoonfuls of her precious china tea into the pot while Sarah and Martineau sat at the table talking and smoking. There was a knock at the door. When Helen opened it, Willi Kleist stood there. "We've brought your Kübelwagen, Standartenführer."

Martineau went out to have a look at it. The canvas was up and the body was camouflaged.

"That seems satisfactory," he said.

"If there's anything else we can do."

"I don't think so."

"By the way, Captain Muller wanted me to tell you that Colonel Heine will be at the town hall this afternoon, if you'd care to call in and see him. I understand he's leaving for Guernsey in the morning for a meeting with General von Schmettow."

"Thank you, I will pay him a visit."

Ernst Greiser was sitting at the wheel of a black Citroën. Kleist got in beside him and they drove away. Martineau went back inside. "Transport taken care of. I'll go into town this afternoon, call on Heine, the military commandant, and then I'll visit Muller and his friends."

"You'd better go in with him and get your hair done," Helen told Sarah. She turned to Martineau. "There's a good hairdresser close to the town hall."

"Fine," he said. "But first I feel like a breath of air. How about showing me round the estate, Sarah?"

"A good idea," Helen said. "I've got things to do. I'll see you both later."

AFTER LEAVING de Ville Place Kleist and Greiser started down the road, but after about a quarter of a mile, the inspector touched the young man on the arm. "Pull in here, Ernst. We'll walk back through the woods."

"Any particular reason?"

"I'd just like to have a look round, that's all."

The cart track was heavily overgrown. Greiser drove halfway along it until they were out of sight of the road and they got out and left the Citroën there, taking a path through the woods of the de Ville estate. It was quiet and really rather pleasant.

Then a young woman carrying a basket appeared unexpectedly a few yards ahead of them. It was impossible to see her face, but her cotton frock was tight enough to reveal, even at that distance, a body that was full and ripe. She didn't notice them and followed the path into the wood.

Kleist said, "Now that's interesting." He turned to Greiser and smiled. "Would you say we should investigate, Sergeant?"

"Very definitely, Herr Inspector," the younger man said eagerly, and they quickened their pace.

The young woman was in fact Mary, the daughter of Helen's housekeeper, Mrs Vibert. The old woman had promised Helen de Ville some eggs for the evening meal and it was these that the girl was taking to the house now.

She was only sixteen and already blossoming into womanhood. She loved the countryside, and was never happier than when walking alone in the woods. Some little way in there was an old granite barn, long disused, the roof gaping. It always made her feel uneasy and yet she was drawn to it by a strange fascination. She paused, then walked across the grass to peer inside.

A harsh voice called, "Now then, what do you think you're doing?"

She turned quickly and saw Kleist and Greiser advancing towards her.

SEAN GALLAGHER was walking down to the south meadow, where he had three cows grazing. They were a precious commodity in these hard times and he stayed with them there in the sunshine for a while before starting back to his cottage.

When he was still two fields away he noticed the Germans walking towards the wood, then he recognised Mary. He paused, shading his eyes against the sun, saw the girl disappear into the trees, the Germans following. Suddenly uneasy, he started to hurry. It was when he was halfway across the field that he heard the first scream. He cursed softly and broke into a run.

THE WEATHER was the best of the spring, delightfully warm as Sarah and Martineau followed the track from the house through the trees. There were daffodils everywhere and camellias blooming.

Sarah held his arm as they strolled along. "God, that wonderful, marvellous smell. Straight back to my childhood and those long hot summers. Did they ever exist, I wonder, or was it all an impossible dream?"

"No," he said. "They were the only true reality. It's the past four years that have been the nightmare."

"I love this place," she said. "It's home. Here I belong. Where do you belong, Harry?"

"A stateless person, that's me," he said lightly. "For years, an American living and working in Europe. No family worth speaking of." He was upset, and it showed in a sudden angry unease. "I just don't belong anywhere. Maybe the man upstairs made a mistake. Perhaps I should have died in the trenches back in 1918."

She pulled him round, angry. "That's a terrible thing to say."

There was a sudden scream. They turned and looked down through the trees to the barn in the clearing, and saw Mary struggling in Kleist's arms, Greiser standing to one side laughing.

"For God's sake, Harry, do something," Sarah said.

He started down the slope as Sean Gallagher ran out of the trees.

KLEIST WAS excited, the supple young body squirming against him. "Shut up!" he told her. "Just be a good girl and I won't hurt you."

Greiser's eyes were shining, his mouth loose. "Don't forget, Inspector, fair shares for all, that's my motto."

Gallagher arrived at the run, shouldering the sergeant out of the way. As he reached Kleist, he kicked hard behind the German's left knee, causing the leg to buckle, and punched him hard in the kidneys. Kleist grunted and went down, releasing the terrified girl.

Gallagher picked up Mary's basket and gave it to her. "It's all right now," he said. "You run on up to the house, to Mrs de Ville."

She ran like a frightened rabbit. As Gallagher turned, Greiser took a Mauser from his pocket, his eyes wild. Kleist called, "No, Ernst, he's mine." He got up, easing his back, and took off his raincoat. "Like all the Irish, you're cracked in the head. Now I shall teach you a lesson."

"Half Irish, so only half cracked." Sean Gallagher took off his jacket and tossed it to one side. "Didn't I ever tell you about my grandfather, old Winter le Brocq? He was sailing in cod schooners at the age of twelve. Twelve times round the Horn by the age of twenty-three."

"Talk away," Kleist said, circling him. "It won't do any good."

He rushed in and swung a tremendous punch which Gallagher avoided with ease. "He was a bosun, and in those days a bosun was only as good as his fists and he was good. Very good." Sean ducked in and landed a punch under the German's left eye. "When I used to come over from Ireland as a kid to stay with him, he gave me boxing lessons. Science, timing, punching, that's what counts, not size."

Every punch the German threw was sidestepped, and in return Gallagher seemed to be able to hit him wherever he wanted. On the hillside a few yards away, Sarah and Martineau watched as the Irishman drove the inspector back across the grass.

And then there was a sudden moment of disaster. As Gallagher moved in, his right foot slipped on the grass and he went down. Kleist seized his chance, kicking Gallagher in the side as he went down. Gallagher rolled away with surprising speed and came up on one knee. "God save us, you can't even kick straight."

Kleist rushed at him. Gallagher slipped to one side, tripping the German so that he went head first into the wall of the barn, then gave him a left and a right in the kidneys. Kleist cried out sharply and Gallagher swung him round. He grabbed him by the lapels and smashed his forehead against the bridge of the German's nose. Kleist swayed and fell.

Gallagher swung round to find Greiser confronting him with the Mauser, but in the same moment a shot rang out, kicking up dirt at Greiser's feet. They turned as Martineau walked into the clearing, Walther in hand.

"Put it away!" he ordered.

Greiser stood there, staring at him, and it was Kleist, getting to his feet, who said hoarsely, "Do as he says, Ernst."

Greiser obeyed and Martineau said, "Good. You are, of course, a disgrace to everything the Reich stands for. This I shall discuss with your commanding officer later. Now leave."

The two men walked rapidly away through the trees.

Sarah came up to Gallagher, took out a handkerchief and wiped blood from his mouth. "I never realised what a deadly combination it could be, Jersey blood mixed with Irish."

"A fine day for it, thanks be to God." Gallagher squinted up at the sun through the trees. "Better times coming." He grinned and turned to Martineau. "You wouldn't happen to have a cigarette on you? I seem to have left mine at home."

CHAPTER 11

MARTINEAU AND Sarah drove down through St Aubin and along towards Bel Royal, passing a number of fortifications and gun positions on the way. The sky was very blue, the sun bright. Sarah leaned back in the Kübelwagen and closed her eyes. "This island has a special smell to it in spring. Nothing quite like it anywhere in the world." She opened her eyes again. "Tell me something. Why have you taken off your uniform?"

He was wearing the leather military trenchcoat, but underneath was a grey tweed suit and white shirt with a black tie. The slouch hat was also in black, the brim down at the front and back.

"Tactics," he said. "I don't need to appear in uniform if I don't want to. SD officers wear civilian clothes most of the time. It emphasizes their power." He pulled in at the side of the road and switched off the engine. "Let's take a walk."

He helped her out and they crossed to the seawall. Below, on the sands, children played, their mothers sitting against the wall, faces turned to the sun. A number of German soldiers swam in the sea, two or three young women among them.

"Unexpectedly domestic, isn't it?" Martineau said.

The soldiers glanced at them, attracted by the girl, but turned from his dark stare. "Yes," she said. "Not what I expected."

"If you look closely you'll see that most of the soldiers on the beach are boys. Twenty years old at most. Difficult to hate. When someone's a Nazi, you know where you stand. But the average twenty-year-old German in uniform . . ." He shrugged.

Neither of them spoke for a time, then Sarah said, "When it's all over, Harry, what will happen to you?" She turned to look at him, her face strained and intense.

He stared out to sea, eyes very dark. "When I was young I used to love railway stations, especially at night. The smell of the steam, the dying fall of a train whistle in the distance, the platforms in those great deserted Victorian palaces, waiting to go somewhere, anywhere. I loved it and yet I also used to get a feeling of tremendous unease. Something to do with getting on the wrong train." He turned to her. "And once the train's on its way, you can't get off."

"The station is ominous at midnight," she said softly. "Hope is a dead letter."

He stared at her. "Where did you hear that?"

"One of your bad poems," she said. "That first day I met you at the cottage the brigadier was reading it. You took it from him, crumpled it up and threw it into the fireplace."

"And you retrieved it?" For a moment she thought he would be angry. Instead he smiled. "Wait here." He left her, crossed to the Kübelwagen and opened the door. When he returned he was carrying a small kodak camera. "Helen gave me this. As the film is four years old she can't guarantee the results."

He walked up to a young soldier standing nearby. There was a brief exchange, then Martineau gave him the camera and returned to stand beside Sarah. "Don't forget to smile."

Sarah took his arm. "What's this for?"

"Something to remember me by."

It made her feel uneasy and she held his arm more tightly. The soldier took the photo and returned the camera, smiling shyly, and walked away. "Did you tell him who you were?" she asked.

"Of course I did." He took her arm. "Let's get going. I've got things to do while you're at the hairdresser's."

KARL MULLER prided himself on his self-control, his remarkable lack of emotion in all situations. He thought of it as his greatest asset and yet, standing by the window in his office at the Silvertide Hotel, it almost deserted him for the first time.

"You *what*?" he demanded.

Kleist's face was in a dreadful state: the flesh around his eyes was purple, his nose was swollen. "A misunderstanding, Herr Captain."

Muller turned to Greiser. "And that's your version also? A mis-understanding?"

"We were only questioning the girl, Herr Captain. She panicked, then Gallagher arrived. He placed entirely the wrong construction on the affair."

"As your face proves, Willi," Muller said. "And Vogel was involved?"

"He arrived at an unfortunate moment," Greiser told him. "And he also placed entirely the wrong construction on things."

Muller was furious. "Leaving me to get you off the hook when he turns up here this afternoon. Go on, get out of my sight!"

He turned to the window and slammed his palm against the wall.

MARTINEAU PARKED near the entrance of the town hall with its Nazi flag flying and a Luftwaffe sentry on the step with a rifle. He and Sarah walked along York Street until they came to a doorway between two shops. The sign indicated that the hairdresser was upstairs. Sarah said, "I remember this place."

"Will you be recognised?"

"I shouldn't think so. The last time I was in here to have my hair cut I was ten years old."

"I must keep my appointment with Colonel Heine at the town hall," Martineau said. "I'll see you later."

He strolled back to the town hall and saw a policeman in traditional British bobby's uniform talking to a sentry. They stopped talking, watching him as he approached.

"Standartenführer Vogel, for the commandant."

The sentry jumped to attention. "The commandant arrived twenty minutes ago, Standartenführer. Please enter."

Martineau moved into the hall and found an army sergeant sitting at the bottom of the stairs. "My name is Vogel. I believe Colonel Heine is expecting me."

The sergeant picked up the phone and within moments there was the sound of boots on the stairs. He turned to find a young man hurrying down, an infantry major, no more than thirty from the look of him.

He was all cordiality, pausing briefly to click his heels before putting out a hand. "Major Felix Necker, Standartenführer."

He'd seen action, that was obvious from the shrapnel scar running into his right eye. As well as the Iron Cross First Class he wore the Infantry Assault Badge. This man was obviously a war hero.

"A pleasure to meet you, Herr Major," he said.

They went upstairs; Necker tapped on a door, opened it and stood to one side as Martineau went in first. The officer who stood up and came round the desk to meet him was a type he recognised instantly. A little stiff in manner, old-fashioned regular army and definitely no Nazi. An officer and a gentleman.

"Standartenführer. A pleasure to see you."

"Colonel Heine." Martineau produced his SD card.

Heine examined it and handed it back. "Please sit down. You've met Felix Necker, of course. My second-in-command. In what way can I serve you?"

Martineau took out the Himmler letter and passed it across.

Heine read it slowly, his face grave, then passed it to Necker. "If I could know the purpose of your visit?"

"Not at this stage." Martineau took the letter as Necker handed it back to him. "All I need is assurance of total cooperation as and when required."

"That goes without saying. I will inform all unit commanders of your presence." Heine hesitated. "There is one thing. I go to Guernsey in the morning. A weekend conference with General von Schmettow."

Martineau turned to Necker. "Presumably you will be left in command?"

"That is correct."

"Then I can see no problem." He got to his feet. "A pleasure to meet you, Herr Colonel. Don't bother to see me out, Major."

The door closed behind him. Heine's whole demeanour changed. "My flesh always crawls when these SD people appear. What in the hell does he want, Felix?"

"God alone knows, Herr Colonel, but his credentials . . .!" Necker shrugged. "Not only signed by Himmler, but by the Führer himself."

"I know." Heine put up a hand defensively. "Just watch him, and at all costs keep him sweet. Trouble with Himmler is the last thing we need."

MARTINEAU HAD time in hand so he walked through the town. There were more civilians than soldiers about. Most people looked underweight and their clothes were well-worn. There were few children because they were at school. The ones he did see were in better shape than he had expected, but then, people always put their children first.

When he went upstairs to the salon, Sarah was adjusting her hat in the mirror. Her hair looked excellent. He helped her on with her coat, and they went outside to the Kübelwagen.

Martineau's next stop was the Silvertide Hotel at Havre des Pas. He parked beside several other vehicles. "I shan't be long."

Sarah smiled. "Don't worry about me. I'll just take a walk along the seawall. I used to come to swim here when I was a kid."

"As you please."

Muller had seen him arrive from the window of his office. When Martineau went inside, a young military policeman was waiting to greet him.

"Standartenführer Vogel? This way, please."

Martineau was ushered into Muller's office. The captain stood up behind the desk. "A great pleasure."

"I wish I could say the same," Martineau said. "You've spoken to Kleist and Greiser?"

"About this misunderstanding at de Ville Place? Yes, they . . ."

"Misunderstanding?" Martineau said coldly. "You will have them in here now, Herr Captain, if you please. My time is limited."

He turned away and stood at the window, hands behind his back, as Muller asked for Kleist and Greiser over the intercom. They came in only a few moments. Martineau didn't bother to turn round, but said softly, "Inspector Kleist, I understand you have put this morning's events at de Ville Place down to a misunderstanding?"

"Well, yes, Standartenführer."

"Liar!" Martineau's voice was low and dangerous. "Both of you are liars." He turned to face Muller. "A child, Captain, barely sixteen, being dragged towards a barn by this animal here while the other stood and laughed. I was about to interfere when General Gallagher came on the scene and gave the bully the thrashing he deserved."

"I see," Muller said.

"Just to make things worse, I was obliged to draw my own pistol and fire a warning shot to prevent this idiot shooting Gallagher in the back." He spoke slowly to Greiser, as if to a child. "The man is Irish, which means he is a neutral, and the Führer's declared policy is good relations with Ireland. We don't shoot people like that in the back. Understand?"

"Yes, Standartenführer."

Now he turned to Muller. "The actions of these men are an affront to every ideal the Reich holds dear, and to German honour."

He was thoroughly enjoying himself, especially when Kleist's anger overflowed. "I'm not a child to be lectured like this."

"Kleist!" Martineau said. "As a member of the Gestapo you took an oath to our Führer, an oath of obedience unto death. Is it not so? Remember from now on that you are here to obey orders. If I give you an order it's '*Zu Befehl*, Standartenführer'."

He turned to Muller. "And you wonder why Reichsführer Himmler thought it worthwhile sending me here?"

He walked out without another word, went through the foyer and crossed the road to the Kübelwagen.

"How did it go?" Sarah asked.

"Oh, I think I put the fear of God in them rather satisfactorily. Now you can take me on a tour of this island of yours."

ROMMEL WAS staying at a villa deep in the countryside near Bayeaux. It had been used as a weekend retreat by the commanding general of the area who had been happy to offer it to the field marshal when he'd expressed a desire for a quiet weekend. The Bernards, who ran the house, were extremely discreet.

Baum and Hofer joined the field marshal in the drawing room.

"Right, let's go over things," Rommel said.

"According to my information the people from Jersey will leave for Guernsey at around ten tomorrow morning," Hofer began. "It's a question of the tide. Berger and I will leave here at nine. We will drive to a Luftwaffe airstrip only ten kilometres away. There is a pilot waiting there now under your personal orders with a Fiesler Stork. He won't know his destination until we join the plane. I estimate we will land in Jersey around eleven o'clock. I've given orders for Berlin to be notified at noon that you've flown to Jersey, the reason for not letting them know earlier being one of security."

"And what happens here?"

"Generals Stulpnagel and Falkenhausen arrive later in the day, stay overnight and leave on Sunday morning. This couple here at the house, the Bernards, know you are here, but then they won't know you're supposed to be in Jersey."

Rommel turned to Baum. "And you, my friend, do you think you can handle it?"

"Yes, Herr Field Marshal. I really think I can," Baum told him.

"Good." Rommel took a bottle of Dom Perignon from the ice bucket that Monsieur Bernard had brought in earlier, and uncorked it. He filled three glasses. "So, my friends, to the Jersey enterprise."

DINNER AT de Ville Place that evening was a strange affair. Martineau and Sarah joined Guido Orsini and several German officers in the main dining room. There was a fresh, lighted candle at each empty place which Sarah found rather macabre, but the young officers were polite and considerate and would obviously have put themselves out even more if it had not been for Martineau's presence. He was wearing his uniform in deference to the formality of the meal and its effect on the others had been definitely depressing.

Helen de Ville passed in and out with the plates. Sarah, bored with the stilted conversation, insisted on helping her to clear the table and joined her in the kitchen where Sean Gallagher sat eating the leftovers.

"Terrible in there. Harry's like a spectre at the feast," she said.

Helen had just prepared a tray for Kelso. "I'll just take this up while they're all still in the dining room."

She went up the back stairs and opened the door to her bedroom at the same moment as Guido Orsini passed the end of the corridor. He hesitated, then tried the door that Helen had just closed behind her. For once, she had omitted to turn the key. He peered inside, saw the secret door ajar and tiptoed across. There was a murmur of voices from upstairs. He listened for a moment, then turned and went out again, closing the door.

Sarah and Gallagher were talking in low voices when he went into the kitchen. "Ah, there you are," he said. "They're into politics now. Can I take you for a walk on the terrace, Anne-Marie?"

"Is he to be trusted?" she asked Gallagher.

"No more than most men I know, especially round a darling like you."

"I'll have to take a chance then. If Colonel Vogel comes looking for me, tell him I'll be back soon," she added formally.

There was a half moon, the sky was bright with stars, and there was a luminosity to everything. Palm trees were etched against the sky. Everywhere there was the smell of flowers, drenched from the rain earlier.

"Azaleas." She breathed deeply. "One of my favourites."

"You are a remarkable girl," he said in English. "You don't mind if we use English, do you? There's no one about."

"All right," she said reluctantly. "But not for long."

"You've never been to Jersey before?"

She lied. "No. I was brought up by my grandmother in Paimpol after my mother died."

"I see. And it was your mother who was English?"

"That's right."

She was wary of his questioning and sat on a low granite wall, the moon behind her. He gave her a cigarette. "You speak French with a Breton accent."

"What's strange about that? My grandmother was Breton."

"And your English is interesting too. Very upper class."

She stood up. "I'd better get back now, Guido. Max can get rather restless if I'm out of his sight too long with another man."

"Of course." He took her arm and they strolled back through the azaleas. "I like you, Anne-Marie Latour. I like you a lot. I want you to remember that."

Martineau appeared on the terrace in the moonlight. "Anne-Marie, are you there?" he shouted in French.

"Coming!" she called and reached to touch the Italian's face. "I'll see you tomorrow," and she ran up the steps to the terrace.

LATER THAT night they were all in the private sitting room at the back of the house, Gallagher, Martineau, Helen and Sarah. Gallagher poured burgundy into four glasses while Helen opened the french window a little. It was very close. She breathed the perfumed air for a few moments, then drew the heavy curtains across.

"So, what happens, now?" Sean Gallagher asked.

"He certainly can't walk at the moment," Helen de Ville said.

"At least he's safe upstairs for the time being," Sarah said.

"He can't sit out the war there," Martineau pointed out. "We need to get him to Granville. Then Cresson can radio London and have a Lysander over, any night we want."

"But how to get him there, that's the thing," Gallagher sighed.

"They've got the small boat traffic under tight control here. Observation posts all along the coast, as you saw for yourself today."

"So what *is* the solution?" Sarah demanded. "We must do something soon."

There was a movement at the window, the curtains parted and Guido Orsini stepped into the room. "Perhaps I can help," he said in English.

CHAPTER 12

WHEN THE phone rang in his office at command headquarters Felix Necker was just about to leave to go riding on the beach at St Aubin. He picked up the receiver and a look of horror appeared on his face. "My God! What's his estimated time of arrival? All right. Arrange a guard of honour. I'll be there as soon as I can."

He slammed down the receiver, then picked it up again and dialled GFP headquarters at Silvertide.

"Herr Major," Muller said when Necker's call was put through, "what can I do for you?"

"Rommel is due at the airport in forty-five minutes. He is arriving from Normandy in a Fiesler Stork, with his aide, a Major Hofer."

"But why?" Muller demanded. "I don't understand."

"Well I do," Necker told him. "It all makes perfect sense. First of all he orders Heine and the others to join General von Schmettow in Guernsey for the weekend, getting them all nicely out of the way, then he flies in out of the blue and takes the place apart. I know how Rommel operates, Muller. He'll go everywhere, check everything."

"At least one mystery is solved," Muller said.

"What's that?"

"The reason for Vogel being here. The whole thing ties in now."

"Yes, I suppose you're right," Necker said. "Anyway, never mind that now. I'll see you at the airport."

He put down the receiver, hesitated, then picked it up again and told the operator to connect him with de Ville Place. Helen answered the phone in the kitchen.

"It's for you," she said to Martineau. "Major Necker."

He took the receiver from her. "Vogel here."

"Good morning," Necker greeted him. "I'm sure it will come as no surprise to you to know that Field Marshal Rommel arrives at the airport in just over half an hour."

Martineau, concealing his astonishment, said, "I see."

"Naturally, you'll wish to greet him. I'll see you at the airport."

Martineau put down the phone slowly as Sarah came in from the garden. "What is it?" she demanded. "You look awful."

"I should do," he said. "I think the roof just fell in on me."

AT SILVERTIDE, Muller was hurriedly changing into uniform in the bathroom next to his office. He heard the outside door open and Kleist called, "Are you there, Herr Captain? You wanted us?"

"Yes, come in," Muller called, as he walked into the office, buttoning his tunic.

"Something up?" Kleist asked. He looked terrible. The bruising around his eyes had deepened and the plaster they had taped across his nose at the hospital didn't improve things.

"You could say that. I've just heard Rommel's flying in on what looks like a snap inspection. I'll have to get up to the airport now. You can drive me, Ernst," he told Greiser.

"What about me?" Kleist asked.

"With a face like that? I don't want you within a mile of Rommel. Take a couple of days off. Let's get moving, Ernst."

After they had gone, Kleist went to the cupboard where the captain kept his drinks, took out a bottle of cognac and poured a large measure into a glass. He swallowed some, went into the bathroom and examined himself in the mirror. He looked awful and his face hurt. It was all that damned Irishman's fault.

He said softly, "My turn will come, you swine, and when it does . . ."

Then he toasted himself in the mirror and emptied the glass.

As the Citroën moved past the harbour and turned along the esplanade Ernst Greiser said, "By the way, I made that call I had booked to my brother in Stuttgart last night."

"What did he have to say?"

"He didn't. He was on leave. Due back today, on the night shift. I'll speak to him then."

"Not that it matters all that much now," Muller said. "Nothing very mysterious about friend Vogel any longer. He obviously came here in advance of the field marshal, that's all."

Konrad Hofer put his hand on Baum's for a moment, in a gesture of reassurance, as the pilot taxied their plane towards the party of officers waiting nervously on the tarmac. Baum turned to nod briefly at Hofer, then adjusted the brim of his cap and tightened his gloves. Showtime, Heini, he told himself, so let's give a performance.

The pilot lifted the door. Hofer got out, then turned to help Baum who had unbuttoned his leather coat to reveal the Blue Max and the Knight's Cross at his throat. Felix Necker advanced to meet him and gave him a punctilious salute. "Field Marshal. A great honour."

Baum casually touched the peak of his cap with his field marshal's baton. "You are?"

"Felix Necker, sir. I'm temporarily in command. Colonel Heine has gone to Guernsey for the weekend. A conference with General von Schmettow."

"Yes, I know about that. Now then, whom have we here?"

Necker introduced the officers, starting with Martineau. "Standartenführer Vogel, whom I think you may know."

"No," Martineau said. "I have never had the pleasure of meeting the field marshal before."

Rommel's surprise at the presence of the SD officer was plain for everyone to see. He passed on, greeting Muller and the other officers and then inspecting the guard of honour. Afterwards he walked across the grass to a hangar where Luftwaffe ground crew waited rigidly at attention. Everyone trailed after him.

Finally he turned to Necker. "I want to see everything. You

understand? I'll be returning tomorrow, so we'll need a suitable billet for tonight. However, that can wait until later."

"The officers of the Luftwaffe mess have had a light luncheon prepared, Herr Field Marshal. It would be a great honour if you would join them."

"Certainly, Major, but afterwards, work. I've a lot to see."

THE OFFICERS' mess was upstairs, in what had been a public restaurant before the war. There was a buffet of salad, roast chicken and ham, served by young Luftwaffe boys in white coats acting as waiters. The officers hung eagerly on the field marshal's every word, conscious of their proximity to greatness.

Halfway through the meal, Baum excused himself and went off to the toilet, followed by Hofer. He checked himself in the mirror and said, "How am I doing?"

"Superbly." Hofer was exhilarated. "There are times when I really think it's the old man himself talking."

"Excellent." Baum combed his hair and adjusted the cheek pads that made his face squarer. He was more than enjoying himself. One thing was certain. He was good. He thought Rommel, so he became Rommel, that was his talent as a performer. "What about the SS colonel?" he said. "I didn't expect that."

"Vogel?" Hofer was serious for a moment. "I was talking to Necker about him. He just turned up on the island yesterday, backed by a special pass signed by Himmler and the Führer himself. So far he's given no information as to why he's here."

"I don't know," Baum said, "those bastards always make me feel funny. You're certain his presence has nothing to do with us?"

"How could it have? Army Group B headquarters only released the news that you were in Jersey an hour ago. So no need to panic. Let's get back to the fray."

IN THE GARDEN at de Ville Place, Sarah sat on the wall looking out over the bay and Guido leaned beside her.

The Italian's entrance through the curtains the night before had been dramatic, and had shocked them all, but his offer had made sense. Helen and Gallagher had assured Martineau of Orsini's trustworthiness, and so had Sarah, the most fervently of all.

Now, the Italian spoke to her in English. "Sarah," he said, shaking his head, "whoever told you that you could pass yourself off as a French tart was gravely mistaken. I knew there was something wrong about you from the start."

"And Harry? Did you think there was something wrong about him, too?"

"No. He worries me, that one. He plays Vogel too well."

"I know." She shivered. "I wonder how he's getting on."

"He'll be fine. The last person I'd ever worry about. You like him, don't you?"

"Yes," she said. "I do." Before they could take the conversation any further, Helen and Gallagher crossed the grass to join them.

"What are you up to?" Helen demanded.

"We were wondering how Harry was getting on," Sarah told her.

"He can take care of himself, that one," Gallagher said. "More important at the moment is the decision on what to do with Kelso. I think we should move him from the Chamber to my cottage."

Guido nodded. "That makes sense. Much easier to take him from there down to the harbour. I've made arrangements to meet Savary. He was picked up after the *Hugo* went down by one of the search and rescue craft from St Malo, and is due over from Granville this evening. He might be willing to smuggle Kelso across to France."

"Do you really think it has a chance of working?" Sarah demanded.

"Sean and I can fix him up some fake papers as a French seaman," Guido told her.

"We'll bandage his face. Say he was in the water after the attack on the convoy and sustained burns," Gallagher added.

"When you look at it, we don't have much choice," Helen said.

Sarah nodded. "I suppose not. It could all go so hideously wrong, though, and so easily."

"Yes, well, we won't think about that," Sean said. "We'll move Kelso late tonight." He smiled reassuringly and put an arm round Sarah. "It's going to work. Believe me."

MARTINEAU JOINED the cavalcade of cars as it left the officers' mess and took the road through the parish of St Peter's. Rommel fascinated him, as did the idea of being so close to one of the greatest soldiers the war had produced. The commander of the Westwall himself, the man dedicated to smashing the Allies on the beaches where they landed.

He was certainly energetic. They visited Meadowbank in the parish of St Lawrence where for two years military engineers and slave workers had laboured on tunnels designed to be an artillery depot. Now it was in the process of being converted into a military hospital.

Afterwards they saw the strong points at Grève-de-Lecq, Plemont and Les Landes. It all took time. The field marshal seemed to want to look in every foxhole personally, visit every gun post.

By the time they reached St Aubin it was evening and most of the party were beginning to flag. Baum, examining the map Necker had provided, noticed the artillery positions on Mont de la Rocque and asked to be taken up there.

Martineau followed, still on the tail of the line of cars climbing the steep hill of the Mont, until they came to a narrow turning that led out on top where there were a number of flat-roofed houses.

"A gun platoon only," Necker assured Baum as he got out. "No civilians living here now."

The house at the end was called Septembertide. In its garden a narrow entrance gave access to a series of underground bunkers and machine-gun posts, which ran along the crest of the hill beyond.

The troops stationed there were overwhelmed to have the Desert Fox in close proximity to them, none more so than the commanding officer, a Captain Heider. It transpired that Septembertide was his personal billet. When the field marshal expressed an interest in it, he eagerly led the way into the garden. The views across the bay were breathtaking. The garden was edged with a low concrete wall and the ground fell almost vertically down to the road far below.

Baum looked up at the house. There was a large terrace in front of the sitting room and balcony above, running the full length at bedroom level. "Nice." He turned to Heider. "I need somewhere to lay my head tonight. Will you lend it to me?"

Heider was beside himself with joy. "An honour, Herr Field Marshal. I can move in with my second-in-command for the night."

"I'm sure you can find us a decent cook amongst your men?"

"That will be no problem, Field Marshal."

Baum turned to Necker. "This will suit me very well indeed. Impregnable on this side and Captain Heider and his boys guarding the front. What more could one ask for?"

"But first it is hoped that you might join us for dinner at the officers' club?" Necker said diffidently.

"Another time. It's been a long day and, frankly, I'd welcome an early night. Call for me in the morning, say at nine, and we can do the other side of the island."

"At your orders, Herr Field Marshal."

They all went round to the front of the house where there was a general leave-taking. When everyone had gone, Baum asked Hofer, "Did I do well?"

"Superb," Hofer said. "You're a genius, Berger."

THE EVENING meal had already started at de Ville Place when Martineau got back. He peered in at the window and saw Sarah sitting with Guido and half a dozen naval officers at the table. He decided not to go in and, instead, went round to the back door and let himself into the kitchen. Helen was washing dishes at the sink and Gallagher was drying for her. "How did things go?" the Irishman demanded.

"Well enough. No problems, if that's what you mean."

Helen poured him a cup of tea and Gallagher said, "We've been making decisions while you've been away." He told him how they'd decided to move Kelso. When he was finished Martineau nodded. "Let's make it a bit later though. Say, around eleven."

He went upstairs and lay on the bed of the room that, for the sake of their cover, he shared with Sarah. He stared at the ceiling, strangely restless, remembering Rommel. What a target! It was nonsense, of course. Shoot Rommel and they'd have the island sewn up tight within an hour. Nowhere to go. They'd probably take hostages until the assassin gave himself up. But in spite of all reason the thought haunted him, would not go away. He lay there thinking about it, then got up, put on his belt with the holstered Walther PPK, found the Carswell silencer and put it in his pocket.

He went downstairs to the kitchen and Helen looked up in surprise. "You're going out again?"

"Things to do." He turned to Gallagher. "Tell Sarah I'll be back soon."

The Irishman frowned, "Is something wrong?"

"Not at all." Martineau assured him. "I'll see you later."

CHAPTER 13

MULLER WAS working late in his office at Silvertide when there was a knock on the door and Greiser looked in. "Working late tonight, Herr Captain?"

"I'm trying to catch up on some paperwork," Muller said. He stretched and yawned. "Anyway, what are you doing here?"

"I phoned my brother in Stuttgart. I've been talking to him about Vogel."

Muller was immediately alert and interested. "What did he have to say?"

"Well, he certainly never came across him at Gestapo head-quarters in Berlin. But he does point out that the SD are housed in a building at the other end of Prince Albrechtstrasse, and it is an open secret that the Reichsführer uses mystery men like Vogel and gives them special powers. Nobody is all that sure who they are."

"Which is exactly the point of the whole exercise," Muller observed.

"Anyway, he says people like that operate out of the SD unit at the Reich Chancellery. As it happens, he knows someone on the staff there rather well. An SS auxiliary named Lotte Neumann."

"And he's going to speak to her?"

"He has a call booked through to Berlin in the morning. He'll get back to me as soon as he can. At least it will tell us just how important Vogel is."

"Excellent." Muller nodded. "Have you seen Willi tonight?"

"Yes," Greiser admitted reluctantly. "At the club, then he insisted on going to a bar in some back street in St Helier."

"He's drinking?"

Greiser hesitated. "Yes, Herr Captain, heavily. I stayed with him for a while, but then he grew morose and angry, as he does. He told me to clear off."

"Damnation!" Muller sighed. "You'd better go to bed. I'll need you again in the morning. Nine o'clock at Septembertide."

KLEIST WAS at that moment parking his car at the edge of the de Ville estate, close to Gallagher's cottage. He was dangerously drunk, way beyond any consideration of common sense, and he had half a bottle of schnapps with him. He took a pull at it, got out of the car and walked unsteadily towards the cottage.

There was a chink of light at the drawn curtains covering one of the sitting room windows. He kicked the front door vigorously. There was no response. He kicked again, then tried the handle and the door opened. He peered into the sitting room. There was an oil lamp on the table, the embers of a fire in the hearth, but no other sign of life. He stood at the bottom of the stairs. "Gallagher, where are you?"

There was no reply. He got the oil lamp and went upstairs to see for himself, but both bedrooms were empty. He descended the stairs again, went into the sitting room and put the lamp on the table.

He took a Mauser from his right-hand pocket and sat down in a wing back chair, nursing the gun in his lap as he waited.

Right, you bastard. You've got to come home some time.

AT SEPTEMBERTIDE, Baum and Hofer had enjoyed a surprisingly good meal, washed down with a bottle of excellent claret. The half moon gave a wonderful view of St Aubin's Bay and they went out on the terrace to finish their wine.

After a while, the corporal who had cooked the meal appeared. "All is in order, Herr Major," he told Hofer. "I've left coffee and milk on the side. Will there be anything else?"

"Not tonight," Hofer told him. "We'll have breakfast at eight sharp in the morning."

The corporal clicked his heels and withdrew.

"My dear Berger, what a day," Hofer said. "The most remarkable of my life."

"And the second act still to come." Baum yawned. "Speaking of tomorrow, I could do with some sleep."

"If you're not already up I'll wake you at seven thirty tomorrow," Hofer told him.

Baum went inside and climbed the stairs. He closed the outer door to his bedroom suite, and walked through the dressing area into the bedroom itself. It was plainly furnished, with heavy velvet curtains at the windows. When he parted them he found a glass door. He opened it and stepped out onto the balcony. The view was even better at this height and he could see down into St Aubin's harbour in the distance. The sea was calm, a white line of surf down there on the beach, the sky luminous with stars in the moonlight.

A night to thank God for.

He raised his glass. "*L'Chayim*," he said softly. Then he turned, parted the curtains and went back inside, leaving the door open.

IT HAD taken Martineau twenty minutes to make his way up through the trees. The going was rough. He still had no idea what he intended as he pulled himself up over the concrete back wall, cautiously, aware of voices. He stood in the shadow of a palm tree, and looked up to see Hofer and Rommel on the terrace in the moonlight.

"My dear Berger, what a day. The most remarkable of my life."

"And the second act still to come."

Martineau stayed in the shadow of the palm tree, astonished at this exchange. It didn't make sense. After they had gone inside, he advanced cautiously across the lawn and paused, because a few seconds later the field marshal reappeared on the balcony and stood alone looking out over the bay.

He raised his glass. "*L'Chayim*," he said softly and went back inside. *L'Chayim* meant "to life", the most ancient Hebrew toast. It was enough. Martineau reached for the railings on the terrace and pulled himself over.

HEINI BAUM took the Blue Max and the Knight's Cross with Oak Leaves, Swords and Diamonds from round his neck, and laid them on the dressing table. He removed his cheek pads and examined his face in the mirror, running his fingers through his hair.

"Not bad, Heini. Not bad. I wonder what the great man would say if he knew he was being taken off by a Jew-boy?"

As he started to unbutton his tunic, Martineau, who had been standing on the other side of the curtain screwing the silencer onto the barrel of his Walther, stepped inside. Baum saw him instantly in the mirror and reached for a Mauser pistol which lay on the dressing table.

"I wouldn't," Martineau told him. "They've done wonders with this new silencer. Now, hands on head."

"Is this some plot of the SS's, to get rid of me?" Baum asked, playing his role to the hilt. "I'm aware that Reichsführer Himmler never liked me, but I didn't realise how much."

Martineau sat on the edge of the bed, took out a packet of cigarettes one-handed and shook one out. As he lit it he said, "I heard you and Hofer talking on the terrace. He called you Berger."

"You've been busy."

"And I was outside a few minutes ago when you were talking to yourself, so let's get down to facts. Number One, you aren't Rommel."

"If you say so."

"All right," Martineau said, "let's try again. If I am part of an SS plot to kill you on Himmler's orders, there wouldn't be much point if you aren't really Rommel. Of course, if you are . . ."

He raised the PPK and Baum took a deep breath. "Very clever."

"What are you, an actor?"

"Turned soldier, turned actor again."

"Incredible," Martineau said. "You fooled me. I saw Rommel in Paris last year and you're exactly like him. Does he know you're Jewish?"

"No." Baum frowned. "Look, what kind of SS man are you?"

"I'm not," Martineau laid the PPK down on the bed beside him. "I'm a colonel in the British army."

"I don't believe you," Baum said in astonishment.

"A pity you don't speak English otherwise I could prove it," Martineau said.

"But I do." Baum broke into very good English indeed. "I played the Moss Empire circuit in London, Leeds and Manchester in 1935 and '36."

"And you went back to Germany? You must have been crazy."

"My parents." Baum shrugged. "Like many old folk they didn't believe it would happen. I hid in the army using the identity of a man killed in an air raid. My real name is Heini Baum."

"Harry Martineau."

Baum hesitated, then shook hands.

"Tell me, what's the purpose of this masquerade?" a curious Martineau asked.

"Rommel's having a quiet get-together in Normandy with Generals von Stulpnagel and Falkenhausen. A highly illegal business, as far as I can make out. Apparently they want to get rid of Hitler and salvage something from the mess while there's still a chance."

"Possible," Martineau said. "There have been attempts on Hitler's life before."

"Now you know all about me. What about you? What are you doing here?"

Martineau told him briefly about Kelso.

"I wish you luck," Baum said. "From the sound of it, it's going to be tricky trying to get him out by boat. At least I fly out tomorrow night. A nice fast exit."

Martineau saw it then, the perfect answer to the whole situation. Sheer genius. "Tell me," he said, "once back, you'll be returned to your regiment?"

"I imagine so."

"Which means you'll have every chance of having your head blown off during the next few months because the invasion's coming and you paratroopers will be in the thick of it. How would you like to go to England instead?"

"You've got to be joking," Baum said in astonishment. "How could such a thing be?"

"Just think about it." Martineau said. "What's the most useful thing about being Field Marshal Erwin Rommel?"

"You tell me."

"The fact that everyone does what you tell them to do. For example, tomorrow evening you go to the airport to return to France in the little Stork you came in?"

"So what?"

"There's a JU52 transport up there, the mail plane, due to leave for France round about the same time. What do you think would happen if Field Marshal Rommel turned up just before take-off with an SS Standartenführer, a wounded man on a stretcher, a young Frenchwoman, and commandeered the plane? What do you think they'd say?"

Baum smiled. "Not very much, I should imagine."

"Once in the air," Martineau said, "the nearest point on the English coast would be no more than half an hour's flying time in that Junkers."

"My God!" Baum said in awe. "You really mean it."

"Do you want to go to England or don't you?" Martineau asked. "Make up your mind." Baum nodded. "That's settled then." Martineau unscrewed the silencer and put the PPK back in its holster.

"So what about Hofer?"

"I'll think of something. I'll join your tour of the east of the island tomorrow morning. At a suitable point, with Necker there, ask me where I'm staying. I'll tell you about de Ville Place. You tell Necker you like the sound of it. That you'd like to have lunch there. Insist on it. I'll finalize things with you then."

"The third act, rewritten at so late a date that we don't get any chance to rehearse," Baum said wryly.

IT WAS JUST after midnight when Sean Gallagher and Guido took Hugh Kelso down the narrow stairway to Helen's bedroom. The back stairs to the ground floor were wider and easier to negotiate and they were in the kitchen within a couple of minutes. They sat Kelso down and Helen closed the door to the stairs, turning the key.

"So far so good," Gallagher said. "Are you all right, Colonel?"

The American looked strained, but nodded eagerly. "I'm feeling great, just to be moving again."

"Fine. We'll take the path through the woods to my place."

Helen motioned him to silence. "I think I hear a car."

Sarah hurriedly turned down the lamp, went to the window and drew the curtains as a vehicle entered the yard. "It's Harry," she said.

Helen turned up the lamp again and Sarah unbolted the back door. Martineau slipped in and closed the door behind him. The excitement was plain to see on the pale face shadowed by the SS cap.

"What is it, Harry?" Sarah demanded. "Has something happened?"

"I think you could definitely say that, but it can wait until later. Ready to go, are we?"

"As ever was," Kelso said.

"Let's get it done then."

"Sarah and I will go on ahead to make sure everything's ready for you." Helen turned down the lamp again, opened the door, and she and Sarah hurried across the yard. Gallagher and Guido linked hands and Kelso put his arms about their necks.

Martineau stood to one side to let them go out, closed the door behind him, and they started across the courtyard.

THE PALE moonlight filtered through the trees and the track was clear before them. Sarah took Helen's arm. For a moment there was intimacy between them, and she was very aware of that warm, safe feeling she had known in the time following her mother's death when Helen had been not only a strong right arm, but the breath of life to her.

"What happens afterwards?" Helen asked. "Back to nursing?"

"Who knows?" Sarah said. "This whole thing's been like a mad dream. I've never known a man like Harry, never known such excitement."

They paused on the edge of the clearing, looking at the cottage a few yards away, bathed in moonlight.

"Temporary madness, Sarah, just like the war. Not real life. Neither is Harry Martineau. He's not for you, Sarah. God help him, he's not even for himself."

In Sean Gallagher's cottage, sitting at the window, Kleist had seen them the moment they emerged from the wood, and it was their intimacy which struck him at once. He got up, moved to the door and opened it a little. It was then that he realised they were speaking English. Helen was saying, "Loving someone is different from being in love, darling. Being in love is a state of heat that passes, believe me. Still, let's get inside. The others will be here in a moment." She put a hand on the door and it moved. "It seems to be open."

And then the door swung, a hand had her by the front of her coat and the muzzle of Kleist's Mauser pressed against her cheek. "Inside, Frau de Ville," he said roughly, "and let us discuss the curious fact that this little French bitch not only speaks excellent English, but appears to be a friend of yours."

For a moment, Helen was frozen, aware only of a terrible fear. Kleist reached and grabbed Sarah by the hair.

"And you are expecting others, I gather. I wonder who?" He walked backwards, pulling Sarah with him. "No stupidities, or I pull the trigger." He released Sarah suddenly. "Go and draw the curtains." She did as she was told. "Good, now come back here."

His fingers tightened in her hair again. The pain was dreadful. She wanted to cry a warning, but was aware of the Mauser pointed at Helen's head. Kleist stank of drink, was shaking with excitement as he waited, listening to the voices approaching. Only at the last moment, as the door swung open, did he push the women away.

"Look out!" Sarah cried, but her anguished cry was too late.

KELSO LAY on the floor and Helen, Sarah and the three men leaned against the wall in a row, arms outstretched. Kleist relieved Martineau of his PPK and slipped it into his pocket. "The SS must be doing its recruiting in some strange places these days." Martineau said nothing, and Kleist moved on to Guido Orsini, running one hand over him expertly. "I never liked you," he said contemptuously. "All you damned Italians have ever done is give us trouble."

Kleist turned to Gallagher, running a hand over him quickly. He found nothing and stood back. "Now then, you bastard, I've been waiting for this." He smashed his right fist into the base of the Irishman's spine. Gallagher cried out and went down. Kleist booted him in the side and Helen screamed, "Stop it!"

Kleist smiled at her. "I haven't even started."

He stirred Gallagher with his boot. "Get up and put your hands on your head." Gallagher stayed on his hands and knees for a moment and Kleist prodded him with a toe. "Come on, move, you thick piece of Irish dung."

Gallagher got to his feet, a half smile on his face. "Half Irish," he said, "and half Jersey. As I told you before, a bad combination."

Kleist struck him backhanded across the face. "I told you to get your hands on your head."

"Anything you say." The bone-handled gutting knife was ready in Gallagher's left hand, skilfully palmed. His arm swung, there was a click as he pressed the button, the blade flickered in the lamplight, catching Kleist in the soft flesh under the chin. Kleist discharged the Mauser once into the wall and fell back against the table. He tried to get up, then tumbled to the floor, kicked convulsively and lay still.

"Oh my God!" Helen said, and turned away.

Martineau crouched down and retrieved his Walther from the dead man's pocket. He looked up at Gallagher. "Where did you learn that trick?"

"Another legacy from my old grandfather," Gallagher said.

Martineau and Guido got Kelso onto the couch while Gallagher picked up his knife. He wiped it on the dead man's coat. "Do you think this was an official visit?"

"I shouldn't imagine so." Martineau picked up an empty bottle of schnapps. "He'd been drinking and he wanted revenge. He came up here looking for you and when you weren't here, he waited."

"What happens now?" Kelso demanded. "I mean, if Kleist doesn't turn up for work in the morning, Muller will turn this island inside out."

"No need to panic." Martineau picked up a rug and covered the body. "There's always a way out. First, we find his car. It's bound to be parked nearby." He nodded to Guido and Gallagher and led the way out. Within ten minutes they had found the Renault.

"Now what do we do?" Guido asked.

"Give him back to them," Martineau said crisply. "He was drunk and ran off the road in his car, it's as simple as that." He turned to Gallagher. "Have you anywhere suitable to suggest? Not too far, but far enough for there to be no obvious connection with the de Ville estate."

"Yes," Gallagher said. "I think I've got just the place."

"Good. I'll go up to the house and get the Kübelwagen. You two take the Renault back to the cottage and put Kleist in the boot." He turned and hurried away through the wood.

WHEN MARTINEAU arrived back at the cottage in the Kübelwagen, they already had Kleist's body in the boot of the car and Gallagher was ready to go. Guido had agreed to remain in the cottage with Kelso, Sarah and Helen.

"How long will it take us to get to this place?" Martineau asked Gallagher.

"About fifteen or twenty minutes at this time in the morning."

"Are we likely to run into anybody?"

"There's the odd military police patrol, but we've every chance of driving to La Moye Point without seeing a soul."

"Right, then let's get moving."

Gallagher was right. Their run along La Route Orange towards Corbière Point passed without incident. Finally, Gallagher turned into a narrow lane. He stopped the Renault and got out.

"The road turns along the edge of the cliffs about two hundred yards from here. It's always been a hazard. No protecting wall."

"All right," Martineau said. "We'll leave the Kübelwagen here."

He got a can of petrol and stood on the running board of the Renault as Gallagher drove along the bumpy road between high hedges. They came out on the edge of the cliffs, where a narrow track ran down to rocks and surf below.

"This will do." Martineau hammered on the roof

Gallagher braked, got out and went round to the boot, leaving the engine running. He and Martineau dragged Kleist out, carried him round to the front and put him behind the wheel.

"All right?" Gallagher demanded in a low voice.

"In a minute." Martineau opened the can and poured petrol over the front seat and the dead man's clothes. "Okay, let him go."

Gallagher released the handbrake, leaving the engine in neutral, and turned the wheel. He started to push and the Renault left the track, moving across the grass.

"Watch yourself!" Martineau called, as he struck a match and dropped it through the open passenger window.

For a moment he thought it had gone out and then, as the Renault bumped over the edge, orange and yellow flame blossomed. They turned and ran back along the lane and behind them there was a grinding crash and then a brief explosion.

When they reached the Kübelwagen, Martineau said, "You get down in the back, just in case."

Five minutes later, as Martineau turned onto the Route du Sud, he saw two military police motorcycles parked at the side of the road. One of the policemen stepped out, hand raised in the moonlight. Martineau slowed at once.

"Military police," he whispered to Gallagher. "Stay low."

He opened the door and got out. "Is there a problem?" At the sight of the uniform, the two policemen jumped to attention. One of them had a lighted cigarette between the fingers of his left hand. "Ah, I see. What we might term a smoke break," Martineau said.

"Standartenführer, what can I say?" the man replied.

"Personally, I always find it better to say nothing. Now, what did you want?"

"Nothing, Standartenführer. It's just that we don't often see a vehicle at this time in the morning in this sector."

"And you were quite properly doing your duty." Martineau produced his papers. "My SD card. Come on, man, hurry up."

The policeman barely glanced at it, hands shaking as he handed it back. "All is in order."

"Good, you can return to your duties then." Martineau got back in the car. "As for smoking, be a little more discreet."

He drove away. Gallagher said quietly, "How the hell do you manage to sound such a convincing Nazi?"

"Practice, Sean, that's what it takes. Lots of practice."

WHEN THEY got back to the cottage, Sarah opened the door instantly. "Everything go all right?"

"Perfect," Gallagher told her as he followed Martineau inside.

"We put the car over a cliff and made sure it burned."

"Was that necessary?" Helen shivered.

"We want him to be found," Martineau said. "On the other hand, we don't want him in too good a condition because then there would be that knife wound to explain."

Kelso said, "So, you had no trouble?"

"A patrol stopped us on the way back," Gallagher replied. "I was well out of sight and Harry did his Nazi bit. No problem."

"So, all that remains now is for Guido to contact Savary in the morning," Sarah said.

"No. There's been a rather significant change of plan."

There was general astonishment. Martineau stood with his back to the fire and said calmly, "If you'll all sit down, I'll tell you."

CHAPTER 14

AT NINE O'CLOCK the following morning, the field marshal's cavalcade left Septembertide, and drove to St Helier. The first stop was Elizabeth Castle. The tide was out. They parked the cars opposite the Grand Hotel and clambered on board an armoured personnel carrier which followed the line of the causeway across the beach. "When the tide is in, the causeway is under water, Herr Field Marshal," Necker explained.

Baum was in his element, filled with excitement at the turn events had taken. He could see Martineau seated at the other end of the truck talking to a couple of young officers, and for a wild moment wondered whether he might have dreamed the events of the previous night. The carrier drove up from the causeway through the old castle gate and stopped. They all got out and Necker said, "The English fortified this place to keep out the French in Napoleon's time. Some of the original guns are still here."

"Now we fortify it further to keep out the English," Baum said. "There's irony for you."

As he led the way to the moat and the entrance to the inner court, Martineau moved to his shoulder. "As a matter of interest, Herr Field Marshal, Sir Walter Raleigh was governor here in the time of Queen Elizabeth Tudor."

"Really?" Baum said. "An extraordinary man. Soldier, sailor, musician, poet, historian."

He strode on ahead, Martineau at his shoulder, talking animatedly, Hofer trailing anxiously behind with Necker. An hour later, after a thorough inspection of every gun and strongpoint Baum could find, they were taken back across the beach to the cars.

ON THE CLIFFS near La Moye Point a group of field engineers hauled on a line, helping the corporal on the other end to walk up the steep slope. He came over the edge and unhooked himself. The sergeant in charge of the detail gave him a cigarette. "You don't look too good."

"Neither would you. He's like a piece of badly cooked meat."

"Any papers?"

"Burnt along with most of his clothes. The car is a Renault and I've got the number."

The sergeant wrote it down. "The police can handle it now." He turned to the other men. "All right, back to the post, you lot."

MONT ORGUEIL at Gorey on the east coast of Jersey is probably one of the most spectacular castles in Europe. Baum stood in the observation post which had been constructed on the highest point of the castle and looked across at the French coast through a pair of fieldglasses. He was for the moment slightly apart from the others. Hofer moved to his shoulder. "Vogel seems to be pressing his attentions," he said softly.

"He wanted to talk so I let him," Baum replied, keeping the glasses to his eyes. "I'm keeping him happy, Major. I'm trying to keep them all happy. Isn't that what you want?"

"Of course. You're doing fine. Just be careful, that's all."

Necker moved up to join them and Baum said, "Fantastic, this place. Now I would like to see something different. The other side of island life. Vogel tells me he's billeted at some manor house called de Ville Place. You know it?"

"Yes, Herr Field Marshal. The owner, Mrs Helen de Ville, is a most charming woman."

"And it's a delightful house, according to Vogel. I think we'll have lunch there. I'm sure Mrs de Ville won't object, especially if you provide the food and wine." He looked up at the cloudless blue sky. "A beautiful day for a picnic."

Minutes later, as the officers moved to where the cars waited, a military police motorcyclist drove up and handed a signal to Muller. Martineau, standing nearby, heard everything.

"The bloody fool," Muller said softly, and crumpled the signal up in his hand. He went to Necker, spoke briefly to him and then got into a Citroën. It moved away quickly, and Martineau walked over to Necker. "Muller seemed agitated."

"Yes," Necker said. "It would seem that one of his men has been killed in a car accident."

"How unfortunate." Martineau offered him a cigarette. "Allow me to compliment you on the way you've handled things at such short notice."

"We do what we can. It's not every day Rommel comes visiting."

THE MESS SERGEANT and his men, who had descended on de Ville Place from the officers' club at Bagatelle, brought ample supplies of food and wine. They simply took the place over, carrying tables and chairs from the house, covering them with the white linen tablecloths they had brought with them, working very fast.

Helen went up to her bedroom, searched through the wardrobe and found a summer dress in pale green organdie which dated from happier days. As she was pulling it over her head, there was a tap on the door and Sarah came in. "Getting ready to play hostess?"

"I don't have much choice, do I?" Helen told her. She brushed back her hair and pushed in side combs.

Sarah said, "You look very nice."

"And so do you." Sarah was wearing a dark coat and tiny black hat, her hair swept up.

"We do our best. I'll be glad when it's all over."

"Not long now, love." Helen put her arms round her and held her for a moment, then turned and moved to the window. "Yes, I thought so. They're here." She smiled. "Don't forget that down there amongst all those officers you and I are formally polite. French only."

"I'll remember."

"Good. Into battle then."

THE WHOLE AFFAIR was obviously a huge success. After lunch Guido Orsini asked permission to take photos to which the field marshal graciously agreed, posing with the assembled officers, Martineau standing next to him.

Necker, on his fourth glass of champagne, was standing by the drinks table with Hofer and Martineau. "I think he's enjoying himself."

Hofer nodded. "Most definitely. A marvellous place and a most charming hostess."

"However reluctant," Martineau commented acidly. "But too well bred to show it. The English upper classes are always the same."

"Perhaps understandably so," Necker said coldly. "Her husband, after all, is a major in the British army."

"And therefore an enemy of the Reich, but then I hardly need remind you of that." Martineau picked up his glass and walked away.

Sarah was surrounded by the naval officers and Guido was taking photos. She waved. "Please, Max," she said in French, "we must have a photo together."

He laughed lightly and handed his glass to Bruno. "Why not?"

The others moved to one side and he and Sarah stood there together in the sunshine.

Guido smiled. "That's fine."

"Good." Martineau retrieved his champagne from Bruno. "And

now I must speak to the field marshal. You'll look after Anne-Marie for me, Lieutenant?" he said to Guido and walked away.

Then he noticed Muller arrive. The policeman looked around as if searching for someone, and when he saw Martineau, crossed the grass towards him.

"May I have a few words in private, Standartenführer?"

"Of course," Martineau said, and they moved away from the others, towards the trees. "What can I do for you?"

"My man Kleist was killed last night. A messy business. His car went over a cliff at La Moye Point."

"Not good," Martineau said. "Had he been drinking?"

"Perhaps," Muller replied cautiously. "The thing is, we can't think of any convincing reason for him having been there. It's a remote sort of place."

"What has it to do with me?" Martineau knew what was coming.

"We ran a routine check with the military police patrols in that sector in case they'd noticed his car."

"And had they?"

"No, but we have got a report that *you* were stopped on the Route du Sud, at approximately two o'clock this morning."

"Correct," Martineau told him calmly. "But what has that to do with the matter in hand?"

"To get to the area of La Moye, where Kleist met with his unfortunate accident, it would be necessary to drive along the Route du Sud. I was wondering what you were doing there at that time?"

"It's quite simple," Martineau said. "I was about my business, under direct orders of the Reichsführer, as you well know. When I return to Berlin he will expect a report on what I have found here in Jersey. I'm sorry to say it will not be all that favourable."

Muller frowned. "Perhaps you'd explain, Standartenführer."

"Security for one thing," Martineau told him. "Or the lack of it. I left de Ville Place at midnight, drove through St Peter's Valley, up to the village and along to Grève-de-Lecq. Just after one o'clock I reached St Ouen's Bay, having taken a back lane around Les Landes. A defence area, am I right?"

"Yes, Standartenführer."

"I then drove along the bay to Corbière lighthouse and was eventually stopped on the Route du Sud by two military policemen who were having a smoke at the side of the road. You do get the point, don't you, Muller?" His face was hard. "I drove around this island in the early hours of the morning close to some of our most sensitive installations and was only stopped once. Would you say that was satisfactory?"

"No, Standartenführer."

"Then I suggest you do something about it." Martineau put his glass down on a nearby table. "And now I think I've kept the field marshal waiting long enough."

As Martineau walked away, Greiser joined Muller. "What happened?"

"Nothing very much. He says he was on a tour of inspection. It fits well enough," Muller said, "but I do hate coincidences. When they get poor old Willi's body up, get it straight in for a postmortem. If he was awash with schnapps when he died, at least we'll know where we are."

"I'll see to it," Herr Captain. Greiser nodded and strode quickly away.

BAUM STOOD talking to Helen and a couple of officers. He turned as Martineau approached. "Ah, there you are, Vogel. I'm in your debt for suggesting my visit to such a delightful spot."

"A pleasure, Herr Field Marshal."

"Come, we'll talk awhile and you can tell me how things are in Berlin these days." He took Helen's hand and kissed it. "You'll excuse us, Frau de Ville?"

"Of course, Herr Field Marshal."

Martineau and Baum strolled away across the grass.

"Right, this is what happens," said Martineau. "The mail plane leaves at eight. They expect you to fly out in the Stork at about the same time. I'll turn up at Septembertide at seven to collect you. I'll

NIGHT OF THE FOX

have Sarah with me, also Kelso, in Kriegsmarine uniform and heavily bandaged."

"What about Hofer?"

"Don't worry about him. I've got a syringe and a strong sedative, courtesy of the doctor who's been treating Kelso. An armful of that and he'll be out for hours. We'll lock him in his bedroom."

"But how do I explain his absence at the airport?"

"I'll come to that in a minute. Necker will be there with his staff to bid you a fond farewell. It's at that point you announce you intend to fly out in the mail plane. Say that the chief medical officer at the hospital has made representations on behalf of this sailor, badly wounded in the convoy attack the other night and in urgent need of special treatment. As you're using the bigger plane, you're giving me and Sarah a lift."

"And Hofer?"

"Tell Necker that Hofer is following behind. That he's going to fly out in the Stork on his own."

"And you think all this will work?"

"Yes," Martineau said, "because nobody says no to Field Marshall Erwin Rommel."

Baum sighed. "I'll never get a role this good again. Ever."

CHAPTER 15

ON A SLAB in the post-mortem room at the hospital, Willi Kleist's corpse looked even more appalling. Major Speer stood waiting while the two medical corporals who were assisting him carefully cut away the burned clothing. Greiser watched in fascinated horror.

The scalpel in Speer's right hand didn't seem particularly large, but when he ran it down from just below the throat to the belly, the flesh parted instantly. The smell was terrible and Greiser could take no more. He removed himself hurriedly to the lavatory.

When he'd recovered, he walked down to the main entrance to phone Muller from the porter's desk.

"It's Greiser, Herr Captain."

"How are things going?" Muller asked.

"Well, it's hardly one of life's great experiences. I'm waiting for Major Speer's conclusions now. They're doing lab tests."

"You might as well hang on for the results. By the way, there's been an interesting development. Your brother phoned. He's heard from this Neumann woman in Berlin. The one who works in the Reichsführer's office."

"And?"

"She's never heard of Vogel. She's kept her enquiries discreet for the moment. Of course, as your brother points out, these special envoys of Himmler are mystery men to everyone else."

"Yes, but you'd think someone like Lotte Neumann would have at least heard of him. What are you going to do?"

"As soon as Speer's ready with those results, give me a ring and I'll come round myself to see what he has to say."

IT WAS JUST before five when the cavalcade of cars returned to Septembertide. Baum and Hofer got out and Necker joined them. "A memorable day, Major," Baum said. "I'm truly grateful."

"I'm pleased everything has gone so well, Herr Field Marshal."

Necker saluted and got back into his car. As the officers dispersed, Martineau stepped forward. "Might I have a word, Herr Field Marshal?"

Hofer was immediately wary, but Baum said cheerfully, "Of course, Standartenführer. Come in."

He went inside, followed by Hofer and Martineau. They went into the living room where Baum took off his leather coat and his cap, and opened the glass door to the terrace. "A drink, Standartenführer?"

"That would be very acceptable."

"Konrad." Baum nodded to Hofer, who poured the drinks. "What an extraordinary view," Baum said, looking down at St

Aubin's Bay. He raised his glass. "To soldiers everywhere, who always bear the burden of man's stupidity." He emptied his glass, smiled and said in English, "All right, Harry, let's get on with it."

Hofer looked suddenly bewildered, and Martineau produced the Walther from his trenchcoat pocket. "It would be stupid to make me shoot you. Nobody would hear a thing with this silencer." He removed Hofer's gun from its holster. "Sit down."

"Who are you?" Hofer demanded.

"Well, I'm certainly not Standartenführer Max Vogel, any more than Heini here is the Desert Fox."

"Heini?" Hofer looked even more bewildered.

"That's me," Baum said. "Heini Baum. Erich Berger was killed in an air raid in Kiel. I took his papers and joined the paratroops. What better place for a Jew to hide!"

"My God!" Hofer said hoarsely.

"Yes, I thought you'd like that. A Jew impersonating Germany's greatest war hero. A nice touch of irony there."

Hofer turned to Martineau. "And who are you?"

"My name is Martineau. Lieutenant Colonel Harry Martineau. I work for SOE. I'm sure you've heard of us."

"Yes. I have indeed." Hofer reached for his glass and finished the rest of his brandy. "So what do you intend to do?" he asked.

"Field Marshal Rommel will fly out in the mail plane tonight, not the Stork, which means I can leave with him, along with a couple of friends, destination England."

"The young lady?" Hofer managed a smile. "So she also is not what she seems."

"One thing more," Martineau said. "Thanks to Heini, I know where Rommel has been this weekend and what he's been up to. The assassination of Hitler would suit the Allied cause very well. Therefore, when I get back to England and tell my people about this business, they'll keep quiet. We wouldn't want to make things too difficult for Field Marshal Rommel, if you follow me. More power to his elbow."

"And how will Rommel explain all this to the Führer?"

"Simple. There's been more than one plot against his life already by the French Resistance and Allied agents. To use Berger to impersonate him on occasion made good sense, and what happened here in Jersey proved it. If he'd come himself, I'd have killed him. The fact that Berger decided to change sides was regrettable, but hardly Rommel's fault."

Martineau stood up. "Now, let's have you upstairs."

Hofer did as he was told and they followed him up to his bedroom. "Do you intend to kill me?" he said.

"Of course not. I need you to tell all to Rommel, don't I?" Martineau replied. "Just keep still and don't make a fuss and you'll be fine." There was a burning pain in Hofer's right arm and he was plunged into darkness. Baum emptied the contents of the syringe before pulling it out and Martineau eased the major down onto the bed.

They went down to the hall. As he opened the front door, Martineau said, "I'll be back at seven o'clock."

Baum nodded. "I'll see you later then, Standartenführer." He turned, walked back into the living room and found the cook corporal awaiting him.

"At your orders, Herr Field Marshal."

"Something simple," Baum said. "Scrambled eggs, I think. Just for me. Major Hofer is having a lie down before we leave."

A SHORT TIME later, Gallagher and Martineau were easing Kelso into a Kriegsmarine uniform which Sean had acquired from the troop supply depot in exchange for black market goods.

Gallagher cut the right trouser leg so that it would fit over the cast. "How's that?" he asked.

"Not bad."

Sarah entered from the kitchen with two large bandage rolls and surgical tape. She went to work on Kelso's head and face, leaving only one eye and the mouth visible.

"That's really very professional," Gallagher said, grinning.

Martineau glanced at his watch. It was almost six o'clock. "We'll go up to the house now, Sean. You keep an eye on him. I'll be back with the Kübelwagen in an hour."

He and Sarah left, and Gallagher went into the hall and came back with a pair of crutches. "Present for you." He propped them against the table. "See how you get on."

Kelso pushed himself up on one leg, got a crutch under one arm, and then the other. He took one hesitant step, paused, then moved on with increasing confidence to the other side of the room.

"Brilliant!" Gallagher told him. "Long John Silver to the life. Now try again."

"ARE YOU certain?" Muller asked.

"Oh, it's quite definite," Speer said. "Something sharp sheared right up through the roof of the mouth into the brain."

"Is it likely such an injury would be explained by the kind of accident he was in?"

"No," Speer said. "Whatever did this was as razor-sharp as a scalpel. The external flesh of the face and neck is badly burned so I can't be certain, but if you want my opinion, he was stabbed under the chin. Does that make any kind of sense?"

"Yes," Muller said. "I think it does. Thanks very much." He nodded to Greiser. "Let's go."

As he opened the door, Speer said, "One more thing."

"What's that?"

"You were quite right. He had been drinking heavily. I'd say, from the tests, about a bottle and a half of spirits."

On the steps outside the main entrance of the hospital, Greiser asked, "What do you think, Herr Captain?"

"That another word with Standartenführer Vogel is indicated, Ernst, so let's go and see him."

IN THE KITCHEN at de Ville Place, Sarah, Helen and Martineau sat round the table. The door opened and Guido came in with a bottle. "Warm champagne," he said. "The best I can do."

"Are you certain the house is empty?" Sarah asked.

"Oh, yes. They're all on tonight's convoy to Granville. Kriegs-marine headquarters haven't come up with a new assignment for me yet."

He pulled the cork and poured champagne into the four glasses Helen provided. She raised hers. "What shall we drink to?"

"Better days," Sarah said.

"Life, liberty and the pursuit of happiness," Guido added. "Not forgetting love."

"You wouldn't." Sarah laughed and turned to Martineau. "And you, Harry, what do you wish?"

"One day at a time is all I can manage," he said as he finished his champagne. "My God, that tastes awful." He put down the glass. "I'll go and get Kelso now. Be ready to leave when I get back, Sarah."

He drove off in the Kübelwagen towards the cottage. At the same time, two hundred yards to the right, the Citroën carrying Muller and Greiser turned into the courtyard of de Ville Place.

IN THE BEDROOM Sarah put on her hat and coat. She heard a car outside, glanced out of the window and saw Muller get out of the Citroën. It was trouble, she knew that instantly. She opened her handbag. The little Belgian automatic Kelly had given her was still there. She lifted her skirt and slipped the gun into the top of her right stocking, then smoothed down her skirt and coat and left the room.

Muller was in the hall talking to Helen. Greiser stood by the front door and Guido was near the door leading to the kitchen. As Sarah came down the stairs Muller looked up and saw her.

"Ah, there you are, Mademoiselle Latour," Helen said in French. "Captain Muller was looking for the Standartenführer. Do you know where he is?"

"I've no idea. Is there a problem?"

"Perhaps. You've no idea when he'll be back?"

"None at all," Sarah said.

"Very well, if the Standartenführer isn't available I'll make do with you." Muller turned to Greiser. "Take her out to the car."

"But I protest," Sarah started to say.

Greiser smiled, his fingers hooking painfully into her arm. "Protest all you like, sweetheart," he said. "I enjoy it," and he hustled her out.

Muller turned to Helen, who tried to stay calm. "Perhaps you would be good enough to tell Standartenführer Vogel on his return that if he wishes to see Mademoiselle Latour, he must come to Silvertide." He turned and walked out.

KELSO WAS doing quite well with the crutches. He made it to the Kübelwagen under his own steam.

"Nice going, me old son," Gallagher said.

As Martineau got behind the wheel, Guido emerged from the trees at the run. He leaned against the car, gasping.

"What is it, man?" Gallagher demanded.

"Muller and Greiser turned up. They're looking for you, Harry. They've taken Sarah. Muller says if you want to see her, you'll have to go to Silvertide. What are we going to do?"

"Get in!" Martineau ordered, and he drove away as the Italian and Gallagher scrambled aboard.

In the courtyard of de Ville Place Helen waited anxiously on the steps. She hurried down to the Kübelwagen as Martineau braked to a halt. "What are we going to do, Harry?"

"I'll take Kelso up to Septembertide and we'll collect Baum. If the worst comes to the worst Baum and Kelso can fly out together. Baum knows what to do."

"But we can't leave Sarah," Kelso protested.

"I can't," Martineau said, "but you can. You're what brought us here in the first place. The reason for everything."

Helen clutched his arm. "Harry!"

"Don't worry. I won't leave her. I'll go down to Silvertide. I'll think of something. Now we must go."

The Kübelwagen moved away across the yard and the noise of the engine faded. Gallagher turned to Guido. "Get the Morris out and you and I'll take a run down to Silvertide."

"What do you have in mind?" Guido asked.

"I never could stand just sitting around and waiting."

MARTINEAU DROVE into the courtyard at Septembertide and helped Kelso out of the Kübelwagen. The American followed him, swinging between his crutches, to the front door which was opened by a corporal. As they went in, Baum appeared from the sitting room.

"Ah, there you are, Vogel! And this is the man you told me about?" He turned to the corporal. "I'll call when I want you."

Baum stood back and as Kelso moved past him into the sitting room, Martineau said quietly, "There's been a change of plan. Muller came looking for me at de Ville Place. I wasn't there but Sarah was. They've taken her to Silvertide."

"Don't tell me," Baum said. "You're going to go to the rescue."

"Something like that." Martineau glanced at his watch. It was just after seven. "You and Kelso keep to your schedule. Getting him out of here is what's important." He walked quickly out, and the Kübelwagen roared away.

Baum poured cognac into a glass. He drank it slowly. "I might have known that under all that surface cynicism he was the kind of man who'd go back for the girl." He pulled on his leather trench-coat and gloves, twisted the white scarf round his neck, adjusted the angle of the cap and picked up his baton.

"What are you going to do?" Kelso demanded.

"Martineau told me that the important thing about being Field Marshal Erwin Rommel was that everyone would do what I told them to do. Now we'll see if he's right. You stay here."

He strode through the courtyard into the road and the men leaning beside the personnel carrier sprang to attention. "One of you get Captain Heider."

A second later Heider hurried out. "Herr Field Marshal?"

"Be ready to go in five minutes. You'll find a wounded sailor indoors. Have a couple of men help him into the personnel carrier. And send a message to the airport to warn them that we shall be flying out in the mail plane."

"But Herr Field Marshal, I don't understand," Heider said.

"You will, Heider," the field marshal told him. "You will."

SARAH SAT on a chair in front of Muller's desk, hands folded in her lap, knees together. They'd made her take off her coat and Greiser was searching the lining while Muller went through her handbag.

"So you are from Paimpol?" he said.

"That's right."

"Sophisticated clothes for a Breton girl from a fishing village."

"Oh, but she's been around, this one, haven't, you?" Greiser ran his fingers up and down her neck, making her flesh crawl.

Muller said, "Where did you and Standartenführer Vogel meet?"

"Paris," she said.

"But there is no visa for Paris amongst your papers."

Her stomach contracted with fear, her throat was dry. "I had one. It ran out." Oh, God, Harry, she thought, fly away. Just fly away. And then the door opened and Martineau walked in.

There were tears in her eyes as Greiser stood back and Harry gently put an arm round her.

The emotion she felt was so overwhelming that she committed the greatest blunder of all. "Oh, Harry," she said in English. "Why didn't you go?"

Muller smiled gently and picked up the Mauser that lay on his desk. "So, you speak English also, mademoiselle. This whole business becomes even more intriguing. I think you'd better relieve the Standartenführer of his Walther, Ernst."

Greiser did as he was told and Martineau said in German, "What do you think you're doing, Muller? There's a perfectly good reason why Mademoiselle Latour speaks English. Her mother was English. The facts are there on file at SD headquarters in Paris."

"You have an answer for everything," Muller said. "What if I told you that a post-mortem has indicated that Willi Kleist was murdered, the time of death being between midnight and two o'clock? I need hardly remind you that it was two o'clock when you were stopped on the Route du Sud, no more than a mile from where the body was discovered. What do you have to say to that?"

"You've been over-working, Muller. When the Reichsführer hears the full facts he'll . . ."

For the first time Muller lost his temper. "Enough of this. It's time we knew the truth about you, Standartenführer. I detest violence. However, Greiser here is different. A strange thing about Greiser. He doesn't like women. He would actually find it pleasurable to extract the truth from Mademoiselle Latour in private, but I doubt that she would."

"Oh, I don't know." Greiser put an arm round Sarah and slipped a hand inside her dress, fondling a breast. "She might like it."

Sarah's left hand clawed down his face, drawing blood. She felt only rage now, more powerful than she had ever known. As Greiser staggered back, Muller's attention was momentarily distracted. Sarah saw her opportunity. She reached under her skirt, and pulled the tiny automatic from her stocking. Her arm swung up and she fired at point blank range, shooting Muller in the temple. The Mauser dropped from his hand to the desk, he reeled back against the wall and fell to the floor. Greiser tried to get his gun from his pocket, but it was too late. Martineau had picked up the Mauser.

GALLAGHER AND Guido were sitting in the Morris on the other side of the road from Silvertide when they heard the sound of vehicles. They turned to see the military column approaching. In front was a Kübelwagen with the top down, and Field Marshal Erwin Rommel standing in the passenger seat for the whole world to see.

The Kübelwagen braked to a halt, Rommel got out and soldiers ran forward in obedience to Heider's shouted orders.

"Right, follow me!" Baum called, and he marched straight in through the entrance of Silvertide. He advanced into Muller's office, with Heider and a dozen armed men behind him, and peered over the desk at Muller's body.

"Herr Field Marshal, this woman has murdered Captain Muller," Greiser whimpered.

Baum ignored him and said to Heider, "Put this man in a cell."

"Yes, Herr Field Marshal." Heider nodded and three of his men grabbed the protesting Greiser. Heider followed them out.

"Back in your vehicles," Baum shouted to the others and he held Sarah's coat for her. "Let's go."

GALLAGHER AND Guido saw them come out of Silvertide and get into the Kübelwagen, Martineau and Sarah in the back, Baum standing up in front. He waved his arm, the Kübelwagen led off, the whole column following.

"Now what?" Guido asked.

"My God, is there no poetry in you at all?" Gallagher demanded. "We follow them of course. I wouldn't miss the last act for anything."

AT SEPTEMBERTIDE, on the bed in the small room, Konrad Hofer groaned and moved restlessly. He opened his eyes, mouth dry, and stared at the ceiling, trying to work out where he was. It was like waking from a bad dream, something you knew had been terrible and yet had already been forgotten. Then he remembered. He tried to sit up, and rolled off the bed onto the floor.

He pulled himself up, head swimming, and reached for the door handle. It refused to budge, so he turned and lurched across to the window. He fumbled with the catch and then gave up the struggle and slammed his elbow through the pane.

The sound of breaking glass brought two soldiers running into the courtyard. They stared up.

"Up here!" Hofer called. "Get me out! I'm locked in!"

He sat on the bed, his head in his hands, and tried to breathe deeply, aware of the sound of boots clattering up the stairs and along the corridor. He saw the handle turn.

"There's no key, Herr Hofer," one of them called.

"Then break it down, you fool!" he replied.

A moment later the door burst open, crashing against the wall, and the two men stood staring at him.

"Get Captain Heider," he said.

"He's gone, Herr Major."

"Gone?" Hofer still had difficulty thinking clearly.

"With the field marshal, Herr Major. The whole unit went with them. We're the only two here."

The effects of the drug made Hofer feel as if he was underwater. He shook his head vigorously. "Can you drive?"

"Of course, sir. Where does the Herr Major wish to go?"

"The airport," Hofer said. "And there's no time to lose, so get me downstairs and let's get moving."

CHAPTER 16

AT THE AIRPORT, the Luftwaffe guard of honour waited patiently as darkness fell. Necker paced up and down anxiously, wondering what on earth was going on. First of all that extraordinary message from Heider about the mail plane, and now this. Twenty minutes past eight and still no sign of the field marshal.

There was the sudden roar of engines. He turned in time to witness the extraordinary sight of the armoured column coming round the corner of the main airport building, the field marshal standing up in the Kübelwagen at the front, hands braced on the edge of the windshield.

The column made straight for the Junkers. Necker saw the field marshal wave to the pilot who was looking out of the side window. The centre engine of the plane coughed into life, and Rommel was barking orders. Soldiers leaped from the trucks, rifles ready, and a bandaged sailor was taken from the personnel carrier to the Junkers by two soldiers.

The whole thing happened in seconds. As Necker started forward, the field marshal came to meet him. Beyond the field marshal, Necker saw Standartenführer Vogel and the French girl dismount from the personnel carrier and go up the short ladder into the plane.

Baum was enjoying himself. He smiled and put a hand on Necker's shoulder. "My deepest apologies for the delay, Necker, but I had things to do. Heider was good enough to assist me."

Necker was bewildered. "But, Herr Field Marshal . . ." he shouted above the noise of the engines.

Baum ignored him. "The chief medical officer at the hospital told me of this young sailor, wounded in the convoy attack the other night and needing treatment at the burns unit in Rennes. He asked if I'd take him with me. In the state he's in we'd never have got him into the Stork. That's why I need the mail plane."

"And Standartenführer Vogel?"

"He was going back tomorrow anyway, so I may as well give him and the young woman a lift." He clapped Necker on the shoulder again. "We must be off now. Again, my thanks. I shall be in touch with General von Schmettow to express my entire satisfaction with the way things are in Jersey."

He saluted and turned to go up the ladder into the plane. Necker called, "But, Herr Field Marshal, what about Major Hofer?"

"He should be arriving later. He'll leave in the Stork, as arranged."

Baum scrambled inside the plane, the crewman pulled up the ladder and closed the door. The Junkers taxied away to the east end of the runway and turned. There was a deepening roar from its three engines as it moved faster and faster, became a silhouette only, in the gathering gloom, and then lifted, climbing out over St Ouen's Bay.

GUIDO HAD parked the Morris a couple of hundred yards along the airport road. He and Gallagher saw the Junkers lift into the evening sky and fly west to where the horizon was tipped with fire.

Guido said softly. "My God, they actually pulled it off."

453

Gallagher nodded. "So now we can go home and get our stories straight for when the questioning starts."

"No problem," Guido said. "Not if we stick together. I am, after all, an authentic war hero, which always helps."

"That's what I love about you, Guido. Your engaging modesty," Gallagher laughed. "Now, let's move. Helen will be worried."

They got into the Morris and drove away.

AT THE AIRPORT, Necker was standing talking to Captain Adler, the Luftwaffe duty control officer, when a Kübelwagen carrying Hofer and the two soldiers came round the corner of the main building and braked to a halt.

Necker knew trouble when he saw it. "Hofer. What is it?"

Hofer was being helped out of the rear of the vehicle. "Have they gone?"

"Less than five minutes ago. The field marshal took the mail plane. He said you'd follow in the Stork."

"No!" Hofer exclaimed. "*Not* the field marshal."

Necker's stomach contracted. "What are you saying?"

"The man you thought was Field Marshal Rommel is his double, a damned traitor called Berger who's thrown in his lot with the enemy. You'll also be happy to know that Standarten-führer Max Vogel is an agent of the British Special Operations Executive."

Necker was totally bewildered. "I don't understand."

"It's really quite simple," Hofer told him. "They're flying to England in the mail plane." He turned to Adler. "Get on the radio. Scramble a night fighter squadron. There's no time to lose."

THE JUNKERS was a workhorse and not built for comfort. Most of the interior was crammed with mail sacks and Kelso sat on the floor propped against them, leg outstretched. Sarah was on a bench on one side of the plane, Baum and Martineau on the other. The crewman came out of the cockpit and joined them.

"My name is Braun, Herr Field Marshal. Sergeant observer. The pilot, Oberleutnant Sorsa, would take it as an honour if you would care to come up front?"

"You don't have a full crew? Just the two of you?" Martineau enquired.

"All that's necessary on these mail runs, Standartenführer."

"Tell Oberleutnant Sorsa I'll be happy to take up his offer a little later," Baum said.

"Certainly, Herr Field Marshal." The observer went back into the cockpit.

Baum turned to Martineau and smiled. "Five minutes?"

"That should be about right." Martineau moved across to sit beside Sarah. "Are you all right?"

"You mean am I going through hell because I just killed a man?" Her face was very calm. "My one regret is that it was Muller instead of Greiser. Greiser was an animal. Muller was just a policeman on the wrong side."

"From our point of view."

"No, Harry," she said. "Whichever way you look at it, we're right and the Nazis are wrong. They're wrong for Germany and they're wrong for everyone else. It's as simple as that."

"Good for you," Kelso said. "A lady who stands up to be counted."

"I know," Martineau said. "It's wonderful to be young." He tapped Baum on the knee. "Ready?"

"I think so."

Martineau took out his Walther and gave it to Sarah. "Action stations. You'll need that to take care of the observer. Here we go."

He opened the cabin door and he and Baum squeezed into the cockpit behind the pilot and the observer.

Oberleutnant Sorsa turned. "An honour to have you here, Field Marshal."

"A pleasure to be here," Baum said.

"If there is anything we can do for you?"

"There is actually," Baum told him. "You can haul this thing round and fly forty miles due west until we are completely clear of all Channel Island traffic."

"But I don't understand?"

Baum took the Mauser from his holster and touched it against the back of Sorsa's neck. "Perhaps this will help you."

"Later on, when I tell you to, you'll turn north," Martineau said, "and make for England."

"England?" the observer said in horror.

"Yes," Martineau told him. "Now, change course to the west."

Sorsa did as he was told and the Junkers ploughed on through the darkness.

Martineau leaned over the observer. "Right, now for the radio. Show me the frequency-selection procedure." Braun did as he was told. "Good, now go and sit down in the cabin and don't do anything stupid. The lady has a gun."

The boy squeezed past him and Martineau got into the co-pilot's seat and started to transmit on the frequency reserved by SOE for emergency procedure.

IN THE CONTROL room at Jersey airport, Hofer and Necker waited anxiously while Adler spoke on the radio. A Luftwaffe corporal came up and spoke to him briefly.

Adler turned to the two officers. "All night fighters in the Brittany area were scrambled an hour ago. Heavy bombing raids expected over the Ruhr."

"There must be something, for God's sake," Hofer said.

Adler waved him into silence, listening, then put down the mike and turned, smiling. "There is. One JU88S night fighter. Its port engine needed a check and it wasn't finished in time to leave with the rest of the squadron."

"And is it now?" Necker demanded eagerly.

"Oh yes. He's just taken off from Cherbourg."

"But can he catch them?" Necker asked.

"Herr Major," Adler said. "That old crate they're flying in can do a hundred and eighty flat out. The JU88S with the new engine-boosting system does better than four hundred."

Necker turned in triumph to Hofer. "They'll have to turn back, otherwise he'll blow them out of the sky."

But Hofer had been thinking about that. If the mail plane returned, it would mean only one thing. Martineau and the others would be flown to Berlin for interrogation. That couldn't be allowed to happen. Berger knew about Rommel's connection with the plot against the Führer, and so did Martineau. He took a deep breath. "No, we can't take a chance on their getting away. Send an order to the pilot of that night fighter to shoot on sight. They mustn't reach England."

"As you say, Herr Major." Adler picked up the microphone.

MARTINEAU LEFT Heini Baum in the cockpit to keep an eye on Sorsa, and went back to join the others.

"Everything okay?" Kelso asked him.

"Couldn't be better. I've made contact with our people in England. They're going to provide an escort to take us in, courtesy of the RAF." He smiled and took Sarah's hand. She'd never seen him so excited. Suddenly he looked years younger. "You all right?" he asked her.

"Fine, Harry. Just fine."

"Dinner at the Ritz tomorrow night," he said.

"By candlelight?"

"Even if I have to take my own." He turned to Braun, the observer. "You said something about coffee, didn't you?"

Braun started to get up, but the plane bucked wildly as a great roaring filled the night, then dropped like a stone. Braun lost his balance, and Sarah screamed. "Harry! What is it?"

The plane regained some sort of stability, and Martineau peered out of one of the side windows. A hundred yards away on the port side, flying parallel with them, he saw a Junkers.

"We've got trouble," he said. "Luftwaffe night fighter." And he turned and wrenched open the door to the cockpit.

Sorsa glanced over his shoulder, face grim and pale in the cockpit lights. "We've had it. What do I do now?" he demanded. "That thing can blow us out of the sky."

Martineau suddenly saw it all. Something had gone wrong, and it had to involve Hofer, and if that were so the last thing he'd want would be to have them back in Gestapo hands, betraying Erwin Rommel.

At that moment the roaring filled the night again, and the mail plane shuddered as cannon shell slammed into the fuselage. Sorsa pushed the control column forward, going down in a steep dive into the cloud layer below. The Junkers roared overhead, passing like a dark shadow.

Martineau scrambled back into the cabin. Several gaping holes had been punched in the fuselage of the plane and two windows were shattered. The observer lay on his back, his uniform soaked with blood.

Sarah looked up, surprisingly calm. "He's dead, Harry."

There was nothing to say. Martineau turned back to the cockpit, hanging on as the mail plane continued its steep dive. They rocked again in the turbulence as the Junkers passed over them.

"Bastard!" Sorsa said, in a rage now. "I'll show you!"

Baum, who was crouched on the cockpit floor, looked up at Harry with a ghastly smile. "He's a Finn, remember? They don't really like us Germans very much."

The mail plane burst out of the clouds at three thousand feet and kept on going down.

"What are you doing?" Martineau cried.

"Just one trick up my sleeve. He's very fast, and I'm very slow, and that makes it difficult for him." Sorsa glanced over his shoulder again and smiled savagely. "Let's see if he's any good."

He was at seven or eight hundred feet when the Junkers came in again on their tail, too fast and banking to port to avoid a collision.

Sorsa took the mail plane down to five hundred feet and levelled off. "Right, you swine. Let's have you," he said.

And when it happened, it was over in seconds. The Junkers

swooped in on their tail again, and Sorsa hauled back the column and started to climb. The pilot of the Junkers banked steeply to avoid what seemed like an inevitable collision, but at that height and speed he had nowhere to go but straight down into the waves below.

"You lost, my friend," Sorsa said softly, and eased back the control column. "All right, let's go back upstairs."

Martineau glanced back into the cabin. "You two all right?" he called.

"Fine. Is it over?" Sarah asked.

"You could say that." Martineau turned back to the cockpit as Sorsa levelled out at six thousand feet. He squeezed into the co-pilot's seat and twisted the radio dial experimentally. Everything seemed to be in working order. "I'll let them know what happened," he said, and started to transmit on the SOE emergency frequency.

"My God," Heini Baum moaned, "what a last act!"

Sorsa said cheerfully, "Tell me, is the food good in British prisoner-of-war camps?"

Martineau smiled. "Oh, I think you'll find we make special arrangements for you, my friend," and then, as he made contact with SOE headquarters, he started to speak into the radio.

IN THE CONTROL room at Jersey airport, Adler sat by the radio, an expression of disbelief on his face. He removed the earphones and turned slowly.

"What is it, for God's sake?" Necker demanded.

"That was Cherbourg Control. They've lost the JU88."

"What do you mean, lost it?"

"They had the pilot on the radio. He'd attacked several times. Then they suddenly lost contact and he disappeared from the radar screen. They think he's gone into the drink."

"And the mail plane?" Hofer said softly.

"Still on radar, moving towards the English coast. No way on earth of stopping her."

There was silence. "What happens now?" Necker asked after a time. "What happens when Berlin hears about this?"

"God knows, my friend," Hofer muttered wearily. "A bleak prospect—for all of us."

ABOUT FIFTEEN minutes after Sorsa had changed course for the second time, Baum suddenly pointed to his left. "Look out there."

Martineau turned and saw, in the moonlight, a Spitfire take station to port. As he checked the starboard side, another appeared. He reached for the co-pilot's headphones.

A crisp voice said, "Martineau, do you read me?"

"Martineau here."

"You are now twenty miles east of the Isle of Wight. We're going to turn inland and descend to three thousand feet. I'll lead and my friend will bring up the rear. We'll shepherd you right in to Hornley Field."

"Our pleasure." Martineau sat back.

"Everything okay?" Baum asked.

"Fine. They're leading us in. Another fifteen minutes, that's all."

Baum was excited. "I can't believe this. I really feel as if I'm breaking out of something."

"I know," Martineau said.

"Do you really? I wonder. I was at Stalingrad, did I tell you that? The greatest disaster in the history of the German army. Three hundred thousand killed. I was lucky. The day before the airstrip closed I was wounded and flown out. Ninety-one thousand taken prisoner, twenty-four generals. Why them, and not me?"

"I spent years trying to find the answers to questions like that," Martineau told him. "In the end, I decided there weren't any answers. No sense, and precious little reason."

He pulled down the earphones as the voice came over the air again, giving new instructions and a fresh course. He passed them on to Sorsa. They descended steadily. A few minutes later, the voice sounded again. "Hornley Field, right in front. In you go."

The runway lights were plain to see, and Sorsa reduced power and dropped his flaps to float in for a perfect landing. The escorting Spitfires peeled away and climbed into the night.

The Junkers touched down. Sorsa taxied towards the control tower and the plane rolled to a halt.

Baum got up and laughed excitedly. "We made it!"

Sarah was smiling. She reached for Martineau's hand and held on tight. Kelso was laughing with relief. Baum got the door open and he and Martineau peered outside.

A voice called over a loudhailer, "Stay where you are." A line of airmen in RAF blue, each one carrying a rifle, moved towards them.

Baum jumped down onto the runway. The voice called again. "Stay where you are!"

Baum grinned up at Harry. "Will you join me, Standarten-führer?" And then he turned and strode towards the line of men. "Put the rifles away," he called in English. "We're all friends here."

There was a single shot. He spun round, took a couple of steps back towards the Junkers, then sank on his knees and rolled over.

Harry ran forward, "No more, you fools!" he shouted. "It's me, Martineau."

He was dimly aware of the squadron leader telling his men to stay back, as he dropped to his knees beside Baum. Heini reached up with his hand and grabbed Martineau by the front of his uniform. "You were right, Harry," he said hoarsely. "No sense, no reason to anything. Say *Kaddish* for me. Promise?"

"I promise," Martineau said. "Don't talk, Heini. We'll get you a doctor."

Sarah crouched beside him. Baum's body seemed to shake and then his hand lost its grip on Martineau's tunic and he lay still. Martineau got up slowly and saw Doug Munro and Jack Carter standing nearby.

"It was an accident, Harry," Munro said. "One of the lads panicked."

"Sometimes I really wonder who the enemy is," said Martineau. "If you're still interested, you'll find your American colonel in the plane."

He went past them, through the line of airmen, and walked aimlessly towards the old aero club buildings. He sat down on the steps of the clubhouse and lit a cigarette, suddenly cold. After a while, he became aware of Sarah sitting a few feet away.

"What did he mean, say *Kaddish* for him?"

"It's a sort of mourning prayer. A Jewish thing. Usually relatives take care of it, but he didn't have any. Now your education's complete. No honour, no glory, only Heini Baum out there, lying on his back," he said.

He got to his feet and she too stood up. Someone had brought a stretcher and they were carrying Baum away. Kelso was crossing the runway on his crutches, Munro and Carter on either side of him.

"Did I remember to tell you how well you did?" Martineau asked Sarah.

"No."

"You were good. So good that Dougal will probably try to use you again. Don't let him. Go back to that hospital of yours."

"Perhaps." They started to walk towards the waiting cars. "And you?" she asked. "What's going to happen to you?"

"I haven't the slightest idea."

She took his arm and held it tightly, and as the runway lights were switched off, they moved through the darkness together.

CHAPTER 17

Jersey 1985

IT WAS very quiet in the library as Sarah Drayton stood at the window peering out. The door opened and Vito, the manservant, came in with a tray which he placed on a low table by the fire. "Coffee, Contessa."

"Thank you, Vito, I'll see to it."

He went out and she sat down and reached for the coffee pot.

"And what happened afterwards?" I asked her.

"Well, Konrad Hofer flew out in the Stork the following morning to brief Rommel on what had happened."

"And how did Rommel cover himself?" I asked.

"Very much as Harry had suggested. He went to see Hitler personally. Told him intelligence sources had warned him of the possibility of plots against his life which was why he'd used Berger to impersonate him. If he'd gone to Jersey himself, Harry would have assassinated him. Berger was dismissed as a rat who'd deserted a sinking ship."

"I'm sure Rommel didn't put it to the Führer in quite those terms."

"Probably not. What must have made his story so believable from the Führer's point of view was Harry himself."

"I don't understand."

"Harry had gone to some pains to tell Hofer who he was. The Gestapo had been after him for a long time. Remember, they only just failed to get their hands on him earlier, at Lyons."

"So Rommel was believed?"

"Oh, I don't think Himmler was too happy with the story, but the Führer seemed satisfied enough. They drew a veil over the whole thing. Hardly wanted it on the front page of national newspapers at that stage of the war. The same thing applied with our people. With D-day coming, Eisenhower was only too delighted to have got Kelso back in one piece and our intelligence people didn't want to publicise the Baum affair, because that would have made things difficult for Rommel and the other generals who were plotting against Hitler."

"And they almost succeeded," I said.

"Yes, the bomb plot in July, later that year. Hitler was injured but survived. Von Stauffenberg and many other conspirators were executed."

"And Rommel?"

"Three days before the attempt on Hitler's life, Rommel's car was machine-gunned by low-flying Allied planes. He was terribly badly wounded. Although he was involved in the plot, that kept him out of things in any practical sense."

"But they caught up with him?"

"In time. Someone broke under Gestapo torture and implicated him. However, Hitler didn't want the scandal of having Germany's greatest war hero in the dock. He was given the chance to take his own life."

"And Hugh Kelso?"

"He didn't return to active duty because that leg of his never fully recovered, but they needed his engineering expertise for the Rhine crossings in March '45. He was killed while supervising work on a damaged bridge at Remagen. A booby trap."

I got up and walked to the window and stared out at the rain. "Amazing," I said. "And the most extraordinary thing is that it never came out, the whole story."

"There was a special reason for that," she added. "After the island was liberated on the ninth of May 1945, it was a difficult time, with accusations and counter-accusations about those who were supposed to have consorted with the enemy. There was a government committee appointed to investigate, and their report was given a special one-hundred-year security classification. You can't read it until the year 2045."

I went back and sat down again. "What happened to Helen de Ville, and Gallagher and Guido?"

"They didn't come under any kind of suspicion. Guido was taken prisoner at the end of the war, but Dougal Munro secured his release. Helen's husband, Ralph, returned in bad shape. He'd been wounded in the desert campaign. He never really recovered and died three years after the war."

"Did she and Gallagher marry?"

"No. It sounds silly, but I think they'd known each other too long. She died ten years ago. He followed her within a matter of months. He was eighty-three and still one hell of a man. I was with him at the end."

I'd been putting off the most important question. "And you and Martineau? What happened there?"

"I was awarded the MBE, Military Division, the reason for the award unspecified, naturally, and Harry received the Distinguished Service Order. But his health deteriorated. That chest wound from the Lyons affair always troubled him, though he worked at Baker Street for a while. There was a lot on after D-day. We had a flat within walking distance of the office."

"Were you happy together?"

"Oh, yes." She nodded. "The best few months of my life. I knew it couldn't last, mind you. He needed more, you see."

"Action?"

"That's right. He needed it like a drug. In January 1945 certain German generals made contact with British Intelligence with a view to bringing the war to a splendid end. Dougal Munro concocted a scheme in which an Arado from the Enemy Aircraft Unit was flown to Germany by a volunteer pilot, with Harry as passenger. The aircraft had German markings and they both wore Luftwaffe uniform."

"And they never got there?"

"Oh, but they did. They landed on the other side of the Rhine, where Harry met with the people concerned, and then flew back. There was a directive to Fighter Command, warning of their return in a German plane. Apparently the message hadn't been forwarded to one particular squadron, and the Arado was attacked by a Spitfire near Margate. Visibility was very bad that day and it was assumed that the Arado had gone down in the sea. Now we know better."

There was silence. She picked a couple of logs from the basket and put them on the fire. "And you?" I said. "How did you manage?"

"Well enough. I got a government grant to go to medical school. Once I was qualified I went to the Cromwell for a year as a house physician. It seemed fitting somehow. For me, that's where it had all started. Guido visited London regularly after the war. Each year I was at medical school he asked me to marry him. I always said no."

"And he still came back and tried again?"

"In between his other marriages. Three in all. I gave in at last on the strict understanding that I would still work as a doctor. One thing he'd omitted to tell me was just how wealthy the Orsini family was. Their estate was outside Florence. I was a partner in a country practice there for years."

"So you really are a contessa?"

"I'm afraid so. Contessa Sarah Orsini. Guido died in a car crash three years ago. Can you imagine a man still racing Ferraris at sixty-four years of age?"

"From what you've told me of him, I'd say it fits."

"After he died I decided to come back to Jersey. This island is a strange place. It has that kind of effect. It pulls people back, sometimes after many years. As a doctor here it's much easier to use my maiden name. The locals would find the other one rather intimidating."

"You and Guido, were you happy?"

"I loved Guido dearly. I gave him a daughter and then a son, the present count, who rings me twice a week from Italy, begging me to return to Florence."

"I see."

She stood up. "Guido understood what he called the ghost in my machine. The fact of Harry would not go away. As Aunt Helen told me, there was a difference between being in love and loving someone."

"She also told you that Martineau wasn't for you."

"She was right enough there. Whatever had gone wrong in Harry's psyche was more than I could cure." She opened the desk drawer again, took out a yellowing piece of paper and unfolded it. "This is the poem he threw away that first day at the cottage at Lulworth. The one I recovered."

"May I see it?"

She passed it across and I read it quickly:

The station is ominous at midnight,
hope is a dead letter,
time to change trains for something better.
No local train now,
long since departed,
no way of getting back to where you started.

I felt inexpressibly saddened as I handed it back to her. "He called it a rotten poem," she said, "but it says it all."

There didn't seem a great deal to say to that. I glanced at my watch. "I've taken enough of your time. I think I'd better be getting back to my hotel."

"I'll run you down there."

"There's no need for that," I protested. "It isn't far."

"It's all right. I want to take some flowers down to the grave anyway."

IT WAS STILL raining heavily as we drove down the hill and parked outside the entrance to St Brelade's Church.

Sarah Drayton got out and put up her umbrella and I handed the flowers to her.

"I want to show you something," she said. "Over here."

She led the way to the older section of the cemetery and finally stopped before a moss-covered granite headstone. "What do you think of that?"

It read:

HERE LIE THE MORTAL REMAINS
OF CAPTAIN HENRY MARTINEAU
LATE OF THE 5TH BENGAL INFANTRY
DIED 7 JULY 1859

"I only discovered it last year, quite by chance. I got one of those ancestor-tracing agencies to check up on it for me. Captain Martineau, Harry's grandfather, came here to retire. Apparently he died at the age of forty from the effects of some old wound or other. His wife and children emigrated to America."

"How extraordinary."

"When we visited this place Harry told me he had this strange feeling of being at home."

We reached the spot where Harry Martineau had been laid to rest earlier that afternoon, and stood looking down at the fresh mound of earth. Sarah laid the flowers on it and straightened up, a curiously indomitable figure, the ancient church behind her, the bay beyond.

"Damn you, Harry Martineau," she said softly. "You did for yourself, but you did for me as well."

There was no answer to that, could never be, and suddenly I felt like an intruder. I turned and walked away and left her there in the rain in that ancient churchyard, alone with the past.

The Eagle
Has Flown

The Eagle
Has Flown

It is winter in wartime London and a cold fog shrouds the city. To Liam Devlin, the fog is a blessing, a cloak for his extraordinary mission: to break a German war hero out of a British fortress. But fog can also be an enemy, veiling the truth and threatening to undo even the best-laid plans.

AT ONE O'CLOCK on the morning of Saturday 6 November 1943, Heinrich Himmler, Reichsführer of the SS and chief of state police, received a simple message: THE EAGLE HAS LANDED. A small force of German paratroopers under the command of Oberstleutnant Kurt Steiner, aided by IRA gunman Liam Devlin, were at that moment safely in England and poised to snatch the British Prime Minister, Winston Churchill, from the Norfolk country house where he was spending a quiet weekend near the sea. By the end of the day—thanks to a bloody confrontation in the village of Studley Constable between American Rangers and the Germans—the mission was a failure, Liam Devlin apparently the only survivor. As for Kurt Steiner...

London–Belfast: 1975

CHAPTER 1

 HERE WAS an Angel of Death on top of an ornate mausoleum in one corner, arms extended. I remember that well because someone was practising the organ, and light drifted across the churchyard in coloured bands through stained-glass windows. The church wasn't particularly old—built on a high tide of Victorian prosperity, like the tall houses surrounding it.

St Martin's Square. A good address once. Now just a shabby backwater in Belsize Park, but a nice, quiet area, where a woman might walk alone at midnight in safety and people minded their own business.

The flat at Number 13 was on the ground floor. My agent had borrowed it for me from a cousin who had gone to New York. It was old-fashioned and comfortable and suited me fine. I was on the downhill slope of a new novel and needed to visit the reading room at the British Museum most days.

That November evening, the evening it all started, it was raining heavily, and just after six I passed through the iron gates and followed the path through the forest of Gothic monuments and gravestones. In spite of my umbrella, the shoulders of my trench coat were soaked—not that it bothered me. I've always liked the rain, the wet city streets stretching into winter darkness, the feeling of freedom it contains.

Things had gone well that day with the work; the end was very definitely in sight.

The Angel of Death was closer now, shadowed in the half-light from the church, the two marble attendants on guard at the mausoleum's bronze doors, everything as usual, except that tonight I could have sworn there was a third figure and that it moved out of the darkness towards me.

For a moment I knew genuine fear, and then as the figure came into the light I saw a young woman, quite small and wearing a black beret and a soaked raincoat. She had a briefcase in one hand. The face was pale, the eyes dark and somehow anxious.

"Mr Higgins? You are Jack Higgins, aren't you?"

She was obviously an American. I took a deep breath to steady my nerves. "That's right. What can I do for you?"

"I must talk to you. Is there somewhere we could go?"

I hesitated, reluctant for obvious reasons to take this any further, and yet there was something quite out of the ordinary about her. Something not to be resisted.

I said, "My flat's just over the square there."

"I know," she said. I still hesitated, and she added, "You won't regret it, believe me. I've information of vital importance to you."

"About what?" I asked.

"What really happened afterwards at Studley Constable. Oh, lots of things you don't know."

Which was enough. I took her arm and said, "Right. Let's get in out of this damn rain before you catch your death, and you can tell me what this is all about."

MY FLAT had a late Victorian decor—mahogany furniture, and red velvet curtains at the bay window. Except for the central heating, the only concession to modern living was the gas fire, which made it seem as if logs burned brightly in a stainless steel basket.

"That's nice," she said, and turned to face me, even smaller than I had thought. She held out her right hand awkwardly, still clutching the briefcase in the other. "Ruth Cohen," she said.

I said, "Let's have that coat. I'll put it in front of the radiator."

"Thank you." She fumbled at her belt with one hand and I laughed and took the briefcase from her.

"Here, let me." As I put it down on the table I saw that her initials were etched on the flap in black. The only difference was that it had PhD at the end of it.

"PhD?" I said.

She smiled. "Harvard, modern history. Six months' post doc at London University."

"That's interesting," I said. "I'll make some tea."

I went to the kitchen and put on the kettle, then turned to find her leaning on the doorway, arms folded.

"Your thesis," I said. "What was the subject?"

"Certain aspects of the Third Reich in World War Two."

"Cohen—are you Jewish?" I turned to make the tea.

"My father was a German Jew. He survived Auschwitz and made it to the US, but died the year after I was born."

I could think of no more than the usual inadequate response. "I'm sorry."

She stared at me for a moment, then went back to the sitting room. I followed with a tray, placed it on a small coffee table by the fire, and we sat opposite each other in wingback chairs.

"Which explains your interest in the Third Reich," I said as I poured the tea.

She frowned and took the cup of tea I handed her. "I'm just a historian," she said. "I have no axe to grind. My particular obsession is with the Abwehr—German military intelligence. That's what brings me to you, and your book *The Eagle Has Landed.*"

"A novel, Dr Cohen," I said. "Pure speculation."

"At least fifty per cent of which is documented historical fact." She leant forward, hands clenched fiercely on her knees.

I said softly, "All right, so what exactly are you getting at?"

"Remember how you found out about the affair in the first place?" she said. "The thing that started you off?"

"Of course," I said. "The tombstone to Steiner and his men that the villagers of Studley Constable had hidden under another tombstone in the churchyard."

"Remember what it said? 'Here lies Lieutenant Colonel Kurt Steiner and thirteen German paratroopers killed in action on six November 1943.'"

"Yes. So what's your point?"

"Thirteen plus one makes fourteen, only there aren't fourteen bodies in that grave. There are only thirteen."

I stared at her incredulously. "How do you make that out?"

"Because Kurt Steiner didn't die that night on the terrace at Meltham House, Mr Higgins." She reached for the briefcase, had it open in a second and produced a brown manila folder. "And I have the proof right here."

Which very definitely called for whisky. I poured one and said, "All right, do I get to see it?"

"Of course. But let me explain. Any study of Abwehr affairs constantly refers to the SOE, the Special Operations Executive, set up by British Intelligence in 1940 on Churchill's instructions to coordinate the Resistance movement in Europe. I thought there might be a book in it. I arranged to come over here to do the research, and one name came up again and again—Brigadier Dougal Munro. Before the war he was an archaeologist at Oxford. At SOE he was head of Section D, the dirty tricks department."

"I had heard of him," I said.

"I did most of my research at the Public Records Office. As you know, few files dealing with Intelligence matters are immediately available. Some are on a twenty-five-year hold, some fifty—"

"And exceptionally sensitive material, a hundred years," I said.

"That's what I have here." She held up the folder. "A hundred-year-hold file concerning Dougal Munro, Kurt Steiner, Liam Devlin and others. Quite a story, believe me."

She passed it across, and I held it on my knees without opening it. "How on earth did you come by this?"

"I checked out some files concerning Munro yesterday. The young clerk on duty got careless, I guess. I found this one sandwiched in between two others—sealed, of course. Since it wasn't on the booking-out form, I slipped it into my briefcase."

"A criminal offence under the Defence of the Realm Act."

"I know. I opened the seals as carefully as I could and read the file. It's a thirty-page summary of events. I photocopied it."

"The wonders of modern technology allow them to tell when that's been done."

"I know; I resealed the file and took it back this morning."

"And how did you manage to return it?" I asked.

"Checked out the same file as yesterday. Took the Munro file back to the desk and told the clerk there'd been an error."

"Did he believe you?"

"I suppose so. I mean, why wouldn't he?"

I sat there thinking about it, feeling uneasy. Finally I said, "Why don't you make us some fresh tea while I have a go at this?"

"All right."

She took the tray and went out. I hesitated, then opened the file and started to read.

I wasn't even aware that she was there, so gripped was I by the astonishing events recorded in that file. When I was finished, I looked up. She was back in the other chair, watching me intently.

I said, "I can understand the hundred-year hold. The powers that be wouldn't want this to come out, not even now."

"That's what I thought."

"Can I hang on to it for a while?"

She hesitated, then nodded. "Till tomorrow if you like. I'm going home on an evening flight. I'd rather be back in my own country."

"Worried?" I asked.

"I'm probably being hypersensitive, but sure. I'll pick the file up tomorrow afternoon. Say three o'clock, on my way to the airport."

The clock on the mantelpiece chimed the half hour, seven-thirty, as I walked her to the door. I opened it, and we stood for a moment, rain driving down hard.

"Of course, there is someone who could confirm the truth of that file," she said. "Liam Devlin. You said in your book he was still around, operating with the Provisional IRA in Ireland."

"Last I heard," I said.

"Well, then." She smiled. "I'll see you tomorrow afternoon."

She went down the steps and walked away through the rain, vanishing in the evening mist at the end of the street.

I sat by the fire and read the file twice; then I went back into the kitchen, made myself more tea and a chicken sandwich and sat at the table eating and thinking about things.

Extraordinary how events coming right out of the blue can change everything. It had happened to me once before—the discovery of that hidden memorial to Steiner and his men. I'd been researching an article for a historical magazine. Instead I'd found something that had changed my life. Produced a book that had made me rich. Now this—Ruth Cohen and her stolen file. I was filled with the same strange, tingling excitement.

Some time later the doorbell rang, shaking me from my reverie. I glanced at the clock. It was just before nine. The bell rang again insistently, and I replaced the file in the folder and put it on the coffee table. When I opened the door, I found a young police constable standing there, his navy-blue mac wet with rain.

"Mr Higgins?" He looked at a piece of paper in his left hand.

"Yes," I said.

"Sorry to trouble you, sir, but I'm making an enquiry relevant to a Miss Ruth Cohen. Would you be a friend of hers, sir?"

"Not exactly," I said. "Is there a problem?"

"I'm afraid the young lady's dead, sir. Hit-and-run accident at the back of the British Museum an hour ago."

"My God!" I whispered.

"We found your name and address on a card in her handbag."

It was so difficult to take in. She'd stood there at the door where he was—such a short time before. I took a deep breath. "What is it you want of me?"

"We've checked the student accommodation she was using at London University. No one there, with it being the weekend. It's a question of official identification. For the coroner."

"And you'd like me to do it?"

"If you wouldn't mind, sir."

I took another deep breath to steady myself. "All right. Just let me get my raincoat."

THE MORTUARY was a depressing-looking building in a side street, more like a warehouse than anything else. When we went into the foyer, there was a uniformed porter on duty at the desk, and a small, dark man in his early fifties standing at the window looking out at the rain. He wore a trilby hat and trench coat.

He turned to meet me, hands in pockets. "Mr Higgins. Detective Chief Superintendent Fox. An unfortunate business, sir."

"Yes," I said.

"Anyway, best to get it over with. If you'd come this way."

They took me into a room walled with white tiles and lit with bright fluorescent lighting. There was a line of operating tables. The body was on the end one, covered with a white rubber sheet.

"Would you formally identify the deceased as Ruth Cohen, sir?" the constable asked, pulling the sheet part-way down.

I nodded. "Yes, that's her." He replaced the sheet.

When I turned, Fox was sitting on the end of the table in the corner. "We found your name in her handbag," he said.

It was then, as if something had gone click in my head, that I came back to reality. Hit-and-run—a serious offence, but when had it merited the attention of a detective chief superintendent? And wasn't there something about Fox, with his saturnine face and dark, watchful eyes? I smelt Special Branch.

It always pays to stick as closely to the truth as possible. I said, "She told me she was over from Boston, working at London University, researching a book."

"About what, sir?"

Which confirmed my suspicions instantly. "Something to do with the Second World War—an area I've written about myself."

"I see. She was looking for advice, that sort of thing?"

Which was when I lied totally. "Not at all. Hardly needed it. A PhD, I believe. The fact is, she simply wanted to meet me. She was flying back to the States tomorrow."

The contents of her handbag and briefcase were on the table beside him, the plane ticket conspicuous. He picked it up. "So it would appear."

We went out into the foyer. He paused at the door. "Damn rain. I suppose the driver of that car skidded. An accident really, but then he shouldn't have driven away. We can't have that, can we?"

"Can I go now?"

"Of course. The constable will run you home."

I'D LEFT the light on in the hall. I went into the kitchen without taking my coat off, put the kettle on and went into the living room. It was then that I saw that the folder I'd left on the coffee table was gone. For a wild moment I thought I'd put it elsewhere, but that was nonsense, of course.

I lit a cigarette, thinking about it. The mysterious Fox, that wretched young woman, my unease when she'd told me how she had returned that file. I thought of her crossing that street in the rain, at the back of the British Museum. It could have been an accident, but I knew that was hardly likely, not with the file missing. Which raised the problem of my own continued existence.

Time to move on for a while, but where? And then I remembered what she had said. There was one person still left who could confirm the story in that file. I packed an overnight bag and checked the street through the curtain. It was impossible to see if I was being watched.

I left by the kitchen door, at the rear of the house, and walked cautiously through a maze of quiet back streets. It had to be a security matter, of course, but would that necessarily mean that whoever had taken care of the girl would have a go at me? After all, the girl was dead, the file back in the records office, the only copy recovered. What could I say that could be proved? On the other hand, I had to prove it to my own satisfaction, and I hailed a cab on the next corner.

THE GREEN MAN was in Kilburn, an area of London popular with the Irish. The bar was full, so I went around to the yard at the rear. The curtains were drawn, and Sean Riley sat at a crowded desk doing his accounts. He owned The Green Man—but, more important, was an organiser for Sinn Fein, the political wing of the IRA. I knocked at the window, and he got up to peer out. He turned away, and a moment later the door opened.

"Mr Higgins, what brings you here?"

"I won't come in, Sean. I'm on my way to Belfast. Get word to Liam Devlin. Tell him I'll be staying at the Europa Hotel and I must see him."

"Now, Mr Higgins, and how would I be knowing such a desperate fella as that?"

Through the door I could hear the music from the bar. They were singing "Guns of the IRA".

"Don't argue, Sean. Just do it," I said. "It's important."

I knew he would, of course, and turned away without another word. I hailed a cab, and minutes later was on my way to the airport.

THE EUROPA HOTEL in Belfast had survived numerous bombing attacks by the IRA and stood in Great Victoria Street next to the railway station. I stayed in my room for most of the day, waiting. Just after six, with darkness falling, the phone rang. A voice said, "Mr Higgins? Reception here, sir. Your taxi's waiting."

It was a black cab, of the London variety, and the driver was a pleasant-faced lady who looked like your favourite aunt. I gave her the ritual Belfast greeting: "Goodnight to you," then added, "Not often I see a lady cab driver, not in London anyway."

"A terrible place that. What would you expect?"

The journey took no more than ten minutes. We passed along the Falls Road, a Catholic area I remembered well from boyhood, and turned into a warren of mean side streets, finally stopping outside a church. She opened the glass panel.

"The first confessional box on the right as you go in."

"If you say so."

I got out, and she drove away instantly. The board said CHURCH OF THE HOLY NAME, and listed the times of Mass and confession in gold paint. I opened the door at the top of the steps and went in. It was not too large and was dimly lit, candles flickering down at the altar.

Instinctively I dipped my fingers into the holy water and crossed myself. I went into the first confessional box on the right and closed the door. I sat there in the darkness for a moment, and then the grille slid open.

"Yes?" a voice asked softly.

I answered automatically. "Bless me, Father, for I have sinned."

"You certainly have, my old son."

The light was switched on in the other box, and Liam Devlin smiled through at me.

HE LOOKED remarkably well. He was sixty-seven, a small man with enormous vitality, hair as black as ever, and vivid blue eyes. There was the scar of an old bullet wound on the left side of his forehead, and a slight ironic smile was permanently in place. He wore a priest's cassock and collar and seemed perfectly at home in the sacristy at the back of the church, to which he'd taken me.

"You're looking well, son. All that success and money." He grinned. "We'll drink to it. There's a bottle here surely."

He opened a cupboard and found a bottle of whisky and two glasses.

"And what would the usual occupant think of this?" I asked.

"Father Murphy?" He splashed whisky into the glasses. "Heart of corn, that one. Out doing good, as usual."

"He looks the other way, then?"

"Something like that." He raised his glass. "To you, my old son."

"And you, Liam." I toasted him back. "You never cease to amaze me. On the British army's most wanted list for five years, and you still have the nerve to sit here in the middle of Belfast."

"Ah, well, a man has to have some fun." He took a cigarette from a silver case and offered me one. "Anyway, to what do I owe the pleasure of this visit?"

"Does the name Dougal Munro mean anything to you?"

His eyes widened in astonishment. "What have you come up with now? I haven't heard that name mentioned in years."

"Or Schellenberg?"

"Walter Schellenberg? There was a man for you. General at thirty. Schellenberg . . . Munro . . . What is this?"

"And Kurt Steiner," I said, "who—according to everyone, including you—died trying to shoot a Churchill look-alike on the terrace at Meltham House."

Devlin swallowed some of his whisky and smiled amiably. "I was always the terrible liar. Now tell me what this is all about."

So I told him about Ruth Cohen, the file and its contents, everything, and he listened intently without interrupting.

When I was finished, he said, "Convenient, the girl's death—you were right about that."

There was an explosion not too far away and, as he went to open the door to the rear yard, the rattle of small-arms fire.

"It sounds like a lively night," I said.

"Oh, it will be. Safer off the streets at the moment." He closed the door and turned to face me.

I said, "The facts in that file. Were they true?"

"A good story."

"In outline."

"Which means you'd like to hear the rest?"

"I need to hear it."

"Why not?" he said, and sat down at a table in the corner. "Sure and it'll keep me out of mischief for a while. Now, where would you like me to begin?"

Berlin–Lisbon–London: 1943

CHAPTER 2

BRIGADIER DOUGAL MUNRO'S flat, in Haston Place, was only ten minutes' walk from the London headquarters of SOE, in Baker Street. As head of Section D, he needed to be on call twenty-four hours a day, and besides the normal phone, he had a secure line routed to his office. It was this phone he answered on that late November evening as he worked by the fire.

"Carter here, Brigadier. Just back from Norfolk."

"Good," Munro told him. "Call in on your way home and tell me about it."

He put the phone down and went back to work, a squat, powerful-looking man with white hair who wore steel-rimmed spectacles. His rank of brigadier was simply for purposes of authority in certain quarters, and at sixty-five, an age when most men faced retirement, even at Oxford, the war had been the saving of him. He was thinking about that when the doorbell rang and he admitted Captain Jack Carter.

"You look frozen, Jack. Help yourself to a drink."

Jack Carter leant his walking stick against a chair and shrugged off his greatcoat. His false leg was a legacy of Dunkirk, and he limped noticeably as he went to pour a whisky.

"So what's the situation at Studley Constable?" Munro asked.

"Back to normal, sir. All the German paratroopers buried in a common grave in the churchyard."

"No marker, of course."

"Not at the moment, but they're a funny lot, those villagers. They actually seem to think quite highly of Steiner."

"Yes, well, one of his sergeants was killed saving the lives of two village children who fell into the mill-race, remember. In fact, that was the thing that blew their cover, causing the failure of the entire operation."

"And he did let the villagers go before the worst of the fighting started," Carter said.

"Exactly. Have you got the file on him?"

Carter got his briefcase and extracted a couple of sheets stapled together.

Munro examined them. "Oberstleutnant Kurt Steiner, age twenty-seven. Remarkable record. Crete, North Africa, Stalingrad. Knight's Cross with Oak Leaves."

"I'm intrigued by his mother, sir. Boston socialite. What they call Boston Brahmin."

"Don't forget his father was a German general, Jack, and a damn good one. Now, what about Steiner? How is he?"

"There seems no reason to doubt a complete recovery. There's an RAF hospital for bomber crews with burn problems just outside Norwich. We have Steiner there under secure guard. The cover story is that he's a downed Luftwaffe pilot."

"And his wounds?"

"He was lucky there, sir. One round hit him in the right shoulder. The second was a heart shot, but it turned on the breastbone. The surgeon doesn't think it will take long. He's in remarkable physical shape."

Munro went and got another small whisky. "Let's go over what we know, Jack. The whole business, the plot to kidnap Churchill, the planning. Everything was done without Admiral Canaris's knowledge?"

"Apparently so, sir—all Himmler's doing. He pressured Max Radl, at Abwehr headquarters, to plan it all behind the admiral's back. At least that's what our sources in Berlin tell us."

"The admiral knows all about it now, though?" Munro said.

"Apparently, sir, and not best pleased. Not that there's anything he can do about it. Can't exactly go running to the Führer."

"And neither can Himmler," Munro said. "Not when the whole project was mounted without the Führer's knowledge. No, Himmler won't want to advertise this one."

"And we don't want it on the front of the *Daily Express*, sir. German paratroopers trying to grab the Prime Minister in an English country village."

"Yes, it wouldn't exactly help the war effort." Munro looked at the file again. "This IRA chap, Devlin. You say he was wounded?"

"That's right, sir. He was in hospital in Holland and simply took off one night. We understand he's in Lisbon."

"Are we keeping an eye on him? Who's SOE's man in Lisbon?"

"Major Arthur Frear, sir. Military attaché at the embassy. He's been notified," Carter told him.

"Good." Munro nodded.

"So what do we do about Steiner, sir?"

Munro frowned, thinking about it. "The moment he's fit enough, bring him to London. We'll house him at the Tower till we decide on a safe house. Anything else?"

"One development. Steiner's father was involved, as you know, in a series of army plots aimed at assassinating Hitler. The punishment is statutory. Hanging by piano wire. By the Führer's orders the whole thing is recorded on film. One of our Berlin sources got us a copy of General Steiner's death. It's not very nice."

Munro got up and paced the room. He paused suddenly, a slight smile on his face. "Tell me, Jack, is that little toad Vargas still at the Spanish embassy here in London?"

"José Vargas, trade attaché. We haven't used him for a while."

THE EAGLE HAS FLOWN

"But German Intelligence are convinced he's on their side?"

"The only side Vargas is on is the one with the biggest bankbook. Works through his cousin at the Spanish embassy in Berlin. Man named Juan Rivera."

"Excellent." Munro was smiling now. "Tell him to pass the word to Berlin that we have Kurt Steiner in the Tower of London. That'll sound dramatic. Make sure that *both* Canaris and Himmler get the information. That should stir them up."

"What on earth are you playing at, sir?" Carter asked.

"War, Jack, war. Now get yourself off home to bed. You're going to have a full day tomorrow."

IN WESTPHALIA, in the small town of Wewelsburg, was the castle of that name that Reichsführer Heinrich Himmler had taken over from the local council in 1934. His original intention had been to convert it into a school for SS leaders, but by the time the architects had finished, he had created a Gothic monstrosity worthy of a Hollywood film set.

The castle had three wings, towers and a moat. In the southern wing the Reichsführer had his own apartments and his special pride, the enormous dining hall, where selected members of the SS would meet in a kind of court of honour. The whole thing had been influenced by Himmler's obsession with King Arthur and the Knights of the Round Table, with a liberal dose of occultism thrown in.

Ten miles away, on that December evening, Walter Schellenberg sat in the back of a Mercedes that was speeding him from Berlin towards the castle. He'd received the order to meet the Reichsführer that afternoon. The reason had not been specified.

He'd been to Wewelsburg on several occasions, so he knew it well. He also knew that the only men to sit around that table with the Reichsführer were cranks like Himmler himself.

Schellenberg had long since ceased to be amused by the excesses of the Third Reich, but in deference to the demands of Wewelsburg, he wore the black dress uniform of the SS, the Iron

Cross First Class pinned to the left side of his tunic. He looked quite charming, although the duelling scar on one cheek hinted at a more ruthless side to his nature. It was a relic of student days at the University of Bonn. He'd started in the faculty of medicine, then switched to law, but times were hard in Germany in 1933, even for well-qualified young men just out of university.

The SS were recruiting gifted young scholars for their upper echelons. Schellenberg had seen it as employment, not as a political ideal. Because of his gift for languages he had been pulled into the Sicherheitsdienst, the SS security service known as the SD. His main responsibility had always been intelligence work abroad, often a conflict with the Abwehr, although his personal relationship with the Abwehr's head, Admiral Wilhelm Canaris, was excellent. A series of brilliant intelligence coups had pushed him rapidly up the ladder. By the age of thirty he was an SS Brigadeführer and major general of police.

The most astonishing thing was that Walter Schellenberg didn't consider himself a Nazi. He looked on the Third Reich as a sorry charade, its main protagonists of a very low order indeed. There were Jews who owed their survival to him, intended victims of the concentration camps rerouted to Sweden and safety. A dangerous game, a sop to his conscience, he told himself, and he had his enemies. He had survived for one reason only. Himmler needed his brains, and that was enough.

The car took the road up to the castle. There was only a powdering of snow in the moat, no water, as the Mercedes crossed the bridge to the gate. Too late to get off the roundabout now, Walter, he told himself. Far too late.

Schellenberg was escorted to the south wing by an SS sergeant and found Himmler's personal aide, a Sturmbannführer named Rossman, sitting at a table outside the door.

"Major." Schellenberg nodded.

"A pleasure to see you, General. He's waiting."

Rossman opened the door, and Schellenberg entered a large room with a vaulted ceiling and flagged floor. There were tapestries on the walls and lots of dark oak furniture. The Reichsführer sat at a table working his way through a mound of papers. He wore a tweed suit, white shirt and black tie. The silver pince-nez gave him the air of a rather unpleasant schoolmaster.

"General Schellenberg, you got here."

"I left Berlin the moment I received your message, Reichsführer. In what way can I serve you?"

"Schellenberg, I am increasingly concerned at the treasonable activities of many members of the high command. Some wretched young major was blown up in his car outside the entrance to the Führer's headquarters at Rastenburg last week. Obviously another attempt on our Führer's life."

"I'm afraid so, Reichsführer."

Himmler stood up and put a hand on Schellenberg's shoulder. "You and I, General, are sworn to protect the Führer, and yet we are constantly threatened by this conspiracy of generals. Stülpnagel, Falkenhausen, Stieff, Wagner, even your friend Admiral Canaris. And Rommel, the Desert Fox himself."

"There is no direct proof, Reichsführer," Schellenberg said, which was not strictly true.

"Proof." Himmler snorted. "I'll have my proof before I'm done. They have a date with the hangman, all of them. But to other things." He returned to the table and sat. "Have you ever had any dealings with an agent named José Vargas?"

"I know of him. An Abwehr contact. A commercial attaché, at the Spanish embassy in London. As far as I know, he has only been used occasionally."

"He has a cousin who is also a commercial attaché, at the Spanish embassy in Berlin. One Juan Rivera, am I right?"

"So I understand, Reichsführer. Vargas would use the Spanish diplomatic bag from London. Most messages would reach his cousin, here in Berlin, within thirty-six hours."

"Operation Eagle, the plan to kidnap or kill Churchill. You are familiar with the details?"

"I am, Reichsführer," Schellenberg said smoothly.

"There is a problem here, General. Although the idea was suggested by the Führer, it was—how shall I put it?—more a flight of fancy than anything else. That is why I personally put the plan into operation, aided by Colonel Radl of the Abwehr, who's had a heart attack, I understand, and is not expected to live."

Schellenberg said cautiously, "So the Führer knows nothing of the affair?"

"My dear General, Operation Eagle, however brilliantly conceived, ended in failure, and who would wish to take failure into the Führer's office and place it on his desk?" Before Schellenberg could reply, he carried on. "Which brings me to this report. It comes to me from Vargas, in London, via his cousin, here in Berlin."

He handed across a signal flimsy, and Schellenberg glanced at it. "Incredible!" he said. "Kurt Steiner alive."

"And in the Tower of London." Himmler took the signal back.

"They won't keep him there for very long," Schellenberg said. "The Tower isn't really suitable to house high-security prisoners long-term. They'll move him to some safe house."

"Have you any other opinion in the matter?"

"Only that the British will keep quiet about the fact that he's in their hands."

"Why do you say that?"

"Operation Eagle almost succeeded."

"But Churchill wasn't Churchill," Himmler reminded him. "Our intelligence people discovered that."

"Of course, Reichsführer, but German paratroopers did land on English soil and fought a bloody battle. If the story was publicised, the effect on the British people would be appalling."

Himmler said, "My sources indicate that Juan Rivera has also passed this news on to Canaris. How do you think he will react?"

"I've no idea, Reichsführer."

"Find out when you get back to Berlin. My opinion is that he will do nothing. He certainly won't go running to the Führer." Himmler examined another sheet in front of him. "I'll never understand men like Steiner. A war hero, a brilliant soldier, and yet he ruined his career to help some Jewish slut in Warsaw. It was only Operation Eagle that saved him and his men from the penal unit they were serving in." He put the sheet down. "The Irishman, of course, is a different matter."

"Devlin, Reichsführer?"

"Yes. A thoroughly obnoxious man. Everything a joke."

"I must say he seems to know his business."

"I agree, but then he was only in it for the money. My reports indicate that he's in Lisbon now." Himmler pushed another sheet across. "You'll find the details there. He's trying to get to America, but has no money. He's been working as a barman."

Schellenberg examined the signal quickly. "What would you like me to do on this matter, Reichsführer?"

"You'll fly to Lisbon tomorrow and persuade Devlin to return with you. I shouldn't think that would prove difficult. Radl gave him twenty thousand pounds for taking part in Operation Eagle, paid into an account in Geneva. Offer him the same—more if you have to. I'll authorise payments up to thirty thousand pounds."

"But for what, Reichsführer?"

"Why, to arrange Steiner's escape, of course. The man is a true hero of the Reich. We can't leave him in British hands."

Remembering how Steiner's father had met his end in the Gestapo cellars at Prinz Albrechtstrasse, it seemed likely to Schellenberg that Himmler might have other reasons. He said calmly, "I take your point, Reichsführer."

"You know the confidence I repose in you, General," Himmler said. He passed an envelope across. "You'll find a letter of authorisation in there that should take care of all contingencies."

Schellenberg didn't open it. Instead he said, "You said you wanted me to go to Lisbon tomorrow, Reichsführer. May I remind you it's Christmas Eve?"

"What on earth has that got to do with anything?" Himmler seemed genuinely surprised. "Speed is of the essence here, Schellenberg, and in reminding you of your oath as a member of the SS, I will now tell you why. In approximately four weeks the

Führer will fly to Cherbourg, in Normandy. January the twenty-first. I shall accompany him. From there we proceed down the coast to a place called Château de Belle-Île.

"May I ask the purpose of the visit?"

"The Führer intends to meet with Admiral Canaris and Field Marshal Rommel personally, to confirm Rommel's appointment as Commander of Army Group B. This will give him direct responsibility for the Atlantic Wall defences. The meeting will be concerned with the strategy necessary if our enemies decide to invade next year. The Führer has given to me the honour of organising the conference and, of course, the responsibility for his safety. It will be purely an SS matter."

"But the urgency on the Steiner affair—I don't understand."

"I intend to introduce Steiner to the Führer at that meeting. A great coup for the SS—his escape and near victory. His presence will make things rather difficult for Canaris, which will be all to the good." His eyes narrowed. "That is all you need to know."

Schellenberg felt that he was hanging on to his sanity by his fingernails. "But what if Devlin doesn't wish to be persuaded?"

"Then you must take appropriate action. To that end, I have selected a Gestapo man I wish to accompany you to Lisbon as your bodyguard." He rang a bell on the desk, and his aide entered. "Ah, Rossman. I'll see Sturmbannführer Berger now."

A moment later Rossman reappeared. With him was a man of about twenty-five, with blond—almost white—hair. Good-looking once, but one side of his face had been badly burnt. Schellenberg could see where the skin graft stretched tightly.

The young man held out his hand. "General Schellenberg. Horst Berger. A pleasure to work with you." He smiled, looking with that marred face like the devil himself.

Schellenberg said, "Major." He turned to Himmler. "May I get started, Reichsführer?"

"Of course. Berger will join you in the courtyard." Schellenberg opened the door, and Himmler added, "One more thing. Canaris is to know nothing of this. You understand?"

"Of course, Reichsführer."

Schellenberg walked along the corridor and found a toilet. He slipped in, then took out the envelope Himmler had given him and opened it.

FROM THE LEADER AND CHANCELLOR OF THE STATE

General Schellenberg acts upon my direct and personal orders in a matter of utmost importance to the Reich. He is answerable only to me. All personnel, military and civil, without distinction of rank, will assist him in any way he sees fit.

ADOLF HITLER

Schellenberg shivered and put it back into the envelope. The signature certainly looked right, but then it would be easy for Himmler to get the Führer's signature on something. Himmler was giving him the same powers as he had given Max Radl for Operation Eagle. But why? There had to be more to the whole business than Himmler was telling him.

He lit a cigarette and left the toilet. Losing his way at the end of the corridor, he hesitated, then realised that the archway at the end led onto a balcony above the great hall. Hearing voices, he moved forward onto the balcony and peered down cautiously. Himmler was standing at the head of the great table, flanked by Rossman and Berger. The Reichsführer was speaking.

"There are those, Berger, who are more concerned with people than ideas. They become sentimental. Unfortunately, General Schellenberg is one of them. That's why I am sending you with him to Lisbon. The man Devlin comes whether he likes it or not."

"Is the Reichsführer doubting General Schellenberg's loyalty?" Rossman asked.

"He has been of great service to the Reich," Himmler said, "but I've always doubted his loyalty to the party. Still, he is too useful for me to discard at the present time, Rossman. We must prepare for Belle-Île while Schellenberg busies himself with the Steiner affair." He turned to Berger. "You'd better be off."

Berger clicked his heels and turned away. When he was

halfway across the hall, Himmler called, "Show me what you can do, Berger."

Berger had the flap of his holster open, and turned with incredible speed, arm extended. There was a fresco of knights on the far wall. He fired at the wall three times very fast, and the heads of three of the knights disintegrated.

"Excellent," Himmler said.

Schellenberg was already on his way. He retrieved his greatcoat and cap and was sitting in the rear of the Mercedes when Berger joined him five minutes later.

"Sorry if I've kept you waiting, General," he said as he got in.

"No problem," Schellenberg said, and nodded to the driver, who drove away. "Smoke if you like."

"No vices, I'm afraid," Berger said.

"Really? Now, that is interesting." Schellenberg turned up his collar and leant back in the corner. "A long way to Berlin. I don't know about you, but I'm going to get some sleep."

SCHELLENBERG'S office at Gestapo headquarters, on Prinz Albrechtstrasse, had a camp bed in one corner, for he often spent the night there. He was in the small bathroom adjacent to it, shaving, when his secretary, Ilse Huber, entered. She was forty-one, a war widow, an attractive woman in white blouse and black skirt. She was devoted to him.

"Juan Rivera is here," she said. "And Admiral Canaris will be riding in the Tiergarten at ten o'clock as usual. Will you join him?"

Schellenberg frequently did, but when he went to the window and saw the powdering of snow in the streets, he laughed. "Not this morning, thank you, but I must see him."

Ilse went and poured coffee from the pot on the tray she had put on his desk.

"Trouble, General?" Dedicated as she was to his welfare, she had an instinct about things.

"In a way, my love." He smiled that dangerous smile of his that made her heart turn over. "But don't worry. Nothing I can't handle.

I'll fill you in on the details before I leave. I'm going to need your help with this one. Where's Berger, by the way?"

"Downstairs in the canteen, last I saw of him."

"All right. I'll see Rivera now."

She paused at the door. "He frightens me. Berger, I mean."

Schellenberg went and put an arm around her. "I told you not to worry. When has the great Schellenberg ever failed to manage?"

His self-mockery, as always, made her laugh. She was out of the door, smiling, as Schellenberg buttoned his tunic and sat down. A moment later Rivera came in—a small man with sallow skin, wearing a dark brown suit. He looked decidedly anxious.

"You know who I am?" Schellenberg asked him.

"Of course, General. An honour to meet you."

Schellenberg held up a piece of paper. "This message you received from your cousin, José Vargas, concerning the whereabouts of a Colonel Steiner. Have you discussed it with anyone?"

Rivera seemed genuinely shocked. "Not a living soul, General. I swear this. On my mother's life."

"Oh, I don't think we need to bring her into it. She's quite comfortable in that little villa you bought her in San Carlos." Rivera looked startled, and Schellenberg said, "You see, there is nothing about you I don't know. There is no place you could go where I couldn't reach you. Do you understand me?"

"Perfectly, General." Rivera was sweating.

"Now, this message from your cousin in London. Why did you also send it to Admiral Canaris?"

"My cousin's orders, General. In these matters there is always the question of payment, and in this case . . ." He shrugged.

"He thought you might get paid twice?" Schellenberg nodded. It made sense, and yet he had learnt never to take anything for granted in this game. "Tell me about your cousin. He isn't married— you are. Does he have a girlfriend in London?"

"As it happens, José's tastes do not run to women, General."

"I see." Schellenberg brooded. Homosexuals were susceptible to blackmail—a weakness for anyone engaged in intelligence work. A point against Vargas, then. "Is he reliable? Any question of him ever having any dealings with our British friends?"

Rivera looked shocked again. "General Schellenberg, I assure you. José, like me, is a good Fascist. We fought together with General Franco in the civil war. We—"

"All right, now listen carefully. We may well decide to attempt to rescue Colonel Steiner."

"From the Tower of London, señor?" Rivera's eyes bulged.

"In my opinion, they'll move him to some sort of safe house. May well have done so already. You will send a message to your cousin today asking for all possible information."

"Of course, General."

"Get on with it, then." As Rivera reached the door Schellenberg added, "If one word of this leaks out, you will end up in the river Spree, my friend, and your cousin in the Thames. I have an extraordinarily long arm."

Rivera started to protest again. "General, I beg of you—"

"Spare me all that stuff about what a good Fascist you are. Just think about how generous I'm going to be. A much sounder basis for our relationship."

Rivera departed, and Schellenberg phoned down for his car, pulled on his overcoat and went out.

ADMIRAL WILHELM CANARIS was fifty-six, a U-boat captain of distinction in World War I. He had headed the Abwehr since 1935 and, despite being a loyal German, had always been unhappy with National Socialism. Although opposed to any plan to assassinate Hitler, he had been involved with the German Resistance for some years, treading a dangerous path.

That morning he was galloping along the path between the trees in the Tiergarten, his horse's hoofs kicking up the powdered snow. He saw Schellenberg standing beside his Mercedes, waved and turned towards him.

"Good morning, Walter. You should be with me."

"Not this morning. I'm off on my travels again."

Canaris dismounted, and while Schellenberg's driver held the horse's reins, they walked to a parapet overlooking the lake.

"Anywhere interesting?" Canaris asked.

"No, just routine," Schellenberg said.

"Come, Walter, out with it. There's something on your mind."

"All right. The Operation Eagle affair."

"The Führer came up with that idea," Canaris told him. "What nonsense! Kill Churchill when we've already lost the war."

"I wish you wouldn't say that sort of thing out loud."

Canaris ignored him. "I was ordered to prepare a feasibility study. I knew the Führer would forget it within days, and he did. Only Himmler didn't. Went behind my back. And the whole thing turned out to be the shambles I knew it would."

"Steiner almost pulled it off," Schellenberg said.

"Pulled what off? Come off it, Walter. I'm not denying Steiner's audacity and bravery, but the man they were after wasn't even Churchill. The look on Himmler's face would have been a joy to see if they'd brought him back."

"And now we hear that Steiner didn't die," Schellenberg said. "That they have him in the Tower of London."

"Ah, so Juan Rivera has passed on his dear cousin's message to the Reichsführer also." Canaris smiled cynically.

"What do you think the British will do?"

"With Steiner? Lock him up tight and keep quiet about it. Wouldn't look too good, just as it wouldn't look too good to the Führer if the facts came to his attention."

"Do you think they're likely to?" Schellenberg asked.

Canaris laughed out loud. "You mean from me? No, Walter. I'm in enough trouble these days without looking for more."

They started to walk back to the Mercedes. Schellenberg said, "I suppose he's to be trusted, this Vargas. We can believe him?"

Canaris took the point seriously. "I admit our operations in England have gone badly. The British secret service came up with a stroke of genius—they stopped having our operatives shot when they caught them, and simply turned them into double agents."

"And Vargas?"

"I don't think so. He has only worked occasionally and as a free-lancer. No contacts with any other agents in England, you see." They had reached the car. He smiled. "Anything else?"

Schellenberg couldn't help saying it, he liked the man so much. "As you well know, there was another attempt on the Führer's life, at Rastenburg. As it happened, the young officer who was involved was carrying a bomb that went off prematurely."

"Very careless of him. What's your point, Walter?"

"Take care, Admiral. These are dangerous times."

"Walter, I have never condoned the idea of assassinating the Führer." The admiral climbed back into the saddle and gathered his reins. "Shall I tell you why?"

"I'm sure you're going to."

"Stalingrad, thanks to the Führer's stupidity, lost us more than three hundred thousand dead. Ninety-one thousand taken prisoner, including twenty-four generals. The greatest defeat we've ever known. One disaster after another, thanks to the Führer." He laughed harshly. "Don't you realise the truth of it, my friend? His continued existence actually shortens the war for us."

He put his spurs to his horse and galloped into the trees.

BACK AT the office, Schellenberg changed into a light grey flannel suit in the bathroom, speaking through the door to Ilse Huber as he dressed, filling her in on the whole business.

"What do you think?" he asked as he emerged. "Like a fairy tale by the brothers Grimm?"

"More like a horror story," she said as she held his coat.

"We'll refuel in Madrid and carry straight on," he told her. "Should be in Lisbon by late afternoon."

He pulled on the coat, adjusted a slouch hat and picked up the overnight bag she had prepared. "I expect news from Rivera within two days at the outside. Give him thirty-six hours, then apply pressure." He kissed her on the cheek. "Take care, Ilse. See you soon." And he was gone.

THE PLANE was a JU-52, with its famous three engines and corrugated metal skin. As it lifted off from the Luftwaffe fighter base outside Berlin, Schellenberg undid his seat belt.

Berger, on the other side of the aisle, smiled. "The Herr Admiral was well, General?"

Now, that isn't very clever, Schellenberg thought. You weren't supposed to know I was seeing him.

He smiled back. "He seemed his usual self."

He opened his briefcase, started to read Devlin's background report and examined a photo of him. After a while he looked out of the window, remembering what Canaris had said about Hitler. *His continued existence actually shortens the war for us.*

Strange how that thought went around and around in his brain and wouldn't go away.

CHAPTER 3

BARON Oswald von Hoyningen-Heune, the minister to the German legation in Lisbon, was a friend and an aristocrat of the old school. He was no Nazi. He was delighted to see Schellenberg.

"My dear Walter. Good to see you. How's Berlin?"

"Colder than this," Schellenberg told him as they sat in his office overlooking a pleasant garden terrace. Schellenberg sighed. "I can understand you hanging on here instead of coming back to Berlin. The best place to be these days, Lisbon."

"I know," the baron told him, pouring the coffee. "A strange time to arrive, Walter — Christmas Eve. It must be important."

"There's a man we want, an Irishman. Goes by the name of Liam Devlin." Schellenberg took Devlin's photo from his wallet and passed it across. "He worked for the Abwehr for a while. The IRA connection. Walked out of a hospital in Holland the other week. Our information is that he's here, working as a waiter at a bar in Alfama."

"The old quarter." The baron nodded. "Captain Eggar, my police attaché here, should be able to assist you." He picked up his phone and spoke to an aide. As he put it down he said, "I caught a glimpse of your companion."

"Sturmbannführer Berger—Gestapo," Schellenberg said.

"Doesn't look your sort."

"A Christmas present from the Reichsführer. Not my choice."

There was a knock at the door, and a man in his forties slipped in. He had a heavy moustache and wore an ill-fitting suit.

"Ah, there you are, Eggar. You know of General Schellenberg?"

"Of course. A great pleasure, sir."

Schellenberg held up Devlin's photo. "Have you seen this man?"

Eggar examined it. "No, General."

"He's Irish, ex-IRA, age thirty-five. He worked for the Abwehr for a while. We want him back. Our latest information is that he's been working at a bar called Flamingo."

"I know the place."

"Good. You'll find my aide, Major Berger of the Gestapo, outside. Bring him in." Eggar went out and returned with Berger. Schellenberg made the introductions. Berger, in his dark suit and with that ravaged face, was a chilling presence as he nodded formally and clicked his heels. "Captain Eggar knows this Flamingo place. I want you to go there with him and check if Devlin still works there. If he does, you will not, I repeat *not*, contact him. Simply report to me." As Berger opened the door Schellenberg called, "Liam Devlin was once one of the IRA's most notorious gunmen. You gentlemen would do well to remember that."

Berger smiled faintly and went out, followed by Eggar.

"A bad one, that. You're welcome to him." The baron checked his watch. "Just after five, Walter. How about some champagne?"

MAJOR ARTHUR FREAR, with his crumpled suit and white hair, was fifty-four and looked older. He'd have been retired by now on a modest pension, leading a life of genteel poverty in Brighton or Torquay. Instead, thanks to Adolf Hitler, he was the military attaché at the British embassy in Lisbon, where he unofficially represented SOE.

The Lights of Lisbon was one of his favourite places. How convenient that Devlin played piano there, although there was no sign of him at the moment. Devlin, in fact, was watching him through a bead curtain at the rear. He wore a linen suit in off-white, dark hair falling across his forehead, the vivid blue eyes full of amusement. The first Frear knew of his presence was when Devlin slid onto the stool next to him and ordered a beer.

"Mr Frear, isn't it?" He nodded to the barman. "Miguel here tells me you're in the port wine business."

"That's right," Frear said jovially. "Been exporting it to England for years—my firm."

"Never been my taste. Now, if it was Irish whisky—"

"Can't help you there, I'm afraid." Frear laughed. Devlin slid off the stool, and Frear said, "Aren't you going to give us a tune?"

"Oh, that comes later." Devlin grinned and was gone.

THE FLAMINGO was a shabby little bar and restaurant. Berger left things to Eggar, who spoke the language fluently. Yes, Devlin had worked there for a while, but he'd left three days ago. He was working another establishment, the Lights of Lisbon, only he was employed not as a waiter but as a pianist in the bar.

"Do you know the place, Eggar?" Berger asked.

"Oh, yes. Quite well. Also in the old quarter."

"Show me the way," Berger said.

THE HIGH WALLS of the Castelo de São Jorge lifted above them as they worked their way through a maze of narrow alleys. As they came into a small square in front of a church Devlin emerged from an alley and crossed the cobbles before them towards a café.

"It's him," Eggar muttered. "Exactly like his photo."

"Is this the Lights of Lisbon?" Berger asked.

"No, Major. Another café. One of the most notorious in Alfama. Gypsies, bullfighters, criminals."

"A good job we're armed, then. When we go in, have your pistol in your right pocket and your hand on it."

"But General Schellenberg gave us express instructions to—"

"Don't argue. Do as I say, and follow me." And Berger led the way towards the café, where they could hear guitar music.

Inside, the place was light and airy, in spite of the fact that dusk was falling. The bar top was marble, the bottles ranged on shelves behind it. The bartender, squat and ugly, with one white eye, sat at a high stool reading a newspaper. Four swarthy, fierce-looking gypsies played poker at a table, and a younger man leant against the wall, fingering a guitar.

The rest of the place was empty, except for Devlin, who sat at a table reading a small book, a glass of beer at his hand. The door creaked open, and Berger stepped in, Eggar at his back. The guitarist stopped playing, and all conversation died as Berger stood just inside the door, death come to visit. Berger moved past the men playing cards. Eggar went closer as well.

Devlin glanced up, smiling amiably, and picked up the glass of beer.

"Liam Devlin?" Berger asked.

"And who might you be?"

"I am Sturmbannführer Horst Berger, of the Gestapo. I must ask you to come with us."

"And me only halfway through my book."

"Now," Berger said.

Devlin drank some more beer. "You remind me of a medieval fresco I saw on a church in Donegal once. People running in terror from a man in a hood. Everyone he touched got the black death, you see."

"Eggar!" Berger commanded.

Devlin fired through the tabletop, chipping the wall beside the door. Eggar tried to get the pistol out of his pocket. The Walther Devlin had been holding on his knee appeared above the table, and he fired again, shooting Eggar through the right hand. Eggar cried out, and one of the gypsies grabbed for his gun as he dropped it.

Berger's hand went inside his jacket, reaching for the Mauser he carried in a shoulder holster there. Devlin tossed the beer into his face and upended the table against him, the edge catching the German's shins, so that he staggered forward. Devlin rammed the muzzle of the Walther into his neck and reached inside Berger's coat, removing the Mauser, which he tossed onto the bar.

"Present for you, Barbosa," The barman grinned and picked up the Mauser. The gypsies were on their feet, two of them with knives in their hands. Devlin slipped his book into his pocket, stepped around Berger, holding the Walther against his leg, and reached for Eggar's hand. "A couple of knuckles gone. You're going to need a doctor." He slipped the Walther into his pocket and turned to go.

Berger's iron control snapped. He ran at him, hands outstretched. Devlin swayed, his right foot flicking forward, catching Berger under the kneecap. As the German doubled over, Devlin raised a knee in his face, sending him back against the bar. Berger pulled himself up, hanging on to the marble top, and the gypsies started to laugh.

Devlin shook his head. "Son, I'd say you should find a different class of work—the both of you." And he turned and went out.

WHEN SCHELLENBERG went into the legation's medical room, Eggar was sitting at the desk while the doctor taped his hand.

"How is he?" Schellenberg asked.

"He'll live." The doctor finished and cut off the end of the tape. "But he may well find that hand rather stiffer in future."

"Can I have a moment?" Schellenberg said. The doctor nodded and went out, and Schellenberg sat on the edge of the desk. "I presume you found Devlin?" he asked Eggar.

"Hasn't the Herr General been told?" Eggar asked.

"I haven't spoken to Berger yet. Tell me what happened."

Which Eggar did, for as the pain increased, so did his anger. "He wouldn't listen, Herr General. Had to do it his way."

Schellenberg put a hand on his shoulder. "Not your fault, Eggar. I'm afraid Major Berger sees himself as his own man. Time he was taught a lesson."

"Oh, Devlin took care of that," Eggar said. "When I last saw it, the major's face didn't look too good."

Schellenberg smiled. "I didn't think it could look worse."

BERGER STOOD in front of the washbasin in the small bedroom he had been given, and examined his face in the mirror. A bruise had already appeared around his left eye, and his nose was swollen.

Schellenberg came in, closed the door and leant against it. "So you disobeyed my orders."

Berger said, "I acted for the best. I didn't want to lose him."

"And he was better than you. I warned you about that."

There was rage on Berger's face as he touched his cheek. "That little Irish swine. I'll fix him next time."

"No, you won't, because from now on I'll handle things myself. Unless, of course, you'd prefer me to report to the Reichsführer that we lost this man because of your stupidity."

Berger swung around. "General Schellenberg, I protest."

"Get your feet together when you speak to me," Schellenberg snapped. Berger did as he was told. "You took an oath on joining the SS. You vowed total obedience to your Führer and to those appointed to lead you. Is this not so?"

"*Jawohl*, Brigadeführer."

"Excellent," Schellenberg told him. "You're remembering. Don't forget again. The consequences could be disastrous." He shook his head. "You look awful, Major. Try and do something about your face before going down to dinner."

He opened the door and went out.

Berger turned back to the mirror. "Bastard!" he said softly.

LIAM DEVLIN sat at the piano in the Lights of Lisbon, a cigarette dangling from the corner of his mouth. It was ten o'clock, and the café was crowded and cheerful. He was playing a slow, haunting number called "Moonlight on the Highway", and he noticed Schellenberg the moment he entered, not because he recognised him, only the kind of man he was. He watched him go to the bar to get a glass of wine, then looked away, aware that the man was approaching.

Schellenberg said, "'Moonlight on the Highway'. I like that. One of Al Bowlly's greatest numbers," he added, mentioning the name of the man who had been England's most popular crooner.

"Killed in the London blitz. Did you know that?" Devlin asked. "Would never go down to the cellars like everyone else."

"Unfortunate," Schellenberg said.

Devlin moved into playing "A Foggy Day in London Town", and Schellenberg said, "You are a man of many talents, Mr Devlin."

"Fruits of a misspent youth." Devlin reached for his wine, continuing to play one-handed. "And who might you be, old son?"

"My name is Walter Schellenberg. You may have heard of me."

"I certainly have." Devlin grinned. "I lived long enough in Berlin for that. Are you something to do with the two idiots who had a try at me earlier this evening?"

"I regret that, Mr Devlin. The man you shot is the police attaché at the legation. The other, Major Berger, is Gestapo. He's with me only because the Reichsführer ordered it."

"Are we into old Himmler again? Last time I saw him, he didn't exactly approve of me."

"Well, he needs you now."

"For what?"

"To go to England for us, Mr Devlin."

"No, thanks. I've worked for German Intelligence twice in this war. The first time, in Ireland, I nearly got my head blown off." He tapped the bullet scar on the side of his forehead.

"And the second time, in Norfolk, you took a bullet in the right shoulder and only got away by the skin of your teeth, leaving Kurt Steiner behind. Operation Eagle."

"Ah, so you know about that? A good man, Colonel Steiner."

"Did you hear what happened to him?"

"Sure—he was killed at a place called Meltham House trying to get at Churchill."

"Two things wrong about that," Schellenberg told him. "It wasn't

Churchill that weekend. He was on his way to the Tehran conference. It was his double. Some music-hall actor."

"Is that a fact?" Devlin stopped playing.

"And more importantly, Kurt Steiner didn't die. He's alive and well in the Tower of London at present, which is why I want you to go to England. You see, I've been entrusted with the task of getting him safely back to the Reich, and I've little more than three weeks to do it in."

Major Arthur Frear had entered the café a couple of minutes earlier and had recognised Schellenberg instantly. He retreated to a side booth, where he summoned a waiter, ordered a beer and watched as the two men went out and sat at a table in the garden.

"General, you've lost the war," Devlin said. "Why do you keep trying?"

"Oh, we all have to do the best we can until the damn thing is over. As I keep saying, it's difficult to jump off the merry-go-round once it's in motion. A game we play."

"Like the old boy inside, in the end booth, watching us now."

Schellenberg looked around casually. "And who might he be?"

"Pretends to be in the port wine business. Name of Frear. My friends tell me he's military attaché at the British embassy here."

"Indeed." Schellenberg carried on calmly. "Interested?"

"Now, why would I be?"

"Money, Mr Devlin. Twenty-five thousand pounds."

Devlin lit another cigarette and leant back. "What do you want him for? Why go to all the trouble?"

"A matter of security is involved."

Devlin laughed harshly. "Come off it, General. You want me to go jumping out of a plane again—at five thousand feet in the dark—and you try to hand me that rubbish."

"All right. There's a meeting in France on the twenty-first of January. The Führer, Rommel, Canaris and Himmler. The Führer doesn't know about Operation Eagle. The Reichsführer would like to produce Steiner at that meeting. Introduce him."

"And why would he want to do that?"

"Steiner led German soldiers in battle on English soil. A hero of the Reich. Added to which the Reichsführer and Admiral Canaris do not always see eye to eye." Schellenberg shrugged. "The fact that Steiner's escape had been organised by the SS—"

"Would make Canaris look bad." Devlin shook his head. "What a crew. I don't much care for any of them, but Kurt Steiner's another thing. A great man, that one. But the Tower of London!"

"They won't keep him there. My guess is they'll move him to one of their London safe houses."

"And how can you find that out?"

"An agent in London, working out of the Spanish embassy."

"Can you be sure he's not a double?"

"Pretty sure, in this case." Devlin frowned, and Schellenberg said, "Thirty thousand pounds." He smiled. "I'm good at my job, Mr Devlin. I'll prepare a plan for you that will work."

Devlin nodded. "I need time to think about it." He stood up. "I've promised to go up-country to a bull ranch a friend of mine runs. I'll be back in three days."

"But time is of the essence. I need to get back to Berlin."

"If you want me, you'll have to wait." Devlin clapped him on the shoulder. "Come on now, Walter. Christmas in Lisbon? Lights, music, pretty girls? I bet it's snowing at this moment in Berlin. Which would you rather have?"

Schellenberg started to laugh, and behind them Major Frear got up and went out.

URGENT BUSINESS had kept Dougal Munro at his office at SOE headquarters on the morning of Christmas Day. He was about to leave when Jack Carter limped in. It was just after noon.

Munro said, "I hope it's urgent, Jack. I'm due for Christmas lunch with friends."

"I thought you'd want to know about this, sir." Carter held up a signal flimsy. "From Major Frear, our man in Lisbon. Guess who friend Devlin was locked in conversation with last night at a Lisbon club. Walter Schellenberg."

Munro sat down at his desk. "Now what in the hell is the good Walter playing at?"

"Lord knows, sir."

"The devil, more like. Signal Frear. If Schellenberg and Devlin leave Portugal together, I want to know at once."

IT WAS RAINING in London on the evening of the twenty-seventh when Jack Carter turned into a small mews. The café was not far from SOE headquarters, which was why he had chosen it when he'd received a phone call from José Vargas. The place was blacked out, but when Carter went in, it was bright with Christmas decorations and holly. There were only three or four customers, including Vargas, who sat in the corner drinking coffee. He wore a heavy blue overcoat and had hollow cheeks and a pencil moustache. His hair was brilliantined and parted in the centre.

Carter said, "This had better be good."

"Would I bother you if it were not, señor?" Vargas asked. "I've heard from my cousin in Berlin."

"And?"

"They want all possible information as to Steiner's whereabouts. They're interested in mounting a rescue operation. They seem to think you will move him from the Tower."

"Who's they? The Abwehr?"

"No. General Schellenberg of the SD is in charge."

Carter nodded, fiercely excited, and got up. "I want you to phone me at eleven, old chum, and don't fail. This is the big one, Vargas. You'll make a lot of cash if you're smart." He turned and went out, and hurried along Baker Street as fast as his game leg would allow.

IN LISBON at that precise moment, Walter Schellenberg was climbing the steep cobbled alley in Alfama towards the Lights of Lisbon. When he went inside, the place was deserted except for the barman, and Devlin at the piano. The Irishman stopped to light a cigarette and smiled. "Did you enjoy your Christmas, General?"

"It could have been worse. And you?"

"The bulls were running well. Wine, grapes and lots of sun, that's what I had for Christmas, General." Devlin started to play "Moonlight on the Highway". "And me thinking of old Al Bowlly in the Blitz. London, fog in the streets. Now, isn't that the strange thing?"

Schellenberg felt excitement rise inside him. "You'll go?"

"On one condition. I can change my mind at the last minute if I think the thing isn't watertight."

"My hand on it."

Devlin got up, and they walked out to the terrace. Schellenberg said, "We'll fly out to Berlin in the morning."

"You will, General, not me. Look down there." Over the wall they could see that Major Frear had come in and was talking to the barman. "He's been keeping an eye on me, old Frear. He's seen me talking to the great Walter Schellenberg. I should think that would figure in one of his reports to London."

"So what do you suggest?"

"You fly back to Berlin and get on with the preparations. Arrange the right papers for me at the legation—travelling money and so on—and I'll come by rail. Lisbon to Madrid, then the Paris Express. Fix it up for me to carry on from there."

Schellenberg nodded. "You're right. So let's have a drink on it. To our English enterprise."

"Holy Mother, not that, General. That's how the Spanish Armada was described, and look what happened to that lot."

DOUGAL MUNRO sat at his desk and listened intently as Jack Carter gave him the gist of his conversation with Vargas.

Munro nodded. "Two pieces of the jigsaw puzzle, Jack. Schellenberg's interested in rescuing Steiner. And where is Schellenberg right now? In Lisbon, hobnobbing with Liam Devlin. Now, what conclusion does that lead you to?"

"That he wants to recruit Devlin to the cause, sir."

"Of course. The perfect man." Munro nodded. "Time to think of moving Steiner. What would you suggest?"

"There's the London Cage, in Kensington," Carter said.

"Come off it, Jack. That's only used for processing transients. Prisoners of war such as Luftwaffe aircrews."

"There's Cockfosters, sir, and the school opposite Wandsworth Prison. A number of German agents have been held there."

"No, that's no good." Munro went to the window and looked out. The rain had turned to sleet now. "Time I spoke with friend Steiner, I think. We'll try and make it tomorrow."

"Fine, sir. I'll arrange it."

Munro turned. "Devlin—there is a photo on file?"

"Passport photo, sir. Special Branch had it. It's not very good."

"They never are, those things." Munro suddenly smiled. "I've got it, Jack. Where to hold Steiner. That place in Wapping. St Mary's Priory."

"The Little Sisters of Pity, sir? It's a hospice for terminal cases."

"They also look after chaps who've had breakdowns, don't they? Gallant RAF pilots who've cracked up. It would be perfect. Built in the seventeenth century. They used to be an enclosed order, so the whole place is walled. Built like a fortress. Yes, I think the priory will do nicely."

"There is one thing, sir. This is a counter-espionage matter, which means it's an MI5 and Special Branch affair."

"Not if they don't know about it." Munro smiled. "When Vargas phones, tell him to wait three or four days, then to notify his cousin that Steiner is being moved to St Mary's Priory."

"Are you actually inviting them to mount this operation, sir?"

"Why not, Jack? We'd bag not only Devlin but any contacts he would have. He couldn't work alone. No. There are all sorts of possibilities to this. Off you go."

"Right, sir."

Carter limped to the door, and Munro said, "Silly me, I'm forgetting the obvious. Walter Schellenberg is going to want a source for this information. It's got to look good."

"May I make a suggestion? José Vargas is a homosexual. Let's say he has picked up one of the soldiers guarding the Tower."

"Oh, very good, Jack," Munro said. "Get on with it, then."

FROM A DISCREET vantage point on the concourse at the airport outside Lisbon, Frear watched Schellenberg and Berger walk across the apron and board the Junkers. He stayed there, watching it taxi away, and only went out to the cab rank when the plane had actually taken off.

Half an hour later he went into the Lights of Lisbon and sat at the bar. He ordered a beer and said to the barman, "Where's our Irish friend today?"

The barman shrugged. "Gone. The boss sacked him. Nothing but trouble. There was a guest here last night. Nice man. A German, I think. Devlin had a row with him. Nearly came to blows. Had to be dragged off."

"Dear me," Frear said. "I wonder what he'll do now."

"Plenty of bars in Lisbon," the barman said.

"Yes, you're certainly right there." Frear swallowed his beer. "I'll be off then."

Devlin stepped through the bead curtain at the back of the bar. "Good man, Miguel. Now let's have a farewell drink together."

IT WAS LATE afternoon, and Munro was at his desk in his office at SOE headquarters when Carter came in.

"Another signal from Frear, sir. Schellenberg left for Berlin by plane this morning, but Devlin didn't go with him."

"If Liam Devlin is as smart as I think he is, Jack, he's been on to Frear from the start. He's probably gone to Berlin by another route. But all to no avail." Munro smiled. "We have Rivera and Vargas in our pockets, and that means we'll always be one step ahead."

"So what happens now, sir?"

"We wait, Jack. We just wait and see what their next move is. Did you arrange the meeting with Steiner?"

"Yes, sir."

Munro went to the window. The sleet had turned to rain and he snorted. "Looks as if we're going to get some fog now. Bloody weather." He sighed. "What a war, Jack, what a war."

CHAPTER 4

THE SMALL hospital room was painted dark green. There was a narrow bed, a cupboard and a wardrobe. There was also a bathroom adjacent to it. Kurt Steiner, in pyjamas and a towelling robe, sat by the barred window reading. From the window he could see out into the inner ward of the Tower. It gave him an illusion of space, and space meant freedom.

There was a rattle of bolts at the stout door. It opened, and a military policeman stepped in. "Visitors for you, Colonel."

Munro moved in, followed by Carter. "You may leave us, Corporal," he told the MP. The man went out, locking the door.

Munro, for effect, was in uniform. He shrugged off his greatcoat, and Steiner took in the badges of rank and red tabs of a staff officer.

"Oberstleutnant Kurt Steiner? Brigadier Munro. This is my aide, Captain Jack Carter."

"Gentlemen, I gave my name, my rank and my number some time ago," Steiner said. "I've nothing to add except to say I'm surprised no one's tried to squeeze more out of me. I apologise for the fact that there's only one chair, so I can't ask you to sit down."

Munro found himself warming to the man. "We'll sit on the bed if we may." They sat down, and Munro said, "Your English is really excellent."

"Brigadier"—Steiner smiled— "I'm sure you're aware that my mother was American and that I lived in London for many years as a boy, when my father was military attaché at the German embassy. I was educated at St Paul's."

"You haven't been pressured into any further interrogation— because of the condition you were in," Munro said. "But we know everything there is to know about Operation Eagle."

"Really?" Steiner said dryly.

"I work for Special Operations Executive, Colonel. Knowing things is our business. I'm sure you'll be surprised to discover that the man you tried to shoot that night at Meltham House wasn't Mr Churchill."

Steiner looked incredulous. "What nonsense is this?"

"Not nonsense," Jack Carter said. "He was one George Howard Foster, known in the music halls as the Great Foster. An impressionist of some distinction."

Steiner laughed helplessly. "But that's wonderful. A music-hall artist. If it had all succeeded and we'd taken him back ... I'd love to have seen Himmler's face." Concerned that he was going too far, he took a deep breath and pulled himself together. "So?"

"Something I've never understood, Colonel," Carter said. "You're no Nazi, we know that. You ruined your career trying to help a Jewish girl in Warsaw, and yet that last night in Norfolk you still tried to get Churchill."

"I'm a soldier, Captain, and the game was in play."

"And in the end the game was playing you," Munro said.

"Something like that."

"Nothing to do with the fact that your father, General Karl Steiner, was being held at Gestapo headquarters in Berlin for complicity in a plot against the Führer?" Carter asked.

Steiner's face shadowed. "Captain Carter, Himmler is noted for many things, but charity and compassion are not among them."

"And it was Himmler behind the whole business," Munro said. "Even the Führer had no idea what was going on. Still hasn't."

"Nothing would surprise me," Steiner said. "Now, gentlemen, what is this all about?"

"They want you back," Munro told him.

Steiner stared at him. "You're joking. Why would they bother?"

"All I know is that Himmler wants you out of here."

"But this is nonsense. German prisoners of war have not been noted for escaping from England."

"You miss the point," Munro said. "We're not talking of a prisoner simply making a run for it. We're talking about a plot, if you like. A meticulously mounted operation masterminded by General Walter Schellenberg, of the SD. Do you know him?"

"Of him only," Steiner replied.

"Of course, it would require the right man to pull it off, which is where your friend Liam Devlin comes in," Carter added.

"Devlin?"

"He also was wounded in Operation Eagle," Carter said. "Walked out of a Dutch hospital and escaped to Lisbon."

Steiner shook his head. "Devlin is one of the most remarkable men I have ever known, but even he couldn't get me out of here."

"Yes, well, it wouldn't be from here. We're moving you to a safe house in Wapping. St Mary's Priory."

"No. I can't believe it. This is some trick," Steiner said.

"What profit would there be in it for us?" Munro demanded. "There's a man at the Spanish embassy here called José Vargas, a commercial attaché. He works for your side on occasion for money. Operates via his cousin at the Spanish embassy in Berlin, using a diplomatic pouch."

"He works for us too, you see, also for money," Carter said. "And they have been in touch—indicated their interest in pulling you out and requested more information as to your whereabouts."

"And we've told him what he needs to know," Munro put in. "Even your new home at the priory."

"Now I understand," Steiner said. "You allow the plan to proceed. Devlin comes to London. He will need help from others, of course, and at the appropriate moment you arrest the lot."

"Yes, that is one way," Munro said. "There is another possibility, of course."

"And what would that be?"

"That I simply allow it to happen. You escape to Germany—"

"Where I work for you?" Steiner shook his head. "Sorry, Brigadier. I'm no Nazi, but I'm still a soldier— a German soldier. I'd find the word traitor difficult to handle."

"Would you say your father and others were traitors because they tried to remove the Führer?" Munro asked.

"That's different. Germans trying to handle their own problem."

"A neat point." Munro turned and said, "Jack."

Carter went and knocked on the door. It opened, and the MP appeared. Munro got up.

"If you'd be kind enough to follow me, Colonel, there's something I'd like you to see."

THE FILM being shown in the large stockroom at the end of the corridor was flickering and rather grainy. The young Intelligence sergeant was using the white-painted wall as a screen. Steiner sat on a chair alone, Munro and Carter behind him.

General Karl Steiner, carried in by two SS men, was already dead from a heart attack. They hung him anyway, and for a little while the camera stayed on that pathetic figure, swaying slightly from side to side. Then the screen went blank.

Kurt Steiner stood and moved to the door without a word. He opened it and walked down the corridor to his room. Munro and Carter followed. When they went into the room, Steiner was standing at the window, gripping the bars and looking out.

"I'm sorry about that," Munro said, "but it was important you knew that Himmler had broken his promise."

Steiner turned, his face very pale. "You're not sorry, Brigadier. You wanted to make your point, and you've made it."

"And what do you think now?" Munro asked.

"Ah, so we come to the purpose of the exercise. Will I now, in a white-hot rage, offer my services to the Allies?" He shook his head. "No, Brigadier. I'll have some bad nights over this—I may even ask to see a priest—but the essential point remains the same. My father's involvement in a plot on Hitler's life was as a German. You must also realise that for me to do what you suggest would be a betrayal of everything he gave his life for."

"All right." Munro stood up. "We're wasting our time. You'll be transferred to St Mary's Priory in the new year, Colonel." He turned to Carter. "Let's get moving, Jack."

Steiner said, "One thing, Brigadier, if I may?"

"Yes?"

"My uniform. I would remind you that under the Geneva convention I am entitled to wear it."

Munro glanced at Carter, who said, "It has been repaired, Colonel, and cleaned. I'll arrange for you to have it later today, together with all your medals, naturally."

"That's all right, then," Munro said, and went out.

Carter went to the door, hesitated and turned. "If it helps at all, Colonel, it was apparently a heart attack your father died of. I don't know the circumstances—"

"Oh, I can imagine them well enough," Steiner answered.

He stood there, hands thrust into the pockets of his robe, quite calm, and Carter, unable to think of anything else to say, stepped into the corridor and went after Munro.

As they drove through the fog along Tower Hill, Munro said, "You don't approve, do you, Jack?"

"No, sir. An unnecessary cruelty in my opinion."

"Yes. Well, at least we know where we stand with friend Steiner now. As for Devlin—let him come whenever he wants. With Vargas tipping us off, we can't go wrong."

IT WAS NEW YEAR'S Day when Devlin finally arrived in Berlin. It had taken him two days to get a seat on the Paris Express from Madrid. In Paris he had got on the Berlin Express, but American bombers had damaged the Frankfurt marshalling yards. This necessitated rerouting of rail traffic into Germany.

The weather was bad, a thin snow changing to sleet and driving rain. Devlin, still wearing a suit more apt for Portugal, was freezing as he trudged through the crowds in the railway station.

Ilse Huber recognised him from his file photo as she stood at the barrier beside the security police. She had already made arrangements with the sergeant in charge, and when Devlin appeared, she intervened at once.

"Herr Devlin?" She held out her hand. "I am Ilse Huber, General Schellenberg's secretary. I have transport waiting."

The car was a Mercedes saloon, with an SS pennant conspicuously on display. "It occurred to the general that you might be caught out by the weather, so I've made arrangements to take you to a second-hand shop. And you'll need somewhere to stay. I have an apartment not too far from headquarters. There are two bedrooms. If it suits, you can have one of them while you're here."

"More to the point, does it suit you?" he asked.

She shrugged. "Mr Devlin, my husband was killed in Russia. I have no children. Life could be difficult except for one thing. Working for General Schellenberg usually takes at least sixteen hours out of my day, so I'm hardly ever home."

She smiled, and Devlin warmed to her. "It's a deal, then, Ilse."

When they emerged forty minutes later from the second-hand shop, Devlin wore a tweed suit, laced boots, a heavy overcoat almost ankle-length, gloves and a trilby hat.

"Where to now—your apartment?"

"No. General Schellenberg wants to see you as soon as possible. He's at Prinz Albrechtstrasse now."

DEVLIN COULD hear the sounds of shooting as they descended the steep stairway. "And what's all this, then?"

Ilse said, "The basement firing range. The general likes to keep in practice."

They opened the door. Schellenberg was firing at a series of cardboard Russian soldiers, watched by an SS sergeant major. He worked his way across three targets, placing two rounds neatly in each heart. As he paused to reload, he noticed Devlin and Ilse.

"Ah, Mr Devlin, so you finally got here. Ilse's taken care of your wardrobe, I see."

"And how did you guess?" Devlin said. "It can only have been the smell of the mothballs."

Schellenberg laughed. "Schwarz," he said to the sergeant major. "Something for Mr Devlin. I believe he's quite a marksman."

Schwarz rammed a magazine into the butt of a Walther PPK and handed it to the Irishman.

"All right?" Schellenberg asked.

Devlin nodded. Fresh targets sprang up, and he fired three rounds so close together that they might almost have been one. A hole appeared between the eyes of all three targets.

He laid the Walther down. Ilse Huber said, "Good Lord."

"A remarkable talent, Mr Devlin," Schellenberg said.

"Remarkable curse more like. Now what happens, General?"

"The Reichsführer has expressed a desire to see you."

Devlin groaned. "He didn't like me the last time around. A glutton for punishment, that man. All right, let's get it over with."

THE MERCEDES turned out Wilhelmplatz and into Voss Strasse and drove towards the Reich Chancellery.

"What's all this?" Devlin demanded.

"Times have changed since Göring said that if a single bomb fell on Berlin, you could call him Meier."

"You mean he got it wrong?"

"I'm afraid so. The Führer has had a bunker constructed below the Chancellery. Thirty metres of concrete, so the RAF can drop as many bombs as they like. The important people have secondary headquarters down there, including the Reichsführer."

The Mercedes drew into the car ramp, and an SS sentry approached and checked their identities thoroughly before allowing them through.

Devlin followed Schellenberg down a seemingly endless passage, with concrete walls and dim lighting. There were SS guards here and there, but no great evidence of people.

Then a door opened further along the passage, and to Devlin's astonishment Hitler emerged, followed by a broad, rather squat man in a nondescript uniform. As they approached, Schellenberg pulled Devlin to one side and stood at attention. The Führer was talking to the other man in a low voice and totally ignored them as he passed and descended the stairs at the other end of the passage.

"So that was the Führer," Devlin said. "And me almost getting to touch the hem of his robe."

Schellenberg smiled. "Sometimes, my friend, I wonder how you've managed to last as long as you have."

"Ah, well, it must be my good looks, General."

Schellenberg tapped on a door, opened it and led the way in. The room was mainly taken up by filing cabinets and the desk behind which Himmler sat working through a file. He glanced up and removed his pince-nez.

"So, General, he's arrived."

"God bless all here," Devlin said cheerfully.

Himmler winced. "I expected you sooner, Herr Devlin."

"Your railway system seemed to be having trouble." Devlin lit a cigarette, mainly because he knew Himmler detested the habit.

Himmler was annoyed, but didn't tell him to stop. Instead he said to Schellenberg, "You seem to have wasted an inordinate amount of time so far, General. Why didn't Herr Devlin return from Lisbon with you?"

"Ah, the general did a fine job," Devlin said. "It was me had plans for Christmas, you see. No, the general was very reasonable. More than I can say for Berger. We didn't get on at all."

"So I understand," Himmler said. "But that scarcely matters, as Sturmbannführer Berger has other duties." He leant back. "So you believe you can get Steiner out?"

"Depends on the plan," Devlin said. "It's getting back in one piece that worries me. I only just made it last time."

"You were well paid then, and I would remind you that you're being well paid this time."

"And that's a fact," Devlin said. "As my old mother used to say, money will be the death of me."

Himmler looked extremely annoyed. "Can't you take anything seriously, you Irish?"

"When I last had the pleasure of meeting Your Honour, I gave you the answer to that one. It's the rain."

"Oh, get him out of here," Himmler said. "And get on with it, General. Needless to say, I expect a regular progress report."

"Reichsführer." Schellenberg ushered Devlin out.

The Irishman was grinning hugely. "I enjoyed that." He dropped his cigarette on the floor and stamped on it as Berger came around the corner, a rolled-up map under his arm.

He was in uniform and wore Iron Crosses First and Second Class. He stiffened when he saw them, and Devlin said cheerfully, "Very pretty, son, but it looks to me as if someone's been spoiling your good looks."

Berger's face was very pale and although the swelling had subsided it was obvious his nose was broken. He ignored Devlin and nodded to Schellenberg. "General." He passed on and knocked at Himmler's door.

"He must be well in there," Devlin observed.

"Yes." Schellenberg nodded. "Interesting."

"Where to now? Your office?"

"No, tomorrow will be soon enough. I'll take you for a meal, then drop you at Ilse's place. You'll get a good night's sleep, and we'll go over things in the morning."

As they reached the mouth of the tunnel, fresh air drifted in, and Devlin took a deep breath, then started to laugh.

"What is it?" Schellenberg demanded.

Devlin pointed to a poster on the wall — a picture of an idealised SS soldier that said AT THE END STANDS VICTORY. Devlin laughed again. "Damn, General, but some people will believe anything."

BERGER CLICKED his heels in front of Himmler's desk. "I have the plan of the Château de Belle-Île here, Reichsführer."

"Excellent," Himmler said. "Let me see."

Berger unrolled the plan, and the Reichsführer examined it.

"Good. Very good." He looked up. "You will be in charge, Berger. Have you visited the place yet?"

"I flew down to Cherbourg the day before yesterday and drove out to the château. It's quite splendid. The owners are French aristocrats who fled to England. There is at the moment only a caretaker and his wife. I've informed him that we'll be taking the place over, but not why, naturally."

"Excellent." Himmler rolled the plan up and returned it to Berger. "After all, the Führer will be our direct responsibility at this conference, Major. A sacred responsibility."

"Of course, Reichsführer."

THE MERCEDES moved along the Kurfürstendamm as snow started to fall again. There was evidence of bomb damage everywhere, and with dusk falling, the prospect was less than pleasing.

"Used to be a great city," Schellenberg said. "Art, music, theatre. Still, let's eat, Mr Devlin. I know a little restaurant not far from here. Black market, but then they know me, which helps."

The place was homely enough, with no more than a dozen tables. It was run by a man and his wife who obviously knew Schellenberg well. They were able to produce a mutton broth, lamb, potatoes, and a bottle of hock to go with it.

The booth Schellenberg and Devlin sat in was quite private, and as they finished the meal Schellenberg said, "Do you really think it is possible, this thing?"

"Anything's possible." Devlin poured the last of the wine into both their glasses. "Vargas is a problem, though. Will he come up with the right information?"

"He always has in the past. This is a Spanish diplomat, Mr Devlin—a man in a privileged position. No ordinary agent. I have had his cousin, this Rivera fellow, thoroughly vetted."

"All right, I accept that. Let's say Rivera's clean as a whistle. But who checks out Vargas? Rivera is just a conduit for messages, but what if Vargas is something else?"

"You mean a British Intelligence plot to entice us in?"

"Well, let's look at the way they would see it. Whoever drops in needs friends in London, some sort of organisation. If I was in charge on the Brit side, I'd give a little rope, let things get started, then arrest everybody in sight. From their point of view, quite a coup."

"Are you telling me you're having second thoughts?"

"Not at all. What I'm saying is that if I go, I have to go on the supposition that I'm expected. That Vargas has sold us out. I'd look a right idiot if we organise things on the basis that Vargas is on our side, and I get there and he isn't."

"Mr Devlin, you are a remarkable man," Schellenberg said.

"A genius on my good days," Devlin replied solemnly.

Schellenberg settled the account, and they went outside. It was still snowing lightly as they walked to the Mercedes.

"I'll take you to Ilse's now." At that moment the sirens started. Schellenberg called to his driver, "Hans, this way." He turned to Devlin. "On second thought, we'll go back to the restaurant and sit in their cellar with the other sensible people. It's quite comfortable. I've been there before."

"Why not?" Devlin said. "Who knows—they may find us a bottle of something in there."

Behind them gunfire was already rumbling like thunder on the edge of the city.

CHAPTER 5

AS THEY approached Schellenberg's office at Prinz Albrechtstrasse, the morning air was tainted with smoke. "They certainly hit the target last night," Schellenberg said.

"You can say that again," Devlin said.

The door opened, and Ilse Huber nodded good morning. "There you are, General," she said. "I was a little worried. Rivera's on his way."

"Oh, good. Send him in when he arrives."

She went out and ten minutes later ushered in the Spaniard. He stood there clutching his hat, nervously glancing at Devlin.

"You may speak freely," Schellenberg said.

"I've had another message from my cousin, General. He says they are moving Steiner from the Tower of London to a place called St Mary's Priory. In Wapping, by the river."

Devlin said, "A remarkable fella, your cousin, to come up with such a prime piece of information so easily."

Rivera smiled eagerly. "José is certain his information is correct, señor. He got it from a friend, a guard at the Tower. My cousin . . ." Rivera shrugged. "A matter of some delicacy."

"Yes, we understand, Rivera." Schellenberg nodded. "All right, you can go. I'll be in touch when I need you."

Ilse showed him out, and came back. "Anything else, General?"

"Yes. Find me one of those gazetteers. You know the sort of thing. London street by street. See if the place is mentioned."

She went out. "I used to know Wapping well at one stage of my career," Devlin said.

"With the IRA?"

"The bombing campaign, 1936. There was an active-service unit who set a bomb or two off in London. Women, kids, passers-by. I was an enforcer in those days, and the men at the top wanted it stopped. Lousy publicity, you see . . . A friend of my mother's, Michael Ryan, ran a safe house there. Not active at all. Very deep cover."

"And you took care of this active-service unit?"

"There were only the three of them." Devlin shrugged. "They wouldn't be told. After that, I went to Spain. Joined the Lincoln-Washington Brigade. Did my bit against Franco till the Italians took me prisoner. Eventually the Abwehr pulled me out. They sent me to Ireland in '41 to pull out one of their agents. Scotland Yard got to him first."

"And this friend of yours, this Ryan—what happened to him?"

"Still in deep, I should imagine. He wouldn't want to know any more. Michael had doubts about the use of violence."

"Could he be of any use?" Schellenberg suggested.

"Hold on, General. You've got the cart before the horse."

Ilse came in with a map book. "I've found it, General. St Mary's Priory. See—right on the edge of the Thames."

Schellenberg and Devlin examined the map. "That isn't going to tell us much," Devlin said.

Schellenberg nodded. "I've just had a thought. Operation Sea Lion, 1940."

"You mean the invasion that never was?"

"Yes. But it was thoroughly planned. One task the SD was given was a comprehensive survey of London. Buildings, I'm talking about. Their usefulness if London were occupied. There was a list of hundreds of such places—and plans, where obtainable." He turned to Ilse. "See what you can do."

"At once, General."

Schellenberg said, "You said last night you preferred to proceed with the notion of Vargas being a traitor. So what would you do? How would you handle it?"

"Easy. We don't tell Vargas I'm going."

"I don't understand."

"We extract what information we need. In fact, we probably have enough already. Then once a week Rivera asks for more information on your behalf—only I'll already be in London."

"Marvellous," said Schellenberg.

"There's another difficulty," Devlin said. "The Special Branch managed to hunt me down when I was in Norfolk. One of the things that helped them was the fact that as an Irish citizen, I had to be entered on the aliens' register by the local police, and that required a passport photo."

"I see. So what are you saying?"

"A complete change in appearance. Hair colour, age . . ."

"I think I can help there," Schellenberg said. "I have friends at the UFA film studios here in Berlin. Some of their make-up artists can achieve remarkable things."

"Another thing. No aliens' register this time. I was born in Ulster, and that makes me officially a British citizen. We'll stick with that when it comes to false papers and so on."

"And your identity?"

"Last time I was a war hero. A gallant Irishman who'd been wounded at Dunkirk and invalided out." Devlin tapped the bullet scar on his head. "This helped the story, of course."

"Good. Something like that, then. What about method of entry?"

"Oh, parachute again. Into Ireland, like last time. A stroll across the border into Ulster, the train to Belfast, and I'm on British soil."

"And afterwards?"

"The boat. Belfast to Heysham, in Lancashire."

"So you get to London. What happens then?"

Devlin lit a cigarette. "Well, if I keep away from Vargas, that means no help from any of your official sources."

Schellenberg frowned. "But you will need the help of others. Also weapons, a radio transmitter—"

"A few things will have to be taken on trust," Devlin said. "Michael Ryan ran a cab, and he worked for the bookies on the side. He had a lot of underworld friends in the old days. The kind who'd do anything for money—deal in guns, that sort of thing."

"Your friend may no longer be in London, you know."

"Or killed in the blitz, General. Nothing is guaranteed. I reach London, I assess the situation. If Michael isn't around, if the whole thing looks impossible, I'm on the next boat back to Belfast, over the border to the south and safe in Dublin before you know it." Devlin grinned. "I'll give you the bad news from your embassy there."

IN THE OFFICE after lunch they started planning again, with Ilse sitting in the corner taking notes.

Schellenberg said, "Say, for argument's sake, that you got Steiner out of the priory one dark evening. That's only the first step. How do you get him back? Do you return the way you came?"

"Not so healthy, that," Devlin said.

Ilse said diffidently, "Surely, the moment the colonel is out, they'll be looking for him."

"Exactly," Devlin said. "Police, army, the security services. Every port watched, especially the Irish routes." He shook his head. "No. Once out, we've got to leave England almost immediately, before they know what's hit them."

Schellenberg nodded. "It occurs to me that one of the cleverest things about Operation Eagle was the way Colonel Steiner and his men were transported to England."

"The Dakota, you mean?" Devlin said.

"An RAF Dakota that had crash-landed in Holland and was put back into service. To all intents, a British plane flying home, if anyone saw it."

"Worked like a charm," Devlin said. "Except on the way back it was shot down by a Luftwaffe night fighter."

"Unfortunate, but an intriguing thought. A small plane flying in under radar. A British plane. A suitable landing place. It could have you and Steiner out and safely in France in no time at all."

"And pigs might fly, General. May I also point out you'd need an exceptional pilot."

"Come now, Mr Devlin. Anything is possible. We have what's called the Enemy Aircraft Flight, where the Luftwaffe tests captured British and American planes." He turned to Ilse. "Get in touch with them at once. Also extend your research on Operation Sea Lion to cover any sites in the London area that we intended to use for covert operations."

"And a pilot," Devlin told her. "Like I said, someone special."

"I'll get right on to it," Ilse said.

As Ilse turned to the door a young woman in SS auxiliary uniform came in carrying a large file. "St Mary's Priory, Wapping. Was that what the general wanted?"

Ilse laughed triumphantly. "Good girl, Sigrid. Wait for me in the office. I've got something else for you." She handed the file to Schellenberg. "I'll get her started on the other thing."

As she reached the door Schellenberg said, "Another possibility, Ilse. Check the files on those British right-wing organisations that flourished before the war, the ones that sometimes had Members of Parliament on their books."

She went out, and Devlin asked, "Who would they be, General?"

"Anti-Semites, people with Fascist sympathies. Many members of the British aristocracy and upper classes rather admired the

Führer, certainly before the war." Schellenberg opened the bulky file and extracted the first plan. "So, Mr Devlin, there you have it in all its glory. St Mary's Priory."

ASA VAUGHAN was twenty-seven. He was born in Los Angeles, his father a film producer. Asa had been fascinated by flying from an early age, even before going to West Point. After he had completed his training as a fighter pilot, he was assigned to take an instructors' course with the navy, at San Diego. Then came the night his world collapsed—the night he'd got into a drunken brawl in a harbour-side bar and punched a major in the mouth.

The fifth of October 1939. The date was engraved on his heart. No scandal, no court-martial. Just his resignation. One week at his parents' house in Beverly Hills was all he could bear. He packed a bag and made for Europe.

The war had started in September, and the RAF was accepting a few Americans, but they didn't like Asa's record. And then on 30 November the Russians invaded Finland. The Finns needed fighter pilots badly, and volunteers from many nations flooded in to join the Finnish air force, Asa among them.

It was a hopeless war from the start, in spite of the gallantry of the Finnish army. The outdated biplanes Asa flew were hopelessly outclassed by the opposition. Only his superior skill as a pilot gave him an edge. Then came that morning of ferocious winds and driving snow when he'd come in at four hundred feet, flying blind, lost his engine at the last moment and crash-landed.

That was in March 1940. His back broken, he'd been hospitalised for eighteen months. He was undergoing final therapy, still a lieutenant in the Finnish air force, when on 25 June 1941, Finland joined with Nazi Germany in going to war against Russia.

Asa returned to flying duties gradually. Then suddenly the roof fell in. First Pearl Harbor, and then the declaration of war between Germany and Italy and the USA.

The Germans held him in a detention camp for three months, and then the officers from the SS came to see him. Himmler was extending the SS foreign legions to prisoners of war. He hadn't had many takers—mostly scum attracted by the offer of good food, women and money. As far as Asa knew, the George Washington Legion, supposedly for American sympathisers to the Nazi cause, never had more than half a dozen members. He had a choice. To join or be sent to a concentration camp. He argued as best he could. The final agreement was that he would serve only on the Russian front. As it happened, his skill as a pilot was so admired he was employed mainly to ferry high-ranking officers.

So here he was, Hauptsturmführer Asa Vaughan, not far from the Russian border with Poland, at the controls of a Stork, forest and snow five thousand feet below. An SS Brigadeführer called Farber was sitting behind him, examining maps.

Farber looked up. "How long now?"

"Twenty minutes," Asa told him. He spoke excellent German, although with an American accent.

"Good. I'm frozen to the bone."

How did I ever get into this? Asa asked himself. And how do I get out? The Stork bucked wildly, and Farber cried out in alarm. A fighter plane took station to starboard for a moment, the red star plain on its fuselage; then it banked away.

"Russian Yak fighter. We're in trouble," Asa said.

The Yak came in fast from behind, firing both cannon and machine-guns, and the Stork staggered, pieces breaking from the wings. Asa banked and went down. The Yak followed, turning in a half circle, punching cannon shell into the Stork, and Farber cried out as a bullet caught him in the shoulder. As the windscreen shattered, he screamed, "Do something, for God's sake."

Asa, blood on his cheek from a splinter, took the Stork straight down to two thousand, waited until the Yak came in, banked and went down again. The forest below seemed to rush towards them.

"What are you doing?" Farber cried.

Asa took her down to a thousand, then five hundred feet, and the Yak, hungry for the kill, stayed on his tail. At the right moment, Asa dropped his flaps. The Yak banked to avoid a collision and ploughed straight down into the forest at three hundred and fifty miles an hour. There was a tongue of flame, and Asa pulled back the column and levelled out at two thousand feet.

"You okay, General?"

Farber clutched his arm. "You're a genius—a genius. I'll see you get the Iron Cross for this."

"Thanks." Asa wiped blood from his cheek. "That's all I need."

AT THE LUFTWAFFE base outside Warsaw, Asa walked into the officers' mess feeling depressed. The medical officer had put two stitches in his cheek but had been more concerned with Brigade-führer Farber's condition.

Asa went in and took off his flying jacket. He wore a beautifully tailored uniform in field grey, SS runes on his collar patch. On his left sleeve was a Stars and Stripes shield. The cuff title on his left wrist said GEORGE WASHINGTON LEGION. He wore the ribbon of the Iron Cross Second Class and the Finnish Gold Cross of Valour.

His very uniqueness made most other pilots avoid him. He ordered a Cognac, drank it quickly and ordered another.

A voice said, "And it's not even lunch time."

As Asa turned, the Gruppenkommandant, Colonel Erich Adler, sat on the stool next to him. "Champagne," he told the barman.

"And what's the occasion?" Asa demanded.

"First, my miserable Yankee friend, Brigadeführer Farber has recommended you for an immediate Iron Cross First Class, which from what he says, you deserve."

"But Erich, I've got a medal."

Adler ignored him. "Second, you're grounded."

"I'm what?"

"You fly out to Berlin on the next available transport. And you report to General Schellenberg at SD headquarters in Berlin."

"Just a minute," Asa told him. "I only fly on the Russian front."

"I wouldn't argue. This order comes by way of Himmler himself." Adler raised his glass. "Good luck, my friend."

"I think I'm going to need it," Asa Vaughan told him.

DEVLIN AWOKE about three in the morning to the sound of distant gunfire. He got up and padded into the living room and peered out through the blackout curtains. He could see the flashes on the far horizon beyond the city.

Behind him Ilse switched on the light in the kitchen. "I couldn't sleep either," she said. "I'll make some coffee."

She was wearing a dressing gown against the cold. He put his overcoat on over his pyjamas and sat at the table, smoking a cigarette.

"Two days, and no suitable landing site for a plane," he said. "I think the general's getting impatient."

"He likes to do things yesterday," Ilse said. "At least we've found a suitable base on the French coast, and the pilot looks promising."

"A Yank in the SS. Not that he had much choice apparently. I can't wait to meet him," Devlin told her.

"My husband was SS. A sergeant major."

"I'm sorry," Devlin said.

"You must think we're all very wicked, Mr Devlin, but you must understand how it started. After the First War, Germany was on her knees, ruined. The Führer seemed to offer so much. Pride again—prosperity. And then it started—so many bad things, for the Jews most of all." She hesitated. "One of my great-grandmothers was Jewish. My husband had to get special permission to marry me. It's there on my record, and sometimes I wake in the night and think what would happen to me if someone decided to do something about it."

Devlin took her hands. "Hush now, girl. We all get that three-o'clock-in-the-morning feeling, when everything looks bad." There were tears in her eyes. "Here, I'll make you smile. My disguise for this little jaunt I'm taking. Guess what it is?"

She was smiling already. "No. Tell me."

"A priest."

"You, a priest?" She started to laugh. "Oh, no, Mr Devlin."

"Wait now. You'd be surprised at the religious background I have." He nodded solemnly. "Altar boy; then, after the British hanged my father in 1921, my mother and I went to live with my old uncle, who was a priest in Belfast. Oh, I can play the priest as well as any priest, if you follow me."

"Well, let's hope you don't have to celebrate Mass or hear confession." She laughed.

"Dear woman, you've given me an idea there. Where's the file we were looking at earlier? The general file."

She went into her bedroom and came back with it. Devlin leafed through it quickly, then nodded. "I was right. The Steiners are an old Catholic family."

"What are you getting at?"

"This St Mary's Priory. It's the sort of place priests visit all the time. The Little Sisters of Pity need confession before they partake of Communion, and both functions need a priest. Then there would be those patients who were Catholic."

"Including Steiner, you mean?"

"They couldn't deny him a priest in a place like that." He grinned.

She nodded. "Let's hope we come up with something in those Sea Lion files." She got up. "Anyway, I think I'll go back to bed."

Outside, the air-raid siren sounded. Devlin smiled wryly. "No you won't. You'll get dressed, and we'll go down and spend another jolly night in the cellars. I'll see you in five minutes."

SCHELLENBERG said, "A priest? Yes, I like that."

"So do I," Devlin said. "It's like a uniform, you see. A soldier, a postman, a railway porter—it's the appearance of things you remember, not the face. Priests are like that. Nice and anonymous."

They were standing at a collapsible map table, the plans of St Mary's Priory spread before them.

"Having studied these on and off for some days, what is your opinion?" Schellenberg asked.

"The most interesting thing," Devlin said, "is the architect's plans for the changes made in 1910, when the Little Sisters took over."

"What's your point?"

"Underneath London is a labyrinth of sewers, underground rivers, tunnels. And nobody knows where half of them are until they're excavating or making changes, as they were at the priory. Look at the architect's plan here. Regular flooding of the crypt beneath the chapel. They were able to deal with the problem because they discovered a stream running into the Thames through an eighteenth-century tunnel next door."

"Very interesting," Schellenberg said.

"They built a grille in the wall of the crypt to allow water to draw into that tunnel. There's a note here on the plan."

"A way out, you mean?"

"It's a possibility. Would have to be checked."

At that moment Ilse Huber came in, very excited. "You were right, General. I found details of a man in one of the British right-wing organisations cross-referenced to Sea Lion. His name is Shaw. Sir Maxwell Shaw." She laid two bulky files on the table.

CHAPTER 6

ROMNEY MARSH, some forty-five miles southeast of London, on the coast of Kent, is a two-hundred-square-mile area reclaimed from the sea by a system of dykes and channels. Much of it is below sea level, and only innumerable drainage ditches prevent it from reverting to its natural state.

Charbury was not even a village, but a hamlet of no more than fifteen houses, a church and a village store. Half the cottages were empty, only the old folk left. The younger people had departed long ago for war work or service in the armed forces.

It was raining as Sir Maxwell Shaw walked down the village street, a black Labrador at his heels. He was a heavily built man of medium height, face craggy, the evidence of heavy drinking there, and the black moustache didn't help. He looked morose and angry much of the time, and most people avoided him.

He wore a tweed hat, a waterproof shooting jacket and Wellingtons. He carried a double-barrelled shotgun under one arm. When he reached the store, he bent down and fondled the Labrador's ears, his face softening. "Good girl, Nell. Stay."

A bell tinkled as he went into the shop. An old man was leaning against the counter, talking to a woman behind it who was even older. "Morning," Shaw said. "You promised me some cigarettes, Mrs Dawson."

The old lady produced a package from beneath the counter. "Managed to get you two hundred Players, Sir Maxwell. Black market, I'm afraid, so they come expensive."

"Isn't everything these days? Put it on my bill."

He placed the package in one of his game pockets and went out. As he closed the door he heard the old man say, "Poor bloke."

He took a deep breath to contain his anger, and touched the Labrador. "Let's go, girl," he said, and went back along the street.

IT WAS Maxwell Shaw's grandfather, a Sheffield ironmaster, who had made the family's fortune. It was he who had purchased the estate, renamed Shaw Place, where he had retired, a millionaire, in 1885. His son had shown no interest in the family firm, which had passed into other hands. A career soldier, the son had died leading his men into battle during the Boer War.

Maxwell Shaw, born in 1890, had followed in his father's foot-steps. Eton, Sandhurst, a commission in the Indian army. In 1917 he returned from France badly wounded and with a Military Cross. His mother was still alive. Lavinia, his younger sister, was married to a pilot in the Royal Flying Corps. During Shaw's convalescence he met the girl who was to become his wife, and married her before returning to France.

It was in 1918, the last year of the war, when everything seemed to happen at once. His mother died, then his wife, when she took a bad fall out with the local hunt. Within a month Lavinia too was alone, her husband shot down over the western front.

After the war it was a different world, and Shaw didn't like it. He and Lavinia had Shaw Place, but as the years went by and the money went, things became increasingly difficult. He was a Conservative member of Parliament for a while, then lost his seat to a Socialist. Like many of his kind, he was violently anti-Semitic, and this, exacerbated by the crushing political blow, led to his involvement with the British Fascist movement.

In all this he was backed by Lavinia, although her main interest lay in keeping their heads above water. Disenchanted with society and their own place in it, they both looked to Hitler as a role model, admiring what he was doing for Germany.

And then at a dinner in London in January 1939 they were introduced to Major Werner Keitel, a military attaché at the German embassy. For several months Lavinia enjoyed a passionate affair with him, and he was frequently a visitor at Shaw Place, for he was a Luftwaffe pilot and shared Lavinia's love of flying. They flew together in a Tiger Moth, a two-seater biplane she kept at the time. Using the south meadow as an airstrip, they covered large sections of the south coast, and Keitel had been able to indulge his interest in aerial photography.

Shaw never minded. Lavinia had had affairs before, although he himself had little interest in women. The Keitel thing was different, however, because of what it led to.

"WERNER KEITEL was an Abwehr agent employed at the time to select deep-cover agents," Schellenberg said. "A war was coming, and there was much forward planning for Sea Lion."

"And the Shaw place was perfect," Devlin observed. "Forty-five miles from London. And a meadow to land a plane on."

"Yes. Keitel found it amazingly easy to recruit both of them. He supplied them with a radio. The sister already knew Morse code. Keitel, by the way, was killed in the Battle of Britain."

"Did they have a code name?"

Ilse, who had been sitting quietly, produced another sheet from the file. "Falcon", Ilse said. "Shaw was to be alerted by the message 'Does the Falcon still wait? It is now time to strike.'"

Devlin said, "So there they were. Waiting for the invasion that never came. And what's the situation now? I wonder."

"As it happens, there is some further information available," Ilse told him. "We have an article here that appeared in an American magazine." She checked the date. "March 1943. 'The British Fascist Movement', it's called. The journalist got an interview with Shaw and his sister. There's a photo."

Schellenberg read the article quickly and passed it to Devlin. "Rather sad. You'll see there that like most of his kind he was detained without trial for a few months under Regulation 18B in 1941."

"Brixton Prison? That must have been a shock," Devlin said.

"The rest is even more sad. Much of the estate sold off, no servants. Just the two of them hanging on in that decaying old house," Schellenberg said. "It could be perfect, you know. Come and look at a map of the Channel." They went to the map table. "Here. Cap de la Hague and Chernay. Used to be a flying club there. It's used as an emergency landing strip by the Luftwaffe. Refuelling, that sort of thing. Only half a dozen men there. It's perfect for our purposes because it's only some thirty miles from the Château de Belle-Île, where the Führer's conference takes place."

"How far to our friends in Romney Marsh?"

"A hundred and fifty miles, most of it over the sea."

"Fine," Devlin said. "Except for one thing. Would the Shaws be willing to be activated?"

"Couldn't Vargas find out?"

"Vargas could drop the lot of us, as I told you. This would be exactly what British Intelligence wants—the chance to pull in everyone they can." Devlin shook his head. "No. The Shaws will have to wait till I get there. If they'll do it, then we're in business."

"But how will you communicate?"

"They may still have that radio."

"And if they haven't?"

Devlin laughed. "Then I'll beg, borrow or steal one. General, you worry too much."

ASA VAUGHAN closed the file and looked up. Schellenberg leant across the desk. "What do you think?"

"Why me?"

"Because they tell me you can fly anything."

"Flattery usually gets you everywhere, General, but let's examine this. When I was—shall we say?—inducted into the SS, the deal was that I only operated against the Russians, that I wouldn't have to take part in any act detrimental to my country's cause."

Devlin, sitting by the window, laughed harshly. "Nonsense. They had you the minute they got you into that uniform, son. Say no, and Himmler will have you in a concentration camp."

"Sounds like no contest, except for one small point," Asa told him. "I end up getting caught in England in this uniform, I'll get the fastest court-martial in American history—and a firing squad."

"No, you won't," Devlin said. "They'll hang you. Now the flight. Do you reckon you could make it in?"

"No reason why not. I'd need to know the Channel approach backwards. From what I can see, I'd stay over the water for almost the whole trip. Turn inland for the last few miles."

"Exactly," Schellenberg said.

"It would mean a night landing. Even with a moon I'd need some sort of guidance." He nodded, thinking about it. "When I was a kid, in California, my flying instructor was a guy who had flown with the Lafayette Escadrille in France. I remember him telling me how they used a few cycle lamps arranged in an inverted L shape, with the crossbar at the upwind end."

"Simple enough," Devlin said.

"And the plane. It would have to be small."

"Yes, well, I'm hoping that's taken care of," Schellenberg said. "I've spoken to the officer in command of Enemy Aircraft Flight, at Hildorf. He thinks he's found us a suitable plane."

THE CHAPEL at St Mary's Priory was cold and damp and smelt of candle grease and incense. In the confession box Father Frank Martin waited until the sister whose confession he had heard was gone. He then left the box, switched off the lights and went out.

He was the pastor of St Patrick's, two streets away, and with St Patrick's came the job of father confessor to the priory. He was seventy-six, a small, frail man with very white hair. If it hadn't been for the war, they'd have retired him, but it was like everything else these days—all hands to the pumps.

He went into the sacristy, removed his alb and carefully folded his violet stole. He reached for his raincoat, debating the virtues of an early night, but compassion and Christian charity won the day as usual. Eighteen patients at the moment, seven of them terminal. A last round of the rooms wouldn't come amiss.

He went out of the chapel and saw the mother superior, Sister Maria Palmer, mopping the floor.

"I'm glad to see you," she said. "They've given us a German prisoner of war again."

"Really?" He walked with her into the entrance hall.

"Yes. A Luftwaffe officer, recently wounded but well on the way to recovery. A Colonel Kurt Steiner. They've put him on the top floor, with half a dozen military police. There's a young second lieutenant called Benson in charge."

At that moment Jack Carter and Dougal Munro came down the main staircase. "Is everything satisfactory?" Sister asked.

"Perfectly," Munro said. "We'll try not to inconvenience you."

"There is no inconvenience," she said. "This, by the way, is Father Martin, our priest."

"Father," Munro said, and turned to Carter. "I'll be off now, Jack. Don't forget to get a doctor in to check him over."

Sister Maria Palmer said, "I am a doctor, Brigadier. Whatever Colonel Steiner's requirements are, I'm sure we can take care of them. In fact, I'll make sure he's settled in properly. And as he is a Catholic, he may need the ministrations of Father Martin here."

"Quite right, Sister," Munro said. "See to it, Jack, will you?"

He went out, and Carter turned and led the way up the stairs. There was a door at the top, heavily studded and banded with steel. An MP sat at a small table beside it.

"Open up," Carter told him. The MP knocked. The door was opened after a moment by another MP. They passed inside. The door to the first room stood open. There was a small desk, and the young lieutenant, Benson, sat at it.

Benson jumped to his feet. "Sir?"

"Sister and Father Martin have access whenever they require it. Brigadier Munro's orders. We'll go and talk to the prisoner now."

Benson unlocked the door, and Steiner, standing by the window, turned to greet them, an impressive figure in the blue-grey Luftwaffe uniform, his medals making a brave show.

Carter said, "This is the mother superior, Sister Maria Palmer. And Father Martin."

Sister Maria Palmer said, "Tomorrow I'll have you down to the dispensary for a thorough check, Colonel Steiner."

"Is that all right, sir?" Benson asked.

"No problem," Carter said. "Anything else, Sister?"

"No. That will do for tonight."

Father Martin said, "I'd like a word with the colonel, in private, if you wouldn't mind."

Carter nodded, and they all went out except for Father Martin, who closed the door and sat on the bed. "My son, you've had a bad time. I can see it in your face. When were you last at Mass?"

"So long ago I can't remember, Father."

"No confession either? A long time since you were able to ease the burden of your sins."

"I'm afraid so." Steiner smiled, warming to the man.

Father Martin got up. "The moment you feel the need for confession and Mass, I'll arrange for you to join us in the chapel."

"I'm afraid Lieutenant Benson would insist on coming too."

"Now, wouldn't that do his immortal soul some good?" The old priest chuckled and went out.

THE FOLLOWING morning at the air base at Hildorf, Asa Vaughan seemed in good spirits as Major Koenig, the officer commanding the Enemy Aircraft Flight, showed him and Schellenberg and

Devlin around. There was a B-17, a Lancaster bomber, a Hurricane, a Mustang, all bearing Luftwaffe insignia. "Now, this is what I thought might suit your purposes," Koenig said. "Here in the end hangar."

The plane standing there was a high wing-braced monoplane, with a single engine and a wingspan of fifty feet.

"Very nice," Asa said. "What is it?"

"A Westland Lysander. Has a maximum speed of two hundred and thirty at ten thousand feet. Short landing and take off. Only needs two hundred and forty yards fully loaded."

"Passengers?" Asa asked.

"Two comfortably. Can manage three. Even four at a pinch." He turned to Schellenberg. "We picked this up in France last month. It was RAF. The pilot caught a bullet in the chest when attacked by a JU night fighter. Managed to land but collapsed before he could destroy it. These planes are used by British Intelligence for covert operations. Perfect plane for such work."

"Good," Schellenberg said. He turned to Asa. "So what are your requirements?"

"Well, obviously I'll want to try it out. And I'll want temporary RAF roundels in place for the flight into England. Canvas covers that can be stripped so that I'm Luftwaffe again for the trip back."

"Easily taken care of," Koenig said.

"Excellent," Schellenberg told him. "Hauptsturmlührer Vaughan will remain to test-fly the plane for the rest of the day. After that, do whatever work is needed and have the aircraft delivered to a destination in France that you will be notified of."

"Certainly, General," Koenig said.

Schellenberg turned to Asa. "I've arranged to borrow a Fieseler Stork from the Luftwaffe. We'll fly down to Chernay and inspect the airstrip tomorrow. I'd also like to have a look at this Château de Belle-Île while we're there."

"And you want me to do the flying?" Asa asked.

"Don't worry, son. We have every confidence in you," Devlin told him as he and Schellenberg went out.

In London, Dougal Munro was working at his desk when Jack Carter came in. "I've had a medical report from Sister Maria Palmer, sir, on Steiner," Carter said.

"What's her opinion?"

"He's still not a hundred per cent. Some residual infection. She asked me to help her get hold of some of this new wonder drug—penicillin. Apparently it's in short supply."

"Then get it for her, Jack, get it."

"Very well, sir. I'm sure I can." He hesitated at the door. "What happens now with the Steiner thing, sir?"

"We wait, Jack. After all, we have Vargas in our pocket. Anything happens, and we'll be the first to know."

"Very well, sir."

As Carter opened the door Munro added, "We've got all the time in the world, Jack. So has Steiner."

When Kurt Steiner went into the chapel that evening, he was escorted by Lieutenant Benson and an MP corporal. The chapel was cold and damp, slightly eerie, with the candles down at the altar and the ruby light of the sanctuary lamp. He dipped his fingers into the holy water, then sat on the end of a bench beside a nun and waited his turn. The mother superior emerged from the confessional box, smiled at him and passed on. The nun went in. After a while she came out, and it was Steiner's turn. He went in and knelt down, finding the darkness surprisingly comforting. He hesitated and then said, "Bless me, Father—"

Father Martin knew it was he. He said, "May the Lord Jesus bless you and help you tell your sins."

"Dammit, Father," Steiner exploded. "I don't even know why I'm here. Maybe I just wanted to get out of that room."

"Oh, I'm sure God will forgive you that, my son. Is there anything you want to say to me? Anything?"

And suddenly Steiner found himself saying, "My father. They butchered my father. Hung him up like a piece of meat."

"Who did this thing, my son?"

"The Gestapo—the bloody Gestapo." Steiner found he could hardly breathe, his throat dry. "Hate, that's all I feel—and revenge. I want revenge, Father. Am I not guilty of a very great sin?"

Father Martin said quietly, "May our Lord Jesus Christ absolve you—and I, by his authority, absolve you from your sins in the name of the Father and the Son and the Holy Spirit."

"You don't understand," Kurt Steiner said. "I can't pray any more."

"That's all right," Father Martin said. "I'll pray for you."

CHAPTER 7

THE FLIGHT from Berlin to Cap de la Hague took just over three hours, Asa charting a course that took them into Chernay from the sea. It was a desolate-looking little place. Not even a control tower, just a grass runway, with three old prewar hangars and several huts. There was also a fuel dump.

Asa made a perfect landing and taxied towards the hangars, where half a dozen men waited in Luftwaffe overalls. As Schellenberg and Devlin got out, a sergeant emerged from the hut with the radio mast and hurried towards them. He took in Schellenberg's uniform and clicked his heels together. "General."

"And your name is?"

"Leber, General. Flight sergeant."

"And you are in charge here?"

"Yes, General."

"Read this." Schellenberg handed him the Führer's directive. "You and your men are now under my command."

Leber handed the letter back. "At your orders, General."

"Hauptsturmführer Vaughan will be making a hazardous and highly secret flight across the English Channel. The aircraft is an unusual one. You'll see that for yourself when it's delivered."

"And our duties, General?"

"I'll inform you later. Is your radio equipment up to scratch?"

"Oh, yes, General. The best the Luftwaffe can offer."

"Good." Schellenberg nodded. "Now find us a Kübelwagen and have the Stork refuelled and made ready for the return trip."

As Leber led them towards a Jeep parked outside the radio hut Devlin said, "Would you look at this place? What a lousy posting. I wonder they can put up with it."

"Better than Russia," Asa Vaughan said.

ASA DROVE, Devlin beside him, Schellenberg in the rear, a map spread across his knees. "Here it is," said Schellenberg. "The road south from Cherbourg goes to Carentan. It's off there somewhere, on the coast."

"What's the purpose of this little trip anyway?" Devlin asked.

"This Belle-Île place intrigues me. I'd like to see what we've got there, as long as we're in the neighbourhood."

Devlin said, "Does the Reichsführer know we're here?"

"He knows about our flight to Chernay, or he will soon. He likes a regular report."

"Ah, yes, General, that's one thing. But this Belle-Île place would be another."

"You could say that, Mr Devlin, you could."

"What a fox you are," Devlin said. "I pity the huntsman when you're around."

THE COUNTRY lanes were so narrow that it would not have been possible for two vehicles to pass each other, but after half an hour Asa cut into the main road that ran south from Cherbourg to Carentan. Here they had trouble with the map, and then a stroke of luck—a sign at the side of the road outside the village of St Aubin that said 12TH PARACHUTE DETACHMENT. There was a spread of farm buildings visible beyond the trees.

"Let's try here," Schellenberg said, and Asa turned off the road.

The men in the yard were all *Fallschirmjäger*—paratroopers— hard young men with cropped hair. Most of them wore camouflaged smocks and jump boots. A number sat on benches against the wall, cleaning weapons; a couple worked on the engine of a troop carrier. They glanced up as the Kübelwagen arrived, rising to their feet when they saw Schellenberg's uniform.

A hard-faced young captain emerged from the farmhouse. He had the Iron Cross First and Second Class, the cuff titles for Crete and the Afrika Korps. He also had a Winter War ribbon.

"You are in charge here?" Schellenberg asked.

"Yes, General. Hauptmann Erich Kramer. May I help you?"

"We're looking for a place called Château de Belle-Île."

"About ten miles east of here on the coast. Let me show you."

They followed him into the farmhouse. The living room was fitted out as a command post, with large-scale maps on the wall. An area map showed the back road to Belle-Île.

"Excellent," Schellenberg said. "Tell me something. What's your unit's purpose here?"

"Security duties, General. We try to keep the French Resistance in place."

"Do you get much trouble from them?"

"Not really." Kramer laughed. "I only have thirty-five men left in this unit. We were lucky to get out of Stalingrad. This is a rest cure for us."

They went outside, and as they got back into the Kübelwagen, Devlin turned to Kramer. "Stalingrad? Did you know Kurt Steiner?"

Even the men cleaning their weapons looked up at the mention of the name.

Kramer said, "Who doesn't in our line of work? A legend in the parachute regiment."

"You've met him, then?"

"Several times. We heard a rumour he was dead."

"You mustn't believe everything you hear," Devlin told him.

"Captain." Schellenberg returned his salute as Asa drove away.

Devlin said, "I sometimes wonder why Steiner doesn't make his own way back across the Channel, walking on water."

BELLE-ÎLE WAS quite spectacular, a castle crowning a hill beside the sea, sand stretching beyond it where the tide had just retreated. Asa took the Kübelwagen up the single winding road. There was a narrow bridge across a gap that was more ravine than moat, and two great doors opened into a cobbled courtyard. Asa braked at the foot of broad steps leading up to the front entrance, walls and towers rising above them.

They got out, and Schellenberg led the way. The door was of oak, buckled with age and studded with rusting iron bolts. Schellenberg pulled the bell hanging from the wall beside it, and a moment later the door creaked open and a very old man appeared, with grey hair down to his shoulders and a black dress coat of velvet that had seen better days.

"*Oui, messieurs?*" he said. "What can I do for you?"

"You are the caretaker?" Schellenberg asked.

"Yes, monsieur. Pierre Dissard."

Schellenberg said, "I wish to inspect the premises." He walked past Dissard into a great entrance hall flagged in granite. There was an enormous fireplace, and a staircase to the first floor, wide enough to take a regiment.

"But the premises have already been inspected, monsieur, by an officer in a similar uniform to your own."

"Do you recall his name?"

"He said he was a major." The old man frowned, trying. "His face was bad on one side."

Schellenberg said calmly, "Was his name Berger?"

"That's it—Major Berger. His French was very bad."

Schellenberg said, "Then you are aware that these premises are required in the near future. I would appreciate a conducted tour. We'll go upstairs and work down."

The old man led them up the staircase. There were innumerable bedrooms, some with four-posters, the furniture draped in sheets, the dust thick on the floor. As they went down, Schellenberg noticed a door at one end of the landing. "What's through there?"

"I'll show you, monsieur. Another way into the dining hall."

They found themselves in a long dark gallery above a massive room. The ceiling had arched oaken beams, and below was an enormous oak table surrounded by high-backed chairs.

They went down the stairs, and Schellenberg looked around, then led the way back into the entrance hall. "I have seen enough," he said to the old man. "What did Major Berger say to you?"

"That he would be back, monsieur." The old man shrugged.

Schellenberg put a hand on his shoulder. "No one must know we have been here, my friend—especially Major Berger."

"Monsieur?" Dissard looked puzzled.

Schellenberg said, "This is a matter of the greatest secrecy. If the fact that we had been here came out, the source of the information would be obvious." He patted Dissard's shoulder with his gloved hand. "This would be bad for you."

The old man was thoroughly frightened. "Monsieur—please. Not a word. I swear it."

They went out to the Kübelwagen and drove away. Devlin said, "Walter, you can be a cold-blooded bastard."

"Only when necessary." Schellenberg turned to Asa. "Can we get back to Berlin tonight?"

The light was already fading, dark clouds dropping towards the sea, and rain drifted in across the wet sands.

"Possible," Asa said. "We might have to overnight at Chernay."

Devlin said, "What a prospect." He pulled up the collar of his overcoat and lit a cigarette. "The glamour of war."

ON THE FOLLOWING afternoon Devlin was delivered to the UFA film studios for his appointment with the chief make-up artist. The man examined a passport-type photo that Devlin had had taken.

"You say this is what they've got on the other side?"

"Something like that."

"It's not much—not for a policeman looking for a face in the crowd. How long would you be away?"

"Ten days at the most. Can you do anything?"

"Oh, yes." The make-up man nodded. "One can change the

shape of the face by wearing cheek pads, that sort of thing, but I don't think it's necessary for you. I think the key is what I do to the hair." He draped a sheet around Devlin's shoulders and reached for a pair of scissors. By the time he was finished, Devlin's dark and wavy hair was cropped close to the skull.

"Now let's have you over the basin." The man washed Devlin's hair, then rubbed some chemical in.

Devlin kept his eyes closed and let him get on with it. When he opened his eyes, he hardly recognised the face that stared out at him from the mirror. The close-cropped hair was grey now, accentuating the cheekbones, putting ten or twelve years on his age.

"That's marvellous."

"One more touch." The make-up man rummaged in his case, took out a pair of spectacles. "Yes, these, I think. Clear glass, naturally." He placed them on Devlin's nose. "Yes, excellent."

"Will it last? The hair, I mean."

"A fortnight, and you said you'd be away ten days at the most."

"Yes," Devlin told him. "I said ten days, and I meant it. It's all one in the end anyway. Any longer, and I'll be dead."

"ASTONISHING!" Schellenberg said.

"I'm glad you think so," Devlin told him. "So let's have the right photos taken. I want to go as soon as possible. Tomorrow or the day after.

Schellenberg looked at him gravely. "You're sure?"

"There's nothing else to hang about for now. We have the set-up at Chernay, Asa and the Lysander. That leaves us with three uncertainties. My IRA friend Michael Ryan, the Shaws and the priory. So the sooner I get there, the sooner we'll know."

"Right," Schellenberg said briskly, and rang for Ilse, who came in. "Papers for Mr Devlin from the forgery department."

"They'll need photos of the new me," Devlin told her.

"Have you decided on your name and circumstances yet?" Schellenberg asked.

"The best kind of lie is the one that sticks closest to the truth. No

sense in trying to sound completely English. So I'm an Ulsterman."
Devlin turned to Ilse. "Are you getting this?"

"Every word."

"Conlon. Now, there's a name I've always liked. My old uncle,
the priest in Belfast I lived with as a boy, was a Conlon. Henry,
though everyone called him Harry."

"Father Harry Conlon, then?" she said.

"Yes, but more than that. Major Harry Conlon, army chaplain,
on extended leave after being wounded."

"Where?" Schellenberg asked.

"In my head." Devlin tapped the bullet scar. "Oh, I see what you
mean. Geographically speaking."

"How about the Allied invasion of Sicily this year?"

"Excellent. I got clipped on the first day. That way I don't need
too much information about the place if anyone asks me."

"I've seen a cross-reference with British army chaplains in the
military documentation file," Ilse said. "I remember because it
struck me as being unusual. May I go and check on it, General?"

Schellenberg nodded. Ilse went out, and he said, "I'll make the
arrangements for your flight to Ireland. I've already checked with
the Luftwaffe. They suggest you take off from the Laville base,
outside Brest."

"Talk about déjà vu," Devlin said. "That's where I left from
before. It wouldn't happen to be a Dornier bomber they suggest?"

"Exactly."

"Ah, well, it worked last time, I suppose."

Ilse came in at that moment. "I was right. Look what I found. It
was taken from a prisoner of war. I'm certain that Forging will have
no difficulty copying it."

The pass was in the name of a Major George Harvey, army chaplain. It had been issued by the British War Office and authorised
unrestricted access to both military bases and hospitals.

"Brilliant," Devlin said. "You're a marvel, Ilse."

"You'll need to see the clothing department as well," she said.
"Will you want a uniform?"

"It could come in useful. Otherwise a dark suit, clerical collar, dark hat, and raincoat. And I'll want a military travel voucher from Belfast to London, just in case I do want to play the major."

"I'll get things started."

She went out, and Schellenberg said, "What else?"

"Cash. Five thousand quid, I'd say, to take care of a few bribes as well as support myself. If you find one of those canvas holdalls officers carry, the money could go in a false bottom."

"I'm sure there'll be no problem. You'll need a code name."

"We'll stick with Shaw's. Falcon. Give me the details for contacting your radio people, and I'll be in touch before you know it."

"Excellent. The Führer's conference at Belle-Île is on the twenty-first. We could be cutting it fine."

"We'll manage," Devlin said.

IT WAS JUST after nine the following night, rain pounding in from the Atlantic, when the Dornier took off with Devlin in it. The pilot made good time, and it was shortly after two in the morning when Devlin jumped at five thousand feet into an area he knew well, adjacent to the Ulster border. He made an excellent landing and within minutes had his suitcase and a trenching shovel out of the supply bag. He scraped a hole, put the supply bag, parachute and flying suit into it, then tossed the shovel into a nearby pond.

He opened the case and put on his raincoat and hat. Underneath the neatly folded uniform was a webbing belt and holster containing a Smith & Wesson .38 revolver and a box of fifty cartridges to go with it. He put on the spectacles, picked up his suitcase and moved on. He followed a network of country lanes and by four fifteen was safe in Ulster and standing on British soil.

And then he had an incredible piece of luck. A farm truck passed him, stopped, and the driver looked out. "Well, Father, and where would you be walking to at this time of the morning?"

"To catch the milk train to Belfast," Devlin said.

"Now, isn't that the strange thing—and me going all the way to Belfast market."

"God bless you, my son." Devlin climbed in beside him.

"Nothing to it, Father," the farmer told him as they drove away. "After all, if a priest can't get a helping hand in Ireland, where would he get one?"

IT WAS ten o'clock at Prinz Albrechtstrasse when Schellenberg knocked on Himmler's door and went in. "I've had confirmation, Reichsführer, that Liam Devlin jumped into southern Ireland at approximately two a.m."

"Really?" Himmler said. "You've moved fast, Brigadeführer. My congratulations."

"Of course, none of this guarantees success, Reichsführer. We have to take even Devlin's safe landing on faith and the whole business when he gets to London is very open ended."

"Of course," Himmler said. "By the way, there's been a change in plans. The Führer's conference at Belle-Île will now take place on the fifteenth."

"But Reichsführer, that only gives us a week."

"Yes. Well, we're in the Führer's hands. It is not for us to query his decisions. I know you'll do your best, Carry on, General."

Schellenberg went out, feeling totally bewildered. "What's the bastard playing at?" he said softly, and went back to his office.

IN BELFAST, Devlin found it impossible to get a ticket for the crossing to Heysham, in Lancashire. There was a waiting list, and the situation was no better on the Glasgow route. He caught the local train to Larne, north of Belfast, went into a public toilet on the docks and locked himself in. When he came out fifteen minutes later, he was in uniform.

It paid off immediately. The special boat train to London was full, but not to military personnel. He produced the travel voucher they had given him in Berlin. The booking clerk hardly looked at it, took in the major's uniform, the ribbon for the Military Cross and clergyman's dog collar and booked him on board immediately. It was the same at Stranraer, where, in spite of the incredible number of people being carried by the train, Devlin was allocated a seat in a first-class carriage.

When Devlin arrived at King's Cross at three o'clock the following morning, the first thing he heard was an air-raid siren. Soon, like thousands of others, he was far below ground, sitting out a hard night in the comparative safety of a London tube station.

CHAPTER 8

MARY RYAN was a girl people remarked on—not because she was particularly beautiful but because there was a strange, almost ethereal look to her. Her face was always pale, with dark smudges beneath her eyes, and she had had a heavy limp since birth. She was only nineteen and looked old beyond her years.

Her father, an IRA activist, had died of a heart attack in a Dublin prison just before the war, her mother of cancer in 1940, leaving Mary with only one relative, her uncle Michael, her father's younger brother. She had moved from Dublin to London and now kept house for him and worked in a large grocery store in the Wapping high street.

No more though, for when she reported for work at eight o'clock that morning, the shop and a sizeable section of the street were reduced to a pile of smoking rubble. After watching the rescue unit sifting through the foundations for those who might still be alive, Mary turned and walked away, a strange limping figure in her black beret and old raincoat. She stopped at a shop, purchased milk and bread, some cigarettes for her uncle, then went out again. It started to rain as she turned into Cable Wharfe.

There had originally been twenty houses backing onto the river. Fifteen were demolished during the blitz. Four more were boarded up. Mary and her uncle lived in the end one. The kitchen door was at the side, opening onto an iron terrace, the waters of the Thames below. She paused at the rail, looking down. She loved the river, never tired of it. The large ships passing to and fro, the constant barge traffic. There was a wooden stairway at the end of the terrace, dropping down to a small private jetty where her uncle kept a motorboat. As she looked over, she saw a man sheltering from the rain. He wore a black hat and raincoat, and a suitcase was on the jetty beside him.

"Who are you?" she called. "It's private property down there."

"Good day to you, colleen," Devlin called cheerfully, and lifted the case and came up the stairs.

"What do you want?" she said.

Devlin smiled. "It's Michael Ryan I'm after. Would you be knowing him? I tried the door, but there was no answer."

"I'm his niece, Mary," she said. "Uncle Michael's not due home yet. He's on a night shift on the cabs. From ten till ten."

He glanced at his watch. "Another hour and a half, then."

She was slightly uncertain. "You know Uncle Michael, then?"

"Oh, yes. Old friends from way back. Conlon's my name. Father Harry Conlon," he added, opening the top of his dark raincoat so that she could see the dog collar.

She relaxed. "Would you like to come in and wait, Father?"

"I don't think so. I'll take a little walk and come back later. Could I leave my suitcase?"

"Of course." She unlocked the kitchen door.

He followed her in and put the case down. "Would you know St Mary's Priory by any chance?"

"Oh, yes," she said. "You go along the Wapping high street to Wapping Wall. It's on the river. About a mile."

He stepped back outside. "The grand view you have here. There's a book by Dickens that starts with a girl and her father in a boat on the Thames, searching for the bodies of the drowned and what was in their pockets."

"*Our Mutual Friend*," she told him.

"My, and aren't you the well-read one."

She warmed to him for that. "Books are everything."

"And isn't that the fact?" He touched his hat. "I'll be back."

He walked away along the terrace, and she closed the door.

Devlin found St Mary's Priory with no trouble. It stood across the road from the river, high walls in grey stone. The roof of the chapel was clear to see, a bell tower rising above it. Below the road there was a narrow band of shingle and mud between the river and the retaining wall. Some little distance away were steps down from the wall. Devlin descended casually and strolled along the strip of shingle, remembering the architect's drawings and the old drainage tunnel. Then he saw it—an arched entrance almost completely flooded, a couple of feet of headroom only.

He went back up to the road and on the next corner from the priory found a public house. He went in. A young woman was mopping the floor. She looked up, saw his dog collar and said, "What can I do for you, Father?"

"I knew I was going to be in the neighbourhood, and a colleague asked me to look up a friend of his. Father confessor at St Mary's Priory. Stupid of me, but I've forgotten his name."

"That would be Father Frank Martin. He's priest in charge at St Patrick's down the road. He handles the priory as well." She smiled. "Lord knows how he manages at his age. Has no help at all, but then there's a war on, I suppose."

"St Patrick's? God bless you," Devlin told her, and went out.

MICHAEL RYAN was a little over six feet and carried himself well for his sixty years. Sitting at the kitchen table, he wore a black leather jacket and white scarf. He was drinking tea from a large mug Mary had given him. "Conlon, you say?" He shook his head. "I never had a friend called Conlon. Come to think of it, I never had a friend who was a priest."

There was a knock at the kitchen door. Mary went and opened it, and Devlin stepped inside. Ryan stared at him, bewilderment on his face. He stood up.

"Liam Devlin—is it you?"

Devlin put his hands on Ryan's shoulders. "The years have been kind to you, Michael."

"But you, Liam — what have they done to you?"

"Oh, don't believe everything you see." He took his hat off and ran his fingers through the grey stubble. "The hair owes more to the chemical industry at the moment than it does to nature."

"Come in, man, come in." Ryan shut the door. "Are you on the run, or what?"

"Something like that. It needs explaining."

Ryan said, "Mary, this is my old friend Liam Devlin."

The effect on the girl was quite extraordinary. It was as if a light had been turned on inside.

"You are Liam Devlin? Good Lord, I've heard of you since I was a little girl. Sit down, please. Will you have some tea? Have you had your breakfast?"

"Come to think of it, I haven't."

While she busied herself at the stove, Devlin took off his coat and sat opposite Ryan. "Have you a telephone here?"

"Yes. In the hall."

"Good. I need to make a call later."

"What is it, Liam? The IRA?"

"No," Devlin told him. "To be frank, I'm from Berlin."

Ryan said, "I'd heard the organisation had had dealings with the Germans, but to what purpose, Liam? Are you telling me you actually approve of that lot?"

"Nazi bastards, most of them," Devlin said. "Not all, mind you. I've had the odd dealing with them, always for money paid into a Swiss account — on behalf of the organisation."

"And you're here for them now? Why?"

"British Intelligence have a man under guard not far from here, at St Mary's Priory. A Colonel Steiner. As it happens, he's a good man and — take my word — no Nazi. It also happens that the Germans want him back. That's why I'm here."

"To break him out?" Ryan shook his head.

"I'll try not to involve you too much, but I do need a little help. I could ask you to do it for old times' sake, but I won't." Devlin picked up the case, put it on the table and opened it. He pushed the clothes out of the way and pulled out the lining. He took out a bundle of five-pound notes and laid them on the table. "A thousand pounds, Michael."

Ryan ran his fingers through his hair. "What can I say, Liam?"

The girl put plates of egg and bacon in front of each of them, saying, "After the stories you've told me about Mr Devlin, you should be happy to do it for nothing."

"Oh, what it is to be young." Devlin put an arm around her waist. "If only life were like that. But hang on to your dreams, girl." He turned to Ryan. "Well, Michael?"

"Hell, Liam, you only live once. But to show I'm a weak man, I'll take the thousand quid."

"First things first. Do you happen to have a gun about?"

"A Luger pistol from before the war, under the floorboards in my bedroom," Ryan said. "And the ammunition to go with it."

"I'll check it over. Is it convenient for me to stay here? It won't be for long."

"Fine. We've plenty of room."

"Transport," said Devlin. "I saw your cab outside. Is that it?"

"No. I have a Ford van in the shed. I use it now and then."

"That's fine. I'll use your phone now if I may."

"Help yourself."

Devlin closed the door and stood alone at the telephone. He rang directory enquires and got the telephone number for Shaw Place, then dialled the operator and gave it to her. After a while the phone was picked up at the other end, and a woman's voice said, "Charbury three one four."

"Would Sir Maxwell Shaw be at home?"

"No, he isn't. Who is this?"

Devlin took a chance. "Would that be Miss Lavinia Shaw?"

"Yes, it is. Who are you?"

"Does the Falcon still wait? It is now time to strike."

The effect was dramatic. "Oh, my heavens," Lavinia Shaw said, and then there was silence.

"Are you there Miss Shaw?" asked Devlin after a moment.

"Yes, I'm here."

"I must see you and your brother as soon as possible. It's urgent."

She said, "My brother's in London. He had to see his solicitor. He's staying at the Army and Navy Club. He told me he'd have lunch there and catch the train back this afternoon."

"Excellent. Get in touch with him and tell him to expect me. Let's say two o'clock. Conlon—Major Harry Conlon."

There was a pause. "Is it coming?"

"Is what coming, Miss Shaw?"

" You know—the invasion?"

He stifled a strong desire to laugh. "We'll speak again, I'm sure, after I've seen your brother."

He hung up and went back to the kitchen, where Ryan still sat at the table. The girl, washing dishes, said, "Is everything all right?"

"Fine," he said. "Every journey needs a first step." He picked up his case. "If you could show me my room. I need to change."

Mary led him upstairs to a back bedroom. Devlin unpacked his case, laid the uniform out on the bed. The Smith & Wesson he slipped under the mattress, with the webbing belt and holster and a leather ankle holster. He had a quick shave, then changed. He went downstairs fifteen minutes later, resplendent in his uniform.

"Liam, I never thought I'd see the day," Ryan said.

"You know the old saying, Michael," Devlin told him. "When you're a fox with a pack on your tail, you stand a better chance if you look like a hound." He turned to Mary and smiled. "And now, girl dear, another cup of tea would go down just fine."

It was at that moment that the poor girl fell totally in love with him. She felt herself blush and turned to the cooker. "Of course, Mr Devlin. I'll make some fresh."

THE ARMY and Navy Club had been renowned since Victorian times for its leniency towards members disgraced or in trouble, and Sir Maxwell Shaw was a case in point. No one had seen the slightest necessity to blackball him over his detention. He was, after all, an officer and a gentleman who had been both wounded and decorated for gallantry in the service of his country.

He sat in a corner of the morning room drinking the scotch the waiter had brought in and thinking about Lavinia's astonishing telephone call. Quite unbelievable that now, after so long, the summons should come. He hadn't felt such a charge in years.

A porter approached him. "Your guest is here, Sir Maxwell. Shall I show him in?"

"Yes—at once, man." Shaw got to his feet, straightening his tie.

The porter returned with Devlin, who held out his hand and said cheerfully, "Harry Conlon. Nice to meet you, Sir Maxwell."

Shaw was dumbfounded, not so much by the uniform but by the dog collar. He shook hands as the waiter brought him another scotch. "Would you like one of these, Major?"

"No, thanks." The waiter departed, and Devlin sat down and lit a cigarette. "You look a little shaken, Sir Maxwell."

"Well, goodness, man, of course I am. I mean, what is all this about? Have you got work for me?"

"There's a job to be done."

"The invasion is finally coming?"

"Not yet," Devlin said smoothly, "but soon. Are you with us?"

Shaw gulped down the rest of his whisky. "Of course I am. What do you require of me?"

"Let's take a little walk," Devlin said. "The park will do."

It had started to rain. For the moment there wasn't a porter in the cloakroom. Shaw found his bowler hat, raincoat and umbrella. Among the jumble of coats there was a military trench coat. Devlin picked it up, followed him outside and put it on.

They went across to St James's Park and walked towards Buckingham Palace. After a while they moved into the shelter of some trees, and Devlin lit a cigarette.

"Before the war your sister used to fly a Tiger Moth," Devlin said. "Does she still have it?"

"No. The RAF took it for training purposes."

"She used a barn as a hangar. Is that still there?"

"Yes."

"And the place she used to land and take off? The south meadow? It's not been ploughed up or anything?"

"No. All the land around Shaw Place is used for sheep grazing. Is that important?"

"You could say so. A plane from France will be dropping in."

Shaw's face became extremely animated. "Really? What for?"

"To pick up me and another man. The less you know, the better, but he's important. Does any of this give you a problem?"

"Good heavens, no. Glad to help, old man." Shaw frowned slightly. "You're not German, I take it?"

"Irish," Devlin told him. "But we're on the same side. You were given a radio by Werner Keitel. Do you still have it?"

"I'm afraid we don't. Back in '41, I was in prison for a few—"

"I know about that."

"Lavinia panicked. Thought the police might turn the house upside down. There's a lot of marsh around our place, some of it bottomless. She threw the radio in, you see." He looked anxious.

"You're going back home today?"

"That's right."

"Good. I'll be in touch. Tomorrow or the next day." Devlin ground out his cigarette and walked away.

WHEN DEVLIN went into the house at Cable Wharfe, Ryan was sitting at the table. He'd covered it with newspaper and was stripping a Luger pistol, oil on his fingers. "Heaven help me, Liam, I've forgotten how to do this."

"Give me a minute to change, and I'll handle it."

Devlin came back wearing slacks and a black polo-neck sweater. He reached for the Luger parts and began oiling them.

"Did it go well?" Ryan asked.

"If meeting a lunatic could ever go well, then yes. Michael, I'm dealing with an English aristocrat so out of his head that he's still eagerly awaiting a German invasion—and that's when he's sober."

He told Ryan about Shaw House, and Shaw and his sister. Then he said, "The trouble is, I need a radio, and they haven't got one."

"So what are you going to do?"

"I was thinking about the old days, when I came over to handle that active-service unit. They got weapons and even explosives from underworld sources, and you were the man with the contacts."

"That was a long time ago."

"Come off it, Michael. There's a war on—black market in everything from petrol to cigarettes. Don't tell me you aren't in it up to your neck, and you a London cabbie."

"All right." Ryan put up a hand defensively. "But it's no good going to some back-street trader. The kind of radio you want would have to be army equipment."

Devlin wiped each piece of the Luger carefully with a rag. "Then who would I go to?"

Ryan said, "There's a fella called Carver—Jack Carver. Has a brother, Eric, who terrifies women. Jack's probably the most powerful gangster in London these days. Not just black market. Girls, gambling, protection. You name it. If he had a grandmother, he'd sell her to the Germans if he thought there was money in it."

"I'm frightened to death," Devlin said. "Where do I find him?"

"Carver owns a dance hall a couple of miles from here called the Astoria Ballroom. Has a big apartment upstairs. He likes that. Convenient for his brother to pick up girls."

Devlin nodded. His hands moved with incredible dexterity, putting the Luger together again. He was finished in seconds.

"You look like death himself when you do that," Ryan said.

"It's just a knack, Michael." Devlin wrapped up the oily newspapers. "And now I think we'll take a little walk down by the river, near the priory. I'd like your opinion on something."

He went down the stairway to the boat and found Mary reading under an awning that stretched over the cockpit. The rain dripped from the edge of the awning, and there was a slight mist on the river. Devlin leant against the rail, hands in his pockets.

Mary stood up. "We're going to have fog in the next few days. A real pea-souper. It's the smell I recognise."

Devlin took her arm. "Your uncle Michael and I are taking a little walk by the river. Why don't you come with us?"

They drove to St Mary's Priory in Ryan's cab. He parked at the side of the road, and they sat looking at the entrance. There was a military police car parked outside. As they watched, Lieutenant Benson came out of the entrance, got into the car and drove off.

"You're not going to get far through the front door," Ryan said.

"More ways of skinning a cat than one. Let's take that walk."

The strip of beach he'd walked along earlier seemed wider, and when he indicated the archway, there was more headroom. "It was almost under the surface this morning," he said.

"The Thames is a tidal river, Liam, and the tide's going out. There'll be times when it's underwater entirely. Is it important?"

"Runs close to the foundations of the priory. According to the plans, there's a grille into the crypt under the priory chapel. It could be a way in."

"You'd need to take a look, then."

"Naturally, but not now. Later, when it's dark."

The rain increased to monsoon-like proportions, and Ryan said, "For heaven's sake, let's get in out of this."

Devlin took Mary's arm. "Would you happen to have yourself a pretty frock tucked away somewhere? Because if you do, I'll take you dancing this evening."

She stared at him, and when she started walking, the limp seemed more pronounced. "I don't dance, Mr Devlin. I can't."

"Oh, yes, you can, my love. You can do anything in the whole wide world if you put your mind to it."

THE ASTORIA was a typical London dance hall of the period, and very crowded. There was a band on each side of the room—one in blue tuxedos, the other in red. Devlin wore his dark suit but with a soft white shirt and black tie he'd borrowed from Ryan. He waited outside the cloakroom for Mary who'd gone in to leave her coat. When she came out he saw that she had on a neat cotton dress and brown stockings. She wore earrings and just a hint of lipstick.

559

"My compliments on the dress," he said. "A vast improvement."

"I don't get a chance to dress up very often," she told him.

"Well, let's make the most of it."

He took her hand and pulled her onto the floor before she could protest. One of the bands was playing a slow fox-trot. He started to hum the tune.

"You do that well," she said.

"Ah, well, I have a small gift for music. I play the piano badly. You, on the other hand, dance rather well."

"It's better in the middle of all these people. Nobody notices."

She was obviously referring to her limp. Devlin said, "Girl dear, nobody notices anyway."

She tightened her grip, put her cheek against his shoulder, and they moved into the crowd, the glitter ball revolving on the ceiling, bathing everything with blue light. The number came to an end, and the other band broke into an upbeat quickstep.

"Oh, no," she protested. "I can't manage this."

"All right," Devlin said. "Coffee it is, then."

They went up the stairs to the balcony. "I'm just going to the cloakroom," she said.

"I'll get the coffee and see you back here."

She went around to the other side of the balcony, passing two young men leaning on the rail. One of them wore a pin-striped double-breasted suit and hand-painted tie. The other was in a leather jacket, with the flattened nose of a prizefighter and scar tissue around the eyes.

"You fancy that, Mr Carver?" he asked as they watched Mary go into the cloakroom.

"I certainly do, George," Eric Carver said.

ERIC CARVER was twenty-two years of age, with thin, wolfish features and long blond hair swept back from the forehead. His father had been a drunken bully who'd died under the wheels of a cart. Jack, fifteen years Eric's senior, had looked after him, and their mother until cancer had carried her off. There was nothing Eric couldn't do—no girl he couldn't have—because he was Jack Carver's brother, and he never let anyone forget it.

Mary emerged from the cloakroom and limped past them, and Eric said, "I'll see you later, George." He moved around the balcony to where Mary leant over the rail, watching the dancers. He slipped his arm around her waist. "Now then, darling, what's your name?"

"Please don't," she said, and started to struggle.

"Oh, I like it," he said, his grip tightening.

Devlin arrived, a cup of coffee in each hand. He put them down on a nearby table.

"Excuse me," he said.

As Eric turned, slackening his grip, Devlin stepped on his right foot, bearing down with all his weight. The young man snarled, trying to pull away, and Devlin picked up one of the cups of coffee and poured it down Eric's shirtfront.

"Sorry, son," he said.

Eric looked down, total amazement on his face. "Why, you little creep," he said, and swung a punch.

Devlin blocked it easily and kicked him on the shin. "Now why don't you go and play nasty little boy elsewhere."

There was rage on Eric's face. "You bastard. I'll get you for this. You see if I don't."

He hobbled away, and Devlin sat Mary down and gave her the other cup of coffee. She took a sip and looked up at him. "That was awful."

"A worm, girl dear. Nothing to worry about. Will you be all right while I go and see this Carver fella?"

She smiled. "I'll be fine." He turned and walked away.

The door at the other end of the balcony said MANAGER'S OFFICE, but when Devlin opened it, he found himself in a small room, with only a desk and chair, on which Eric's friend George sat reading a newspaper, while piano music played on the radio.

"Nice that." Devlin leant on the doorway. "Carroll Gibbons, from the Savoy."

George looked him over coldly. "And what do you want?"

"A moment of Jack Carver's valuable time."

"What's it about? Mr Carver don't see just anybody."

Devlin took out a five-pound note and laid it on the table. "That's what it's about, my old son—that and another one hundred and ninety-nine like it."

George put the newspaper down and picked up the bank note. "All right, wait here." He got up and knocked on a door behind him, then went in. After a while he looked out. "All right, he'll see you."

Jack Carver sat behind a walnut Regency desk that looked genuine. He wore a navy worsted suit, tailored in Savile Row, and a discreet tie. To judge by outward appearances, he could have been a prosperous businessman, but the jagged scar that ran from the corner of the left eye into the dark hairline, and the cold, dangerous-looking eyes belied that.

"All right, so what's it about?" he said, holding up the fiver.

"Aren't they beautiful, those things?" Devlin said. "A work of genuine art, the Bank of England five-pound note."

Carver said, "According to George, you said something about another hundred and ninety-nine. That came to a thousand quid when I went to school."

At that moment Eric entered, wearing a clean shirt and fastening his tie. He stopped dead, astonishment on his face. "That's him, Jack—the little squirt who spilt coffee down me."

"Oh, an accident surely," Devlin told him.

Eric started towards him, and Jack Carver snapped, "Leave it out, Eric. This is business." Eric stayed by the desk, rage in his eyes, and Carver said, "Now, what would I have to do for a thousand quid? Kill somebody?"

"Come off it, Mr Carver. We both know you'd do that for fun," Devlin said. "No. What I need is an item of military equipment. The IRA thinks you're a man who can get anything. I wonder what Special Branch at Scotland Yard might make of that titbit."

Carver smoothed the fiver between his fingers, his face blank. "You're beginning to sound right out of order."

"Me and my big mouth. I'll never learn," Devlin said. "And all I wanted was to buy a radio. There's a rather nice one the army uses. It's called a Mark Four. Fits in a wooden box with a handle." Devlin took a piece of paper from his pocket and put it on the desk. "I've written the details down. Now, can you handle it?"

"Jack Carver can handle anything. A thousand, you said?"

"But I must have it tomorrow."

Carver nodded. "All right, but I'll take half in advance."

"Fair enough." Devlin had expected as much. He took the money out and dropped it onto the table. "There you go."

Carver scooped it up. "And it'll cost you another thousand. Tomorrow night, ten o'clock. Black Lion Dock. There's a warehouse with my name over the door. Be on time."

"Sure and you're a hard man to do business with," Devlin said. "But then we have to pay for what we want in this life."

"You can say that again," Carver said. "Now get out of here."

Devlin left, George closing the door behind him. Eric said, "He's mine, Jack. I want him."

"Leave it out, Eric. I've got this." Carver held up the five hundred pounds. "And I want the rest of it. Then he gets squeezed. Now get out. I want to make a phone call."

MARY WAS sitting quietly watching the dancers when Devlin joined her. "Did it go all right with Carver?" she asked.

"I'd rather shake hands with the devil. That little rat I chastised turned out to be his brother, Eric. Would you like to go now?"

"All right. I'll get my coat."

When they went out, it was raining. She took his arm, and they walked down the wet pavement towards the main road. There they took the turning down to Harrow Street.

"Shall I try and get a cab?" Devlin asked.

"Oh, no. It's not much more than a mile and a half, and I like walking in the rain."

She kept her hand lightly on his arm as they walked in companionable silence alongside the river, towards Wapping. There was a heavy mist on the Thames, and a large cargo boat slipped past them, green and red navigation lights plain in spite of the blackout.

"I'd love to be like that boat," she said. "Going to sea, to faraway distant places, something different every day."

"You're only nineteen, girl. It's all waiting for you out there, and this bloody war can't last for ever."

"I wish we had time to walk down to the Embankment," said Mary.

"Too far surely?"

"I saw this film once. I think it was Fred Astaire. He walked along the Embankment with a girl, and his chauffeur followed along behind in a Rolls-Royce. It was very romantic."

"Ah, there's a woman for you."

They turned along Cable Wharfe and paused on the little terrace before going into the house.

"I've had a lovely time."

He laughed out loud. "You must be joking, girl."

"No, really. I like being with you." She still held his arm and leant against him.

He put his other arm around her, and they stayed there for a moment. He felt a sudden dreadful sadness, remembering a girl in Norfolk just like Mary Ryan, a girl he had hurt very badly indeed.

He sighed, and Mary looked up. "What is it?"

"Oh, nothing. I was just wondering where it had all gone. It's a touch of that three o'clock in the morning feeling when you feel past everything there ever was."

"Not you, surely. You've got years ahead of you."

"Mary, my love. You are nineteen and I am an old thirty-five who's seen it all and doesn't believe in much any more. In a few days I'll be on my way, and a good thing." He gave her one small hug. "So let's get inside before I lose what few wits I have entirely."

JACK CARVER said, "I phoned Morrie Green. He knows more about surplus military equipment than any man in London."

"Does he have this radio the little creep wanted?" Eric asked.

"No, but he can get one. No trouble. The interesting thing is what he said about it. It's no ordinary radio. Sort of thing the army would use operating behind enemy lines."

Eric looked bewildered. "But what's it mean, Jack?"

"That there's a lot more to our friend than meets the eye. I'm going to have some fun with him tomorrow night."

RYAN, SITTING on the other side of the table, said, "Jack Carver's bad news, Liam. How can you be certain he'll play straight?"

"He couldn't if he wanted to," Devlin said. "The radio I need is an unusual piece of equipment, and when Carver realises that, he's going to want to know what's going on."

"So what are you going to do?"

"I'll think of something, but that can wait. What can't is an inspection of that drainage tunnel under the priory."

"I'll come with you," Ryan said. "We'll go in the motorboat. Only take fifteen minutes to get there."

Mary turned from the sink. "Can I come?"

Before Devlin could protest, Ryan said, "A good idea. You can mind the boat."

"But you stay on board," Devlin told her. "No funny business."

"Right. I'll go and change." She rushed out.

Ryan said, "She likes you, Liam."

"And I like her, Michael old friend, and that's where it will end. Now, what do we need?"

"The tide is low, but it's still going to be wet. I'll dig out some overalls and boots," Ryan told him, and went out.

THE SMALL motorboat moved in towards the beach, its engine muted. The prow dug into mud, and Ryan cut the engine. "Right, Mary. Keep an eye on things. We shouldn't be long."

He and Devlin, in their dark overalls and boots, went over the side and faded into the darkness. Ryan carried a bag of tools and Devlin a large torch. There was three feet of water in the tunnel.

Ryan said, "We'll have to wade."

As they moved into the water the smell was pungent. Devlin led the way, the tunnel stretching ahead of them in the rays of the torch. The brickwork was very old and corroded. There was a sudden splash, and two rats leapt from a ledge and swam away.

"Filthy creatures," Ryan said in disgust.

"It can't be far," Devlin said. "A hundred yards maybe."

Suddenly there it was, an iron grille perhaps four feet by three, just above the surface of the water. They looked into the crypt, and Devlin played the light across the interior. There were a couple of tombs almost completely covered with water, and stone steps in the far corner going up to a door.

Ryan got a crowbar from his bag of tools. Devlin held the bag while the other man pushed into the mortar in the brickwork beside the grille. The wall buckled, and five or six bricks tumbled into the water. "The whole place is ready to come down," said Ryan. "We can have this grille out in a fast ten minutes, Liam."

"No. I need to know what the situation is upstairs. We've found out all we need for the moment, which is that the grille can be pulled out any time we want. Now let's get out of here."

DOUGAL MUNRO was still in his office, on Baker Street, standing at a map table, charts of the English Channel spread before him, when Carter limped in.

"The invasion, sir?"

"Yes, Jack. Normandy. They've made their decision. Eisenhower wants a blanket report on the strength of the French Resistance units in this general area. Let's hope the Führer still believes the landing will be at the Pas de Calais."

"I understand his personal astrologer's convinced him of it."

Munro laughed. "Anything new?"

"Vargas gave me a call. Another message from his cousin in Berlin. Could he send as much information as possible about St Mary's Priory."

"All right, Jack. Cook something up in the next couple of days, staying as close to the truth as possible, and pass it on to Vargas."

"Fine, sir." Carter went out, and Munro returned to his maps.

CHAPTER NINE

THE FOLLOWING morning Father Martin knelt at the altar rail, eyes closed, and prayed. He was tired, that was the trouble, and he prayed for strength to the God he had loved all his life.

"I bless the Lord who gives me counsel; in the night also my heart instructs me. I keep the Lord always before me . . ." He spoke the words aloud and faltered, unable to think of the rest.

A strong voice said, *"Because He is at my right hand, I shall not be moved."*

Father Martin half turned and found Devlin standing there in uniform. "Major?" The old man tried to get off his knees, and Devlin put a hand under his elbow.

"Or Father. The uniform is only for the duration. Conlon — Harry Conlon."

"And I'm Frank Martin. Is there something I can do for you?"

"Nothing special. I'm on extended leave. I was wounded in Sicily," Devlin told him. "Spending a few days with friends not too far from here. I saw St Pat's and thought I'd look in."

"Well, then, let me offer you a cup of tea," the old man said.

Devlin sat in the small, crowded sacristy while Martin boiled water in an electric kettle and made the tea.

"So you've been in it from the beginning?"

Devlin nodded. "November 'thirty-nine, I got my call."

"Has it been bad?" Father Martin poured the tea.

"Bad enough. Just as bad for you, though. The blitz, I mean. You're rather close to the London docks."

"Yes, it was hard." Father Martin nodded. "And it doesn't get any easier. I'm on my own here these days."

He suddenly looked very frail, and Devlin felt a pang of conscience, yet he knew that he had to take this as far as it would go. "I called in at the local pub for some cigarettes. I was talking to a girl there who told me you were father confessor at the hospice near here. St Mary's Priory?"

"That's right."

"Must give you a lot of extra work, Father."

"It does indeed, but it must be done." The old man looked at his watch. "In fact, have to be there soon. Rounds to do."

"Do you have many patients there?"

"It varies. Fifteen, sometimes twenty. Many are terminal. Some are special problems. Servicemen who've had breakdowns. Pilots occasionally. You know how it is."

"I do indeed," Devlin said. "But when I walked by earlier, I saw a couple of military policemen going in. It struck me as odd."

"Ah, well, there's a reason for that. Occasionally they keep German prisoners of war on the top floor."

"Oh, I see. There's someone there now?"

"Yes, a Luftwaffe colonel. A nice man. I've even persuaded him to come to Mass for the first time in years."

"Interesting."

"Well, I must make a move." The old man reached for his raincoat.

As they went out Devlin said, "I've been thinking, Father. Here's me with time on my hands and you carrying all this burden alone. Maybe I could give you a hand? Hear a few confessions at least."

"Why, that's extraordinarily kind of you," Father Martin said.

Liam Devlin had seldom felt lower in his life, but he went on. "And I'd love to see something of your work at the priory."

"Then so you shall," said the old man.

THE PRIORY CHAPEL was as cold as could be. Near the altar, Devlin said, "It seems very damp. Is there a problem?"

"Yes. The crypt has been flooded for years. Sometimes quite badly. No money available to put it right."

Devlin could see the stout oak door banded with iron in the shadows in the far corner. "Is that the way in, then?"

"Yes, but no one goes down there any more."

"I once saw a church in France with the same trouble. Could I take a look?"

"If you like."

The door was bolted. He eased it back and ventured halfway down the steps. Flicking on his lighter, he saw the dark water around the tombs and lapping at the grille. He retraced his steps and closed the door. "There's not much to be done for it," he called.

"Yes. Well, make sure you bolt it again," the old man called back. "We don't want anyone injuring himself down there."

Devlin rammed the bolt home, the solid sound echoing through the chapel, then quietly eased it back. He rejoined Father Martin, and they moved up the aisle. As they opened the outer door Sister Maria Palmer came out of her office.

"Ah, there you are," Father Martin said. "I looked in when we arrived, but you weren't there. I've been showing Father—Major—Conlon the chapel. He's going to join me on rounds."

Devlin shook her hand. "A pleasure, Sister."

"Major Conlon was wounded in Sicily."

"I see. Have they given you a London posting?" she asked.

"No. I'm still on sick leave. In the neighbourhood for a few days. I met Father Martin at his church."

"He's been kind enough to offer to help me out at the church. Hear a few confessions and so on," Father Martin said.

"Good. You need a rest. We'll do the rounds together." As they started up the stairs she said, "By the way, Lieutenant Benson's gone on a three-day pass. That young Sergeant Morgan's in charge."

"I called in on Steiner last night," Father Martin said. "Did you?"

"No, I didn't have time. I'll see him now, though. I'm hoping the penicillin's finally cleared his chest infection."

They worked their way from room to room, talking to various patients, and it was half an hour before they reached the top floor. The MP on duty outside the outer door jumped up and saluted when he saw Devlin. The door was opened by another MP, and they passed through. The young sergeant sitting at Benson's desk stood up and came out. "Sister—Father Martin."

"Good morning, Sergeant Morgan," Sister Maria Palmer said. "We'd like to see Colonel Steiner."

Morgan took in Devlin's uniform and the dog collar. "I see," he said uncertainly.

Devlin took out his wallet and produced the fake War Office pass Schellenberg's people had provided, the one that guaranteed unlimited access. He passed it across. "I think you'll find that takes care of it, Sergeant."

Morgan examined it. "I'll just get the details for the admittance sheet, sir." He did so and handed it back. "If you'll follow me."

He led the way to the end of the corridor, nodded and the MP on duty unlocked the door. Sister Maria Palmer went in, followed by Father Martin and Devlin. The door closed behind them.

Steiner, sitting by the window, stood up, and Sister Maria Palmer said, "And how are you today, Colonel?"

"Fine, Sister."

"I'm sorry I couldn't see you last night. I had an emergency, but Father Martin tells me he called in."

"As usual." Steiner nodded.

The old priest said, "This is Major Conlon, by the way. As you can see, an army chaplain. He's on sick leave. Like yourself, recently wounded."

Devlin smiled amiably and put out his hand. "A great pleasure, Colonel."

Kurt Steiner, making one of the most supreme efforts of his life, managed to keep his face straight. "Major Conlon." Devlin gripped the German's hand hard, and Steiner said, "Anywhere interesting? Where you picked up your wound, I mean."

"Sicily," Devlin said.

"A hard campaign."

"Ah, well, I wouldn't really know. I got mine the first day there." He walked to the window and looked out down to the road beside the Thames. "A fine view you've got here. You can see right down to those steps and that little beach, the boats passing. Something to look at."

"It helps pass the time."

"So we must go now," Sister Maria Palmer said, and knocked at the door to signal the MP to open it.

Father Martin put a hand on Steiner's shoulder. "Don't forget I'll be hearing confessions tonight. All sinners welcome."

Devlin said, "Now then, Father, didn't you say I'd take some of the load off your shoulders? It's me who'll be sitting in the box tonight." He turned to Steiner. "You're still welcome, Colonel."

As the door opened, Father Martin said, "Just one thing. I usually start at seven. The MPs prefer to bring Steiner down at eight because everyone's gone by then. I see him last."

"No problem," Devlin said.

They reached the foyer, and the porter handed them their raincoats. Sister Maria Palmer said, "See you tonight, then, Major."

"I'll look forward to it," Devlin said, and went down the steps with the old priest.

"TALK ABOUT Daniel in the lion's den," Ryan said. "You've the cheek of Old Nick himself."

Mary, sitting at one end of the table, said, "But Mr Devlin, to sit there in the box and hear people's confessions—and some of them nuns. That's a mortal sin."

"I've no choice, Mary. It doesn't sit well with me to make a fool of that fine old man, but it's my one chance of speaking to Steiner."

"Well, I still think it's a terrible thing to be doing." She left the room, came back a moment later in her raincoat and went outside.

"The temper on her sometimes," Ryan said.

"Never mind. We've things to discuss. My meeting tonight with Carver. Black Lion Dock. Could we get there in your boat?"

"I know it well. Take about thirty minutes. Ten o'clock, you said."

"I'd like to be there earlier. To review the situation."

"Leave at nine, then."

Devlin nodded. He lit a cigarette. "I can't go down to Shaw Place in your taxi, Michael. A London cab would look out of place in Romney Marsh. I'll need your van the night I get Steiner out. It'll be a one-way trip. It's not a good idea for you to try and get it back."

Ryan smiled. "I took it as payment for a bad debt from a dealer in Brixton two years ago. The logbook's crooked, and so is the licence plate. No way could it be traced back to me."

"Ah, well, a bob or two extra for you for that." Devlin got up. "I'll go and make my peace with your niece now."

She was sitting under the awning in the boat, reading again, as he went down the steps.

"What is it this time?" he said.

"*The Midnight Court*," she told him reluctantly.

"I used to be able to recite the whole of it in Irish. My uncle gave me a Bible for doing that. He was a priest."

"I wonder what he'd say about what you're doing tonight."

"Oh, I know very well," Devlin told her. "He'd forgive me." And he went back up the steps.

DEVLIN SAT in the confession box in uniform, a violet stole about his neck, and listened patiently to four nuns and two male patients as they confessed their sins. He honestly did the best he could, tried to say the right thing, but it was an effort. His last client departed, and then the chapel door opened and he heard the ring of army boots on the stone floor.

The confessional door opened and closed. From the darkness Steiner said, "Bless me, Father, for I have sinned."

"Not as much as I have, Colonel." Devlin switched on his light and smiled through the grille at him.

"Mr Devlin," Steiner said, "what have they done to you?"

"A few changes, just to put the hounds off." Devlin ran his hands through his grey hair. "How have you been?"

"Never mind that. The British were hoping you would turn up. Brigadier Munro of Special Operations Executive told me they'd made sure my presence in London was known in Berlin. They passed the information through a man at the Spanish embassy called Vargas. He works for them."

"I knew it," Devlin said.

"They told me that General Walter Schellenberg was in charge of organising my escape and that they expected him to use you. They're waiting for you."

"Yes. But I allowed for British Intelligence handling it this way. Vargas is still getting messages asking for more information. They will be thinking I'm still in Berlin. How many MPs escort you down here?"

"Two. Usually Lieutenant Benson, but he's on leave."

"Right. I'm going to have you out of here in the next two or three days. We'll exit through the crypt. There'll be a boat waiting on the river. After that, a two-hour drive to a place where we'll be picked up by plane from France. The evening we go, you'll come down to confession just like tonight. Usual time."

"How will I know?"

"A fine view from your window and the steps down to the little beach by the Thames. Remember?"

"Ah, yes."

"The day we decide to go, there'll be a young girl standing by the wall at the top of those steps. She'll be wearing a black beret and an old raincoat. She'll be there at noon exactly, and she has a pronounced limp. You can't miss her."

Steiner hesitated. "The MPs?"

"A detail only." Devlin smiled. "Trust me. Now three Hail Marys and two Our Fathers, and be off with you." He switched off the light. The door banged; there was the sound of boots again and the outer door opening and closing.

Devlin came out and moved towards the altar. "God forgive me," he murmured.

He checked that the bolt of the crypt door was still open, then got his trench coat and left.

RYAN STOOD at the door as Devlin changed quickly from the uniform into dark slacks and sweater. Devlin pulled up his right trouser leg and strapped the ankle holster to it, slipped the Smith &

Wesson .38 in and pulled down his trouser. Then he opened his suitcase, took out a wad of fivers and put them into his pocket.

They went downstairs and found Mary sitting at the table reading. "Are we going now?" she asked.

Devlin opened the kitchen-table drawer, took out the Luger, checked it and slipped it inside his jacket. "You're not going anywhere, girl dear—not this time," he told her.

She started to protest, but her uncle shook his head. "He's right, girl. It could get nasty. Best stay out of it."

"The same applies to you, Michael," Devlin said. "Stay out of it. My affair, not yours."

Jack and Eric Carver arrived at the Black Lion Dock at nine forty-five in a Humber limousine. Carver's man, George, was driving. The dock was almost completely dark except for the shaded light over the main warehouse doors. The sign on the warehouse said CARVER BROTHERS—EXPORT AND IMPORT, and Jack Carver looked up at it with satisfaction as he got out of the car. Eric followed him, and George went around to the back of the car. He opened the boot and took out the radio set in its olive-green wooden case.

Eric unlocked the Judas gate in the main door, stepped inside and found the light switch. His brother and George followed him. The warehouse was stacked with packing cases of every kind. There was a table in the centre and a couple of chairs.

"Right. Put it on the table," said Jack. George did as he was told, and Carver added, "You've got the shooter?"

George took a Walther PPK from one pocket, a silencer from the other, and screwed it into place.

Carver lit a cigar. "Look at that, Eric. Bloody marvellous. With the silencer on, it just sounds like a cork popping."

"I can't wait for that little bastard to get here," Eric said.

But Devlin had been there for some time, hidden in the shadows, having gained access through an upstairs window. He watched George position himself behind a packing case, the brothers sitting at the table; then he slipped out the way he had come.

A couple of minutes later he approached the main door, whistling cheerfully, opened the Judas gate and went in. "Hello," he called, and neared the table. "You got it, then, Mr Carver?"

"I told you. I can get anything. You didn't mention your name last night, by the way."

"Churchill," Devlin said. "Winston."

"Very funny."

Devlin opened the case. The radio fitted inside — headphones, Morse tapper, aerials, everything. It looked brand-new. He closed the lid again.

"Satisfied?" Carver asked.

"Oh, yes."

"Then cash on the table," Carver said.

Devlin took the thousand pounds from his pocket and passed it over. Carver dropped the money onto the table. "Of course, we now come to the other matter."

"And what matter would that be?"

"Your insulting treatment of my brother and your threats to me. IRA and Special Branch. I can't have that. You need chastising." He blew cigar smoke into Devlin's face. "George."

George had the Walther at the back of Devlin's neck in a second. Eric reached inside his jacket and relieved him of the Luger.

Devlin spread his arms. "All right, Mr Carver, so you've got me. What happens now?" He walked across to a packing case, sat down and took out a cigarette.

Carver said, "You're a cool bastard, I'll give you that."

"I'll tell you what happens now," Eric said, taking a cutthroat razor from his pocket. "I'm going to slice your ears off."

"While George holds the gun on me?" Devlin asked.

"That's the general idea," Eric told him.

"Only one problem with that," Devlin said. "That gun is a Walther PPK, and you have to pull the slider back to put yourself in business, and I don't think George has done that."

George pulled at the slider desperately. Devlin hitched up his trouser, yanked the Smith & Wesson from the ankle holster and fired, all in one smooth motion, drilling him through the upper arm, so that he cried out and dropped the Walther.

Devlin picked it up. "Nice," he said. "Thanks very much." He pushed it into his waistband.

Carver sat there, a look of total disbelief on his face. Eric looked frightened to death as Devlin put first the money and then the Luger inside his leather jacket. He picked up the case containing the radio and walked away.

As he reached the door he turned. "Oh, Eric, I was forgetting. You said something about slicing my ears off?"

His arm swung up, he fired, and Eric screamed as the lower half of his right ear disintegrated. He grabbed at it, blood spurting.

Devlin said, "A good job you don't wear earrings."

He stepped out, and the Judas gate banged behind him.

SCHELLENBERG was in his office at Prinz Albrechtstrasse when the door burst open and Ilse appeared. Asa Vaughan was at her shoulder, excitement on his face.

"What is it?" Schellenberg demanded.

"You must come to the radio room now." She could hardly get the words out. "It's Devlin, General, calling from London."

THE RADIO was open on the kitchen table, the aerials looped all the way around the walls. Ryan and Mary sat watching in fascination as Devlin tapped away in Morse code.

"Damn," he said, frowning. There was a little more action, and then he stopped. "That's it. Get the aerials down."

Mary moved around the kitchen coiling up the wires.

Ryan said, "Is everything all right, Liam?"

"All wrong, old son. We were supposed to be back in France for the twenty-first. Now they say the great occasion is on the fifteenth, and as tonight is the twelfth, that doesn't give us much time."

"Is it possible, Liam?"

Devlin said, "First thing in the morning we'll take a run down to Romney Marsh and see what the situation is at Shaw Place." He turned to Mary. "How would you like a day out in the country?"

"It sounds just fine to me."

"Good. I'll give the Shaws a call and warn them to expect me."

BACK IN his office, Schellenberg sat at his desk studying the message in front of him, Asa Vaughan and Ilse watching.

"So," Schellenberg said. "He's there at his IRA friend's house; he's made contact with Shaw and now with Steiner."

"Everything fits," Asa said.

"Perhaps, but he can't make the fifteenth. It would be impossible, even for Devlin."

"I'm beginning to wonder if anything is impossible to that guy," Asa said.

"Well, we shall see." Schellenberg stood up. "I doubt whether the canteen runs to champagne, but whatever they have is on me."

CHAPTER 10

THEY TOOK the road to Maidstone, Ryan driving, Devlin squeezed in beside him. Mary was sitting in the back of the van, reading a book. Devlin wore his trench coat, the black trilby slanted over one ear.

In Maidstone, Ryan drove around the centre of the town until he found a cycle shop. Devlin went in and bought half a dozen standard bicycle lamps with fresh batteries.

"I've cleaned him out," he said when he returned. "Told him I wanted them for my church Scout troop."

"And why would you want those?" Mary asked.

"A plane coming in through the darkness at night needs a little welcome light, girl dear."

Beyond Ashford they pulled in at the side of the road and had tea from a thermos. There was a path leading to a little copse, and Mary and Devlin strolled along it. The rain had stopped, but the sky was still dark and threatening all the way to Romney Marsh and to the sea beyond. They stood under a tree, taking it all in.

He nodded at her book. "What this time?"

"Robert Browning," she said. "Do you like poetry?"

"I had some published once. I could make the stuff up at the drop of a hat, and then I realised one day just how bad it was."

"I don't believe you. Make something up about me."

"All right." He thought for a moment, then said, *"Now voyager sail thou forth to seek and find."*

"That's marvellous," she said. "Did you write that?"

"Not exactly. A Yankee fella called Walt Whitman thought of it first." It started to rain, and he put a hand on her elbow. "But I wish I'd written it for you. Let's get moving." They hurried back to the van.

AT THE APARTMENT over the Astoria, Jack Carver was sitting at the table by the window having a late breakfast when Eric came in. His ear was heavily bandaged, and he looked terrible.

"How do you feel?" Carver asked.

"The pain's bloody awful, Jack." Eric poured coffee, his hand shaking. "That little creep. We've got to get our hands on him."

"We will, son," Jack said. "And then it'll be our turn. I've put his description out all over London. He'll turn up. Now drink your coffee and have something to eat."

USING THE road map, Ryan found Charbury easily enough, and an enquiry at the little village store led them to Shaw Place. The great rusting iron gates at the end of the drive stood open. The drive, stretching towards the old house, had grass growing through the gravel.

"This place has seen better days," Ryan commented.

Devlin stepped out, opened the van doors and got the radio and the bag of cycle lamps out. "You can leave me here," he said. "I'll walk up to the house."

"What time shall we call back?" Ryan asked.

"Give me four hours, and if I'm not here, just wait. Go and have a look at Rye or one of those places."

"Fine," Ryan said. "Take care, Liam." And he drove away.

Devlin picked up the radio case and started up the long drive. The house showed every evidence of lack of money. The shutters at the windows badly needed a coat of paint, as did the front door. He gave the bell pull a heave and waited, but there was no response. After a while he went around to the rear of the house. One of the stable doors stood open, and there were sounds of activity. He put the case down and looked in.

Lavinia Shaw, wearing riding breeches and boots, was rubbing down a large black stallion.

"Miss Lavinia Shaw?" Devlin enquired.

His voice startled her, and she looked around. "Yes."

"Harry Conlon. Your brother is expecting me."

"Major Conlon." There was a sudden eagerness about her. She put down the brush she was using and ran her hands over her breeches. "Of course. How wonderful to have you here."

The well-bred upper-class voice, her whole attitude, was quite incredible to Devlin, but he took the hand she offered, and smiled. "A pleasure, Miss Shaw."

"Maxwell is out on the marsh with his gun. You know how it is. Food shortages. Anything's good for the pot." She didn't seem to be able to stop talking. "We'll go into the kitchen, shall we?"

The kitchen was very large, with an enormous pine table, and chairs around it. There were unwashed dishes in the sink, and the whole place was cluttered and untidy, the lack of servants evident.

"Tea?" she asked. "Or would you like something stronger?"

"No. Tea would be fine."

He put the case on the table with the bag of cycle lamps, and she made the tea quickly. He poured a little milk in, and she sat on the other side of the table, excited and nervous, eyes glittering now, never leaving him.

"I can't tell you how absolutely thrilling all this is. Have you been in Germany recently?"

"Oh, yes," he told her. "I was in Berlin only the other day."

"How marvellous to be part of all that. People here are so complacent. They don't understand what the Führer's done for Germany."

"For all of Europe, you might say," Devlin told her.

"Exactly. Strength, a sense of purpose, discipline. Whereas here—" She laughed contemptuously. "That drunken fool Churchill has no idea what he's doing. Just lurches from one mistake to another."

"Ah, yes, but he would, wouldn't he?" Devlin said drily. "Do you think we could have a look round? I'd like to see the old barn you used for your Tiger Moth, and the south meadow."

"Of course." She jumped up so eagerly that she knocked over the chair. As she picked it up she said, "I'll just get a coat."

The meadow was larger than he had expected and stretched to a line of trees in the distance. "How long?" Devlin asked. "Two fifty or three hundred yards?"

"Oh, no," she said. "Getting on for three fifty. The grass is so short because we leased it to a local farmer to graze sheep, but they've gone to market now."

"You used to take off and land here a lot?"

"All the time. Great fun."

"And you used the barn over there as a hangar?"

"That's right. I'll show you."

The place was quite huge, but like everything else, it had seen better days, dry rot very evident, planks missing. Devlin helped her open one of the massive doors slightly so they could go inside. It was empty, rain dripping through holes in the roof.

"You'd want to put a plane in here?" she asked.

"Only for a short while, to be out of sight. A Lysander. Not too large. It would fit in here, and no trouble."

"When exactly?"

"Tomorrow night."

"My goodness, you are pushing things along."

"Yes, well, time's important."

They went out, and Devlin closed the door. Somewhere in the far distance a shotgun was fired.

"My brother," Lavinia said. "Let's go and find him, shall we?" As they walked across the meadow she said, "We had a German friend who used to come here in the old days—Werner Keitel. We used to fly together. Do you happen to know him?"

"He was killed in the Battle of Britain."

She paused for a moment only, then carried on. "Yes. I thought it would be something like that."

"I'm sorry," Devlin told her.

She shrugged. "A long time ago, Major." And she started to walk faster.

They followed a dyke through the small reeds, and it was Nell, the dog, who appeared first, gambolling around them before running away again. There was another shot, and then Shaw emerged from the reeds and came towards them, holding a couple of rabbits.

"See who's here," Lavinia called.

"Conlon, my dear chap. Nice to see you. Won't shake hands. Blood on them." He might have been welcoming Devlin to a weekend in the country. "Better get home and find you a drink."

They started back along the dyke. Devlin looked out across the expanse of reeds intersected by creeks.

"Desolate country this."

"Dead, old man. Everything about the damn place is dead. It was different in my grandfather's day. Twenty-five servants in the house alone. People don't want to work these days—that's the trouble. Bolshies all over the place. That's what I admire about the Führer. Gives people some order in their lives."

"Makes them do as they're told, you mean," Devlin said.

Shaw nodded enthusiastically. "Exactly, old man, exactly."

DEVLIN SET up the radio in a small study behind the library. Shaw had gone to have a bath, and it was Lavinia who watched intently as the Irishman explained the set to her.

"Is it much different from the one you had before?" he asked.

"A bit more sophisticated, that's all."

"And your Morse code. Can you still remember it?"

"Good heavens, Major Conlon, you never forget something like that. I was a Girl Guide when I first learnt it."

"Right," Devlin said. "Let's see what you can do, then."

IN THE radio room at Prinz Albrechtstrasse, Schellenberg studied Devlin's message, then turned to Ilse and Asa. "Incredible. He intends to pull Steiner out tomorrow evening. He wants you at Shaw Place in time to leave no later than midnight."

"Then we'll have to get moving," Asa told him.

"Yes." Schellenberg said. "The Lysander was delivered to Chernay yesterday. It's only a matter of getting ourselves down there." He said to the radio operator, "Send this message to Falcon, 'Will meet your requirements. Departure time will be confirmed tomorrow night.'"

He started to walk out, and the operator called, "I have a reply, General."

Schellenberg turned. "What is it?"

" 'A pleasure to do business with you.'"

LAVINIA TURNED from the radio set. "Did I do all right?"

Her brother was sitting by the fireplace, eyes already glazed, a tumbler of whisky in his hand. "Seemed fine to me."

"You were excellent," Devlin said. "Now, this set has a direct voice capacity for short ranges only. That was why I gave them the frequency reading. I've adjusted it, and all you do is switch on. That means you can talk to the pilot when he's close."

"Marvellous. Anything else?"

"After they contact you to confirm the departure time, place the cycle lamps in the meadow as I described."

"I will. You may depend on it."

Devlin got up. "On my way, then. See you tomorrow night."

Shaw mumbled something, and Lavinia took Devlin back to the kitchen, where he got his coat and hat.

"Will he be all right?" Devlin asked.

"Who, Max? Oh, yes. No need to worry there, Major."

"I'll see you, then."

It started to rain as he went down the drive. He stood there, hands in pockets, for thirty minutes before the van turned up.

"Did it go well?" Ryan asked.

Mary cut in. "We've had a lovely time. Rye was a fine place."

"Well, I'm happy for you," Devlin said sourly. "Those two didn't even offer me a bite to eat."

ASA VAUGHAN was just finishing a late lunch in the canteen when Schellenberg hurried in. "A slight change in plan. I've had a message saying the Reichsführer wants to see me. I'm to bring you. It seems you've been awarded the Iron Cross First Class, and the Reichsführer likes to pin them on SS officers himself."

Asa said, "I wonder what my old man would say. I went to West Point, for Pete's sake."

"The other complication is that he's at Wewelsburg. You've heard of the place, of course?"

"Every good SS man's idea of heaven. What does this do to our schedule?"

"No problem. Wewelsburg has a Luftwaffe base only ten miles away. We'll fly there in the Stork and carry on to Chernay afterwards." Schellenberg glanced at his watch. "The appointment's for seven, and he takes punctuality for granted."

AT SIX-THIRTY it was totally dark on the Thames as Ryan nudged the motorboat in towards the shingle beach. He said to Mary, "Just sit tight. It shouldn't take long."

Devlin picked up the bag of tools and the torch and went over the side. The water in the tunnel was chest-high, but they pressed on and reached the grille in a few minutes.

"Are you sure about this?" Ryan asked.

"Now, wouldn't I look the fool if I turned up to grab Steiner tomorrow night and found the grille wouldn't budge?"

"All right, let's get on with it," Ryan said.

"And no banging. I don't want someone on their knees up there in the chapel wondering what's happening down here."

Which is what made the whole thing rather more difficult than it had at first appeared. The slow, careful probing between the brick-work took time. On occasion several bricks fell out of place at once, but others proved more difficult. It took half an hour to clear the grille out of the way.

Devlin took the torch and peered inside, then handed it to Ryan. "You hold the light while I go and take a look."

"Watch your step now."

Devlin went through the hole and waded inside. The water was now up to his armpits, covering the tombs. He made it to the steps and started up. He paused on the top step, then gently tried the handle. There was the faintest of creaks, and the door eased open. He peered around it cautiously. The chapel was quite deserted. Very quietly Devlin closed the door and retreated down the steps.

"Perfect," he said to Ryan as he clambered through the hole. "Now let's get out of here."

AT THE Luftwaffe base, Schellenberg commandeered the station commander's Mercedes and set out for Wewelsburg with Asa. It started to snow, and as they approached, Asa looked up at the castle and its towers.

"It's incredible," he said in awe.

"I know." Schellenberg closed the glass partition so that the Luftwaffe driver couldn't hear what they were saying. "Looks like a film set. Actually, it's a personal retreat for the Reichsführer and a home away from home to the elite of the SS."

"But what do they do there?"

"The Reichsführer is obsessed with King Arthur and the Knights of the Round Table, so he has his twelve most trusted lieutenants sit at a round table. They have a memorial hall, with a swastika in the ceiling and a pit in which the remains of these special ones will be burnt on death. There are twelve pedestals and urns waiting for

THE EAGLE HAS FLOWN

the ashes." Schellenberg shook his head. "And people like these are handling the destinies of millions."

They signed in at the entrance hall and left their greatcoats and caps with the sergeant of the guard, who checked his register.

"Yes, General, the Reichsführer is expecting you in his private sitting room. I'll take you up, sir."

"No need. I know the way."

Asa followed Schellenberg across the hall. As they turned along a corridor the general checked his watch. "We've got fifteen minutes. Come on, I'll show you the memorial hall. There's a little gallery just along here. Yes, here we are."

There were perhaps a dozen steps up to an oak door. It opened easily, and Schellenberg immediately heard voices. He turned to Asa and put a finger to his lips, then led the way in.

The circular room was a place of shadows, only dimly lit. Asa was aware of the pedestals and urns Schellenberg had described, but it was the people who were most interesting. The Reichsführer stood in the pit beneath the ceiling swastika, face to face with Sturmbannführer Horst Berger. Rossman, Himmler's aide, stood to one side waiting. They all wore black dress uniforms.

"I have brought you to this holy place, Berger, before you depart on what I can only describe as your sacred mission."

"An honour, Reichsführer."

"Now let's go over the details. You will meet the Führer's plane at the Luftwaffe base at Cherbourg at six tomorrow night. I shall be with him. You will escort us to Château de Belle-Île, where we will spend the night. At seven o'clock the following morning the Führer will have breakfast with Rommel and Admiral Canaris. You will take action at the end of the meal. How many men will you have in the guard?"

"Thirty. Handpicked, Reichsführer."

"Good—the fewer involved in this, the better. There are some who would not agree with what we intend. General Schellenberg, for instance. That's why I gave him this ridiculous mission, to occupy him elsewhere these past three weeks. To bring Steiner out of England. An impossibility. I happen to know that the agent working for us in London—Vargas—also works for the British. We didn't tell Schellenberg that, did we, Rossman?"

"No, Reichsführer."

"So we may deduce that the Irishman Devlin will not last long."

"I couldn't be more pleased, Reichsführer," Berger said.

"We could have won this war at Dunkirk, Berger, if the Führer had allowed the panzers to roll onto the beaches. Russia, one disaster after another. Stalingrad, a catastrophic defeat. Blunder after blunder, and he still won't listen."

"I see, Reichsführer," Berger said. "All men of sense would."

"And so, inexorably, Germany sinks deeper into the pit of defeat, and that is why the Führer must die, Berger. To accomplish that is your sacred task. It will look like a dastardly attack on the part of Rommel and Canaris, leading to the Führer's unfortunate death, followed by their own deaths at the hands of loyal SS men."

"And afterwards?" Berger said.

"We of the SS will naturally assume all governmental powers. The war may then be continued as it should be. No weakness." He put a hand on Berger's shoulder. "We belong to the same sacred brotherhood, Major. I envy you this opportunity."

Schellenberg nodded to Asa and edged him out.

"Now what happens?" Asa said.

"We keep the appointment. If he finds out we overheard that lot, we'll never get out of here alive." As they hurried along the corridor Schellenberg said, "Follow my lead, and not a mention that Devlin's got things to the stage they are."

He quickly led the way to the door of Himmler's sitting room in the south wing. "Now we wait. They'll probably come up by the back entrance to his room."

A moment later the door opened, and Rossman looked out. "Ah, there you are."

"Right on time." Schellenberg led the way in.

Himmler, behind his desk, looked up. "So, General—and this is Vaughan, the pilot you recruited for the Steiner affair?"

"Yes, Reichsführer."

"Any news of your Mr Devlin?"

Schellenberg said, "I'm afraid not, Reichsführer."

"Ah, well, it was always a problematical mission, to say the least. The Führer arrives at Belle-Île tomorrow night. Canaris and Rommel are to breakfast with him the following morning. The idiots have a crazy idea the invasion will come in Normandy and hope to persuade the Führer to agree with them."

"I see, Reichsführer."

"However—to the reason for your visit." Himmler stood up and opened a medal case, then took the Iron Cross it contained, came around the table and pinned it to Asa's tunic.

"To you, Hauptsturmführer Asa Vaughan, in acknowledgment of supreme valour in aerial combat over Poland."

"Reichsführer," said Asa.

"And now you may go. I have work to do."

Schellenberg and Asa hurried down the stairs, retrieved their greatcoats and caps and went out to the waiting Mercedes.

"Back to the base," Schellenberg told the driver.

As they drove away Asa closed the glass partition and said, "What do you make of it?"

"I know one thing," Schellenberg said. "Killing Hitler is the worst thing that could happen. At least with him making one foul-up after another, there's a prospect of a reasonably early end to the war, but Himmler would be another story."

"So what are you going to do? Warn Rommel and Canaris?"

"First of all, Asa, I don't know exactly where they are, and second, why should anyone believe me? My word against that of the Reichs-führer of the SS?"

"Come off it, General. According to Liam Devlin, you're a very smart guy. Surely you can come up with something."

"I'll put my heart and soul into it," Schellenberg promised him. "But for the moment, let's concentrate on getting back to the airfield and the Stork. We fly out at once. The sooner we're at Chernay, the happier I'll be."

CHAPTER 11

THE DUTY MP usually brought Steiner a cup of tea at eleven each morning. Today he was late.

"There you go, Colonel."

"Thank you, Corporal."

"I suppose you'd prefer coffee, sir," the corporal said, lingering, for he rather liked Steiner.

"But I was raised on tea, Corporal," Steiner told him. "I went to school right here in London. St Paul's."

"Is that a fact, sir?"

The MP turned to the door, and Steiner said, "Is Lieutenant Benson back yet?"

"His leave is up at midnight, sir, but if I know him, he'll look in this evening. You know these young officers. Dead keen."

He left, the bolt rammed home, and Steiner went back to his seat by the window, waiting for noon as he had on the previous day, drinking his tea and trying to compose himself to patience.

It was raining again, and there was fog in the city—so heavy that he could barely see the other side of the river. As he watched, a large cargo boat eased down from the London docks. Then he saw the girl, just as Devlin had described—black beret and shabby raincoat. She limped along the pavement, collar up, hands thrust deep into her pockets. She stopped and leant on the wall, watching the boats on the river. She stayed there for ten minutes, then turned and walked away.

Steiner steadied himself. The door opened behind him, and the corporal reappeared.

"If you're finished, Colonel, I'll take your tray."

"Yes, I am, thank you." The MP picked up the tray and turned to the door. "Oh, by the way, I'll be going down to confession this evening," Steiner added.

"Right, sir. I'll make a note of it."

He went out and locked the door. Steiner listened to the sound of his boots receding along the corridor, then turned.

"Now we pray, Mr Devlin," he said softly. "Now we pray."

DEVLIN WASN'T really sure why he had come to St Patrick's. Conscience again, he supposed. He only knew he couldn't leave without a word with the old priest. He'd used him, and it didn't sit well. What was worse was the fact that they would meet for the last time in the chapel at St Mary's that evening. No avoiding that, or the distress it would cause.

Frank Martin was down at the altar arranging a few flowers. He turned at the sound of Devlin's approach, and there was genuine pleasure on his face.

"Hello, Father."

Devlin managed a smile. "I just dropped in to tell you I'm on my way. I got my orders this morning. I'm to report to a military hospital in Portsmouth."

"Ah, well, as they say, there's a war on."

Devlin nodded. "The war, the war, the bloody war, Father. It's gone on too long, and we all of us have to do things we normally would never do. Things to shame us."

The old man said, "You're troubled, my son. Can I help?"

"No, Father, not this time. Some things we have to live with ourselves." Devlin put out his hand, and the old priest took it. "It's been a genuine pleasure, Father."

"And for me," Frank Martin said.

Devlin walked away. The old priest stood there for a moment, puzzled, and then he turned back to his flowers.

THERE WAS the merest hint of fog at Chernay at four o'clock, when Schellenberg went in search of Asa. He found him in the hangar with the Lysander and Flight Sergeant Leber. The Lysander had the RAF roundels in place on canvas strips, and the swastika on the tail plane had been blocked out with black canvas.

"How is it?" Schellenberg asked.

"Perfection, General," Leber told him.

"And the weather?"

"Uncertain," Leber said. "Visibility could be restricted. There are a couple of conflicting fronts moving in. I've checked with our base at Cherbourg, and they don't really know."

"But the plane is ready?"

"Oh, yes," Asa told him.

"Good. Let's go for a walk. I feel like the air."

It was raining only slightly as they walked along the airfield. Schellenberg smoked a cigarette, not speaking for a while. They reached the end and looked out to sea.

Asa said, "Assuming I put down here with our friends some time early tomorrow morning, what happens then? What about the Belle-Île situation? Have you any ideas?"

"Only one, and it would be a desperate venture. The Führer will be having breakfast with Rommel, the admiral and the Reichsführer. Berger will strike at the end of the meal. What if you and I and Mr Devlin arrived to join them for breakfast and exposed the plot?"

"But we'd go down the hole too—that's obvious," Asa said. "Even if you said your piece to the Führer, Berger and his chums would just get on with it."

"Yes." Schellenberg nodded. "But there is a wild card I haven't mentioned. Remember when we were driving to Belle-Île? The Twelfth Parachute Detachment, outside St Aubin? Hauptmann Erich Kramer and thirty-five paratroopers?"

"Sure I do."

"What do you think would happen if Colonel Kurt Steiner, the living legend of the parachute regiment, appeared and told them he needed their services because there was an SS plot ten miles up the road to kill the Führer?"

"Of course! Those guys would follow Steiner anywhere."

"Exactly. And the *Fallschirmjäger* have always been notorious for their dislike of the SS."

"Let me get this straight. We'd go in first? Steiner would follow?"

"Yes. Let's say fifteen minutes later."

Asa said, "That could be one hell of a breakfast."

IN RYAN'S KITCHEN, Devlin had various items laid out on the table. "Let's see what I've got here," he said. "Those MPs carry handcuffs, but I'll take a little twine for emergencies, just in case."

"I've made up three gags," Ryan said. "Bandages and sticking plaster. You've the priest too, remember."

"I'd prefer to forget him," Devlin said.

"And a weapon?"

"I'll take the Luger, the Smith & Wesson in the ankle holster and that Walther with the silencer I got from Carver."

"Would you anticipate any killing?" Ryan looked troubled.

"The last thing I want. Have you got that sap of yours?"

Ryan opened the kitchen-table drawer and produced a leather cosh. It was loaded with lead, and there was a loop for the wrist. It was a thing carried by many London cab drivers for self-protection. Devlin put it down beside the Walther.

"That's everything, then," Ryan said.

Devlin smiled lightly. "All we need is Steiner now."

The door opened, and Mary came in. Her uncle said, "I'm starving, girl. Bacon and eggs all round if you can manage it."

"No problem," she said. "But we're out of bread and tea. I'll just run along to the shop. I shan't be long." And she took her beret and raincoat and went out.

THE FOG was rolling in when Mary left the shop carrying the bread and tea, and she stopped cautiously on the corner before crossing the road.

Eric Carver, at the wheel of his brother's Humber, had stopped at the traffic lights. She was only a yard or two away as she passed, and he saw her clearly. As the lights changed, he pulled the Humber in at the kerb, got out and followed her.

Mary turned into Cable Wharfe, walking as quickly as she

could, and crossed to the house. As she went around the corner Eric hurried across and peered around.

The kitchen door opened, and he heard Devlin say, "Ah, there you are, girl. Will you come in out of that?"

The door closed. Eric said softly, "Right. I've got you." And he turned and hurried away.

JACK CARVER was in his bedroom dressing when Eric burst in.

"I've found him, Jack. I've found where that bastard's shacked up. I saw the girl. I followed her home, and he was there. A place called Cable Wharfe, in Wapping."

"Right." Carver nodded in satisfaction. "We'll sort him."

"When?"

"I've got a big game on tonight. We'll pay him a call after that, when he thinks he's nicely tucked up for the night." Carver smiled, opened a drawer and took out a Browning. "Just you and me and our friend here."

"I can't wait, Jack," Eric said, an unholy look on his face.

LIEUTENANT BENSON returned from his leave just before seven. As soon as he arrived at the priory, he went straight upstairs, where he found a corporal sitting in his office. The man jumped to his feet.

"Where's Sergeant Morgan?" Benson asked.

"Went off about an hour ago, sir."

"Everything calm while I've been away?" asked Benson.

"I think so, sir."

"Let's have a look at the log." Smith handed it over, and Benson leafed through it. "What's this entry here on the admittance sheet? Major Conlon?"

"Oh, yes, sir—the padre. He did a tour of the place with the sister and Father Martin."

"Who gave him permission?"

"He had a War Office pass, sir. You know, one of those unrestricted access things. I think you'll find Sergeant Morgan put the details down."

"I can see that. The point is, what was he doing here?"

"Search me, sir. Nice-looking man. Grey hair, glasses. Looked like he'd had a hard time."

"Yes, well, that doesn't mean anything," Benson said sourly. "I'm going down to see Sister."

Sister Maria Palmer was in her office when he went in. She glanced up and smiled.

"You're back. Did you have a good leave?"

"Yes, not bad. There was a Major Conlon here when I was away."

"Ah, yes, the army chaplain. A nice man. On sick leave. I understand he was wounded in Sicily last year."

"Yes, but what was he doing here?"

"Nothing. We just showed him round, and he took over for Father Martin one evening."

"Has he been back?"

"No. I understand from Father Martin that he's been posted." She looked slightly bewildered. "Is anything wrong?"

"Oh, no. It's just that when unexpected guests turn up with War Office passes, one likes to know who they are."

"You worry too much," she said.

"Probably. Goodnight, Sister."

But it wouldn't go away—the nagging doubt—and when he got back upstairs to his office, he phoned Dougal Munro.

Jack Carter had gone to York for the day, so Munro was working alone in his office when he took the call. He listened patiently to what Benson had to say.

"You were right to call me," he said. "I don't much like the idea of officers with War Office passes sticking their noses into our business, but there it is."

"I've got Conlon's details here on the admission sheet, sir. Do you want them?"

"Tell you what," Munro said. "I'm packing up here soon and going home. I'll call in and see you. About an hour and a half."

"I'll expect you, sir."

Benson put down the phone, and Corporal Smith, standing at the door, said, "You'll see Colonel Steiner's booked for chapel, sir. Eight o'clock as usual. Shall I do it with Corporal Ross?"

"No. We'll do it together. I'm expecting Brigadier Munro, but he won't be here until half past eight. Now get me a cup of tea."

AT CHERNAY, the elements were very definitely against them, fog rolling in from the sea, and rain with it. Schellenberg and Asa Vaughan stood in the radio room waiting while Flight Sergeant Leber checked the situation with the Cherbourg base.

After a while he turned to them. "The Führer's plane got in all right, General. Landed just before this started."

"So what's the verdict?" Asa demanded.

"Parts of the Channel you'll find winds gusting up to force eight. Fog over southern England, from London down to the Channel coast. Another thing. They say it will get worse here during the night." He looked worried. "To be frank, sir, it stinks."

"Don't worry, Sergeant. I'll find a way."

There was silence; then Schellenberg said, "Look, if you think it's not on, if you don't want to go . . ."

"Don't be silly," Asa told him. "Of course I'm going. Devlin's depending on me. Wind doesn't bother me. But let me tell you about fog. Taking off in it's nothing, but it worries me that I might not be able to land when I get there."

"So what do you want to do?"

"Leave it as late as possible. Devlin wanted me there for a midnight departure. Let's cut it really close. I won't leave until ten o'clock. That will give the weather a chance to clear."

"Fine. I'll send a signal to that effect to Shaw Place now."

LAVINIA SHAW, seated at the radio in the study, tapped out a quick reply: MESSAGE RECEIVED AND UNDERSTOOD. She took off her headphones and turned. Her brother sat by the fire cleaning his shotgun, a tumbler of scotch beside him.

"They won't be leaving until ten o'clock, Max. It's this damn

594

weather." She went to the french windows, pulled back the curtains and looked out at the fog.

Shaw stood up and moved to her side. "I should have thought this stuff was all to the good for this kind of secret landing."

Lavinia said, "Don't be silly. It's the worst thing for a pilot."

Rain started to spot the terrace in front of them in the light from the window.

"There you are," Shaw said. "That should help clear the fog. Now let's have another drink."

"YOU'VE GOT EVERYTHING?" Michael Ryan asked as the motorboat coasted into the little beach.

Devlin, wearing loose blue overalls and boots, tapped at his pockets. "Everything in perfect working order."

Ryan said, "I wish you'd let me come with you."

"My affair, Michael, and if there's the slightest hint of trouble, you and Mary get out of it. This fog is a blessing in a way." He smiled at Mary through the darkness. "You were right about that."

She reached up and kissed him on the cheek. "God bless you, Mr Devlin. I've prayed for you."

"Then everything will be all right." And he went over the side.

The water was not quite as deep, which was something, and he moved on, the light from his torch splaying against the tunnel until he reached the hole in the wall. He checked his watch. It was a couple of minutes past eight. He climbed in and waded through the water, then started up the steps.

DOUGAL MUNRO had finished a little earlier than he had intended, so he called a staff car and told the driver to take him to St Mary's Priory. It was a difficult journey in the fog, and it was just after eight o'clock when they arrived.

"I shan't be long," the brigadier said as he got out.

"I'll get off the road, sir, while I'm waiting," his driver replied. "I'll just turn up the side. There's a yard there."

"I'll find you." Munro went up the steps and rang the bell.

The night porter opened it. "Good evening, Brigadier," he said.

"Lieutenant Benson about?" Munro asked.

"I saw him go into the chapel a few minutes ago, sir, with one of the corporals and that German officer."

"Really?" Munro hesitated, then crossed to the chapel door.

DEVLIN EASED the door open and got the shock of his life. Corporal Smith was standing with his back to him, no more than six feet away. Benson was up by the door. Devlin didn't hesitate. He pulled out the cosh and lashed Smith across the back of the neck, and moved back into the shelter of the door as the corporal went down with a clatter.

Benson called, "Smith, what's going on?" He ran along the aisle and paused, staring down at the body. Then, sensing too late that something was very wrong indeed, he reached for the Webley revolver in his holster.

Devlin stepped out, the silenced Walther in his left hand, the cosh in his right.

"I wouldn't do that, son. Now turn round."

Benson did, and Devlin gave him the same as Smith. The young lieutenant fell across the corporal. Devlin searched them for handcuffs, but only Smith appeared to be carrying them.

"Are you there, Colonel?" Devlin called.

Steiner stepped out of the confessional box, and Father Martin joined him.

The old priest looked shocked and bewildered. "Major Conlon? What's happening here?"

"I'm truly sorry, Father." Devlin turned him around and handcuffed his wrists behind him. He sat the old man down in a pew and took out one of his gags.

Father Martin said, "You're not a priest, I take it."

"My uncle was, Father."

"I forgive you, my son," Frank Martin said, and submitted himself to the gag.

At that moment the door opened and Dougal Munro walked in.

Before he could say a word, Kurt Steiner had him turned around, an arm like steel across his throat.

"And who might this be?" Devlin demanded.

"Brigadier Dougal Munro," Steiner told him. "Of SOE."

"Is that a fact?" Devlin held up the Walther. "This thing is silenced, Brigadier, so be sensible."

Steiner released him, and Munro said bitterly, "Good Lord, Devlin—Liam Devlin."

"As ever was, Brigadier."

"What happens now?" Steiner asked.

Devlin was excited, a little cocky. "A short trip downriver, a gentle drive through the country—and you'll be away while this lot are still running round in circles looking for us."

"Which means you intend to fly," Munro said. "Interesting."

"Me and my big mouth," groaned Devlin. "If I leave you, you'll have the RAF on the job before we know where we are. I could kill you, but I'm in a very generous mood."

"Which leaves what alternative?"

"We'll have to take you with us." He nodded to Steiner. "Watch him." He eased open the door. "We're going straight out of the front door and across the road. It's thick fog, so no one will notice a thing." He urged Munro across the hall, the Walther at his back. "Don't forget, Brigadier, a wrong word and I blow your spine out."

It was Steiner who led the way down to the pavement. The fog was thick and brown and tasted sour at the back of the throat. They didn't see a soul. They went down the steps to the beach. At the bottom Devlin paused and passed the gun to Steiner.

"I've got friends I don't want this old bugger to see, or he'll be hanging them for treason."

Devlin quickly tied the brigadier's hands with the twine he'd brought. Munro was wearing a silk scarf and the Irishman took that and bound it around his eyes, then started along the beach, a hand at Munro's elbow. The motorboat loomed out of the darkness.

"Is that you, Liam?" Ryan called softly.

"As ever was," Devlin replied. "Now let's get out of here."

In Ryan's bedroom, Devlin changed quickly into the clerical suit and dark polo-neck sweater. He collected his few belongings and put them into a holdall, together with the Luger and the Walther. He checked the Smith & Wesson in the ankle holster, picked up the bag and went into the kitchen. Steiner was sitting at the table with Ryan, Mary watching him in awe.

"Are you fit, Colonel?" Devlin demanded.

"Never better, Mr Devlin."

Devlin tossed him the military trench coat he'd stolen from the Army and Navy Club the day he'd met Shaw. "That should do to cover the uniform. Now let's move it."

He opened the cupboard under the stairs to reveal Munro sitting in the corner with his hands tied, still wearing the scarf around his eyes. He pulled Munro up and out and walked him to the front door. The van stood at the kerb. They put Munro into the back, and Devlin checked his watch.

"Nine o'clock, Michael, me old son. We'll be off now."

They shook hands. When he turned to Mary, she was in tears. Devlin put his bag into the van and opened his arms. She rushed into them, and he embraced her. "A wonderful girl you are."

"I'll never forget you," she said. She was really crying now.

He was too full to speak himself. He got in beside Steiner and drove away. The German said, "A nice girl."

"Yes," Devlin said. "I shouldn't have involved them or that old priest, but there was nothing else I could do."

"The nature of the game we're in," Munro said from the rear. "Tell me something, just to assuage my idle curiosity. Vargas."

"Oh, I smelt a rat there from the beginning," Devlin said. "It always seemed likely you were inviting us in, so to speak. I knew the only way to fool you was to fool Vargas. That's why he's still getting messages from Berlin."

"Clever. Mind you, as that fine old English saying has it: *There's many a slip between the cup and the lip.*"

"And what's that supposed to mean?"

"Fog, Mr Devlin, fog," Dougal Munro said.

CHAPTER 12

JACK CARVER'S big game in the back room at the Astoria Ballroom had not gone his way at all, and if there was one thing guaranteed to put him in a bad mood, it was losing money. He broke off the game angrily at eight thirty and went down to the ballroom. Eric, dancing there with a young girl, saw him at once.

"Sorry, sweetness, another time," he said, and went up the stairs to join his brother. "You've finished early, Jack."

"Yes, well, I got bored, didn't I?"

Eric, who knew the signs, didn't pursue the matter. Instead he said, "I was thinking, Jack. You're sure you don't want to take some of the boys along when we pay that call?"

Carver was furious. "What are you trying to say? That I can't take care of that little squirt on my own?"

"I didn't mean anything, Jack. I was just thinking—"

"You think too bloody much," his brother told him. "Come on. Let's go."

The Humber, Eric at the wheel, turned into Cable Wharfe no more than ten minutes after the van had left.

"That's the house, at the far end," Eric said.

"Right. We'll leave the motor here and walk." Carver took the Browning from his pocket and pulled the slider. "Got yours?"

"Sure I have, Jack." Eric produced a Webley .38 revolver.

"Good boy. Let's go and give him some stick."

MARY WAS sitting at the table reading and Ryan was poking the fire when the kitchen door burst open and the Carvers entered. Mary screamed, and Ryan turned, poker in hand.

"No, you don't." Carver extended his arm, the Browning rigid in his hand. "You make one wrong move, and I'll blow your head off. See to the bird, Eric."

"A pleasure, Jack." Eric slipped his revolver into his pocket, stood behind Mary and put his hands on her shoulders. "Now you be a good girl."

He kissed her neck, and she squirmed in disgust. "Stop it!"

Ryan took a step forward. "Leave her alone."

Carver tapped him with the barrel of the Browning. "I give the orders here, so shut your face. Where is he?"

"Where's who?" Ryan demanded.

"The little bastard who shot half my brother's ear off."

Mary answered defiantly, "You're too late. They've gone."

"Leave her," Carver said to Eric. "Check upstairs, and make sure you have your shooter in your hand."

Eric went out, and Carver gestured at the other chair. "Sit," he ordered Ryan. The Irishman did as he was told. "She didn't say we'd missed him—she said we'd missed them."

"So what?" Ryan said.

"So who was that pal of yours, and who's he mixed up with?"

"Don't say a word, Uncle Michael," Mary cried.

"Not me, girl."

Carver hit him across the face with the Browning, and Ryan went over backwards in the chair. Mary screamed again, and Eric came back. "Here, what have I missed?"

"Just teaching him his manners. Anything?"

"Not a sausage. But there was a major's uniform in one of the bedrooms."

"Is that a fact?" Carver turned back to Ryan, who was wiping blood from his face. "All right, I haven't got all night. Watch the girl, Eric."

Eric moved behind her, pulled her up from the chair, his arms about her waist.

"You like that, don't you? They all do."

She moaned, trying to get away, and Carver picked up the poker from the hearth and put it into the fire. "All right, hard man, either you tell me what I want to know, or I put this to your niece's face once it's nice and hot."

Mary tried to move, but Eric held her, laughing. Ryan said, "You bastard."

Carver took the poker out. It was white hot. He put it to the tabletop, and the dry wood burst into flame. Then he moved towards Mary, and the girl screamed in terror.

"All right, I'll tell you," Ryan cried out.

"Okay," Carver said. "His name."

"Devlin—Liam Devlin."

"Who was with him? IRA?" Ryan hesitated, and Carver touched the girl's woollen cardigan so that it smouldered. "I ain't kidding, friend."

"He was doing a job for the Germans. Breaking out a prisoner they had here in London."

"And where is he now?"

Ryan hesitated again, and Carver touched the poker to the girl's hair. The stench of burning was terrible, and she screamed again.

Ryan broke completely. "Driving to a place near Romney. He's going to be picked up by a plane."

"Don't, Uncle Michael," Mary cried.

"A village called Charbury. Shaw Place is the house."

"Marvellous." Carver put the poker down on the hearth and turned to Eric. "Fancy a little drive down to the country?"

"I don't mind, Jack." Eric kissed Mary on the neck again. "As long as I can have ten minutes upstairs with this little madam."

Mary cried out in revulsion and reached back, clawing his face. Eric released her with a howl of pain, then slapped her. She backed away as he advanced on her slowly. She reached behind her and managed to get the kitchen door open. He grabbed at her. She kicked out at him, then staggered back against the rail. There was an ugly snapping sound as it gave way, and she disappeared into darkness.

Ryan gave a cry and started forward, and Carver had him by the collar, the barrel of the Browning at his ear. "Go and check on her," he called to Eric.

Ryan stopped struggling and waited in silence. After a while

601

Eric appeared, his face pale. "She's croaked, Jack. Fell on a jetty down there. Must have broken her neck."

Ryan kicked back against Carver's shin, shoving him away. He picked up the poker from the hearth, turned with it raised above his head, and Carver shot him in the heart.

There was silence.

Eric wiped blood from his face. "What now, Jack?"

"We get out of here, that's what," said Jack.

He led the way, and Eric followed. They turned along the wharf and got into the Humber. Carver lit a cigarette. "Where's that map?" Eric found it in the glove compartment, and Carver flipped through it. "Here we are, Romney Marsh. There's Charbury. Let's get going."

"To Charbury?" Eric said.

"Why not? There's one aspect to all this that doesn't seem to have occurred to you. We take care of Devlin and this German, we'll be bleeding heroes."

At Chernay, visibility was no more than a hundred yards. Schellenberg and Asa stood in the radio room and waited while Leber checked the weather. The American wore a leather helmet, flying jacket and boots. He smoked a cigarette nervously.

"Well?" Asa demanded.

"They've listened to RAF weather reports for the South of England. It's one of those situations, Captain—thick fog, but every so often the wind blows a hole in it."

"Okay," Asa said. "Let's stop monkeying around."

He went out, Schellenberg following, and walked to the plane. Schellenberg said, "Asa, what can I say?"

Asa laughed and pulled on his gloves. "Don't worry, General, I've been on borrowed time ever since I crash-landed in that blizzard in Finland. Take care of yourself."

He clambered into the cockpit, pulling down the cupola.

Schellenberg stepped back out of the way. The Lysander started to move. It turned at the end of the field and came back into the wind. Asa boosted power and gave it everything, rushing headlong into that wall of fog, darkness and rain. He started to climb, turning out to sea.

Schellenberg watched him go in awe. "Dear God," he murmured. "Where do we find such men?"

GETTING OUT of London was the worst part, as Devlin discovered, crawling along in traffic at fifteen miles an hour.

"A devil this," he said to Steiner.

"It will make us late, I presume," Steiner said.

"A midnight departure was the aim. We're not done yet."

Once they were through Greenwich, there was much less traffic, and Devlin was able to make better time. He lit a cigarette with one hand. "We're on our way now."

"I wouldn't count your chickens," Munro said from the back.

Devlin said, "You're a great man for the sayings, Brigadier. What about one from the Bible? *The laughter of a fool is like the crackling of thorns under a pot.*" And he increased speed.

THE CARVER brothers had exactly the same problem getting out of London, and Eric managed to take the wrong turning in Greenwich, going three miles in the other direction. It was Jack who checked their route and sorted him out.

"It's bleeding simple. Greenwich to Maidstone, Maidstone to Ashford. From there you take the road to Rye, and we turn off halfway for Charbury."

"But there's hardly any road signs these days, Jack."

"Yes, well, there's a war on, isn't there, so just get on with it."

ASA CHARTED a course that took him along the Channel in a straight line. There were strong crosswinds, and that slowed him down, but it was good, monotonous flying. All he had to do was check for drift every so often. He stayed at eight thousand, well above the fog, keeping an eye cocked for other planes.

When one came, it took even an old hand like him by surprise. A

Spitfire lifted out of the fog, banked and took up station to starboard. Up there, visibility was good, and Asa could see the pilot clearly in the cockpit. The American raised a hand and waved.

A cheerful voice crackled over his radio. "Hello, Lysander. What are you up to?"

"Sorry," Asa replied. "Special Duties Squadron, operating out of Tempsford."

"A Yank, are you?"

"In the RAF," Asa told him.

"Saw the movie, old man. Terrible. Take care." The Spitfire banked away to the east and disappeared into the distance.

Asa said softly, "That's what comes of living right, old buddy."

He went down into the fog until his altimeter showed a thousand feet, then turned in towards Romney Marsh.

SHAW HAD had a considerable amount of whisky. He was slumped in his chair beside the sitting-room fire, his shotgun on the floor, when Lavinia put a hand on his shoulder. He stirred and looked up. "Hello, old girl. Everything all right?"

"I'm going to go down to the barn, Max. It must be close now — the plane, I mean."

"All right, old girl." He closed his eyes again.

She went into the study, hurriedly took down the radio's aerial and packed everything into the carrying case. Then she found the bag of cycle lamps and got her shooting jacket. When she opened the front door, Nell slipped out beside her, and they went down to the south meadow together.

She stood outside the barn listening. There was no sound, the fog embracing everything. She went in and switched on the light. On a workbench by the door she set up the radio, running the aerial wires along the wall, looping them over rusting old nails. When she put on the headphones and switched to the voice frequency, she heard Asa Vaughan's voice instantly.

"Falcon, are you receiving me? Again — Are you receiving me?"

It was eleven forty-five, and the Lysander was only five miles away. Lavinia stood in the entrance to the barn, holding the head-phones in one hand. Of the plane, there was no sound.

"Am receiving you, Lysander. Am receiving you."

"What are your conditions?" Asa's voice crackled.

"Thick fog. Visibility fifty yards. Wind gusting occasionally, strength four to five. It only clears things intermittently."

"Have you placed your markers?" he asked.

She'd totally forgotten. "Oh, no. Give me a few minutes."

She put down the headphones, got the bag of cycle lamps and ran out into the meadow, Nell chasing after her. She arranged them in an inverted L shape, the crossbar at the up-wind end, and switched them on so that their beams shone straight up into the sky. She was panting for breath when she returned to the barn and reached for the mike. "Falcon here. Markers in place."

She stood in the doorway of the barn looking up. She could hear the Lysander clearly. It seemed to pass at a few hundred feet and move away. "Falcon here," she called. "I heard you. You were directly overhead."

"Can't see a thing," Asa replied. "It's bad."

At that moment Maxwell Shaw appeared from the darkness. He was not wearing a raincoat or hat, and his speech was slurred and halting. "Ah, there you are, old girl. Everything all right?"

"No, it isn't," she told him.

Asa said, "I'll keep circling, just in case things change."

"Right. I'll stand by."

Strangely enough, it was Maxwell Shaw who came up with the solution. "Needs more light," he said. "Lots more light. I mean, he'd see the bloody house if it was on fire, wouldn't he?"

"Of course!" Lavinia said, and reached for the mike. "Falcon here. Now listen carefully. I'm a pilot, so I know what I'm talking about."

"Let's hear it," Asa said.

"My house is three hundred yards south of the meadow—and downwind. I'm going to go and put on every light in the place."

"Isn't that what they call advertising?" Asa said.

"Not in this fog, and there isn't another house for two miles. I'm going now. Good luck." She put down her headphones and mike. "You stay here, Max."

She ran all the way to the house, gasping for breath, and got the front door open. She climbed the stairs first, going into every room, switching on the lights and yanking back the blackout curtains. Then she went down to the ground floor and did the same thing. She left quickly, and when she stopped to look back, the house was ablaze with lights.

"Bloody place looks like a Christmas tree," Max told her when she returned. She ignored him and reached for the mike.

"Right. I've done it," she said to Asa. "Is that any better?"

"We'll take a look," Asa said.

He took the Lysander down to five hundred feet, suddenly filled with a strange fatalism. He went in hard, and now the fog was suffused with a kind of glow, and a second later Shaw Place, every window alight, came into view. He had always been a fine pilot, but for a moment greatness took over as he pulled back the column and lifted over the house with feet to spare. And there on the other side were the lights of the meadow, the open barn door.

The Lysander landed perfectly, turned and taxied towards the barn. Lavinia got the doors fully open and gestured Asa inside. He switched off the engine, took off his flying helmet and got out.

"I say, that was a bit hairy," she said, and stuck out her hand. "I'm Lavinia Shaw, and this is my brother, Maxwell."

"Asa Vaughan. I really owe you one."

"Good heavens, the fellow sounds like a Yank," Max said.

"Well, you could say I grew up there." Asa turned to Lavinia. "Where are the others?"

"No sign of Major Conlon, I'm afraid. Fog all the way from London to the coast. I expect they've got held up."

Asa nodded. "Okay. Let's get a message out to Chernay right now, telling them I'm down in one piece."

After they had tapped out their message to Schellenberg, Asa helped Lavinia put out the extra lights in the house. Shaw was slumped in his chair by the fire, eyes glazed.

"Come into the kitchen," Lavinia told Asa. "I'll make some tea or coffee if you'd like it."

"Coffee would be great." He sat on the edge of the table smoking a cigarette, while she made the coffee. He took off his flying jacket, and she saw the cuff title on the sleeve of his SS uniform.

"I say, the George Washington Legion. I didn't know there was such a thing. My brother was right. You are an American."

"I hope you won't hold it against me," he said.

"We won't, you beautiful Yankee bastard," said Liam Devlin, coming through the door. He threw his arms around Asa. "How the devil did you manage to land in that stuff, son? It took us all our time to make it from London by road."

"Genius, I suppose," Asa said modestly.

Munro appeared behind Devlin, still with his wrists bound and the scarf around his eyes. Steiner was at his shoulder. "Colonel Kurt Steiner, the object of the exercise, plus a little excess baggage we acquired along the way," Devlin said.

"Colonel, a pleasure." Asa shook Steiner's hand.

Lavinia said, "Why don't we all go into the living room and have a cup of coffee? It's just made."

"Well, if it's made, there's no harm," Devlin said. "But five minutes, and we're away."

"I wouldn't count on that," Asa said to him as they moved through. "The weather was just as bad at Chernay when I left."

In the living room, Devlin pushed Munro down into the other chair by the fire and looked at Maxwell Shaw in disgust. "Hell, if you struck a match, he'd catch fire."

Shaw woke up and opened his eyes. "What's that, eh?" He focused on Devlin. "Conlon, that you?"

"As ever was," Devlin answered.

Shaw sat up and looked across at Munro. "Who's that? What's he got that thing round his eyes for?" He reached across and pulled off the scarf before anyone could stop him. Munro shook his head, blinking in the light. Shaw said, "I know you, don't I?"

"You should, Sir Maxwell," Dougal Munro told him. "We've

been fellow members of the Army and Navy Club for years."

"That's torn it, Brigadier," Devlin told him. "I'd intended to dump you somewhere in the marsh before we left, to find your own way home, but now you know who these people are."

"Which means you have to shoot me or take me with you."

It was Steiner who said, "Is there room, Captain?"

"Oh, sure. We could manage," Asa said.

Steiner turned to the Irishman. "It's up to you, Mr Devlin."

Munro said, "Never mind, my friend. I'm sure your Nazi masters will pay well for me."

Asa said, "I haven't filled you in on what the score is over there yet. You'd better know now because you'll be up to your necks in it if we get back over there in one piece."

"You'd better tell us, then," Steiner said.

So Asa did.

THE FOG was as bad as ever as they all stood around the radio in the barn, Lavinia scribbling on the pad in front of her. "They suggest you delay take-off for another hour," she said. "There's a slight chance conditions at Chernay might improve by then."

Devlin glanced at Steiner. "We don't seem to have much choice."

"Well, I can't say I'm sorry for you." Munro turned to Lavinia with a charming smile. "I was wondering, my dear. Do you think when we get back to the house, I might have tea this time?"

SHAW WAS sprawled in his chair by the fire, asleep. Munro sat on the sofa, wrists bound. Asa was in the kitchen helping Lavinia.

Devlin said to Steiner, "I was thinking, Colonel, you might need a side arm." He put his holdall on the table and opened it. The silenced Walther was lying inside on top of a couple of shirts.

"A thought," Steiner said.

There was a gust of wind, a creaking at the french windows, and then Jack and Eric Carver stepped into the room, guns in their hands.

CHAPTER 13

DEVLIN SAID, "Look what the wind's blown in."

Steiner said calmly, "Who are these men?"

"Well, the big, ugly one is Jack Carver. He runs most of London's East End. Makes an honest bob out of protection, gambling, prostitution. The other one—the one who looks as if he's just crawled out of his hole—is his brother, Eric."

"I'll teach you." Eric advanced on him, his face pinched. "We'll give you what we gave that pal of yours and his niece."

Devlin went cold inside. "What are you telling me?"

"No funny stuff this time," Carver said. "Check to see if he has that bleeding gun up his trouser leg."

Eric dropped to one knee and relieved Devlin of the Smith & Wesson. "It won't work twice, you cunning bastard."

"My friends," Devlin said calmly. "What happened to them?"

Carver was enjoying himself. He took a cigar from his pocket and stuck it into his mouth. "We paid them a visit not long after you left. A little persuasion was all it took, and here we are."

"And he talked—my friend—as easily as that?" Devlin asked. "I find that hard to believe."

Carver lit his cigar. "I wouldn't think too badly of him. It was his niece he was concerned about. He had to do the decent thing."

"Not that it did either of them much good." Eric smiled sadistically. "Want to know what happened to her? She made a run for it, went over the rail down to that jetty. Broke her neck."

"And Michael?" Devlin asked Carver, his voice choking.

"I shot him, didn't I? Isn't that what you do with dogs?"

Devlin took a step towards him, and the look on his face was terrible to see. "You're dead, the both of you."

Carver stopped smiling. "Not us—you."

It was at that moment that Shaw came back to life. He opened his eyes, stretched and looked around him. At the same moment, the double doors were flung open, and Lavinia appeared holding a tray, Asa beside her.

"Tea everyone," she said, then froze.

"Just hold it right there," Carver told them.

She looked absolutely terrified, but didn't say a word.

Dougal Munro said, "Steady, my dear. Just keep calm."

Shaw, on his feet, swayed drunkenly, eyes bloodshot, speech slurred. "You bloody swine. Who do you think you are — coming into my house, waving guns about?"

"Another step, and I'll blow you away," Carver told him.

Lavinia shouted, "Do as he says, Max." She dropped the tray with a crash and took a step forward.

Carver turned and shot her, more a reflex action than anything else. Maxwell Shaw, with a cry of rage, jumped at him, and Carver fired again, shooting him twice at close quarters.

Asa, on his knees beside Lavinia, looked up. "She's dead."

"I warned you, didn't I?" Carver said, his face contorted.

"You certainly did, Mr Carver," Kurt Steiner told him.

His hand went into Devlin's open holdall, found the Walther, brought it out and fired in one smooth motion. The bullet caught Carver in the forehead, and he went back, into the chair.

"Jack!" Eric screamed as he took a step forward.

Devlin grabbed for his wrist, twisting it until Eric dropped the revolver.

Eric backed away, and Devlin said, "You killed that girl — is that what you're telling me?" He leant down and picked up Maxwell Shaw's shotgun from the floor beside the chair.

Eric was terrified. "It was an accident. She was running away." The curtains billowed in the wind from the open french windows, and he backed out onto the terrace.

"But what made her run? That's the thing," Devlin said, thumbing back the hammers.

"No!" Eric cried, and Devlin gave him both barrels, lifting him over the balustrade.

AT CHERNAY, it was almost two o'clock. Schellenberg was dozing in the chair in the corner of the radio room.

Leber called to him. "Falcon coming in on the radio, General."

Schellenberg hurried to his side. "What is it?"

"Another check on the weather. I've told him how bad things are here." He listened intently, then looked up. "He says he's not prepared to wait any longer. He's leaving now."

Schellenberg nodded. "Just say good luck." He opened the door and went out. The fog rolled in from the sea remorselessly, and he turned up the collar of his greatcoat and started to walk aimlessly along the side of the airstrip.

HORST BERGER was sitting by the open window in his room at Belle-Île. He had found himself unable to sleep, so he sat there in the darkness listening to the rain falling through the fog. There was a knock at the door, it opened, and light fell into the room.

One of the SS duty sentries stood there. "Sturmbannführer, the Reichsführer wants you. He's waiting now at his apartment."

"Five minutes," Berger told him, and the man went out.

In the sitting room of his apartment, Himmler was standing by the fire in full uniform when Berger knocked and entered. The Reichsführer turned.

"Ah, there you are. The Führer can't sleep. He's sent for me. Asked particularly that I bring you."

"I see, Reichsführer. But why am I commanded?"

"Who knows? Some whim or other." Himmler consulted his watch. "We are due at his suite in fifteen minutes. There's fresh coffee on the table. Time for you to have a cup before we go."

IN THE BARN at Shaw Place, everyone waited while Devlin tapped out his message on the radio. He put down the headphones, switched off the radio and turned to Steiner and Asa who stood there, Dougal Munro, his hands still bound, between them.

"That's it," he said. "I've told Schellenberg we're leaving."

"Then let's get the plane out," Asa said.

Munro stood against the wall, his hands still bound, while the others rolled the Lysander some distance away from the barn. Asa got the cupola up and reached for his helmet.

"What about our friend in the barn?" Steiner asked.

"He stays," Devlin said.

Steiner turned to him. "You're sure?"

"Colonel," Devlin said, "I may be on your side at the moment, but I haven't the slightest intention of handing over the head of Section D at SOE to German Intelligence. Now you two get in and start up. I'll be with you in a minute."

When he went into the barn, Munro was struggling with the twine around his wrists. He paused as the Irishman took a small pocket knife from his pocket and opened the blade.

"Here, let me, Brigadier."

He sliced through the twine, freeing him, and Munro rubbed at his wrists. "What's this?"

"You didn't really think I was going to hand you over to those Nazi bastards, now did you? There was a problem for a while, Shaw exposing you to things, but there's no one left you could hurt."

"Lord help me, Devlin, I'll never understand you."

"And why should you, Brigadier, when I don't understand myself most of the time." The engine of the Lysander started up, and Devlin said, "We'll be going now. You could alert the RAF, but they'd need the luck of the devil to find us in this fog."

"True," Munro agreed.

"On the other hand, you just might think Walter Schellenberg has the right idea."

"Strange," Munro said. "There have been moments in this war when I'd have jumped for joy at someone killing Hitler."

"A great man once said that as the times change, sensible men change with them." Devlin moved to the door. "Goodbye, Brigadier. I don't expect we'll be seeing each other again."

"I wish I could count on that," Munro said.

The Irishman hurried across to the Lysander, where Steiner was stripping the canvas with the RAF roundels from the wings, revealing the Luftwaffe insignia. Devlin ran to the tail plane, did the same there, then scrambled inside after Steiner. The Lysander taxied to the end of the meadow and turned into the wind. A moment later it roared down the runway and took off.

Munro stood there listening to the sound of it disappear into the night. There was a sudden whimper, and Nell slipped out of the darkness and looked up at him. When he turned and started back to the house, she followed him.

JACK CARTER, in the outer office at SOE headquarters, heard Munro's phone and rushed in at once to answer it.

"Jack?" Munro said.

"Thank heaven, sir. I've been worried as hell. I got in from York and found all hell broken loose at the priory. The porter said you were there, sir. At the priory, I mean. What happened?"

"It's quite simple, Jack. Liam Devlin made fools of the lot of us and is at this very moment flying back to France with Steiner."

"Shall I alert the RAF?" Carter asked.

"I'll take care of it. More important things to do. Number one, there's a house on Cable Wharfe, in Wapping, owned by a man called Ryan. You'll find him and his niece dead. I want a disposal team there as soon as possible."

"Right, sir."

"I also want a disposal team here, Jack. Shaw Place, outside Charbury, in Romney Marsh. Come yourself. I'll wait for you."

Munro put the phone down. No question of phoning the RAF, of course. Schellenberg was right, and that was that. He left the study, went to the front door and opened it. The fog was as thick as ever. Nell whined and sat on her haunches, staring up at him.

Munro bent down and fondled her ears. "Poor old girl," he said. "And poor old Devlin. I wish him luck."

WHEN HIMMLER and Berger were admitted to the Führer's apartment, Adolf Hitler was sitting beside an enormous stone fireplace in which a log fire burned brightly. He had a file open on his knees, which he continued to read as they waited. After a while he looked up, a vacant expression in his eyes.

"Reichsführer?"

"You wished to see me and Sturmbannführer Berger."

"Ah, yes." Hitler closed the file and put it on a table. "The young man who has so brilliantly organised my security here at Belle-Île." He stood and touched Berger's Iron Cross First Class with one finger. "A brave soldier too, I see." He turned to Himmler. "Obersturmbannführer would be more appropriate, I think."

"I'll take care of it, my Führer," Himmler told him.

"Good." Hitler turned back to Berger and smiled indulgently. "Now off you go. The Reichsführer and I have things to discuss."

Berger clicked his heels and raised his right arm. "Heil Hitler," he said, turned on his heel and went out.

Hitler returned to his chair and indicated the one opposite. "Join me, Reichsführer." Himmler sat down, and Hitler said, "Insomnia can be a blessing in disguise. It gives one extra time to ponder the important things. This file, for example." He picked it up. "A joint report from Rommel and Canaris in which they try to persuade me that the Allies will attempt an invasion by way of Normandy. Nonsense, of course. Any idiot can see that the Pas de Calais will be the target."

Himmler said carefully, "And yet you still intend to confirm Rommel as commander of Army Group B, with full responsibility for the Atlantic Wall defences?"

"Why not?" Hitler said. "A brilliant soldier, we all know that. He'll accept my decision in this matter and follow orders."

"But will he, my Führer?"

"Rommel will do as he is told," Hitler said serenely. "I am well aware of the existence of those extremists in the army who would destroy me if they could. I am also aware that it is a distinct possibility that Rommel is in sympathy with such aims. At the right moment there will be a noose waiting for all such traitors."

"And richly deserved, my Führer."

Hitler got up and stood with his back to the fire. "Before you go," he said calmly, "remember one thing." Himmler stood up. "Since I took power, how many attempts on my life? How many plots?"

Himmler for once was caught. "I'm not sure."

"At least sixteen," Hitler said. "And this argues divine intervention. The only logical explanation."

Himmler swallowed hard. "Of course, my Führer."

Hitler smiled benignly. "Now be off with you. Try and get a little sleep, and I'll see you at breakfast."

THE ENGLISH CHANNEL was fogged in for most of the way to Cap de la Hague. Asa used it as cover, making good time, finally turning in towards the French coast just after three.

He called Chernay over the radio. "Chernay, Falcon here. What's the situation?"

In the radio room at Chernay, Schellenberg sprang from his chair and crossed to Leber.

The flight sergeant said, "We've had some clearance with wind, but not enough. Ceiling zero one minute; then it clears to maybe a hundred feet, then back again."

"Is there anywhere else to go?" Asa demanded.

"Not around here. Cherbourg's totally closed in."

Schellenberg took the mike. "Asa, it's me. Are you all there?"

"We sure are, only we don't seem to have anywhere to go."

"What's your fuel position?"

"I figure I'm good for about forty-five minutes. What I'll do is stooge around for a while. Keep on the line, and let me know the second there's any kind of improvement."

Leber said, "I'll have the men light runway flares, General."

"I'll take care of that," Schellenberg told him. "You stay on the radio." And he hurried out.

AFTER TWENTY MINUTES Asa said, "This is no good. Sit tight, and I'll give it a shot." He took the Lysander down, his wheel spots on, and the fog enveloped him, just as it had done at Shaw Place. At six hundred feet he pulled the column back and went up, coming out of the mist and fog at around a thousand. The moon was low, dawn streaking the horizon.

Asa called Chernay. "It's suicide to try and land. I'd rather put her down in the sea."

"The tide's out, Captain," Leber answered.

"Is that a fact? How much beach do you get down there?"

"It runs for miles."

"Then that's it. It's some sort of a chance anyway."

Schellenberg's voice sounded. "Are you sure, Asa?"

"The only thing I'm sure of, General, is that we don't have any choice. We'll see you or we won't. Over and out."

Schellenberg turned to Leber. "Can we get down there?"

"Yes, General. There's a road leading to an old slipway."

"Good. Then let's get moving."

"If I HAVE to land in the sea, this thing's not going to float for very long," Asa said over his shoulder to Steiner and Devlin. "There's a dinghy pack there behind you. The yellow thing. Get it out fast, pull the red tag and it inflates itself."

Steiner smiled. "You swim, of course, Mr Devlin."

Devlin smiled back. "Some of the time."

Asa started down, easing the column forward, sweat on his face, all the way to five hundred. The Lysander bucked in a heavy gust of wind, and they passed three hundred.

Devlin cried, "I saw something."

The fog seemed to open before them, as if a curtain were being pulled to each side, and there were great waves surging in from the Atlantic, half a mile of wet sand stretching towards the cliffs of Cap de la Hague. Asa heaved the column back, and the Lysander levelled out no more than fifty feet above the whitecaps that pounded on the shore.

Asa slammed the instrument panel with one hand. "You beautiful, beautiful girl. I love you," he cried, and turned into the wind to land.

THE TRUCK containing Schellenberg, Leber and several Luftwaffe mechanics had reached the slipway at the very moment the Lysander burst into view.

"He made it, General," Leber cried. "What a pilot!"

Schellenberg felt totally drained. He waited as the Lysander taxied towards the end of the slipway. It came to a halt, and Leber and his men cheered as Asa switched off the engine. Devlin and Steiner got out first and Asa followed, tossing his flying helmet into the cockpit.

Schellenberg stood waiting as Steiner and Devlin came towards him. He held out his hand to Steiner.

"Colonel, a pleasure to see you here."

"General," Steiner said.

Schellenberg turned to Devlin. "As for you, my mad Irish friend, I still can't believe you're here."

"Well, you know what I always say, Walter, me old son. All you have to do is live right." Devlin grinned. "Would you think there might be a bit of breakfast somewhere? I'm starved."

THEY SAT around the table in the canteen, drinking coffee. Schellenberg said, "So the Führer arrived safely last night."

"And Rommel and the admiral?" Devlin said.

"They will be joining him soon."

Steiner said to Schellenberg, "This plan of yours makes a wild kind of sense, but there is a considerable uncertainty."

"You don't think the men of this parachute detachment will follow you?"

"Oh, no. I mean what happens to the three of you in the château before we arrive."

There was a moment's silence, and Schellenberg said, "Are you with me in this, Colonel, or not? There isn't much time."

Steiner got up and moved to the window. It had started to rain heavily. He stared out for a moment and turned. "I have little reason to like the Führer, and not just because of what happened to my father. I could say he's a disaster for the human race, but for me the important thing is that he's bad for Germany. Having said that, Himmler as head of state would be infinitely worse."

"So you will join with me in this?" asked Schellenberg.

"I don't think any of us have a choice," said Steiner.

Asa shrugged. "What the hell, you can count me in."

Devlin stood up and stretched. "Right. Well, let's get on with it." And he opened the door and went out.

WHEN SCHELLENBERG went into the hut he and Asa had been using, Devlin had a foot on the bed, his trouser leg rolled up as he adjusted the Smith & Wesson in the ankle holster.

"Your ace in the hole, my friend?"

"And this." Devlin took the silenced Walther from his holdall and put it into his waistband at the rear. Then he took out Ryan's Luger. "This is for the pocket. I doubt those SS guards will let us through the door armed, so best to have something to give them."

"Do you think this whole thing will work?" Schellenberg asked.

"Uncertainty—and from you at this stage, General?"

"Not really. You see, the Allies have made one thing clear. No negotiated peace. Total surrender. The last thing Himmler wants."

"Yes. There's a rope waiting for him one of these days."

"And me also, perhaps. I am, after all, a general of the SS."

"Don't worry, Walter." Devlin smiled. "If you end up in a prison cell, I'll break you out—and for free. Now let's get moving."

FIELD MARSHAL Erwin Rommel and Admiral Canaris left Rennes at five a.m. in a Mercedes limousine driven by Rommel's aide, a Major Carl Ritter. Two military police motorcyclists were their only escort as they twisted and turned through the narrow French lanes in the early morning gloom.

"The only reason we've had to turn out at such a ridiculous time is because he wants us at a disadvantage," Canaris said.

"The Führer likes all of us at a disadvantage, Admiral," Rommel said. "I learnt that long ago."

"I wonder what he's up to," Canaris said. "We know he's going to confirm your appointment as Commander of Army Group B, but he could have made you fly to Berlin for that."

"Exactly," Rommel said. "And there are such things as telephones. No. I think it's the Normandy business."

"But surely we can make him see sense about that," Canaris said. "The report we've put together is really quite conclusive."

"Yes, but unfortunately, the Führer favours the Pas de Calais, and so does his astrologer."

"And Uncle Heini?" Canaris suggested, using the nickname common in the SS behind Himmler's back.

"Himmler always agrees with the Führer, you know that."

Beyond, through a break in the rain, they saw Belle Île. "Very Wagnerian," Canaris said dryly. "The castle at the end of the world. The Führer and Himmler must be enjoying themselves."

"Have you ever wondered how it came to happen, Admiral?" Erwin Rommel asked. "How we came to allow such monsters to control the destinies of millions of people?"

"Every day of my life," Canaris replied.

CHAPTER 14

IT WAS JUST after six a.m., and Hauptmann Erich Kramer, commanding the 12th Parachute Detachment, was having coffee in his office when he heard a vehicle drive into the farmyard. He went to the window and saw a Kübelwagen, its canvas hood up against the rain. Asa got out first, followed by Schellenberg and Devlin.

Kramer recognised them instantly from the last visit, and frowned. "Now what in the hell do they want?" he said softly.

And then Kurt Steiner emerged. He stood there in the rain in his blue-grey flying blouse, jump trousers and boots. Kramer took in the Knight's Cross with Oak Leaves, the silver-and-gold eagle of the paratrooper's badge, the Crete and Africa Korps cuff titles. He recognised him, of course.

He reached for his cap and opened the door, buttoning his blouse. "Colonel Steiner." He clicked his heels together and saluted, ignoring the others. "I can't tell you what an honour this is."

"A pleasure. Captain Kramer, isn't it?" Steiner took in Kramer's cuff titles, the ribbon for the Winter War. "So we are old comrades, it would seem."

"Yes, Colonel."

Several paratroopers had emerged from their canteen, curious about the arrivals. At the sight of Steiner they all jumped to attention. "At ease, lads," he called, and said to Kramer, "What strength have you here?"

"Thirty-five only, Colonel."

"Good," Steiner told him. "I'm going to need everyone, including you. Let's get them together, and I'll explain."

IN THE FARMYARD, in the rain, the thirty-five men of the 12th Parachute Detachment stood to attention in four ranks. Most of them had Schmeisser machine-guns slung across their chests. Steiner addressed them, with Schellenberg, Devlin and Asa Vaughan behind him, Kramer at one side.

Steiner hadn't bothered with niceties, only facts. "So there it is. The Führer is to meet his death very shortly at the hands of traitorous elements of the SS. Our job is to stop them. Any questions?"

There wasn't a word, only the heavy rain drumming down. Steiner turned to Kramer. "Get them ready, Captain." Kramer saluted, and Steiner turned to Schellenberg. "Will fifteen minutes be enough for you?"

"Then you arrive like a panzer column," Schellenberg told him. "Very fast indeed."

He and Asa got into the Kübelwagen.

Devlin turned to Steiner, "In a way, we've been here before."

"I know and the same old question. Are we playing the game, or is the game playing us?"

"Let's hope we have better luck than we did last time, Colonel." Devlin smiled and got into the Kübelwagen, and Asa drove away.

AT THE CHÂTEAU DE BELLE-ÎLE, Rommel, Canaris and Major Ritter went up the steps to the main entrance. One of the two SS guards opened the door, and they went inside. There seemed to be guards everywhere.

Berger came down the stairs and advanced to meet them. "Herr Admiral, Herr Field Marshal, a great pleasure. Sturmbannführer Berger, in charge of security."

"Major." Rommel nodded.

"The Führer is waiting in the dining hall," said Berger. "He has requested that no one bear arms in his presence."

Rommel and Ritter took their pistols from their holsters. "I trust we're not late," the field marshal said.

"Actually you are early by two minutes." Berger gave him a good-humoured smile. "May I show you the way?"

He opened the great oak door, and they followed him in. The long dining table was laid for four people only. The Führer was standing by the stone fireplace, looking down into the burning logs. He turned and faced them.

"Ah, there you are."

Rommel said, "I trust you are well, my Führer."

Hitler nodded. His eyes flickered to Ritter, who stood rigidly at attention, clutching a briefcase.

"And who have we here?"

"My personal aide, Major Carl Ritter, my Führer. He has further details on the Normandy situation," Rommel said.

"More reports?" Hitler shrugged. "If you must, I suppose." He turned to Berger. "Have another place laid at the table, and see what's keeping the Reichsführer."

As Berger moved to the door it opened, and Himmler entered. He wore the black dress uniform, and his face was pale, a faint edge of excitement to him that he found difficult to conceal. "I apologise, my Führer—a phone call from Berlin as I was about to leave my room." He nodded. "Herr Admiral—Field Marshal."

"And the field marshal's aide, Major Ritter." Hitler rubbed his hands together. "I feel extraordinarily hungry. You know, gentlemen,

621

perhaps we should do this more often. The early breakfast, I mean. It leaves so much of the day for matters of importance. But come. Sit."

He himself took the head of the table. Rommel and Canaris sat on his right, Himmler and Ritter on the left. "So," he said, "let's begin. Food before business."

He picked up the small silver bell at his right hand and rang it.

IT WAS no more than ten minutes later that the Kübelwagen arrived at the main gate. Schellenberg leant out. The sergeant who came forward took in his uniform and saluted.

"The Führer is expecting us," Schellenberg told him.

"I've orders to admit no one, General."

"Don't be stupid, man," Schellenberg said. "That hardly applies to me." He nodded to Asa. "Drive on, Hauptsturmführer."

They drove into the inner courtyard and stopped. Schellenberg said, "Let's just keep going," and he got out of the car, marched up the wide steps and reached for the handle of the front door.

In the dining hall, Hitler was enjoying himself, working his way through a plate of toast and fruit. The door opened, and an SS sergeant major entered.

It was Himmler who spoke to him. "I thought I made it clear we were not to be disturbed for any reason."

"Yes, Reichsführer, but General Schellenberg is here with a Hauptsturmführer and a civilian. Says it is imperative he see you."

Himmler said, "Nonsense. You have your orders!"

Hitler cut in at once. "Schellenberg? Now, I wonder what that can be about. Bring them in, Sergeant Major."

SCHELLENBERG, Devlin and Asa waited in the hall, by the door. The sergeant major returned. "The Führer will see you, General, but all weapons must be left here."

"Of course." Schellenberg took his pistol from its holster, slapping it down on the table.

Asa did the same, and Devlin took his Luger from a coat pocket, saying, "All contributions graciously given."

The sergeant major said, "If you would follow me, gentlemen." He turned and led the way across the hall.

When they went in, Hitler was still eating. Rommel and Canaris looked up curiously. Himmler was deathly pale.

Hitler said, "Now then, Schellenberg, what brings you here?"

"I regret the intrusion, my Führer, but a matter of the gravest urgency has come to my attention. Another attempt on your life."

"Impossible," Himmler said.

Hitler waved him to silence and glanced at Devlin and Asa Vaughan. "And who have we here?"

"If I may explain. The Reichsführer recently gave me the task of planning the safe return to the Reich of a certain Colonel Kurt Steiner, who was held prisoner in the Tower of London. Herr Devlin here and Hauptsturmführer Vaughan delivered Steiner to me at the small Luftwaffe base nearby a short time ago."

Hitler said to Himmler, "I knew nothing of this."

Himmler looked quite wretched. "It was to be a surprise."

Hitler turned again to Schellenberg. "This Colonel Steiner— where is he?"

"He'll be here soon. The thing is, I received an anonymous telephone call only a couple of hours ago. I regret to have to say this in the presence of the Reichsführer, but whoever it was spoke of treachery within the ranks of the SS."

Himmler was almost choking. "Impossible."

"An officer named Horst Berger was referred to."

Hitler said, "But Sturmbannführer Berger is in charge of my security here. I've just had him promoted."

"Which just goes to show—you can't trust anyone," Berger called. He moved out of the shadows at the end of the dining hall, an SS man on either side of him holding a machine-gun.

STEINER AND KRAMER led the way up the hill to the château in a Kübelwagen, the top down in spite of the rain. The paratroopers followed in two troop carriers. Steiner had a stick grenade tucked into one of his jump boots and a Schmeisser ready in his lap.

Kramer slowed at the outer gate, and the SS sergeant came forward. Steiner raised the Schmeisser, lifted him back with a quick burst, and was swinging to cut down the other guard as Kramer took the Kübelwagen forward with a surge of power.

As they reached the steps leading to the front door more SS appeared from the guardhouse on the right. Steiner pulled the stick grenade from his boot and tossed it into the centre of them; then he leapt from the Kübelwagen and started up the steps. Behind him the paratroopers jumped from the troop carriers and stormed after him, firing across the courtyard at the SS.

"YOU DARE to approach me like this, a gun in your hand?" Hitler said to Berger, his eyes blazing.

"I regret to have to say it, my Führer, but your moment has come. You, Field Marshal Rommel here, the admiral . . ." Berger shook his head. "We can no longer afford any of you."

"You can't kill me, you young fool," Hitler told him calmly. "It is not my destiny to die here."

Somewhere in the distance was the sound of shooting. Berger glanced at the door, and Major Ritter leapt to his feet, threw his briefcase at him and ran for the door. "Guards!" he shouted. One of the SS men fired his Schmeisser, shooting Ritter in the back several times.

Schellenberg said, "Mr Devlin."

Devlin's hand found the butt of the silenced Walther in his waistband against the small of his back. His first bullet caught the man who had just machine-gunned Ritter, in the temple; the second took the other SS man in the heart. Berger swung to face him, his mouth open in a terrible cry of rage. Devlin's third bullet hit him between the eyes.

Devlin walked across and looked down at him, the Walther slack in his hand. "You wouldn't be told, son, would you? I said you needed a different class of work."

Behind him the doors burst open, and Kurt Steiner rushed in at the head of his men.

WHEN SCHELLENBERG knocked, and entered Himmler's room, he found the Reichsführer standing at the window. It was instantly evident that he intended to brazen it out.

"Ah, there you are, General. A most unfortunate business. It reflects so terribly on the SS. Thank goodness the Führer sees Berger's abominable treachery as an individual lapse."

"Fortunate for all of us, Reichsführer."

Himmler sat down. "The anonymous phone call you mentioned. You've absolutely no idea who it was?"

"I'm afraid not."

"A pity. Still . . ." Himmler looked at his watch. "The Führer wants to see you and the other three at noon. I believe he thinks decorations are in order."

"Reichsführer."

Schellenberg turned to the door, and Himmler said, "Better for all of us if this never happened. You follow me, General? Rommel and Canaris will keep their mouths shut, and a posting back to the Russian front will take care of those paratroopers."

"I see, Reichsführer," Schellenberg said carefully.

"Which, of course, leaves us with Steiner, Vaughan and the man Devlin. I feel they could all prove a serious embarrassment."

"Is the Reichsführer suggesting—" Schellenberg began.

"Nothing," Himmler told him. "I'm suggesting nothing. I simply leave it to your own good sense."

SCHELLENBERG, Steiner, Asa and Devlin waited in the library. Just before noon the door opened, and the Führer entered, followed by Himmler, who carried a leather briefcase.

"Gentlemen," Hitler said.

The three officers jumped to attention, and Devlin, sitting on the window seat, got up awkwardly. Hitler nodded to Himmler, who opened the case, which was full of decorations.

"To you, General Schellenberg, the German Cross in Gold, and also to you, Hauptsturmführer Vaughan." He pinned on the decorations, then turned to Steiner. "To you, Colonel Steiner, I now award the Swords. And to you, Mr Devlin," the Führer said, turning to the Irishman, "the Iron Cross First Class."

Devlin couldn't think of a thing to say. He stifled an insane desire to laugh as the cross was pinned to his jacket.

"You have my gratitude, gentlemen, and the gratitude of all the German people," Hitler told them. He turned and went out, Himmler trailing behind.

The door closed. Devlin said, "What happens now?"

"The Führer returns to Berlin at once," Schellenberg said. "Canaris and Himmler go with him."

"What about us?" Asa Vaughan asked.

"There's a slight problem," Schellenberg said. "The Reichsführer has made it plain he doesn't want you three around."

"I see," Steiner said. "And you're supposed to take care of us?"

"Something like that. Of course, there is the Lysander waiting on the beach at Chernay," Schellenberg said. "Leber will have had it checked out by now and refuelled."

"But where in the hell do we go?" Asa Vaughan demanded.

Schellenberg glanced enquiringly at Devlin, and the Irishman started to laugh.

"Have you ever been to Ireland?" he asked.

IT WAS COLD on the beach, the tide much higher than it had been that morning, but there was still ample space to take off. Schellenberg shook hands with Steiner and Asa. "Gentlemen, good luck." They got into the Lysander, and he turned to Devlin. "You are a truly remarkable man."

Devlin said, "Come with us, Walter. Nothing for you back there."

"Too late, my friend. As I've said before, far too late to get off the merry-go-round now."

"And what will Himmler say when he hears that you let us go?"

"Oh, I've thought of that. An excellent marksman like you should have no difficulty in shooting me in the shoulder. Let's make it the left one. A flesh wound, naturally."

"Damn—it's the cunning old fox you are."

Schellenberg walked away, then turned. Devlin's hand came out of his pocket holding the Walther. It coughed once. Schellenberg staggered, clutching at his shoulder. There was blood between his fingers. He smiled. "Goodbye, Mr Devlin."

The Irishman scrambled in and pulled down the cupola. Asa turned into the wind; the Lysander roared along the beach and lifted off. Schellenberg watched as it sped out to sea. After a while he turned and walked back towards the slipway.

LOUGH CONN, in the county of Mayo and not too far from Killala Bay, on the west coast of Ireland, is better than ten miles long. On that evening in the failing light, as darkness swept down from the mountains, its calm surface was like black glass.

Asa made a masterly landing several hundred yards from the shore, dropping the Lysander's tail at the last moment. They skidded to a halt, and then water started to come in. He got the cupola up and heaved the dinghy package out. It inflated at once.

"How deep is it here?" he asked Devlin.

"Two hundred feet."

"That should take care of her, then. Let's get moving."

He was into the dinghy in a moment, followed by Steiner and Devlin. They started to paddle towards the darkening shore, then paused to look back. The Lysander's nose went under, only the tail plane showing, with the Luftwaffe swastika, and then that too disappeared below the surface.

Steiner said, "What now, Mr Devlin?"

"A long walk before us, but the whole night to do it in. My great-aunt Eileen O'Brien has an old farmhouse above Killala Bay. Nothing but friends there."

"And then what?" Asa demanded.

"We'll have to see, my old son," Liam Devlin told him.

The dinghy drifted into a small beach. Devlin went first, knee-deep, and pulled them into shore.

"*Céad mile fáilte*," he said, putting out a hand to Kurt Steiner. "A hundred thousand welcomes."

Belfast: 1975

CHAPTER 15

IT WAS ALMOST four in the morning. Devlin stood up and opened the sacristy door. The city was quiet now, but there was the acrid smell of smoke. It started to rain, and he shivered.

"Nothing quite like a bad night in Belfast."

I said, "Tell me something. Did you ever have dealings with Dougal Munro again?"

"Oh, yes." He nodded. "Several times over the years. He liked his fishing, did old Dougal."

As usual I found it difficult to take him seriously, and tried again. "All right, what happened afterwards? How did Dougal Munro manage to keep it all under wraps?"

"Well, you must remember that only Munro and Carter knew who Steiner really was. To poor old Lieutenant Benson, Sister Maria Palmer and Father Martin he was just a prisoner of war. A Luftwaffe officer."

"But Michael Ryan and his niece? The Shaws?"

"The Luftwaffe had started on London again at the beginning of that year. The little blitz, it was called, and that was very convenient for British Intelligence because people died in bombing raids. People like Sir Maxwell Shaw and his sister, Lavinia, killed in London during a raid in January nineteen forty-four. Look up *The Times* for that month. You'll find an obituary."

"And Michael Ryan and Mary? Jack and Eric Carver?"

"They didn't rate *The Times*, but they all ended up in the same crematorium in north London. Listed as victims of the bombing."

"And the others?"

"Canaris was arrested when the attempt to kill Hitler in July failed. They hanged him in the last month of the war. The Führer thought Rommel was involved, but couldn't bear to have the people's hero revealed as a traitor, so the general was allowed to commit suicide. We all know what happened to Hitler, holed up in his bunker at the end. Himmler tried to make a run for it, but didn't make it. He took cyanide when they caught him."

"And Schellenberg?"

"Now, there was a man, old Walter. He became head of the combined secret services before the end of the war. Outlasted the lot of them. When it came to the war-crimes trials, the only thing they could get him for was being a member of an illegal organisation, the SS. All sorts of witnesses came forward to speak for him at the trial, Jews amongst them. He only served a couple of years in jail. He died in Italy in fifty-one—cancer."

"So that's it," I said.

He nodded. "We saved Hitler's life. Did we do right?" He shrugged. "It seemed like a good idea at the time, but I can imagine why they put a hundred-year hold on that file."

He opened the door again and looked out. I said, "What happened afterwards to you and Steiner and Asa Vaughan? I know you were a professor at some American college in the years after the war, but what happened in between?"

"And haven't I talked enough? I've given you enough for another book. The rest will have to wait. You should be getting back to your hotel. I'll go a step of the way with you."

He wore a hat and a raincoat over his cassock and sheltered us with his umbrella as we walked through the mean streets, passing here and there the devastation of a bombing.

"Would you look at this place?" he demanded. "Rat's alley, where the dead men left their bones."

"Why do you keep on with it?" I asked him. "The bombings, the killings?"

"To be honest with you, son, I'm getting tired, and I never did like soft-target hits—the indiscriminate bomb that kills passers-by, women, children. My old aunt Eileen left that farmhouse to me, and there's a job waiting as professor of English at Trinity College in Dublin whenever I want." He stopped on the corner and sniffed the smoky air. "Time to get the hell out of this and let those who want to get on with it."

"You mean you've finally got tired of the game playing you instead of you playing the game?"

He nodded. "That's what Steiner always says."

"Interesting," I commented. "You said, 'Steiner says'."

He smiled. "Is that a fact?" We were on the corner of the Falls Road. In the distance was a foot patrol and a Saracen armoured car. "I think I'll leave you here, son."

"A wise decision." I took his hand.

"You can look me up in Killala any time." He turned away and paused. "One thing."

"What's that?" I asked.

"The Cohen girl—the hit-and-run accident. Convenient for someone, that. I'd watch my back if I were you."

I lit a cigarette in cupped hands and watched him go, the cassock like skirts around his ankles, the umbrella against the rain. I glanced down the Falls Road. The patrol was nearer now, but when I turned to take a last look at Liam Devlin, he'd gone, disappeared into the shadows, as if he had never been.

About the Author

In the days before he did army service, a young man named Harry Patterson once entered a short story competition. He did not win it, but a judge recognised promise in his work and encouraged him to keep on writing fiction. "I think if he hadn't said that, maybe I would've dropped the whole idea." It was a fragile beginning to a stunning career, for that young man would go on to be one of the most prolific and most widely read authors on the globe, best known to readers worldwide by his famous pseudonym: Jack Higgins.

Higgins, pictured here with Tarquin, the mascot of the fighter-pilot hero in one of his novels, *Flight of Eagles*, was born and grew up in working-class Belfast, where he spent countless hours in the library. "I read all the time because there wasn't much else to do." Despite this, he admits he "did really badly" at school and left at age fifteen. It was during national service in the Royal Horse Guards that he became aware of his own special capabilities. "They were fighting soldiers, very elite … my squadron leader was the